THE DEBACLE

THE DEBACLE

Emile Zola

Introduction by
ROBERT BALDICK

DUFOUR
1969

Published by Dufour Editions, Inc.
Chester Springs
Pennsylvania 19425

This translation © 1968 Elek Books Ltd.

Library of Congress Catalog Card Number: 69–14377

Translated by
John Hands

Printed in England by
A. Wheaton & Co., Exeter

INTRODUCTION

BY ROBERT BALDICK

WHEN, in 1868, Emile Zola first planned the cycle of novels which were to become the saga of the Rougon-Macquarts, 'the natural and social history of a family under the Second Empire', he decided that one of the ten books he intended to write should be a 'military novel' set during the war in Italy. If we are to judge by the articles he wrote at that time attacking the concept of the 'armed peace', this novel would have implicitly condemned the Emperor's militaristic policies and suggested that a republic would be better able to keep the peace. But the Franco-Prussian War of 1870–71 radically altered not only the character of Zola's 'military novel', but also its place in the Rougon-Macquart saga, and indeed the saga itself. Since the collapse of the Second Empire had created a specific time-span within which to set the Rougon-Macquart cycle, it became almost inevitable that Zola should abandon the idea of a novel on the Italian War for one on the Franco-Prussian War; that he should make this book the concluding novel of the saga proper; and that as the story of a national disaster it should acquire far greater significance and scope than Zola could ever have given to the story of a military adventure. This book was written twenty years after the war it described : the nineteenth novel in a greatly enlarged saga (the twentieth and last, *Doctor Pascal*, merely rounded off the series); it was entitled *La Débâcle*.

In April 1891 a journalist called Gaston Calmette reported that Zola was hard at work making notes for a new novel provisionally entitled *War*, and that his study in the Rue de Bruxelles was littered with maps, plans, memoirs and historical works. It is clear from Calmette's article that Zola had already read many of his major sources and that for once his documentation was taking precedence over his outline of the novel, or *ébauche*. The task facing him was a daunting one, and he later admitted that *The Debacle* had given him infinitely more trouble than any of his previous works. 'When I began writing it', he told Robert Sherard, 'I had no conception of the immensity of the task which I had imposed on myself. The

v

labour of reading up all that has been written on my subject in general, and on the battle of Sedan in particular, has been enormous, and the work of condensation of all that I have had to read has been all the more laborious in that on no subject has more divergence of opinion been expressed.'

Another difficulty he faced was that he had not taken part himself in the fighting, and for information about the experiences of the French troops he had to rely on the testimony of those who had actually served in the 1870 campaign. 'As soon as it became known,' he wrote later, 'that I was writing a book about the war and about Sedan, I received from all parts of France manuscript accounts written by people of all classes who had been present at that battle, and who sent me their recollections. That was most excellent material – indeed the best, because not to be found anywhere else. An "Anecdotal Account of the Battle of Sedan" was sent me by a gentleman who is now a professor at one of the Universities in the South. A long, ill-spelt letter came to me from a gamekeeper in the North, who was a private soldier in the Seventh Army Corps at the time, in which he gave me a full account of the battle as it impressed him. I have masses of such documents, and it was my duty to go through everything that could throw any light on my subject.'

After studying what documents he had collected, Zola proceeded to make a draft outline of the novel and at the same time to choose the characters he intended to portray. First of all, and quite exceptionally, he decided not to give any woman a major role, but instead to provide a comprehensive and moving study of 'all the friendship that can exist between two men'. One of these two men was to be Jean Macquart, the hero of Zola's earlier novel, *Earth*, and was to stand for 'the very spirit of France, sane and courageous, though attached to the earth'; the other, provisionally called Paul but later given the name of Maurice Levasseur, was to represent the shallow, decadent section of French society – 'the mistakes, the head in the clouds, the vain egoism of the other part of France'. Zola intended the interplay of these two characters to be as symbolic as the characters themselves : Paul would save Jean's life at Sedan, but in the 'Bloody Week' of May 1871 which ended the rule of the revolutionary Commune of Paris, Jean would kill Paul just as a doctor would cut a gangrened limb off a healthy body.

Zola now had to visit the sites to be described in his novel. 'With my rough draft in my pocket,' he told Sherard later, 'and my head teeming with the shadows of my marionettes, and of the things that they were to do and to explain, I set off for Reims and went carefully over the whole ground, driving from Reims to Sedan, and following foot by foot the road by which the Seventh Corps – already then decided upon as the *milieu* in which my novel was to develop – marched to their disaster. During that drive I picked up an immense quantity of material, halting in farmhouses and peasants' cottages, and taking copious notes.' Leaving Reims on 17 April 1891, accompanied by his wife, Zola reached Sedan on Sunday the 19th, and spent a week in and around the town, with Charles Philippoteaux, the brother of the late mayor of Sedan, acting as his guide. 'After a careful study of the place and the people,' he wrote, 'I saw that my novel must deal largely, for the full comprehension of my story, not only with the locality, but with the people of the town. This gave me the bourgeois of Sedan, who play an important part in my tale.' Philippoteaux himself, who was to be portrayed as Delaherche in *The Debacle*, was especially useful to Zola, for not only did he introduce him to fellow citizens who had lived through the events of September 1870, but he recalled his own memories of that time and took the novelist to see the various places connected with the disaster of Sedan. These included his own estate, just outside Sedan, and the little town of Bouillon, where Napoleon III had spent the night of his surrender, and where, in the Emperor's hotel room, Zola saw the same engravings that he had seen in 1870 : ironically enough, *The Last Judgement* and *Rouget de l'Isle Singing the Marseillaise*. Zola returned to Paris on 26 April, so deeply moved by what he had heard of the battle of Sedan and seen of the battlefield that the last entry in his notebook reads : 'My hallucination, coming back from Givonne on a fine moonlit evening. The dead waking up. An immense cemetery . . .'

Back in Paris, as he later explained, 'I was in an immense workshop or yard surrounded with huge mountains of hewn stones, mortar and bricks, and all that remained then to do was to build the best structure that I could build of these materials'. After planning every chapter in detail, in accordance with his usual method, he began writing the novel on 18 July 1891, only to discover that the enormous amount of material he had amassed raised serious problems of condensation. 'I had to reduce to one page,' he told Sherard, 'what I could easily, and without prolixity, have treated in a dozen pages; so that with each page, nay with each sentence, I have been confronted with the question of what to leave out and what to say. Then, when each page was written, I began to torture myself with the doubt whether I had left unsaid things I ought to have said, whether I had sacrificed good to inferior materials.'

Most of his letters at this period expressed the same scruples, and some mentioned a fresh anxiety : fear that his accuracy and objectivity might be questioned. 'I have endeavoured,' he wrote, 'to speak the truth without fear or favour. The reader will be aroused to compassion with the sufferings, bodily and mental, of the heroic and martyred army, just as he will be aroused to indignation at the conduct of its chiefs, which fell little short of downright dementia. It has been my duty to be severely critical, and I have not shrunk from the responsibility of wounding, where it was right and just to do so, susceptibilities which I see no reason for respecting. I dare say there will be some outcry at my blame, but I do not care, having spoken the truth.' And after finishing the novel in May 1892, he told a Dutch friend : 'I should be quite happy if, in France and Germany, people recognized the great effort I have made to tell the truth.'

In the event, as he should have guessed, the press as a whole denied him this recognition. True, some of France's leading literary critics praised *The Debacle* highly when it was published in book form on 24 June 1892, Anatole France eulogising its 'epic quality', Gaston Deschamps calling it 'a masterpiece', and Émile Faguet declaring that it was 'a very great work, the greatest, I believe, in the whole library of books Monsieur Zola has written'. Soon, however, there came a mounting wave of criticism. This began innocuously enough with letters and articles cavilling at points of detail in the novel which the writers maintained to be inaccurate : there were no hop-gardens between Mulhausen and Altkirch as stated in the second chapter of the novel (Zola had to admit that he had mistaken the local vineyards with their tall poles for hop-grounds); the uniform of the Prussian Royal Guard was wrongly described (Zola referred his critics to the illustrated books on German uniforms sent to him from Berlin); Napoleon III was not in the habit of using rouge (Zola retorted that he had not suggested that the Emperor normally used rouge, but only that he rouged his cheeks on the morning of the battle of Sedan).

There was more serious and damaging criticism to come. In the *Revue des Deux Mondes* the Academician Eugéne-Melchior de Vogüé reproached Zola with having denigrated and belittled both the French Army and the French nation, and this accusation was the signal for an avalanche of hostile articles and pamphlets. Jules Arnaud condemned Zola's novel as 'demoralising, perfidious, lying and misleading'; an army captain reviled 'the errors of *The Debacle*' in a pamphlet entitled *Gloria Victis*; and the Abbé Théodore Delmont described the book as 'a hideous nightmare as unhealthy as it is unpatriotic'. Already, in fact, the Army and the Church had joined forces, as they would again during the Dreyfus Affair, to denounce Zola as a traitor to his country.

The irony of these accusations was that in *The Debacle* Zola had not only written, for once, a didactic novel, but a didactic novel with a specifically patriotic purpose : to teach the French that heroism and tradition were not enough, and that their only hope of a *revanche* lay in organising their army on scientific lines, like the Prussians. Zola had stated this purpose repeatedly in his private correspondence, and now he did so publicly in his reply to de Vogüé :

'In writing this book I believe I acted as a moralist and a patriot. I exposed the faults and failings of our dear country. I revealed the mistakes made in the course of that terrible war of 1870, so that they might serve as a lesson to us. . . . I have the satisfaction and the conviction of having written a book calculated to raise our soldiers' spirits : it is a book of courage and revival, a book insisting on the need for revenge. . . .'

Didactic works of literature, however popular they may be – and *The Debacle* was a bestseller in Zola's day – are usually doomed to rejection by later generations, either because their purpose has been achieved or abandoned, or because their style of appeal has lost its power of persuasion. *The Debacle* is a notable exception to this rule. As Zola's sometime disciple Henry Céard wrote to him, 'the whole of your book condemns your theories and belies your paradoxes. It certainly does not inspire a taste for battle. On the contrary, it inspires a horror of war, not so much through the blood that flows and the corpses that pile up, as through the immense stupidity revealed even by the victors.' Without knowing what he was doing, and without meaning to do it, Zola had written in *The Debacle* one of the most moving and impressive modern indictments of the cruelty and stupidity of war.

ROBERT BALDICK

I

THE camp lay a mile or two eastwards of Mulhouse, towards the
Rhine, at the heart of the fertile plain. In the dwindling light of
that August evening the shelter-tents stood in rows beneath the
black, lowering sky and the flares glinted at regular intervals along
the front. Sentries mounted guard with loaded rifles, never stirring,
keeping their eyes trained lifelessly on the purplish haze mounting
from the great river on the far horizon.

They had arrived here from Belfort at about five. It was now
eight, and the men had only just been allowed to draw rations. The
firewood must have gone astray, though – none had been issued and
they had no means of cooking the evening meal. They had had to
make do with cold dry biscuit, munching it as best they could and
washing it down with long swigs of brandy which took the last
ounce of stamina from their weary legs. Over by the canteen, however, behind the flares, two soldiers were persevering in an attempt
to conjure a blaze from a pile of unseasoned wood; the logs, hacked
from young boughs with the aid of the men's sword-bayonets, were
stubbornly refusing to burn up. A column of thick black smoke
mounted slowly in the evening air – an infinitely cheerless sight.

Barely twelve thousand men were mustered here under General
Félix Douay, a mere skeleton of his 7th Army Corps. The first
division, called to the front the day before, had set off for Froeschwiller; the third was still at Lyons; and somewhat reluctantly he
had decided to leave Belfort and move forward with only the second
division, the reserve artillery and a cavalry division – this last below
strength. Camp fires had been spotted at Lorrach. A telegram from
the Sub-Prefect of Schelestadt brought news that the Prussians were
about to cross the Rhine at Markolsheim. The general felt that he
was too isolated at the extreme right of the other army corps, and
so decided to reach the frontier as quickly as possible, a decision
which had been strengthened the day before, when reports had
arrived of the appallingly effective surprise attack on Wissembourg.
He might at any moment have to withstand an attack on his own

1

lines, or have to go to the assistance of the 1st Corps. On this tense, stormy Saturday, August 6, 1870, there must have been fighting somewhere over towards Froeschwiller : the fact was written plain in the unquiet, oppressive sky, traversed by mighty blasts and sharp, unheralded gusts of wind laden with a sense of foreboding. And for two whole days the troops had felt sure of being on their way to battle and had expected to find the Prussians waiting for them at the end of their forced march from Belfort to Mulhouse.

Daylight was fading as the "retreat" sounded in some remote corner of the camp – a roll of drums followed by a bugle-call, faint as yet, borne away on the air. And Jean Macquart, hammering the pegs deeper into the ground to make the tent secure against the wind, scrambled to his feet. At the first hint of war he had set out from Rognes, still grieving over the tragedy of losing his wife Françoise and the farmland which she had brought to him in marriage, and re-enlisted at the age of thirty-nine. They had made him a corporal again and posted him forthwith to the 106th Regiment of the Line, which was being brought up to strength. At times he was still amazed to find himself back in uniform – he, the man who after Solferino had been so glad to leave the service, to be released from the sabre-rattling role of the hired killer. But what else was a man to do when he suddenly had no trade to ply, no wife, no property, and when his heart was bursting with grief and anger ? He might as well take it out on his country's enemies, if they were causing trouble. And Jean remembered his cry : damn it – since he no longer had the heart to till the old soil of France, he would fight as its defender !

Having stood up, Jean glanced at the main body of the camp, where the drum and bugle band was leaving a hustle of activity in its wake. A few men were running. Others, who had already begun to doze, were picking themselves up and stretching themselves with a look of weary annoyance. He himself stood patiently awaiting roll-call with the splendid unexcitability and level-headedness which made him such an admirable soldier. His comrades were always saying that if only he were educated he might have gone far. But he could barely read or write, and so he did not even aspire to the level of sergeant. Once a peasant, always a peasant.

But suddenly the smouldering logs drew his attention and he hailed the two men, who were still desperately trying to get the fire going. Their names were Loubet and Lapoulle, both members of his squad.

"Stop that, now! What are you trying to do – poison us?"

Loubet, lean and lively, with the look of a born joker, greeted the words with a scoffing laugh.

"It's beginning to burn up, Corporal – honest it is. . . . Blow, can't you!"

And he gave Lapoulle a shove. Lapoulle, an absolute giant of a man, was wearing himself out in his attempts to unleash a hurricane from cheeks bulging like goatskins. His face was deeply flushed, and his eyes were red and full of tears.

Two other members of the squad, Chouteau and Pache – the first lying flat on his back with his usual sluggishness and self-indulgence, the second squatting on his haunches and conscientiously darning a tear in his trousers – burst into laughter at the terrible facial contortions of that clod Lapoulle.

"You might do better if you turned round and blew at the other end!" cried Chouteau.

Jean let them laugh. There might not be much to laugh at from now on; besides, for all the weighty earnestness of his full, regular features he was no killjoy – he was always ready to turn a blind eye when his men were enjoying themselves. But at this point his eye was drawn to a second group. For the best part of an hour Maurice Levasseur, another of Jean's men, had been in conversation with a civilian, a red-haired gentleman aged thirty-six or thereabouts with the face of a well-trained spaniel and a pair of big blue goggle-eyes whose shortsightedness had earned him exemption from military service. A battery sergeant in the reserve artillery, looking jaunty and self-assured with his dark pointed beard and flowing moustache, had walked over to join them. And there they lingered, a cosy trio, as unconcerned as if they were at home.

Jean thought it his duty to intervene. He had no wish to see them hauled over the coals. He went up to the civilian and said civilly: "I'd be on my way, *monsieur*, if I was you. The 'retreat' is being sounded, and should the lieutenant see you . . ."

Maurice did not give him time to finish.

"There is not the slightest reason for you to leave, Weiss," he said. And turning to the corporal he added curtly: "This gentleman is my brother-in-law. He is here by special permission of the colonel, with whom he is personally acquainted."

Why did one have to suffer such interruptions from a peasant whose hands still stank of manure? Maurice had enlisted as a volunteer, after being admitted to the bar only the previous autumn;

3

thanks to the colonel's influence he had been posted direct to the 106th without serving a preliminary spell at the depôt. He was willing enough to shoulder a pack; but from the very first a feeling of repugnance, of silent revolt, had set him against this illiterate bumpkin from whom he had to take orders.

"Suit yourselves," replied Jean, with his usual quiet control. "Go ahead and get caught – why should I care?"

Then he turned away, realizing that Maurice had been telling the truth; for at that moment the colonel, M. de Vineuil, went by – aristocratic as ever, with thick white mustachios spread across his long yellow face – and conferred a smile of acknowledgment on Weiss and the private soldier. The colonel was hurrying towards a farmhouse which showed between the branches of some plum trees, two or three hundred yards away to the right, where headquarters had been set up for the night. No one could say whether the corps commander was in there or not; he was still bowed with grief at the death of his brother, killed in the attack on Wissembourg. But Brigadier Bourgain-Desfeuilles, who controlled the movements of the 106th, was sure to be present – vociferous as ever, his massive trunk rolling about on top of his short legs, his cheeks ruddy from the continual good living of a man unencumbered with brains. There were signs of ever-increasing activity in and around the farmhouse; messengers were coming and going all the time; altogether there was the tense atmosphere of waiting for despatches, which were too slow in coming but which would bring news of the great battle which, ever since morning, had seemed close-by and decisive. Where had it been fought and what, so far, had been the outcome? As the night came down it was as though a black lake of agonized anticipation stretched and rumbled above the orchards and over the haystacks that stood dotted about the cowsheds. It was rumoured that a Prussian spy had been caught prowling around the camp and taken to the farmhouse for interrogation by the general. Could it be the arrival of some important telegram that was causing Colonel de Vineuil to hurry so?

Meanwhile Maurice had resumed his conversation with his brother-in-law, Weiss, and his cousin, Sergeant Honoré Fouchard. The "retreat" band, gradually growing louder as it drew near, passed close to them, blaring and thudding in the moody peacefulness of the spreading dusk; yet they acted as though they did not hear. Grandson of one of the heroes of the Grande Armée, the

4

young man had been born at Le Chêne-Populeux, in the Argonne, of a father who – turning away from the paths of glory – had sunk to the lowly and ill-paid status of tax-collector. His peasant mother had died giving birth to him and his twin sister Henriette who, from a tender age, had attended to his upbringing. His presence here as a volunteer was the aftermath of years of general dissipation and wrongdoing, resulting from a weak, impetuous nature. Oh, the money he had thrown away on gambling and on women and on all the wild pleasures of Paris, that predatory city where he had been sent to complete his studies at the expense of a family which had pinched and scraped in their efforts to make a gentleman of him. His behaviour had brought about the death of his father. His sister, after losing all she owned, had been lucky enough to find a husband – the worthy Weiss, a native of Mulhouse, here in the Alsace, who after many years as a book-keeper at the refinery in Le Chêne-Populeux was now a foreman working for M. Delaherche, one of the leading cloth manufacturers in Sedan. Today Maurice regarded himself as thoroughly reformed; he was highly strung, full of high hopes at one moment and of dark despondency at the next; although a man of generous enthusiasms, he had no more consistency than a weathercock. He was a short, fair-haired figure; beneath the bulging brow, the narrow face showed a small nose and chin and a pair of soft grey eyes which at times took on a somewhat crazed look.

Weiss had hastened to Mulhouse on the eve of hostilities, filled with a sudden desire to attend to some family business. He had approached Colonel de Vineuil in order to have a brief word with his brother-in-law, encouraged by the fact that the colonel happened to be an uncle of young Madame Delaherche, the attractive widow whom the cloth manufacturer had taken to wife a year ago. Maurice and Henriette had known her as a child, as they had happened to be neighbours. Maurice had recently found another of Gilberte Delaherche's connections – in addition to the colonel – in the person of Captain Beaudoin, his company commander: she and the captain had been friends (intimate friends, so rumour had it) in the days when she was Madame Maginot of Mézières, wife of M. Maginot, inspector of forests.

"Give all my love to Henriette," the young man said to Weiss, not once but several times, for he adored his sister. "Tell her I mean to gladden her heart and make her proud of me at last."

Tears came into his eyes at the thought of his past follies. His

5

brother-in-law, hardly less moved, checked the tide of sentiment by turning to Honoré Fouchard, the artilleryman.

"And the next time I'm over at Remilly I'll call in and tell Uncle Fouchard that I saw you here and that you're doing well."

Uncle Fouchard, a peasant who owned a few acres of land and earned his living as an itinerant butcher, was an uncle of Henriette and Maurice, on their mother's side. He lived in Remilly, up on the hill, four miles outside Sedan.

"Right you are," Honoré returned calmly. "The old man could not care less, but carry on if it gives you any pleasure."

At that moment there was a sudden commotion over by the farmhouse. From the front door, walking free and escorted by a single officer, emerged the prowler, the man who had been accused of spying. Presumably he had succeeded in establishing his identity and giving a satisfactory account of himself, for he was simply being turned out of the camp. At that distance, in the thickening gloom, it was impossible to make out much apart from his huge square frame and auburn hair.

Maurice, however, let out a cry.

"Why look, Honoré . . .! That looks like that Prussian. *You* know who I mean – Goliath!"

The artilleryman jumped visibly at the sound of this name and brought his fiery eyes to bear on the figure in question. Goliath Steinberg, a farmhand, the man who had robbed him of Silvine and brought about the rift between him and his father, the man responsible for that whole ghastly story, for every aspect of the terrible situation from which he was still suffering! He would have raced over to the man and choked the life out of him. But the figure was already on the far side of the flares and fast disappearing into the dusk.

"Oh, Goliath!" he muttered, "I shouldn't think so. He's over there with the rest of them. . . . But if ever our paths should cross – !"

He had flung out a threatening arm, pointing to the dark horizon, to the whole of that purple East which to him was Prussia. In the silence which followed his words, the "retreat" sounded again. But it came from somewhere in the far distance, somewhere right at the other end of the camp, the soft notes dying away in the blurred landscape.

"Blast!" Honoré went on. "I'll be pinched if I miss roll-call. . . . Goodnight all!"

6

Whereupon he gave each of Weiss's hands a final clasp and went striding away towards the hillock on which the reserve artillery was parked. He had made no further mention of his father, nor had he asked for any message to be sent to Silvine, though her name was burning on his lips.

A few more minutes went by; then somewhere to the left of them, where the 2nd Brigade was camped, a bugle sounded the call. Another, closer at hand, responded. Then came a third, a long way off. They were sounding on every side when Gaude, the company bugler, let out a peal of clear, ringing notes. He was a tall, thin, beardless lad with a woebegone face, but who blew into his bugle with gale force.

At this, Sergeant Sapin – a small, prim man with large, vacant eyes – began to call the roll. He rapped out the names in his thin voice while the soldiers, who had gathered round, answered in tones that varied from deep 'cello to high flute. But suddenly there was a break in the flow.

"Lapoulle!" repeated the sergeant, shouting at the top of his voice.

Still no answer. Jean had to dash over to the pile of smouldering logs which Fusilier Lapoulle, egged on by his cronies, was doing his obstinate best to set aflame. Now, lying flat on his belly with his face well cooked, he was blasting the smoke horizontally across the ground. The wood was beginning to turn black.

"Saints preserve us!" yelled Jean. "Let it be, can't you! Answer to your name when it's called!"

Lapoulle scrambled up, bewildered, and appearing to understand what was wanted, he bellowed "Here!" in such a raucous tone that Loubet fell over backwards, overcome with laughter. Pache, who had finished his darning, answered the roll in a barely audible voice, as though muttering a prayer. Chouteau acknowledged his own presence disdainfully, without even rising, and spread himself even more comfortably than before.

Meanwhile the orderly officer, Lieutenant Rochas, stood waiting, motionless, a few yards away. When, at the end of roll-call, Sergeant Sapin went up to him and reported all present and correct, the lieutenant jerked his chin in the direction of Weiss, who was still deep in conversation with Maurice.

"We even have a supernumerary," he growled into his whiskers. "What's that civilian doing here?"

"Special permission of the colonel, sir," Jean explained, who had overheard the question.

7

Rochas shrugged his shoulders with annoyance and, without another word, began to stroll along the line of tents, waiting for lights-out; while Jean, his legs stiff and aching from the long day's march, sat down within a few paces of Maurice. He could hear what was being said, but at first the words merely droned in his ears. He did not listen, for at the back of his dense, slow-moving mind he was a prey to certain shadowy, ill-defined musings of his own.

Maurice was an apologist of war, regarding it as inevitable and as essential to the very life of a nation. He had accepted this idea ever since he had committed himself, unreservedly, to the theory of evolution which was then already exciting all educated young men. What was life itself but a war that had to be waged at every moment? And did not the very laws of nature point to continuous fighting, to the survival of the fittest, to the maintenance and renewal of strength through action, and to the replenishment and rejuvenation of life through death? And he recalled the wonderful sense of exhilaration which had taken hold of him at the thought of enlisting as a soldier and going off to fight at the frontier. Perhaps the electorate, however willingly they might have surrendered France to the Emperor's keeping, did not want this war. He himself, only a week ago, had condemned it as being wrong and idiotic. An argument had arisen over the decision of a Prussian prince to offer himself as a candidate for the Spanish throne; in the confusion which had gradually followed, everyone appeared to be in the wrong – with the result that nobody was in a position to say which side had been guilty of the original act of provocation; all that now remained intact was that fatal law which, at the appointed hour, sets one people against another. A great wave of patriotic feeling had swept through Paris : he thought back to that hot summer evening, to the huge crowds flowing along the boulevards, to the groups of men brandishing torches and shouting : "To Berlin! To Berlin!" He could still hear that woman singing the Marseillaise from the box seat of a carriage outside the Hotel de Ville – a tall, beautiful woman with the profile of a queen, standing draped in the flag of France. Had it all been a meaningless charade, had the heart of Paris not palpitated that night? And then, as always with Maurice, this spell of highly charged enthusiasm had given way to hours of hideous unsureness and revulsion. It was the latter mood which had attended his arrival at the barracks, his official reception by the C.S.M. and his kitting-out under the supervision of a sergeant; it had been intensified by the offensive fug and dirtiness of the barrack room, by the cross familiarity of his new companions and by the soulless drilling which taxed his limbs and dulled his mind. In less than a week, however, he had grown inured to it. And he had regained his enthusiasm when the regiment had at last set out for Belfort.

From the very first, Maurice had felt utterly convinced of victory. As he saw it, the Emperor's plan was clear : the intention was to dispatch four hundred thousand men to the banks of the Rhine, cross the river before the Prussians were ready, and launch a vigorous spearhead attack which would sever communications between northern and southern Germany; a dramatic success of this kind would promptly force Austria and Italy to throw in their lot with France. Had there not been rumours for a while that the 7th Corps, to which his own regiment formed part, was to sail from Brest and be landed in Denmark where it would carry on a diversionary campaign that would keep an entire Prussian army pinned down? The enemy was to be caught unawares, overpowered on every flank and brought to his knees in a matter of weeks. A mere route march from Strasbourg to Berlin. But the long delay at Belfort had left Maurice seriously worried. The 7th Corps, whose mission was to stand guard over the Black Forest "gap", had reached the area in an indescribable state of confusion, well below strength and lacking everything. The third division had yet to arrive from Italy; the second cavalry brigade had been left behind in Lyons, for fear of local riots; and three batteries of artillery had gone astray, no one knew where. In addition, there was an incredible shortage of equipment. The shops in Belfort, which were to have supplied everything, turned out to be empty : no tents, no mess-tins, no cholera-belts, no field medical chests, no portable forges, no hobbles . . . Not a single medical orderly or mechanic. Not until the last moment did it dawn on anyone that thirty thousand spare parts were missing, and that without them it was impossible to service any of the rifles; an officer had been dispatched post-haste to Paris; he had returned with five thousand, and even those had been obtained with the utmost difficulty. Then again, Maurice was distressed that the days should be so inactive. Two whole weeks they had been there : why weren't they moving forward? How clearly he sensed that every day wasted in Belfort was an irreparable blunder, a chance of victory tossed away. And instead of the ideal plan, there was the sad reality of what was

9

being done in practice; even then he was harassed by intimations of this truth, though the details were not clear to him until much later. It alarmed him to think of the seven army corps diffused – "echeloned", to use the official term – all the way along the frontier, from Metz to Bitche and from Bitche to Belfort; of unit after unit so gravely undermanned that the total force was reduced from four hundred thousand to, at most, two hundred and thirty thousand; of the generals eaten up with jealousy for one another, each determined to win his baton of Maréchal de France without lending support to his neighbour; of the most fearful lack of foresight; of mobilization and concentration "synchronized" in the interests of speed, a process which resulted in inextricable muddle; and finally of the creeping paralysis which began at the very top, in the person of the sick Emperor who was incapable of coming to quick and firm decisions. This paralysis was to invade the whole army, disorganizing it, annihilating it, plunging it into the worst disasters without a chance to defend itself. And yet, apprehensive as he was in this dull waiting period, Maurice still felt an intuitive thrill when he thought of the ultimate prospect. His confidence in victory was an unwavering as ever.

Suddenly, on August 3, had come the startling news of the previous day's victory at Saarbrucken. Whether it was a great victory remained to be seen. But the newspapers were brimming over with enthusiasm : this marked the invasion of Germany, the first step in the triumphant advance. And a legend was born – of the young Prince Imperial who had calmly picked up a bullet on the field of battle. Then, two days later, reports had come in of the surprise destruction of Wissembourg, and a cry of rage went up throughout France. Five thousand men, caught in a trap, had held out for ten hours against thirty-five thousand Prussians : that cowardly massacre was simply crying out to be avenged! No doubt those in authority had been guilty of seeing no further than their noses and taking inadequate precautions. But all that was about to be set right! MacMahon had summoned the first division of the 7th Corps, and the 1st Corps was to be supported by the 5th : the Prussians must have scurried back across the Rhine by this time, with the bayonets of French infantryman prodding their backs. And the idea of there having been furious fighting that day gave rise to an ever-intensifying longing for news, so that a general feeling of restless concern was spreading moment by moment beneath the fading sky.

"No doubt about it," Maurice was insisting, "we'll have given them a real good hiding today!"

Weiss did not answer, but merely nodded his head with a look of concern. He too was gazing eastwards towards the Rhine, which was now completely enveloped in night – a dark wall enshrouded in mystery. Since the final bugle calls, a deep silence had settled upon the benumbed camp, broken solely by the voices and footsteps of a few soldiers still astir. A light twinkled in the main room of the farmhouse where the staff officers put off going to sleep while they waited for the despatches which came in hour after hour – though as yet these brought no definite news. And the pile of unseasoned wood, abandoned at last, was still smouldering dismally; a light breeze wafted the smoke over the unquiet house, blotting out the first stars in the sky.

"A real good hiding," Weiss repeated at long last. "God grant you are right!"

Jean, still sitting only a few yards away, pricked up his ears; while Lieutenant Rochas, who had overheard this tremulous admission of doubt, stopped in his tracks and listened.

"What!" cried Maurice. "You mean to say you are not absolutely confident? Do you really believe in the possibility of defeat?"

His brother-in-law flung out his arms to stem the flow of words. Weiss's hands were quivering, and his kindly face had turned pale and acquired a look of consternation.

"Defeat? Heaven forbid . . .! I come from these parts, don't forget. Both my grandparents were butchered by the Cossacks in 1814; and whenever I think of the invasion I clench my fists and would willingly go off and fight as a common soldier, dressed exactly as I am tonight. . . . Defeat? Oh, no! I won't accept the possibility of that!"

He recovered his composure; but then his shoulders sagged, as though beneath an intolerable burden.

"Only . . . well, how can you expect me to have an easy mind? I know all there is to know about my Alsace; I've just crossed the length of it again, and wherever our business took us we saw things that the generals have preferred to shut their eyes to. . . . Oh, we wanted this war with Prussia right enough : for years we've been patiently biding our time till we had the chance to pay off old scores. But that didn't stop us from living on friendly terms with Baden and Bavaria, and we all of us have friends or relatives across the Rhine. We even thought that they, like us, were secretly longing

11

to break the unbearable arrogance of the Prussians. You know that ordinarily we are a calm and disciplined people, and yet for over a fortnight we have been filled with impatience and alarm by the way in which things have gone from bad to worse. Ever since war was declared, enemy horsemen have been allowed to terrorize villages, carry out reconnaissance and cut telegraph wires. The whole of Baden and Bavaria are rising and enormous troop movements are being carried out in the Palatinate. Information coming in from markets and fairs all over the countryside make it quite obvious that the frontier is seriously threatened. But when villagers and local mayors at last begin to panic and go along to lay these facts before passing officers, what happens? The officers shrug their shoulders and dismiss all such talk as fanciful and lily-livered; the enemy is miles and miles away. . . . It's hard to credit! Here we are without a moment to lose, and yet day after day is going to waste! What are we waiting for? For the whole might of Germany to come crashing down on us?"

He spoke in quiet, disconsolate tones, as though voicing for his own benefit thoughts which had long been maturing in his mind.

"Ah! I know Germany almost as well as I know Alsace, and the terrible thing is that to the rest of you, apparently, it's as big a mystery as China. . . . Listen, Maurice, you will probably remember my cousin Gunther – he paid me a brief visit in Sedan last spring. His mother is my mother's sister. She married a Berliner and the son could hardly be more German : he feels nothing but hatred for France. Today he is serving as a captain in the Prussian Guards. I've never forgotten the way he snapped at me, the evening I saw him off at the station : 'If France declares war on us, she is in for a beating.' "

So far Lieutenant Rochas had succeeded in containing himself, but at these words he strode forward angrily. He was a tall, thin fellow, almost fifty years of age, with a long, bony, weather-beaten face. His huge hooked nose descended to a greying, bristly moustache and a wide, fierce-willed but kindly natured mouth. His temper was up.

"Now see here!" he thundered. "What the hell do you mean by undermining the men's morale?"

Jean held aloof from the quarrel, but in his heart he felt that the lieutenant was right. He too, even though he was beginning to be shocked by the long delays and by the chaotic nature of their movements, had never been in any doubt that the Prussians were in for a terrible hiding. Could anything be more certain, when he and his comrades had come all this way for no other purpose?

"Why, lieutenant," answered Weiss, much taken aback, "I have no intention of undermining anybody's morale. On the contrary, I should like everyone to know what I know – forewarned is fore-armed. . . . Just think how Germany . . ."

And with admirable clarity he went on to explain his fears. He talked of the greater might of Prussia since Sadowa; of the upsurge of nationalist feeling which was placing her at the head of the other German states; of that whole vast Empire-in-the-making, which had on its side youth, enthusiasm, and the irresistible force of its united determination to conquer. He spoke too of the system of compulsory military service which was turning the country into an armed camp, well-trained, thoroughly disciplined, endowed with a huge reserve of arms and ammunition, prepared for war on a large scale, still preening itself over its crushing defeat of Austria. Then there was the intelligence and resourcefulness of the Prussian army: its senior officers were young, almost without exception, and its commander-in-chief seemed destined to revolutionize the techniques of war – where was the man who could match him for vigilance and farsightedness or equal his perfect clarity of vision?

When he had finished painting this daunting picture of Germany, Weiss turned his attention to France. The Empire was old and worn: it might continue to be acclaimed by popular vote but it was rotted at its very foundations. Having blurred all sense of patriotism by its attacks on human freedom, it now – once again, but this time too late – seemed liable to collapse the moment it ceased to gratify the self-indulgent cravings which it had fostered. True, the army had retained its traditional gallantry and was still resplendently wreathed in the laurels of Italy and the Crimea, but even here there were faults: rich young men could still purchase the right to have others serve in their stead; attitudes formed in North Africa were too rigidly clung to, and so great was the general confidence in victory that no one could be bothered to master the new techniques of war. And last but not least there were the generals, mediocre for the most part, consumed by their personal rivalries, in a few cases quite stunningly ignorant, under the leader-ship of the Emperor, sick and vacillating, duping himself and duping others as to the nature of this fearful enterprise – into which they were all plunging like blind men, without any preparation

13

worthy of the name, but rather in the panicky confusion of cattle driven to the slaughter-house.

Rochas stood listening, wide-eyed and open-mouthed. His awesome nose had wrinkled up. Then, suddenly, he opted in favour of laughter – of laughter so unrestrained that it creased his jaws from side to side.

"What the devil are you talking about? Where's the sense in what you say? Why, there isn't a grain of sense in the whole long rigmarole – it's too absurd for a man to bother his head about. . . . You may get a raw recruit to listen to you, but not me. Oh no! Not an old soldier with twenty-seven years' service!"

And he thumped his chest with his fist. Born in Paris, the son of a bricklayer's mate from Limousin province, he had been so appalled by his father's lot in life that he had enlisted when he was still only eighteen. He had worked his way up from the ranks, serving first as a common soldier, then as a corporal in Africa and a sergeant at Sebastapol. Only after Solferino did he obtain a commission : it had taken him fifteen years of rough living and heroic bravery to rise thus far, but he had had so little formal education that he could never be promoted captain.

"You talk as though you knew everything, *monsieur,* but here's something you don't know . . . I fought at Mazagram when I was barely turned nineteen; there were only a hundred and twenty-three of us, all told, and for four whole days we held out against twelve thousand Arabs. . . . Oh yes, you should have been out in Africa with us, at Mascara and Biskra and Dellys, and later on in Grand Kabylia and at Laghouat; year in, year out, you would have seen those dirty niggers run like hares whenever we showed our faces. . . . And you ought to have been with us at Sebastapol, *monsieur* – damn it, no one can pretend life was easy. Gales strong enough to loosen every hair in your head; freezing cold, day and night; the bugler sounding the alarm again and again and again. And when it was all over, those ruffians blew everything sky-high! But that didn't stop us blowing *them* sky-high and frying them alive . . .! And Solferino! You weren't there, my friend, so what right have you to talk about it? Solferino! That day was a real scorcher, even though the skies shed more water than you're ever likely to have seen. Solferino! We gave the Austrians such a drubbing – if only you could have seen how they ran from our bayonets, falling over one another, as though someone had set fire to their breeches!"

He was jubilant. All the old gaiety of France's military traditions rang in his laughter. He was exulting in the myth of the gallant French soldier wandering the length and breadth of the earth with his lady-love on one arm and a bottle of good wine under the other, of the whole wide world put in its place to the merry sound of drinking songs. One corporal, a squad of four, and mighty armies bit the dust.

"Beaten!" he roared with sudden fury. "Are you seriously suggesting that France could be beaten? Do you really think those Prussian pigs could beat such men as us?"

He stepped briskly forward and seized one of the lapels of Weiss's frock-coat. Every inch of his tall, slim, knight-errantly frame conveyed unmitigated contempt for any foe, at any time, in any place.

"Take my word for it – if the Prussians have the gall to show themselves, we'll soon boot their behinds back where they belong. . . . Do you hear me? We'll boot their behinds all the way to Berlin!"

So saying, he flung his arm out haughtily with the easy assurance of a child, the openhearted conviction of a simpleton who knows nothing and fears nothing.

"By heaven, yes! There are no two ways about it!"

Weiss, nonplussed and almost convinced, was quick to declare that he asked for nothing better. As for Maurice, he had held his peace till now, not wishing to speak out of turn in the presence of his superior; but at this point he added his voice to Rochas's gale of laughter. As a rule Maurice looked upon him as a brainless fool, but at the moment he found him heartwarming. Similarly Jean had been nodding his head in approval of the lieutenant's every word. He too had fought at Solferino, where it had rained so hard. Here was the kind of talk that a man could understand! If only the rest of the officers had talked like this, the men would have shut their eyes to the shortage of mess-tins and cholera-belts!

Night had closed in long ago – but Rochas went on waving his long arms and talking in the dark. He had only ever struggled through one book : a pedlar had sold him a volume celebrating the victories of the first Napoleon, and he had carried it round in his knapsack for years. Tonight he could not still his feelings, and all his learning came surging out in an impetuous cry.

"Austria trounced at Castiglione and Marengo, at Austerlitz and Wagram! Prussia trounced at Eylam and Jena and Lutzen! Russia trounced at Friedland, Smolensk, Moscow! Spain and England

15

trounced wherever we have encountered them! The entire globe trounced from side to side and pole to pole. . . . Why should we be trounced now? You must think this a topsy-turvy world if you can imagine such a thing!"

He drew himself up to an even greater height, raising his arm like a flagstaff.

"Listen, there has been heavy fighting today and over at headquarters they're all waiting for news. Well, I'll tell you the news here and now . . .! The Prussians have been licked, torn to shreds, blown to smithereens!"

At that moment a loud, doleful cry swept past beneath the sombre heavens. Was it the squeal of some night bird? Was it a voice of mystery, come from afar, laden with tears? The whole camp, enfolded in darkness, resounded with it; it extended and intensified the general mood of anxiety that resulted from the long wait for dispatches. Inside the distant farmhouse the candle-flame lighting the anxious vigil of the senior officers was burning taller, as still and upright as the flame of a taper in church.

It was ten o'clock – and Gaude, the bugler, springing up from the dark earth into which he had vanished, was first to sound lights-out. The other bugles responded, dying away by degrees in a dwindling fanfare, as though the players were already benumbed with sleep. Then Weiss, who had stayed so long, gave Maurice an affectionate hug and bade him be of good heart. He promised to give Henriette her brother's love and deliver good wishes to Uncle Fouchard. But just as he was leaving, a sudden excited rumour swept through the camp : the Crown Prince of Prussia had been taken prisoner with twenty-five thousand men and the enemy army had been driven back and destroyed, leaving its artillery and supplies in the hands of the French.

"There – what did I tell you?" boomed Rochas.

And delightedly pursuing Weiss, who was heading rapidly back towards Mulhouse : "I told you we'd kick 'em in the arse, and so we shall, *monsieur* – all the way to Berlin!" But a quarter of an hour later another dispatch reported that the army had been compelled to abandon Wörth and was falling back.

What a night! Rochas, broken with fatigue, wrapped himself in his greatcoat and fell asleep on the ground, as he often did, with no thought of sheltering his head. Maurice and Jean had crept into the tent, where Loubet and Chouteau and Pache and Lapoulle already lay huddled together, using their knapsacks as pillows. A

16

tent could hold six men, provided they slept with their legs curled up. At first Loubet had played havoc with their hunger by kidding Lapoulle that chicken was on the menu next morning. But they were too tired; already they were snoring away – the Prussians could come, for all they cared. For a moment Jean lay pressed against Maurice, without moving. Weary as he was, it was taking him a long time to get to sleep. Every point that the civilian had made was going round and round in his brain : Germany an armed camp, with troops beyond number, ready to devour everything in their path. . . . And Jean sensed that his companion was as wide-awake as he, and thinking the same thoughts. Then Maurice fidgeted and drew away, and Jean realized that he was causing annoyance. The instinctive hostility between peasant and man of education, the feeling of disgust inspired by different class and different upbringing, constantly gave rise to a sense of almost physical discomfort. The knowledge of this made Jean ashamed and sad at heart; he did his best to render himself inconspicuous and thereby evade the hostile contempt which he could sense in Maurice. Although the night air was turning cool, the atmosphere in the crowded tent was so stifling that Maurice, feeling intolerably hot and restless, suddenly darted out and lay down several yards away. Jean, feeling wretched, sank into a half-waking nightmare in which his sorrow at being disliked was mingled with forebodings of a terrible disaster, which he seemed to hear galloping towards him out of the depth of the unknown.

Several hours must have gone by. It was as though the entire camp, dark and still as ever, were being crushed out of existence by the boundless, gloomy night which was heavy with the presence of something monstrous but as yet without a name. The sound of violent twitching emerged from a pool of deep shadow, a sudden gurgle came from an unseen tent. These noises were followed by others which could not be identified – the snorting of a horse, the sudden clatter of a sword, the fleeing footsteps of a late prowler; each was accountable and unremarkable, yet seemed full of sinister overtones. Then, without warning, a powerful light flared up beside the canteens, casting a fierce glow upon the weapons stacked along the colour-lines and giving the bright, smooth rifle-barrels a red glint, as though they had been smeared with fresh blood. The sentries loomed dark and upright in the unexpected glare. Could it be the enemy, whom the staff had announced two whole days ago, and for whom they had come from Belfort to Mulhouse? But

17

at that moment the flame died down amid a great shower of sparks. It was merely the pile of unseasoned wood which Lapoulle had tussled with for so long; after smouldering for hours it had blazed up like a bundle of straw.

Now it was Jean's turn to hurry out of the tent, startled by the glare, and he nearly stumbled over Maurice, who had propped himself up on one elbow and was looking at the scene. Already darkness had fallen again, thicker than ever. The two men remained stretched out on the bare ground, a few feet apart. There was nothing to be descried, in the dense gloom confronting them, apart from the light of the candle still burning forlornly in the parlour window of the farmhouse, as if guarding a corpse. What time could it be? Two o'clock, or three perhaps. . . . The staff officers had certainly not yet gone to bed. The booming voice of General Bourgain-Desfeuilles could be heard quite clearly; he had been put out of temper by this long vigil, and would have been unable to endure it without the support of drinks and cigars. New telegrams were coming in; presumably the position was deteriorating, for the shadowy figures of dispatch riders were coming and going with panicky haste. There was a stamping of feet, a volley of oaths, and then a sound like the stifled scream of a man at the moment of death. The subsequent silence was appalling. Could it really be that the end had come? An icy blast had swept across the camp, as it lay prostrate with sleep and dread.

Just then a tall, slim figure hurried past, instantly recognizable to Jean and Maurice as Colonel de Vineuil. It became apparent that he was with Major Bouroche, a man of bulky figure and leonine head. They were exchanging fragments of conversation, as disjointed and hard to hear as words uttered in a bad dream.

". . . the news from Basle . . . the whole of our first division destroyed . . . twelve hours' fighting . . . the entire army in retreat . . ."

The colonel came to a standstill and hailed another figure who – slight and dapper – was fast approaching them.

"Is that you, Beaudoin?"

"Yes, colonel."

"Oh, what news! MacMahon beaten at Froeschwiller, Frossard beaten at Spickeren, de Failly pinned down helplessly between them. . . . At Froeschwiller a single corps did wonders against a complete army. But all our defences have been swept away. There is rout and panic everywhere. France is wide open to attack . . ."

Tears were choking him, and his next words were lost as the shadowy trio moved on and melted into the darkness.

Maurice had scrambled up, quivering in every fibre of his being.

"My God!" he gasped.

It was all he could find to say – while Jean, his heart turned to ice, muttered: "Ah, the tragedy of it! Seems your brother-in-law was right, after all, when he said they were more than a match for us."

Maurice was so beside himself that he could have strangled Jean. The Prussians more than a match for the French! The very idea was a bludgeon to his pride. But already the peasant was adding, with his old calm obstinacy: "Makes no difference, mind. A man doesn't give in just because he has been hit once. . . . This mustn't stop us hitting back."

But by this time a tall human shape had drawn itself erect immediately in front of them. They saw that it was Rochas, still enfolded in his greatcoat. He had been roused from his heavy slumbers by the stray sounds, and perhaps even by the whiff of defeat. He interrogated them, impatient to learn the truth.

When he had at last groped his way to an understanding of the facts, a look of utter stupefaction appeared in his vacant, child-like eyes.

More than a dozen times he repeated: "Beaten! What do you mean, 'beaten'? Why ever should we be beaten?"

Now, in the East, the first pallor of day was appearing; an infinitely sad, dank greyness showed above the slumbering tents and began to reveal, within one of them, the ashen faces of Loubet, Lapoulle, Chouteau and Pache, still snoring away, open-mouthed. A grief-stricken dawn was breaking among the black haze that had mounted from the distant river.

II

AT ABOUT eight o'clock the sun dispersed the heavy clouds and a hot and flawless August sun shone over Mulhouse, at the centre of the broad, fertile plain. From the camp, wide-awake now and buzzing with life, the bells of every parish church for miles around could be heard pealing out in the clear air. The disasters of this Sunday morning were hidden behind the cheerful blue sky of a holiday.

All of a sudden Gaude sounded his bugle : it was time to collect rations. Loubet looked astonished. What could possibly be in store for them? Not, by any chance, the chicken which he had promised Lapoulle the night before? The casual offspring of a Les Halles barrow-woman, Loubet had joined the army "so as to make a bit of money", after trying his hand at everything else. He was the resident glutton, a man forever scenting out titbits, and he hurried off to take a look while Chouteau, the resident artist – a house-painter from Montmartre, handsome and full of revolutionary ideas (how furious he was at being called up again, when he had already served his time!) – subjected Pache to a bout of merciless taunting; he had just caught him down on his knees, praying, at the back of the tent. So they had a Holy Joe among them! Why couldn't he ask his God for a hundred thousand a year? But Pache – a puny little man with a sharply pointed head, who came from some remote village in Picardy – endured these jibes with the long-suffering silence of a martyr. He was the resident butt – together with Lapoulle, the wild man from the Salogne who had sprouted to giant proportions somewhere in that marshy province (he was so completely ignorant that on the day he joined the regiment he had asked to see the King). And although the disastrous news from Froeschwiller had been going the rounds since reveille, the four men were laughing and setting about their usual tasks with their habitual and mechanical lack of feeling.

A few minutes later, however, a jeer of surprise rang out. It was prompted by the sight of Jean and Maurice returning with some firewood. At last the regiment was receiving the supply of wood for which it had waited in vain the day before, when the time had come round for the evening meal. Only twelve hours late.

"Ah, where would we be without the supply wallahs?" mocked Chouteau.

"Never mind, it's done now," said Loubet. "Just wait till you savour the lovely stew I'm going to cook for you!"

As a rule he gladly took charge of the cooking; and this earned him general thanks, for his meals were delicious. On all such occasions, however, he would subject Lapoulle to a series of weird and wonderful demands.

"Go and fetch the champagne," he would say, "go and fetch the truffles . . ."

On this particular morning an exceptionally weird idea came into his head, with which this Paris street-urchin could tease the life out of the simpleton.

"Buck up, now!" he said. "Hand me the chicken."

"Chicken?" said Lapoulle. "What chicken? Where?"

"Why, there on the ground beside you. . . . The chicken I promised you. The chicken the corporal brought back with him just now."

He was pointing at a large white pebble which lay at their feet. Lapoulle was too startled, at first, to say or do anything; but in the end he picked up the pebble and began to turn it this way and that.

"What the devil are you gawking at? Wash that chicken, can't you! Get on with it – wash its feet, wash its neck. Give it a thorough soaking, you lazy hound!"

And just for a joke, because the prospect of a good meal had awakened his humour, he tossed the pebble into the boiling pot so that it lay with the meat.

"*That* ought to give the stew a bit of flavour! Don't tell me you weren't alive to the idea, you great dolt! Why, you can't be alive to anything . . .! You shall have the parson's nose – that'll show you how tender it is!"

The rest of the squad were shaking their sides with laughter at the expression of Loubet's face: he was quite won over to the idea, by this time, and licking his chops in anticipation. What a good chap Loubet was – never a chance of getting bored with him around! And when the fire crackled in the sunlight and the pot began to sing, they all gathered round like gladdened worshippers,

21

watching the meat dance and inhaling the pleasant aroma that was already starting to spread. They had been ravenously hungry ever since the day before, and the thought of eating was driving all else from their minds. The army might be beaten, but a man still had to satisfy the needs of his stomach. Fires were blazing and pots bubbling throughout the length and breadth of the camp. Everyone was singing, eagerly and cheerfully, while the clear peal of the bells continued to ring out from every parish church.

But shortly before nine o'clock a commotion spread through the camp. Officers began to rush about and Lieutenant Rochas, in response to an order from Captain Beaudoin, came striding along the line of tents erected by his platoon.

"Come on, get everything stowed away. We're pulling out."

"But what about the meal?"

"The meal will have to wait. We're pulling out at once."

Gaude's bugle was ringing out imperiously. The order gave rise to a general mood of consternation and suppressed fury. What! March away on empty stomachs? Surely they could wait another hour, until the meal was ready! Well, thought Loubet and the others, at least we'll drink the broth. But as yet the broth was no more than hot water, and the uncooked meat was as resistant to the teeth as leather. Chouteau stood growling angrily. Jean had to intervene and make them hurry with their packing. Why the sudden urgency? What possible justification was there for rushing people off their feet like this, before they'd had time to restore their energies? Maurice heard some of the men claiming that they were setting off to meet the Prussians and get their own back, but he greeted the words with an incredulous shrug. In less than a quarter of an hour the entire force had struck camp; all tents had been dismantled, folded away, fastened to knapsacks, all rifles had been redistributed, and the ground was bare once more except for the dying embers of the mess-fires.

General Douay had grave reasons for deciding in favour of immediate retreat. The dispatch from the Sub-Prefect of Schelestadt, already three days old, was now confirmed : later reports stated that the camp-fires of the Prussian units threatening Markolsheim had been observed again, while another telegram announced that an enemy army corps was crossing the Rhine at Huningue. Precise details were pouring in : cavalry and artillery sighted, infantry converging on their rallying-point from every direction. There seemed to be no doubt about it : even an hour's delay and the line of retreat to Belfort would be cut off. In the aftermath of the defeats at Wissembourg and Froeschwiller, the general – isolated and exposed – had no choice but to fall back as quickly as possible, especially as this morning's news was even worse than last night's.

The staff had ridden on ahead, digging their spurs in hard for fear that the Prussians might have stolen a march on them and be lying in wait at Altkirch. General Bourgain-Desfeuilles, foreseeing a hard day's march, had taken the precaution of proceeding by way of Mulhouse where he had eaten a hearty breakfast, inveighing bitterly against the unseemly bustle. And the people of Mulhouse were sick at heart when they saw the officers riding away. As soon as they got wind of the retreat, the inhabitants poured into the streets, bewailing the precipitous departure of troops for whose presence they had clamoured. Could it really be that the untold wealth of material assembled in the railway station was to be abandoned to the enemy, and that they themselves would be reduced to the level of a captive community by nightfall? In the same way the families living in the villages and isolated houses along the country roads had stationed themselves in their doorways, overcome with fear and confusion. Only yesterday they had seen these same regiments going by on their way to battle; now they were pulling out, running away without even firing a shot! The commanders wore gloomy expressions and urged their horses on, fighting shy of all questions as though disaster were in hot pursuit of them. So it was true that the Prussians had crushed the army and were pouring into France on every hand, like the floodwaters of a river? And already the peasants, gripped by a mounting sense of panic, imagined that they could hear, in the silent air, the distant but swelling rumble of invasion; and carts were being loaded with possessions, whole houses were being emptied, and a long procession of families was fleeing along the roadways in the path of this sudden terror.

So great was the confusion of the retreat that on reaching the bridge over the Rhine-Rhône Canal the 106th was brought to a standstill before it had covered even a mile. The marching orders, poorly phrased and still more poorly executed, had resulted in the pile-up of the entire second division at one point; and the bridge was so narrow – barely sixteen feet from side to side – that the operation seemed likely to go on for ever.

Two hours went by, and still the 106th waited, unbudging, as the never-ending stream flowed past. The men stood in the hot sunshine, with their arms at the order and the full weight of their kit on their backs. Their impatience boiled over at last.

"Seems we're to act as rearguard," said Loubet, as sarcastically as ever.

But Chouteau flew into a rage.

"They just want to muck us about – that's the only reason we've been left to stew. We got here first; we ought to be miles away by now."

As the units on the other side of the canal proceeded along the flat roads that divided the hop-fields from the acres of standing corn, it became obvious that the army was in full retreat and marching back along the selfsame route as it had traversed the day before. The realization was giving rise to angry derision.

"Ah, so we're making a run for it!" added Chouteau. "They keep on about 'advancing to meet the enemy'; this is a damned funny way of doing it, I must say. . . . Seriously though, our generals take the palm for sheer pluck. First they march us here, then they march us back – before we've even had time to eat our soup."

At this the men's aggravated laughter grew louder than ever. And Maurice, standing next to Chouteau, had to admit that he was right. They had spent two whole hours stationed here like gate-posts, so why couldn't they have been allowed to cook their meal and eat it in peace? Hunger was tightening its hold again, and their thoughts were dark and bitter as they recalled how the uncooked ingredients had been tipped from the pot. They could not fathom the need for this extraordinary haste, which to their way of looking was stupid and cowardly. What were they supposed to be? Hares?

But at this point Lieutenant Rochas let fly at Sergeant Sapin, accusing him and his men of outrageous conduct. And Captain Beaudoin wandered over, his attention attracted by the noise.

"Silence in the ranks!"

Jean meantime had held his peace, as befitted a veteran of the Italian campaign; no one could be more thoroughly used to discipline. But he stared at Maurice, who appeared to find Chouteau's angry and resentful jibes amusing; and this shocked him – for how could a gentleman, a young fellow of so much education, possibly lend his approval to thoughts which, even if they turned out to be true, ought never to be voiced aloud? If every private soldier started condemning the generals and setting forth his own ideas, the outlook for the army would indeed be a bleak one.

Finally, after another hour's wait, the 106th received the order to move forward. The bridge, however, was still so congested by the tail-end of the division that the direst confusion resulted. Several regiments became hopelessly entangled; some companies were swept hurriedly across the bridge, despite the chaos, while others were pushed to the edge of the roadway and had to mark time. And just to add to the mess, a squadron of cavalry insisted on riding across; the stragglers already being shed by the infantry were forced back into the neighbouring fields. The result was that by the end of the first hour of the withdrawal, a considerable number of men were lagging behind, strung out at the rear of the main force as though deliberately taking their time.

Which was how Jean and his squad – for he would not abandon them – found themselves far adrift, in the hollow of a sunken road. The 106th had vanished : there was not a man or officer in sight who belonged to the same company. The only troops in the vicinity were individual soldiers, a haphazard assembly of strangers, each of them exhausted almost at the outset of the day's march and each of them proceeding at his own pace, bound for wherever his footsteps guided him. It was an extremely hot day and the sun beat down relentlessly. The men's packs, made heavier by the tents and all the complicated equipment with which they were crammed, were a terrible weight on their shoulders. Many of them were quite unused to carrying such a load, and for them the thick greatcoats, like leaden shrouds, were quite heavy enough. All of a sudden a small, pale soldier, his eyes filled with tears, stopped and flung his pack into a ditch, with a deep sigh and the heavy breathing of a man shaking off a mortal illness and returning to the world of the living.

"Now there's a soldier with the right idea," murmured Chouteau.

He kept on the move, however, rounding his back under the weight. But when he saw two others shed their loads, he could hold out no longer.

"Ah, to hell with it !" he cried.

And with a jerk of the shoulders he heaved his pack on to the grassy bank. He had been trudging about quite long enough, thank you, with half a hundredweight on his back. Anyone would think they were beasts of burden, the way they were expected to cart all that with them !

Almost at once, Loubet followed his example and coerced Lapoulle into doing the same. Pache, who blessed himself each time they went past a stone cross, undid his webbing and carefully laid the entire bundle at the foot of a low wall, as though he anticipated coming back for it. And Maurice was the only member of the squad still wearing a pack when Jean, glancing round, saw what his men had been up to.

"Pick those packs up. . . . What are you trying to do? Get me courtmartialled?"

But the squad, though not rebelling openly as yet, marched onwards with looks of mute resentment, thrusting the corporal ahead of them, farther along the narrow lane.

"Kindly pick up your packs or I shall put you on a charge."

It was as though Maurice had been lashed across the face with a whip. A charge! That clod was going to put them on a charge because, poor devils, they had sought to bring relief to their aching muscles. And in a paroxysm of blind anger, he in turn unbuckled his webbing and, staring defiantly at Jean, let his pack fall by the roadside.

"Very well," the corporal said quietly, realizing that physical compulsion was not a practical possibility. "We'll deal with it this evening."

Maurice's feet were causing him dreadful pain. He had not yet grown used to these big, heavy boots and they had chafed the skin until it bled. He was of a rather delicate constitution, and the heavy bruising caused by the pack on his spine was like a raw wound. He no longer knew which arm to use for carrying his rifle; the weight of it was enough to take his breath away. But he was even more distressed by his anguish of mind, having fallen into one of those fits of despair to which he was prone. Suddenly – so suddenly that he had no chance to offer any resistance – his willpower would collapse and he would give way to evil impulses, to a spell of complete self-abandon which would afterwards reduce him to tears of shame. His misdeeds in Paris had never been anything but the acts of madness committed by what he termed his "other self", by the weakling he turned into at moments of desperation – a creature capable of the vilest conduct. And now that he was shuffling along under the fierce sun, taking part in this retreat which was so akin to a rout, he felt he was no more than an animal in this sluggish, broken herd strewn about the country roads. It was a nervous reaction from the news of defeat, from the thunder which had rolled miles and miles away, in a distant corner of the sky; and the echo of that thunder continued to pursue these men as they fled without having set eyes on a single enemy soldier. What hope could they

26

entertain now? Surely it was all over? They were beaten, and there was only one thing to do : lie down and go to sleep.

"What does it matter?" cried Loubet, shouting at the top of his voice and laughing like the barrow-boy he had once been. "Wherever else we may be bound for, it isn't Berlin!"

"Ber – lin! Ber – lin!" Maurice still seemed to hear the sustained roar of the crowds thronging the boulevards on that night of wild enthusiasm which had decided him in favour of enlisting. The wind had veered round, turning squally. How horrifying was its change of direction, and how typical of the Gallic temperament was the manner in which the nation's mood of heady confidence had given way abruptly, at the first setback, to the sense of despair which hounded these troops – beaten and disorganized before a shot had been fired.

"This bloody gun isn't half making my arms ache!" continued Loubet, transferring once again his rifle from one shoulder to the other. "Fancy having to lug a thing like this about!" Then, alluding to the sum of money which he had received for doing another man's military service : "Say what you like, fifteen hundred francs is a damned poor reward for a job like this . . .! Think of the rich lay-about I'm to get crocked for! I bet he's sitting with his feet up, having a good old smoke. . . ."

"What about me!" growled Chouteau. "I'd served my time and they were just about to send me on release. . . . Ah, you're right – it's a black day for anyone, getting sucked into a mess like this!"

He was swinging his rifle back and forth with every sign of anger. Then, in a fit of fury, he hurled it over the hedge.

"There! And good riddance to the blasted thing!"

The rifle spun round twice before thudding into a furrow, where it lay flat and still as a corpse. Already other rifles were following in its wake. Soon the field was full of discarded weapons lying stiff and forlorn in the taxing heat of the sun. A contagious fit of madness had taken hold of the men; it stemmed from their footsore condition, from the hunger gnawing within them, from the humiliation of marching back along these roads and from the unexpected defeat which continued to resound menacingly behind them. What had they to look forward to? The generals had bolted, there were no food supplies; they were so angry and depressed that they simply longed for the whole thing to be over and done with – although as yet it had not even started. So the rifles might as well go the same way as the packs. And in a mindless outburst of fury, to the

27

accompaniment of snickers that would have been more appropriate to lunatics at play, rifles went flying through the air along the whole length of the line of stragglers which spread like a tail as far as the eye could see.

Before ridding himself of his gun, Loubet twirled it round and round like a drum-major's baton. To Lapoulle, the antics of the others must have suggested that throwing away one's rifle was all part of the drill; and he quickly followed their example. But Pache was deterred from doing so by the obscure sense of duty which he owed to his religious upbringing. He continued to carry his rifle despite the abuse showered upon him by Chouteau, who called him a "priest's pet".

"Did you ever see such a goody-goody . . .? And all because his old peasant mother made him swallow Gentle Jesus every Sunday . . .! Why don't you clear off and serve Mass? There's not much spunk in a man who won't stand by his mates!"

Maurice plodded on in silence, looking very gloomy and bowing his head beneath the blazing sky. By this time the landscape surrounding his monstrously tired limbs was that of a bleak, ghost-ridden nightmare. It was as though he were advancing towards an abyss in the full knowledge that it lay somewhere ahead, waiting to engulf him. The experience was undermining his whole outlook as an educated man; it was dragging him down to the level of the wretches who surrounded him.

"Do you know," he said suddenly, turning to Chouteau, "you're absolutely right!"

And Maurice had already set his rifle down on a pile of stones when Jean, who was vainly trying to make a stand against this appalling breach of regulations, turned round and caught him. He came rushing over.

"Pick that rifle up! Pick it up this minute, do you hear?"

A terrible wave of anger had suddenly coursed through Jean, bringing the blood to his cheeks. He was so placid as a rule, always ready to smooth things over, but now his eyes were blazing and his voice had grown loud and dictatorial. His men had never seen him like this before. They halted in surprise.

"Pick that rifle up this minute, or you'll have me to answer to!"

Maurice was quivering with rage. He confined his answer to a single word, making it sound as abusive as possible.

"Peasant!"

"That's it – you've hit the nail right on the head. I *am* a peasant. Whereas you, of course, are a gentleman. . . . And for that very reason you're a pig – yes, a dirty pig. And I make no bones about it."

This provoked a number of boos and jeers, but the corporal raged on with extraordinary intensity : "If a man has the good fortune to be educated, he shows it. . . . We may well be a set of louts and bumpkins – all the more reason for you to set us a good example, seeing that you know so much more than we do. . . . Pick that rifle up, by God, or I'll have you in front of a firing squad as soon as the regiment makes camp."

Maurice was crushed. He picked his rifle up. Tears of anger blurred his vision. He stumbled forward, lurching about like a drunk. The men around him were scoffing at him, now, for knuckling under. Oh, that Jean! The hate Maurice felt for him was imperishable. He had been cut to the quick by the ferocity of the reprimand, though in his heart he knew that it was merited. And when Chouteau, marching at his side, growled that the best thing to do with a corporal like that was get him on the battlefield and put a bullet through his brains, Maurice saw red and pictured himself, quite clearly, cornering Jean one dark night and battering his skull in.

But suddenly the attention of the squad was diverted to another quarter. Loubet noticed that while the quarrel was going on Pache had at last disposed of his weapon, setting it down quietly and carefully at the foot of a bank. Why had he changed his mind? He made no attempt to explain it, but merely laughed to himself with a mixture of relish and bashfulness, like a normally well-behaved schoolboy caught up to mischief. He looked much more cheerful and frisky as he marched along with his arms dangling free. And so the shambling retreat continued along the interminable, sun-strewn roads, past the changeless succession of cornfields and hopfields. Without their packs and rifles, the stragglers were merely a wandering horde of tramps and beggars at whose approach every cottage door was bolted in panic.

At that moment an incident occurred which brought Maurice to the ultimate pitch of fury. There was a low rumbling sound somewhere in the distance. It was the reserve artillery. The gunners had been last to leave camp, but suddenly the first of them rounded a bend in the road and the stragglers barely had time to jump out of the way into the adjoining fields. The column drove by at a lordly trot. It was a complete regiment of six batteries, impeccably grouped, with the colonel riding on the outside and the other officers, in their appropriate places, on the inside. The field-guns went thudding past at unfailingly regular intervals, each accompanied by its own ammunition waggon, its own horses and its own men. And in the fifth battery Maurice spotted his cousin Honoré, the battery-sergeant's field-gun. There he sat, proudly erect on his horse, to the left of the leading driver of the team – a handsome, fairhaired man named Adolphe, mounted on a sturdy chestnut admirably paired with the off-wheeler trotting at its side. Occupying his rightful position among the half-dozen members of the gun-crew seated two by two on the ammunition boxes was Louis the gun-layer. Louis, short and dark, was Adolphe's friend and opposite number; it was general practice in the artillery to pair a horseman and a foot-soldier so that they formed a "couple". To Maurice, who had been introduced to them back at the camp, they looked much taller; and the field-gun, drawn by its four horses and closely followed by its ammunition waggon, drawn by six more, seemed resplendent as a sun, so beautifully tended and richly burnished, so fawned upon by its entire retinue, animal and human alike, who clustered round it with the tenderness and discipline of a happy family. What pained Maurice most of all was the contemptuous stare which cousin Honoré directed at the stragglers – though contempt changed suddenly to stupefaction when he recognized the young lawyer among this gang of unarmed men. But the procession was already coming to an end; the supply waggons drove past, and the field ambulance. Then, amid a final cloud of dust, came the spare horses and men. They rounded another bend in the road and were lost, amid a gradually diminishing clatter of hooves and wheels.

"They'd be a darned sight less ready to show off," declared Loubet, "if they had to use shanks's pony."

Altkirch had turned out to be unoccupied on the staff's arrival. No Prussians yet. But General Douay, still haunted by the fear that the enemy was in hot pursuit and liable to appear at any moment, decided to press on as far as Dannemarie. It was five o'clock before the first detachments got that far – and eight o'clock, with dusk already beginning to settle, before any serious preparations were made for setting up camp. The regiments were reduced to half-strength and in an appalling state of confusion, the men ready to drop with hunger and fatigue. And for another two hours the late-comers trickled in, individually or in small groups, the whole

30

lamentable, interminable tail of the lame and the mutinous – searching for their companies and unable to find them.

As soon as he had located his regiment, Jean went off in search of Lieutenant Rochas; his first duty was to report what had happened. He found the lieutenant outside a small inn, deep in conversation with Captain Beaudoin and the colonel. They were seriously worried about the roll-call and anxious to find out where their men had got to. Barely had Jean begun to address his platoon commander than Colonel de Vineuil beckoned him forward and made him tell the whole story. There was a look of mute desolation in the colonel's brown eyes; those eyes, set in his yellow face, had remained dark, almost black, long after the thick hair and drooping moustache had turned pure white.

"There is only one course open to us, colonel!" cried Captain Beaudoin, not waiting for his superior to voice an opinion. "Half a dozen of these blackguards will have to be lined up and shot."

Lieutenant Rochas nodded his head in agreement. But the colonel threw up his hands to convey his powerlessness in the matter.

"There are too many of them. Close on seven hundred. How can we hope to deal with them? Which of them would we pick . . .? Besides, the general would never stand for it. He's like a father to his men. All the time he was in Africa he never ordered a single punishment. No, no! My hands are tied, I'm afraid. But it's monstrous."

"Monstrous is the right word," the captain rejoined boldly. "Things have come to a pretty pass!"

Jean was already walking away when he heard Major Barouche, whose presence he had not noticed before, growling moodily from the doorway of the inn : no more discipline, no more punishments, the army might as well disband; at this rate every officer could expect a kick in the backside before the week was out; but if a few of those ruffians were to be dealt with here and now, it might give the others something to think about. . . .

No one was punished. With commendable foresight some officers in the rearguard had salvaged most of the packs and rifles from the roadside. Only a small number were missing and the men were rearmed at daybreak, almost furtively, so that the incident should not attract attention. Orders were given for camp to be struck at five, but in fact the troops were roused a full hour earlier and the retreat to Belfort was speeded up – for the staff were certain that

31

the Prussians were by this time no more than five or six miles away. As on the previous morning the men had to be content with dry biscuits. Deprived of a warming meal, they had as little energy as ever, especially after the much-too-short, sweltering night. Once again the orderliness of the journey ahead was imperilled by unreasonable haste in setting out.

It was a profoundly dispiriting day, even worse than the day before. The physical appearance of the countryside had altered : they had come to a hilly area. The roads dipped and climbed over fir-clad slopes, and the slender valleys, covered in broom, were a mass of flowering gold. But a gale of panic blew across this vivid landscape, lurid in the strong August sunlight, and grew shriller with every passing hour. The latest dispatches urged all mayors to alert local inhabitants to the wisdom of storing their valuables in a safe place; and this had brought the mood of terror among the people to its highest pitch. So the enemy was upon them! Would they even have time to make their escape? Every one of them felt that they could hear the mounting roar of invasion, a low rumble like that of a river bursting its banks, a sound which was increased, in village after village, by one outburst after another of panic fraught with wailing and ranting.

Maurice had taken on the gait of a sleepwalker. His feet bled, his shoulders felt crushed beneath the weight of his pack and rifle. He had given up thinking and succumbed to the nightmare of what met his eyes. Awareness of his comrades, trudging behind and in front of him, had receded; only of Jean – immediately to his left, and beset by the same weariness, the same sense of sorrow as himself – was he still dimly conscious. A heartbreaking sight, these villages they passed through. As soon as the retreating units came into view – that straggling column of tired, limping troops – the villagers would bestir themselves and quicken their preparations for escape. They had been so calm, even a fortnight ago; the whole of Alsace had waited for war with a smile, quite convinced that all the fighting would be in Germany! And now France was invaded, and it was over their own soil, around their own houses, upon their own fields, that the storm was breaking – like one of those terrible outbreaks of hail, wind and lightning which can lay waste a whole province in the space of two hours. There was chaos at front-doors as the menfolk loaded their carts with family possessions, piling sticks of furniture on top of one another until the entire edifice was in danger of falling and shattering. From upstairs windows, women would lower one last mattress or the cradle which they had so nearly forgotten. Then the baby would be strapped in, and the cradle perched at the top of the pile, among the legs of the upturned chairs and tables. And being lashed to a cupboard on the cart behind was the ailing old grandfather, ready to be borne away like an inanimate object. Those who had no cart laid a few goods and chattels across a wheelbarrow; some set off with a bundle of old clothes in their arms; still others had no thought of saving anything but the clock, clutching this one possession to their hearts as they might have clasped a child. It was impossible to carry everything : odds and ends of furniture and unmanageable bundles of linen lay discarded by the roadside. Some people were careful to lock and bolt everything before they left, and the well-secured doors and windows gave their houses a dead look; but the majority, in their haste and in the despairing conviction that everything was bound to be destroyed, made no attempt to hide or guard the gaping emptiness of the stripped rooms. And these, standing open to the four winds, were the saddest-looking of all – with the sadness of a captured town depopulated by fear; even the cats had fled, in shuddering apprehension of what was to come. Village by village, the pitiful spectacle darkened and more and more families took to the road. The hustle increased, and so did the oaths and the tears and the clenching of fists.

But Maurice's distress was most agonizing of all as they plodded along the highway, through open country. The closer they drew to Belfort, the bigger the trail of refugees became, stretching out to form a dense, uninterrupted procession. How many poor people dreamed of finding a place to shelter beneath the walls of the old fortress! The menfolk belaboured the horses and the womenfolk followed behind, dragging the children after them. Whole families hurried along the white, dazzling, sunbaked roads, overburdened and advancing in a state of straggling confusion – for the little ones were unable to keep up. Many people had taken their shoes off and were walking barefoot in the hope of getting along faster; and there were nursing mothers giving suck to their squalling brats, laying half their bodies bare but not allowing their pace to slacken even for a moment. Scared faces were turned to rearward. Frenzied hands were flung out, as though to obliterate the horizon. And all the time the panic-bearing wind was tousling heads of hair and bringing disarray to the clothes which had been so hurriedly donned. Others, farmers with all their hired men, were racing across the fields and driving their loosed flocks and herds before them – the sheep and cows, the oxen and horses which had been driven out of their sheds and stables. They were making for the ravines, the uplands, the virgin forests, and the dust they raised was reminiscent of those great migrations of old, when the inhabitants of invaded regions were forced to give ground to the conquering barbarians. They were going to live under canvas, surrounded by a ring of lonely crags so far from all charted tracks that no enemy soldier would ever venture there. Already the dust-cloud was disappearing behind the clumps of firs, already the lowing of the cattle and the thud of their hooves were dying away – but still the refugees streamed along the road, impeding the progress of the troops. On the outskirts of Belfort there were so many of them, driven by so strong a current, that the troops were several times brought to a standstill.

It was during one of these brief halts that Maurice witnessed a scene which afterwards haunted his mind like the memory of a blow.

Standing at the side of the road was an isolated house, the home of some poor peasant, with a meagre plot of land at the back. This man had been unwilling to leave his small property: he was too deeply rooted to the soil. And so he had stayed behind, since departure would have torn his flesh from his body. The troops could see him, sitting huddled on a bench and staring empty-eyed as the men poured past; how well he knew that by their retreat they were making his ripe corn over to the enemy. His wife stood at his side; she was still quite young and she had two children with her, one of them in her arms and the other clinging to her skirts. She and they were sobbing and wailing. But suddenly the door was flung open and the grandmother appeared on the threshold. She was tall, thin and extremely old. Her bare arms were knotty as ropes and she was waving at the soldiers furiously. Grey hair spilled from beneath her bonnet, flapping about her gaunt face, and her anger was so extreme that she could not get the words out – she was choking with fury.

At first the soldiers laughed. What a face she had on her, poor old loon! Then the syllables began to cohere.

"You rabble!" she was shouting. "You riffraff! You cowards! You cowards!"

Her voice grew shriller and shriller as she spat the insult at them with all the strength of her lungs. And the laughing stopped. The

34

men felt their bodies go cold. They bowed their heads and kept their eyes averted.

"You cowards! You cowards! You cowards!"

All at once she seemed to grow even taller. She drew herself up, a tragically spare figure in her tattered dress, and swung her long arms from west to east in a gesture so sweeping that it seemed to fill the sky.

"You cowards! That isn't the way to the Rhine. . . . The Rhine is over there, you cowards! Oh, you cowards!"

At long last the troops began to move forward again. As they did so, Maurice, happening to gaze in Jean's direction, saw that the corporal's eyes were brimming with tears. He was violently taken aback, and his sense of misery was worsened by the thought that even the clods around him had been hurt by an insult which had to be endured, however unmerited it might be. It was as though everything were giving way within his poor aching head; afterwards he could never remember how he got through the rest of the march.

It had taken the 7th Corps all day to cover the fifteen miles from Dannemarie to Belfort, and once again night was falling by the time the troops were able to set up a temporary camp – beneath the walls of the old fortress, on the very spot from which they had set out four days earlier to meet the enemy. Despite the late hour and their extreme tiredness, the soldiers insisted on lighting fires and cooking a meal. At last, for the first time since leaving here, they had a chance to eat something hot. And around the camp fires, beneath the cool night sky, noses were being thrust into bowls and preliminary grunts of satisfaction emitted when a rumour spread through the camp, shocking and horrifying all who heard it. Two more telegrams had arrived in quick succession : the Prussians had never crossed the Rhine at Markolsheim and there was no longer a single Prussian in Huningue. The crossing of the Rhine at Markolsheim, the erection of a pontoon bridge by the light of giant electric furnaces . . . all these alarming tales had been no more than a nightmare, an unaccountable hallucination on the part of the Sub-Prefect of Schelstadt. And as for the army corps which was allegedly threatening Huningue – that celebrated army corps from the Black Forest which had prompted so much terror throughout Alsace – it consisted solely of a tiny detachment of Wurtembergers, two battalions and one squadron, who by their clever tactics, by an endless series of marches and counter-marches and of sudden and unexpected sallies, had given people the impression of being confronted by a force of between thirty and forty thousand men. To think that, only that morning, the French had nearly blown up Dannemarie Viaduct! Fifty miles of rich countryside had been ravaged for no reason whatever, as a result of really foolish panicking. And as their minds went back to what they had seen in the course of that dreadful day – to the local people fleeing in panic and heading their livestock into the mountains, to the endless line of carts heading for the city, stacked with furniture and surrounded by herds of women and children – the soldiers lost all temper and vented their rage in sneers of exasperation.

"Well, if that doesn't beat all!" spluttered Loubet, talking with his mouth full and waving his spoon about. "So we were sent all that way simply to chase shadows! There was no one about . . .! Twenty-five miles there, twenty-five miles back, and not a living soul confronting us! All for nothing, except the pleasure of having the fear of God put into us!"

Whereupon Chouteau, who was noisily wiping his bowl, began to rail against the generals – though without mentioning them by name.

"Why, the daft devils! We've been lumbered with a pack of prize hares! If they bolt like this when there's nobody about I'd give a lot to see them if ever they came up against a real army."

Another bundle of wood had been tossed on to the fire for the sheer joy of watching the tall flames. Jean had turned a deaf ear up to this point. Only when Lapoulle, blissfully warming his legs, let out a roar of mindless, uncomprehending laughter did the corporal break his self-imposed silence.

"Shut up, now," he said, in an almost parental tone. "If anyone were to hear you it might lead to trouble."

Even he, with his unassuming common sense, was indignant that the staff should have displayed such stupidity. Still, it was imperative that they be respected; and when Chouteau went on with his grumbling, Jean was quick to silence him.

"Keep quiet, I say . . .! Here comes the lieutenant. If you've any comments to make, I suggest you address them to him."

Maurice was sitting on his own, in silence. He hung his head. Things had indeed come to a pretty pass! The nation's resistance was at an end almost before it had begun. Already, at the first setback, the men's rebelliousness and lack of discipline were turning the army into a broken, disorganized rabble which must surely meet with disaster. They had not so much as set eyes on a Prussian in the area below Belfort, and yet they were beaten.

The days ahead, however monotonous, were aquiver with uneasy anticipation. General Douay was determined that his men should not be idle; he made them toil at the outworks surrounding the fortress, which were still far from complete. Resentfully they dug up soil and hacked their way through rock. And not a word of news reached them! Where was MacMahon's army? What was happening below Metz? The most extravagant rumours circulated. Only a handful of newspapers arrived from Paris, and these, by their very contradictions, served merely to add to the black doubts which were besetting everyone. The general had twice written urgently for orders, without even getting a reply. Meanwhile, on 12th August, the 7th Corps was at last brought nearer to its full strength by the arrival of the third division from Italy. But one division – the first – was still missing. Beaten at Froeschwiller, it had been swept along in the undisciplined withdrawal and even at this late stage no one knew for certain where the tide of retreat had deposited it. Then, after a week of neglect and total isolation from the rest of France, a telegram brought orders for the corps to move on. How happy the men were : anything was preferable to the cooped-up life they had been leading. And as they made ready, conjecture started all over again. Nobody knew where they were bound for; some said they were off to defend Strasbourg, while others even talked of a bold thrust into the Black Forest aimed at cutting the Prussians' line of retreat.

The 106th was one of the first regiments to be crowded into the cattle trucks and sent on its way. No truck could have been more crowded than the one in which Jean and his squad found them-selves; it was so full, indeed, that Loubet claimed there wasn't room for a man to sneeze. The distribution of rations had been as chaotic as ever, and the troops had received in brandy what they ought to have received in food. In consequence nearly all of them were drunk, with a violent, uproarious drunkenness which vented itself in lewd songs. As the train rattled along, the pipe-smoke became so thick inside the truck that the men could hardly see one another. They were so restless and packed so close together that the heat was soon all but unbearable, and the hubbub that emerged from the dark, careering vehicle was sufficient to drown the rumbling of the wheels before dying away over the bleak countryside. It was only when they got to Langres that they realized they were being taken back to Paris.

"Mother of God!" cried Chouteau, who by his unrivalled glibness of tongue had already established his supremacy in that corner of the truck. "We're obviously going to be formed up at Charenton-neau, just to make sure Bismarck doesn't take to spending his nights at the Tuileries."

The others shook with laughter at the idea; they found it intensely funny, though they could not have said why. Indeed, even the most trivial incidents in the journey were treated as an occasion for deafening hoots and shouts and guffaws: the peasants lining the railway track; the tense crowds waiting for the trains to pass through the small country stations in the hope of gleening some news; a glimpse of France as a whole, shaking and terrified at the prospect of invasion. And so as the train thundered past, the crowds which had gathered in such haste received nothing for their pains except the crude bawlings of the cannon fodder inside. But during a halt at one of the stations, three well-dressed ladies – the wives of prosperous townsmen – achieved a great personal triumph by distributing mugs of broth among the troops. The men were weeping as they thanked the women and kissed their hands.

Before long, however, the disreputable singing and shouting started all over again. And a short distance beyond Chaumont the train happened to pass another, laden with artillerymen who were presumably bound for Metz. Both engines had slackened speed, and there was terrible pandemonium as the trainloads of men called back and forth to one another. The artillerymen won the day – no doubt they were the drunker of the two. They were shaking their fists as they bawled, with such desperate ferocity that all else was drowned: "Off to the slaughter! Off to the slaughter! Off to the slaughter!"

An ice-cold wind, carrying more than a hint of the grave, seemed to blow along the railway track. There was a sudden startling silence, broken only by the jeering voice of Loubet.

"Cheerful beggars, aren't they!"

"They're right, though," rejoined Chouteau, in his mob-orator's voice. "It's a rotten trick, sending a bunch of decent lads to the slaughter – all on account of a bit of hanky-panky that doesn't mean a thing to them personally."

And he said a great deal more. He was the resident corruptor, this shoddy workman from Monmartre, this idle, roistering house-painter who – fed on the undigested scraps of speeches heard at public meetings – mingled the most outrageous rubbish with the noble principles of liberty and equality. He knew everything and was bent on indoctrinating his comrades. Especially Lapoulle : he had promised to put some spunk into Lapoulle. "Seems plain enough to me – doesn't it to you, old friend? If Badinguet and Bismarck are having a private quarrel, let them settle it between themselves with their bare fists. Why should they upset the lives of hundreds of thousands of men who don't even know one another and have no desire to come to blows?"

The whole truckload was laughing again, amused and won over by his remarks. Lapoulle had no idea who Badinguet was and could not even have said whether it was an emperor or a king he was fighting for; but his face lit up.

"That's the answer," he kept saying, looking more than ever like a child-giant, "yes, that's the answer. Fight it out with bare fists and then have a friendly drink together. . . ."

But by this time Chouteau had turned his head away and begun to tackle Pache.

"And what about you? You're supposed to believe in God, and He says fighting is forbidden. So what are you doing here, you goat?"

"You surely don't think I'm here for the fun of it," replied Pache, considerably taken aback. "But the police . . ."

"Police? Who gives a damn about the police . . . ! Do you know what we'd all do if we had an ounce of gumption in us? Do a bunk the moment we're let out of this train. That's it – do a quiet bunk and leave that fat slug Badinguet and his crew of tupenny-ha'penny generals to cope with the blooming Prussians as best they can."

Loud cheers greeted his words. Corruption was taking its toll and Chouteau, visibly exultant, trotted out his theories – a dark, churning torrent of slogans about the Republic and Human Rights and the rottenness of the Empire (it must be overthrown) and the treasonableness of France's military leaders, each of whom had turned traitor for a million (it had been proved). He made no bones about being a revolutionary, whereas the others did not even know whether they were Republicans – nor, indeed, what being a Republican really amounted to. Only Loubet, the food-fancier, knew exactly where he stood, never having been loyal to anyone or anything except his stomach. They were all so carried away, however, that they needed no further encouragement to start railing against their Emperor, their officers and the whole blessed structure – a structure which they would break with, and fast, at the first sign of real trouble. And as he continued to fan the flames of their discontent,

39

Chouteau kept a close eye on Maurice. He was conscious of amusing the young "gentleman" and proud to think that they were on the same side. Eager to rouse him to the same degree as the others, he suddenly decided to pitch into Jean. Up to this point the corporal had sat quite still in the midst of the shindy, keeping his eyes half-closed like a man dead to the world. Surely Maurice must still have a grudge against his superior for the way the latter had let fly at him and made him pick up his rifle? Now was the time to set the two men against one another.

". . . And then there's *some* people I could mention who talked of having us shot," Chouteau went on, in menacing tones, "*some* curs who treat us worse than animals and don't realize that a man can grow sick and tired of his pack and rifle, and that when he does – why, he'll chuck them into the nearest field to see whether they'll sprout others . . . ! Well, comrades : what would those same people say if at a time like this, when we've got them where we want them, we were to chuck *them* out – right out on to the railway track . . .? Are we all agreed? We must make an example of one of them, just to make clear we are going to have no further truck with this rotten war. Death to Badinguet's bugs ! Death to the bastards who would have us fight !"

Jean had turned very red; his rare moments of anger unfailingly brought the blood rushing to his face. Though enclamped by the bodies of the men around him, he rose and thrust out his clenched fists and flushed face in a manner so daunting that Chouteau turned pale.

"By all that's holy ! When are you going to shut that damned mouth of yours? For hours I've sat silent, since there are no officers left and I can't pack you off to the glasshouse. Oh yes, I'd be doing the regiment a mighty favour by ridding it of a dirty blackguard like you. . . . But listen to me : now that punishments have been made nonsense of, you'll have to start reckoning with me on a man-to-man basis. You're not dealing with a corporal any more – just a poor harmless devil who's tired of being got at and who intends to shut you up once and for all. . . . Ah, so you won't fight, you bloody coward ! Just say that again and I'll clump you."

By this time everyone in the truck was changing loyalties, stirred by Jean's fine show of mettle. Suddenly Chouteau found himself without an ally. Stammering confusedly, he backed away from the stout fists of his adversary.

"And Badinguet means as little to me as you do, d'you hear . . .?

40

I've never bothered my head about politics or empires or republics. I feel just as I did in the old days when I was tilling my plot of land : all I ask is a quiet life and happiness and prosperity for all. . . . Do you really think anyone welcomes the thought of having to fight? Be that as it may, though, there's only one way of dealing with the kind of scum who try to get at us when we've a hard enough time trying to do the right thing. Stand them against a wall and shoot them. Damn it lads, doesn't it stir your blood to know that the Prussians are here on your native soil, waiting to be booted out !"

Whereupon, with the readiness of audiences everywhere to discard one passionate commitment in favour of another, the soldiers cheered the corporal as he reiterated a threat to knock the living daylights out of the first man who said anything about not fighting. Hooray for the corporal ! They'd soon put paid to Bismarck !

And as the wild cheering continued, Jean turned to Maurice. His anger had left him and the courtesy with which he spoke conveyed little sense of a non-commissioned officer addressing a member of his squad.

"I can't imagine you ever siding with cowards, sir," he said. "Come, we're not beaten yet – we'll trounce those Prussians before we're done, you mark my words !"

At that moment Maurice felt a warm ray of sunshine flow right through him, all the way to the heart. It left him feeling abashed. What? Had he been wrong to look upon the man as a mere boor? And he remembered the scalding hatred which had consumed him as he picked up his rifle after flinging it away in an unthinking moment. But he also remembered how startled he had been to see those two great tears in the corporal's eyes when the old woman – grey hair tossed by the wind – had stood hurling her words of abuse at them and pointing to the Rhine, far away to the rear, beyond the horizon. What could be cleansing him of his bitterness? Was it a sense of kinship, born of sharing the same aches and the same hardships? He came from a Bonapartist home and his Republican aspirations had always been entirely theoretical. He even felt a certain affection for the Emperor as a human being. He was an advocate of war, without which no nation could survive. All of a sudden he felt hope revive within him – another of those unexpected changes of mood which were so familiar to him. And the enthusiasm that had prompted his enlistment began to pulsate anew, flooding his heart with an unshakeable confidence in victory.

41

"Why, there's no two ways about it, corporal," he said cheerfully. "We'll trounce them, right enough!"

The truck rattled onwards, ever onwards, conveying its human cargo amid a mass of pipe-smoke and the stifling heat of close-packed bodies; and each time it passed through a tense railway station or swept by one of the distraught rows of peasants lining the hedgerows, it imparted snatches of its lewd singing and drunken bawling. On 20th August they arrived at Pantin station, on the outskirts of Paris. By evening they were on their way again; and the following day they left the train at Rheims, ostensibly bound for Châlons camp.

III

NOTHING could have surprised Maurice more than that the 106th should detrain at Rheims and be given orders to make camp there. Did it mean that they were not, after all, on their way to join the main body of the army at Châlons? And when, two hours later, his regiment piled arms a couple of miles outside the city – over towards Courcelles, in the vast plain which stretches along the banks of the Aisne-Marne Canal – his astonishment increased. For now he learned that the entire Châlons army had been falling back since early morning and was going to bivouac on this very spot. Indeed, tents were going up from one end of the horizon to the other, all the way to Saint-Thierry and La Neuvillette and even beyond the main Laon road. The fires of four army corps would be blazing there that evening. The generals had clearly decided in favour of taking up positions below Paris and there awaiting the Prussians. And of this he was very glad, for it was surely the wisest course?

Maurice spent the afternoon of the 21st wandering about camp in search of news. The men were left to their own devices : discipline appeared to have grown more lax than ever and they all came and went just as they pleased. In the end Maurice himself quietly made his way back to Rheims, with the intention of cashing a postal order for a hundred francs sent by his sister Henriette. In one of the cafés he overheard a sergeant talking of the spirit of rebelliousness rife among the eighteen battalions of the Seine-District Militia, which had just been posted back to Paris; the 6th Battalion had, for instance, come close to killing its officers. Out at the camp the generals were abused daily, and since the defeat at Froeschwiller the men had even given up saluting Marshal MacMahon. The café was beginning to fill with voices and a violent quarrel broke out between two placid-looking civilians as to how many men the marshal would have at his disposal. One of them talked in terms of three hundred thousand, which was ridiculous. The other, more sensibly, considered the four army corps one by one. The 12th, after much effort, had been brought up to strength here at the camp with

43

a division of marines and men from the mobile infantry regiments. The scattered remains of the 1st had been trickling in ever since 14th August and were now being pieced together again after a fashion. The 5th, defeated without ever fighting, had been swept away and broken up in the general rout. And the 7th had only recently arrived at Rheims, where it had been reunited at last with the bits and pieces of its "lost" first division. A hundred and twenty thousand men at most, even including the Bonnemarie and Margueritte divisions of the reserve cavalry. But when the sergeant broke in on the argument, furiously and contemptuously dismissing the army as a disorganized rabble, as a herd of innocents being led to the slaughter by idiots, the two civilians beat a hasty retreat for fear of being implicated in a treasonable outburst.

Back in the street, Maurice set about obtaining newspapers. He stuffed his pockets with as many issues as he could lay hands on and started to read them as he strolled beneath the tall trees lining the magnificent walks on the edge of town. Where on earth were the German armies? The defenders seemed to have lost track of them. Two of them, presumably, were in the vicinity of Metz – the first, under General Steinmetz, covering the fortress; the second, under Prince Frederick Charles, trying to work its way up the right bank of the Moselle and cut the main Paris road at Bazaine. But as for the third army – commanded by the Crown Prince of Prussia and now, after its victories at Wissembourg and Froeschwiller, in hot pursuit of the 1st and 5th Corps – the maze of conflicting reports was valueless to anyone wishing to ascertain its true position. Was it still camping at Nancy? Or was it almost at Châlons, which would account for the French decision to pull out in such haste and set fire to magazines, forage-waggons and supplies of every description? Moreover there was the usual conflict of opinion as to the nature and purpose of the generals' plans. To all intents and purposes, Maurice had been living quite cut-off from the rest of the world; only now did he learn what had been happening in Paris – the unnerving shock of defeat, sustained by a city utterly confident of victory; the appalling street-disturbances; the convening of the upper and lower Houses; the fall of the liberal government which had been responsible for the Plebiscite; the transference of supreme command from the Emperor to Marshal Bazaine. For the past five days the Emperor had been at Châlons camp, and all the papers spoke of a high-level meeting on 17th August, attended by Prince Napoleon and several generals; but there was little agreement as to

44

what decisions had actually been taken. It was plainly as a result of this meeting, however, that General Trochu had been appointed Governor of Paris and Marshal MacMahon put in charge of the Châlons army – a step which seemed to portend the total eclipse of the Emperor. Maurice's reading afforded him a glimpse of terrible bewilderment and irresolution, of ever-changing plans resulting in self-defeat. And still the question remained : where on earth were the German armies? Who was right? The people who maintained that Bazaine still enjoyed freedom of movement and was even now falling back along the line of the northern fortresses? Or the others, who said he was already surrounded somewhere below Metz? There were persistent rumours of tremendous confrontations, of heroic, week-long stands between 14 and 20 August – though the only thing to emerge from them was the mighty and unattainably distant roar of battle.

Maurice's legs felt ready to give way, so he sat down on a park bench. The city, all around him, appeared to be living its normal life. Nursemaids kept an eye on the children playing under the beautiful trees, and men of means enjoyed their usual leisurely stroll. Maurice returned to his papers and almost immediately came across an item which had previously escaped his attention. It appeared in an organ passionately committed to the cause of the Republican opposition. Instantly, all became clear. According to this report, the meeting at Châlons camp on August 17 had decreed that the Army of Paris should fall back and General Trochu's appointment as governor was merely a preliminary to the Emperor's return to the capital. But the paper went on to say that both aims had been frustrated by the attitude of the Empress-Regent and the new administration. In the view of the Empress, there was bound to be a revolution if the Emperor came back. She was alleged to have remarked : "He would never reach the Tuileries alive." And so the full weight of her stubborn determination was still directed towards getting the army to advance and join up with the units at Metz; and in this she was supported by General de Palikao, the new war minister, who had devised a plan to relieve Bazaine by means of a lightning push. Maurice lowered the newspaper and stared vacantly ahead of him. He felt that he was now able to understand it all : the two conflicting plans of campaign; Marshal MacMahon's reluctance to carry out this highly dangerous flanking movement with forces that could not be relied on; the impatient and ever more vexed orders from Paris, urging the marshal to shut his eyes to the rash folly of such a venture. And then, quite suddenly, he had a clear vision of the Emperor at the centre of this tragic struggle. Shorn of his imperial powers (which he had entrusted to the Empress-Regent), stripped of his rank as generalissimo (which he had just conferred on Marshal Bazaine), he had become a nobody, a vague, indeterminate shadow of an emperor, a nameless, useless encumbrance whom nobody knew what to do with, whom Paris was rejecting and who no longer had any place in the army now that he had even undertaken to stop giving orders of any kind.

Next morning, however, after a stormy night in the open, with only a blanket over him, Maurice was relieved to learn that the plan to fall back on Paris was definitely in the ascendant. Apparently another meeting had been held the evening before. Among those attending was the former "vice-Emperor", M. Rouher. The Empress had sent him, hoping that he would persuade the army to advance to Sedan without delay; but the marshal seemed to have convinced him of the dangers of that or any similar move. Could it be that bad news had arrived from Bazaine? No one had the heart to say so. But the very absence of news spoke for itself and there was unanimous support, among all but the more stupid officers, for the idea of awaiting the enemy below Paris – which would enable them to go to the defence of the capital in case of need. And convinced, to his delight, that a general withdrawal would begin the very next day (the appropriate orders were said to have been given), Maurice decided to satisfy a childish longing to escape the communal meal for once and enjoy the luxury of a table cloth, a bottle, a glass, a plate. . . . All these things, as it seemed to him, had been missing from his life for months past. Well, he had money in his pocket; so he hurried away, his heart thudding with a sense of adventure, and began to search for a suitable inn.

It was across the canal, on the outskirts of the village of Courcelles, that he found the kind of meal he had been longing for. The day before, someone had told him that the Emperor was staying in a private house thereabouts and he had strolled over to satisfy his curiosity. It was then he had noticed this tavern built on a street corner. It had an arbour with beautiful bunches of grapes hanging from the trelliswork, already ripe and golden. Green-topped tables were set beneath the spreading vine. The door leading into the huge kitchen stood wide open, affording a glimpse of the loud-ticking pendulum clock and the cheap coloured prints on the tiled walls – and also of the innkeeper's wife, a really buxom woman busy with

46

the roasting-jack. It was all so cheerful and cosy and pretty, summing up all the virtues of traditional French hospitality.

A handsome, big-bosomed girl appeared, flashed her fresh young teeth at him and asked: "Will the gentleman be wanting something to eat?"

"Indeed he will. . . . I'd like two eggs, a chop and some cheese. . . . And a bottle of white wine!"

He called her back.

"Tell me, isn't the Emperor staying in one of these houses?"

"Why yes, sir – in the one just across the way. You can't see the house itself: it's hidden behind those trees and the high wall beneath them."

Whereupon he settled in the arbour, undoing his belt to make himself more comfortable and choosing a table on which the sunlight, filtering through the vine-branches, cast splashes of gold. And his eyes kept stealing back to that high yellow wall which lent shelter to the Emperor of France. It was certainly a quiet and secluded place to live: not even the rooftop was visible. The entrance was on the other side, facing the village street – a narrow street which, devoid of shops and even of windows, wound its way between two rows of drab-looking walls. The grounds at the rear of the building provided a small green oasis amid the neighbouring buildings. And at this point his attention was drawn to a spacious courtyard at the other end of the street. It was surrounded by stables and coach-houses and contained a wide variety of vans and carriages. The place was a hive of activity: men and horses were coming and going all the time.

"Are they all for the use of the Emperor?" he asked the waitress, intending to make a joke of it, as she spread a crisp white cloth over the table.

"Indeed they are – for his use and no one else's," she replied with all her fetching cheerfulness, only too glad of the opportunity to show her flawless teeth.

Then she treated him to an itemized list; presumably she owed her information to the stablemen, who had been buying drinks at this inn ever since their arrival the day before. First came the staff of twenty-five officers, the sixty members of the household cavalry, the platoon of Guides and the half-dozen military police; then came the household, seventy-three strong – chamberlains, valets and footmen, cooks and scullions; next, four saddle-horses and two carriages for the Emperor, ten horses for the equerries and eight for the

47

grooms and outriders, to say nothing of the forty-seven post-horses; next, a brake and twelve baggage waggons – two of which, set aside for use of the cooks, had aroused the girl's admiration by the extraordinary number of utensils, plates and bottles which were to be seen inside them, all in perfect order.

"Oh sir – you've never seen such saucepans! Shine like the sun they do. . . . And all kinds of dishes and receptacles and things I can't even tell the use of . . .! And you should see all the different wines! Bordeaux and Burgundies and Champagnes. What a wedding-breakfast you could give with all those!"

Entranced at the sight of the spotless tablecloth and the pale golden wine sparkling in his glass, Maurice ate the two boiled eggs with a hearty relish quite outside his normal experience. Away to his left, whenever he turned his head towards one of the arbour gates, he had a clear view of the broad plain studded with tents: a whole teeming township had risen from the stubblefields between Rheims and the canal. The only touches of green in the vast grey expanse were conferred by a few meagre clumps of trees. Three windmills raised their slender arms aloft. But above the jumbled rooftops of Rheims, which were lost among the leafy chestnuts, the great pile of the cathedral stood out against the blue sky, looking – in spite of the distance – gigantic beside the low-built houses. The sight of it took him back to the lessons drummed into him at school: the coronations of the Kings of France, the Holy Ampulla, Clovis, Joan of Arc, all the bygone glories of France. . . .

Once again Maurice's thoughts were drawn to the Emperor, living in that modest and sequestered house. Returning his gaze to the high yellow wall, he was surprised to discover the slogan "Vive Napoleon!" scrawled in huge charcoal characters, side by side with crude obscenities which were magnified out of all proportion. The lettering had been almost washed away by rain; obviously the inscription was an old one. What an extraordinary thing to find written here on this wall – an expression of martial fervour, doubtless intended as a tribute to the uncle, the conquering hero, rather than to the nephew! By this time, the whole of Maurice's childhood was being brought to life again. His mind filled with memories of the days in Le Chêne-Populeux, when – even in the cradle – he had listened to the stories of his grandfather, who had served as a soldier in the Grande Armée. His mother was dead; his father had been forced to become a tax-collector, as part of the inglorious heritage which had befallen the heroes' sons following the overthrow of the Empire. And the grandfather was reduced to living in these drab surroundings with only a tiny pension to support him. His sole consolation lay in recounting his experiences to his grandchildren – the two twins, boy and girl, both with the same flaxen hair. In a sense, he was a mother to them. He would perch Henriette on his left knee and Maurice on his right, and for hours at a time he would treat them to homeric tales of battle.

Times and periods would become confused : everything seemed to take place outside of history, in an awesome confrontation of every race in Europe. The British, the Austrians, the Prussians and Russians . . . they all paraded through the children's minds separately and jointly, depending on the state of alliances at any given moment, though it was not always possible to say why some were beaten rather than others. But in the final reckoning they were all beaten, inescapably, before ever a shot was fired; nothing and nobody could withstand a surge of patriotism and genius which swept whole armies away like chaff. There was Marengo, the classic engagement on level ground, with its long lines of troops skilfully deployed and its chequerwise withdrawal, battalion by battalion, silent and impassive under fire; the legendary battle, lost at three o'clock and won at six, when the eight hundred grenadiers of the Consular Guard broke the charge of the entire Austrian cavalry, when Desaix came out to meet his death and turn impending rout into immortal victory. . . . There was Austerlitz, with its lustrous sunlight amid the winter fog – Austerlitz, opening with the capture of the Pratzen plateau and closing with the terrifying disintegration of the frozen ponds; a thunderous cracking of the ice, that drowned an entire Russian army, men and beasts; and the godlike Napoleon (who, naturally, had foreseen all this) finished off the disaster with his bullets. There was Jena, that graveyard of Prussia's military might : the skirmishers firing through the October mists; Ney almost jeopardizing the situation by his impatience; then Augereau moving in and extricating his colleague; then the head-on clash, which by its very ferocity swept away the enemy's centre; and finally the headlong flight of an overrated cavalry – the French hussars cut them down like ripe oats, strewing the romantic-looking valley with the scythed bodies of men and horses. . . . There was Eylau, Eylau the vilest and bloodiest battle of all, a ceaseless piling-up of hideously mutilated corpses, Eylau blood-red beneath the snowstorm, a bleak heroic burial-ground, Eylau still re-echoing from the smash-attack of Murat's eighty squadrons, which thrust

49

clean through the Russian army, littering the soil with such a thick layer of corpses that even Napoleon wept at the sight. . . . There was Friedland, the great and terrible trap into which the Russians blundered anew like a flock of bemused sparrows, the strategic masterpiece of the Emperor whose knowledge and capabilities surpassed all limits; his left hung back while Ney, after capturing the town street by street, destroyed the bridges; then the French left charged the enemy's right and trapped it against the river bank and proceeded to annihilate it; so many had to be slaughtered that the killing went on until after ten at night. . . . There was Wagram, where the Austrians tried to stop the French from reaching the Danube; they kept reinforcing their right wing in an attempt to beat the wounded Masséna, who was commanding his troops from an open barouche; the shrewd, titanic Napoleon let them continue undisturbed until suddenly the dreadful firepower of a hundred cannon shattered their depleted centre and drove it back two or three miles; in the meantime Masséna had succeeded in turning the tables, and in horror at its isolated position the Austrian right fell back, dragging the remainder of the army with it amid scenes of devastation that were more akin to a dam-burst. . . . Lastly there was the battle of the Moskva, where the bright sunlight of Austerlitz reappeared for the last time, a terrifying melee rendered chaotic by the great numbers of men involved and the obstinate courage displayed on all sides; hillocks changed hands beneath incessant hail of fire, redoubts were stored at bayonet-point and every inch of ground was disputed in a never-ending series of attacks and counter-attacks; the Russian Guard fought with such ferocity and valour that victory could never have been wrested had it not been for the merciless charges conducted by Murat, for the combined thunder of three hundred cannon and for the gallantry shown by Ney, whose greatest triumph this was. And whatever the battle, the flags would flutter in the evening air with the same panache, and the same cries of "Vive Napoleon!" would ring out as camp-fires were lighted on the conquered positions. France was at home from one end of Europe to the other, wherever she elected to parade her invincible eagles. She had only to set foot inside foreign kingdoms for the vanquished races to sink into the soil.

Maurice was finishing his chop, less intoxicated by the white wine sparkling at the bottom of his glass than by the reverberations of all this remembered glory, when he suddenly saw a pair of ragged and mud-bespattered soldiers. They looked like a couple of footsore bandits tired of the road and he heard them asking the waitress for information as to the exact positions of the regiments camped alongside the canal.

He called them over.

"Why," he said, "you're from the 7th Corps!"

"Aye – from the first division. By God I am! If it's proof you want, I was at Froeschwiller – and it was a long way from cold there, take my word for it. . . . I'm forgetting myself, though. Our friend here is from the 1st Corps and he was at Wissembourg, another filthy hole."

They described what had happened to them, how they had been caught up in the rout and panic and how they had stumbled into a ditch and lain there, both slightly wounded and half-dead with exhaustion. In consequence they had lagged behind the main body of the army. Bouts of fever had laid them low and compelled them to linger in towns. Small wonder they had only just got here. Now, feeling in slightly better condition, they were searching for their respective platoons.

Maurice listened with heavy heart. He was about to bite into a piece of gruyère when he observed the hungering looks which the two men were directing at his plate.

"Waitress!" he called. "Let's have some more bread and cheese and wine . . . ! You will join me, won't you comrades? Let me drink your health."

They were only too glad to join him. He, for his part, sat and stared at them with a growing sense of chill. How low they had been brought : soldiers deprived of their weapons, soldiers whose greatcoats and red trousers were so darned and strung together as to give them the appearance of gipsies getting a few last days of wear out of garments pilfered from some battlefield.

"No," resumed the taller of the two, talking with his mouth full, "it was no damned picnic, I can tell you . . . ! Nobody who wasn't there to see it would ever believe it. Go on, Coutard, tell him your part of the story."

And the shorter man did as he was urged, gesticulating and waving his bread about.

". . . There was I, rinsing my shirt out while the meal was stewing. We were in a blasted hole – a real crater, with woods all round – so those Prussian bastards were able to creep up on us unawares. Suddenly, at seven o'clock, the shells started plopping into our boiling pots. Well we didn't just sit there, believe you me!

51

We made a rush for our rifles, and from then until eleven we really thought we were knocking the stuffing out of them. . . . But you must realize there were less than five thousand of us and those devils kept on coming. I was up on a small hill, crouching behind a bush, and I could see them swarming out right, left and centre. Like columns of black ants they were. More and more and more of them. Honestly, we all thought the brasshats were downright fools to have landed us in such a hornet's nest, a long way from any of our comrades, and then to let us stew, without lifting a finger to help. . . . Well, all of a sudden our own general (poor old General Douay – neither a fool nor a coward, that one) stopped a bullet and fell flat on his back, with his arms and legs in the air. That was the end of him! Not that it made any difference, mind: we still stood our ground. There were too many of them, though, and eventually we had to skedaddle. We fought in an orchard for a while, then fell back and defended the railway station – the pandemonium was enough to deafen anybody. . . . I can't rightly remember what happened after that. The town must have fallen. Anyway, next thing we knew, we were on a mountainside – the Geissberg, I think they call it; we took up our positions in a sort of castle and managed to kill no end of the swine! It was a treat to see them leap in the air and fall flat on their faces. But . . . well, what else can you expect? They kept coming at us and coming at us; we were outnumbered ten to one and they had all the artillery support they wanted. In a situation like that there's only one thing courage can lead to: getting yourself killed stone dead. They pounded us to a jelly, and all we could do was pull out. . . . But I still say our officers showed themselves up as complete and utter dolts – didn't they, Picot?"

There was a pause. Picot, the taller one, drained his glass, wiped himself with the back of his hand and replied: "They certainly did. . . . It was just the same at Froeschwiller: a man would have to be crazy to fight in such conditions. My captain is a knowing little beggar, and he said so himself. . . . The plain fact is, those in command simply can't have known what they were doing. A whole army of the devils swooped on us, and we were barely forty thousand. We weren't expecting to have to fight that day, but the battle began shortly afterwards – against the generals' wishes, apparently. Of course, there was a lot I didn't see with my own eyes. But this I can tell you: each time we thought it might be over the fighting would start up again, worse than ever; it just went on and

52

on and on. . . . It all began at Wörth, a lovely little village with a strange-looking steeple, tiled like a stove. Why they ever ordered us out of the place I can't imagine, for afterwards we fought tooth and nail to get back – and didn't succeed. Oh, we had a terrible time of it, lads! You'd never believe how many men had their bellies ripped open or their brains crushed to pulp. After that we had a set-to on the outskirts of another village, Elsasshaussen – what a mouthful! We were under fire from a mass of heavy guns, all blazing away from a bloody hilltop which we'd left only that morning. And then, true as I'm talking to you now, I saw the cuirassiers make their charge. Poor devils – a terrible number of them rode to their deaths. It was a crying shame to send horses and men into action on sloping ground like that, with all those bushes and ditches. Especially as it could do no earthly good. Never mind, though – it was plucky, it gave your heart a lift. . . . After that, the best thing seemed to be to pull out. The village was burning like a box of matches; in the end we had the Wurttembergers and Prussians and the lot from Baden, all round us. The whole pack of them. Later on someone worked out there were more than a hundred and twenty thousand of the bastards. But that still wasn't the end of it: around Froeschwiller, things grew hotter than ever. For you can take my word for it: MacMahon may be dense but he's got courage. You should have seen him on his big horse, with the shells raining down all round him! Anyone else would have bolted at the word go, and see no disgrace in refusing to fight when you were so heavily outnumbered. But once the battle started he made up his mind to take whatever was coming to him. And he certainly did that . . .! At Froeschwiller, it wasn't men but wild beasts eating each other up. For the best part of two hours the gutters ran with blood. . . . And then – why, there was no help for it: we had to take to our heels. You can imagine how we felt when he heard we'd bashed the daylight out of the Bavarians at the other end of the line. Good God! If we'd had the proper artillery support they had and generals who knew their stuff – you should have seen us then!"

Still caught up in the violence and exasperation of those hours of fighting, Coutard and Picot – sitting there in their torn, grimy uniforms – helped themselves eagerly to slices of bread and wolfed great lumps of cheese, shedding their nightmarish memories beneath the charming trelliswork, with the bunches of ripe grapes riddled by the golden arrows of the sun. Now they came to the dreadful rout that followed: the muddled, demoralized, famished regiments

fleeing across country; the highways packed with a frightful confusion of men, horses, carts, heavy guns; the total disintegration of
a wrecked army lashed by a wild gale of panic. Having forfeited
the opportunity of making a prudent withdrawal and defending the
Vosges passes, where ten thousand men could have halted a
hundred thousand, the French ought at least to have blown up
the bridges and blocked the tunnels. But the generals had let themselves be stampeded by events, and victors and vanquished alike
were blown about by such a storm-wind of bewilderment that for
a while the two armies entirely lost track of one another, groping
about in the full light of day: MacMahon went hurrying towards
Lunéville while the Crown Prince of Prussia carried out a futile
hunt in the neighbourhood of the Vosges. On August 7 the ruins
of the 1st Army Corps poured through Sauverne like a murky river
in flood and full of driftwood. On August 8, at Sarrebourg, the
5th Corps chanced upon the 1st like one raging torrent meeting up
with another; it too was in full retreat, beaten without ever fighting,
dragging its commander along with it – the melancholy General
de Failly, who was beside himself when he heard that his failure
to take positive action was being looked upon as the main cause of
the general defeat. On August 9 and 10 the mad rush continued, a desperate headlong flight: there was no time for a man
to glance back over his shoulder. On the eleventh, in heavy rain,
they made their way down towards Bayon, bypassing Nancy because
of a rumour that the town was in enemy hands. On the twelfth
they camped at Haroué and on the thirteenth at Vicherey.
August 14 found them at Neufchâaateau, where the railway at last
absorbed this seething human mass; for three whole days the men
were shovelled into trains for conveyance to Châlons. Twenty-four
hours after the last train departed, the Prussians arrived.

"Ah, they properly rushed us off our feet!" concluded Picot.
"And there was me and Coutard, stranded in hospital."

Coutard was tipping the last of the wine into their two glasses.

"Yes, we cleared out as quick as we could, and we've been on
the road ever since. . . . Still, things are better than they were –
at least we can drink a toast to the boys who came through it
unscathed."

And now Maurice understood. After the stupid ensnarement at
Wissembourg, the defeat at Froeschwiller had come as a thunder-
bolt – and the glare of it shed clear light on the appalling truth.
The French had been ill-prepared, with inadequate artillery, wide-

spread undermanning and incompetent generals; whereas the enemy, previously regarded with so much condescension, appeared to be well-organized, strong and almost numberless – and his discipline and strategy were alike exemplary. The three German armies had driven mighty wedges through the thin protective screen afforded by the seven French army corps strung out between Metz and Strasbourg. And so France was left all alone : neither Austria nor Italy would come in on her side, for the Emperor's plan had fallen through because of the slowness of his military operations and the incompetence of the army chiefs. Even fate was against her. She had suffered a series of misfortunes and disastrous coincidences, all of which made for the success of the Prussians' secret plan – to cut the defending armies in two, to thrust one half back to a position below Metz, thereby isolating it from France, and to march on Paris after annihilating the remainder. The success of this plan now looked a mathematical certainty : France was bound to be beaten, and the many reasons for it were as obvious as the inevitable outcome. The world was witnessing a clash between mindless bravery on the one hand, numerical superiority and cold method on the other. Whatever arguments might rage afterwards, defeat was as inescapable as the law of gravity.

All of a sudden, as he gazed uncertainly about him, his eyes settled once more on the slogan "Vive Napoléon !" scrawled on the high yellow wall. And the sight occasioned him a feeling of intolerable unease, a pain so scorching that it seemed to burn right through his heart. So it was true, then : for all its legendary victories, France – a nation which had drummed and trumpeted its way across Europe – had been felled at a single blow, and by a people on which it had always looked down ! Fifty years had been long enough to transform the world : defeat, with all its horrors, was being visited upon the unfailing victors of yesteryear. And Maurice thought back to that night of tense anticipation outside Mulhouse, remembering all that Weiss, his brother-in-law, had said. Yes, he had been the only one to see things clearly at the time, fathoming the deep, long-term causes of France's decline and scenting the new wind of youthfulness and vitality which was blowing from Germany. Surely this marked the close of one martial era and the opening of another. Woe betide any nation that falters in the continuous effort which all must make : victory belongs to those which march in the van, to the ablest, the fittest, the strongest !

But at that moment they were disturbed by the squeals and

laughter of a girl being teased by some man. The noise was occasioned by Lieutenant Rochas who was standing in the smoky old kitchen, with its bright cheap pictures, and clasping the pretty waitress to him; he looked every inch the victorious campaigner. He stepped into the arbour and ordered coffee. Obviously he had overheard the closing remarks of Coutard and Picot.

"Bah, lads!" he countered cheerfully. "It's nothing to fret about. Those were early days : now you'll see us turn the tables and no mistake. . . . Oh yes, up to now we've been outnumbered five to one; but now we're three hundred thousand. The moves we're making may seem hard to understand, but they all have one purpose : our aim is to lure the Prussians towards us so that Bazaine, who is keeping a close watch on the situation, can pounce on them from the rear. And then – got you! – we shall squash them just as I'm squashing this fly!"

With a resounding crack he brought his two hands together and caught a passing fly; and he talked on in the same bright vein, even louder than before, believing with childlike fervour in this marvellously simple plan and backing it up with his faith in the insuperability of sheer physical courage. He was kind enough also to explain to the two soldiers exactly where they would find their regiments; then, wearing a contented look and clenching a cigar between his teeth, he sat down in front of his small black coffee.

"The pleasure was mine, comrades!" said Maurice as Coutard and Picot took their leave, thanking him for the cheese and the bottle of wine.

He too had called for a cup of coffee and he sat staring at the lieutenant, quite won over to his expansive mood, though somewhat taken aback by his mention of three hundred thousand men, when the force assembled amounted to little more than a hundred thousand, and by the remarkable ease with which he envisaged crushing the enemy between the Châlons army and the Metz army. But he was equally in need of illusion. Why not go on hoping, when the glorious past still sang so clear in his memory? The little hostelry was such a joyous sight, with its trelliswork and the bright grapes of France, golden from the sun! Once again he felt a wave of confidence rise within him, temporarily obliterating the great unvoiced sadness which had gradually built up inside him.

Maurice's attention had been momentarily drawn to an officer in the Chasseurs d'Afrique who, with an orderly riding at his side, had just disappeared round the back of the silent house where the

56

Emperor was staying. Now the orderly reappeared alone, leading both horses. As the man paused at the door of the inn, Maurice let out a cry of surprise.

"Prosper . . . ! Why, I thought you were at Metz!"

The newcomer hailed from Remilly – an ordinary farm labourer whom he had known as a child when he used to go and spend the holidays with Uncle Fouchard. Conscripted by ballot, he had been in Africa for three years when war broke out; and with his long, lean face and wonderfully lithe and sturdy limbs, he looked quite splendid in his sky-blue jacket, red leather belt and broadcut trousers – red, with blue stripes.

"Monsieur Maurice . . . ! Fancy meeting you here!"

But he did not hurry over; instead he led the steaming horses to the stable, treating his own mount, especially, to a look of almost fatherly concern. A love of horses, no doubt acquired in his boyhood days when he had often minded the plough-teams, had made him elect to join the cavalry.

"Sorry about that," he added when he returned, "but we've just ridden all the way from Monthois – twenty-five miles non-stop – and Zephyr will be mighty glad to get something inside him."

Zephyr was his horse. Prosper himself declined the offer of food and would take no more than a cup of coffee. He was waiting for his officer, who in turn was waiting for the Emperor. It might take five minutes, it might take two hours. So his officer had told him to tether the horses in the shade. Maurice's curiosity was aroused, but Prosper met his inquiries with a blank expression.

"No use asking me. . . . Some message of other. . . . Documents to be delivered."

Rochas, meanwhile, was eyeing the cavalryman with special interest and regard: the uniform brought back memories of his own days in Africa.

"Where were you serving, lad?" he asked.

"In Medeah, sir."

Medeah! The very name established a bond between them, despite their difference in rank. Prosper had grown inured to that life of uninterrupted active service: they were forever in the saddle, riding off to battle as though to a day's hunting, flushing Arabs in lieu of game. There was only one mess-tin to each "tribe" of ten men; and each tribe was a family, one man cooking the meals, another doing the washing, the rest pitching the tents, looking after the horses and keeping the equipment clean and polished. They

57

rode all morning and all afternoon with enormous packs on their shoulders and the sun beating down. At night they lit huge fires to keep the mosquitoes at bay and sat round the blaze singing songs that reminded them of home. Often, beneath the mass of stars in the clear night sky, they had to get up and pacify the horses which, lashed by the hot wind, would suddenly begin to bite one another and break free, whinneying furiously. And then there was the coffee, the delicious coffee, the big event of the day : they used to grind it at the bottom of a mess-tin and sift it through a regulation red sash. But there were the black days also, days when they were brought face to face with the enemy far from all human habitation. No singsongs or drinking-bouts then. Sometimes they suffered monstrously from thirst or hunger or lack of sleep. But they still loved the life for its adventurousness and unpredictability, and with its never-ending skirmishes the war was well-suited to spectacular acts of personal bravery. It was fun, this life of subduing a wilderness, enlivened by the razzias, or wholesale looting-raids, or by the milder raids of the local thieves, whose legendary feats made even the generals laugh.

"Ah!" said Prosper, turning solemn, "it's a different story over here : they don't fight the same way at all."

And prompted by a further question from Maurice, he told of their landing at Toulon and their long and arduous journey to Lunéville. Only there did they learn what had been happening at Wissembourg and Froeschwiller. There was some confusion in his mind as to the exact route they had followed after that – the names of the towns were all jumbled together; but from Nancy they had trudged to Saint-Mihiel, and from Saint-Mihiel to Metz. On 14th August there must have been a great battle : the horizon was ablaze. But all he had seen of it was four Uhlans crouching behind a hedge. On the sixteenth there was more fighting. The artillery thundered away all day, from six in the morning onwards. By all accounts, even worse horrors were to follow on the eighteenth. But by that time the Chasseurs were far away – for on the sixteenth, while lined up beside a road at Gravelotte, waiting to be sent to the front, the Emperor drove by in a barouche and commandeered them as his escort on the journey to Verdun. A charming ride that turned out to be! Twenty-five miles at the gallop, ceaselessly haunted by the fear of being cut off by the Prussians. . . .

"What about Bazaine?" asked Rochas.

"Bazaine? They say he was only too glad to get the Emperor out from under his feet."

But the lieutenant wanted to know whether Bazaine was on his way here. At this, Prosper shrugged helplessly : who could say? Since the sixteenth their days had been entirely given over to marches and counter-marches in the rain, to reconnaissance expeditions and outpost duties; and in all that time they had never set eyes on a Prussian. Now he was an accredited member of the Châlons army. His regiment, together with two other regiments of light cavalry and one of hussars, was incorporated in one of the divisions of reserve cavalry – the 1st Division under General Margueritte, of whom he spoke with liking and enthusiasm.

"Aye – he's a plucky devil, that one. But what's the use? So far, the only thing the other generals have been any good at is landing us in the mire."

After that they were silent for a while. Then Maurice mentioned Remilly and Uncle Fouchard, and Prosper said how sorry he was that he could not go and pay his respects to Honoré, the artillery sergeant, whose battery was presumably stationed three or four miles away on the Laon road. But suddenly Prosper pricked his ears up : somewhere a horse had snorted. He left the table and went off to make sure that Zephyr was not in need of anything. Gradually soldiers of every rank and regiment were trickling into the tavern, for it was the hour for coffee and liqueurs. Not one table was left vacant : there was a cheerful medley of uniforms amid the green of the sun-dappled vine-leaves. Barouche, the medical officer, had just sat down beside Rochas when Jean came up and saluted.

"The captain presents his compliments, sir, and asks you to attend a meeting at three."

Rochas nodded and said he would be there sharp on time. Jean was in no hurry to leave. He smiled at Maurice, who was lighting a cigarette. Since the scene in the cattle-truck there had been a tacit truce between the two men, a kind of mutual stock-taking which grew more amicable with every passing day.

Prosper showed signs of impatience when he came back.

"If my officer is stuck in that place much longer, I'm going to treat myself to a meal. . . . What a mess-up : the Emperor may not be back before evening."

"Oh !" said Maurice, his curiosity reawakened. "So the chances are you've brought news of Bazaine?"

"Could be. There was a lot of talk about him at Monthois."

But there was a sudden commotion. And Jean, who had lingered at one of the arbour gates, looked round and said : "The Emperor !"

Instantly every man there was on his feet. A platoon of life-guards came in sight between the rows of poplars lining the white roadway. How splendidly crisp and glittering their uniforms were : the breastplates shone like golden suns. A second platoon followed some distance behind, and in the considerable gap between the two rode the Emperor, mounted on horseback and accompanied by his staff.

Heads were bared and a few cheers rang out. And as he rode by, the Emperor glanced up – looking extremely pale and drawn, with dim, wavering, watery eyes. Like a man waking from a nap, he directed a faint smile at the sunny little inn and saluted.

At this point Jean and Maurice distinctly heard Barouche, who had been subjecting the Emperor to a long, hard professional stare, grunt : "No doubt about it, the man's got the gravel." Then in two brief words he delivered his prognosis : "Done for !"

Jean, reacting with his instinctive common sense, nodded his head in agreement : a wretched misfortune for an army, having such a leader ! And when, ten minutes later, delighted with the tasty meal he had eaten, Maurice shook Prosper by the hand and went off for a quiet stroll and smoke, he also bore away the memory of that remote, white-faced Emperor trotting by on his horse. His features and bearing had been those of a conspirator, a dreamer, whose energy fails him when the moment for action arrives. He was said to be extremely goodnatured, with a capacity for thinking in broad, generous terms and with the unshakeable determination of a man of few words; in addition he was very brave, with the instinctive contempt for danger of a fatalist who is prepared to accept whatever comes his way. But major crises seemed to knock him into a daze; it was as though the fulfilment of destiny had a paralyzing effect on him, rendering him helpless once it turned against him. And Maurice found himself wondering whether this was not some special physiological condition, aggravated by pain, and whether the illness from which the Emperor was clearly suffering was not the cause of the indecisiveness and mounting incompetence which he had displayed ever since the campaign began. That would explain everything. A stone in the bladder, and empires tottered.

After rollcall that evening there was a sudden stir and bustle in the camp. Officers hurried about, passing on orders, making

60

arrangements for departure at five next morning. And it was with a start of surprise and alarm that Maurice realized the entire position had been transformed yet again : they were no longer falling back on Paris; they were going to move forward to Verdun and link up with Bazaine. There were rumours that a dispatch had arrived in the course of the day, announcing the latter's intention of carrying out a withdrawal; and the young man's thoughts went back to Prosper and his officer who had ridden all the way from Monthois, possibly to bring a copy of that very dispatch. So the Empress-Regent and the newly formed cabinet were having their way after all, thanks to the constant vacillating of Marshal Mac-Mahon; still horrified at the idea of the Emperor's returning to Paris, they were stubbornly determined to impel the army forward in a final bid to save the dynasty. And this wretched Emperor, this poor man who had no further place in his own empire, was about to be borne away like a useless and burdensome bundle, among the baggage-train of his own forces; and as a final irony, he would drag in his wake his imperial household, his lifeguards, his carts, his horses, his cooks, his vans with their choice wines and silver saucepans, all the pomp of his bee-spangled imperial robes trailing over the blood and mud of the road to defeat.

Midnight found Maurice still awake. A feverish restlessness, interspersed with bad dreams, made him toss and turn beneath the canvas. In the end he went outside. It was a relief to stand up and breathe in the cool air and the wind. The sky had clouded over and the darkness was growing very black, an endless gloom lit here and there by the last dying fires along the colour-lines. And in the overpowering stillness of these black silent acres it was possible to sense the slow breathing of the hundred thousand men who were lying there. At this, Maurice's unrest was allayed; he was invaded by a powerful sense of a fellow-feeling and indulgent fondness for every one of these sleeping beings, thousands of whom would soon be sleeping the sleep of the dead. Say what you like, they were a good crowd. They hadn't much discipline; they stole and they drank. But what sufferings they had already endured – and what a wealth of excuse there was for them, with the whole nation tumbling about their ears ! By this time the golden veterans of Sebastapol and Solferino formed only a tiny nucleus at the heart of a force which was in the main too young and incapable of prolonged resistance. These four army corps, hastily assembled and reconstituted, with so little co-ordination, were the army of despair, the atoning flock sent to the sacrifice in a bid to appease the wrath of destiny. They must endure their martyrdom to the last, redeeming the sins of the whole community with the red river of their blood, ennobled by the very horror of the disaster bearing down on them.

And as he stood there, in the depths of the quivering dark, Maurice was suddenly filled with a powerful sense of duty. He was no longer swayed by the vainglorious hope of repeating the legendary victories of the past. By going to Verdun they were going to their deaths, and he accepted the fact with a rugged and cheerful determination – since they had to die.

IV

AT SIX O'CLOCK in the morning on Tuesday August 23, the camping ground was cleared and the hundred thousand men of the Châlons army began to surge forward like a mighty river resuming its course after temporarily widening into a lake; and despite the rumours which had circulated the night before it was a great surprise to many to find that, instead of continuing the withdrawal, the army was turning its back on Paris and heading away eastwards, into the unknown.

As late as five o'clock the 7th Corps had still been without cartridges. For the past two days the artillerymen had toiled furiously in the cluttered railway station, unloading the supplies that were pouring in from Metz. Only at the last moment were a few vanloads of cartridges discovered among the hopeless confusion of trains; a fatigue party – Jean was a member – took away two hundred and forty thousand, using vehicles which had been hurriedly requisitioned. Jean issued the regulation hundred cartridges to every member of his squad just as Gaude began to sound his bugle.

The 106th was not destined to pass through Rheims. Its orders were to skirt the town and head for the main road to Châlons. But once again no attempt had been made to organize a phased withdrawal : all four army corps set off at the same time, which led to extreme confusion as the units tried to emerge from the byways. Artillery and cavalry were constantly cutting across the lines of infantrymen and bringing them to a standstill. Entire brigades were kept waiting for an hour, arms at the order. And to complete their discomfort, a terrible storm broke barely ten minutes from the start, a torrential downpour which soaked the men to the skin, making their packs and greatcoats weigh even heavier on their shoulders. The 106th was able to move forward again, however, just as the rain stopped. A column of Zouaves were less fortunate : compelled to go on waiting in an adjoining field, they decided to while away

63

the time by flinging mud-pies at one another; how they laughed as the dirt splashed over their uniforms!

Almost at once the sun blazed forth again in the hot August morning, restoring the men to their earlier mood of cheerfulness. They steamed like washing on a line and very soon they were dry, resembling muddied dogs pulled out of a pond, full of jokes about the lumps of dried earth which stuck to their red trousers. Each new cross-roads brought them to a standstill. Finally the column came to a halt outside a busy tavern on the very edge of Rheims.

Maurice took it into his head to stand a round of drinks and toast the other members of the squad.

"If you don't mind, corporal. . . ."

Jean hesitated for a moment, then said he wouldn't object to a nip. Loubet and Chouteau joined them, the latter slyly respectful ever since the corporal had stood up to him. And Pache and Lapoulle were there too – not much harm in either of them as long as other people didn't put ideas into their heads.

"Good health, corporal!" said Chouteau, as though butter would not melt in his mouth.

"Same to you, and may we all come back in one piece!" Jean returned civilly, and the others laughed and seconded his wish.

But they were already on the move again. Captain Beaudoin came over to them with a shocked expression on his face, although Lieutenant Rochas turned a blind eye, understanding the men's thirst. They hurried along the Châlons road, a straight, endless, tree-lined ribbon drawn across the immense plain, with stubble-fields as far as the eye could see, broken here and there by tall hayricks and wooden mills with rotating sails. Farther northwards, lines of telegraph poles indicated where other roads lay, and the dark lines of tramping regiments showed clearly on them. Some units were even advancing in bulk across the fields. At the head of the column and a little to the left, a brigade of cavalry trotted along, looking resplendent in the sunlight. And the sad, empty reaches of the entire horizon were brought to life by these streams of men issuing from every direction like the outpourings of some inexhaustible anthill.

At about nine o'clock the 106th left the Châlons highway and turned left on to the Suippe road, another unvarying ribbon stretching away into the far distance. The men were advancing in open file, leaving the middle of the roadway free. The officers progressed at their own pace, away from the rest, and Maurice could not help noticing the worried looks on their faces, so much at variance with the high spirits and cheery contentment of the men, who were happy as sandboys to be on the march again. Since the squad was almost at the head of the column, he even had a distant view of the colonel, M. de Vineuil, whose sombre bearing and tall stiff frame, rocking in time with his horse, made a profound impression on him. The band had been relegated to the rear, among the sutlers' carts. Then, attached to the division, came the ambulance teams and the commissariat, and these in turn were followed by the convoy catering for the needs of the whole army corps; it stretched for over three miles and was made up of forage waggons and provision vans and baggage carts, vehicles of every kind; glimpses of this enormous tail were afforded on the rare occasions when there was a slight bend in the road. Last of all, bringing up the rear, came a herd of cattle – a straggling drove of large oxen trampling along in a cloud of dust, the unslaughtered meat of a migrating warrior tribe.

Every so often Lapoulle would heave his pack higher on to his back. The others were always using his outstanding strength as an excuse to burden him with heavy items which were used by the squad as a whole – the boiling pot and the can containing the water supply. On this occasion they had entrusted him with the company spade – as a special honour, they explained. And far from complaining, he laughed as he listened to the song with which Loubet, the resident tenor, sought to relieve the tedium of the long straight road. Loubet himself was the owner of a much-renowned pack which held something of everything : linen, spare shoes, needle and thread, brushes, chocolate, knife and fork, tin mug, to say nothing of regulation rations and biscuits and coffee. . . . In addition to all this and the hundred cartridges, there was the weight of the rolled blanket resting on top of his pack, as well as of the shelter-tent with its ropes and pegs. Yet he was, to use his own words, such a deft hand at packing that the load seemed a light one.

At long intervals Chouteau would grumble : "Filthy rotten place !" and dart a look of contempt at these drab plains of barren Champagne. The vast expanses of chalky soil stretched away and away in unrelieved monotony. Never a glimpse of a farmhouse or a human being, nothing but flocks of crows on the wing, black specks against the immeasurable greyness. Over on the left, in the far distance, dark green pinewoods capped the gentle undulations that rimmed the sky; over on the right the course of the river Vesle

65

could be divined from an unbroken line of trees. And for the past two or three miles a considerable quantity of smoke had been observed rising from the back of the hills beyond the river, until at last the billows blotted out the horizon with undeniable evidence of a major conflagration.

"What can be burning over there?" voices were asking on every side.

But soon the explanation sped through the column. It was Châlons camp, and it had been ablaze for the past forty-eight hours, fired by order of the Emperor so that the wealth of supplies gathered there should not fall into enemy hands. Apparently the rearguard cavalry had been instructed to ignite a shambling wooden building known as the Yellow Magazine, full of tents and pegs and matting, and also the New Magazine, a giant shed piled high with mess-tins and shoes and blankets, sufficient to equip another hundred thousand men. Hayricks had been fired too and were going up in smoke, like giant torches. And at the sight of all this, at the spectacle of these live swirling masses pouring out from behind the distant hills and filling the sky with an emblem of unrelieved mourning, the army was reduced to a pained silence as it moved across the great bleak plain. There was no other sound beneath the sky except the rhythmic tramp of feet, and time and again heads were turned involuntarily in the direction of the ever-growing pall which, like a portent of disaster, seemed to pursue the marching column for a couple of miles or more.

Cheerfulness returned at the midday halt. The troops enjoyed a snack in a field, cushioning themselves with their kit. The thick square-shaped biscuits were all right for dipping in stew; but the small round ones, light and crisp, were a real titbit. There was only one thing wrong with them: they induced a terrible thirst. Now it was Pache's turn to sing: at the invitation of his comrades he broke into a hymn – and soon the whole squad joined in. Jean smiled goodnaturedly, voicing no protest, while Maurice's confidence revived as he considered the general animation, the perfect orderliness and high spirits of this first day on the march. And the remainder of the allotted distance was covered with the same alacrity, though the last eight miles were hard going. They had left the village of Prosnes behind and to the right of them and abandoned the highway in favour of some sandy wastes, quite empty except an occasional pine spinney. The entire division, with its endless supply column in tow, was twisting and turning among these spinneys, and the men sank up to their ankles as they trudged through the sand. Here the country was even more lonely than before : the only living creatures they encountered were a meagre flock of sheep guarded by a big black dog.

Finally, at about four o'clock, the 106th stopped at Dontrien, a village standing beside the Suippe. The small river meanders among clumps of trees; the old churchyard is shaded throughout its length and breadth by an enormous chestnut tree. And it was on the left bank, in a sloping meadow, that the regiment pitched its tents. According to the officers, all four army corps would be making camp that night along a twelve-mile stretch of the Suippe, all the way from Auberive to Heutrégiville, an area that included Dontrien, Bétheniville and Pont-Faverger.

Gaude lost no time in sounding the call to rations, and Jean went hurrying off with Lapoulle at his side – for the corporal was the great provider, always on the alert. They came back half an hour later with a raw rib of beef and a bundle of firewood. Of the herd of cattle at the rear of the army, three animals had already been killed and sliced up in the shade of an oak. Lapoulle had to make a second journey for the bread, which had been baking in the village ovens from midday onwards. On this first leg of the journey there was plenty of everything except wine and tobacco – of which, indeed, no distribution was ever to be made.

When Jean returned he found Chouteau and Pache putting the tent up. He watched them for a while with the eye of a veteran; clearly he did not think much of their workmanship.

"Good job it's going to be a fine night," he said at last. "If a wind got up, we'd all be blown straight into the river. I'll have to show you the right way of doing it."

He was on the point of sending Maurice to fill the big water-can. But Maurice was sitting on the grass with his shoe off, examining his right foot.

"Hullo, what's the matter?"

"The counter has rubbed the skin off my heel. . . . My other shoes were wearing out and I was fool enough to buy these in Rheims. They seemed a good fit at the time, but I was wrong."

Jean knelt down, took hold of the injured foot and turned it this way and that as gingerly as if it were a child's. He shook his head.

"I don't like the look of it," he said. "You'll have to watch out. Without the use of his feet, a soldier is no good to anyone. My

67

captain in Italy never tired of saying it was legs that won or lost battles."

So Pache was sent for the water instead – no great hardship, in fact, for the river was only sixty yards away. While he was gone, Loubet dug a hole in the ground and lit the wood so that as soon as the water arrived he was able to start cooking. Into the big pot went the skilfully skewered hunk of beef. And then came the blissful sight of the meal beginning to boil and bubble. It was like a family picnic : the whole squad, released from duties, lay sprawled on the grass surrounding the fire, full of fond solicitude for the stewing meat while Loubet gravely skimmed the pot with his ladle. In this futureless race to the unknown they had become like children or savages, with no thought for anything but eating and sleeping.

At this point, however, Maurice opened his pack and fished out one of the newspapers which he had bought in Rheims.

"Any news of the Prussians?" asked Chouteau. "If there is, you'd better read it out to us."

They were all getting on well together, thanks to the growing weight of Jean's authority. Maurice obligingly read out all the news that was likely to interest them while Pache, the resident seamster, put a darn in his greatcoat and Lapoulle gave his rifle a clean. First came an account of a great victory for Bazaine, who had sent an entire Prussian army corps flying into the quarries at Jaumont; and this fanciful tale was enriched by dramatic accounts of men and horses being crushed to death among the rocks – annihilation so complete that there was nothing left to bury except unrecognizable bits and pieces. Then came copious details of the pitiful condition of the invading armies : ill-fed and ill-equipped, the German troops were on their last legs and dying off fast from hideous diseases. Another news item recorded that the King of Prussia was suffering from diarrhoea and that Bismarck had broken his leg by jumping out of the window of an inn where he was very nearly captured by a party of Zouaves. The squad revelled in every word of this. Lapoulle laughed as though he would never stop, while Chouteau and the others, their minds untroubled by the smallest seed of doubt, were cock-a-hoop at the thought of gathering in the Prussians as easily as sparrows felled in a hailstorm. And they really fell about when they heard of how Bismarck had come a cropper. Ah – those Zouaves and Turcos were plucky devils, and no mistake ! Currency was being given to legendary stories of every kind. The Germans were apparently quaking in their boots and objecting angrily that it was disgraceful for any civilized nation to employ "savages" in defence of its soil. Despite the fact that the French had already been mown down at Froeschwiller, the impression was given that the Algerian units were still intact and invincible.

The clock in the little belltower of Dontrien church struck six.

"Grub up!" shouted Loubet, without a moment's delay.

The squad gathered round like worshippers. At the last minute Loubet had managed to procure some vegetables from one of the local peasants. All the right ingredients had gone into the pot to yield a stew that melted in the mouth and smelled sweetly of carrots and leeks. The spoons scraped and clattered in the little mess-tins. Sharing the food out was Jean's responsibility and today he had to allocate the meat with special care, for all eyes were upon him and there would have been a tremendous outcry if any one portion had been larger than the rest. The men gorged themselves till not a scrap was left.

When Chouteau had finished he lay back in the grass and let out a contented sigh.

"Ah," he said, "that was a darned sight better than a kick in the pants!"

Maurice was feeling equally well-fed and cheerful. He gave no further thought to his foot : the smart was wearing off. He was ready now to accept this rough-and-ready comradeship; the physical demands of living as one of a group had induced an easy-going sense of equality. Similarly at night he slept the same deep sleep as his tent-mates; they all huddled together, pleased by the warmth which they gave and received under the heavy dew. It must be added that at Loubet's instigation Lapoulle had appropriated several generous armfuls of straw from a nearby rick – the six fellows could not have slept more comfortably in a feather bed. And beneath the clear night sky, from Auberive to Heutrégiville, along the pleasant willowed banks of the slow-moving Snippe, the camp-fires of these hundred thousand slumberers illumined the twelve-mile expanse of plain like a trail of stars.

At sunrise they made coffee, crushing the beans with a rifle-butt and tipping them into the boiling water, then precipitating the grounds by adding a drop of cold. That morning the sun-rise was unusually magnificent, amid a cluster of purple-and-gold clouds. But even Maurice no longer had eyes for these brilliant skies and Jean – with his peasant wariness – was the only one to gaze uneasily at the red dawn foretelling rain. Which was why, just before they set off, he berated Loubet and Pache for tying the squad's daily bread-ration to the outside of their packs. But by then they had folded the tents away and fastened their packs, so they paid no attention. The church clocks in all the neighbouring villages were striking six as the whole army moved off, blithely resuming its march in the pristine confidence of the new day.

The aim now was for the 106th to rejoin the Rheims-Vouziers road. For more than an hour it cut along by-roads and made its way uphill through the stubblefields. Below them and to the north, Béthiniville was visible among trees – the Emperor was reputed to have slept there. And when they reached the Vouziers road, yesterday's plains began all over again; barren Champagne unfolded the remainder of its poor fields, dispiriting in their monotony. Now they had the meagre Arne on their left, while on their right the bare fields stretched away as far as the eye could see – the uniform lines extending to the horizon. They passed through some villages : Saint-Clément, whose single winding street bisects the highway; Saint-Pierre, a market-town whose wealthy inhabitants had barricaded their doors and windows. . . . The column halted for a long rest at about ten o'clock, close to another village, Saint-Etienne, where to their joy the men were able to lay in some more tobacco. The 7th Corps had divided into several columns. The 106th was now on its own, with nothing to rearward except one battalion of Chasseurs and the reserve artillery. Maurice looked back in vain whenever they came to bends in the road : there was no sign of the huge supply column which had captured his interest the day before. The cattle had disappeared; only the artillery remained, rumbling along, the guns so magnified by these bare flat plains that they looked like dark, long-legged grasshoppers.

Beyond Saint-Etienne, however, the going became atrocious – the road undulating slowly uphill amid broad barren fields where nothing grew save the inevitable dark-capped pine spinneys which looked so dismal among the colourless tracts of soil. Here was desolation such as they had never yet encountered. Inadequately metalled and thoroughly softened by the recent rain, the roadway was a bed of mud – liquified grey clay that stuck to the feet like pitch. Progress became so difficult that the men soon felt too exhausted to go on. And to make matters worse a series of heavy showers began, of alarming ferocity. The artillery got stuck and nearly had to be left behind.

Eventually Chouteau, who was carrying the rice issue, grew out

70

of breath. He was so furious at the crushing burden that had been inflicted on him that he discarded the bundle in the fond belief that the action would pass unnoticed. But Loubet caught him.

"Don't go doing things like that : it will mean empty bellies for the rest of us."

"Don't you believe it!" returned Chouteau. "There's plenty more where that lot came from. We can stock up again tonight."

And Loubet, who was carrying the bacon ration, was sufficiently convinced by this argument to jetison his own burden.

Meanwhile Maurice's foot had been growing more and more painful : the heel must have become inflamed again. He was limping so badly that Jean, giving way to his mounting concern, asked : "Beginning to trouble you again, is it?"

And when, shortly afterwards, the man were granted a short breather, he proffered a word of advice : "Take your shoe off and march barefoot. The cool mud will ease the smart."

Maurice complied with the suggestion and afterwards, sure enough, he was able to keep up without too much difficulty. He was filled with a profound sense of gratitude. It was a real stroke of luck for any squad, having a corporal like Jean with plenty of service behind him and real knowledge of the various tricks of the trade. He was only a rough peasant, but there was a lot to be said for him just the same.

Not until late in the day did they reach Contreuve, where they were due to make camp. First they had to cross the Châlons-Vouziers highway and make the steep descent into Semide gully. The landscape was changing : already they were in the Ardennes. And from the vast bare hills, selected as camping ground for the 7th Corps and overlooking the village, they had a distant view of the Aisne valley under pale smokey rain.

Six o'clock came and still Gaude had not sounded the call to rations. So Jean, eager for a task that would occupy his brain and hands, and genuinely worried about the strong wind that was getting up, decided to demonstrate the proper method of pitching a tent. He explained how important it was to choose a site that was somewhat on the slope, to drive the pegs in at an angle, and to dig a small trench round the circumference as a trap for rainwater. Maurice was excused all duties on account of his foot, and he merely looked on, taken aback by the dexterity of this stolid, clumsy-looking man. He himself was dog-tired, yet borne up by the mood of optimism which was now returning to every heart. They had

71

been marched off their feet since Rheims, covering the best part of forty miles in two days. If they continued at this rate, marching straight ahead all the time, they would unquestionably send the German second army reeling and establish contact with Bazaine before the third army under the Crown Prince of Prussia – reputedly at Vitry-le-François – had time to make its way up to Verdun.

"Looks like they're going to let us starve," said Chouteau, when seven o'clock came and still no rations had been distributed.

To be on the safe side, Jean had bidden Loubet light the fire and set the water to boil just as usual; and since they had no wood he had been forced to shut his eyes when, as a means of obtaining some, the latter calmly ripped the trelliswork from a neighbouring garden. When he talked about cooking some rice and bacon, however, his subordinates had no choice but to admit that both these foodstuffs had been left behind in the muddy wastes of the Saint-Etienne road. Chouteau lied brazenly, insisting that the bundle must have worked loose and fallen from his pack unbeknown to him.

"You worthless louts!" roared Jean. "Throwing good food away when there are thousands of poor devils crying out for a meal!"

They were in no better luck with the three loaves which had been issued to them that morning. Loubet and Pache had obstinately refused to listen when he had told them to cover the bread, and now the rain had watered it down till it was all pap and quite unchewable.

"Now we're really up the creek," shouted Jean. "We had everything we needed, yet here we are without a crumb between us. . . . Ah, you worthless louts!"

Just then the platoon leaders were called together. Sergeant Sapin, gloomy as ever, returned with the news that it was quite impossible to get any rations to the men : they would have to make do with what they had with them. Apparently the supply column had been held up by the bad weather. As for the cattle, conflicting orders must have led to their being herded to the wrong place. Afterwards it came to light that the 5th and 12th Corps had been making for Rethel, where the army was to set up its headquarters; consequently all the produce of the local villages had been pouring into the town – and so had the inhabitants, fired with enthusiasm at the thought of seeing the Emperor. Which was why the countryside in the path of the 7th Corps came to be empty : no meat, no bread, no villagers even. And as a crowning misfortune, the food already in the hands of the commissariat had been misrouted to

72

Le Chêne-Populeux. Throughout the campaign the wretched supply officers were in constant despair; they were the target of every fighting man's abuse, yet as a rule their only error was to keep to schedules which the troops themselves did not observe.

"You worthless louts!" said Jean yet again, beside himself with rage. "Serves you darned well right! And now I've got to rack my brains and find you something. You don't deserve it, but it's my duty to see you don't peg out on the road."

He went reconnoitring, as every good corporal should; with him he took Pache, liking him for his gentleness, even though he considered him over-addicted to priests.

By this time, however, Loubet had spotted a small farmhouse some two or three hundred yards away, on the farthest outskirts of Contreuve. A good deal of activity seemed to be going on there. He called Chouteau and Lapoulle over and said. "Let's do some reconnoitring of our own. I reckon there's some grub going over there."

So Maurice was left in charge of the boiling-pot, which was beginning to bubble, and given strict orders to keep the fire going.

He sat on his blanket, leaving his shoe off in the hope that the air might dry up the sore. The camp was an engrossing sight: a certain topsy-turviness had prevailed since the news that no rations were forthcoming. He was beginning to realize that some squads were always hard up for everything while others lived in unfailing plenty; it depended on the degree of skill and foresight shown by each corporal and the men under him. Ignoring all the stir and bustle that surrounded him and staring past the tents and the piled arms, he observed some squads which had not even succeeded in lighting a fire; others had already given up the struggle and settled down for the night; a number, on the other hand, were enjoying a good meal – heaven knew what they were eating, but it must have been something good. Another thing that impressed him was the impeccable turn-out of the reserve artillery encamped on the hill-side above him. The sun, as it went down, appeared among the clouds and lent a glow to the heavy guns, which the artillerymen had already washed clean of mud.

Meanwhile, in the little farmhouse which Loubet and his com-panions had their eyes on, General Bourgain-Desfeuilles – their brigade commander – was making himself at home. After finding himself a reasonable bed, he had just sat down to an omelet and a roast chicken – the sight of which put him in an excellent frame of mind. Colonel de Vineuil happened to pay a duty call just then, so the general invited him to dinner. The two men were being waited on by a tall, flaxen-haired fellow who had been in the farmer's service for only three days and who was, he said, from Alsace – a refugee from the rout at Froeschwiller. The general talked freely in front of this man, commenting on the army's movements and then asking him where various towns and villages were, and how far away, forgetting that the servant was not a local man. Eventually the colonel was quite unnerved by the utter ignorance which these questions revealed. He himself had lived in Mézières for a time. He imparted a few clear directions, which prompted the general to exclaim : "Could anything be more senseless ! How can a man be expected to fight in strange surroundings?"

The colonel shrugged despairingly. Survey maps of Germany had been issued to all French officers as soon as war was declared; but did even one of them have a map of France in his possession? The colonel had been utterly confounded by what he had seen and heard during the past month. Now he was shorn of everything except his courage, for his authority carried little weight. As a leader of men he was rather weak and unimaginative, inspiring affection rather than fear.

"Can't a man even have dinner in peace?" the general shouted suddenly. "Why should I have to endure that hullabaloo. You," he said to the man from Alsace, "go and find out what's happening !"

But at this point the farmer burst into the room, incensed, gesticulating, sobbing. The army was thieving his property : the building was being looted by Chasseurs and Zouaves. In a moment of weakness he had begun to offer his wares, being the only man in the village with eggs and potatoes and rabbits to dispose of. He had demanded a price that was not unduly extortionate, pocketed the money, handed over the goods. And what had happened? The purchasers – coming in ever greater numbers, more than he could cope with without confusion – had finally pushed him out of the way and taken the lot without paying. The fact that a great many peasants were hiding everything they owned and refusing even requests for glasses of water was attributable to their alarm at the steady and irresistible military force which was driving them from their homes and possessions.

"Don't come whining to me, my good man !" the general replied in vexation. "By rights we ought to shoot a dozen of the scoundrels every day. But how can we?"

And with that he demanded that the door be shut, so that he should not be embroiled. It was left to the colonel to explain that no rations had been issued and the men were hungry.

Outside, Loubet had quickly detected a potato field. He and Lapoulle hurried over to it and began to rummage with both hands, uprooting the potatoes and stuffing them into their pockets. But suddenly Chouteau, who had been gazing over a low wall, let out a summoning whistle. They raced to his side and gasped when they saw what he was looking at : a flock of geese, a dozen magnificent geese, strutting majestically in a narrow yard. The men put their heads together and Lapoulle was persuaded to hop over the wall. A terrible scuffle ensued : the goose which Lapoulle had seized nearly sliced his nose off with its tough shear-like beak. Whereupon he grabbed its neck and tried to strangle it while the bird belaboured his arms and midriff with its powerful webbed feet. In the end he had to batter its head in with his fist, and even then it went on struggling. He took to his heels – pursued by the rest of the flock, which were tearing at his legs.

The trio hurried away, keeping their booty hidden in a sack. On their return they ran into Jean and Pache, who were equally well contented with their expedition and laden with four fresh loaves and a cheese which they had bought from a kindly old woman.

"Water's boiling – we'll make some coffee," said the corporal. "We've bread and cheese – the makings of a real banquet."

But all of a sudden he caught sight of the goose lying at his feet and he could not help laughing. He prodded it like an expert and was overwhelmed with admiration.

"Well, that's a damned fine bird if ever I saw one! Must weigh nigh on twenty pounds."

" 'Twas a chance encounter," explained Loubet with his usual waggishness. "She seemed so eager to make our acquaintance."

Jean held up his hand as much as to say : tell me no more. Men had to live. Besides, why shouldn't they feast themselves for once? Poor devils, they had forgotten what poultry tasted like.

Loubet was already stoking the fire up. Pache and Lapoulle were ripping the feathers off the bird. Chouteau rushed away to borrow a length of string from the gunners; on his return he hung the goose before the blazing fire, with bayonets as twin supports; and Maurice was given the job of turning it from time to time with a flick of his fingers. The fat dripped into the large mess-tin which had been carefully positioned beneath the bird. It was a triumph

75

of outdoor roasting. The whole regiment gathered round, lured by the delicious smell. What a banquet! Roast goose, boiled potatoes, bread, cheese . . .! No sooner had Jean finished carving the bird than the squad fell to. This was no time for fussing over the size of portions : everyone was stowing away as much as he could hold. They even dispatched a helping to the gunners who had given them the string.

That evening, as it happened, there was no food for the officers. The provision van had gone astray, presumably following the same route as the main supply column. True, any breakdown in distribution was likely to result in hardship for the men; but as a rule they managed to find something or other to eat – they helped one another, they pooled their resources. Whereas an officer was helpless if the canteen failed him; left to his own devices, he had no means of staving off hunger.

Chouteau had heard Captain Beaudoin inveighing against the disappearance of the provisions van. So when, burrowing deep into the carcass of the goose, he glanced up and saw the captain walking stiffly and proudly by, he quickly drew the others' attention to the sight.

"Just look at him!" he jeered. "See his nostrils twitching? He'd give a week's pay for the parson's nose."

They all relished the thought of the captain's hunger. He had failed to win the affection of his men, being too young and too harsh – "a proper little martinet", as they called him. For a second or two he seemed about to rebuke the squad for creating such a commotion. But something – presumably the fear of betraying his own hunger – made him change his mind and he strode away with his head held high, as though he had seen nothing.

Lieutenant Rochas's hunger-pangs were just as severe, but he laughed manfully as he strolled near the well-satisfied squad. He, for his part, was worshipped by his men, firstly because he loathed the captain – that puppy from Saint-Cyr – and secondly because he knew what it was like to serve in the ranks. Not that he was always an easy man to deal with : sometimes he reprimanded them in terms so crude that they could have hit him.

Jean, after a quick exchange of glances with his comrades, stood up and led Rochas round to the back of the tent.

"No disrespect intended, sir, but we wondered whether you might fancy a little of this . . ."

And he handed him a hunk of bread and a mess-tin, in which a leg of goose lay atop half a dozen potatoes.

76

Once again they needed no rocking to sleep when they settled down for the night. The six of them slept off the effects of the meal, lying with their fists clenched like children. And they had good reason to be grateful to the corporal for pitching the tent so securely, even though they never noticed the violent squall which got up at about two o'clock, bringing a violent downpour with it. A number of tents were blown away and their occupants, waking with a start, were soaked to the skin and forced to scurry about in the dark. Whereas their own stood firm and they were kept safe and dry thanks to Jean's simple but effective system of drainage.

Maurice woke at first light, and as the day's march was not due to begin until eight o'clock it occurred to him that he might as well walk up to the hillside encampment of the reserve artillery and pay his respects to cousin Honoré. A good night's sleep had eased the pain in his foot. Once again he found himself marvelling at the skill and efficiency with which the gunners had parked their transport and equipment : the six heavy guns were impeccably aligned, and neatly drawn up behind them were the ammunition carts, the forage waggons and the field smithies. In the background the tethered horses were whinneying, with their nostrils turned towards the rising sun. He immediately located Honoré's tent, for the entire team associated with a particular gun is lodged in a single line of tents; which makes it possible to tell at a glance how many guns there are in any given camp.

When Maurice arrived, the gunners were already up and about. They were drinking coffee and there was a quarrel in progress between Adolphe, the front driver, and Louis, the gunner – his "mate". Throughout the three years they had been paired they had got on well except at mealtimes. Louis, better educated and highly intelligent, accepted the subordinate role which any horse-soldier foists upon any foot-soldier. He was willing enough to pitch the tent, do all the chores and keep an eye on the cooking, while Adolphe – with an air of utter superiority – merely attended to his two horses. All the same, Louis (dark and thin, with an inordinate appetite) used to rebel when Adolphe (an extremely tall figure, with a fair bushy moustache) adopted a lordly attitude towards food and drink. That morning the quarrel had been sparked off when Louis, who had made the coffee, accused Adolphe of drinking it all. The others had to mediate between them.

Honoré always started the day by going and taking a look at his gun. He would superintend the removal of the night dew, as

77

though giving a favourite horse a rub-down for fear of its catching cold. And he was beside the gun, looking on with proprietary contentment in the cool dawn air, when he caught sight of Maurice.

"Well, well!" he said. "I knew the 106th was somewhere in the vicinity. I had a letter from Remilly yesterday and I was intending to come down and see you. Let's go and have a glass of wine together."

So that they could be alone he led Maurice towards the little farmhouse which the soldiers had raided the day before. The farmer, with an incorrigible eye for profit, had broached a cask of wine and set up a makeshift bar : he was dispensing his merchandise from a plank outside the front door, at a price of four sous a glass. He was assisted in this enterprise by the young man whom he had engaged four days earlier – the flaxen-haired giant from Alsace.

Honoré was already drinking Maurice's health when his gaze encountered this man. For a moment he stared at him in stupefaction. Then he let out a terrible cry.

"By all that's holy! Goliath!"

And with that he sprang forward, aiming to grab him by the throat. But the peasant, imagining that his home was about to be ransacked again, darted back through the doorway and barricaded himself in. For a moment there was utter confusion; all the soldiers sitting or standing round about came rushing forward, while the artillery sergeant – choking with fury – shouted : "Open up! Open up, you blasted fool. . . . The man's a spy – he's a spy, I tell you!"

By this time, all Maurice's doubts had deserted him. The man he had just seen was, indisputably, the man who had been allowed to leave Mulhouse camp because there was insufficient evidence against him. And that man was Goliath, whom old Fouchard had at one time employed as a farmhand in Remilly. When the peasant at last consented to open his door, there was no sign of the fellow – that same amiable-looking, flaxen-haired giant whom General Bourgain-Desfeuilles had questioned in vain the day before, speaking quite openly in front of him as he was having dinner. Presumably he had jumped out of a window at the rear of the building : one of them was found to be open. But a thorough search of the neighbouring fields was of no avail – tall though he was, he had disappeared like a puff of smoke.

Maurice was compelled to take Honoré to one side. The artilleryman's despair was becoming all too apparent to his comrades, and there was no point in embroiling them in these private tribulations.

78

"By all that's holy!" he exclaimed a second time. "I'd willingly have wrung his neck with my own bare hands. If anything more was needed to rouse my fury against him, this letter certainly did the trick!"

The two men had sat down by now and rested their backs against a hayrick within a few yards of the farmhouse. He handed the letter to his cousin.

There was nothing unusual about this star-crossed love of Honoré Fouchard for Silvine Morange. A dark-haired girl with beautiful submissive eyes, Silvine had been no more than a child when she lost her unmarried mother – who had been put in the family way while working as a factory hand in Rancourt. The idea of placing her in service with old Fouchard was conceived by her foster-father, Dr. Dalichamp, an admirable man who was always ready to adopt the offspring of the unfortunate women whom he attended in childbirth. True, old Fouchard was basely avaricious and inhumanly exacting : the urge to make money had made him turn butcher and hawk his wares round a score of neighbouring parishes. But he kept a fatherly eye on the child, and if she worked hard her future was assured. At all events she would be spared the debauchery of factory life. And nothing could have been more natural than that, living under old Fouchard's roof, employer's son and servant girl should fall in love. When she first went to work in the house, Silvine was twelve and Honoré sixteen. Four years later he drew lots for conscription. To his great delight he drew a blank. He was determined to marry the girl. Throughout these years the young man had shown a rare restraint, born of his calm and serious-minded disposition : nothing had ever occurred between them, beyond a few heartfelt embraces and kisses in the barn. But when he voiced the question of marriage to his father, the latter was much incensed and declared stubbornly that if a marriage took place it would be over his dead body. He offered no objection to keeping the girl in his service, though; he was confident that they would gratify their desires and that all thought of marriage would fade. For almost eighteen months after that the two young people continued to worship one another and want one another, yet still they held back. Finally, as a consequence of a terrible scene between the two men, the son decided that he could not remain at the farm any longer. He enlisted in the army and was posted to Africa. The old man kept the girl in his employ, being well-content with her services. Then the terrible thing happened : one evening a fortnight later Silvine, who had sworn that she would wait for Honoré, found herself in the arms of a farmhand who had been taken on a few months earlier – this same Goliath Steinberg, "the Prussian" as he was generally known, a tall genial-looking fellow with short fair hair and broad rosy features set in a permanent smile; Honoré had always treated him as his comrade and confidant. Had old Fouchard engineered it? Had Silvine succumbed in an unthinking moment or had she been half-ravished while still sick with grief and weak from crying over her departed loved-one? Even she could not have said; she was dumbfounded. Soon she was with child and prepared to accept the necessity of marrying Goliath. He – as ever – was all smiles: he did not say no, but merely talked of postponing the ceremony until the child was born. Then, on the very eve of the birth, he disappeared. Later it was rumoured that he had found a job on another farm, somewhere in the vicinity of Beaumont. That was three years ago, and today no one was in any doubt but that Goliath – such an affable figure, such a lad with the girls – was one of the host of spies whom the Germans had established in Eastern France. When news of these events reached Honoré in Africa he spent three months in hospital, like a man felled by sunstroke; and never once did he take home leave, for fear that he might set eyes on Silvine and the child.

The gunner's hands shook all the time Maurice was reading the letter. It was a letter from Silvine, the first and only letter she had ever written him. What emotion had impelled her to write – that reticent, subservient creature, whose dark beautiful eyes occasionally took on an expression of unshakeable resolve, in spite of having been a servant all her life? All she said was: she knew he was fighting in the campaign, and if she was destined never to see him again she could not bear to think of his dying in the belief that she no longer loved him. She loved him as much as ever and had never loved anyone else; she said the same thing over and over again for four whole pages, with little variation, not seeking to make excuses, not even attempting to explain what had happened. And not a word about the child: the letter was no more than an inexpressibly tender message of farewell.

Maurice was deeply affected. In the old days Honoré had been in the habit of opening his heart to him. He glanced up and, seeing him in tears, hugged him like a brother.

"My poor Honoré!"

But already the artillery sergeant was mastering his feelings. He carefully returned the letter to its place next to his heart. Then he buttoned his jacket.

"Yes, that kind of thing can drive one mad. . . . Oh, what wouldn't I have given for the chance to wring his neck . . . ! Anyway, we shall see."

The bugles gave warning of impending departure and they had to race back to their respective tents, though in the event there was considerable fuss and delay, so that the troops were kept waiting in full kit until nearly nine o'clock. A mood of vacillation seemed to have taken hold of the commanders : gone already was the admirable resoluteness of the first two days, when the 7th Corps had covered forty miles with only a single night's rest. And a strange, disquieting piece of news had been going the rounds since early morning : apparently the other three army corps had been striking northwards, the 1st as far as Juniville, the 5th and 12th as far as Rethel. There was no logic in this; it was being accounted for in terms of supply difficulties. Were they to assume that they were no longer bound for Verdun? Why was this day being allowed to go to waste? The position was made even more worrying by the fact that the Prussians must be close at hand by now. Indeed the men had been warned not to dawdle : any stragglers might well fall into the hands of the reconnaissance parties sent out by the enemy cavalry.

It was August 25 – and afterwards, when he recalled the manner of Goliath's disappearance, Maurice was convinced that he was one of the men who kept the German High Command informed of the exact movements of the Châlons army and who were responsible for the dramatic change of front effected by the German third army. Within twenty-four hours the Crown Prince of Prussia had left Revigny and sent his forces speeding across the Champagne region and the Ardennes in a vast enveloping movement, perfectly carried out. While the French marked time and dithered like men suddenly afflicted with the palsy, the Prussians were advancing at a rate of almost twenty-five miles a day, tracking down their human quarry and driving it towards the borderland forests.

At long last they set out, and sure enough the army wheeled to the left. The 7th Corps marched only two short leagues that day, from Contreuve to Vouziers, while the 5th and 12th stayed put at Rethel and the 1st stopped short at Attigny. Between Contreuve and the Aisne valley the plains began again, growing barer than ever. As the road drew nearer to Vouziers it wound among grey

81

tracts of soil and desolate hillocks with never a sign of a tree or a house. The place was as cheerless as a desert waste and, short though it was, the journey seemed hideously magnified by the boredom and weariness of the men's minds and bodies. It was barely midday when they halted on the left bank of the Aisne and bivouacked on the barren slopes. The last spurs overhung the valley, affording a clear view of the Monthois road, which – running parallel with the river – was the route by which they expected the enemy to appear.

Nothing could have had a more stunning effect on Maurice than the sight of the Margueritte Division riding along this same Monthois road. Margueritte's large force of reserve cavalry was supposed to be supporting the 7th Corps and reconnoitring the army's left flank. Now there were rumours that it was on its way up to Le Chêne-Populeux. Why were the generals weakening the very flank that was vulnerable to attack? What was the point of transferring these two thousand horsemen to the centre, where they would surely be utterly superfluous? They ought to be sent out on wide-ranging scouting missions. To make matters worse, their present manoeuvre was so mistimed that they had all but ploughed through the columns of the 7th Corps, giving rise to an inextricable muddle of men, guns and horses. Some of the Chasseurs d'Afrique were kept waiting almost two hours on the outskirts of Vouziers.

Which was how Maurice chanced to meet Prosper. The cavalryman had led his horse to the side of a pond, and they were able to converse for a few moments. Prosper was looking quite dazed and bewildered; he knew nothing and had seen nothing since leaving Rheims. No, that wasn't quite true : he had seen another couple of Uhlans; the devils kept on appearing and disappearing and no one ever found out where they came from or where they afterwards went to. Already there were stories of how four Uhlans had galloped into a town and captured it at gun-point, a full fifteen miles from the main body of their army corps. They were everywhere, buzzing like bees, always well to the fore of the main columns, providing a moveable screen behind which the infantry could advance unhampered as in time of peace. And Maurice felt heartbroken when he considered what poor use was being made of the Chasseurs and Hussars who now cluttered the roadway.

"Well, I'll be seeing you," he said, shaking Prosper by the hand. "Perhaps you really *are* needed further north."

But the Chasseur looked utterly out of patience with the class of work that was being thrust upon him. He stroked Zephyr forlornly and replied : "Don't you believe it ! The horses are being ridden to death and the men might as well not be there. It's downright disgusting !"

As the day wore on, Maurice's heel began to throb feverishly. When, that evening, he took his shoe off to examine the sore, he broke the skin. The blood came spurting out and he gave a cry of pain. Jean happened to be standing close by, and he looked visibly alarmed and sorry for the young man.

"Here," he said, "that needs attention or you'll be laid up with it. Just you leave it to me. . . ."

He knelt down, bathed the wound and bound it up with a spotless bandage which he took from his pack. His actions were almost motherly : into them went all the gentleness of a man of experience whose thick fingers were capable of extreme delicacy when the occasion arose.

Maurice felt quite overcome with emotion; his vision grew blurred. He felt an irresistible impulse to display affection, as though recognizing a long-lost brother in this peasant whom he had once loathed and whom, even yesterday, he had been inclined to look down on.

"What a good chap you are," he said. "You're a true friend and I thank you for it."

Jean looked very happy and he was wearing his usual smile as he responded with equal warmth : "Now, young fellow, I've still got a bit of tobacco left – how about a cigarette?"

V

WHEN Maurice got up next morning, August 26, he was stiff-backed and aching all over from his night under canvas. He had still not grown used to sleeping on hard ground. Furthermore the men had been given strict orders, the previous night, not to take their shoes off; the sergeants had gone round, feeling in the dark, making sure that everyone was properly shod and gaitered. So his foot showed little improvement – it was still painful and feverishly hot, and in addition he seemed to have caught a chill in the legs, from rashly stretching them outside the canvas in the hope of taking the stiffness out of them.

Jean's reaction was immediate : "Listen, if there's a full day's march ahead of us you'd better see the M.O. and get put aboard one of the ambulances."

But as yet there was no telling what was likely to happen. The most conflicting rumours were flying about. For a while the general supposition was that the advance was to continue. The whole army corps moved on through Vouziers : the left bank of the Aisne was abandoned except for a brigade from the second division, which was to continue to keep close watch on the Monthois road. Then suddenly, on the far side of the town, the units were brought to a standstill and ordered to pile arms in the fields and meadows stretching away on either side of the road to Grand-Pré. A few moments later, the sight of the 4th Hussars galloping away along that same road gave rise to all kinds of conjectures.

"If we remain here for any length of time, I'll stay with the rest of you," declared Maurice. He balked at the idea of the medical officer and the ambulance.

Sure enough, they learned soon afterwards that they were to camp there until General Douay had obtained definite information as to the enemy's movements. Ever since, the day before, he had seen Margueritte's division heading up towards Le Chêne, the general had been in a state of ever-increasing anxiety; this derived from the knowledge that his units no longer enjoyed the benefit of even the thinnest protective screen – with no one to guard the Argonne passes, he might well be attacked at any moment. And he had just sent the 4th Hussars out on reconnaissance, as far as the Grand-Pré and La Croix-aux-Bois passes, with orders to bring back news without fail.

The day before, thanks to the initiative shown by the mayor of Vouziers, there had been a distribution of bread, meat and fodder; and at about ten o'clock that morning the men were given permission to cook a hot meal, for fear that later there might not be time. But when, shortly afterwards, General Bordas's brigade went cantering off along the same road as that taken by the hussars, all minds were set astir again. What now? Could it be that they were leaving? Could it be that they were to lose the chance of eating in peace, just as the pots were beginning to simmer? But the officers explained that Bordas's brigade had been dispatched to occupy Buzancy, only a few miles away. Others, however, maintained that the hussars had clashed with a considerable number of enemy squadrons and that the brigade's real mission was to extricate them.

The result, for Maurice, was several delightfully restful hours. He lay full-length on the hillside where the regiment was bivouacking, and benumbed with fatigue he gazed at the greenness of the Aisne valley, at the meadows dotted about with clumps of trees and at the river threading its way idly among them. Straight ahead of him the town of Vouziers rose in tiers, sealing off the valley with an array of rooftops, dominated by the church with its slender spire and dome-capped bell-tower. Farther down, by the bridge, smoke was pouring from the tall chimneys of the tanneries, while at the other end the buildings of a large mill showed clearly, white with flour against the green foliage by the water's edge. And this sky-line view of a small town hemmed with leafy growth seemed to Maurice full of tender charm, as though his eyes were once again the eyes of a dreamer, a man of sensitivity. The days of his youth were coming back to him : he was reliving the journeys he had made to Vouziers during his early years in Le Chêne. For a whole hour he forgot everything else.

The meal had long since been digested, and time had begun to hang heavy again, when at about half-past two signs of renewed activity – limited at first, but gradually increasing in scope and volume – began to spread through the entire camp. Orders flew about, the meadows were evacuated and the troops, after working their way higher, were finally drawn up on the hills between two

85

villages, Chestres and Falaise, which lay a couple of miles apart. Already the engineers were digging trenches and establishing breastworks, while away to the left the reserve artillery was positioned atop a hillock. And the rumour spread that General Bordas had just sent dispatch rider to report that, having run into superior odds at Grand-Pré, he had no choice but to fall back on Buzancy – which gave rise to fears that his line of retreat to Vouziers might soon be cut off. So the 7th Corps commander, regarding an attack as imminent, had instructed his men to take up combat positions so as to withstand the first brunt of the attack until the rest of the army moved up in support of him; one of his aides-de-camp had been sent off with a letter addressed to the marshal, telling him of the situation and asking for assistance. Finally, for fear that he might be encumbered by the endless supply column (which had caught up with the fighting units during the night and was once again trailing in their wake), he sent it on its way again, directing it – more or less at random – towards Chagny. All of which suggested that a battle was imminent.

"So it's the real thing this time, is it, sir?" Maurice ventured to ask Lieutenant Rochas.

"By Christ it is!" replied the lieutenant, waving his big arms about. "Won't be long before all hell breaks loose!"

All the men were delighted. Since the formation of the line of battle between Chestres and Falaise, excitement had grown even greater and a feverish impatience was taking hold of everyone. So at last they were to set eyes on these Prussians whom the newspapers described as worn out from marching, dropping with sickness, starving, clad only in rags. . . . And the hope of trouncing them at the first encounter put new heart into every man.

"A good thing too!" said Jean. "We've been playing hide-and-seek quite long enough – ever since we lost sight of them back at the frontier, after things had gone their way. . . . Only, I wonder whether these are the same ones that beat MacMahon?"

Maurice did not know what to say; he was in two minds about it himself. If what he had read in Rheims was anything to go by, it was hard to see how the third army – and its commander, the Crown Prince of Prussia – could be in Vouziers, when only two days ago it had, by all accounts, been camping as far off as Vitry-le-François. Certainly there had been talk of a fourth army, led by the Prince of Saxony and earmarked for operations along the line of the Meuse : presumably this was it – though it was amazing that Grand-Pré should have fallen so early, in view of the distances involved. Maurice's view of the situation was robbed of any last attempt at clarity, however, when to his utter bewilderment he heard General Bourgain-Desfeuilles questioning one of the local peasants as to whether the Meuse did not flow through Buzancy and whether there were not some stout bridges there. Moreover, in his blissful ignorance the general insisted that they were about to be attacked by a column of a hundred thousand men advancing from Grand-Pré, whilst another – this time of sixty thousand – was moving up via Sainte-Menehould.

"How's the foot?" asked Jean, glancing at Maurice.

"It isn't bothering me now," he answered, with a laugh. "And it won't if we're going to fight."

This was true : he was buoyed up by such intense nervous excitement that it was as though he had been lifted right off the ground. To think that he had not fired a shot at anytime in the whole campaign! He had marched all the way to the frontier and spent that night of agonizing suspense outside Mulhouse without setting eyes on a Prussian or unloosing a single bullet; he had been forced to retreat to Belfort, and then to Rheims; and now once again he had been trudging towards the enemy for five whole days – and his rifle was still virginally intact, a useless encumbrance. A slow anger was mounting within him : he wanted to level the thing and fire it for the sake of firing, simply as a means of soothing his nerves. It was now almost six weeks since he had enlisted, in a moment of wild enthusiasm, with visions of fighting on the morrow; and all he had done was wear out his unsturdy legs and frame by running away and marking time far from the field of battle. All his comrades were in a state of feverish anticipation, but none of them stared with a greater degree of impatience than he at this main road to Grand-Pré, stretching straight ahead, mile after mile, between two beautiful lines of trees. The valley unfurled at his feet and the Aisne was like a ribbon of silver among the willows and poplars; but it was the road that now preoccupied him.

At about four o'clock there was a general alert. The 4th Hussars were returning after a lengthy detour, and stories began to circulate (growing wilder and wilder as they spread) of a number of clashes with Uhlans. This bore out the widespread feeling that an attack was imminent. Two hours later another dispatch rider appeared, helter-skelter, and reported that General Bordas was reluctant to leave Grand-Pré lest the road to Vouziers had been cut. His fears were without foundation, since the dispatch rider had got through without any difficulty. Yet they might well be realized at any moment – and the divisional commander, General Dumont, set out immediately with his one remaining brigade, in the hope of extricating his other brigade, which was still in difficulties. The sun was going down behind Vouziers, whose line of rooftops stood out black against a large red cloud. The brigade remained in sight for a long time as it advanced between the double row of trees; then at last it was hidden in the early dusk.

Colonel de Vineuil came along to make sure that his regiment was correctly positioned for the night. Much to his astonishment, he found Captain Beaudoin missing from his post. The captain happened to return from Vouziers just then and explained that he had been having luncheon with Baroness de Ladicourt. He was treated to a sharp reprimand – and endured it in silence, with his air of the true officer.

"Listen, lads," said the colonel as he passed among his men, "we shall almost certainly be attacked tonight, or at latest by dawn tomorrow. . . . Steel yourselves and remember : the 106th has never given ground."

They all cheered : in the mood of tiredness and dejection which had been welling up in them since leaving Rheims, there was not a man among them who did not welcome the prospect of a "real dust-up" which would settle matters once and for all. Rifles were overhauled and firing-pins changed. As they had eaten a hot meal that morning, they made do with coffee and hard biscuit. Instructions were given that they were not to lie down for the night. Outpost pickets were stationed about a mile away, and sentries posted all the way to the banks of the Aisne. The officers kept vigil around the camp fires. And over against a low wall there could be distinguished at moments, by the dancing lights of one of these fires, the braided uniforms of the corps commander and his staff, whose shadowy figures bestirred themselves anxiously, darting towards the road, straining for the sound of horses' hooves – so intense was their disquiet concerning the fate of the third division.

At about one in the morning Maurice was stationed as an advanced sentry on the edge of a field of plum-trees midway between road and river. The darkness was inky-black. No sooner was he alone in the overpowering silence of the still countryside than he fell victim to an appalling sense of fear such as he had never before experienced; he could not master it and he began to tremble with shame and anger. He looked round, hoping to find reassurance in the sight of the camp fires. But these were, apparently, hidden from him by a small wood, and there was nothing to the rear of him but a sea of darkness. The only points of light were a few lamps and candles burning late in Vouziers: the inhabitants, forewarned no doubt and quaking at the thought of the coming battle, had decided against going to bed. What finally made him cold with horror was the realization, as he practised taking aim, that he could not even see the sight of his rifle. Then began a really taxing period of waiting. All his physical and mental resources were concentrated in the sense of hearing; his ears were so responsive to even the faintest sounds that in the end they seemed filled with a thunderous roar. The trickle of distant water, a faint rustle of leaves, the hopping of an insect – each of these acquired an extraordinary fullness of sound. Surely he could hear galloping hooves straight ahead of him, and the ceaseless rumble of artillery? And had he not caught, away to his left, the carefully lowered voices of an advanced guard crawling through the blackness in preparation for a surprise attack? Three times he was on the point of firing a warning shot which would raise the alarm. The fear of being misled and making a fool of himself only served to heighten his sense of physical unease. He knelt down and rested his left shoulder against a tree. It seemed to him that he had been out here for hours: the army must have forgotten him and gone away without him. And then, quite suddenly, he ceased to be afraid. From down on the road – which, as he knew, was only two hundred yards away – he caught the unmistakable rhythmic tread of soldiers on the march. At once he knew beyond all doubt that here were the beleaguered troops whose return had been so impatiently awaited – General Dumont was on his way back with the Bordas brigade. At that moment his replacement arrived. He had been on guard for barely the statutory hour.

It was indeed the third division marching in. The sense of relief was tremendous. But security precautions were made tighter than ever, for information now brought back confirmed all previous suppositions as to the enemy's movements. The handful of prisoners who had been taken – sullen Uhlans, draped in their huge greatcoats – refused to talk. And the suspense was as great as ever, giving rise to an impatience that was physically tiring, as the morning twilight appeared: a livid dawn, bringing rain. For almost fourteen hours the men had not dared to sleep. At about seven o'clock

Lieutenant Rochas claimed that MacMahon was on his way to them, with the whole army. The true situation, however, was rather different: in reply to his dispatch of the previous day, reporting that a conflict below Vouziers was now inevitable, General Douay had received a letter from the marshal bidding him stand firm until it was possible to get support to him; the 1st Corps was proceeding to Terron and the 5th to Buzancy, while the 12th would stay behind at Le Chêne and form a second line of defence. All of which sharpened the men's impatience: the fight in store was no mere isolated engagement but a great battle involving every division in the army which had been turned back from the Meuse and was now moving southwards into the Aisne valley. And still it was more than they dare do, to cook a meal; again they had to be satisfied with coffee and dry biscuits. For the "big dust-up" was due at midday: they were all sure of that, though they could not have said why. An aide-de-camp had again been sent to the marshal, to make sure that the reinforcements were moved up as quickly as possible – for the certainty was growing that the two enemy armies were closing in. Three hours later a second officer went galloping off to Le Chêne, where general headquarters were, with instructions to return with immediate orders; for the situation had become ever more tense as the result of a claim by one of the local mayors that he had seen a hundred thousand men in Grand-Pré, while a hundred thousand more were moving up by way of Buzancy.

Midday came and went – still no sign of any Prussians. One o'clock, two o'clock – nothing whatever happened. And by that time weariness was beginning to set in, and so was doubt. Derisive remarks were made at the generals' expense. Perhaps they had been scared by the sight of their own shadows. The widespread opinion was, they could do with spectacles. A fine pack of jokers they would look if nothing were to happen, after they had messed everyone around like this!

"So it's to be the same story as at Mulhouse!" shouted one wiseacre.

The very name caused Maurice's heart to shrink at the memories it aroused. He recalled the senseless, panicky flight of the 7th Corps at a time when there had been no Germans within twenty miles of the place. And now it was going to be the same story all over again: by now he could feel it in his bones, he was utterly convinced of it. There was only one explanation for the fact that the enemy had not attacked them within twenty-four hours of the skirmish at Grand-

Pré – the Prussians with whom the 4th Hussars had clashed must have been no more than a cavalry reconnaissance group. The main columns must still be a long way off, possibly two days' march. Quite suddenly this notion struck terror into him, when he thought of all the time that had just been wasted. In three whole days they had progressed only from Contreuve to Vouziers, a distance of only a few miles. On August 25 and 26 the other army corps had headed northwards, allegedly because of supply requirements, while now – on the twenty-seventh – they were making their way south-wards again to take up a challenge which had never been thrown down. Heading towards the unprotected passes of the Argonne, in the wake of the 4th Hussars, Bordas's brigade had mistakenly regarded itself as trapped and brought the entire division rushing to its rescue, and then the entire 7th Corps, and then the entire army – all to no purpose. And Maurice reflected on the incalculable value of every hour in this madcap scheme to re-establish contact with General Bazaine at Metz, a plan which only a general of genius would have been capable of carrying out, with troops of proven worth – and even then they would have to put their heads down and charge straight ahead, oblivious to every obstacle.

"We're done for!" he said to Jean, overcome with despair as a clear view of their real situation was suddenly and briefly revealed to him.

The corporal opened his eyes wide in amazement and incomprehension, and for his benefit Maurice lowered his voice and continued – referring to the generals – "No getting away from it: their minds are empty rather than twisted, and nothing seems to go right for them. They've no knowledge, no foresight, no guiding plan, no ideas, no luck. . . . Ah, everything is against us! We're done for!"

And this mood of dejection – which Maurice, with his intelligence and education, was able to rationalize – gradually began to weigh on all the troops, kept there on tenterhooks without rhyme or reason. Doubt and an inkling of their true position were beginning to affect the workings of their slow minds; and before long there was not a man among them, however limited his intellectual horizons, who was not disturbingly aware of being badly led, uselessly deployed and pitched blind into an enterprise which could only result in disaster. What in God's name were they doing here, since there was no sign of the Prussians? They wanted either to fight at once or go away and sleep in peace. They'd had enough. Ever since the last aide-de-camp had hurried off for orders, the tensions within the camp had been mounting moment by moment; the troops stood in small groups, talking aloud and airing their views. The officers, succumbing to the unrest, did not know how to deal with the questions that were boldly directed at them. So when, at five o'clock, word went round that the aide-de-camp had returned with instructions for a withdrawal, there was a lightening of all hearts, a sigh of real joy.

So at last the apostles of good sense were to have their way. The Emperor and the marshal had never been in favour of the advance to Verdun and now, alarmed by the knowledge that they had again been outpaced and were about to be confronted by the combined forces of the Crown Prince of Saxony and the Crown Prince of Prussia, they were abandoning this unlikely attempt to reach Bazaine's army; instead they were going to retreat along the line of the northern fortresses with the eventual aim of falling back on Paris. The 7th Corps was to make its way up to Chagny by way of Le Chêne, while the 5th Corps was to make for Poix and the 1st and 12th for Vendresse. In which case – since they were now falling back – why had they ever pressed on as far as the Aisne, why had they wasted all those days and all that energy, when it would have been so easy and so logical to have proceeded directly from Rheims to vantage points in the Marne valley? Could it be that there was a total lack, not only of strong leadership and military planning but even of plain common sense? But the men were no longer in the mood for such questions : they were ready to forgive all in their delight at this eminently sensible decision, the only decision that could extricate them from the hornets' nest into which they had stumbled. All of them, from general to common soldier, had the feeling that the army was about to be restored to its former strength; it would prove invincible below Paris and could not fail to defeat the Prussians. But it was essential to evacuate Vouziers at first light and be on the move towards Le Chêne before any attack came. And immediately the camp became a scene of extraordinary animation. Bugles rang out, waves of orders overlapped. Already the baggage train and the service-corps vehicles were setting out ahead, so as not to be a burden to the rearguard.

Maurice was delighted. But as he tried to make the significance of this withdrawal clear to Jean, a cry of pain escaped his lips. Now that his mood of excitement had passed he was again conscious of his foot weighing like lead at the end of his leg.

"What, is it giving trouble again?" asked the corporal, with genuine commiseration. And it was he, with his practical turn of mind, who saw an answer to the problem. "Listen, lad, you told me yesterday that you knew some people over in the town. What you ought to do is see the M.O., get someone to drive you into Le Chêne and have a good night's sleep in a comfortable bed. Tomorrow, provided you are able to get along better, we'll pick you up on our way past. . . . What do you say to that?"

It so happened that right here in Falaise – the village they were camping by – Maurice had come across an old friend of his father's; he owned a small farmstead and was about to drive his daughter into Le Chêne, where she was to stay with an aunt. His horse stood harnessed to a light cart, all ready for departure.

But Maurice's appeal to the medical officer nearly misfired at the outset.

"I've rubbed the skin off my foot, doctor . . ."

Instantly Bourouche, shaking his massive leonine head, roared: "Don't you dare call me a doctor! What in Christ's name have I done, that I should have a man like you inflicted on me?"

And as Maurice, greatly startled, stammered out an excuse the officer continued: "I'm to be addressed as sir, you clod, do you hear me?"

When he realized whom he was dealing with he must have felt rather ashamed, for he grew angrier than ever.

"Rubbed the skin off your foot, indeed . . .! All right, all right, permission granted. Get on your cart and go – you can fly away in a balloon for all I care. We've more than enough sluggards and shirkers."

As Jean was helping Maurice into the cart, he turned to thank him and the two men embraced as though they were never going to see one another again. And how could they be certain of doing so, amid all the confusion of the retreat, and with the Prussians waiting to pounce? Maurice could not get over his surprise at the warm affection which he had already begun to feel for the corporal. Twice he turned and waved goodbye as he left the camp. He saw that huge fires were being laid, in the hope of misleading the enemy while the units stole away before daybreak.

As they drove towards Le Chêne, the farmer moaned on and on about the awfulness of the times they were living in. He had not had the heart to stay in Falaise, yet already he regretted not being there – insisting again and again that he was a ruined man if the enemy burned down his house. His daughter was a tall, pale creature and she was crying. But Maurice was so drunk with fatigue that he did not hear; he slept sitting upright, lulled by the trotting hooves of the little horse which negotiated the ten miles from Vouziers to Le Chêne in less than an hour and a half. It was not yet seven, and the light had hardly begun to fade, when – startled and shivering – the young man got down in the main square, beside the bridge over the canal, opposite the narrow, yellow-walled house in which he had been born, and where he had spent the first twenty years of his life. It was for this house that he made instinctively, even though it had been sold eighteen months ago to a veterinary surgeon. And in reply to the farmer's questions he remarked that he knew perfectly well where he was going; he could never, he added, thank him enough for his kindness.

And yet he remained stock-still in the centre of the triangle that formed one half of the main square. He was utterly bewildered, like a man who had lost his memory. Where *was* he going? All of a sudden he remembered that he was making for the lawyer's house, which was next door to the one in which he had grown up; the lawyer's mother – the extremely aged and kindly Mme. Desroches – exercised the neighbourly perogative of spoiling him as a child. But he scarcely recognized Le Chêne. As a rule the little town was lifeless; but now – as a result of having an army corps encamped at its gates – it was full of stir and bustle, and apart from all the officers and messengers the streets were thronged with prowlers, stragglers and hangers-on of every kind. He had no difficulty in placing the canal which flowed through the whole length of the town, bisecting the main square, whose narrow stone bridge served to connect the two triangular halves; and that building with the moss-grown roof, over on the other bank, was unmistakably the market, flanked by the Rue Beroud on the left and, on the right, by the main road to Sedan. From where he was standing, however, he had to look up and identify the slated belfry above the lawyer's house before he could be certain of knowing the once deserted spot where he used to play hopscotch. In the square itself, an area was apparently being kept clear : there were troops to ensure that on-lookers did not advance too close. And to his amazement he found that a broad expanse of ground behind the well had been turned into a kind of depot for an array of carts and vans and waggons which he had certainly seen somewhere before.

The sun had just vanished into the smooth, blood-red waters of the canal and Maurice was about to move on when a woman who had been standing beside him and staring at him for some time past cried : "Lord love us – it can't be! And yet I'd swear it was young Levasseur!"

Whereupon he in turn recognized Mme. Courbette, whose husband owned the chemist's shop in the square. No sooner had he begun to explain his intention of seeking a night's rest under Mme. Desroches's roof than she dragged him away in agitation.

"Oh, no! Just you come along to our house and I'll explain matters to you. . . ."

She led him to the chemist's shop, shut the door carefully and then asked : "Why, lad, haven't you heard? The Emperor has moved into the Desroches'. . . . The house has been requisitioned for his use – and they're none too glad of the honour, I can tell you. She's in her seventies, poor old thing, and they've turned her out of her room and made her go and live in the maid's quarters, right at the top of the building . . .! Everything you can see out there in the square is the Emperor's – his luggage, as you might say."

Of course! Maurice's mind went back to the day in Rheims when he had first seen this superb fleet of vehicles belonging to the imperial household.

"My, you should have seen what it contained : silver plate and basket-loads of provisions and fine linen . . . something of everything! The unloading went on for two hours, without pause. I can't help wondering where they managed to put it all, for the house isn't a large one. . . . Here, just look at the size of the fire burning in the kitchen!"

He gazed at the small, white, two-storey house on the corner of the square and the Rue de Vouziers. Quiet and ordinary-looking. In his mind's eye he could see, as clearly as if he had visited it only yesterday, the four rooms on each floor and the central passageway running right through the house. There was already a light in the corner window on the first floor, the one overlooking the square – *that*, explained the chemist's wife, was the Emperor's room. But just as she had said, the biggest blaze of all came from the kitchen, whose window – on the ground floor – looked out on to the Rue de Vouziers. The people of Le Chêne had never seen anything like it. The street was filled with a never-ending stream of onlookers, come to gape at this fiery furnace where an emperor's dinner was roasting and boiling. So as to get a little air, the cooks had thrown the windows wide. There were three of them in immaculate white jackets, bustling about before a line of chickens on a giant spit, and stirring sauces in huge saucepans whose copper shone like gold. And the old men could not recall ever having seen – not even in the Lion d'Argent inn, in preparation for the grandest wedding feasts – such leaping flames or so much food cooking at once.

Courbette the chemist – a short, wiry figure, always on the go – returned home in a state of high excitement at all he had seen and heard. As deputy mayor, he seemed fully acquainted with the situation. It was at about half past three that MacMahon had wired Bazaine to the effect that the Crown Prince of Prussia's arrival in Châlons made it imperative for him to fall back on the northern fortresses; and a further dispatch was about to be sent to the War Minister, informing him of the retreat and explaining the appalling danger of the army being cut off and annihilated. The dispatch to Bazaine might just get through – though all communications with Metz appeared to have been cut for several days. But the second dispatch was a more serious matter; lowering his voice, the chemist told how he had heard a senior officer say : "If they get word of this in Paris, we're finished !" It was common knowledge that the Empress-Regent and the cabinet were ruthlessly determined to have the army move forward. And things were becoming more confused with every passing hour; the most extraordinary reports were reaching the town concerning the advance of the German armies. Could the Crown Prince of Prussia really be in Châlons? And what was the identity of the units with which the 7th Corps had clashed in the Argonne passes?

"The people at headquarters don't know *what's* happening," continued the chemist, waving his arms in despair. "Oh, what a mess to be in. . . . Still, everything will be all right so long as the army begins to fall back tomorrow. Well now, my young friend," he went on, showing his natural kindness, "I'll just put something on your foot – and then afterwards, when we've all had dinner together, you shall go and sleep upstairs in my apprentice's little room. The boy has fled the town."

But Maurice was so tormented by the need to look around and find out things for himself that he could not be dissuaded from following his original intention of calling on old Mme. Desroches. He was surprised not to be stopped at the door, which – despite the tumult in the square – stood wide open and was not even guarded. People were going in and out all the time – officers, household staff. . . . And it was as though the stir and bustle in the overheated kitchen were spreading right through the building. There was no light on the stairs, however, and he had to grope his way up. At the first landing he paused for a few moments, with thudding heart, outside the door of the room which he now knew to be the Emperor's; but there was not a sound to be heard from within – the silence of death prevailed. And one floor higher, lurking on the threshold of the maid's quarters to which she had been banished, old Mme. Desroches was at first afraid of him.

"Oh, my dear lad!" she exclaimed when she recognized him. "What a terrible moment for us to meet . . .! I'd have been only too willing to turn my house over to the Emperor – but some of the people with him are so ill-bred! You should have seen the way they grabbed everything. And they bank the fires so high – they'll burn the house down before they are done. . . . He, poor man, looks as though he had just stepped out of the grave – and there is such a sad expression on his face. . . ."

Before he took his leave, the young man did his best to reassure her. She walked with him to the top of the stairs and leaned over the banister.

"Look!" she muttered, "You can see him from here. . . . Ah – we're lost, every one of us, and no mistake. Goodbye, my boy."

Maurice halted abruptly on one of the shadowy steps. Craning his neck and peering through a fanlight, he beheld a sight which remained indelibly stamped on his memory forever after.

For there was the Emperor, at the far end of that chilly, undistinguished room, seated at a small table laid for dinner and lighted by two candles – one on either side. A pair of aides-de-camp were positioned silently in the background. A major-domo hovered expectantly beside the table. The Emperor's glass was unused, his bread untouched. He was staring motionlessly down at the tablecloth with those same dim, wavering, watery eyes which had characterized his appearance in Rheims. But tonight he gave the impression of being even more tired; and when – as though it cost him a mighty effort – he at last resolved to carry a couple of mouthfuls to his lips, he immediately pushed all the rest aside. The Emperor had dined. An expression of privately endured suffering made his face look whiter than ever.

As Maurice was walking past the dining room, downstairs, the door opened unexpectedly, and amid the flaring candles and steaming dishes he perceived a tableful of equerries and aides-de-camp and chamberlains, all rowdily engaged in guzzling the wine from the vans, demolishing the fowls and lapping up the sauces. Ever since the marshal's dispatch had gone off, these people had been revelling in the conviction that the imperial forces were about to retreat. Another week and they would be back in Paris, sleeping in clean and comfortable beds again.

Only then was Maurice aware, all of a sudden, of how intolerably tired he was. The matter was settled: the whole army was going to withdraw, and the best thing he could do was sleep until the 7th Corps passed through the town. He walked back across the square and somehow found his way to the chemist's house, where he ate his dinner like a man in a dream. Afterwards he sensed rather than knew that his foot was being dressed and bandaged and, later, that he was being led upstairs to a bedroom. Then everything went black. He slept on and on, exhausted, with never a murmur. Some incalculable time later – it might have been hours, it might have been centuries – he shuddered awake and sat up amid the shadows. Where on earth was he? What could account for the unending, thundering roar which had interrupted his sleep? A split second later it all came back to him and he rushed to the window to see what was happening. In the darkness of the square below, usually so peaceful at night, a regiment of artillery was going by – a ceaseless procession of men, guns and horses, moving at such a fast trot that the walls of the lifeless little houses shook perceptibly. The sight of this unheralded departure provoked an instinctive sense of alarm. What time could it be? The clock above the town hall struck four. He sought reassurance in the view that what he was witnessing was merely the first phase of the withdrawal ordered the day before; but as he turned his head away he saw something that brought his irrational panic to an ever higher pitch: the light was still burning in the corner window of the lawyer's house, and at regular intervals the figure of the Emperor was darkly but distinctly silhouetted in the frame.

Maurice hurriedly drew his trousers on, intending to go downstairs. But at that very moment Courbette appeared in the doorway, holding a candlestick and gesticulating with his free hand.

"I saw you from the street, on my way back from the town hall, and I decided to come and tell you the news. . . . Would you believe it? They've kept me out of bed all night. For the past two hours the mayor and I have been busy trying to cope with the new requisition orders. . . . Yes, it's all been turned back to front again. Ah, that officer knew only too well what he was talking about when he said Paris ought never to have been told of the new plan!"

The chemist went on for a long time, haltingly and disjointedly, and when at last he realized what had happened the young man was too crestfallen to speak. At about midnight the Emperor had received a dispatch from the War Minister, in reply to the marshal's message. The exact wording was not known as yet, but one of the aides-de-camp had remarked aloud in the town hall that the Empress and the cabinet feared there would be a revolution in Paris were the Emperor to abandon Bazaine and return to the capital. The dispatch revealed a false appreciation of the latest movements of the German armies and implied a belief in a positional advantage which the Châlons army no longer possessed; it insisted, in extraordinarily heated terms, that the forward movement be resumed come what may.

"The Emperor summoned the marshal," added the chemist, "and they were closeted together for the greater part of an hour. I don't know what can have passed between them, of course, but every officer I have spoken to says the same thing : instead of falling back, the army is now once again making for the Meuse. We have just requisitioned all available ovens for the use of the 1st Corps, which will be arriving in town tomorrow morning as a replacement for the 12th – whose artillery, as you can see for yourself, is already leaving for La Besace. This time the die is cast – you're bound for the battlefield!"

He broke off. He too was staring at the lighted window in the lawyer's house. Then, speaking in an undertone, in the manner of a man eaten up with curiosity, he asked : "What *can* they have said to one another . . .? There's no getting away from the fact : it's rum to fall back at 6 p.m. and then to advance at midnight in the face of a threat that hasn't changed one bit."

But Maurice was still listening to the artillery as it rumbled through the dark little town below them – an incessant human flow pouring towards the Meuse and the dreadful unknown of the coming day. And silhouetted against the thin commonplace curtains at the window he saw the shadowy figure of the Emperor coming and going at regular intervals – an invalid kept out of bed by insomnia, driven by a need to remain on the move despite his physical suffering, half-deafened by the sound of these horses and men whom he was allowing to be sent to their deaths. So a few hours had been sufficient time for the disaster to be decreed, and accepted. What indeed could they have said to one another, the Emperor and marshal? Both men were fully alive to the tragic fate that would befall the army if it continued to move forward. Both men – as late as the previous evening – had felt certain it would meet with defeat, granted the appalling conditions in prospect. They could not conceivably have changed their minds that morning, when the peril was mounting hour by hour. General de Palikao's plan for a lightning advance to Montmédy had been a hazardous proposition even on August 23. By the twenty-fifth it might still have been practicable, provided it was executed by forces of proven worth under a commander of genius. On the twenty-seventh it was taking on the character of an act of sheer lunacy, in view of the continual vacillations of the high command and the accelerating decline in the troops' morale. If both men knew this, why were they yielding to the implacable voices of people who were clearly playing on their indecisiveness? Perhaps the marshal was after all only a dutiful, unenterprising soldier, excelling in self-sacrifice. And the Emperor, no longer exercising command, was passively awaiting the fulfilment of destiny. They were being asked to surrender their lives and the lives of the army, and they *were* surrendering them. This was the night of the great crime, the loathsome night when a nation was knowingly put to death; for from that time forward the army was in desperate straits – a hundred thousand men were being sent to the slaughter.

As he pondered these matters, shuddering with despair, Maurice kept his eyes trained on the shadowy figure behind Mme. Desroches's light muslin curtains – that frantically pacing figure which seemed to be driven by the merciless voice from Paris. Surely the Empress must have wished death on the father that night, so that the son might reign. "On, on!" she seemed to be bidding him. "On, with never a glance over your shoulder! On through the rain and mud to extermination, so that this last despairing bid by the dying Empire may be played out to the last! On, On! Die like a hero upon the heaped-up corpses of your people! Touch the heart of the whole wide world and fill it with admiration if you would win forgiveness for your descendants!" And no doubt the Emperor *was* bound for death if he obeyed her. . . . Downstairs, there was no longer any sign of the blazing fire in the kitchen; the equerries and aides-de-camp and chamberlains were asleep; the whole house was in darkness, save that one window where the shadowy figure came and went, came and went, resigned to the inevitability of the sacrifice which had been demanded. And still the 12th Corps roared by in the dark.

Suddenly it occurred to Maurice that if the advance were resumed the 7th Corps would not pass through Le Chêne; and he had visions of being left behind, cut off from his unit through having deserted his post. His foot no longer bothered him – a skilful dressing and a few hours' untroubled rest had stilled the fever. Courbette found him a pair of broad-fitting, comfortable shoes, and he expressed the desire to leave there and then in the hope that he might yet encounter the 106th on the road between Le Chêne and Vouziers. All the chemist's attempts to dissuade him were in vain, and Courbette was within an ace of offering to drive him back in his gig when Fernand, his apprentice, walked into the house. He explained that, far from fleeing the town, he had merely been keeping an assignation with his cousin. So this tall, pale, spineless-looking fellow was given the task of harnessing the horse to the gig and delivering Maurice to his destination. It was not yet five o'clock. Torrential rain poured from the ink-black sky and the vehicle's lamps were too weak to be of any great avail in lighting the way through the wet, sprawling countryside full of tremendous echoes, which made them pull up at least once a mile for fear of colliding with an entire army.

Jean, meantime, had not slept at all in the encampment outside Vouziers. Ever since Maurice had explained how the promised withdrawal was about to redeem the entire situation he had been on the watch, ensuring that his men did not wander away and awaiting the order to strike camp, an order which he expected the officers might give at any moment. At about two o'clock, when the pitch-black night was pierced only by the red stars of the camp fires, a prodigious rumble of horses' hooves resounded through the camp : it was the cavalry setting out ahead and making for Ballay and Quatre-Champs so as to keep watch on the roads to Boult-aux-Bois and La Croix-au-Bois. An hour later it was the turn of the infantry and artillery to move off, thus finally abandoning a line which, for two long days, they had obstinately defended against an enemy who never came. The sky had clouded over, making the night blacker than ever, as the various regiments moved off in strict silence – a procession of shadowy figures stealing away under cover of darkness. But all hearts were beating joyously, as though the army had narrowly avoided being led into a trap. Already the men were picturing themselves below the walls of Paris, on the eve of a triumphant counter-attack.

Jean stared about him in the heavy gloom. The road was lined with trees, and he had the impression that it ran between broad meadows. Then came a series of dips and climbs. They were approaching a village, presumably Ballay, when there was a sudden violent cloudburst. The men had endured so many previous soakings that they did not even show resentment, but simply squared their shoulders; soon Ballay was behind them, and as they drew close to Quatre-Champs a terrific wind got up; on the far side of the village they came out on to the vast plateau whose barren acres extend all the way to Noirval. There the full gale burst upon them, driving the rain mercilessly into their faces. And it was in the midst of these open spaces that, one after another, the regiments were brought to a standstill. The whole of the 7th Corps – thirty-odd thousand men – remustered there as the dawn came up, a murky dawn streaked grey by the heavy rain. What was going on? Why had they been halted? A wave of alarm was already surging through the ranks; some of the men were claiming that the marching orders had suddenly been reversed. They had been told to stand at ease, but forbidden to break ranks or sit down. At times the wind sweeping across the high plateau was so fierce that they had to cling to one another to avoid being blown away. The rain was blinding them and cutting into their skin, an icy rain that seeped inside their clothing. Two hours went by. Nobody knew the reason for this seemingly interminable wait, and once again everyone was overcome by a sense of acute anxiety.

As the light strengthened, Jean did his best to take his bearings. Someone pointed out the road to Le Chêne; it led uphill, in a north-westerly direction, on the other side of Quatre-Champs. In which case, why had they turned right instead of left? Next his attention was drawn to the temporary headquarters – set up in a farmhouse at La Converserie, on the very edge of the plateau. A good deal of panicky activity seemed to be going on there : officers were rushing about, arguing and gesticulating. Yet nothing happened – what could they be waiting for? The plateau formed a kind of amphitheatre. The countless acres of stubble were overhung to North and East by wooded hills. Southwards lay areas of dense forest land, while an opening on the western side afforded a glimpse of the Aisne valley and the small white houses of Vouziers. Below La Converserie rose the slated steeple of Quatre-Champs, drenched by the furious downpour which seemed sure to wash away the poor, moss-grown rooftops that constituted the remainder of the tiny village. And then, as Jean glanced along the hilly road, he spotted a gig hurrying over the flinty surface now awash with rain-water.

Sitting in the gig was Maurice, who – at long last – had just caught sight of the 7th Corps while rounding a bend on the hillside. For two whole hours he had been scouring the countryside, seriously delayed by a peasant's misleading directions and by the sullen incompetence of his driver, who was eaten up with fear of the Prussians. As soon as he reached the farm, he leaped down from the vehicle and lost no time in finding his regiment.

Jean was amazed to see him.

"What on earth are you doing here?" he cried. "I thought we were going to collect you on our way through the town?"

Maurice threw up his hands in a gesture fully expressive of his anger and distress.

"Oh yes, but the army is no longer bound for Le Chêne. *That's* where we're going – and it means death for all of us!"

The corporal turned quite pale.

"Ah well," he said after a time. "At least we'll cop it together."

And they greeted one another just as they had parted – with an embrace. In the heavy rain, the private returned to his place in the ranks while the corporal, anxious to set a good example, maintained a stoical silence even though he was soaked to the skin.

But the news had begun to circulate, and now it was official. Instead of falling back on Paris, they were to make for the Meuse again. One of the marshal's aides-de-camp had just arrived with instructions for the 7th Corps to proceed to Nourat and make camp there. Meantime the 5th would be striking towards Beauclair, to take up its position on the right wing of the army, while the 1st headed for Le Chêne so as to relieve the 12th which had been ordered forward to La Besace, for service on the left wing. That thirty-odd thousand men had been kept standing in the wind and rain for almost three hours was due to the fact that General Douay, amid the appalling confusion of this further change of front, was on tenterhooks as to the fate of the supply column sent on ahead the previous day with orders to make for Chagny. He had no choice but to wait until it returned to the fold. There were rumours that it had become entangled with the 12th Corps's supply column in Le Chêne. Then again, some of the service-corps vehicles – including all the field smithies – had taken a wrong turning and were now heading back from Terron along the Vouziers road, where they would almost certainly fall into German hands. Never was chaos more complete or anxiety more taxing.

At this, the majority of the troops succumbed to open despair. Many of them were ready to squat down in the rain and mud and await their deaths on that sodden plateau. They began to hurl jibes and abuse at their commanders. Damned fine commanders – brainlessly undoing at the end of the day what little they had done at the beginning, loitering to no purpose when the enemy was miles away and taking to their heels as soon as he appeared! A fit of utter despondency was finally turning the army into a dispirited and undisciplined herd that was being led haphazardly to the slaughter. Over towards Vouziers, rifle-fire had broken out – shots were being exchanged between the rearguard of the 7th Corps and the vanguard of the German forces. And for the past few moments all eyes had been turned in the direction of the Aisne valley, where a thick black column of smoke was spiralling upwards into a small patch of clear sky. To their fury the men learned that it was Falaise village, set ablaze by the Uhlans. So the Germans were here now! For two whole days the corps had hung about waiting for them, giving them time to arrive, and now it was creeping away. Even in the dullest minds there was a mounting sense of anger at the irreparable blunder that had been committed, at the foolishness of this long delay, at this trap they had fallen into: the scouts of the German fourth army were holding Bordas's brigade and bringing corps after corps of the Châlons army to a standstill, while the Crown Prince of Prussia was able to race forward with his third army. And even at this moment the junction was being effected between the enemy forces, thanks to the ignorance of Marshal MacMahon who still did not know what units were confronting him. The 5th and 7th Corps were going to be harassed continually and subjected to the constant threat of disaster.

Maurice stood watching Falaise burn on the horizon. But there was a moment of relief: the supply column which they had all given up at last now emerged from the road to Le Chêne. Immediately – while the 1st Division remained at Quatre-Champs to await and give protection to the interminable baggage-train – the 2nd Division moved off and cut through the forest to Boult-aux-Bois, and the 3rd took up positions on the Belleville hills with the aim of safeguarding communications. And as the rain began to fall harder than ever and the 106th left the plateau at last, resuming its criminally misguided advance to the Meuse, Maurice's mind went back to the shadowy figure of the Emperor grimly coming and going in the little window of the old lady's house. Ah, it was indeed an act of desperation to sentence an army to certain death in the faint hope of saving a dynasty! On, on, with never a backward glance, on through the rain and mud to final extermination!

VI

"GOOD God!" said Chouteau, when he woke aching and shivering in the tent next morning. "What wouldn't I give for a mugful of strong broth!"

The evening before, at Boult-aux-Bois where they had made camp, there had been only a miserly issue of potatoes – for the supply people had become increasingly confused and disorganized by all the marching and counter-marching, and so had never managed to meet the fighting units at the pre-arranged rendezvous. There was such chaos on the roads that no one knew where the droves of cattle had got to, and the army now faced the prospect of famine.

Loubet unleashed a despairing gibe as he stretched and yawned.

"And so bloody well say all of us! No more roast goose anyway!"

The squad was in a sullen mood. An empty belly is not good for a man's spirits. And in addition there was the incessant rain to contend with, and the mud beneath their bodies.

The sight of Pache, making the sign of the Cross at the end of his silent morning prayer, redoubled Chouteau's fury.

"While you're at it," he raged, "perhaps you wouldn't mind asking him to send every one of us a couple of fat, juicy sausages and a good measure of wine!"

"I'd settle for a single loaf of bread, provided it was big enough for all of us," sighed Lapoulle. In him the pangs of hunger were sharpest of all, for he had the appetite of a horse.

But Lieutenant Rochas soon called them to order. They ought to be ashamed of themselves, always thinking of their insides! For him the solution was simple : he merely tightened his belt. Now that things looked really black and occasional gunfire could be heard in the distance, he had recaptured all his stubborn confidence. With the enemy here at last, it all became so simple – they would trounce the Prussians, and that would be that. And he stood shrugging his shoulders over the pale, tight-lipped, crestfallen air of Captain Beaudoin. *He,* the young whipper-snapper, had been like a bear with a sore head ever since his kit had gone astray. He could put up with not eating, but it made his blood boil that he should be denied a change of shirt.

When Maurice opened his eyes he was dog-tired and quivering with cold. So far, thanks to the broad fit of the borrowed shoes, his foot had not swollen up again. But his greatcoat was still heavy from its drenching the day before, and he was aching in every limb. When he was sent to fetch the water for their coffee, he examined the plain which Boult-aux-Bois abuts upon. Forests rose to West and North, while southwards the village of Belleville stood atop a slope. In the East lay mile after mile of open country, with just a few hamlets concealed in its gentle dips. Was *that* the direction from which the enemy was expected? As he trudged back from the stream with his canful of water, a family of tearful peasants hailed him from the doorway of a small farmhouse and inquired whether the troops were at last going to stand their ground and defend them. Thrice already had the 5th Corps come and gone through the area like a shuttlecock. The day before, they had heard heavy gunfire from the general direction of Bar; so the Prussians could not be more than five or six miles away. When Maurice admitted that the 7th Corps was unlikely to remain here any longer than the 5th, the poor devils really began to wail. So they were to be forsaken? So, instead of fighting, the troops were merely going to scamper back and forth giving the enemy the slip?

"If anyone prefers it sweetened," said Loubet, as he poured out the coffee, "I suggest he dips his thumb in and waits for it to melt."

Nobody even smiled. There was nothing funny about coffee without sugar. If only they had something to chew! The day before, nearly all of them had sought to allay the boredom of the long wait outside Quatre-Champs by nibbling the few dry biscuits left in their knapsacks. Luckily, however, the squad came across a dozen potatoes and these were quickly shared out.

Maurice's stomach was in a bad way.

"If only I'd known!" he cried ruefully. "I could easily have bought some bread in Le Chêne!"

Jean sat there listening in silence. He had begun the day by quarreling with Chouteau, who had insolently refused to collect the firewood, arguing that it was not his turn. In the ever-worsening situation, discipline was declining so sharply that the officers and N.C.O.s could no longer afford the risk of issuing reprimands. And Jean, with his usual commendable calm and restraint, had realized that he must cease to make his rank felt if he wished to avoid provoking open acts of rebellion. He was matey towards his men, while they, on their side, were able to benefit from his long experience. His squad might not be as well-fed as before, but at least it wasn't starving yet – as so many others were. But nothing touched his heart more than the sight of Maurice's distress. He could sense that the young man was growing weaker and he looked on with anxious eye, wondering how his delicate constitution would ever stand up to the days ahead.

When Jean heard Maurice complain because there was no bread he got up, disappeared for a moment and came back after rummaging in his pack.

"Here," he said, quietly slipping a biscuit into the private's hand, "keep it out of sight. I haven't got any for the others."

"But what about yourself?" the young man asked, very touched.

"Oh, you needn't worry your head about me. . . . I've a couple more."

Which was no lie. He had carefully saved up three biscuits in case the regiment should be sent into action, for he knew how hungry a man gets on the battlefield. Besides, he had only just eaten a potato. That was enough to be going on with.

At about ten o'clock the 7th Corps moved off again. Presumably the marshal's original intention had been for it to proceed via Buzancy to Stenay, and there across the Meuse. But the Prussians, always outpacing the Châlons army, were certainly in Stenay by this time – and some people reckoned they were even in Buzancy. As a result the corps had been driven farther north, and it had just received orders to make for La Besace (some fifteen miles from Boult-aux-Bois), whence it was to continue next day as far as Mouzon before crossing the river. The long march was begun in low spirits. The men were full of grumbles : there was not enough food in their bellies and not enough rest in their limbs; they were worn out from the exertions and delays of the campaign so far. As for the officers, they were downcast and on edge at the thought of the catastrophe for which they were heading; they fretted at being kept idle; they fumed because they had not been sent to Buzancy in support of the 5th Corps, when they were within sound of its artillery fire. The 5th must now also be falling back and making its way up towards Nouart, while the 12th was leaving La Besace for Mouzon and the 1st was making for Raucourt. They trudged on like a harassed herd with the dogs snarling at its heels, knocking into one another in their hurry to reach the Meuse, longing to get to it after the endless delays and dawdlings of the recent past.

As the 106th left Boult-aux-Bois, in the wake of the cavalry and artillery, almost lost in the long straggling columns that consisted of three full divisions, the sun went in again and the mournful, sombre, slow-moving clouds served to complete the men's gloom. The regiment was keeping to the Buzancy highway, which was lined with magnificent poplars. In the village of Germond, heaps of manure stood smoking outside the doors on either side of the street and the women sobbed and picked their children up and held them out to the passing troops, as though beseeching the men to carry them away. There was not a scrap of bread left in the place, not even a potato. Afterwards, instead of proceeding any farther in the direction of Buzancy the 106th wheeled to the left and headed towards Authe; and when they saw Belleville standing on its hill on the other side of the plain, the men were distinctly aware of going round and round in circles. Belleville! Why, they had marched through Belleville the day before!

"Good God!" growled Chouteau. "What do they think they are doing, making us spin like tops?"

And Loubet chimed in with: "That's the kind of twopenny-halfpenny generals we have! Their left hand doesn't know what their right is doing. What do our aching legs mean to *them*?"

They were all roused to anger. Intolerable that men should be marched off their feet like this, just for the fun of it! They advanced across the gently dipping ground of the open plain, marching in open column, with a line of men on each side of the road and the officers in the middle. But gone now were the joking and singing which had cheered them on their way through the Champagne region, after leaving Rheims. In those days they had borne the weight of their packs cheerfully; their shoulders had been lightened by the hope of outmanoeuvring the Prussians and defeating them. Today they shuffled along in silence, full of hatred for the rifles that bruised their shoulders and the kits that broke their backs. They had lost all faith in their commanders and had given way to so powerful a mood of despair that their progress was that of a resentful and brutalized herd. The wretched army was on the road to martyrdom.

For some minutes past, however, Maurice had been deeply engrossed. Away to their left rose a series of ridges, and he had just seen a horseman appear from a small wood in the distance.

Almost at once a second horseman came into view, and then a third. All three came to a halt and kept quite still, like sharply defined toys no bigger than a man's hand. He supposed they must be a detachment of hussars returning from a scouting mission; but suddenly, to his amazement, he saw something glitter on their shoulders, something which could only be the flash of brass epaulettes.

"Look over there!" he said, nudging Jean who was marching along beside him. "Uhlans!"

The corporal opened his eyes wide.

"Well, well," he said, "would you believe it!"

They were indeed Uhlans – the first Prussians the 106th had seen. After almost six weeks in the field, the men had still not fired a shot in anger or even clapped eyes on an enemy soldier. The news was hurriedly passed along the line and soon, amid mounting curiosity, every face was turned in the direction of the wood. They made rather a handsome sight, those three Uhlans.

"One of them looks mighty well-fed," observed Loubet.

But suddenly an entire squadron appeared on an expanse of raised ground to the left of the little wood – an ominous sight which quickly brought the column to a halt. Orders arrived, and the 106th took up position behind the trees growing along the bank of a stream. By this time, sections of artillery were galloping back along the path they had previously travelled and establishing themselves on a hillock. For almost two hours after that, the regiment lurked beside the stream in battle formation. Nothing further happened. The force of enemy cavalry remained in exactly the same position on the skyline. And at long last the French realized that they were wasting valuable time.

"Ah well," Jean murmured regretfully, as the 106th moved forward again, "once more we've been done out of a fight!"

Maurice felt the same way about it: he was itching to pull the trigger at least this once. And his mind began to dwell again on the blundering failure, the day before, to move up in support of the 5th Corps. The Prussians' decision not to attack could only stem from the fact that they had as yet insufficient infantry at their disposal; therefore their sole object in making a show of cavalry, at a safe distance, must be to slow down the movements of the marching columns. Once again the French had fallen into a trap. And from then on, indeed, the 106th had to endure the sight of the Uhlans, away to the left, whenever the features of the landscape

110

permitted : they were following it, keeping close watch on it, disappearing behind a farm only to reappear round the side of a wood.

The men were slowly but surely unnerved by the sensation of being enveloped at long range, as though caught in the meshes of an invisible net. Even Pache and Lapoulle began to grumble : "This is getting to be too much of a good thing ! It would be easier to bear if only we could bang away at them for a while."

But they trudged on and on, with a heavy step that soon wearied. Amid the tension and discomfort of the march they could sense the enemy approaching from every direction, as one can sense the coming of a storm before it looms over the horizon. Strict orders were given to ensure proper vigilance on the part of the rearguard, and there were no stragglers now – everyone knew for certain that the Prussians were immediately behind the corps, waiting to pounce on all and sundry. The enemy's infantry was moving up at a lightning pace, whereas the French regiments, ceaselessly harassed and halted, were more or less marking time.

Just as they reached Authe, the sky cleared; and Maurice, who was taking his bearings from the sun, noticed that instead of proceeding any further towards Le Chêne – three long leagues away – they were wheeling round and marching due East. It was two o'clock, and after two days of shivering and shuddering in the rain the stifling heat was almost more than they could endure. The road wound and climbed slowly through empty plains. Never a house, never a living soul – only an occasional small, cheerless-looking wood relieved the drab monotony of these open spaces, and the dismal silence of these lonely expanses had begun to infect the troops as they slouched along, sweating and hanging their heads. Finally Saint-Pierremont came into view – just a few empty houses perching on a hillock. They did not pass through the village, however; Maurice took note of the fact that they immediately wheeled to the left, heading northwards again in the direction of La Besace. At this he realized that this route had been adopted in a bid to reach Mouzon before the Prussians. But could it possibly succeed, when the troops were so tired and so demoralized? At Saint-Pierremont the three Uhlans had reappeared in the distance, at the bend of a road leading from Buzancy; and just as the rearguard was leaving the village a battery was unmasked and a number of shells rained down, without causing any damage. The fire was not returned; instead the march went on, more arduous than ever.

111

It is a good eight miles from Saint-Pierremont to La Besace, and on learning the fact from Maurice, Jean made a gesture of utter despair : the men would never make it; he could tell as much from the dazed looks on their faces and from the way they were puffing and blowing. The road was still an uphill one, running between two slopes which gradually grew closer together. Eventually they had to pause for rest. But the brief halt served only to increase the numbness of the men's limbs; and when the time came for them to move on, they fared even worse. The regiments no longer made any real headway, and men were beginning to fall to the ground. Glancing at Maurice, Jean saw that his face was becoming increasingly pale and that his eyes were rolling with tiredness. As a rule Jean never permitted himself to chatter while on the march, but now he did his best to rouse the young man with a ceaseless flow of words, hoping to keep him awake amid the mechanical trudge-trudge to which he had grown oblivious.

"So your sister lives in Sedan? Perhaps we shall pass through there . . ."

"Through Sedan? Not a chance of it! Sedan is miles out of our way. The generals would need to be mad."

"I suppose she's quite young?"

"Why, she's the same age as me. I told you : we're twins."

"Does she look like you?"

"Well, we're both fair. . . . She has soft, curly locks. She's short and slim, with a little face and such quiet and gentle ways. Dear Henriette !"

"Then you're attached to one another?"

"Oh, yes. . . ."

There was silence for a while, and when Jean glanced at Maurice again he found that his eyes were closing and that he was about to fall.

"Hey there – bear up, mate! Hand me your rifle for a while, that'll lighten the load for you. . . . At this rate, half the regiment is going to fall by the roadside. It just isn't possible for us to go any farther today !"

He had just caught sight of the village of Oches – a few tumble-down cottages dotted about on the hillside confronting them. The yellow-stone church was perched among the tree-tops, high above the rest of the buildings.

"That's where we shall kip down – you take my word for it."

He had guessed right. Witnessing the exhaustion of his troops,

112

General Douay saw little hope of ever reaching La Besace that day. But what weighed with him most of all was the arrival of the baggage train – that same bothersome baggage train which he had been forced to drag after him ever since leaving Rheims. What a terrible encumbrance it was to him, with its eight-mile procession of horses and vehicles. He had given orders for it to proceed straight from Quatre-Champs to Saint-Pierremont; yet only at Oches did the teams catch up with the corps, and the horses were in such a state of exhaustion that they refused to budge any farther. It was already five o'clock. The general, loath to venture into the Stonne pass at so late an hour, decided that he would give up any attempt to complete the day's march as laid down by the marshal. They all halted and made camp. The baggage train stayed down in the meadows, with a whole division mounting guard. The artillery took up its position on the slopes behind, while the brigade which was to act as rearguard next day occupied an eminence facing Saint-Pierremont. Another division – the one that included General Bourgain-Desfeuille's brigade – bivouacked behind the church, on a broad plateau edged with a wood of oak trees.

There was so much fuss and confusion as to which regiment was to go where that darkness was falling by the time the 106th was at last able to settle down on the very fringe of the wood.

"Damned if I'm interested in food," Chouteau said furiously. "Sleep is all I care about!"

It was the same cry with all the others. Many had not sufficient energy to pitch their tents; they fell asleep wherever they happened to drop, like mounds of earth. Besides, how could they eat without drawing rations? And there were no rations in Oches – the commissariat was awaiting the 7th Corps at La Besace. Organization had become so haphazard and lackadaisical that there was not even a bugle-call to assemble the squad-leaders so that they could be told the bad news. It was a case of every man for himself. From then on there were to be no further issues of supplies. The men were to subsist on the foodstuffs which they were supposed to have in their knapsacks. And their knapsacks were empty. Precious few could even lay hands on a crust of bread, the paltry remains of the plenty they had briefly had at Vouziers. They still had some coffee though, and the less weary among them once again tasted the delights of unsweetened coffee.

Jean took out his last two biscuits, intending to eat one of them himself and give the other to Maurice. But Maurice was fast asleep.

113

For a moment the corporal toyed with the idea of waking him; then, stoically, he returned both biscuits to the bottom of his pack with the same infinite care as if he were hiding gold. He made do with coffee, like his comrades. He had insisted on pitching the tent and they were all lying down inside when Loubet returned from a foraging mission, armed with a bunch of carrots from a nearby field. Since there was no means of cooking them, the men munched them raw. But the carrots merely served to aggravate their hunger. Pache was sick.

"No, no, let him sleep," said Jean, when Chouteau made as if to rouse Maurice and hand him his share.

"Ah well," said Lapoulle, "we can look forward to having some bread tomorrow, when we get to Angoulême. . . . I've a cousin garrisoned in Angoulême and he speaks highly of the food."

His remark was greeted with general astonishment.

"What do you mean, 'when we get to Angoulême'?" cried Chouteau. "We've got a real dolt here – he thinks he going to Angoulême!"

And it was impossible to get a word of explanation out of Lapoulle. He quite simply believed that they were on their way to Angoulême. That morning also the sight of the Uhlans made him say that they were some of Bazaine's troops!

Then an inky blackness came down on the camp, bringing the silence of death. Though the night was a cool one, orders had been given forbidding the lighting of fires. The Prussians were known to be only a few miles away, and all noise was kept to a minimum for fear of alerting them. Already the officers had warned the troops that the march was to be resumed at four, or thereabouts, so as to make up for lost time. Stunned with fatigue, they all fell asleep like men impatient to leave the waking world behind them. Above the widely scattered encampments, the heavy breathing of those close-packed thousands ascended into the darkness like the exhalation of the earth itself.

Suddenly the squad was disturbed by the sound of a gunshot. It was still very dark, and the time could not have been more than three o'clock. They were all on their feet at once and cries of alarm spread through the camp in the belief that the enemy was launching an attack. All it was, however, was Loubet who, having woken up, had taken it into his head to explore the neighbouring wood, where there were bound to be some rabbits. What a feast it would make, for him and his mates, if he were to return with a couple at first

114

light! But as he was looking for a suitable hiding-place he heard some men coming towards him. He caught their whispers and the sound of cracking twigs and he promptly panicked and fired, assuming they were Prussians.

Maurice, Jean and some of the others were already on their way to the spot when someone shouted hoarsely: "For God's sake don't shoot!"

And there, on the edge of the wood, they saw a tall, thin man with a bushy beard that was just distinguishable in the darkness. He wore a grey loose-fitting outergarment secured at the waist by a red sash, and he had a gun slung over his shoulder. He lost no time in explaining that he was French, a sergeant in the irregular Francs-tireurs, and that he and two of his men had come all the way from Dieulet woods with information for the general.

"Hey ...! Cabasse! Ducat!" he shouted, turning round to look for them. "Come on, you sluggards! Where are you hiding yourselves?"

The pair must have been afraid up to then, but at his words they hurried forward. Ducat was short and fat, with a white face and thinning hair. Cabasse, on the other hand, was tall and spare, with swarthy features and a long, blade-like nose.

Meanwhile Maurice had been staring intently at the sergeant, with obvious surprise. Finally he said: "Listen, aren't you Guillaume Sambuc from Remilly?"

The man hesitated for a moment, wearing an uneasy look; then he said yes. Maurice could not help recoiling, for this same Sambuc had the reputation of being a tremendous rough, the true son of a degenerate family of woodcutters. The father, an habitual drunkard, had been found in a quiet corner of a wood one night with his throat slit from ear to ear. The mother and daughter were notorious beggars and thieves and had both ended up in a brothel. Guillaume himself went in for poaching and smuggling, and there was only one white sheep in the family – Prosper, the cavalryman, who in the days before good fortune had led to his joining the Chasseurs d'Afrique, had become a farmhand, in bitter rejection of the woodland life.

"I saw your brother in Rheims and again in Vouziers," added Maurice. "He was in good fettle."

Sambuc made no answer to this. Instead he returned briskly to the business which had brought him here.

"Take me to the general. Tell him a party of Francs-tireurs

115

from the Dieulet woods have something important to communicate to him."

As they walked back towards the camp, Maurice turned his thoughts to these independent fighting groups in which such high hopes had been invested, but which were already provoking complaints all over the country. They were supposed to be waging war by stealth, from behind hedgerows, harassing the enemy, slaying his sentries, keeping a tight grip on the forest-lands so that never a Prussian should emerge alive. But instead they were fast becoming a nightmare to the peasants, providing them with scant protection yet ruining their crops. For the Francs-tireurs attracted the riffraff. Shying away from the discipline of ordinary military service, these men were only too happy to roam the countryside like bandits on the spree, sleeping and carousing wherever their paths happened to lead them. Some of the groups were even made up of really dangerous characters.

After every step Sambuc would turn round and call: "Hey, Cabasse! Hey, Ducat! Buck up, you pair of layabouts!"

Maurice sensed at once that these two were as bad as any. Cabasse – a tall, wiry fellow – was a native of Toulon. For a time he had worked as a waiter in Marseilles, but eventually he had turned up in Sedan as a commission agent for a firm down south. An act of larceny, never quite cleared up, had nearly put him on the wrong side of the law. Ducat – short and fat, on the other hand – had once served as court bailiff in Blainville, but had been forced to resign following a number of improprieties with small girls. He had recently come close to prosecution on the same revolting charges at Raucourt, where he had been employed as a book-keeper in one of the factories. While Ducat was full of Latin tags, Cabasse could scarcely read; but they were well-matched, a really shifty and alarming couple.

But this time the camp was beginning to show signs of life. Jean and Maurice conducted the irregulars to Captain Beaudoin, who in turn conducted them to Colonel de Vineuil. The latter began to interrogate them, but Sambuc self-importantly insisted on speaking to the general. It so happened that General Bourgain-Desfeuilles had just appeared in the doorway of the priest's house, where he had been sleeping. He was thoroughly out of temper at having to get up in the middle of the night and face another day of hunger and fatigue, and when the three men were brought before him he gave them an unfriendly welcome.

"Where are they from? What do they want? . . . Oh, so it's you irregulars! More idlers and dawdlers!"

Sambuc was entirely unabashed.

"General," he explained, "we and our comrades are guarding Dieulet woods . . ."

"Where the blazes are Dieulet woods?"

"Between Stenay and Mouzon, sir."

"Stenay? Mouzon? Never heard of them! How can I be expected to find my bearings, with all these new names?"

Much embarrassed, Colonel de Vineuil quietly intervened to remind the general that Stenay and Mouzon were towns on the Meuse; the enemy had succeeded in isolating Stenay and the defending army was now on its way to Mouzon bridge, which lay farther to the north, in the hope of crossing the river there.

"Well now, sir," Sambuc continued, "we are here to warn you that Dieulet woods are now full of Prussians. . . . As the 5th Corps was leaving Bois-les-Dames yesterday there was an engagement over towards Nouart . . ."

"What's that? You say there was fighting yesterday?"

"Why yes, sir. The 5th Corps was under attack as it withdrew. By this time it must be at Beaumont. . . . Some of our comrades have gone to inform its commander of the enemy's movements. It occurred to us three that we ought to come and tell you the situation so that you can go to help him, for he will have fully sixty thousand men to reckon with in the morning."

General Bourgain-Desfeuilles merely shrugged his shoulders when he heard this figure.

"Sixty thousand men my eye! Why don't you make it a hundred thousand? Pure imagination, man! You're in a funk and seeing double. There couldn't possibly be sixty thousand men so close to us. If there were, we'd know all about it."

He was not to be budged. Sambuc sought in vain to corroborate his statement with the eye-witness accounts of Ducat and Cabasse.

"We saw their artillery," insisted the southerner. "And they must be raving mad, the devils, to risk moving heavy guns along the forest tracks. There's been so much rain of late that the mud comes up to over your ankles."

"They've got someone to guide them, you can stake your life on it," declared the one-time bailiff.

But after their experience at Vouziers the general had abandoned all belief in the junction rumoured to have taken place between

117

the two German armies. He was, he said, sick and tired of hearing about it. He saw no point in bothering the corps commander with the three men; and they, in fact, thought it was with the commander that they had spoken. Had the staff lent an ear to every peasant and prowler who had come to them with so-called information, they would never have advanced a single step without being pitched right and left into mythical encounters. He did, however, instruct the three irregulars to remain with the column and accompany it, since they evidently knew the area.

"No getting away from it," said Jean, as he and Maurice walked back to the tent, "there must be a lot of good in them or they wouldn't have hiked ten miles to warn us."

The young man agreed. In his view the Francs-tireurs were talking sense. Like them he knew the area, and it alarmed him terribly to think of the Prussians striking through Dieulet woods and making for Sommauthe and Beaumont. He sat down, exhausted even before the day's march began. His stomach was empty, his heart was tight with anxiety. As the dawn broke, he knew that the day ahead could not be other than appalling.

In desperation at seeing him so pale, the corporal asked with fatherly concern: "Still feeling rough, are you? What is it – your foot again?"

Maurice shook his head. His foot was much better, thanks to the broad-fitting shoes.

"What is it, then – are you hungry?"

And seeing that he made no answer, Jean surreptitiously extracted one of the two remaining discuits from his knapsack.

"Here, I kept your share for you," he said, lying artlessly. "I ate the other one just now."

It was barely light when the 7th Corps left Oches and began to move towards Mouzon – via La Besace, where it should have spent the night. The monstrous baggage train had gone on ahead, escorted by the 1st Division, and although the service-corps vehicles kept up a good pace, pulled by strong teams, the requisition vans – empty for the most part, and serving no purpose – dawdled unaccountably amid the slopes of the Stonne pass. The road is an uphill one, especially on the far side of the hamlet of La Berlière, surrounded as it is by wooded heights. At about eight o'clock, just as the other two divisions were at last beginning to move forward, Marshal MacMahon rode up. He was furious at finding them this far back; they were supposed to have set out from La Besace this morning, only a few short miles from Mouzon. His discovery led to a sharp altercation with General Douay. It was decided that the 1st Division and the supply column should be allowed to continue towards Mouzon, but that the other two divisions should proceed via Raucourt and Autrecourt and cross the Meuse at Villers, so that they should not be held up any further by this extremely cumbersome and slow-moving vanguard. Once again they were to strike farther northwards as a result of the marshal's eagerness to put the river between himself and the foe. They must at all costs be on the right bank by the end of the day. And yet the rearguard was still only at Oches when a Prussian battery opened fire from a distant hilltop, over towards Saint-Pierremont, starting the same tricks which had been used the day before. At first the French were rash enough to reply; then the last units fell back.

Until eleven o'clock, or thereabouts, the 106th laboured along the road which winds between the tall mounds on either side of the Stonne pass. On the left the ridges are steep and bare, whereas the wooded slopes on the right afford a gentle ascent. The sun had reappeared and it was extremely hot in that narrow, oppressively lonely valley. On the far side of La Berlière, which is overhung by a high, bleak-looking Way-of-the-Cross, there is nothing to be seen, not a farmhouse, not a living being, not even an animal grazing in the meadows. And the men were so tired and hungry that already they were beginning to walk lame. There was no heart left in them and they were simmering with rage.

Then, quite suddenly, as they were resting beside the road, there came a roar of artillery from the right. The reports were so crisp and full that the fighting could not have been more than five miles away. The effect on these men – worn out from retreating, on edge with suspense – was quite extraordinary. In a trice they were all on their feet, quivering, raring to go, without a thought for their tiredness. They longed to fight and kill or be killed – anything rather than go on with this straggling flight which seemed wholly without purpose or destination.

Taking Colonel de Vineuil with him, General Bourgain-Desfeuilles had, as it happened, just climbed one of the hillocks on the right with the aim of reconnoitring the area. They were visible from below, standing midway between a pair of copses and making ample use of their field-glasses. They immediately sent down an aide, demanding the presence of the three Francs-tireurs if they were still with the regular troops. A number of men, Jean,

Maurice and a few others, accompanied the trio in case any help should be needed.

"Damned awful place !" shouted the general, as soon as he caught sight of Sambuc. "Nothing but woods and hills. Well, you've got ears," he added. "Where's it coming from? Where's the fighting?"

Sambuc did not answer for a while. Instead, with Ducat and Cabasse close behind him, he stood and listened, examining every part of the enormous sky-line. Maurice, within a few feet of him, followed his example and was filled with wonder at the sight of the immense rolling expanse of woods and valleys. It was like an endless sea of giant, slow-moving waves. The forests showed as dark-green stains on the yellowy soil, and under the hot sun the distant slopes were bathed in a red-brown haze. And although not even a puff of smoke appeared in the cloudless sky, the roar of guns continued; it was like listening to a storm growing louder and louder in the distance.

"That's Sommauthe over on the right," Sambuc said finally, pointing to a high hill capped with foliage. "And that's Yoncq over on the left. . . . Beaumont is where they're fighting, general."

"That's it," said Ducat, backing him up, "either Varniforet or Beaumont."

The general stood quietly fuming.

"Beaumont? Beaumont? This whole damned area is a mystery to me. . . ." Then he said aloud : "And how many miles are we from Beaumont or whatever you call it?"

"About six if you take the Le Chêne–Stenay road over there."

The gunfire thundered on and on. It seemed to be advancing from West to East.

"By God !" added Sambuc, "things are hotting up. I thought they would. I warned you this morning, general. You can bet your life those are the batteries we saw in Dieulet woods. By this time the 5th Corps must be under attack from the massive forces that were seen moving up through Buzancy and Beauclair."

In the ensuing silence the roar of battle grew louder than ever. And Maurice stood clenching his teeth, filled with a wild urge to raise his voice in protest. Why didn't they march straight towards the sound of gunfire, without all this hemming and hawing? Never in his life had he been brought to such a pitch of excitement. Every shot that was fired reverberated in his chest, stirring his feelings, making him long to be over there in the thick of it, so that the whole thing should be over and done with at last. Were they really going to lurk on the fringes of yet another battle, without even once squeezing the trigger? It was inconceivable that they should have been tugged hither and thither like this, always on the run, ever since the outbreak of war! At Vouziers, all they had heard was the rifle-fire of the rearguard. At Oches just now, the enemy had merely subjected them to a few short salvoes from the rear. And yet they were going to scamper away, forfeiting once again the opportunity of racing to the assistance of their comrades! Maurice looked at Jean : like himself, the corporal had turned extremely pale and his eyes shone feverishly. All hearts were beating hard in response to the violent summons of the artillery fire.

But now came a further spell of waiting. A party of staff officers was on its way up the narrow path which led to the top of the hillock. Chief among them was General Douay. There was a worried look on his face and he was hurrying. And when he had finished firing his own series of questions at the three Francs-tireurs, a cry of despair escaped his lips. Even if he had been aware of the situation that morning, what could he possibly have done? The marshal's decision was unshakeable : the Meuse must be crossed before nightfall, regardless of the cost. Besides, the units under his command were spaced out all the way to Raucourt; how, at this juncture, was he to remuster them for a rapid advance on Beaumont? Were they not bound to arrive too late? By now the 5th Corps must be falling back towards Mouzon – as indeed was clear from the artillery fire, which was moving farther and farther eastwards like a cataclysmic hailstorm moving on and away. General Douay cast up his two arms, extending them above the great panorama of hills and valleys, forests and meadows, in a gesture of enraged helplessness; and then he gave orders for the march on Raucourt to be continued.

Oh, what a march that was through the depths of the Stonne pass, with the high ridges on either side and the continuous rumble of artillery from behind the woods on the right. At the head of the 106th rode the stiff, upright figure of Colonel de Vineuil; his face was set and pale and his eyelids kept fluttering as though to hold back the tears. Captain Beaudoin nibbled at his moustache, saying nothing, while Lieutenant Rochas poured out a muted but uninterrupted flow of foul language, aimed at everyone including himself. And even among those men who had no taste for a fight, even among the most faint-hearted, there was a mounting need to hit out at the enemy and open their lungs in a battle-cry, a mounting anger born of constant defeat, a fury that they should still be retreating in lame confusion when the damned Prussians were within earshot of them, slaughtering their comrades.

Below Stonne the road coiled downwards between a series of hillocks and then broadened out. Soon the columns were advancing across a huge expanse of open land dotted about with a few woods and copses. The 106th was in the rearguard now, and ever since leaving Oches it had been in constant expectation of attack; for the enemy was following the column step by step, keeping close watch on it and presumably waiting for the most opportune moment to fall on it from the rear. Detachments of cavalry, taking advantage of the slightest dip in the ground, were attempting to steal up on both flanks. Several squadrons of Prussian Guardsmen were observed coming out from behind a wood, but they stopped short when a regiment of hussars moved forward in a show of strength. And thanks to this respite the withdrawal continued in a fairly orderly manner; the regiment was almost at Raucourt when the men were treated to a sight which greatly increased their tension and alarm and took away what little morale they had managed to retain until then. For suddenly they observed a wild throng rushing along a side road towards them – wounded officers; disbanded, unarmed men; service-corps vehicles careering along; men and animals alike were fleeing in panic, driven by a gale of disaster. These were the shattered remnants of a brigade belonging to the 1st Division, part of the escort for the baggage train which had set out for Mouzon that morning, via La Besace. By an appalling mischance, this brigade – together with a section of the baggage train itself – had taken a wrong turning and at Varniforet, near Beaumont, it had blundered straight into the disorganized retreat of the 5th Corps. Caught unawares by a flank attack and obliged to yield to numerical superiority, they had turned and run. They came back panic-stricken, covered in blood, wearing wild, half-crazed looks on their faces, instilling an ungovernable sense of horror into their comrades. The accounts they gave of their experience spread a feeling of terror; it was as though they had been swept into their path by the thunderous barrage which had continued uninterrupted since noon.

As a result, their march through Raucourt was done in a tense and desperate hurry. Ought they to turn right towards Autrecourt as a preliminary to crossing the Meuse at Villers, as had been decreed? Worried and undecided, General Douay was afraid that the Villers bridge might turn out to be congested or even in enemy hands. And he decided in favour of forging straight ahead through the Haraucourt pass so as to be in Remilly before nightfall. First Mouzon, then Villers, now Remilly : they were heading farther and farther north, with the Uhlans hard on their heels. There were only four miles to go, but it was already five o'clock and the men felt thoroughly worn-out. They had been on the march since dawn and it had taken them twelve hours to cover barely eight miles as the result of endless marking-time and interminable halts, during which they had been subjected to the most intense fears and emotions. For the past two nights they had been allowed much too little sleep, and they had gone hungry ever since Vouziers. They were ready to drop. In Raucourt, things were really distressing.

It is a prosperous little place, with a good number of factories, a smart-looking church and town hall, and a high street lined on both sides with attractive shops and offices. The only trouble was : it had been drained of all its resources. The grocers' and bakers' had been stripped bare and there was not so much as a crumb of bread left in the private houses. The Emperor and Marshal MacMahon had spent the night there, cluttering it with staff-officers and the count-less members of the imperial household, and then the entire 1st Corps had passed through the town, flowing through the high street like a never-ending river. Now there was no sign of bread or wine or sugar or any of the things a man can eat or drink. Ladies had been observed standing in their doorways and distributing glasses of wine and cups of broth until barrels and pots were dry. At last it was all over; and when at about three o'clock the leading regiments of the 7th Corps began to file through, the townspeople were overcome with despair. Unbelievable ! It was starting all over again. There were as many troops as before. The high street was aflow a second time with exhausted men, everyone of them covered in dust and sick with hunger, and nobody had a scrap of food to offer them. Many of the soldiers were stopping, knocking on doors and stretching their hands out imploringly for a hunk of bread. And women stood at open windows, sobbing in desperation and signalling that they were powerless to help, since they had nothing whatever left.

At the corner of the Rue des Dix-Potiers, Maurice came over giddy and nearly lost his footing.

"No, leave me be," he said, as Jean hurried to his side. "This is the end . . . I'd as soon die here."

And with that he sank down on to a milestone.

"Jesus! How do I come to have a man like you in my squad?" asked Jean, simulating the gruffness of a riled superior. "Do you want the Prussians to collar you? Come along, now – get up on your feet!"

But the young man did not answer. His face looked bloodless, his eyes were closed and he was only half conscious. Looking at him, Jean swore again – but this time there was a note of immeasurable compassion in his voice.

"Jesus! Oh, Jesus!"

There was a drinking-fountain not far away. Jean hurried over to it, filled his mess-tin with water and bathed the private's face and forehead. Then – and this time he made no attempt to conceal his movements – he took the last preciously guarded biscuit from his knapsack, broke it into small pieces and began to feed them to Maurice, who opened his eyes and nibbled hungrily.

"You were supposed to have eaten it this morning," Maurice said suddenly, remembering Jean's words early in the day.

"Oh, you needn't worry about me," said Jean. "I can wait – I'm made of harder stuff. A swig of Adam's ale, and I'll be right as rain."

He refilled his mess-tin and gulped down the contents, smacking his lips. He was deadly pale too, and the pangs of hunger were so intense that his hands shook.

"Come on now, we must catch up with the others."

Maurice leaned heavily on Jean's arm and allowed himself to be led along like a child. Never had the touch of a woman's arm brought such warmth to his heart. The world was collapsing about him; he was forced to endure extreme privation and the strong possibility of death – yet how delightfully consoling was the awareness of another human being loving and caring for him. And it may have been that his gratitude was considerably sweetened by the fact that the man whose heart he had won was an unsophisticated peasant, of an earthiness which had at first inspired repugnance in him. Here, surely, was the spirit of brotherliness which had existed in the early days of the world, the brand of friendship which had preceded all barriers of class and education – an affection binding two men united in their mutual need for help against the implacably threatening forces of nature. He could hear his own humanity in the sound of Jean's heartbeats and he took pride in the feeling that the other man was stronger than he, and in the awareness that the corporal was sustaining him even to the point of self-sacrifice. Jean, for his part, did not analyze his feelings; but he rejoiced in the opportunity to shield his friend's intelligence and refinement, knowing that in his own case these qualities had never progressed beyond the rudimentary. Since the violent death of his wife, carried off in circumstances of appalling tragedy, he had imagined that his heart was closed for ever; he had vowed that he would always keep away from any of those creatures who cause a man so much pain, even when there is no malice in them. And to both men the friendship was becoming a kind of enlargement; indeed they had difficulty not to embrace each other, they felt so close to each other at that moment; and however dissimilar their natures, like and concern went so deep that on this atrocious march to Remilly they were as one – a single human being imbued with pity and suffering.

Even as the rearguard left Raucourt, the Germans were entering the town from the other end. They at once set up a pair of batteries on the hills that rise on the left, and the guns promptly opened fire. By then the 106th was hurrying away down the road which follows the course of the Emmane, and in consequence they were an obvious target. One shell blasted a poplar growing on the river bank; another buried itself in a meadow beside Captain Beaudoin, but it did not explode. Between there and Haraucourt the pass grows narrower and narrower, and soon they plunged into a tight passageway overhung by two lines of ridges with plenty of trees. It needed only a handful of Prussians lying in wait up there, and disaster would be inescapable. Shelled from behind and threatened with the possibility of attack on both sides, the troops were a prey to ever-increasing alarm as they pressed forward; they could not wait to get out of this death-trap. And so a final surge of energy took possession of even the weariest among them. Spurred on by the thought of the peril confronting them, the same men who, only a short time earlier, had staggered through Raucourt, lurching from door to door, were now stepping out with a new vigour. Even the horses seemed to realize that the wasting of a single moment might cost them dear. The head of the column must already have been in Remilly when, suddenly and unexpectedly, the troops were brought to a standstill again.

"What now, for God's sake!" said Chouteau. "Are they going to leave us stranded?"

The 106th had not yet reached Haraucourt and the shells were still raining down. As the regiment marked time, waiting to move

125

forward again, one of the shells exploded to the right of the road-way – luckily without injuring anybody. Five minutes went by – an appalling, seemingly endless expanse of time. Even then they did not budge. Somewhere out in front, an obstacle was barring the way; it was as though a high wall had been built in their path. The colonel rose in his stirrups, staring about him, all aquiver, conscious of the mounting panic of the men behind him.

"We've been betrayed," Chouteau added vehemently. "Everyone knows that!"

At this, loud murmurings broke out – a mounting rumble of exasperation whipped up by fear. Yes, that was the plain truth of the situation : the generals had brought them here so as to betray them and sell them into the hands of the Prussians. Misfortune had dogged them so persistently, and blunder had succeeded blunder with such incredible regularity, that to these narrow intelligences betrayal had suddenly come to seem the only possible explanation for the series of disasters which had overtaken them.

"We've been betrayed!" they cried in panic-stricken voices.

At this point a fanciful idea suddenly occurred to Loubet.

"It's that swine of an Emperor holding us up," he said. "He's blocking the way with all his luggage."

The news spread rapidly. It was put about as a fact that the hold-up had been caused by the imperial household cutting across the head of the column. And at this the troops cursed and swore in the foulest language, venting all the hatred aroused within them by the insolence with which the Emperor's staff had assumed control of towns where fighting men might have slept, flaunting their wines and rich foods and silver plate in front of human beings who had to go without everything, setting kitchens ablaze with light and heat when thousands of poor devils were pinched with hunger. Oh, wretched Emperor! Ousted from his throne and stripped of his authority, he was like a lost child in his own Empire, a useless bundle consigned to be baggage-train, an invalid forced to display the ironic trappings of his resplendent household, his life-guards, his carriages, his horses, his cooks, his provision vans, all the pomp of his bee-spangled state robes trailing in the blood and mire of the road to defeat!

Two more shells exploded in rapid succession. Lieutenant Rochas had his cap knocked off by a piece of shrapnel. And the ranks closed with a violent pushing and shoving which, like a sudden big wave, made itself felt far and wide. There were choking cries and

126

Lapoulle bellowed furiously, calling on the soldiers in front to move forward. Another minute and an appalling catastrophe might have ensued, a wild stampede that would crush the life out of the human being trapped in the constricted pass.

The colonel turned round. His face was white.

"Try and be patient, lads, try and be patient. I've sent someone to find out what is happening. . . . We're on our way again now."

But these were empty words, and the seconds seemed like centuries. By this time Jean had taken hold of Maurice's hand and was quietly explaining, with admirable calm and clearheadedness, that if the pushing started again they would dart to the left and then work their way up through the woods on the other side of the river. He looked about him for the Francs-tireurs, reflecting that they were bound to know the roads; but he was told that they had disappeared on the way through Raucourt. And then, all of a sudden, the column began to move forward again; very soon it rounded a bend in the road and was safely screened from the German batteries. Afterwards it was learned that the procession which had cut across the path of the 7th Corps, in the confusion of that disastrous day, was in fact Bonnemain's division – four full regiments of Cuirassiers.

Night was coming on when the 106th marched through Angecourt. The high ridges continued on the right, but on the left the pass was beginning to broaden and a bluish valley was visible in the distance. And at long last, from the Remilly hills, a pale silver ribbon showed through the evening haze amid the unfurling expanse of meadows and farmland. It was the Meuse, the longed-for Meuse where victory apparently awaited them.

And Maurice, extending his arm in the direction of a few points of light shining cheerfully at the far end of this rich green valley, exquisite in the twilight, turned to Jean and with the joyous relief of a man returning to a place he loves cried: "Look . . .! Over there . . .! That's Sedan!"

127

VII

In Remilly itself, the street winding downhill to the Meuse was hopelessly congested with men, horses and vehicles. Half-way along the slope, a number of heavy guns were stranded outside the church; their wheels had become interlocked and they were not to be budged, despite all the kicking and swearing on the part of their crews. Down by the spinning mill, where there is a constant roar from a water-fall, a whole string of forage-waggons was blocking the roadway; while an ever-growing mob of soldiers was brawling outside the Croix-de-Malte inn, though none of them succeeded in obtaining even a glass of wine.

This tremendous jam extended all the way to the southern end of the village, which is separated from the river by a clump of trees. Here, early in the day, the army engineers had erected a pontoon bridge. On the right was a ferry, the boatman's house providing a solitary touch of white among the tall grass. Big fires had been built on both banks; and the flames, stirred up at intervals, set the darkness ablaze, covering the water and the two stretches of shore with what was almost daylight. These moments of extreme brightness showed how great was the throng of troops waiting to get across. Yet the footbridge would take only two at a time, and on the main surface of the temporary structure – ten feet wide at most – cavalry, artillery and supply waggons were kept to a snail's pace. An ammunition convoy and an entire 1st Corps brigade were reported to be still in Remilly, to say nothing of the four regiments of cuirassiers belonging to Bonnemain's division. And moving into position behind all these was the whole of the 7th Corps – thirty-odd thousand men who, believing the enemy hard on their heels, were clamouring to reach the safety of the far shore.

For a time they were in utter despair. To think they should have marched all day on empty stomachs, battling their way through the Haraucourt pass, only to meet with a dead end and be pitched into this scene of chaos and alarm. It might well be hours before their turn came; and every one of them was acutely aware that, even if the Prussians were not so bold as to keep up the pursuit overnight, they would be under attack first thing next morning. Nevertheless they were ordered to pile arms and make camp on the broad bare hillsides which, hugged by the Mouzon road, sloped down to the Meuse-side meadows. Up on a plateau behind them, the reserve artillery was deployed in battle formation, with its guns trained in readiness on the exit from the pass. And so another long wait began, in a mood of considerable anxiety and rebellion.

The 106th was stationed above the road, in a stubble-field that afforded a clear view of the vast plain. The men had been reluctant to part with their rifles and they kept glancing back over their shoulders, haunted by the fear of an attack. There were hard, set, remote looks on all their faces, and they did not speak except to grunt and growl from time to time. Nine o'clock was about to strike : they had been here two whole hours. Yet many of them, despite their appalling physical fatigue, were unable to sleep. They lay flat on the ground, shuddering and pricking up their ears at the slightest sound from the countryside behind them. They had given up all thought of stilling the hunger that gnawed at their bellies : they would eat when they were safely across the water and they would eat grass if nothing else came to hand. In the meantime, however, the congestion seemed to be growing worse than ever. The officers whom General Douay had positioned down by the bridge returned at twenty-minute intervals with the same unvarying, irritating news – it would take hours and hours yet. In the end the general decided to make his own way down to the bridge. He could be seen struggling in the midst of the turmoil, clearly doing his best to hurry things along.

Maurice and Jean sat resting against a bank. Maurice was pointing his finger northwards, just as he had done earlier.

"Sedan is at the far end. . . . And look – there's Bazeilles. . . . Then Douzy and then Carignan, over on the right. . . . Carignan is almost bound to be our rallying-point. . . . Oh, if only it were daylight you'd be able to see how spacious the valley is !"

And his gesture embraced the whole dusky scene. The sky was not so black as to conceal the pale course of the river amid the dark rolling meadows. The clumps of trees composed heavier masses – not least a row of poplars eerily damming the horizon on the left. Then, in the far distance, behind the cluster of bright dots that indicated Sedan, the blackness was intensified as though all the

129

forests of the Ardennes had rung down the curtain of their ancient oaks.

Jean's attention had returned to the pontoon bridge below them. "Look at that . . .! The whole thing is going to give way. We shall never get across."

The fires on either bank were burning higher, and just then the brightness was so intense that the whole terrible scene was lit up with the startling clarity of an apparition. Under the collective weight of all the cavalry and artillery which had driven over since early morning, the pontoons supporting the planks had eventually foundered – and now the main surface of the bridge was several inches under water. At the moment it was the cuirassiers who were making their way across, advancing two by two in an uninterrupted procession, emerging from the darkness of one bank only to sink into the darkness of the other; and the bridge was no longer to be seen – they appeared to be walking on water, water which had turned into a dancing fire. The horses were whinneying as, shock-haired and stiff-legged, they braved the terrors of the swaying surface, which seemed to be about to give way beneath them. The cuirassiers sat upright in their stirrups and kept a tight hold on their reins as they moved forward, pair after pair, draped in those long white cloaks which concealed all but their helmets, glinting red from the blaze. They might have been phantom knights with flaming hair, on their way to war against the spirits of darkness.

A low moan issued from Jean's dry, constricted throat.

"Oh, I'm so hungry!"

In the meantime the men around them had fallen asleep, despite the pain in their bellies. Excessive tiredness had finally overcome fear and laid them all flat on their backs, crushed and open-mouthed beneath the moonless sky. All along these bare hillsides, the hum of apprehension had given place to a death-like silence.

"Oh, I'm hungry – so hungry I could eat a lump of earth!"

Inured and uncomplaining as he was, Jean was no longer able to check this outburst. The words came out of their own accord, in the delirium brought on by hunger – he had eaten nothing for almost thirty-six hours. Whereupon Maurice, realizing that it might well be two or three hours before their regiment crossed the Meuse, made up his mind to speak.

"Listen," he said, "I've an uncle living in these parts. You know who I mean. Uncle Fouchard. I've told you about him. . . . It's about half a mile back, and I wasn't sure whether to mention it;

130

but as you're so hungry. . . . Hang it, he's bound to find a bit of bread for us!"

Without more ado, he led his unresisting companion away. Old Fouchard's little farmhouse stood close to the exit from the Haraucourt pass, beside the plateau where the reserve artillery was deployed. It was a low-roofed structure with ample outbuildings – barn, cowshed, stable. . . . Across the road was a kind of coachhouse, the centre of the peasant's activities as an itinerant butcher; it was here that he personally slaughtered the animals which he afterwards hawked through the villages in his cart.

As they drew nearer, Maurice was surprised to see no light in the house.

"Ah, the old miser! He must have barricaded himself against all comers."

But he was stopped in his tracks when he saw what was happening outside the farmhouse. A party of ten or a dozen marauding soldiers were there whose hunger had presumably proved too much for them, and who were out for whatever they could lay their hands on. At first they had called out, then they had knocked; now, observing that the house was as black and silent as ever, they were thumping the door with their rifle-butts in an attempt to force it. Gruff shouts flew about in the darkness.

"Hammer away, lads! There's no one here, so let's smash the damned thing down!"

At this, the shutter of one of the attic windows banged open without warning and an old man appeared. Tall, bare-headed and clad in a smock, he had a candle in one hand and a shotgun in the other. Beneath the shock of white hair, his foursquare features were heavily lined; he had a prominent nose, big pale eyes and a resolute chin.

"Are you robbers, that you should smash everything like that?" he shouted in a hoarse voice. "What do you want?"

The soldiers backed away, somewhat disconcerted.

"We're starving, we want something to eat."

"I haven't got anything, not even a crust. . . . Do you seriously think we can feed hundreds of thousands of men just like that? You're not the first lot we've had today – oh no! General Durcot's men passed through here this morning, and they took all I owned."

One by one the soldiers were gathering round again.

"That needn't stop you letting us in. We can rest for a while, and you're bound to find something. . . ."

131

And they had already returned to their hammering when the old man, setting the candlestick down on the windowsill, levelled his shotgun.

"As true as I'm standing here, I'll put a bullet through the first man who lays a finger on my door."

The threat very nearly resulted in bloodshed. The troops began to curse and fume, and someone bellowed the suggestion that they should do the bastard in. For he was just like all the other peasants: he would rather throw his bread in the lake than offer a bite to a soldier. And their rifle-barrels were trained at him, they were about to shoot him down at point-blank range – for he was so furious and stubborn that instead of backing away he stood full in the light of the candle.

"I've nothing left, I tell you! Not even a crust! They took all I owned!"

Deeply alarmed, Maurice rushed forward with Jean close behind. "Comrades, comrades . . ."

He pushed the soldiers' rifles aside; then he stared up at the window and said with a note of entreaty: "Come now, be sensible. . . . Don't you recognize me? It's me."

"Who's 'me'?"

"Maurice Levasseur, your nephew."

By this time old Fouchard had picked up the candle again. Doubtless he did recognize Maurice. But he refused to be budged from his determination not to part with even a glassful of water.

"How can a man tell who's a nephew and who isn't, on a devilish black night like this . . .? Clear off, the whole pack of you, or I'll fire!"

And amid the loud chorus of abuse and the constant threats to shoot him down and set fire to his hovel, he kept on bawling the same thing, twenty times or more: "Clear off, or I'll fire!"

Suddenly a loud, clear voice resounded above the general din.

"Even at me, father?"

The others had stepped aside and an artillery sergeant came forward in the dancing light of the candle. It was Honoré, whose battery was positioned less than two hundred yards away and who for hours had been trying to fight down the irresistible desire to come and knock on this door. He had sworn never to set foot inside it again; and not once, during four whole years of army service, had he exchanged letters with the father, to whom he now called so curtly. Already the marauders were putting their heads together

132

and reappraising the position. So the newcomer was the old man's son, and an N.C.O. for good measure! The outlook was a poor one; they had better go and try their luck elsewhere! And with that they scurried away into the thick darkness.

When old Fouchard realized that the danger to his property had passed, he was content to remark as imperturbably as if he had seen his son the day before: "So it's you. . . . All right, I'll come down."

This took him a long while. From within came the sounds of locking and unlocking, the slow ritual of a man making sure that nothing has been left lying about. Then, at long last, the door opened – only a few inches, though, and he kept a sturdy grip on it.

"In you come – but nobody else, mind!"

He could hardly refuse shelter to his nephew, however, even though his reluctance was clear enough.

"All right, you as well!"

And implacably he began to shut the door in Jean's face. Maurice had to parley with him. Even then he would not yield: oh no, he didn't want any thieving strangers forcing their way into his home and breaking up the furniture. Finally Honoré managed to heave their comrade inside and the old man had to submit, though he continued to issue threats in a low growl. He was still gripping his shotgun. After leading the way to the living-room, he stood the firearm against the sideboard and set the candle down on the table; then he fell into a stubborn silence.

"Now see here, father, we're starving. Surely we're welcome to some bread and cheese?"

He did not answer; he seemed not to hear; he kept going back to the window and listening hard in case another party of men should be preparing to lay siege to his house.

"Oh, come on uncle – Jean is like a brother to me. He sacrificed his own bits and pieces so as to keep me going. And we have been through such hard times together!"

The old man just shambled about the room, making sure that nothing was missing, not even looking at them. Finally he came to a decision, still without a word. All of a sudden he picked up the candle and left them in total darkness, carefully locking the door after him to ensure that he could not be followed. They heard him going down the cellar steps. Once again his mission took a very long time. Then he came back, conscientiously re-establishing his

133

barricade. He laid a large loaf and a cheese on the centre of the table. He was as silent as ever; but now that his anger had worn off, the silence was merely a matter of general policy – a man never knew where talking might lead. In any case, the three soldiers fell to with a vengeance and for a while their furious munching was the only sound to be heard.

Eventually Honoré rose to fetch a jug of water that was standing close to the sideboard.

"Father, you might have spared us some wine."

At this, Fouchard – calm and self-assured – found his tongue.

"Wine, d'you say? I've none left – not a drop . . . ! Ducrot's men ate and drank and looted everything!"

He was lying; and this, despite his attempts at concealment, was obvious from the way he stood blinking his large pale eyes. Two days ago he had spirited his cattle away, not only the small number which he maintained as a farmer, but even those meant for his slaughter-house; he had led them out at night and hidden them heaven knew where, in the depths of some wood or an abandoned quarry. And since then he had spent hours concealing all trace of food and drink, even such things as salt and flour. As a result even a wholesale ransacking of the cupboards would have proved unprofitable. The house was clean as a whistle. He had even refused to sell to the first soldiers who had come knocking at his door. Who could say whether better opportunities might not present themselves? Visions of far more lucrative trading had begun to form in his shrewd, grasping, time-biding head.

Maurice, still eating his fill, was the first to speak.

"Have you seen anything of my sister Henriette?"

The old man was still walking about the room. From time to time he directed a long, hard stare at Jean, who was tucking away enormous mouthfuls of bread.

"Henriette," he replied unhurriedly, as though he had given the question a great deal of thought. "Oh yes, I saw her in Sedan a month or two ago. But I had a glimpse of Weiss, her husband, only this morning. He was with his employer, Monsieur Delaherche. They were driving to Mouzon together. They wanted to see the army march through the town, just for the fun of the thing. . . ."

A look of deepest irony flickered across the peasant's normally impassive face.

"I wouldn't be surprised if they've seen a bit too much of the army and found it less fun than they hoped – for by three o'clock the streets were so packed with fleeing troops that it was impossible to move."

In the same calm, seemingly indifferent voice he gave a few details of the defeat of the 5th Corps. A surprise attack at Beaumont, launched while the men were cooking their midday meal, had forced the French to give ground; then the Bavarians had driven them all the way back to Mouzon. A group of survivors, trudging panic-stricken through the streets of Remilly, had alleged at the tops of their voices that de Failly had done a deal with Bismarck and sold them into the enemy's hands. And Maurice's mind went back to the frenzied marching of the past forty-eight hours and to how, in his implacable determination to cross the Meuse, Marshal MacMahon had given orders for the retreat to be accelerated – after all those precious days had been squandered in incomprehensible dithering. The decision had come too late. Admittedly, to the Marshal (who had flown into such a rage at finding the 7th Corps still at Oches, when he had imagined it to be in La Besace) it must have seemed certain that the 5th was safely encamped at Mouzon by the time the Germans wiped them out at Beaumont. Yet what was to be expected of troops who were ill-led, demoralized and dying of starvation and fatigue?

In his astonishment at the speed with which Jean was disposing of mouthful after mouthful, Fouchard had eventually come to a standstill beside the corporal's chair.

"Feel better now, do you?" he inquired with heavy humour.

The corporal glanced up, and with the same rustic stolidity replied : "Beginning to, thanks."

Honoré was just as hungry. But ever since he had sat down to table, he had been pausing from time to time and looking round as though he fancied he heard a sound. Only after a long tussle with his conscience had he gone back on his oath never to set foot inside this house again, and his change of heart was due entirely to the irresistible desire to see Silvine. Inside his shirt, right next to his skin, he continued to carry the letter which he had received from her in Rheims – that wonderfully tender letter in which she told him that she still loved him and would never love anyone else, despite the bitter events of the past, despite Goliath and the son she had borne him. And now all his thoughts were for her, and it worried him that he should have seen no sign of her – even though he braced himself, to avoid betraying his anxiety to his father. But the strength of his feelings proved too great.

135

"What about Silvine?" he asked, doing his best to make his voice sound natural. "Isn't she with you any longer, then?"

Fouchard directed a sidelong glance at his son, and there was a gleam in his eyes as though he were laughing inwardly.

"Oh, yes."

Then he promptly fell silent again and enjoyed a good spit. After a period of silence, the artilleryman was compelled to return to the attack.

"In bed then, is she?"

"Oh, no."

Eventually the old man condescended to explain that he had driven to Raucourt just as usual that morning, and taken his servant-girl with him. Troops might be passing through the town, but that was no reason for the world to stop eating meat or for a man to neglect the call of business. So, the same as every other Tuesday, he had gone into town with a sheep and a hunk of beef; and he was in process of completing the transaction when the arrival of the 7th Corps had unleashed pandemonium all about him. There was a great deal of rushing and pushing and shoving. Whereupon, fearing that his horse and cart might be misappropriated, he had driven off and abandoned Silvine who was running a few errands at the time.

"Oh, she'll be back," he concluded calmly. "She must have gone to her godfather's for shelter – old Dr. Dalichamp. . . . She may be placid but she's got pluck, that girl. No getting away from it : she's many good points."

Was he joking? Was he trying to explain why he kept the girl on despite the fact that it was she who had come between him and his son and despite the encumbrance of the Prussian's child, with whom she refused to part? Again he gave Honoré a sidelong glance and a soundless laugh.

"Charlot is here, fast asleep in her room – so you can rest assured she won't be long."

Honoré's lips were trembling and he stared at his father with such intensity that the latter began to pace about the room again. And silence returned, total and apparently endless, while the artilleryman helped himself to another slice of bread and went on eating. Jean continued to do the same, too, without feeling any desire or need to utter a single word. Maurice had eaten his fill; he sat with his elbows on the table, gazing at the furniture – same old sideboard, same old clock – and daydreaming about the holidays which he and his sister Henriette had spent here in days gone by. The minutes ticked away until all of a sudden the clock struck eleven.

"Good heavens!" he murmured. "We mustn't let the others move off without us."

And, meeting with no objection from Fouchard, he walked over to the window and threw it open. The whole of the dark valley opened out before them like a black rolling sea. As soon as their eyes grew acclimatized, however, they had no difficulty in making out the bridge, lit by the fires on both banks. The Cuirassiers were still riding across in their long white cloaks, like ghost-horsemen whose steeds – lashed onwards by a gale of terror – appeared to be walking on water. On and on went the procession, as though it would never end, and the tempo was forever that of a slow-moving vision. And the stillness of death prevailed along the bare hillsides on the right, where the army lay asleep.

"Well, that's that," said Maurice, with a gesture of desperation, "we shan't get across till morning."

He had left the window wide open, and old Fouchard – snatching up his gun – swung his leg over the sill and hopped out with the nimbleness of a young man. For a while they heard him clumping up and down as regularly as a sentry; then there was no further sound save the loud, distant rumble from the crowded bridge. Presumably he had sat down at the edge of the road, calmer for being out in the open with a clear view of any approaching threat, ready at a moment's notice to hop in again and defend his house and home.

By now, not a minute went by without Honoré's looking at the clock. He was growing more and more worried. Raucourt was only four miles away – little more than an hour's walk for a girl as young and sturdy as Silvine. Why wasn't she here? It was hours since the old man had deserted her; and there had been chaos ever since, with an entire army corps swamping the countryside and blocking the roads. No doubt about it: something terrible had happened. He pictured her roaming the fields, dazed and lost, and the horses' hooves thudding into her body.

But suddenly the three men in the cottage leaped to their feet. There was a patter of footsteps from the road and they heard Fouchard cock his gun.

"Who's there?" the old peasant shouted gruffly. "Is that you, Silvine?"

No answer. He repeated his question and threatened to open fire. At this a tight, breathless voice replied: "Yes, yes – it's me, Monsieur Fouchard."

"Is Charlot all right?" the girl asked a moment later.

"He's in bed and asleep."

"Ah, that was kind of you. . . ."

At once she stopped hurrying and vented all her alarm and weariness in a single heavy sigh.

"Climb in through the window," said Fouchard. "We've got visitors."

As she lowered herself into the parlour, she was considerably taken aback by the sight of the three men. Even in the wavering light of the candle, her extreme darkness was plain to behold. She had thick black hair and large, appealing eyes which were, in themselves, sufficient to make her oval face beautiful. Her expression was placid, almost submissive. At that particular moment, however, the sudden sight of Honoré had brought all the blood to her cheeks, even though she was hardly astonished to find him here : he had been on her mind all the way home from Raucourt.

The artilleryman, though he felt faint and ready to choke, tried to appear completely calm.

"Hullo, Silvine."

"Hullo, Honoré."

Then, to avoid bursting into tears, she turned her head away and smiled at Maurice, whom she had just recognized. And Jean made her feel awkward. She was suffocating, so she took off the silk scarf which she wore round her neck.

Honoré spoke again, with greater reserve than he had shown in the old days : "We were worried about you, Silvine. With all those Prussians moving up behind us . . ."

She suddenly turned very pale, and a look of utter consternation and distress appeared on her face. She could not keep from glancing towards the room where little Charlot lay asleep. Then, fluttering her hand as though to dispel a monstrous vision, she murmured : "Yes, they are – they *are* ! I've seen them."

She sank exhausted into a chair and related how, when the 7th Corps had surged into Raucourt, she had taken shelter in the house of her godfather, Dr. Dalichamp, hoping that old Fouchard would have the sense to call there for her before he started home. The high street was a scene of such frantic hustling and bustling that not even a dog would have ventured into it. And until four

o'clock or so she had waited with reasonable patience and unconcern, helping a group of ladies prepare some lint; for the doctor –
impelled by the notion that wounded might be dispatched from
Metz or Verdun, if there was fighting in those areas – had spent
the past fortnight organizing a dressing-station in the town hall.
Some people who called at the house said the dressing-station might
well be needed for immediate use; and indeed, as early as noon
artillery fire had been heard coming from the general direction of
Beaumont. But it was still a long way off and no one was particularly afraid. And then, all of a sudden, just as the last French
troops were leaving Raucourt, there was a terrifying roar and a
shell burst through the roof of one of the neighbouring houses. Two
more followed – it was a German battery bombarding the rearguard of the 7th Corps. By this time some of the wounded from
Beaumont were inside the town hall, and there was a general fear
that a shell might finish them off as they lay on the straw waiting
for the doctor to come and operate on them. Wild with terror, the
wounded men were scrambling up and trying to reach the cellars,
though their shattered limbs made them groan with pain.

"And then," continued Silvine, "I don't know how it came about,
but suddenly all was quiet. . . . I had gone to one of the upstairs
windows which gives a good view of the street and the countryside.
There was no one in sight, not a single French uniform, and then
I heard the tramp of heavy boots, and there was a shout, and all
the rifle-butts struck the ground at the same moment. There, at
the lower end of the street, was a column of short, black, dirty-
looking men with big ugly heads and helmets just like our firemen
wear. They were Bavarians, someone said. . . . And then, looking
up, I saw – oh, thousands and thousands of them heading towards
us along the roads and across the fields and through the woods in
endless, close-packed columns. The whole countryside had turned
black with them. It was like an invasion of black locusts – more and
more and more of them, so that in next to no time the soil was
completely hidden."

She was shaking all over, and once again she fluttered her hand
as though warding off the horror of her recollections.

"What happened after that is beyond your power to imagine. . . .
It appears these men had been on the march three whole days and
had just fought like madmen at Beaumont. So their eyes were
starting from their heads with hunger and exhaustion; they were
three parts insane. . . . The officers didn't even try to stop them;

139

they charged straight into the shops and houses, smashing windows, breaking down doors, wrecking furniture. . . . In their wild search for food and drink, they swallowed anything – whatever came to hand. At Monsieur Simonnot's, the grocer's, I saw one man scooping treacle out of a tub with his helmet. Others were gnawing hunks of raw bacon. The townsfolk had previously told them there was nothing left – for hadn't our own troops been streaming through the town for the past forty-eight hours? Yet despite this the Germans still chanced upon hidden supplies. And so they set about demolishing everything, in the belief that food was being deliberately withheld from them. Within an hour there wasn't a grocer's shop or a baker's or a butcher's or even a private house which hadn't had its windows smashed in, its cupboards emptied, its cellars stripped bare. . . . At the doctor's own house, I even – can you believe such a thing? – saw a big fat man eating all the soap. Down in the cellar, though : that was where they wreaked most havoc of all. We could hear them from upstairs, roaring like wild beasts, smashing every bottle and turning on every tap till it was like listening to a waterfall. When they showed themselves again, their skin and clothes were red from splashing about in all that wine. . . . And to give you some idea of what it's like when human beings revert to savagery : try as he did, Dr. Dalichamp couldn't stop one soldier from drinking a litre of syrup of opium which he happened to lay his hands on. The poor wretch can't but be dead by now, considering the state he was in when I left."

She shuddered violently and put both hands over her eyes so that she should not have to go on seeing.

"No, no! I've seen too much – the memory of it is suffocating me!"

Old Fouchard, still mounting guard beside the road, had come closer and was standing just outside the window, where he could hear. The girl's story worried him. He had been assured that the Prussians always paid for everything; surely they wouldn't turn out to be robbers? Maurice and Jean were no less engrossed by these particulars concerning an enemy whom this girl had just set eyes on and whom they themselves had yet to meet, although they had been on active service for a whole month. Honoré, for his part, sat deep in thought, his mouth drooping dolefully. He was concerned solely with the girl herself; he had no mind for anything but the tragic event which had parted them so long ago.

But at that moment the door of the adjoining room opened and

140

little Charlot appeared. He must have heard his mother's voice and now, clad in his night-shirt, he came running out to kiss her. He was a child of uncommonly heavy build, with fair skin, rosy cheeks, big blues eyes and a mop of curly flaxen hair.

Silvine shivered in response to the boy's sudden, unheralded entrance. She seemed almost startled at the sight of him. Could it be that for a moment she failed to recognize the child she worshipped? She was staring at him in terror, as if at the living embodiment of her nightmare. Then she burst into tears.

"My poor darling!"

And she clasped him to her desperately, while Honoré – all trace of colour driven from his face – took full stock of Charlot's extraordinary likeness to Goliath. The square head was the same, and so was its covering. Here in the full bloom of childhood, carefree and pristine, were all the characteristics of the Teutonic breed. The Prussian's child – "the little Prussian", as the wags of Remilly dubbed him! And here was his French mother, hugging him to her heart, still feeling dazed and lacerated by what she had seen of the invasion!

"My poor darling, be good now and go back to bed . . .! Go to bye-bye, my poor darling!"

She carried him into the bedroom. When she returned to the living-room she had stopped crying and her face wore its familiar look of calm courage.

Honoré was first to speak.

"You were telling us about the Prussians," he prompted, with a tremor in his voice.

"Oh yes, the Prussians. . . . Well, not content with smashing and eating and drinking everything in sight, they stole the household linen – towels, sheets, even the curtains, tearing them into long strips and bandaging their feet with them. I saw some men whose feet were raw all over from the marching they had done. There were quite a few sitting on the kerb outside the doctor's; they had taken their boots off and were binding their heels with some lace-trimmed shifts which they must have stolen from beautiful Madame Lefèvre, the mill-owner's wife. . . . The looting and plundering went on till nightfall. The houses had lost all their doors and windows; at street level there was nothing but gaping holes, and you could see the battered remains of the furniture inside. Oh, the havoc they'd wrought! Even the calmest townsfolk were roused to anger. For my own part, I was almost out of my mind – I simply couldn't stay there a minute longer. They did their best to dissuade me, arguing that the roads were blocked and that I would be killed for certain; but I ran off and immediately took to the fields on the right as you leave Raucourt. I saw several carts on their way from Beaumont, piled high with French and Prussian wounded. Two of them passed quite close to me in the dark, and at the sound of all the screaming and groaning I took to my heels and ran, charging through woods and fields with no thought for where I was going. I went miles out of my way, right over towards Villers. . . . Three times I hid, thinking I heard soldiers. But I didn't meet anyone, except another woman. She was running away too. From Beaumont. Some of the things she told me made my hair stand on end. . . . Well, now I'm here – and I feel so upset, so terribly upset!"

Her voice grew choked with tears again. Her mind was obsessed with the story which the woman from Beaumont had told her. The woman lived in the main street of the village, and from dusk onwards she had watched the German artillery trundle past. Troops lined the street, holding blazing torches which turned the roadway a fiery red. And between the two rows of men and torches poured a torrent of horses and guns and caissons, all of them driven at an infernally fast and furious gallop. The scene suggested an insane determination to achieve victory; there was something diabolical about the way the Prussians were pursuing the French forces, as though they longed to finish them off and annihilate them at the bottom of a deep pit. Nothing was spared; every obstacle was battered down as the artillery sped on regardless of cost. Whenever a horse fell, its traces were cut at once and it was crushed and mangled until it looked like flotsam soaked in blood. Likewise, any human being who tried to cross the road was knocked down and cut to pieces by the wheels. So irresistible was the force of the hurricane that the starving drivers did not even stop to eat, but simply caught loaves of bread as they were flung to them and seized hunks of meat that had been impaled on the tips of the torch-bearers' bayonets. Afterwards, the men lining the road used those same tips to prod the horses, which would writhe and kick in frenzy and then gallop faster than ever. And the night wore on, and still the artillery stormed through the village, to the accompaniment of wild cheering and shouting.

For all the attentiveness with which he had been following Silvine's account, Maurice was so knocked out by fatigue after eating so much that his head had slumped forward on to the table,

142

so that it lay between his arms. Jean struggled for a moment or two longer; then he too was compelled to give way, dropping off to sleep at the other end of the table. Old Fouchard had gone down the road again. So Honoré was to all intents and purposes alone with Silvine as she sat, quite still now, in front of the open window.

Observing this, the artillery sergeant stood up and walked over to the window. The night was still deep and black, its gloom intensified by the heavy breathing of the troops camped nearby. But now the noises that carried to them from the half-submerged bridge below were louder and more sonorous. There were rumblings and cracklings. Artillery units were making their way across. Horses were rearing at the frightening sight of moving water. Occasionally one of the ammunition waggons would half slip from the bridge and have to be toppled over into the river. And at the sight of the withdrawal being so slowly and arduously effected on the far bank, a withdrawal which had been going on ever since the day before and would certainly not be completed by daybreak, the young man's thoughts turned to those other artillery units coursing through Beaumont like a wild torrent, overturning everything in its path, crushing animals and human beings alike so that it might go faster.

Honoré moved closer to Silvine and stood beside her, looking out towards the wildly quivering darkness.

"Are you really unhappy?" he asked gently.

"Oh, yes, of course I am!"

She sensed that he was about to speak of the terrible affair which had come between them, and she hung her head.

"Tell me, how did it happen . . .? I should like to know."

But she was incapable of answering.

"Did he make you – or was it of your own free will?"

She was nearly choking, but in reply to this she managed to stammer out: "O dear Lord, I don't know! I swear I don't. Even I don't know that. . . . But it would be wrong to lie, wouldn't it? And I can't say I'm not to blame. Oh no, he didn't knock me about. . . . You had gone away, and I was out of my mind, and somehow it happened. I can't explain it, I simply can't explain it. . . ."

She was overcome by a fit of sobbing, and he, white-faced and hampered by a tightening of the throat, hung fire for a moment. The fact that she clearly was unwilling to lie soothed him, however, and he returned to his questioning; his mind was obsessed by the many things which continued to baffle him.

143

"My father let you stay here then?"

She did not even look up. The turmoil had subsided. Once again she wore her familiar expression of courageous resignation.

"I'm a good worker. I never cost him much in food and drink; and the presence of two mouths, rather than one, gave him an excuse to cut my wages. . . . Now he can be sure that I will obey his every bidding."

"But you were free to go."

She was so taken aback by this observation that she stared up at him.

"Free to go where, pray? At least my child and I get enough to eat here and are allowed to live in peace."

There was another silence between them. They were looking straight into one another's eyes now. From the distance, floating along the darkened valley, came the sound of the waiting troops, louder now than before. The guns continued to rumble across as though they would never stop. Suddenly a loud, despairing cry – perhaps human, perhaps animal – went through the night air with a note of inexpressible sorrow.

"Listen, Silvine," Honoré resumed slowly, "you sent me a letter which brought me great happiness. I had made up my mind never to come back here. But then I received that letter. I read it again last evening, and it says things which could not be said better. . . ."

When she heard him speak of this letter, she turned pale at first. Perhaps he was angry with her for daring to write to him so brazenly. Then, as he made his feelings plain, she grew quite red in the face.

"I know you have no intention of lying," he went on, "and so I believe what you wrote. . . . Yes, now I believe every word of it. . . . You were right : nothing could have pained me more deeply than to have died in this war without ever seeing you again, convinced that you did not love me. . . . Well then, since you still love me, since you have never loved anyone but me . . ."

He grew tongue-tied; the right words eluded him; he was shaking from the extraordinary intensity of his feelings.

"Listen, Silvine – if these damned Prussians don't kill me, I still want you. Do you hear? We'll get married as soon as I'm released from the army."

She sprang up, let out a cry and fell into the young man's arms. She was speechless; all the blood in her body had rushed to her face. He sat down on the chair and pulled her on to his knee.

144

"I've thought it over carefully, and I came with that proposal in mind. If my father refuses his consent, we'll move away. The world is a big place. . . . As for the child, well darn it we can't just wring his neck! You'll have many more, and in time to come I shan't know which is which."

She had his forgiveness. She had to struggle against the over-whelming happiness it brought her. At last she murmured : "No, it's too good to be true. You might rue your words one day. . . . But how good you are, Honoré, and how I love you !"

With a kiss on the lips he silenced her. And already she was shorn of the strength to resist the happiness ahead – a complete return to the happy life which she had looked upon as dead and gone for ever. Giving way to an impulse that was too strong to withstand, she flung her arms right round him; now it was her turn to kiss and hug him with all her might, behaving as though he were a private possession which she had won back and which nobody was going to take from her, ever again. He was hers, exactly as he had been before she lost him, and she would die rather than forfeit him a second time.

But at that moment there was uproar : the heavy darkness was filled with all the pandemonium of an early reveillé. Orders were being shouted, bugles were ringing out and a bustling confusion of shadowy figures rose from the bare hills in a murky, shifting sea which was already beginning to spill towards the road. Down below, the fires on either bank were almost out and nothing could be seen but a blur of slow-moving conglomerations; it was not even possible to tell whether the bridge was still in use. And never before had the black night contained such a degree of alarm and terrified bewilderment.

Old Fouchard hurried back to the window and announced, at the top of his voice, that the army was on the move. His words roused Jean and Maurice and they rose, stiff and shivering. Honoré, mean-while, had swiftly clasped Silvine's hands in his.

"You have my oath on it. . . . Wait for me."

She could not think of a word to say, but simply looked at him with an expression that conveyed her every feeling – one long, last look as he vaulted over the window-sill before racing off to his unit.

"Goodbye father !"

"Goodbye son !"

And that was that. Peasant and soldier were parting precisely as

145

they had met – without any show of affection, in the manner of a father and son who felt no vital need of one another's presence.

When they in turn had left the farm, Maurice and Jean scurried away down the steep slopes. At the foot there was no sign of the 106th : like all the other regiments, it was already on the move; and they had to hurry on, directed now to right and now to left. Finally, bewildered from the appalling confusion all around them, they chanced upon their company. It was under the leadership of Lieutenant Rochas and had evidently come adrift from Captain Beaudoin and the remainder of the regiment. And at this point Maurice was stunned by the realization that this press of men, horses and guns was leaving Remilly and making its way up towards Sedan, along the left-hand side of the river. What the devil was happening? The units were no longer crossing the Meuse, but retreating northwards!

For some unaccountable reason there was a cavalry officer among them.

"For Christ's sake !" he said aloud. "If we were going to bolt we should have bolted on the 28th, back at Le Chêne !"

Other voices spoke up, passing on scraps of news and providing an explanation for this sudden movement. At about two in the morning, one of Marshal MacMahon's aides had brought word to General Douay that the whole army was to fall back on Sedan without a moment's delay. After its crushing defeat at Beaumont, the 5th was pulling the other three corps down. When the aide arrived the general, who had been keeping watch beside the pontoon bridge, was in despair at the fact that only his third division had managed to get across the river. It would soon be daylight, and they were liable to be attacked at any minute. He therefore instructed his battalion commanders to make independently for Sedan by the most direct routes. He himself, abandoning the bridge and giving orders for its destruction, hurried away along the left bank with his first division and the reserve artillery, while the third division proceeded along the right bank and the second – battered and disintegrated after the onslaught at Beaumont – fled heaven knew where. Of the 7th Corps, which had yet to fight an engagement, all that remained was so many bits and pieces scurrying about the dark roads.

It was not yet three o'clock, and the night was as black as ever. Even Maurice, familiar as he was with the area, lost all sense of direction as he blundered on amid the wild press, which surged along the roadway in an uncontrollable torrent. A good many survivors from Beaumont – men belonging to every branch of the service, clad in rags and covered with blood and dust – mingled with the regiments, spreading terror. From the entire stretch of valley beyond the river came the identical din of other herd-like trampings, other panic retreats : the 1st Corps, which had just set out from Carignan and Douzy; the 12th Corps, on its way from Mouzon with the remnants of the 5th. . . . All these had been set in motion and swept along by the same logical and irresistible force which, ever since 28th August, had been driving the army northwards and deep into the impasse where it was to perish.

Meanwhile, first light appeared as Beaudoin's company was marching through Le Pont-Maugis; and Maurice recovered his bearings as he saw the Liry hills away to the left and the Meuse on the right, running parallel with the road. Yet how bleakly Bazeilles and Balan showed in this grey dawn, as they lay suffused in mist at the far end of the meadows; while the Sedan that took shape on the horizon, against the broad dark curtain of trees, was nightmarish, funereal, in its total absence of colour. And when, on the far side of Wadelincourt, they at last reached the Torcy gate they had to parley and entreat and threaten – had, in fact, almost to besiege the fortress – before the governor would agree to lower the drawbridge. It was then five o'clock. The 7th Corps entered Sedan, drunk with fatigue, hunger and cold.

VIII

AT THE point where the main road from Wadelincourt flows into the Place de Torcy, the crush was so great that Jean got separated from Maurice. He rushed about, lost in the press, unable to find him. This was a really bad stroke of fortune, for he had accepted the young man's offer to take him to his sister's house – where they would be able to rest and even enjoy the comforts of a good bed. So great was the confusion, with all the different regiments jumbled together, no clear directions and no senior officers to impart them, that the men were more or less free to do as they liked. There was time to snatch a few hours' sleep and then find their way back to their comrades.

Jean, considerably flustered by then, found himself hurrying across the Torcy viaduct; the broad meadows underneath had been flooded with river water, by order of the governor. Then, after negotiating another gateway, he crossed the bridge over the Meuse; and despite the spreading dawn it seemed to him that night was returning to this confined town, choking within its ramparts, where so many tall houses lined the damp streets. He could not even remember the surname of Maurice's brother-in-law; all he knew was, the sister was called Henriette. Which way was he to turn? Whom was he to ask for? It was only his mechanical gait that kept him upright; he felt sure he would fall if he stopped. A dull buzzing filled his ears, as though he were a drowning man; the only sound he could make out came from the uninterrupted stream of animals and human beings in which he was being swept along. Since the meal at Remilly, shortage of sleep had become his main cause of suffering; and it was the same with the men around him – tiredness was proving stronger than hunger as the shadowy herd stumbled through the unfamiliar streets. At every step a man would slump on to a stretch of pavement or collapse into a doorway and go on lying there, as though in the sleep of the dead.

Glancing upwards, Jean saw a street-sign which read: Avenue de la Sous-Prefecture. At the far end there was a monument standing in a public garden. And on the corner of the avenue there was a horseman belonging to the Chasseurs d'Afrique. He had a familiar look – surely it was Prosper, the fellow from Remilly whom he had seen Maurice talking to back at Vouziers? The man had dismounted, and his horse – wild-looking, emaciated and shaking all over – was suffering such agonies of hunger that it was stretching its neck and nibbling the woodwork of a van parked beside the kerb. It was two days since the horses had received any fodder and they were dying of exhaustion. The cavalryman stood crying as the big teeth rasped away.

Jean walked on for a while, then retraced his steps thinking : he is sure to know where Maurice's sister lives. But to his despair he found the cavalryman gone. He wandered from street to street; eventually he found himself back at the Sub-Prefecture, and from there he pressed on as far as the Place Turenne. At this point he had a momentary sense of being saved – for outside the town hall, immediately below the statue, he observed Lieutenant Rochas surrounded by a few members of the company. If he could not reach his friend, he might as well return to the fold and enjoy a good rest under canvas. Of Captain Beaudoin there was no sign – evidently the tide of events had deposited him elsewhere; so the lieutenant was endeavouring to remuster his men and doing his best to find out which area had been set aside for the division to make camp. But as it progressed through the town, the company grew smaller instead of bigger. One soldier, gesticulating wildly, strode into a tavern and was never seen again. Three others came to a halt by the door of a grocer's shop, accosted by a party of Zouaves who had succeeded in battering a hole in a small barrel of brandy. Several of these Zouaves already lay in the gutter; others attempted to leave, but at once sank into a stupor like men pole-axed. Chouteau and Loubet, after an exchange of nudges, had just disappeared down a dark lane in pursuit of a fat woman who was carrying a loaf. In the end the lieutenant was left with no one except Pache and Lapoulle and about a dozen of their comrades.

Under the bronze figure of Turenne, Rochas was making a considerable effort to stay upright and keep his eyes open.

"Ah, it's you, corporal!" he murmured, when he recognized Jean. "Where are your men?"

Jean threw up his hands in a gesture that was intended to convey his ignorance. But Pache answered for him.

"We're here," he said, pointing at Lapoulle and giving way to

149

tears. "There's only us two left. . . . Lord have pity on us, it's more than human beings can stand!"

His gluttonous companion was staring greedily at Jean's hands: how indignant he was that they should always be empty nowadays! In his present sleepy state, he may even have been cherishing the illusion that the corporal had gone to collect the squad's rations.

"Oh, blast!" he growled. "We've to tighten our belts again."

Gaude the bugler had been standing with his back to the railings, awaiting orders to sound the general fall-in. But now he fell asleep, slipping down with a single uninterrupted movement until he lay flat on his back. They were all succumbing, one after another, gradually closing their fists and starting to snore. In the end Sergeant Sapin was the only man with his eyes wide open; he stood with his nose wrinkled up in his small white face, as though reading his own impending doom in the vistas afforded by this unfamiliar town.

Meanwhile Lieutenant Rochas had yielded to the irresistible urge to sit on the ground. He endeavoured to give an order.

"Corporal, we shall have to . . . shall have to . . ."

No other words would come: tiredness was clogging his mouth. And all of a sudden it was his turn to slump back, knocked out by sleep.

Jean walked away, least he too should sink to the pavement. He was still obstinately determined to find himself a bed. Glancing across the square, he had caught sight of General Bourgain-Desfeuilles standing at one of the windows of the Croix d'Or hotel; the general was in his shirt-sleeves and would shortly be slipping between a pair of soft white sheets. What was the point of being over-zealous and enduring further suffering? And he had a sudden sense of relief and exhilaration: a name had come into his head, the name of the cloth manufacturer for whom Maurice's brother-in-law worked – Monsieur Delaherche. Yes, that was it! He stopped an old man who happened to be going by.

"Can you tell me where Monsieur Delaherche lives?"

"In the Rue Maqua, practically on the corner of the Rue au Beurre – a fine big house with a carved front. . . ."

A moment later, the old man came running after him.

"Listen though," he said, "I see you belong to the 106th. If it's your regiment you're after, it just marched out of town by way of the castle. . . . I happened to bump into your colonel, Monsieur de

150

Vineuil. Used to know him well when he was stationed in Mézières."

But Jean hurried on with a gesture of furious impatience. Oh no! Now that he could be sure of finding Maurice, he had no intention of sleeping rough! And yet in his heart he was troubled by a sense of remorse, for he had visions of the colonel – tall, upright, truly indefatigable in spite of his years – sleeping under canvas just like his men. Without delay he turned into the high street, lost his bearings again amid the noise and bustle and finally made inquiries of a small boy who led him to the Rue Maqua.

It was here, in the seventeen hundreds, that a great-uncle of the present Delaherche had erected the monumental factory which had now been in the family's hands for a hundred and sixty years. There are several such mills in Sedan, all dating back to the early years of Louis XV's reign and all as big as the Louvre itself, with regal façades. The one in the Rue Maqua had three rows of tall windows, each window decorated with severe carvings; inside was a palatial courtyard where old trees grew – giant elms which had been planted there when the mill was first opened. Three generations of Delaherches had made substantial fortunes out of it. The father of Jules, the current proprietor, had inherited the factory from a cousin who had died without having any children of his own; so it was now a junior branch that held sway. Jules's father had added to the firm's prosperity, but he was a man who took his pleasures where he could find them and he had made his wife unhappy. As a result this woman, after she became a widow, had lived in dread of seeing her son get up to the same tricks; she had married him off to a woman of unexceptionably simple and godfearing ways and kept him tied to her apron-strings till he was past fifty. Alas, life is apt to get its own back in the most terrible ways. The wife died and Delaherche, now well past his prime, fell head over heels for a young widow living in Charleville – the pretty Madame Maginot; she was the subject of a good many whispered stories but eventually he had married her, late in '69, despite his mother's remonstrances. Sedan, a highly puritanical place, had always frowned on Charleville as a haunt of the frivolous and self-indulgent. And indeed the wedding would never have taken place if Gilberte had not been the niece of Colonel de Vineuil, who stood a fair chance of being promoted to general. The thought of marrying into a distinguished military family was extremely flattering to the cloth manufacturer.

That morning, hearing that the army was about to pass through

Mouzon, Delaherche had driven there in his gig together with Weiss, his book-keeper, exactly as old Fouchard had described to Maurice. Tall, thickset and ruddy-faced, with a prominent nose and thick lips, he was of an exuberant disposition and had all the cheerful curiosity of the typical French bourgeois, who enjoys nothing better than a dashing and colourful military parade. At Mouzon the local chemist had told him that the Emperor was at Baybel farm, and so he had gone out there, set eyes on him and very nearly exchanged words with him – an unbelievable adventure, and one which he had been retailing to all and sundry ever since his return. And what a terrible experience that return journey had been! First the scenes of panic at Beaumont, and then road after road congested with fleeing troops! A score of times the gig had narrowly escaped landing upside-down in a ditch. Obstacle had succeeded obstacle, and it was dark by the time the two men arrived home. And Delaherche's little outing had ended so unexpectedly and so miserably that on the homeward drive, forced back by the retreating waves of the army which he had hoped to admire at his leisure, he had exclaimed a dozen times: "And there was I, fondly imagining it was on its way to Verdun and *so* anxious not to miss seeing it . . .! Well, now I have seen it; and if you ask my opinion, we people of Sedan are going to see a good deal more of it than we'll want!"

Today, awakened at 5 a.m. by the tidal roar of the 7th Corps surging through the town, he had hurriedly put on his clothes; and whom should he meet in the Place Turenne but Captain Beaudoin. In Charleville, the year before, the captain had been on close terms with pretty Madame Maginot, and naturally she had introduced the two men before she married Delaherche. At the time, the story ran that the captain – his own desires completely satisfied – had tactfully withdrawn in favour of the mill-owner, not wishing to deprive his lady friend of the very considerable fortune that was in store for her.

"Good God! Fancy seeing you here!" exclaimed Delaherche. "And look at the state you're in!"

Beaudoin, as a rule so immaculately and stylishly dressed, was indeed a pitiful sight. His uniform was grubby and his face and hands were black. He was fuming, for he had been compelled to make the journey with a party of Algerian riflemen; how he had come to lose his company, he had no idea. Like everyone else, he was ready to drop with hunger and fatigue; but he was reduced to

152

even lower depths of despair by the fact that he'd been unable to change his shirt since Rheims. He lost no time in bewailing the fact.

"Would you believe it? They mislaid all my personal effects at Vouziers! The idiots, the scoundrels – ah, if only I could get my hands on them . . .! They've left me without a single thing. I haven't so much as a handkerchief or a pair of socks! It's enough to make a man mad!"

Delaherche immediately pressed his hospitality on him. But the captain fought shy. No, no, no! He didn't look human, he had no intention of frightening the wits out of people. The mill-owner had to give his word that neither his mother nor his wife would be up and about yet. Besides, he would provide him with soap, water, fresh linen . . . everything a man needed.

Seven o'clock was striking as Captain Beaudoin, looking newly scrubbed and wearing one of his host's shirts under his uniform, walked into the dining room with its grey wainscoting and uncommonly high ceiling. Madame Delaherche senior was already in the room – for she invariably rose at dawn, even though she was seventy-eight. Her hair was completely white; age had thinned the nose set in the long narrow face, and the mouth had lost all trace of humour. She rose, welcomed the captain with great courtesy and bade him sit down to one of the cups of white coffee which had already been set on the table.

"Though perhaps, monsieur, you would rather have meat and wine in view of the ordeals you have suffered?"

He was quick to deny it.

"How very kind of you, madame, but a little milk and some bread and butter will suit me best of all."

At that moment one of the doors was gaily flung open and Gilberte hurried in with outstretched hand. Delaherche must have told her of the captain's arrival, for generally she never rose before ten. She was tall, lithe and sturdy-looking, and her splendid dark hair and splendid dark eyes provided a charming and unexpected contrast with her rosy complexion. Her merry face suggested a certain light-headedness, but was entirely free of malice. Her beige dressing gown, covered with red silk embroidery, came from Paris.

"Why, captain!" she cried with animation, shaking hands with the young man. "How kind of you to honour us with a visit in our dull backwater."

It is only fair to say that she was the first to laugh at her own absurdity.

153

"What a silly ass I am! You would a good deal rather not be in Sedan in such circumstances. . . . But I *am* very glad to see you!"

And sure enough her beautiful eyes were sparkling with pleasure. Madame Delaherche senior, who could hardly fail to be familiar with the stories put about by the Charleville scandalmongers, sat and stared at the two of them, her face as inflexible as ever. The captain behaved with considerable restraint however, acting like a man inspired solely by fond memories of an hospitable household in which he used to be a welcome visitor.

They began to eat, and Delaherche at once returned to the excursion he had made the day before. The craving to describe it again was too strong to be resisted.

"You know I saw the Emperor over at Baybel . . .?"

He was off, and there was no stopping him. First came a description of the farmhouse, a big square-shaped building; it was perched on a hillock overlooking Mouzon, to the left of the Carignan road. Then he turned his attention to the 12th Corps, relating how he had driven past it while it was camping among the hillside vineyards. Grand-looking troops, resplendent in the sunlight; it had given him a patriotic thrill, just to look at them. . . .

"So there I was, captain, when all at once the Emperor came out of the farmhouse, where he had stopped for a meal and a rest. He wore an overcoat draped over his general's uniform, although it was extremely hot in the sun. A manservant walked along behind him, holding a campstool. . . . The Emperor wasn't looking at all well – dear me, he wasn't! He was stooping and shuffling, and his face was a yellowy colour. A sick man if ever I saw one. . . . And that didn't surprise me, for when the chemist at Mouzon advised me to make the journey out to Baybel he told me that an aide-de-camp had just arrived poste-haste for something to relieve . . . something to relieve . . . well, you know what I mean. . . ."

The presence of his wife and mother prevented him from referring more explicitly to the dysentery from which the Emperor had been suffering ever since he had left Le Chêne and which was the cause of his frequent stops at farmhouses along the line of retreat.

"Anyway, the manservant positioned the stool at one end of a cornfield, beside a copse, and the Emperor sat down. And there he remained, still and bowed, for all the world like some ordinary local squire sunning his aches and pains. With his gloomy eye he surveyed the vast horizon. Beneath him lay the Meuse, flowing through the valley; facing him were line after line of wooded hills.

On his left, the treetops of Dieulet; on his right, the rich green slopes of Sommauthe. . . . He was surrounded by aides-de-camp and senior officers. One of these, a colonel of dragoons, had been asking me various questions about the district. He turned and signalled to me that I was not to go away. And then, all of a sudden . . ."

Delaherche stood up, for he was approaching the powerful climax of his narrative and he intended to strengthen word with mime.

". . . all of a sudden there was a series of loud reports, and what do you think I saw? Shells arcing across the stretch of sky directly in front of us, this side of Dieulet woods! Believe me, it was like watching a firework display in broad daylight, and I need hardly add it caused a good deal of alarm and confusion among the Emperor's party. My colonel of dragoons came hurrying over to ask whether I could tell him exactly where the fighting was. 'It's at Beaumont,' I said, without a moment's hesitation, 'there can't be any doubt as to that.' He went back to the Emperor, who was now sitting with a map spread open on his knee. His Majesty wouldn't believe that the fighting was at Beaumont. Well, it wasn't for me to argue – especially as the shells were getting nearer every minute, following the line of the Mouzon road. . . . And then – plain as I see you now, captain – I saw the Emperor turn his sickly face towards me. Yes, he stared at me for a moment through those cloudy eyes of his, full of sadness and suspicion. And then his head drooped over the map, and he did not move again."

Delaherche had been an ardent Bonapartist at the time of the plebiscite. Following the initial setbacks in the war, he had been ready to admit that the Empire had made mistakes. But he continued to speak in defence of the dynasty and felt very sorry for Napoleon III, who was a very ill-used man. In his view, the men really responsible for the disasters now befalling France were really those Republican deputies on the opposition benches who had voted against the provision of adequate manpower and funds.

"And what did the Emperor do?" asked Captain Beaudoin. "Go back to the farmhouse?"

"Heaven only knows, captain. I left him sitting there on his stool. . . . It was noon, the battle was drawing closer and I was beginning to have fears about getting home. I can only add this: when I pointed out Carignan, lying in the plain far to the rear of us, one of the generals seemed quite thunderstruck to hear that the town is but a few miles from the Belgian border. . . . Ah, poor Emperor! Those are the men he has to rely on!"

Meanwhile, Gilberte was dispensing hospitality with the same smiling composure as in the days of her widowhood. She fussed over the captain, passing the toast, passing the butter. . . . She did her utmost to talk him into accepting a room and a bed; but he declined and it was arranged that he should simply take a couple of hours' rest on the sofa in Delaherche's study and then go back to his regiment. As he was taking the sugar-basin out of the young woman's hands, old Madame Delaherche – still keeping a sharp eye on them – distinctly saw them clasp fingers. All her suspicious were confirmed.

But at that moment one of the maids appeared.

"Excuse me, sir, but there's a soldier downstairs asking for Monsieur Weiss's address."

Delaherche was no snob, for he had a gossipy pleasure in being popular, so that he was always ready to exchange words with the poor and humble.

"Wants Weiss's address, does he? That's a bit odd. . . . You had better show this soldier in."

Jean entered the room, almost reeling from exhaustion. He jumped when he saw his captain seated at table between two ladies and withdrew the hand with which he had instinctively clutched at one of the chairs. Then he briefly answered the questions put to him by the mill-owner, who was careful to sound affable and kind. In a few short words he explained his attachment to Maurice and why he was looking for him.

"The corporal here is a member of my company," the captain broke in finally.

Then it was his turn to ask questions, for he was anxious to know what had become of the regiment. And when Jean reported that someone had just seen the colonel marching the remainder of his men out of town, prior to making camp on the north side, Gilberte once again let her tongue run away with her.

"Oh, why didn't Uncle come and have breakfast with us? We could have made up a bed for him. . . . What say we send a messenger?"

But Madame Delaherche senior waved the suggestion aside with an authoritarian sweep of her arm. The blood in her veins was imbued with all the stolidity of the old border towns, where the patriotism of every respectable citizen is vigorous and unyielding. She maintained a stern silence, except to remark : "Leave Monsieur de Vineuil be – he is where duty demands."

This gave rise to an awkward silence. Delaherche took the captain along to his study, anxious to reassure himself that Beaudoin would be comfortable on the sofa. As for Gilberte, in spite of the rebuke she went away with all her usual perkiness – like a bird fluttering its wings, cheerful even though the day had turned stormy. Meanwhile the maid, who had been told to act as Jean's guide, led him across the factory yard and through a maze of passageways and staircases.

The Weisses lived in the Rue des Voyards; but the house, which belonged to Delaherche, communicated directly with the monumental building in the Rue Maqua. In those days, this Rue des Voyards was one of the strangest in Sedan – a dank, narrow lane, robbed of light by the city wall which ran alongside it. The eaves over the tall façades very nearly touched, and the dark passages were like the mouths of vaults – especially at that end of the street where the wall of the College rose high. But Weiss could account himself lucky; he had the use of the entire third floor, with no rent to pay and no fuel to buy, lived within easy reach of his office, and could shuffle along in his slippers without needing to show himself in the street. Marriage to Henriette had made a happy man of him after all those years of longing for her in Le Chêne, where from her seventh year onwards she had kept house for her father, the tax-collector, in place of her dead mother. Weiss, who had joined the staff of the local refinery as little more than a general labourer at first, had set about educating himself and steadily worked his way up to the position of book-keeper. Even then, his dreams would never have been realized had it not been, first, for the death of her father and then for her twin-brother's wild living in Paris. She had sacrificed herself to Maurice without reserve, waiting on him hand and foot in the hope of turning him into a gentleman. Brought up to a life of household drudgery, able to read and write but possessing little else by way of education, she sold up house and home and even then could not repay all the debts which the young man had so recklessly incurred. Whereupon Weiss, with his warm heart and sturdy arms, hurriedly stepped forward and offered her all he owned; and she agreed to marry him, moved to tears by his quiet and thoughtful affection, which, while it was not passionate, was full of loving regard. And now fortune was smiling on them. Delaherche had talked of offering Weiss a partnership. Once children began to arrive, their happiness would be complete.

157

"Mind how you go," the maid said to Jean. "The stairs are very steep."

And indeed he was stumbling about in the dark when all at once a door was flung open and a shaft of light flew across the steps. Then he heard a soft voice say : "It's him."

"Madame Weiss," called the maid, "there's a soldier here asking for you."

At this there was a chuckle of satisfaction from the head of the stairs, and the same soft voice observed : "That's all right, that's all right – I know who it is." Then, as the corporal lingered by the door, feeling awkward and out of breath : "Come in, Monsieur Jean. We've been dying for you to come ever since Maurice got here, two whole hours ago !"

As he stepped into the pale light of the room he observed her remarkable likeness to Maurice, that extraordinary likeness which, in the case of twins, makes one face seem the exact duplication of the other. Though she was shorter than he and even thinner – more frail-looking – she had the same rather big mouth and small features under the splendid blonde hair, bright and pale as ripe oats. The chief difference between brother and sister lay in her grey eyes, in whose calm courage the heroic spirit of her grandfather – that hero of the Grande Armée – seemed to live again. With her reticence and her quiet movements, she was so lithe and gentle and serene that she seemed to impart a caress to the surrounding air.

"This way, Monsieur Jean, this way. . . . Everything will soon be ready."

He stood and stammered, so overcome at being given such a friendly welcome that he could not think of a way to express his thanks. Besides, his eyelids were closing; in the insuperable drowsiness that gripped him she managed to hover freely in the air, surrounded by haze. Could it be that the kind and thoughtful young woman smiling at him with such simple directness was no more than a delightful vision? And yet he distinctly had the impression that she was taking him by the hand and that he could feel her hand, small and firm, as reassuring as the trusty grip of an old friend.

Jean had no clear awareness of anything that happened after that. They were in the dining room and there was bread and butter on the table, but he would never have had the strength to carry the pieces to his mouth. There was a man in the room, sitting in a chair. Eventually he recognized the man as Weiss, whom he had

158

seen at Mulhouse. But he could not make out what Weiss was saying with such a careworn face and such slow, despondent gestures. On a camp-bed in front of the stove lay Maurice, his features as motionless in sleep as they would have been in death. And Henriette was busy making up a divan. A mattress had already been laid on it, and she came into the room armed with a bolster, a pillow, some blankets. . . . Then, with great speed and deftness, she spread a pair of white sheets, marvellous white sheets, sheets white as snow.

Ah, those white sheets – they were a sight for which he had longed, and now he had eyes for nothing else! It was six weeks since he had taken his clothes off and slept in a bed. He felt a wild urge, a childlike impatience, an irresistible craving to sink into that coolness and whiteness and be lost. No sooner had his host and hostess gone than he was standing in his bare feet, naked but for his shirt. He got into bed and snuggled down with the grunt of a contented animal. The pale morning light came in through the tall window; and when, already toppling into sleep, he half-opened his eyes, he was treated to another vision of Henriette – even less distinct and corporeal this time – as she tiptoed back into the room and set on the table beside him a glass and a water-jug which she had forgotten to set there before. She appeared to linger for a few seconds, looking at both of them – himself and her brother – with that characteristically serene smile, full of goodness and kindness. Then she faded away and Jean, all resistance gone, sank into a deep sleep among the cool white linen.

Hours, years went by. Jean and Maurice had ceased to be : no dreams, no awareness even of the quiet throbbing of their arteries. Ten years or ten minutes – time was no longer of any account; it was as though their overtaxed bodies were finding revenge and gratification in the extinction of their entire being. Then, suddenly and simultaneously, both men came to with a start. Good Lord – what was happening? How long had they been asleep? The same pale light was flowing down from the tall window. They ached all over; their joints had stiffened up; their limbs were even more tired, their mouths even more bitter-tasting than when they had gone to bed. Fortunately they could not have slept for more than an hour. And they were not unduly surprised to find Weiss still sitting on the same chair, in the same despondent attitude, as though he had been waiting for them to open their eyes.

"Damn it!" gasped Jean. "We must hurry up and get back to the regiment before noon."

He groaned slightly as he sprang out on to the tiled floor. He began to pull on his clothes.

"Before noon!" repeated Weiss. "Do you realize that it's seven o'clock at night and that you've been asleep for the best part of twelve hours?"

Seven o'clock? Good God! The news filled them with alarm. Jean, already fully dressed, wanted to rush from the house; while Maurice, still in bed, was bewailing the discovery that he could not move his legs. How were they ever going to get back to their comrades? The army must surely have left hours ago. . . . And both men grew angry: they should never have been allowed to sleep for so long. But Weiss threw up his hands in despair.

"Considering how little has been achieved in the meantime, you were in the best possible place!"

He had been scouring Sedan and the surrounding area ever since morning. He had only just got back, sick at heart over the fact that the troops had not budged: the whole of this valuable day, August 31st, had been wasted in inexplicable delays. There was only one possible excuse, the men's extreme tiredness and undeniable need of rest; even so, he could not understand why the withdrawal should not have continued after the bare minimum of sleep.

"For my own part," he continued, "I can't claim any expert knowledge, but I've a feeling – yes, a very definite feeling – that Sedan is a very bad place for the army to be. . . . The 12th Corps is at Bazeilles, where there was a little fighting this morning; the 1st is strung out along the Givonne, all the way from La Moncelle village to the Garenne woods; while the 7th is encamped on the Floing plateau, and the 5th – or what's left of it – is huddling under the city wall, over by the castle. . . . And that's what frightens me – to know that they're all spread round the town like that, simply waiting for the Prussians. If it had been up to me, I'd have pressed on as far as Mézières without delay. I know the lie of the land and there's no other path of retreat that will safeguard you from being driven into Belgium. Besides . . . come over here and I'll show you something.

He took Jean by the hand and led him to the window.

"Look what's happening on those hilltops."

The window faced southwards and looked out over the ramparts and the neighbouring rooftops at the whole of the Meuse valley. There was the river, winding its way through the broad meadows; there was Remilly, over on the left, with Pont-Maugis and Wadelincourt straight ahead and Frénois on the right. And there were the hills, parading their green slopes – first the Liry, then the Marfée, then the Croix-Piau, all of them heavily wooded. In the dwindling light, the immense skyline was wonderfully soft and pellucid.

"See? All those dark columns on the move. Like lines of black ants."

Jean stared in dismay, while Maurice – kneeling up – craned his neck for a better view.

"Oh yes!" they exclaimed, each at the same moment. "There's one column, there's another . . . *and* a third . . . *and* a fourth! They're everywhere."

"Well," continued Weiss, "those are the Prussians. . . . I've been watching them all day long and there is never a moment's break in the flow. One thing is certain : if our troops are waiting for them, they for their part can't get here soon enough . . .! And every civilian in town has seen them as plainly as I have. It's only the generals who can't see for looking. I had a few words with one of them, a while ago. All he did was shrug his shoulders and assure me that Marshal MacMahon was positive he had a force of only seventy thousand to reckon with. God grant his information is correct. Just look at them, though! The earth is covered with them. On and on and on they come. Like black ants, I tell you!"

At this point Maurice flung himself back on the bed and began to sob wildly. Henriette, looking as cheerful as the evening before, happened to come into the room just then. She hurried over to him in alarm.

"Why, whatever is it?"

But already he was waving her aside.

"No, no, leave me be, shut your mind to me. I've never brought you anything but sorrow and distress. When I think of how you used to go without new clothes so that I might finish my education. Much good they've done me, all those years at college . . .! And to cap everything, I nearly brought dishonour on our family name. I don't know where I'd be today if you hadn't bled yourself dry redeeming my follies."

Her smile had returned.

"Poor darling, you don't seem to have woken in a very cheerful frame of mind. . . . Why fret over things which are over and done

161

with and long since forgotten? Aren't you now doing your duty as a Frenchman? Since you enlisted, I've been very proud of you – you needn't have any doubts about that."

She had turned her face towards Jean, as though begging him to come to her aid. He was staring at her, slightly startled by the discovery that she was less beautiful than she had seemed that morning; she looked thinner and paler now that his mind had been cleared of the hallucinatory effects of physical exhaustion. He was still impressed by her likeness to her brother, and yet the total dissimilarity of their natures could not have stood out with greater clarity than at that moment – he, on his side, as highly strung as a woman, unsettled by the sickness of the times, a victim of the historical and social crisis through which the French race was passing, as capable of rising to the noblest enthusiasm, at a moment's notice, as of sinking into the blackest depression; she, on her side, so frail and self-effacing, a resigned little Cinderella, but with a broad brow and steady eyes – of such stuff as martyrs are made.

"Proud of me!" exclaimed Maurice. "You have no cause to be, really you haven't! For the past month we've done nothing but run like the cowards we are."

"Well, what else could we do?" said Jean (commonsensical as always). "We're not the only ones – we're simply doing as we're bidden."

But at this the young man's paroxysm of despair grew wilder still.

"That's just it, and I've had my fill . . .! Isn't it enough to make a man shed tears of blood? These constant defeats, these scatter-brained generals, thousands of troops led mindlessly to the slaughter as if they were herds of cattle. . . . And now we are caught in a blind alley from which there can be no escape. You can see for yourself – the Prussians are moving up from every direction. The army is done for; it's only a question of time before we are annihilated. . . . No, no! I'm staying here, I'd rather be shot as a deserter. . . . Jean, you can return by yourself if you must. I shan't go back, I'm staying here."

A renewed fit of sobbing laid him low again. He was in the grip of one of those ungovernable and self-destructive bouts of despera-tion into which he so easily fell, one of those unpredictable plunges into despair and contempt for everything and everyone, including himself. His sister, knowing him of old, was not unduly perturbed.

162

"Maurice dear, it would be terribly wrong to desert your post in time of danger."

He sat up with a jolt.

"All right then, hand me my gun and I'll blow my brains out. That way, it will be over and done with quicker."

Then, reaching out his arm and pointing at Weiss, who sat there still and silent : "Well, well, well ! He's the only one with any sense. Yes, he's the only one who saw things in their true light. Remember, Jean? Remember what he said at Mulhouse, a whole month ago?"

"That's true," admitted the corporal. "The gentleman said we would be beaten."

And that tense night-scene came back to them, with all its grim suspense : the cheerless sky already providing an augury for the disaster at Froeschwiller, while Weiss expressed his fears of Germany, fully prepared, better led, better armed, uplifted by a powerful surge of patriotism; and of France flustered and disorganized, caught napping, gone to seed, lacking the right leaders, the right number of men, the right arms and ammunition. And now his terrible prophecy was coming true.

Weiss held up his trembling hands. There was a look of deepest sorrow on his good-natured face.

"Oh, I don't glory in the fact that I've been proved right," he muttered. "I'm just an ignorant dolt, but it was so obvious once one knew the facts . . .! But even if we *are* beaten, we can still kill some of those blasted Prussians. That must be our consolation. If we die, and I think we're going to, let's see to it that a whole host of Prussians die with us – so many that the ground out there will be thick with their bodies."

He had risen from his chair and was pointing at the Meuse valley. A bright flame shone in those big short-sighted eyes which had kept him out of the army.

"By God yes, I'd fight if I had the chance. . . . I don't know whether it's because they're lording it over my own part of the country – as though poor Alsace hadn't suffered enough at the hands of the Cossacks ! But I can't bear to picture them strutting about our land and setting foot inside our homes. It makes me long to get my hands on a dozen of them and let daylight into their bodies. . . . Oh, if only I hadn't been turned down, if only I were a fighting man !" Then, after a short silence, he added : "Besides, who knows . . .?"

With these words he was expressing the hope, the need to believe

163

that victory was still possible, which existed even in the minds of the most disillusioned. And Maurice, already ashamed of his own tears, lay listening to him and clutching at this dream. After all, had there not been rumours the day before that Bazaine was in Verdun? Fortune certainly owed a miracle to France, to which she had at one time given glory for so long.

Henriette, preferring to say nothing, had left the room; when she returned, she was not in the least surprised to find her brother up and dressed and ready to leave. She was determined that he and Jean should eat a meal before they set out. But although she made them sit down to table, the food almost choked them and made them feel sick, for they were still feeling half-asleep. With characteristic foresight, Jean cut a loaf of bread in two and put one half in Maurice's knapsack and the other half in his own. The light was fading; they must be on their way. Henriette had paused beside the window and was watching the Prussians as they continued to advance ant-like along the top of the distant Marfée hill; they were becoming gradually less distinct as the dusk closed in on them. She groaned despite herself.

"Oh, this war! This horrible war!"

Instantly Maurice poked fun at her, getting his own back.

"Come, come, dear! You're the one who's so keen for us to fight – yet here you are running the war down!"

She turned and looked him straight in the eye, with all her natural frankness.

"It's true I loathe and detest it," she replied. "I look upon it as unjust and repulsive. . . . Perhaps it's simply because I'm a woman, but all this killing sickens me. Why not talk things over and come to an understanding?"

Jean, excellent fellow, nodded his head in agreement. His untutored mind responded in the same way: it seemed the most natural thing in the world that everyone should reach agreement, if only things were thrashed out fully and fairly. But Maurice, swayed by his reading again, was reflecting on the plain need for war – since war was synonymous with life itself, an unchallengeable law of the universe. It was puny man, surely, who introduced the notions of peace and justice; left to itself, impartial nature had bred nothing but slaughter.

"Come to an understanding!" he cried. "Yes, in a few hundred years' time. If all nations were but one, it is just conceivable that such a golden age might come about; though wouldn't the ending

164

of war mean the ending of humanity as well . . .? I talked and acted like a fool just now: one *must* fight, since it is the law."

It was his turn to smile as he reiterated what Weiss had said: "Besides, who knows . . .?"

Once again he was caught in the trap of self-delusion. He was so highly strung that he needed continual self-deception.

"By the way," he continued brightly, "what news of cousin Gunther?"

"Cousin Gunther?" said Henriette. "Why, he's in the Prussian Guards. . . . Are *they* fighting in these parts?"

Weiss shrugged his shoulders helplessly, and the two soldiers did the same. How could they possibly say, when even the generals did not know what units they were up against?

"It's time we left," said Weiss. "I'll show you the way. I found out earlier where the 106th is encamped."

Then he told his wife that he would not be back that night; instead he would sleep in Bazeilles, where he had recently bought a little house. He was in the last stages of decorating it and furnishing it, so that they would be able to live there until the cold weather came. It stood next to a dyeworks belonging to M. Delaherche. And he was beginning to grow concerned about the provisions which he had already installed in the cellar: a barrel of wine, a couple of sacks of potatoes. . . . The building was bound to be looted, he said, if it was left standing empty; whereas he would probably keep it safe from intruders by spending the night there. His wife stared at him intently all the time he was talking.

"Don't worry," he added with a smile, "all I propose to do is keep an eye on our bits and pieces. And I promise you: should the village be attacked, should there be the slightest danger, I'll return at once."

"All right," she said. "Mind you do though, or I shall come and fetch you."

At the door, Henriette kissed Maurice with warm affection. Then she took Jean's hand and held it in a long and friendly clasp.

"Well, I'm entrusting my brother to your safekeeping again. . . . Yes, he's told me how kind you've been to him – and you have won a place in my heart."

His feelings were so powerfully stirred that he could find nothing to say; he merely returned the clasp of that small sturdy hand. And his first impression of her was reborn: with her retiring ways and her pale golden hair, she was so light and serene that she seemed to caress the air around her.

The atmosphere of Sedan, closing in on them as soon as they left the building, was no less gloomy than it had been that morning. Twilight was already descending on the narrow streets, where all was bustle and confusion. Most of the shops were closed and the houses had a lifeless look, whereas out-of-doors there was a dreadful crowd. They got as far as the main square, however, without too much difficulty, and there, quite by chance, they met Delaherche, who was out seeing what was going on. He greeted them with a gasp of surprise, looked delighted when he recognised Maurice and related how he had just been escorting Captain Beaudoin as far as Floing, where the regiment was; and his habitual contentment became ampler than ever when he learned that Weiss was intending to sleep at Bazeilles; for he himself – as he had been telling the captain only a few minutes ago – had made up his mind to spend the night at his dyeworks there, so as to keep an eye on things.

"We'll make the journey together, Weiss. . . . But in the meantime let's take a stroll as far as the Sub-Prefecture. We may catch a glimpse of the Emperor."

Ever since he had come so close to speaking to him, on that farm at Baybel, he had no thought for anything or anyone but Napoleon III; and in the end he even persuaded the two soldiers to join them. The square in front of the Sub-Prefecture was empty except for a few isolated groups of men and women who hung about whispering and for a number of officers flurrying past from time to time. The melancholy dusk was already robbing the trees of their colour. The Meuse could be heard roaring by on the right, below the walls of the houses. Among the crowd there were stories of how the Emperor – who had not left Carignan until eleven the previous night, and only then with extreme reluctance – had adamantly refused to drive on as far as Mézières, not wishing to demoralize the troops by deserting the danger zone. Others were insisting that he was no longer in Sedan but had fled, leaving one of his lieutenants to act as his double; the resemblance, allegedly, was so great that the entire army was taken in. Still others were willing to swear on oath that they had seen vehicles laden with the imperial fortune drive into the grounds of the Sub-Prefecture – a hundred million in mint twenty-franc gold pieces. In fact these vehicles were merely those of the Emperor's household – the break, the two barouches and the twelve vans which had caused such a stir in Courcelles and Le Chêne and Raucourt, swelling in people's imaginations until they were thought of as forming a huge procession which had dragged the army to a standstill and which had finally come to rest, monstrous and shameful objects, deservedly hidden from all eyes behind the lilac bushes of the Sub-Prefecture.

Beside Delaherche, who was craning his neck and scanning the ground-floor windows, stood an old woman – just a poor local working-woman with a twisted frame and gnarled hands eroded by toil.

"An Emperor, eh?" she was muttering through her teeth. "Ah well, I wouldn't mind clapping eyes on him . . . just so I can say I've seen one."

All of a sudden Delaherche grabbed Maurice's arm and exclaimed : "Look, that's him. . . . Over there – see? At that window on the left. . . . Oh, I couldn't be wrong, not after standing so close to him yesterday. I'd know him anywhere. . . . He's lifted the curtain now. . . . Aye, there's our man – that sickly face by the window. . . ."

When the old woman overheard these words she simply gaped. For there sure enough, close to the grating, was the haunting vision of a cadaverous-looking face – the eyes grown dim, the features blurred, the whiskers faded in these final hours of agonizing suspense. The old woman was so stupefied that she immediately turned her back and walked away with a gesture of utter scorn.

"Are you telling me that's an Emperor! Don't talk daft !"

A Zouave was standing near them, one of the many who had been forced to break ranks and were in no hurry to return to their units. He was brandishing his gun and swearing and spitting out threats; suddenly he turned to another soldier and said : "Just hang on while I put a bullet through his blasted brains !"

Delaherche intervened indignantly. But already the Emperor's face had vanished. The loud rushing of the Meuse went on. A horribly dispiriting wail seemed to have found its way into the thickening dusk, while a scattering of further shouts were rumbling in the distance. Could it be that terrible order "Forward, forward . . ." from Paris which had driven this man from one halting-place to another, impelling him along the road to defeat, with the irony of his imperial escort in tow, and which had now brought him face to face with the appalling disaster that he had foreseen and had almost come here to find? How many decent people were about to die for his mistakes, and what a complete inward defeat

167

he had to endure in every particle of his being, this invalid, this soulful dreamer, as he waited so silently and cheerlessly for fate to take its course!

Weiss and Delaherche accompanied the two soldiers as far as the plateau of Floing.

"Well . . . a last goodbye!" said Maurice, as he hugged his brother-in-law to him.

"Oh come now, come!" the mill-owner exclaimed cheerfully. "Till we meet again, you mean!"

Jean lost no time in scenting out the 106th, whose tents were spread out along the slope of the plateau, at the back of the grave-yard. The darkness was almost complete by this time, but it was still possible to make out great black clusters of city rooftops. Beyond these lay Balan and Bazeilles, among the meadows which stretched away as far as the line of hills between Remilly and Frénois. Spreading in a darker patch on the left were La Garenne woods, while lower down and to the right gleamed the broad pale ribbon of the Meuse. For a moment Maurice stood watching this vast horizon as it slowly merged into the darkness.

"Ah, here's the corporal!" said Chouteau. "Perhaps he's been collecting our rations. . . ."

There was uproar. All day long men had been returning to their units, some singly, others in small groups; there was so much confusion that officers had quickly given up trying to call men to account. They shut their eyes to faults and offered a ready welcome to anyone obliging enough to report back.

Moreover Captain Beaudoin had arrived only a short while ago, and not until two o'clock had Lieutenant Rochas marched the depleted company into camp, shorn of two-thirds of its number. Now it was almost up to strength. A few of the men were drunk; others were still very hungry, having failed to get so much as a hunk of bread – and once again there had been no organized distribution of rations. True, Loubet had contrived to cook some cabbages culled from a neighbouring garden; but as there was no salt or lard to make them palatable, the troops' bellies were still crying out for sustenance.

"Come on then, corporal, let's see the fruits of your skill and experience!" joked Chouteau. "Not that I want anything, mind. Loubet and I met a generous lady and had a darned good lunch."

Anxious faces were turned towards Jean. The squad had been waiting for him – especially Lapoulle and Pache who, unlucky in their own endeavours, had placed all their reliance in him, seeing him as a man quite capable of extracting flour from a stone. And Jean, moved to pity and tormented with remorse over the manner in which he had forsaken his men, shared out the half-loaf of bread in his knapsack.

"Jesus Christ," Lapoulle kept saying as he wolfed his share, "Jesus Christ . . ." He could think of no other means, apart from occasional grunts, of conveying his satisfaction. Pache very quietly said an Our Father and a Hail Mary, to ensure that Heaven would send him his daily bread again on the morrow.

Gaude the bugler had just sounded a flourish, summoning the men to roll-call. But there was no retreat: the camp was immediately plunged into deepest silence. And when he discovered that his half-section was all present and correct, Sergeant Sapin, with his pinched nose and unwholesome looks, remarked softly: "There'll be some absent tomorrow night."

Then, feeling Jean's eyes upon him, he added with calm conviction as he stared into the dark: "Oh, I'll be one of them – I shall be killed tomorrow."

It was nine o'clock. The night threatened to be a really cold one, for a heavy mist had risen from the Meuse and was hiding the stars. And Maurice, stretched out next to Jean under a hedge, shivered and observed that it might be better for them to go and lie in the tent. But they were so worn out – they felt even worse as a result of those twelve hours in bed – that neither of them was able to sleep. How they envied Lieutenant Rochas, who, uninterested in shelter, with nothing but a blanket wrapped round him, was snoring away like a hero on the damp ground beside them. For a long while after that they were intrigued by the small flame of a candle burning in a large tent where the colonel and a few other officers were sitting up late. All evening, Colonel de Vineuil had looked very worried: no orders had arrived for next morning. He felt that his regiment was perilously far forward, though it had already withdrawn from the advanced position which it had occupied that morning. General Bourgain-Desfeuilles had not put in an appearance; he was said to be ill in bed at the Croix-d'Or Hotel, and only after long deliberation did the colonel dispatch an officer to him, alerting him to the apparent dangers of the new position – for the 7th Corps was too thinly distributed over too long a defensive line, extending all the way from the Meuse loop to La Garenne woods. Battle would commence at first light; of that there could be no doubt. The most they

169

could now look forward to was seven or eight hours of this black spacious calm. At last the little light in the colonel's tent went out, and a moment later Maurice was startled to see Captain Beaudoin creep along the hedge beside him and then vanish in the direction of Sedan.

The darkness was growing thicker and thicker, gloomily enshrouded by the heavy mist from the river.

"Are you asleep, Jean?"

Jean was asleep, and Maurice felt all alone in the world. The thought of joining Lapoulle and the others in the tent induced a feeling of great weariness. He heard the rhythm of their snores respond to Rochas's and he envied them. He thought: if great captains sleep well on the eve of battle, it may be simply due to tiredness. The only sound he could hear, from the whole of that vast, night-enfolded camp, was the slow, heavy breath of sleep; it was like a single exhalation, at once mighty and gentle. Nothing else existed; he was merely aware that the 5th Corps must be camping over there beneath the ramparts, that the 1st was strung out from La Garenne woods to the village of La Moncelle, and that the 12th was occupying Bazeilles, on the far side of Sedan; and all was asleep, the slow throbbing ascending from every tent, from the nearest to the farthest, lost somewhere in the blackness, almost three miles away. And beyond that lay another unknown region, full of noises of its own, which carried to him from time to time, so faint and distant that he might have supposed they were merely a buzzing in his ears: cavalry galloping; artillery rumbling; above all the heavy tramp of armed men as the black human swarm advanced over the hilltops in that process of encroachment and envelopment which even the night had been unable to still. And he was almost certain he had seen the flash of signals down there in the distance, and heard unconnected shouts – all symptoms of mounting panic as the night dragged on towards the terrible day to come.

Maurice groped in the dark until his fingers closed on Jean's hand. Only then did he feel assured enough to fall asleep. All seemed quiet now, in the distance, except for a steeple in Sedan from which the hours rang out one by one.

170

PART TWO

I

IN HIS dark little room at Bazeilles, Weiss was startled out of bed by a heavy thump. He listened : it was artillery-fire. He had to grope for the candle and light it before he could see the time by his watch. Four o'clock : day was barely dawning. He snatched up his pince-nez and stared along the high street, the main road to Douzy, which runs through the village; but it was filled with a kind of thick dust and nothing was distinguishable. So he went into the other bedroom, where the windows looked out on to the meadows lying in the general direction of the Meuse; and then he realized that a morning mist was rising from the river and blotting out the horizon. The artillery was thundering louder beyond this natural veil, on the far side of the water. All of a sudden a French battery fired back, from so close and with such ferocity that the walls of the little house shook.

The Weisses' houses stood near the centre of Bazeilles, on the right as one approaches the church. It was set back a little from the street, which it overlooked – just a single row of windows with an attic above. Round the back was a surprisingly big garden sloping down towards the meadows and affording a view of the vast range of hills between Remilly and Frénois. Displaying a keenness that stemmed from the novel experience of being a householder, Weiss had been up until almost two in the morning; he had hidden all his provisions in the cellar and barricaded the windows with mattresses, so as to keep the furniture as safe as possible from bullets. He was filled with mounting rage at the thought that the Prussians might come and ransack this house. He had wanted it so badly; it had provided so difficult to acquire; he had barely begun to enjoy the ownership of it. . . .

But a voice was summoning him from the roadway.

"Weiss! Weiss! Do you hear what I hear?"

Down below he found Delaherche, who had insisted on spending the night at his dyeworks, a large brick building which was attached directly to the house. All the workers had fled through the woods

171

into Belgium, and the only person who had stayed behind to keep an eye on the place was the concierge, Françoise Quittard, widow of a mason. And she, trembling and distraught, would have bolted with the rest had it not been for Auguste, her ten-year-old son. The child was so sick with typhoid that he could not be moved.

"Do you hear that?" insisted Delaherche. "Our wisest course would be to return to Sedan at once."

Weiss had promised his wife firmly that he would leave Bazeilles at the first sign of real danger, and he was quite determined to keep that promise. But as yet this was no more than a somewhat random artillery duel being fought at long range through the early-morning mist.

"Oh, let's wait a bit," he replied. "There's no hurry."

And in fact Delaherche's curiosity was so keen and so anxious that it was making him brave. He had not slept a wink all night; he had been far too interested in the preparations for the town's defence. After warnings that he would be attacked at first light, General Lebrun – commander of the 12th Corps – had spent the hours of darkness digging in; for his orders were that Bazeilles must at all costs be prevented from falling into enemy hands. Barricades had been set up in the high street and the roads leading off it; small detachments of men had been assigned to each house; every lane and garden had been turned into a fortress. And on the stroke of three, when it was still pitch dark, the troops had been wakened noiselessly and sent to their posts. Their rifles were newly oiled, their pouches contained the regulation issue of ninety cartridges. The enemy's opening salvo had come as no surprise, and the French batteries, stationed in the rear, between Balan and Bazeilles, had started firing back at once, merely to make their presence felt, for in the poor visibility aim was a matter of guess-work.

"You know that the dyeworks are going to be stoutly defended," said Delaherche. "They've allotted me a whole section. Come and have a look."

Sure enough, forty-odd marines had moved in. They were commanded by a lieutenant, a tall fair-haired boy, extremely young but with a look of resourcefulness and determination. By this time his men had taken over every inch of the building. Some were drilling holes in the shutters on the first floor, facing the street; others were crenellating the low wall of the factory yard, overlooking the meadows at the rear.

It was in the middle of this yard that Delaherche and Weiss

172

found the lieutenant, vainly trying to peer through the morning mist.

"Blast this fog!" he muttered. "It will be like playing blind man's buff. . . ." Then, after a silence but without any apparent mental connection, he asked: "What day of the week is it?"

"Thursday," answered Weiss.

"Thursday – so it is. . . . God, we're living in a vacuum. It's as though the world had come to an end!"

But at that moment, amid the incessant roar of artillery, there was a lively burst of rifle-fire from the very edge of the meadows, only three or four hundred yards away. And just then a sudden dramatic change came over the scene – as the sun rose, the mist from the Meuse broke up and blew away like shreds of finest muslin and the blue sky was revealed in all its flawless clarity. Here was the exquisite beginning of a really splendid summer day.

"Ah!" cried Delaherche, "they're coming across the railway bridge. See them trying to advance along the line . . .? How stupid of us, not to have blown the bridge up!"

The lieutenant made a gesture of silent anger. The charge had been laid, he explained; but yesterday, after a four-hour battle to regain control of the bridge, they had forgotten to set fire to the fuse.

"Just our luck," he added in his clipped tones.

Weiss was staring about him, trying to take stock of the situation. The French were strongly placed in Bazeilles. Built on either side of the Sedan–Douzy road, the village afforded a clear view of the plain. There was only the one road leading directly to the village; it curved to the left and ran past the château as far as the village square, where another road branched off in the direction of the railway bridge. So the Germans were obliged to advance across the meadows and the ploughed fields, whose vast open spaces ran alongside the Meuse and the metal track. They were known for their canniness and it seemed unlikely that the real attack would be made from this direction; yet huge clusters of them were still moving up by way of the bridge, despite the slaughter being inflicted among their ranks by the French machine-gun batteries on the outskirts of Bazeilles. Those who were successful in getting across immediately flung themselves down in skirmishing order among the few willows. Already columns were forming up again and beginning to press forward. It was from this direction that the mounting rifle-fire was coming.

173

"Hallo!" remarked Weiss. "They're Bavarians. I can clearly make out the crests on their helmets."

At the same time he had the impression that additional columns were heading swiftly to the right in an endeavour to reach the distant trees, so that they could afterwards make an angled descent on Bazeilles. Were they to succeed in their bid to shelter in Mont-villiers park, the village might well be captured. Of this he had a swift if hazy realization; but as the frontal assault intensified, so the realization faded.

All of a sudden he turned to look at the Floing hills, which were clearly visible in the north, beyond and above the town of Sedan. A battery had just opened fire up there : puffs of smoke were lifting in the bright sunlight and the reports could not have been more distinct. It must have been about five o'clock."

"Well, well," he murmured, "the attack looks like being a general one."

To which the lieutenant of marines, following the direction of his gaze, replied with a gesture of total conviction : "Ah, but Bazeilles is the focal point. It is here that the battle will be decided, one way or the other."

"Do you really think so?" exclaimed Weiss.

"No doubt about it. The marshal himself must think so – he came here last night and told us to die to the last man rather than let the village fall to the enemy."

Weiss shook his head and surveyed the whole skyline; then, speaking in a hesitant voice, as though addressing himself, he said : "No, no, no, that can't be right. . . . What I'm afraid of is something quite different, something I daren't quite put a name to. . . ."

And with that he broke off, merely spreading his arms wide like the jaws of a vice; then he turned towards the North and brought his hands together again, as though the jaws had suddenly closed.

This fear had been with him ever since the day before, stemming from his knowledge of the region and from his appreciation of the movements of both armies. And even now, with the vast plain spread out before him in the radiant light, his eyes kept returning to the hills on the left bank; it was on those hills that, for a whole day and a whole night, a black swarm of German troops had poured past. There was a battery firing from the top of Remilly hill. Another, whose shells were now beginning to land, had taken up position at Pont-Maugis, by the bank of the river. He folded his pince-nez so that one lens was directly over the other, hoping this

174

would give him a clearer view of the wooded slopes; but all he could see was the small pale puffs of smoke with which the guns were capping the hills minute by minute. What had become of the human torrent which had washed over them? In the end, his prolonged searchings brought to light only a cluster of uniforms and horses – some general and his staff, no doubt – on the corner of a pinewood of the Marfée hill, high above Noyers and Frénois. Farther off was the bend in the river, barring the West; and in that direction the only possible line of retreat upon Mézières lay along the narrow road following the course of the Saint-Albert pass, between the Meuse and the Ardennes forest. Only the day before he had ventured to speak of this one and only path of retreat to a general whom he happened to encounter along a sunken road in the Givonne valley; later he had learned that it was General Ducrot, commander of the 1st Corps. If the army did not withdraw at once by the route in question, if it waited for the Prussians to cut it off after crossing the Meuse at Donchery, it could not fail to be brought to bay against the frontier. Even by that evening it had been too late, for the Uhlans were reported to be in possession of the bridge – another bridge which had not been blown up, this time because it had not occurred to anyone to bring any dynamite. And in despair Weiss told himself that the great stream of men, the black swarm, must be in Donchery plain by now, on its way to Saint-Albert pass; already its forward units must be striking at Saint-Menges and Floing, where he had conducted Jean and Maurice only the night before. In the dazzling sunlight, Floing steeple looked a very long way off to him, like a thin white needle.

To eastward lay the other jaw of the vice. Whereas looking north, all the way from the plateau of Illy to the plateau of Floing, he could see the battle-line of the 7th Corps (inadequately supported by the 5th, which had been placed in reserve below the ramparts), he had no means of telling what was happening in the East, where the 1st Corps was ranged along the Givonne valley from La Garenne woods to the village of Daigny. But there was a roar of artillery-fire from that direction too, and the fight was presumably taking place in Chevalier wood, on the near-side of the village. His alarm was the greater because, according to some of the local peasants, the Prussians had got as far as Francheval the day before; so that the movement being effected in the West by way of Donchery was duplicated in the East by way of Francheval, and the jaws of the vice could not fail to close – up there in the North, at the Calvary of Illy – unless this dual flanking movement were checked. He knew nothing of military science, he had only his own common sense to guide him; yet he trembled at the sight of this huge triangle, one side of which was formed by the Meuse and the other two by, respectively, the 7th Corps in the North and the 1st Corps in the East; meanwhile the 12th, down here at Bazeilles in the South, occupied the farthermost corner; and all three were positioned with their backs to one another, waiting – heaven alone knew why or how – for an enemy who was closing in from every direction. And there, right in the middle, as though trapped in the depths of a dungeon, lay the town of Sedan, armed with obsolete guns, devoid of ammunition or food supplies.

"Don't you see?" said Weiss, repeating his earlier gesture, spreading his two arms wide and bringing his two hands together. "*That's* the way it will be if your generals don't watch out. . . . The enemy are only playing with you here at Bazeilles. . . ."

But he was expressing himself badly and confusedly, and the lieutenant, not being familiar with the area, could make no sense of his remarks. So he dismissed them with an impatient shrug, scornful of this civilian with his overcoat and pince-nez who was trying to make out that he knew better than the marshal. And when Weiss repeated that the attack on Bazeilles could well be purely diversionary, he was so annoyed that he finally burst out: "Oh, stop bothering us. . .! We're going to boot your Bavarians into the Meuse – that'll show them whether we're to be played with!"

The German riflemen seemed to have drawn nearer in the past few moments; bullets were slapping into the bricks of the dyeworks and the marines had started firing back from the shelter of the little wall in the factory yard. Not a moment went by but a rifle-shot rang out crisp and clear.

"Boot them into the Meuse! Why yes, I don't doubt it!" murmured Weiss. "And afterwards use them as stepping-stones which will put you back on the road to Carignan. That would be splendid!" Turning to Delaherche, who had hidden behind the pump so as to screen himself from the bullets, he added: "No escaping it, the proper plan was to race on to Mézières last night; and if I were them, I'd rather be there than here. . . . Still, they must fight now that retreat is out of the question."

"Are you coming?" asked Delaherche. For all his burning curiosity, he was beginning to blanch. "If we leave it any longer, we'll never get back to Sedan."

176

"All right, hold on a minute and I'll be with you."

Despite the risk involved, he was standing on tiptoe and obstinately trying to keep track of what was happening. To the right lay the meadows which had been flooded by order of the governor. These formed a vast lake stretching all the way from Torcy to Balan and providing the town with a defensive screen. In the morning sunlight the water was still and a delicate shade of blue; but it gave out on the outskirts of Bazeilles, and sure enough the Bavarians had succeeded in moving forward across the grassland by taking advantage of every ditch and tree, however small. They were about three hundred yards away and the thing that struck him most was the slowness of their movements, the patience with which they gradually gained ground, exposing themselves as little as possible. Moreover they enjoyed the support of heavy artillery-fire : increasingly the cool clean air was disturbed by the whine of shells. Glancing up, he saw that the battery at Pont-Maugis was not the only one that was firing on Bazeilles; two others, positioned half-way up Liry hill, had opened fire and were not only pounding the village but raking the bare landscape at La Moncelle, where the 12th Corps reserves were, and even the wooded slopes of Daigny, which were occupied by a division of the 1st Corps. Indeed, flashes were issuing from every ridge on the left bank. Guns seemed to spring up from out of the soil, forming an ever-widening belt of fire. There was a battery at Wadelincourt firing on Sedan; there was another – a really powerful one – at Frénois, below Marfée hill, aiming its shells clean over the town so that they burst among the troops of the 7th Corps on the plateau of Floing. Weiss had always loved those hills, fondly imagining that the succession of green humps were there solely to delight the eye and set a gay seal on the valley; but he stared at them in terror and alarm now that they had turned, all of a sudden, into a monstrous stronghold battering down the useless fortifications of Sedan.

A light fall of plaster prompted him to lift his head : a bullet had chipped the front of his house, which was clearly visible above the party-wall. He was extremely put out.

"What are they trying to do, the ruffians? Destroy my home?"

But just then he was startled by another short soft sound, this one directly behind him. And as he turned, he saw a soldier fall down on his back after being hit in the heart. His legs twitched for a moment, but death had struck with such lightning speed that his face continued to look young and calm. This was the first man to die, and what upset Weiss most was the clatter of the rifle as it hit the stonework and bounced.

"Oh no, I'm off!" gasped Delaherche. "If you don't come, I shall make a dash for it by myself."

The lieutenant was quick to back him up – they were getting on his nerves.

"Yes, gentlemen, you had better go. . . . We are liable to be attacked at any moment."

It was these words which – after one last look at the meadows, where the Bavarians were still gaining ground – finally persuaded Weiss to leave with Delaherche. But as soon as they got outside into the street, he decided that he ought to go and double-lock the door of his house; and when eventually he returned to his companion, a new spectacle caused them both to stop in their stride.

At the end of the street, some three hundred yards away, the village square was coming under attack from a large troop of Bavarians emerging from the Douzy highway. The regiment of marines responsible for defending the square seemed to reduce their rate of fire for a moment, as though deliberately allowing the Bavarians to move forward. All of a sudden, when the attacking force was clustered together immediately ahead of them, the marines carried out an extraordinary and quite unexpected manoeuvre. First the riflemen rushed to one or other side of the street, where many of them threw themselves flat; then the machine-guns, grouped together at the back, discharged a hail of bullets across the area which had been cleared with such speed. It was as if the attackers had been struck by blast. At once the marines leaped to their feet and bayonet-charged the scattered survivors until they too were either knocked to the ground or driven back. Twice more was this manoeuvre carried out, each time with the same success. In a small house on the corner of a lane, three women who had chosen to remain in the village were calmly stationed at one of the windows; they were laughing and clapping in undisguised amusement as if they were at the theatre.

"Oh, damn!" Weiss said suddenly, "I forgot to lock the cellar and take the key from the door. . . . Would you mind waiting? I shan't be a minute."

The initial attack had apparently been warded off, and Delaherche – curiosity getting the better of him again – was no longer in such a hurry. He stood outside the dyeworks and chatted with

178

the concierge, who had ventured as far as the doorway of the room which she occupied on the ground floor.

"Poor Françoise, you ought to come with us. I hate to think of a woman enduring such horrors alone."

She threw up her trembling arms in despair.

"Oh sir, I'd have gone like a shot if it weren't for young Auguste being so ill. Why don't you step inside, sir, and see for yourself?"

He did not go in, but merely looked round the side of the door. He shook his head at the sight of the burning red face on the clean white pillow; the boy's flaming eyes stared intently at the mother.

"Well, why not bring him with you?" asked Delaherche. "I'll see to it that you have a roof over your head in Sedan. . . . Wrap him in a warm blanket and come with us."

"Oh no, sir, it's out of the question. That would be the death of him – the doctor told me straight. If only his poor father was still alive! But there's only the two of us, and each must keep safe and sound for the sake of the other. . . . And after all, there's a chance these Prussians won't harm a lone woman and sick child!"

Weiss came back, content in the knowledge that all his possessions were safely under lock and key.

"There – if anyone wants to get in, he'll have to wreck the building first. . . . And now off we go; though that's easier said than done. We shall have to stay close to the walls if we're to avoid being hit."

And indeed it seemed likely that the enemy was preparing to launch another attack, for the small-arms fire was intensifying and the whine of shells had become incessant. Two had already landed in the roadway, about seventy yards away; another had just buried itself in the soft garden soil, without exploding.

"Why, Françoise!" Weiss exclaimed, "I must just peep inside and say hullo to little Auguste. . . . Oh, he isn't as bad as all that – another couple of days and he'll be out of danger. . . . Well, keep your spirits up, and for heaven's sake hurry back indoors and stay out of sight."

The two men were leaving at last.

"Goodbye, Françoise."

"Goodbye, gentlemen."

But at that very moment there was a terrifying roar as a shell took away one of the chimney-pots on Weiss's house and landed on the pavement, exploding with such force that all the windows in the vicinity were broken. There was so much dust and such a heavy pall of smoke that nothing else was visible for a while. Then the front of the building reappeared. It had been ripped open, and there – sprawled dead in the doorway – lay Françoise; her back had been broken and her skull crushed; she was just a human rag, red all over, an appalling sight.

Weiss rushed to her side in a fury. "God Almighty!" he gasped. "God Almighty!" Oaths were all he could utter. Stooping over her, he felt her hands. Yes, she was dead all right. And as he straightened up, he encountered the deeply flushed face of little Auguste, who was craning his neck to look at his mother. He neither spoke nor wept, but his big feverish eyes opened inordinately wide as he gazed at that unrecognizably mangled body.

"God Almighty!" shouted Weiss, finding other words at last, "So now they've taken to slaughtering women!"

He stood shaking his fist at the Bavarians, whose helmets were coming in sight again on the far side of the church. And when he saw how big a hole had been torn in the roof of his house, he fell into a frenzy.

"You bastards! Kill defenceless women, would you! Wreck my house, would you! . . . Oh no, I can't just turn my back and run. After this, I'm staying!"

He raced back into the factory yard and reappeared a moment later with the dead soldier's rifle and ammunition. For special occasions (when he needed to see things clearly) he always carried a pair of spectacles about with him, though he was disarmingly shy of wearing them in the presence of his young wife. Now he snatched the pince-nez from his eyes and put the spectacles on instead. And this plump, overcoated civilian, his kindly round face transfigured with anger, looking almost comical yet at the same time wonderfully heroic, started to shoot, firing into the mass of Bavarians at the far end of the street. It was in his blood, as he had so often said in the past; he had been itching to do a few of them in ever since, as a small child back home in Alsace, he had been lulled to sleep by tales of 1814.

"Oh, you bastards! You dirty bastards!"

And still he fired, so rapidly that in the end the barrel of his rifle was burning his fingers.

The attack showed every sign of being on a terrible scale. Down in the meadows, the small-arms fire had ceased. The Bavarians were now in full control of the narrow stream lined with poplars and willows and were getting ready to storm the houses commanding the village square. Their skirmishers had carried out a wary withdrawal and nothing slept but the sunlight, spread in a cloth of gold over the great tracts of grassland where occasional dark specks marked the bodies of dead soldiers. In consequence, the lieutenant had now abandoned the factory yard, leaving only one sentry behind; he realized that the street had become the principal source of danger. He swiftly aligned his men along the pavement and told them that if the enemy succeeded in taking the square they were to barricade themselves in, on the first floor, and fight until the last round of ammunition had been expended. Lying flat on the ground, sheltering behind milestones, taking full advantage of even the smallest salient, the men were firing as and when they chose; and along that broad, deserted, sunstrewn highway sped a hurricane of lead streaked with smoke, like a downpour of hail driven by a high wind. A girl was seen to race panic-stricken across the street without being hit. Then an old man – a peasant in a smock frock who obstinately insisted on returning his horse to its stable – was struck right in the forehead, and the blow was such a mighty one that he was projected into the middle of the road. The church roof had just been smashed in by a shell. Two others had set fire to some houses, whose timberwork crackled and blazed in the strong sunlight. And the sight of poor Françoise lying crushed and mutilated beside her sick child, and of the old peasant with a bullet through his head, and of all this wreckage and conflagration, was sufficient to complete the wrath of the villagers who had preferred to stay and die here rather than escape into Belgium. People of every class, some in smart coats, others in shabby overalls, were firing hot-temperedly from the windows.

"Ah, the ruffians!" shouted Weiss. "They've worked their way round. I saw them stealing along behind the railway. . . . There – hear them? Over on the left."

He was right : heavy firing had just broken out behind Mont-villiers Park, whose trees grew alongside the road. If the enemy won control of that park, Bazeilles was as good as captured. But the very ferocity of the exchanges indicated that the 12th Corps commander had foreseen this development and taken steps to defend the park.

"Mind out, you oaf!" roared the lieutenant, shoving Weiss flat against the wall. "Do you want to be cut in two?"

Plump, bespectacled Weiss had finally intrigued him by his courage, even though he could not help smiling at his appearance;

so when he heard a shell coming, he gave him this friendly push. The missile landed a dozen paces away and exploded, showering them both with shrapnel. The civilian went on standing there without a scratch; the lieutenant got both his legs smashed.

"There now!" he murmured. "It had *my* name on it."

He had been knocked flat on the pavement, and so he had himself set with his back against the door, beside the dead woman, who was lying across the threshold. And his young face still had the same resourceful and determined look.

"It makes no odds, lads. Listen carefully. . . . Take your time and don't hurry your aim. I'll tell you when to move in and use your bayonets on them."

Thus he continued to direct them, holding his head up and watching every movement made by the distant enemy. Across the way, another house had caught fire. The roar of bursting shells and the patter of rifle-shots rent the air and filled it with dust and smoke. Soldiers were being blown off their feet at every corner; dead bodies – some of them isolated, others heaped together – appeared as dark patches spattered with blood. And above the village there rose an ever-increasing din, the ominous clamour of thousands of troops charging a few hundred courageous men who had made up their minds to die.

At this, Delaherche – who had been calling out to Weiss repeatedly – asked one last time: "Aren't you coming . . .? Well, I'm sorry but I must leave you to it. Goodbye!"

It was about seven o'clock and he had tarried too long. While there were still houses alongside him he took every advantage of the doorways and jutting walls, wedging himself in the smallest cranny each time a shot rang out. Never would he have imagined himself capable of the youthful agility with which he wormed his way forward. But when he reached the end of Bazeilles he had to follow the exposed, deserted road for almost two hundred yards at a point where it was being raked by the batteries on Liry hill. He was conscious of shivering all over, even though he was bathed in sweat. For a moment or two he stumbled along a ditch with his body bent double. Then he set off like a madman, galloping straight ahead with the exploding shells echoing in his brain like bursts of thunder. His eyes were burning; he felt as if he were advancing through flames. This seemed to go on for an eternity. Suddenly he saw a little house on his left; he rushed forward until he reached shelter, and felt as if an enormous weight had been lifted from his chest. There was life around him, men and horses; at first he could not make out what he was looking at, but what he eventually saw amazed him.

For it was the Emperor with a full staff of officers. He was not quite sure, even though he had boasted that he would know the Emperor anywhere after so nearly speaking to him at Baybel; then he gaped. It really was Napoleon III. He looked taller mounted on horseback and his moustaches were so heavily waxed, his cheeks so highly coloured, that Delaherche at once concluded that, like an actor, he had made himself up to look younger. Obviously he had had this done so that his army should not be demoralized by the sight of those cadaverous features drawn with suffering, that pinched-looking nose, those bleary eyes. And as soon as he heard that fighting had broken out at Bazeilles, he had ridden straight here, but as subdued, doleful and ghastly as ever, despite the rouge with which he had touched up his cheeks.

By chance this brickworks afforded a temporary haven. The walls on the other side were being riddled by an incessant stream of bullets, and not a second went by but a shell burst on the road. The entire escort had come to a halt.

"Sire," murmured one of its members, "you really are taking a risk. . . ."

But the Emperor turned and with a wave of the hand instructed his staff to align themselves along the narrow lane which ran past the brickworks. There, men and horses alike would be completely hidden.

"Believe us, sire, this is madness. . . . Sire, we beg of you . . ."

He merely waved his hand again, as though to indicate that the sudden emergence of a uniformed party on this bare stretch of road could not fail to attract the attention of the batteries on the left bank. Then, all alone, he rode out among the bullets and shells – quite unhurriedly, with his usual air of dolefulness and unconcern, going forward to meet his destiny. Doubtless he could hear at his back the implacable voice which was thrusting him forward, that voice which bellowed from Paris : "On, on, on . . . die like a hero upon the heaped-up bodies of your people, fill the whole wide world with compassion and admiration so that your son may reign !" And on he dutifully went, slowly walking his horse. For a hundred yards or so he kept going. Then he stopped, awaiting the end for which he sought. The bullets whistled by like an equinoctial gale; a shell burst, covering him with earth. Still he waited. His horse's mane stood on end, its coat twitched all over as it intuitively recoiled from the death which flashed past at every moment without choosing to touch steed or rider. At last, after this timeless period of waiting, bowing as always to the inevitable and realizing that his ultimate destiny was not to be found here, the Emperor rode calmly back as though he had simply wanted to locate the exact positions of the German batteries.

"Sire, what bravery . . .! For pity's sake don't expose yourself again. . . ."

But with a third wave of the hand he bade his staff follow him. This time he spared them as little as he spared himself, setting off through open country in the direction of La Moncelle. A captain was killed and two horses fell to the ground. As he rode past the regiments of the 12th Corps, the men neither cheered nor saluted; they stared at him as if he were a spectre appearing and then vanishing.

Delaherche had witnessed all this. And it made him shudder, especially when he reflected that as soon as he left the brickworks he too would be fully exposed to the bullets and shells. He bided his time, listening to some unseated officers who were sheltering there.

". . . I tell you he was killed outright. A shell cut him clean in two."

"No, no, I saw them carry him away. . . . Just a wound, a bit of shrapnel in the backside. . . ."

"What time was this?"

"About half past six – an hour ago. Happened in a dip near La Moncelle."

"So now he's back at Sedan?"

"Where else?"

Who could they be talking about? All of a sudden Delaherche realized that they were referring to Marshal MacMahon, wounded while on his way to inspect the forward positions. The marshal wounded! "Just our luck," as the lieutenant of marines had put it. And Delaherche was still pondering the consequences of the mishap when a messenger rode past at full tilt, calling out to a comrade whom he happened to recognize : "General Ducrot has been made C.-in-C. . . . The whole army is to muster at Illy and then fall back on Mézières !"

The messenger was riding at such a gallop that he was already entering Bazeilles, where the shooting had greatly intensified. Meanwhile Delaherche, bewildered by these extraordinary tidings which had come to his ear in such rapid succession, decided that – rather than risk being trapped in the general retreat – he would proceed to Belan as fast as his legs would carry him; and from there he eventually got back to Sedan without too much difficulty.

In Bazeilles, the messenger was still riding at a gallop as he sought out the officers and gave them their orders. And the news was galloping too – Marshal MacMahon wounded; General Ducrot appointed commander-in-chief; the entire army told to muster at Illy.

"What! What are they saying?" shouted Weiss, already black with powder. "Fall back on Mézières at this stage in the proceedings? Why, that's insane – the army will never get through!"

He was in despair and overcome with remorse at the thought that he himself had counselled such a move only the day before – and counselled it to this same General Ducrot who had now been invested with supreme authority. Admittedly the only feasible plan, the day before, had been to retreat without delay along the Saint-Albert pass. But by this time the route was sure to be blocked – for the great black swarm of Prussians had headed in that direction, making for the Donchery plain. And now – countering one mad stroke for another – there was only one last desperate chance open to the French: they must hurl the Bavarians into the Meuse and march over their dead bodies until they were back on the road to Carignan.

Weiss, continually hitching up his glasses in his excitement and agitation, explained the position to the lieutenant, who was still sitting propped against the door with both his legs blown off; he looked extremely pale and was dying from loss of blood.

"I'm right, lieutenant, I assure you I am. . . . Tell your men to keep it up. We're winning – you can see that with your own eyes. One final effort, and we really *shall* boot them into the Meuse!"

True enough, the Bavarians' second attack had just been repulsed. The machine-guns had raked the village square again: piles of bodies covered the cobbles in the strong sunlight, and bayonet-charges, launched from every side-turning, were thrusting the enemy back into the meadows; this headlong flight towards the river would unquestionably have turned into a rout if only fresh troops had moved up in support of the marines, who were worn out and depleted by this time. Moreover the shooting in Montvilliers park

185

was not coming appreciably closer, a sure sign that the woods could have been cleared had reinforcements been available.

"Order a bayonet-charge, lieutenant, for heaven's sake order a bayonet-charge!"

Though his cheeks had turned white as wax and his voice was fast fading, the lieutenant still found the strength to mumble : "You heard, lads. Bayonets at the ready, now . . .!"

And that was the last breath he drew. He died – face set and determined, eyes open, still watching the battle. Flies were already buzzing about and settling on poor Françoise's broken head. Little Auguste was delirious with fever; in a low, pleading voice he was calling from his pillow and asking for something to drink.

"Mama, wake up. . . . Get up from there, Mama. . . . I'm thirsty. I'm ever so thirsty. . . ."

But the orders were categorical : the officers had no choice but to withdraw, however aggrieved they might feel at not being allowed to benefit from the advantages which they had just won. Obviously General Ducrot, impelled by an obsessive fear of the enemy's pincer movement, was sacrificing everything to the present hectic bid to escape his clutches. So the village square was evacuated, the troops fell back lane by lane and soon the high street was empty. Women began to scream and sob; men swore and shook their fists at the soldiers when they saw how they were being abandoned. A considerable number shut themselves away in their houses, determined to fight until they were dead.

"Well, I'm damned if *I* have any intention of bolting!" roared Weiss, who was quite beside himself. "No, I'd rather stay here and be buried in the rubble. . . . So come on, you Prussians – let's see you start smashing my furniture and drinking my wine!"

He was no longer conscious of anything except his raging impatience to do battle, brought on by the thought of the invader strutting into his house and sitting down on his chair and drinking from his glass. The notion roused him in every fibre of his being, making him forget the familiar pattern of his days – his wife, his job, his sensible petit-bourgeois cautiousness. And he barricaded himself in and prowled about his house like an animal in its cage, going from room to room, making sure that every opening was well and truly sealed. He counted his ammunition : he still had about forty rounds. Then, as he took one last look in the direction of the Meuse, to make sure there was no risk of attack from the meadows, he was once again momentarily arrested by the sight of the hills on the left bank. Mounting puffs of smoke clearly indicated the positions of the French batteries. And above the particularly powerful battery at Frénois, at the corner of a small wood on Marfée hill, he observed the uniformed party which had captured his attention earlier; it had grown in number and was so resplendent in the sunlight that when he fitted his pince-nez over his spectacles he could make out the gold of their epaulettes and helmets.

"You bastards! You filthy bastards!" he cried, shaking his fist.

It was King William and his staff. At seven o'clock the Prussian King had set out from Vendresse, where he had spent the night, and now he was up on Marfée hill, safely out of harm's reach, with the whole Meuse valley – the whole sprawling battle-zone – spread out before him. The huge relief map stretched from one side of the sky to the other while he looked on from his hill-slope, as though from the seat of honour in a gigantic royal box.

In the centre, standing out against the dark green backdrop of the Ardennes forest, lay Sedan with the geometrical lines of its fortifications, covered in the South and West by the river and the flooded meadows. In Bazeilles a number of houses were already ablaze and the whole village was enshrouded in the dust of battle. In the East, between La Moncelle and Givonne, there were no signs of hostilities except for a few regiments of the 1st and 12th Corps, resembling lines of insects as they trudged through the fields of stubble and disappeared at times into the slender valley with its smattering of concealed villages. On the rising ground directly facing the King and his party, the Chevalier woods showed as a heavy green stain on the pale meadows. But the clearest view of all was that afforded of the 7th Corps – so many black dots moving about on the plateau of Floing, that broad band of reddish soil sloping down from La Garenne woods to the grassland at the water's edge. Beyond lay Floing and Saint-Menges and Fleigneux and Illy, villages lost in the undulations of this contorted landscape, cut about by sudden escarpments. And away to the left was the loop in the Meuse, whose slow-moving waters shone like new silver in the bright sunshine; that slow, languorous bend completely blocked the way to Mézières, and between the farthermost bank and the impassable entanglement of forests there was one exit only, the Saint-Albert pass.

Cooped up within this triangle were the hundred thousand men and five hundred pieces of artillery which constituted the French army; and when the King of Prussia turned his eyes westward, he was treated to the view of another plain, the plain of Donchery, an endless series of grey, empty fields stretching out in the direction of Briancourt and Marancourt and Vrignes-aux-Bois, turning to dust beneath the blue sky; and when he turned his eyes eastward he could see – directly facing the inordinately cramped French lines – another untrammelled expanse teeming with villages : first Douzy and Carignan, then in succession Rubécourt, Pourru-aux-Bois, Francheval, Villers-Cernay, all the way to La Chapelle, next to the Belgian frontier. The whole of the surrounding area was his : he was free to direct wherever he wished the two hundred and fifty thousand men and eight hundred guns at his disposal, and he could take in their various encroaching movements at a single glance. On the one hand, XI Corps was already advancing on Saint-Menges, while V Corps was at Vrignes-aux-Bois and the Wurttemberg Division was waiting near Donchery; and on the other hand, even if the hills and trees obstructed the view he could guess what was happening, for he had just seen XII Corps advance into the Chevalier wood and he knew that the Guard must by this time have reached Villers-Cernay. These were the two jaws of the vice – the army of the Crown Prince of Prussia on the left, the army of the Crown Prince of Saxony on the right – opening and reaching out with irresistible force while the two Bavarian corps hurled themselves upon Bazeilles.

At King William's feet the almost unbroken line of batteries between Remilly and Frenois were thundering away without respite, unloading shell after shell on La Moncelle and Daigny and firing clean over the top of Sedan so as to rake the plateaux to the north of the town. It was still only a little after eight o'clock and already he was awaiting the inevitable outcome of the battle, eyes trained on the giant chessboard, mind engrossed in the task of steering this human dust, of controlling this handful of black dots as they scurried about amid nature's cheerful and everlasting presence.

II

GAUDE'S bugle resounded at full blast as the first light of day appeared among the heavy mist that had closed on Floing plateau. But the air was so damp that the joyful peal of notes was sadly muffled and quite failed to rouse the troops. They had not even had the heart to pitch their tents the night before, but had simply lain down in the mud with the canvas wrapped around them. They were already like corpses, their wan faces were set hard with sleep and exhaustion, and they had to be shaken one by one, to rouse them from their temporary death. They got up like men recently risen from the grave; their skin was the colour of ashes and their eyes were full of the terror of being alive.

"What? What's happening?" cried Maurice when Jean shook him awake.

He stared about him in bewilderment, seeing nothing but the shadowy figures of his comrades swimming about in a sea of grey. Visibility was down to less than twenty yards; there was nothing by which he could take his bearings, and he would not even have been able to say in what direction Sedan lay. But at that moment the rumble of artillery fire somewhere in the far distance reached him.

"Oh yes, today the fight's on, and thank God for that! At last we can get it over and done with."

All around him, other voices were saying the same. The men were sombrely conscious of a sense of relief, so great was their longing to shake off the nightmare of the past few weeks and come face to face with these Prussians whom they had sought everywhere, yet from whom they had fled for such an unendurable length of time! So at last they were going to blaze away at the enemy and shed some of these cartridges which until now had been a useless encumbrance on their never-ending journey. This time, as everyone sensed, a pitched battle could not be shirked.

"Where's the gunfire coming from?"

189

"My God!" replied Maurice, "I guess it must be somewhere near the river, but I'm damned if I've any idea where I am."

"Listen, lad," the corporal went on, "you're to stick by me today, for it takes experience to keep out of trouble. . . . I've been through all this before, so I'll watch out for both of us."

Meanwhile the squad was beginning to grumble. They were furious at being denied the chance to get something warm inside them. There could be no question of lighting a fire when they had no dry wood and the weather was so foul. Even as battle was about to start, the problem of filling their stomachs was reasserting itself, imperious and all-absorbing. Heroes they might be, but their insides came first. Eating was the only thing that really mattered. How lovingly they skimmed the pot on days when there was a proper meal, and what childish and barbarous fits of anger they indulged in at times when they had to go short!

"If we don't eat, we don't fight," declared Chouteau. "You won't blasted well catch me risking my neck today!"

He was showing his revolutionary side again, this big brute of a house-painter and bar-room theorist from Montmartre who ruined his smattering of more-or-less reasonable ideas with an appalling admixture of lies and stupidities.

"Besides," he continued, "look at the way they pulled the wool over our eyes about the Prussians. The Prussians were supposed to be dying of disease and starvation; they were supposed to be roaming about like tattered, filthy tramps, without so much as a shirt on their backs. . . ."

Loubet roared with laughter, looking every inch the barrow-boy from the Paris markets.

"A likely story! It's *us* who are on our last legs, *us* who are so mucky and down-at-heel that people would give us charity-money just to look at us. . . . And these great victories we hear about! They were simply having us on with their stories of Bismarck being taken prisoner and a whole army being hurled into a quarry. . . . My, they've been making mugs of us!"

Pache and Lapoulle – all ears – were clenching their fists and nodding their heads furiously. Some of the others were getting angry too, for the everlasting lies in the newspapers had ultimately brought disastrous repercussions. All trust was gone: people no longer believed in anything. The minds of these overgrown children, which had once brimmed over with wild and wonderful hopes, were now beset by mad nightmares.

190

"Well, it doesn't take much explaining, does it?" insisted Chouteau. "It's obvious, isn't it, when we all know we've been betrayed."

Lapoulle's simple, rustic brain grew incensed whenever he heard this expression.

"Betrayed! It takes blackguards to betray people!"

"Betrayed, exactly as Judas betrayed his Master," murmured Pache, still obsessed with the Scriptures.

"There's no mystery attached to it!" crowed Chouteau. "Everyone knows the facts and figures. MacMahon was paid three million, and the other generals a million apiece, to deliver us here. It was all settled in Paris last spring, and last night they fired a rocket to announce that all was ready and that the enemy could move in and take us."

The crass stupidity of this allegation was too much for Maurice. At one time he had been entertained and almost won over by Chouteau's metropolitan working-class gusto. But nowadays he could not bear to listen to this trouble-maker who, by his abusiveness, tried to put others off doing what had to be done.

"What makes you talk such rubbish?" he cried. "You know quite well there isn't a word of truth in what you are saying."

"Not a word of truth in it? Are you trying to make out we haven't been betrayed . . .! What's this then, toff? Are you in with them? Maybe you're a slimy traitor yourself. . . ." He strode forward menacingly. "If that's the case you've only to say so, Bighead, and we'll attend to you without waiting for your friend Bismarck."

The others were beginning to growl, and Jean thought the time had come to intervene.

"Quieten down, will you! The first man to make a move will find himself on the report-sheet."

Chouteau simply scoffed at this. To hell with the report-sheet! Whether he'd fight or not fight was entirely up to him, and people had better mind their p's and q's because he had bullets for others besides Prussians. Now that the battle had begun, such little discipline as had been preserved through fear would crumble. What could they possibly do to him? He intended to clear off as soon as he'd had enough. And then he became really offensive, working up strong feelings against the corporal, who was – he said – deliberately allowing them to die of hunger. Yes, it was Jean's fault that the squad had gone without food for three whole days while their

191

comrades had been enjoying good meat and good broth. But his lordship and the toff had done themselves well: some girls had looked after them in Sedan. This had not escaped notice.

"You've been enjoying yourself at our expense – you haven't the nerve to deny it, you dirty crook!"

At this, matters showed every sign of getting out of hand. Lapoulle stood clenching his fists, while Pache – for all his usual gentleness – was so beside himself with hunger that he insisted the charge be answered. Loubet was the only one to behave with moderation; shrewd as ever, he pointed out that it was idiotic for the French to fall out among themselves when the Prussians were within striking distance. Personally, he was against settling disputes either with bare fists or with rifles, and harking back to the few hundred francs which he had been paid for doing another man's military service he added: "I mean it! If *that's* all the value they place on my hide, I'll see they get no more than their money's worth!"

Maurice and Jean, however, had been sorely stung by this unprovoked attack. They were hotly rejecting Chouteau's allegations when all at once a loud voice issued from the fog.

"What's this I hear? What's this I hear? Who are those idiots shouting their heads off?"

A moment later, Lieutenant Rochas appeared on the scene. The continual rain had caused his cap to fade; there were several buttons missing from his greatcoat; hardship and neglect were pitifully apparent in every inch of his thin, gawky figure. Not that this stopped him from putting on a bold front: his moustaches were bristling and the light of victory was in his eyes.

"It's these men here, sir," replied Jean, unable to contain himself. "They say our own generals have sold us into the hands of the enemy. They keep on about it, at the tops of their voices."

In Rochas's circumscribed brain the suggestion of betrayal was not wholly unacceptable, for it would account for defeats which otherwise made no sense to him.

"Well, what the blazes is it to them whether they've been sold down the river or not . . .? Is it any concern of theirs . . .? It doesn't alter the fact that the Prussians are here, and that we're going to give them the kind of drubbing we used to hand out in the past."

In the distance, beyond the thick curtain of mist, the gunfire at

Bazeilles went on and on. He flung out his arms in a commanding gesture.

"This time we've got them where we want them! Now we can thump them back into Germany with the butt-ends of our rifles!"

Since the first rumble of artillery-fire, his mind had been closed to everything else – to the delays and vacillations of the long march, to the demoralization of the troops and the disaster at Beaumont and the final agony of the enforced retreat to Sedan. Now that the fight was on, victory could surely be accounted as certain. He had neither learned anything nor forgotten anything: he still had the same blustering contempt for the enemy, the same total ignorance of the altered nature of warfare, the same stubborn conviction that no veteran of the Algerian, Crimean and Italian campaigns could ever be beaten. What could be more preposterous than for a man to start losing battles at his age!

Suddenly his face creased with laughter. He yielded to one of those kind and generous impulses for which his men worshipped him, even if he did sometimes bite their heads off.

"Listen, boys, a nip of something special will do you far more good than squabbling with each other. . . . Here, have one on me and drink to my health."

And from one of the capacious pockets in his greatcoat he drew a bottle of brandy – adding, with the air of a conqueror, that it was a present from a lady. Only the day before, in fact, someone had seen him in Floing with a barmaid on his knee, with whom he seemed to be having a very good time. By this time the troops were laughing heartily and queueing up for their tots of brandy, while he cheerfully poured a good measure into each tin mug.

"Lads, you must drink to your lady-loves, if you have any, and you must drink to the glory of France. Those are the only things I care about, so here's to happiness!"

"Quite right, sir – here's to your health and everyone else's!"

They all drank, and the toast induced warmth and reconciliation. Nothing could have been more welcome, in the chill of early morning, than this nip of brandy just before going into battle. And Maurice could feel it working its way into his bloodstream, restoring him to the cosy half-drunk state of self-delusion. Why shouldn't they beat the Prussians? Didn't battles sometimes turn out surprisingly, due to reversals of fortune so astonishing that they were assured of a permanent place in the history books? And this incorrigible man Rochas went on to say that Bazaine was on the march

193

and would be with them by nightfall; oh yes, he had it on the best authority, straight from one of the general's aides-de-camp. And even though the lieutenant pointed towards Belgium to indicate the direction from which Bazaine would be coming, Maurice succumbed to one of those ungovernable bouts of optimism without which his life would hardly have been possible. Perhaps they really were going to get their own back at last.

"What are we waiting for, sir?" he asked, deciding to speak up boldly. "Shouldn't we be on the move?"

Roches gesticulated as if to say : I cannot act without orders. Then, after a pause, he inquired : "Has anyone seen the captain?"

Nobody answered. Jean remembered that he had seen him steal off towards Sedan under cover of darkness; but a wise soldier should never observe a superior except in the course of duty. He was therefore tactfully refraining from speech when, happening to glance round, he saw a shadowy figure advancing along the hedgerow.

"Here he is," he said.

And indeed it was Captain Beaudoin. They were all amazed to see him so immaculately turned out : his well-brushed uniform and highly polished shoes could not have been in more glaring contrast to the lamentable condition of the lieutenant's clothes. Moreover there was something decidedly foppish about the whiteness of his hands and the curliness of his moustaches; they gave off a faint aroma of Persian lilac, redolent of the well-appointed boudoir of some pretty woman.

"Well, well!" jeered Loubet. "So the captain's found his luggage!"

But nobody smiled, for they all knew the captain was not a man to joke with. How they loathed him for his aloofness. A proper little martinet, as Rochas put it. Ever since the early defeats he had gone about with a thoroughly scandalized look, and the disaster which was generally forecast struck him as inconvenient rather than anything else. An ardent Bonapartist, with really good prospects of advancement and any number of friends in high places, he was very conscious that his own fortunes would be dragged down in this quagmire. Rumour had it that he possessed a very pleasing tenor voice, to which he already owed a great deal. Not that he was unintelligent, he just happened to know nothing about his trade; all he was concerned with was being pleasant, and although he could be very decent when he had to be, he was never over-zealous.

"Quite a fog!" he said casually, feeling better now that he had

194

found his company. He had spent the past half-hour searching for it, haunted by the fear that he might have lost them completely.

A few moments later (orders having arrived at last) the battalion moved forward. Streaks of mist were rising from the Meuse, for the men had to pick their way almost blindly through a sort of off-white dew which was coming down in a slow drizzle. And then Maurice suddenly became aware of a scene which made a great impression on him: on Colonel de Vineuil looming out of the fog at the point where two roads met. The colonel sat quite motionless in the saddle, very tall and very pale, like a marble statue of despair, while his horse shivered in the cold morning air, flaring its nostrils and straining them in the direction of the artillery fire. But what impressed Maurice even more was the sight of the regimental colours, ten paces behind the colonel, already unfurled and borne aloft by the ensign; among the soft spiralling mists it was a fantastic heavenly vision, trembling and already beginning to fade. The gilded eagle was drenched, while the silk tricolor, embroidered with the names of victories, was faded, smoke-blackened, holed with ancient wounds; and the generally subdued tones of the flag were enlivened only by the glittering enamel arms of the cross surmounting the bow and tassels.

Colonel and colours disappeared, drowned beneath another wave of mist, and the battalion continued to grope its way forward as if through an ocean of wet cotton-wool. After negotiating a downhill slope, they were now going up a narrow path. Then a shouted order brought them to a standstill. And there they remained, arms at the order, packs pressing down on their shoulders, with strict orders not to move. Presumably they were on a plateau, but visibility was still below twenty yards and they could not see a thing. It was seven o'clock; the artillery fire seemed to be getting nearer; other batteries were firing from the other side of Sedan and they sounded more and more close-packed.

"Well, I know what's going to happen to me," Sergeant Sapin observed without warning, addressing his words to Jean and Maurice. "I shall be killed today."

He had not opened his lips since reveille, and with his thin face, large handsome eyes and small pinched-looking nose he had given the impression of being lost in reverie.

"What a thing to say!" protested Jean. "How can anyone know? Either a bullet has got your name on it or it hasn't."

But the sergeant shook his head with a vigour that suggested absolute conviction.

"Oh, it's got *my* name written on it all right. I shall be killed today."

Faces were turned towards him and someone asked whether he had seen his death in a dream. No, he hadn't dreamed anything; but he could sense its presence.

". . . And the thought of it riles me, I can't pretend otherwise, for I was going to marry when I got home."

His eyes went away again; he was thinking back over his life. His family had run a small grocery business in Lyons; he had been spoilt by his mother (whom he had lost) and he had never been able to get on with his father. As a result he had stayed in the army, feeling a general aversion towards it yet unwilling to be bought out. And then, during a spell of leave, he had come to an understanding with one of his cousins; the engagement had given him a new lease of life and with mutual enthusiasm they had planned to open a business of their own, with the help of her small dowry. He had received a certain amount of education: he could write, he could spell, he could add up. For an entire year he had been living solely for the happy future that now lay ahead of him.

His body shook, as though he were physically casting off his obsession. Then he added with every appearance of calm: "Yes, the thought of it riles me – but die I shall."

Nobody spoke after this. The tension persisted. They did not know whether they were facing the enemy or whether they had their backs to him. Every so often indistinct sounds emerged from the mysterious depths of the fog: the rumble of wheels, the tramp of many feet, the distant trot of horses, each sound indicating hidden troop-movements as the units of the 7th Corps advanced to their combat positions. In the course of the past few moments, however, the fog had shown signs of lifting. Here and there it was coming away in shreds, like muslin, and a few odd corners of the skyline were beginning to reveal themselves – blurred as yet, and of the same cheerless blue as deep water. In one of these clearer moments they saw the light cavalry riding along in a ghostly procession: these were the regiments of Chasseurs d'Afrique which formed part of Margueritte's division. Sitting extremely upright in the saddle, in those easily distinguishable tunics with the broad red sash, they urged their horses on, small and three-parts hidden beneath all the paraphernalia they had to carry. Squadron after squadron went by, and all of them – as they returned to the gloom from which they had emerged – looked as though they were melting under the fine rain. No doubt they were in the way and the generals had bundled them off, not knowing what to do with them, as had happened time after time since the start of the campaign. Little enough use had been made of them even as scouts, and as soon as any fighting broke out they were hustled from valley to valley, invaluable, and yet of no apparent use.

As Maurice stood and watched, his thoughts turned to Prosper. "There!" he said quietly. "That might be him."

"Might be who?" asked Jean.

"That fellow from Remilly. You remember: we met his brother at Oches."

But the Chasseurs had gone, and now suddenly there was another sound of galloping hooves as a general and his staff came hurrying down the slope. Jean was able to identify their brigade commander, Bourgain-Desfeuilles, who was waving his right arm about in a ferocious manner. So he had finally condescended to leave the Croix-d'Or Hotel! His present show of temper was ample proof of his annoyance at having to get up so early after being so poorly lodged and fed.

His thunderous voice carried to them quite distinctly: ". . . the Moselle or the Meuse or whatever its blessed name is . . . the stretch of water ahead of us, God damn it!"

The fog continued to lift, however. The end came as suddenly here as it did at Bazeilles, like the curtain going up in a theatre and laying bare the scenery. A bright stream of sunlight was descending from the blue sky. And at once Maurice recognized the spot where they were waiting.

"Aha!" he said to Jean, "We're on what they call the Algerian plateau. . . . See that village directly across the valley from us? That's Floing. And the one over there is Saint-Menges, with Fleigneux to the rear of it. . . . And right at the very back, in the Ardennes forest – see? those thin trees on the horizon – that's the frontier. . . ."

He continued to point out landmarks. The Plateau de l'Algérie, a two-mile strip of reddish soil, sloped gently down from La Garenne woods to the meadows bordering on the Meuse. It was here that General Douay had deployed the 7th Corps, desperately conscious of the fact that he did not have enough men either to hold so broad a line or to establish firm links with the 1st Corps,

197

whose positions – perpendicular to his own – extended along the Givonne valley, from La Garenne woods to Daigny.

"Just look at the size of it!" cried Maurice.

He turned and with a sweep of the arm embraced the length and breadth of the surrounding scene. From the Plateau de l'Algérie, the battle zone ranged far to the south and west. First came Sedan, with the fortress clearly visible above the rooftops; next Balan and Bazeilles, indistinct among a lingering haze of smoke; then, in the background, the high ground on the left bank – the Liry, Marfée and Croix-Piau hills. But the outlook on the westerly side, towards Donchery, was even more extensive. The loop of the Meuse drew a pale ribbon round the Iges peninsula; and here the narrow road to Saint-Albert showed plainly between the river-bank and a steep hill which, farther back, was surmounted by the small wood of Le Seugnon, a spur of the larger woods at La Falizette. At the top of the slope, the cross-roads of La Maison-Rouge opened the way to Vrignes-aux-Bois and Donchery.

"There lies our one hope of falling back on Mézières."

But at that very moment came the first artillery report from Saint-Menges. Shreds of fog were still clinging to the low-lying areas, and all they could make out was a body of men on the march in the Saint-Albert pass.

"Ah, there they are!" said Maurice, instinctively lowering his voice and avoiding any direct mention of the Prussians. "It's all up with us – our line of retreat is cut off!"

It was not yet eight o'clock. The gunfire, growing louder than ever over towards Bazeilles, was also beginning to resound on the eastern side – in the Givonne valley, which was hidden from view. It was at this stage that the Crown Prince of Saxony's army emerged from the Chevalier woods and clashed with the 1st Corps on the near side of Daigny. And now that the Prussian XI Corps – marching on Floing – had begun to fire on General Douay's units, battle was engaged on all sides, from north to south, along the whole of this vast perimeter.

Maurice had just realized the irreparable mistake that had been made of not withdrawing during the night to Mézières. The full consequences of this omission were not as yet clear to him, but an inkling of the dangers to which they were exposed caused him to stare in alarm at the distant hills rising above the Plateau de l'Algérie. Assuming there had not been sufficient time for the army to fall back on Mézières, why hadn't the generals moved their forces on to this high ground? There they could have fought with their backs to the frontier, and if they were toppled from those positions they could have crossed into Belgium. Two points seemed to constitute a particular threat: on the left, the rounded hillock of Le Hattoy, above Floing; on the right, the Calvary of Illy, a stone cross standing between two lime trees. The day before, General Douay had posted a regiment to Le Hattoy; but it had fallen back at first light because it was too exposed and isolated. As for the Calvary of Illy, it was to be defended by the left wing of the 1st Corps. The vast bare acreage of undulating land stretched all the way from Sedan to the Ardennes forest; and the key to the situation was manifestly here, at the foot of the cross and the two lime trees, from which the whole of the surrounding area could be raked with gunfire.

Three other heavy reports rang out. Then came a complete salvo. This time a puff of smoke was seen to ascend from a small hill to the left of Saint-Menges.

"Aha!" said Jean. "It's our turn next."

Nothing happened though. As the men continued to stand there, quite motionless and with their arms at the order, their only amusement was to look at the splendid array of the 2nd Division, drawn up before Floing; its left, set back at right-angles to the remainder, was facing the Meuse so as to parry any attack from that quarter. On the eastern side, the 3rd Division was deployed as far as La Garenne woods, below Illy; while the 1st, after its battering at Beaumont, formed a second line of defence. The engineers had been hard at work throughout the night. Even now, with the Prussian shells beginning to fall, they were still digging trenches and raising gun-banks.

But just then a short burst of rifle-fire broke out in the lower part of Floing, and Captain Beaudoin's company was ordered to fall back two hundred yards. They had reached the middle of a huge cabbage-patch when all at once the captain barked: "Get down, all of you!"

They had to lie flat. The cabbages were covered with dew: it clung to the thick, greenish-gold leaves in drops as clear and bright as big diamonds.

"Range three hundred yards!" shouted the captain.

In response, Maurice rested the barrel of his rifle on a cabbage growing directly in front of him. They all had their eyes so close to the ground, though, that they couldn't see a thing: the earth

199

stretched away in front of them, quite featureless except for occasional areas of green vegetation. Maurice gave Jean a nudge and asked what the devil they were here for; and Jean, experienced in such matters, drew his attention to a battery which was being set up on a nearby mound. Obviously they had been assigned to this position with the object of giving supporting fire to the battery. Maurice's curiosity was so great that he stood up. He was eager to find out whether Honoré, and the other members of his team, were up on the mound; but the reserve artillery was farther back, in the shelter of a clump of trees.

"For God's sake, man!" bellowed Rochas. "Get down, will you!"

And Maurice had no sooner complied than a shell came whining past. From then on the shells came over without pause; their range was all wrong at first, completely overshooting the French battery, which had already begun to fire back. In addition a good many of them had their impact deadened by the softness of the soil and did not explode at all; so at first there was an incessant flow of jibes about the ineptness of the Kraut gunners.

"Dud display of fireworks if ever I saw one!" said Loubet.

"I reckon they must have pissed on 'em first," jeered Chouteau.

Even Lieutenant Rochas joined in.

"Didn't I tell you those good-for-nothings haven't the first idea how to fire a gun?"

But a shell burst ten yards away, covering the company with earth; and though Loubet tried to make a joke of it, by calling to his mate to get out their clothes brushes, Chouteau turned pale and said nothing. He had never been under fire before, nor Pache, nor Lapoulle either; Jean was the only member of the squad who had been. Eyelids blinked nervously, voices grew shrill, throats contracted. But Maurice retained sufficient control of himself to study his own reactions : he was not yet frightened, for he did not believe himself to be in danger; yet he felt an uneasy sensation in the pit of his stomach, while his mind went blank, incapable of consecutive thought. Moreover, amazed by the composure of the other men, his hopes rose, and he felt convinced that if only they could attack with the bayonet victory would be assured.

"Why," he muttered, "the place is full of flies."

Three times he had heard a sound like a flight of bees.

"No, no," said Jean, laughing, "that's bullets."

Again there was a faint hum of wings overhead, and the whole squad looked up, interested. The sound was irresistible, the men could not stay still. Loubet, making fun of Lapoulle's simple-mindedness, advised him:

"Listen, when you see a bullet coming, all you have to do is to hold your finger in front of your nose like this: it cuts the air, so that the bullet swerves aside."

"But I can't see them," said Lapoulle.

At this, there was a loud burst of laughter.

"What d'you mean, can't see them . . .? You want to keep your eyes open, booby . . .! Look, there's one . . . and another. You must have seen that one, it was bright green."

And, gazing straight ahead of him, Lapoulle held his finger in front of his nose, while Pache fingered the medallion he wore round his neck, wishing it was big enough to cover his whole chest like a breastplate.

Rochas, who had remained standing up, shouted to the men in his sarcastic way:

"It's all right ducking when you see a shell, lads, but with bullets it's no use, there are too many of them."

At that moment, a shell splinter shattered the head of a soldier lying in the front rank. He did not even cry out: there was a spurt of blood and brains, and that was all.

"Poor sod!" said Sergeant Sapin simply, calm but very pale.

But you could no longer hear yourself speak, and it was this terrible din that most upset Maurice. A nearby battery was firing incessantly, making a continual rumbling sound that shook the ground; but, worst of all, was the intolerable scream of machine-guns, rending the air. How long would they have to stay like this, stretched out amongst the cabbages, unable to see anything and not knowing what was going on? It was quite impossible to have any idea of how the battle was going, even to tell whether it was really an important one. All Maurice could see, standing out above the flat line of fields, was the round, wooded summit of Le Hattoy, far away in the distance and still unoccupied. But, so far, there was not a Prussian in sight, only puffs of smoke, rising in the air and floating for a moment in the sunlight. Looking over his shoulder, he was surprised to see, in a remote valley protected by steep hills, a peasant at work in the fields, patiently walking behind his plough, which was drawn by a big white horse. Why waste time? Just because there was a battle on, the corn wouldn't stop growing, people still had to live.

Growing impatient, Maurice rose to his feet; and, as he looked

201

around, he could see the batteries at Saint-Menges that were bombarding them capped by a dark haze of smoke; and, more significantly, the road from Saint-Albert, black with Prussians, looking for all the world like a swarm of invading insects. Then Jean caught hold of him by the leg, and pulled him down violently.

"Are you crazy? That's the way to get yourself killed!"

And Rochas shouted angrily:

"Can't you damn well keep down! You're a bright lot, trying to get yourselves killed before anyone's ordered you to!"

"But you're standing up, sir," said Maurice.

"Oh, that's different. I have to see what's going on."

Captain Beaudoin, too, boldly remained standing. But, since he was quite out of touch with his men, he never so much as opened his mouth: unable to stay still, he kept walking up and down from one end of the field to the other.

Still the waiting went on, and still nothing happened. Maurice felt almost suffocated by the weight of his haversack, which crushed his back and chest as he lay there in a position that became more and more uncomfortable as time went on. The men had received strict orders not to throw away their packs, except as a last resort.

Presently he asked Jean:

"Here, are we going to spend the rest of the day like this?"

"It could be. . . . At Solferino, they kept us lying like this, flat on our faces, for five hours – only then it was a field of carrots."

Then he added, like the practical fellow he was:

"Anyhow, what are you grousing about? It's not so bad here, and we shall have plenty of time to expose ourselves later on. Everybody has to take his turn. If we were all to get ourselves killed at the start, by the end there wouldn't be anyone left to finish things off."

"Hi," Maurice broke in, "just look at that smoke over La Hattoy. . . . They must have taken it. That'll soon liven things up!"

And for a time his curiosity, shot through with anxiety and a first flutter of fear, had found something to feed on. He kept his eyes fixed on the rounded summit of the hillock, the only rising ground in sight, and dominating the huge fields that ran away into the distance on a level with his eye. Le Hattoy was too far away from him to make out the men firing the guns that the Prussians had just brought up; in fact, all he could see were the puffs of smoke that rose, at each discharge, above the copse where the battery was concealed. As he had already realized, it was a serious matter for the enemy to have taken this position, which General Douay had just had to abandon, for it commanded the whole surrounding plain. Straight away, the battery had opened fire on the second division of the 7th Corps, cutting it to pieces. They had soon found the range, and, in quick succession, two of the gunners belonging to the French battery nearest to Beaudoin's company were killed. A shell splinter even wounded one of the men belonging to the company, a quartermaster-sergeant; his left heel had been shot away, and he was howling with the pain, as though suddenly demented.

"Can't you shut up, you idiot," shouted Rochas. "There's no need to yell like that, just because you've been hit in the foot!"

Immediately the man stopped screaming, and sat there, dazed and motionless, holding his foot in his hand.

And the formidable artillery duel continued, growing louder and louder above the heads of the regiments lying there, in that dreary, sweltering countryside, with not a soul to be seen beneath the blazing sun. There was only the thunderous roar of this destructive hurricane, surging above an empty solitude. And for hour after hour it would go on and on. But the superiority of the German artillery soon became apparent. Almost all their percussion shells exploded, at a tremendous distance; whereas the French shells, detonated by fuse and with a much shorter range, more often than not exploded in the air before reaching their target. And all they could do was to go on lying there, pressing themselves to the earth in an effort to make themselves as small as possible, without even the relief, the deafening intoxication, of firing their rifles, for in that vast empty expanse there was no one to shoot at!

"Aren't we ever going to get a chance to shoot?" Maurice kept saying, almost beside himself. "I'd give a hundred sous just to set eyes on one of the sods. It's maddening having to lie here being machine-gunned, without a chance to answer back."

"Hang on, our time will come," Jean told him, calm as ever.

But the sound of galloping horses on their left made them turn round. They recognized General Douay, accompanied by his staff. He had hurried over to find out how his troops were standing up to the terrible bombardment from Le Hattoy. He seemed to be satisfied, and was giving some orders, when General Bourgain-Desfeuilles suddenly emerged from a sunken road. The latter, a real barrack-yard soldier, was trotting about, heedless of the hail of bullets, sticking to the routine he acquired in Africa and refusing to learn from experience. He was bawling and gesticulating just like Rochas:

"I'm ready for them, just you wait till we get to close quarters!"

Then, seeing General Douay, he rode over to him.

"Is it true, sir, this story of the marshal being wounded?"

"Unfortunately, it is. . . . I've just had a note from General Ducrot, informing me that the marshal had appointed him as his successor."

"Oh, so it's to be General Ducrot . . .! And what are his orders?"

The general shrugged his shoulders despairingly. Ever since yesterday he had felt convinced the army was finished; in vain he had insisted that Saint-Menges and Illy should be occupied, to secure the retreat to Mézières.

"Ducrot now accepts our plan, and all the troops are to be concentrated on the Illy plain."

And again he shrugged his shoulders, implying that it was already too late. The noise of the guns drowned his words, but Maurice had grasped their meaning all too clearly, and felt utterly dismayed. So Marshal MacMahon was wounded, General Ducrot was taking his place and the whole army to the north of Sedan was in retreat! Yet the wretched soldiers who had to risk their lives were quite unaware of these serious matters, and, purely as a result of an accident, the whole ghastly business was to be handed over to the whim of a new commander! He could sense the confusion, the utter disarray the army was falling into, leaderless, without a plan, pulled in every direction, while the Germans, with the disciplined precision of a machine, made straight for their objective.

General Bourgain-Desfeuilles was already almost out of sight when General Douay, having just received a new message that had been brought to him by a hussar covered with dust, yelled to him to come back. His voice was so loud, so full of surprise and emotion, that he was able to make himself heard above the noise of the artillery.

"General, it's not Ducrot who's taking command, it's de Wimpffen . . .! Yes, he turned up yesterday, right in the middle of the break-through at Beaumont, to replace de Failly as commander of the 5th Corps. . . . He says he had received a letter from the Minister of War, appointing him as commander of the army in the event of the post becoming vacant. . . . And there's to be no more retreating. His orders are to win back our first positions and defend them."

204

General Bourgain-Desfeuilles listened to him in wide-eyed astonishment.

"Good God!" he said at length, "we might have known. . . . All I can say is, to hell with the lot of them!"

And he galloped off, not really worried in the slightest, for he regarded the war simply as the quickest way of getting promoted to the command of a division, and his one concern was to get this wretched campaign over as soon as possible, since everybody was already fed up with it.

To the soldiers in Beaudoin's company the whole thing was a joke. Maurice said nothing, but he agreed with Chouteau and Loubet who were cynically playing the fool. This way, that way, what difference does it make! Why, they're all in it up to their necks, and all just looking after number one! With leaders like this lot, we might as well have stayed at home in bed! Three commanders-in-chief in less than two hours, three gormless idiots that haven't the slightest idea what to do, and all giving different orders! No, really, it's enough to make God himself go off the handle! And once again the inevitable accusations of treachery were revived: Ducrot and de Wimpffen were out to get Bismarck's three million francs, the same as MacMahon.

General Douay had stayed behind, apart from his staff, gazing into the distance at the Prussian lines, in a mood of profound sadness. For a long time he examined Le Hattoy, from where the shells were falling almost at his feet. Then, turning towards the plain of Illy, he summoned an officer, and dispatched him with orders to the 5th Corps, which, on the previous day, he had asked General de Wimpffen to let him have, and which now formed his liaison with General Ducrot's left flank. And they distinctly heard him say:

"If the Prussians capture the calvary, we shouldn't be able to hang on here for an hour . . . we should be thrown back on Sedan."

And, with that, he rode away, disappearing with his escort round a bend in the sunken road; whereupon the firing redoubled. They must have seen him. The shells, which had so far only been coming from the front, were now pouring in from the left as well. These came from the batteries at Frénois, and another mounted in the Iges peninsula, whose line of fire crossed that of the Le Hattoy guns. The whole plateau of Algeria was swept by them, so that now the position of the company was becoming terrible. The men, already concerned with what was happening in front of them, now had this further anxiety behind them. In quick succession, three men were killed; two, who had been wounded, were screaming. And it was in this way that Sergeant Sapin met the death he had been expecting. Turning round, he had seen a shell coming towards him, but too late to avoid it. He merely said:

"Here it comes!"

On his small face, with its large, fine eyes, there was no trace of fear, only sadness. His stomach was ripped open.

"Don't leave me here," he moaned, "get me to an ambulance. . . . For pity's sake, get me to an ambulance."

Intending to make him be quiet, Rochas was on the point of telling him brutally that, with a wound like that, there was no point in risking two men's lives, when he suddenly took pity on him.

"There, there, lad," he said. "Hang on a bit till the stretcher-bearers get here."

But the wretched man went on, tears running down his face, overcome at the thought of the happiness oozing away with his blood:

"Get me out of it, get me out of it. . . ."

And Captain Beaudoin, whose exasperated nerves could no longer stand the sound of his moaning, called for two volunteers to carry him away to a nearby wood. Before any of the others could move, Chouteau and Loubet sprang to their feet, seized the sergeant by the arms and legs and bore him away at the double. But, before they had got halfway, they felt his body suddenly go stiff, and with a final gasp he expired.

"Look, he's dead," declared Loubet. "We may as well leave him here."

But Chouteau insisted furiously:

"Keep going, you lazy good-for-nothing! If we leave him here, we shall only be called back!"

And they went on as far as the wood, where they dropped the body at the foot of a tree and made off. They were not seen again until evening.

The firing was growing louder, the nearest battery had just been reinforced by two more guns and, in the growing din, Maurice was overwhelmed with fear, crazy fear. To begin with he had not experienced this cold sweat, this horrible fainting sensation at the pit of his stomach, this irresistible need to get up and rush away as fast as he could, screaming. Probably even now, it was simply a reflex reaction, as often happens with nervous, sensitive people. But Jean, who was watching him closely, and could tell from the uneasy, wavering look in his eyes that he was in a critical state, seized him in his powerful arms and held him close. Then, quietly, in a fatherly way, he began swearing at him, trying to make him feel ashamed by the violence of his language, for he knew that, sometimes, the best way to restore a man's courage was to kick him hard. Some of the others were also quaking with fear, and Pache, his eyes full of tears, kept moaning to himself, quietly, helplessly, like a baby that can't stop crying. Then Lapoulle was so ill with such terrific churning in his stomach that, before he could reach the hedge, he had to pull down his trousers, whereupon they all started booing him, pelting him with clods of earth as he squatted there, his nakedness exposed to the shells and bullets. Several of the others suffered in the same way, and relieved themselves to an accompaniment of the coarsest pleasantries, which served to restore everyone's courage.

"You bloody coward," Jean was saying to Maurice. "You're surely not going to shit yourself like them. . . . If you don't pull yourself together I'll fetch you such a clout, my boy."

Then suddenly, just as these insults were beginning to take effect, there, four hundred yards in front of them, they noticed a dozen or so men in dark uniforms emerging from a little wood. It was the Prussians, at last! They could recognize them by the spikes on their helmets, the first Prussians they had seen since the beginning of the campaign, and well within range. This first squad was followed by others; and, just ahead of them, they could see the little spurts of dust thrown up by the falling shells. The whole thing was neat and precise. There was a trim elegance about the Prussians, like rows of little lead soldiers drawn up on parade. Then, as the rain of shells grew heavier, they withdrew, disappearing once more behind the trees.

But, having once seen them, Beaudoin's company was convinced they were still there. Their rifles went off of their own accord. Maurice was the first to pull the trigger. Jean, Pache, Lapoulle, and the others followed suit. As no orders had been given, the captain tried to stop the firing, and only refrained from doing so when Rochas pointed out emphatically the value of giving the men this safety-valve. So they went on firing, using up the ammunition they had been dragging about for the past month without ever getting a shot! Maurice especially was cheered by it; the deafening noise provided an outlet for his fears. The outskirts of the wood

207

had a mournful appearance, not a leaf stirred, not a Prussian showed himself; and they went on firing at the motionless trees.

Looking up for a moment, Maurice was surprised to see Colonel de Vineuil, seated on his charger, man and beast impassive as figures carved out of stone. Facing the enemy under the hail of bullets, the colonel waited. The whole of the 106th must have withdrawn to this area, other companies were already lying in the neighbouring fields, the firing came nearer and nearer. And the young man also noticed, a little to the rear, the regimental colours, borne by a burly second-lieutenant. But it was no longer a mere ghost of a flag, half hidden in the morning mist; in the hot sunlight the golden eagle glittered and, battle-stained though it was, the vivid colour of the silk tricolour shone bright. In the wind caused by the bombardment, it streamed out against the blue sky like a flag of victory.

Now they had begun to fight, why shouldn't they win? And Maurice and the rest of them furiously used up their ammunition, firing at the distant wood, producing a steady, silent rain of tiny branches.

III

HENRIETTE was unable to sleep. The thought of her husband at
Bazeilles, so near the German lines, tormented her. In vain she kept
telling herself that he had promised to come back at the first sign
of danger; and every few moments she pricked her ears, thinking
she could hear him. Towards ten o'clock, instead of getting into
bed, she opened the window and, leaning on the sill, lost all count
of time.

It was so dark that she could scarcely make out the Rue des
Voyards, a narrow passage winding its way between the ancient
houses. In the distance, towards the College, the one street lamp
was a hazy star. A smell of saltpetre rose from the cellars, a cat
miaowed angrily, and she could hear the heavy footsteps of a
soldier who had lost his way. Behind her the whole town of Sedan
was full of unaccustomed noises, furious galloping, endless rumbling, that faded away like the rustle of death. Her heart was beating
wildly, but though she strained her ears to listen she still could not
hear her husband's footsteps turning into the street.

As the hours went by, she grew more and more uneasy about the
lights she could see, far away in the country beyond the ramparts.
It was so dark that she kept trying to make out where places were.
That large white expanse over there must surely be flooded
meadows, and that fire she had seen, shooting up into the sky and
dying down again, must have been at La Marfée. And all around
other fires were burning, at Pont-Maugis, at Noyers, at Frénois,
mysteriously flickering above crowds of people swarming in the
darkness. And then, on top of this, the unusual sounds made her
shudder, the tramp of people on the march, animals panting, the
clash of swords, a vast cavalcade in that pit of darkness. Suddenly,
a single cannon shot rang out, overwhelming, terrifying, followed by
complete silence. It froze the blood in her veins. What could it be?
Doubtless a signal that some movement had succeeded, announcing
that they were ready, that the sun would soon be up.

Towards two o'clock Henriette flung herself on the bed, without

209

undressing or even bothering to close the window. She was over-come with fatigue and anxiety. What was the matter with her, that her teeth should be chattering as though she had a fever – she, usually so calm and light-footed that one scarcely knew she was alive? And she fell into a deep, uneasy sleep, haunted by the per-sistent feeling of misfortune that hovered in the darkness. Then, suddenly, in the depths of this restless sleep, the guns began again, dull, far away detonations; and this time they went on and on, stubbornly, at regular intervals. She sat up, trembling. Where was she? At first, the bedroom seemed to be so full of smoke that she did not recognize it; then she realized that it must be the mist, blowing in from the river. The noise of the cannon grew louder. She leapt out of bed and ran to the window, listening.

The town clock was striking four. Shafts of strange, ugly day-light were struggling to pierce the russet-coloured fog. It was still too dark to see anything. She could not even make out the College buildings a few yards away. Where was the firing, for heaven's sake? Her first thought was for her brother Maurice, for the sound of the guns was so muffled that it seemed to come from the North, beyond the town. Then she decided that the firing was there, right in front of her. Yes, there could be no doubt about it; and she began worrying about her husband. Yes, surely, it must be at Bazeilles. Yet, for a minute or two, she felt reassured, for now the explosions seemed to be coming from the right . . . perhaps the fighting was at Donchery, where she knew they hadn't succeeded in blowing up the bridge. The difficulty of making up her mind was driving her crazy: Donchery? Bazeilles? With this incessant buzzing in her ears, how on earth could she tell? Presently her anxiety reached such a pitch that she felt she couldn't wait a moment longer. The urgent need to find out made her tremble and, throwing a shawl over her shoulders, she left the house in search of news.

Outside, in the Rue des Voyards, the town was still so dark beneath the dense, enveloping mist that for a moment Henriette was at a loss. The early morning light had not yet penetrated as far as the damp pavement between these old, smoke-grimed houses. In a café in the Rue au Beurre, she caught sight of two drunken Turcos, sitting with a prostitute beside a flickering candle. It was not until she turned into the Rue Maqua that she found any signs of life : soldiers furtively hurrying along in the darkness, deserters, perhaps, looking for somewhere to hide; a tall cavalry man, who had lost his way and was banging angrily at the doors, looking for his officer;

a group of townsfolk sweating with fear at the thought that they might be too late, then finally deciding to pile into a cab, in the hope of getting to Bouillon, a town across the Belgian border, to which half the population of Sedan had emigrated during the last couple of days. Instinctively, she was making for the Sub-Préfecture, where she felt sure of being able to obtain information; and, anxious to avoid meeting anyone, she decided to cut through the side streets. But the Rue du Four and the Rue des Laboureurs were both blocked by artillery, a long train of guns, with their limbers and forage-waggons, that must have been parked there out of the way the previous day, and seemed to have been forgotten. There was not even a soldier on guard. The sight of all these pitifully useless guns, abandoned in an empty side street, made her feel cold with apprehension. She had to retrace her steps through the Place du Collège, back to the Grande-Rue where, in front of the Hotel de l'Europe, orderlies were walking horses up and down, waiting for their officers, whose loud voices could be heard from the garishly lighted dining-room. In the Place du Rivage and the Place Turenne, the crowds were thicker, groups of anxious people, women and children mixed up with disorderly bodies of frightened soldiers; and she caught sight of a general, swearing at the top of his voice, who came out of the Croix d'Or Hotel and galloped away, scattering people left and right. For a moment it seemed as though she meant to go to the Town Hall, but eventually she turned into the Rue du Pont-de-Meuse, which led to the Sub-Prefecture.

Never before had Sedan impressed her as being such a tragic city as it did now, sunk in fog beneath the unclean morning light. The houses seemed dead; many of them empty and abandoned in the last two days, others hermetically sealed in contrast to the sort of frightened insomnia around them. The very morning itself shuddered with fear, with its still half-deserted streets, peopled only by anxious ghosts, traversed by sudden departures, amidst the piles of rubbish left over from the previous day. As the light grew stronger the town was becoming more congested, submerged in disaster. It was half-past five; the noise of the guns, muffled by the high black walls, could scarcely be heard.

At the Sub-Prefecture, Henriette was acquainted with the concierge's daughter Rose, a pretty, fair-haired, frail little creature who worked at the Delaherche mill. She went straight to the concierge's office. The mother was not there, but Rose greeted her in a friendly manner.

"You must excuse us, ma'am, but we're almost worn out. Mama has just this minute gone to lie down. There's been such a continual stream of people that we've been kept on the go all night."

And without waiting to be questioned she went on talking and talking, excited by all the extraordinary things she had seen since yesterday.

"The marshal at least managed to get some sleep. But the poor Emperor, you'd never believe what he's been through . . .! Just imagine, yesterday evening I was upstairs, helping get the beds ready, and as I was going into the room next to his dressing-room, I heard the most terrible groans, as if somebody was dying. I stood there trembling all over, terrified, for I knew it must be the Emperor. . . . It seems he's got some horrible illness that makes him cry out like that. He manages not to when there are people about, but when he's by himself he can't help himself. He just shouts and groans, it's enough to make your hair stand on end."

"Do you know where the fighting is this morning?" Henriette asked, in an attempt to interrupt her.

But Rose simply waved the question aside, and continued:

"After that, I wanted to know what was happening. So during the night I went upstairs four or five times, and listened at the door. . . . He kept on groaning, almost without stopping. I'm quite sure he never closed his eyes all night. . . . Mustn't it be terrible to suffer like that, with all the worries he must have on his mind? You simply can't imagine what a scurry and bustle there was, you'd think they were all out of their minds – more people arriving every moment, doors banging, people angry, others crying, officers drinking out of bottles and getting into bed with their boots on . . . a regular mad-house. Really, the Emperor's better than any of them, and makes the least fuss, just hidden away so that no one can hear him groaning."

Then, as Henriette repeated her question:

"Where they're fighting? Why, at Bazeilles. It's been going on since first thing this morning . . .! A soldier arrived on horseback to tell the marshal, and he immediately went to the Emperor's room to inform him. . . . The marshal left about ten minutes ago, and I'm pretty sure the Emperor means to catch him up. . . . They're getting him ready now. . . . I saw them a moment ago, combing his hair and dolling him up, putting all sorts of stuff on his face."

212

But Henriette, having found out what she wanted to know, made her escape.

"Thank you, Rose. I must hurry."

And the young girl obligingly accompanied her as far as the street, calling after her :

"I'm glad I could be of service to you, Madame Weiss. With you, I know one can always speak freely."

Henriette made her way back to the Rue des Voyards as quickly as she could. She was convinced that she would find her husband waiting for her, and imagining how worried he would be if he found she was not there, she quickened her pace. As she approached the house she looked up, expecting to see him leaning out of the window, watching for her to get back. But, although the window was still wide open, there was no one there. And going upstairs, glancing hurriedly into the three rooms, she was seized with panic to find them empty, save for the icy fog amid the incessant roar of the guns. She went back to the window for a moment. Now that she knew what was happening, although the wall of morning mist was still impenetrable she could envisage quite clearly the battle that was being fought at Bazeilles; the rattle of the machine-guns, the deafening volleys from the French batteries, answering the distant fire of the German guns. It sounded as though the explosions were coming nearer, as though every moment the battle was growing worse.

Why hadn't Weiss returned? He'd promised so explicitly that he would, at the first sign of an attack ! And her uneasiness increased, she began imagining what could have prevented him : the road had been cut, the bombardment made it too dangerous, perhaps, even, something terrible had happened to him. But she brushed the thought aside, pinning her hopes on action. For a moment she thought of setting out to look for him. But she could not make up her mind. Supposing they missed one another on the way, what would become of her? Or supposing he arrived home and didn't find her there? He'd be worried to death. Apart from these doubts, the temerity of visiting Bazeilles at a time like this seemed to her to be perfectly natural, not at all heroic, merely befitting her role as an active woman, silently determined to do what was necessary to run her household properly. Wherever her husband was, she must be with him – it was as simple as that.

Then, with a sudden gesture, she turned away from the window, and said aloud :

"Why, M. Delaherche. . . . I must go and find out. . . ."

She had just remembered that the mill-owner had also spent the night at Bazeilles. If he had returned, he would have news for her. She hurried downstairs. Instead of going into the Rue des Voyards, she crossed the narrow courtyard in front of the house and took the passage that led to the huge factory buildings, whose splendid façade faced the Rue Maqua. As she came out into what had once been the great central garden, but was now paved over, except for a lawn surrounded with superb trees, great elms planted in the previous century, she was astonished to see a sentry posted outside the closed doors of a shed. Then she remembered : yesterday she had heard that all the funds belonging to the 7th Corps had been deposited there. And she thought that all this gold, millions of francs, people said, was hidden away in this shed, while all around men were killing one another, made a strange impression on her. Then, as she was going up the backstairs to Gilberte's room, she had another surprise; an encounter so utterly unforeseen that she retreated to the bottom of the stairs, scarcely knowing whether she dared knock at her door. An army captain had hurried past her, swift as a ghost, and immediately disappeared; but not before she had recognized him; it was a man she had seen in Gilberte's house at Charleville, when she was still only Madame Maginot. Stepping back into the courtyard she looked up at the two tall windows of the bedroom, the blinds of which were still drawn; then decided to go upstairs all the same.

Reaching the first floor, she intended to knock at the door of the dressing-room, like an intimate friend in the habit of dropping in for a morning chat. But, in the haste of departure, the door had not been properly shut, she only had to push it to find herself in the dressing-room, then in the bedroom itself. It was a room with a very high ceiling, from which hung long red velvet curtains completely surrounding the big double bed. And not a sound, only the clammy silence of a night of happiness; nothing but the peaceful, scarcely perceptible murmur of breathing and the faint odour of lilac scent.

"Gilberte !" Henriette called softly.

The young woman had immediately fallen asleep again, and there she lay, in the feeble light coming through the red window blinds, her pretty little round head, which had slipped from the pillow, resting on one naked arm amongst the tumbled tresses of her black hair.

214

"Gilberte !"

Without opening her eyes, she stirred restlessly, murmuring :
"Yes, yes, goodbye . . . please, please. . . ."

Then, looking up and recognizing Henriette, she exclaimed :
"Why, it's you. . . . Whatever's the time . . .?"

Embarrassed to discover that it was barely six o'clock, she tried
to disguise her dismay by jokingly remarking that this was no time
to wake people up. And when Gilberte asked her about her husband,
she replied :

"But he's not back yet. I'm not expecting him before seven. . . .
Why do you want him back so soon?"

Seeing her face, still drowsy with happiness, Henriette insisted :
"Don't you realize they've been fighting at Bazeilles since early
this morning? I'm worried about my husband. . . ."

"Oh, but you shouldn't be, my dear," Gilberte exclaimed. "Mine
is so cautious that if there'd been the slightest danger, he'd have
been back long ago. . . . Since he's not, you can put your mind at
rest."

This reflection impressed Henriette, for it was quite true that
Delaherche was not the man to run unnecessary risks. Heartened
at the thought, she got up, pulled back the curtains and raised the
blinds, and the sun, which was beginning to break through the mist,
tinging it with gold, lit up the whole room. Now, through the half-
opened window, the sound of the guns could be distinctly heard in
this big warm room, recently so shut in and stifling. Propped up
on her elbow amongst the pillows, Gilberte looked up at the sky.

"So they're fighting, then," she murmured.

Her nightdress had slipped from one shoulder, revealing the
delicate pink flesh beneath the scattered strands of hair, and now
that she was awake her body exuded a penetrating odour, the odour
of love.

"Do they really have to start fighting so early, my God? How
ridiculous it is, all this fighting !"

But Henriette had just caught sight of a pair of military gloves,
left behind on the bed table, and seeing her start Gilberte blushed.
She held out her arms, and drew her towards her with a shy,
caressing gesture. Then, hiding her face on her shoulder, she said :

"I felt sure you knew about it, that you'd seen him. . . . Don't
judge me too harshly, my dear, he's an old friend. Don't you
remember, in the old days at Charleville, I told you how fond of
him I was?"

Lowering her voice she continued, speaking tenderly and half-laughing :

"Yesterday, when I saw him again, he begged so hard. . . . Just imagine, this morning he'll be fighting, perhaps he'll be killed. . . . Could I really refuse?"

She spoke with such tender gaiety that it sounded heroic and delightful, this last gift of pleasure, this one night of happiness on the eve of battle. And despite her embarrassment, the thought of it made her smile, artlessly as a little bird. How could she have had the heart to refuse him, seeing that circumstances conspired to make it all so easy?

"Do you blame me?"

Henriette listened to her gravely. Such matters surprised her, for she could not understand them. She must be different. All morning her heart had been with her husband and her brother, out there amongst the bullets. How could anybody sleep so peacefully, look so gay and tender, when those one loved were in danger?

"But what about your husband, my dear, and this fellow himself? Doesn't it break your heart to be parted from them . . .? Don't you realize that at any minute they may be brought back wounded?"

With a swift movement of her enchanting bare arm, Gilberte brushed the ghastly picture aside.

"Oh heavens, whatever are you saying, you wicked creature? Do you want to spoil my whole morning . . .? No, no, no, I refuse to think about it, it's too sad !"

Despite herself, Henriette could not help smiling. She remembered, when they were children, how Gilberte's father, Naval Commander de Vineuil, had been appointed Director of Customs at Charleville on account of his wounds; and how he had sent his daughter to a farm near Chêne-Populeux, worried at the sound of her cough, haunted by the memory of his wife, who had just died of tuberculosis. The little girl was only nine years old, but already wildly flirtatious, always wanting to act, dressing up as the queen, decking herself out with bits of material, saving up the silver paper from chocolates to make crowns and bracelets. And later on, when she had married M. Maginot, a forestry inspector, at the age of twenty, she had still been the same. She had never liked Mézières, shut away behind its ramparts, and continued to live in Charleville, enjoying its easy-going life and gay parties. Since her father had died, she had enjoyed complete freedom, with an accommodating husband who was such an utter nonentity that she did not even feel remorse. At the time, local gossip had credited her with plenty of lovers, but although she had always been surrounded by army officers as a result of her father's early connections and her relationship to Colonel de Vineuil, her only real affair had been with Captain Beaudoin. She was neither vicious nor ill-natured, but simply liked enjoying herself; and, in taking a lover, she had most likely simply been yielding to her irresistible need to be admired and gay.

"It was very bad of you to take up with him again," Henriette eventually said, in her serious way.

At which, with one of her pretty, affectionate gestures, Gilberte pressed her hand to her mouth.

"But, my love, I simply couldn't help it, and it was only this once. . . . Nowadays, as you know, I'd rather die than deceive my present husband!"

Neither of them said any more, and though they were so unalike, they embraced affectionately. They could both feel the beating of their hearts, even if the language they spoke was so different, the one full of happiness, always ready to give and share, the other absorbed by a single, steady passion, with all the silent heroism of a steadfast soul.

"They really are fighting," Gilberte exclaimed. "I must hurry up and get dressed."

During their silence, the noise of the explosions did, indeed, seem to grow louder. She jumped out of bed and, without calling her maid, hurriedly began dressing, ready to go downstairs and receive visitors if necessary. As she finished doing her hair, there was a knock at the door, and she ran to open it, recognizing the voice of her mother-in-law, Mme. Delaherche.

"But of course you can come in, mother dear."

Thoughtless as ever, she ushered her into the room, oblivious of the pair of gloves that were still lying on the night table. In vain Henriette rushed to pick them up and hide them behind an armchair: Mme. Delaherche must have seen them, for she stood there for some moments, scarcely able to breathe. Involuntarily she glanced round the room, and her gaze came to rest on the red curtained bed, which had not yet been made.

"So it was Mme. Weiss who came up to call you. . . . You managed to sleep then, my dear. . . ."

Clearly, she had not come simply to say this. Oh this marriage that her son had insisted upon making, against her wishes, when he was already in his fifties and had been unsatisfactorily married for twenty years to a sullen, skinny creature . . . he, who had been so sensible up to then, only to be swept away now by this youthful passion for this pretty widow, so flighty and gay! She had been determined to keep an eye on things, but she could scarcely have expected the past to turn up like this! Should she say anything? Already her presence in the house was little more than a silent reproach, always shut up in her room, leading a life of the strictest piety. This time, however, it was such a serious matter that she decided to tell her son about it.

Blushing, Gilberte replied:

"Yes, I managed to get a few hours of good sleep. . . . You know Jules isn't back yet . . .?"

Mme. Delaherche cut her short with a wave of her hand. Ever since the guns had started booming she had been anxiously awaiting her son's return, but she refused to betray her fears. Then suddenly she remembered the reason for her coming upstairs.

"Your uncle, the colonel, has sent Major Bouroche with a note, written in pencil, asking whether it wouldn't be possible for us to have a first-aid post here. . . . He knows we have plenty of room in the factory, and I have already put the yard and the drying-room at their disposal. . . . Only, you ought to come down."

"Yes, yes, at once," said Henriette, reproaching herself. "We must come and help."

Gilberte herself appeared to be very excited by the thought of playing a new part, as a hospital nurse. She quickly snatched up a piece of lace to tie up her hair, and followed the other two women downstairs. As they reached the great portico, they could see through the open gates a crowd gathering in the street. A low-slung waggon was slowly approaching, drawn by a single horse, which a lieutenant in the Zouaves was leading by the bridle; and they assumed this was the first wounded man being brought in.

"That's right, bring him in here, please!"

But they soon realized their mistake. The wounded man lying on the floor of the waggon was none other than Marshal MacMahon. His left leg had been almost shot away, and they were taking him to the Sub-Prefecture, after putting a rough dressing on his wound in a gardener's little house. He was bareheaded and half undressed, the gold braid on his uniform dulled with dust and blood. He said nothing, but, raising his head, he looked at them with a vague expression in his eyes. Then, catching sight of the three women, stunned by the terrible sight of the commander-in-chief struck down at the very start of the battle, he bowed slightly to them and gave them a faint, fatherly smile. Some of the onlookers took off their hats; others were busily explaining that General Ducrot had just been appointed commander-in-chief. It was half-past seven.

"But what's happened to the Emperor?" Henriette asked a book-seller, standing outside the door of his shop.

"He passed by almost an hour ago," the man replied. "I followed him, and saw him leave by the Balan gate. . . . They say he's been wounded in the head by a bullet."

But this angered the grocer on the other side of the street:

"Get along with you, that's all lies! It's only brave men that get killed!"

Near the Place du Collège the waggon disappeared amongst the increasing crowd, amongst whom the most extraordinary stories about the battle were already circulating. The fog had cleared, and the streets were filled with sunlight.

But someone in the courtyard shouted roughly:

"It's not out there you're needed, ladies, but in here!"

The three women returned to the yard, where they found Major Bouroche, who had already thrown his uniform into a corner and put on a large white apron. With his enormous head, his wiry, bristling hair, his snub-nosed face gleaming with energy, and above all, that huge, still spotless apron, he presented such a terrifying appearance that they were only too ready to do anything he asked them, almost knocking one another down in their efforts to please him.

"There's simply nothing here. . . . Get me some bandages. . . . Find some more mattresses. . . . Show my men where the pump is. . . ."

The women rushed hither and thither, waiting on him hand and foot.

It had been a good idea to select the factory as a hospital. In the first place there was the drying-room, a huge room with windows all along one side, where a hundred beds could easily be installed; and, next to it, was a shed which was just right for an operating theatre: a long table had been brought in, the pump was only a few feet away, and those who were not dangerously wounded could wait outside on the lawn. Moreover it was pleasantly situated, beneath the shade of the fine old elm trees.

Bouroche had decided straight away to establish his hospital in Sedan, foreseeing the inevitable massacre and the terrible attack the enemy would launch against it. He had been content to leave two field ambulances with the 7th Corps, to the rear of Floing, where the wounded could receive first-aid before being sent on to him. A squad of stretcher-bearers would also remain there, with orders to collect the wounded under fire and take them to the waggons they had with them. Apart from two assistants he had left on the battlefield, Bouroche had brought with him his entire staff, two majors and three assistants, who would doubtless be able to deal with all the operations, and, in addition, three dispensers and a dozen nurses.

Yet he remained like a bear with a sore head, for he could do nothing unless he was in a passion.

"What the devil d'you think you're up to? Put those mattresses closer together. . . . If necessary, we can put some straw down, over there in the corner."

The guns went on rumbling, he knew that at any moment more carts filled with bleeding flesh would be arriving, and, furiously, he went on getting the room ready. In the operating shed other preparations were being made : boxes of dressings and medical supplies were opened and laid out on a shelf, packets of lint, slings, compresses, bandages, splints; while on another shelf, in addition to a large pot of wax ointment and a bottle of chloroform, the instruments were set out, probes, forceps, knives, chisels, saws, a whole arsenal of gleaming instruments for piercing, probing, slashing, cutting. But there were no basins.

"Surely you must have some pans, buckets, cauldrons? Anything will do. . . . We don't want to be smothered in blood. . . . And sponges, try to get hold of some sponges!"

Mme. Delaherche hurried off, and returned with three servants, carrying all the receptacles she had been able to find. Gilberte beckoned to Henriette to come and look at the instruments, shuddering as she pointed them out to her. And holding each other's hands, they stood there without saying a word, mutely expressing the terror and anxious pity that overwhelmed them.

"Imagine, my dear, having to have a limb amputated!"

"Poor creatures!"

Bouroche had just put a mattress on the operating table, and was covering it with a sheet of oilcloth, when they heard the sound of horses beneath the portico. It was the first ambulance arriving.

But there were only ten lightly wounded men in it, sitting facing one another, most of them with their arms in slings, some hit in the head and wearing bandages. They were helped down, and the doctors began their work.

As she was gently assisting a young soldier, who had been shot through the shoulder, to pull off his greatcoat, Henriette noticed his regimental number.

"So you are from the 106th! Do you belong to Captain Beaudoin's company?"

No, he was in Ravaud's company. All the same, he knew Corporal Jean Macquart, and he was pretty sure his squad had not yet been in action. And vague as it was, this information was enough to cheer the young woman up : her brother was alive, if only she could embrace her husband, whom she was still expecting to turn up at any moment, how relieved she would feel. At this moment, Henriette, chancing to look up, was amazed to see Delaherche, surrounded by a group of people a few paces away, describing the terrible risks he had run on the way from Bazeilles to Sedan. How had he got here? She had not noticed him come in.

"Isn't my husband with you?"

But Delaherche, who was being questioned by his wife and his mother, told her to wait a moment, and went on with his story :

"Between Bazeilles and Balan, I was almost killed about twenty times. There was a continual hail of bullets and shells . . .! I saw the Emperor there, a brave fellow. . . . Then, from Balan onwards, I just kept going. . . ."

"But my husband?" Henriette said, tugging at his arm.

"What, Weiss? Why, he stayed behind! He took a rifle from a dead soldier, and started fighting."

"Fighting? Whatever for?"

"Oh, he's crazy! As he refused to come with me, naturally I just left him."

Henriette gazed at him, her eyes fixed and staring. There was a moment's silence. Then, quite tranquilly, she made up her mind.

"Good, then I'm going to him."

But how could she? It was impossible, mad! Once more Delaherche described how the bullets and shells were sweeping the road. Gilberte seized her by the hand again, trying to prevent her, and old Mme. Delaherche did her best to convince her that she was being completely reckless. In her gentle, straightforward way, she merely repeated however :

"It's no use trying to stop me, I'm going."

And she persisted, accepting the black lace scarf that Gilberte was wearing. Still hoping to dissuade her, Delaherche finally declared that he would go with her, at least as far as the Balan gate. But he had just caught sight of the sentry, who, despite all the commotion of installing the hospital, was still walking up and down in front of the shed where the funds belonging to the 7th Corps were locked up; recalling this, he was seized with alarm, he went to make sure that all those millions of francs were still there. Meanwhile Henriette had already reached the porch.

"Do wait for me a minute. Upon my word, you're as crazy as your husband!"

Besides, another ambulance was just coming in, and they had to wait for it to pass. It was smaller than the first, with only two wheels, and the two men in it, who were badly wounded, were lying in pools of blood. The one they lifted out first, as carefully as they could, was little more than a mass of bleeding flesh; one hand smashed, his thigh ripped open by a shell splinter. The second one had his right leg completely crushed. And immediately, Bouroche, telling them to lay the latter on the operating table, began his first operation amidst all the coming and going of nurses and assistants. Sitting on the lawn, Mme. Delaherche and Gilberte were rolling bandages.

Outside, Delaherche caught up with Henriette.

"Now look, my dear Mme. Weiss, this is utter madness. How on earth do you hope to find your husband? He's certain not to be there any longer. He's probably set out across country, and is now making his way home. . . . I assure you, it's absolutely impossible to get to Bazeilles."

But she paid no attention to him, and, walking more quickly, turned into the Rue Ménil to get to the Balan gate. It was nearly nine o'clock, and Sedan no longer had that air of shivering darkness, of lonely groping, awakening beneath the early morning fog. The dark outlines of the houses stood out clearly in the sunlight, and dispatch riders were continually galloping through the streets, packed with anxious people. They crowded round the soldiers, some of whom had already returned, some slightly wounded, others gesticulating and shouting in a state of extraordinary nervous excitement. And yet, had it not been for the shutters over the shop windows and the dead house fronts with their lowered blinds, the town would still have had its more or less everyday appearance.

And then there was the firing, the unceasing firing, which made every stone in the place, the ground itself, the walls, even the slates on the roofs, tremble.

Delaherche was experiencing a most unpleasant inner struggle, torn between his duty as a decent man, urging him not to leave Henriette, on the one hand, and on the other, his terror at the thought of making his way back to Bazeilles through the shells. As they reached the Balan gate, they were separated by a stream of mounted officers, who were returning to the town, while at the gate itself a crush of people was waiting for news. He hurried hither and thither, looking for the young woman, but it was no use, she must have left the town and already be on her way to Bazeilles. And without pursuing his search any further, he was surprised to hear himself say aloud:

"Oh well, it can't be helped! She's really being too stupid!"

And, with this, Delaherche began wandering around the town, determined not to miss anything, yet beset by increasing anxiety. What was going to become of all this? If the army was defeated, wasn't the town bound to suffer terribly? But the answers to his questions remained obscure; too much depended upon what happened. None the less, he shuddered at the thought of what might happen to his factory, to his house in the Rue Maqua, although he had already stripped it of his most valuable belongings and hidden them somewhere safe. He made his way to the Town Hall, where he found the Municipal Council in permanent session; and he hung about there, without discovering anything new except that the battle was going very badly. The army no longer knew whom to obey, having been ordered to retreat by General Ducrot in the short time he was in command, then sent in to the attack by General de Wimpffen, who had just succeeded him. And this meaningless vacillation, all these positions abandoned and then having to be recaptured, the complete lack of planning and vigorous leadership were leading inevitably to disaster.

Delaherche now pushed on as far as the Sub-Prefecture, to find out if anything had been seen of the Emperor. But the only news he could get was about Marshal MacMahon: a surgeon had treated his wound, which was not serious, and now he was safe in bed. Then, towards eleven o'clock, still wandering around, he was held up for a moment in the Grande-Rue, outside the Hotel de l'Europe, by a slow procession of cavalrymen, covered with dust, their exhausted horses no longer even able to trot. At their head

223

he recognized the Emperor, who was returning after spending four hours on the field of battle. Evidently, death had rejected him. The anxiety of his journey through defeat had made the sweat pour down his face and washed away his make-up and melted his waxed moustache, while his ashen face had assumed the mournful, bewildered expression of a man on the point of death. An officer, who had dismounted outside the hotel, turned to the group of people who collected and explained how they had come, from La Moncelle to Givonne, along the little valley filled with soldiers belonging to the 1st Corps, whom the Saxons had driven back across the stream; and after this, they had taken the sunken road leading from Givonne, where there were already such masses of people that, even if the Emperor had wanted to return to the front, he would have had the greatest difficulty in doing so. In any case, what was the use?

As Delaherche was listening to these details, a violent explosion shook the whole neighbourhood. It was a shell that had just demolished a chimney stack in the Rue Sainte-Barbe, near the Keep. There was a mad scramble, women began shrieking, and no sooner had he flung himself down against a wall than another explosion broke all the windows in a nearby house. This was becoming terrible. What if they were to bomb Sedan? And he set off at full speed for the Rue Maqua, so obsessed with the desire to find out what was happening that, without stopping, he rushed upstairs and climbed out on to the roof, where he had built himself a platform from which one could see over the whole town and the country around.

Immediately, he was reassured. The battle was going on above the town, the German batteries at La Marfée and Frénois were firing over the houses into the plain of Algeria; and he found himself taking an interest in the flight of the shells, in the huge smoky curves that they drew in the sky above Sedan, like invisible birds leaving a slender trail of grey feathers. At first it seemed that the few shells that had fallen upon the houses round about were the result of misfires; as yet, they were not bombarding the town. Then, watching them more closely, he realized that they must be in response to the few shots fired from the city's guns. He turned towards the North, and examined the citadel, that great mass of complicated and formidable fortifications, the blackened surface of the walls, the green slopes of the ramparts, the geometrical maze of bastions, especially the three giant forts, the Écossais, the Grand

Jardin and the Rochette; and further on, like some cyclopean prolongation to the West, the Nassau fort, followed by the Palatinate
fort, above the suburb of Ménil. They made a melancholy impression upon him, an impression both of vastness and of childishness.
What purpose did they serve now, with these cannons that could
hurl their missiles so easily from one end of the sky to the other?
Besides, the fortress was unarmed, it had neither the requisite guns
nor the munitions, nor the men. It was scarcely three weeks since
the governor had started organizing a volunteer militia to man the
few guns that were still in working order. And this was why only
three guns were firing from the Palatinate fort, while at the Paris
gate there were at least half a dozen. The trouble was, each gun had
only seven or eight rounds of ammunition, so that they had to
economize, firing only one shot every half-hour, and then merely
as a point of honour, for the shells did not carry, but fell in the
meadow opposite. And so the enemy batteries only replied at long
intervals, disdainfully, as though out of charity.

It was these batteries that interested Delaherche. He was scanning the slope of La Marfée, when he remembered the telescope
he had at one time amused himself with. He went off to look for it,
brought it back and set it up; and, as he found his bearings, his
gaze presently alighted on the same group of uniforms that Weiss
had seen from Bazeilles, at the corner of a pinewood beyond the
Frénois battery. Delaherche, however, thanks to the glass, could
distinguish the officers attached to this command post so clearly that
he could actually count them. Several of them were half lying in
the grass, others were standing about in groups and, in front of
them, one man stood by himself, a slim, wiry figure in a plain
uniform, in whom, nevertheless, he recognized the master. It was,
of course, the King of Prussia, scarcely half an inch high, like one
of those tiny leaden soldiers that children play with, although it was
not until later that he could be quite sure. He hardly took his eyes
off him, continually coming back to this infinitely small figure,
whose face was little more than a white speck beneath the vast,
blue sky.

It was not yet midday, and since nine o'clock the King had been
watching the mathematical, inexorable advance of his armies. On
and on they went, following the exact course laid down for them,
completing the circle step by step, investing Sedan in a great wall
of men and guns. After leaving the flat plain of Donchery, the
army on the left flank, streaming endlessly through the Saint-Albert

gorge, had passed Saint-Menges, and was already nearing Fleigneux; and now, behind the XIth Corps, violently engaged with
General Douay's troops, he could distinctly see the Vth, advancing
under cover of the woods in the direction of the Calvary of Illy,
while battery after battery took up its position, forming an endless
line of thundering guns, until gradually the whole horizon was
aflame. By this time, the army on the right flank had occupied the
whole valley of the Givonne, the XIIth Corps had taken La Moncelle, and its advance guard, having passed through Daigny, was
already ascending the stream, also making for the Calvary after
forcing General Ducrot to fall back behind the Garenne forest. One
more effort, and the Crown Prince of Prussia would join hands with
the Crown Prince of Saxony, in those naked fields on the very edge
of the forest of Ardennes. To the South of the town, Bazeilles could
no longer be seen, hidden by the smoke of burning houses and the
tawny dust-clouds of furious battle.

Since early morning the King had tranquilly been watching and
waiting. An hour, two hours, maybe three, it was now only a
question of time; one cog was turning another, the pulverizing
machine was on the move, and nothing could stop it. Beneath the
vast expanse of sun-bright sky the battlefield contracted, the whole
scurrying surge of black specs was converging, ever closer and closer,
upon Sedan. In the town, window-panes gleamed in the sun, and
to the left, towards the suburb of La Cassine, a house seemed to be
on fire. And further on still, in the once more deserted fields, out
towards Donchery and Carignan, all had become peaceful again,
warm and luminous, with the clear waters of the Meuse, the trees
happy to be alive, the great fertile fields, the large green meadows
beneath the burning midday heat.

The King turned to ask for a report. He wanted to know what
was happening on this gigantic chess board, to maintain control of
these swarms of men under his command. Away to his right, a flight
of swallows, scared by the noise of the guns, spiralled high into the
air, and disappeared towards the South.

IV

AT FIRST, Henriette was able to walk quickly. It was scarcely ten o'clock, and the broad highway to Balan, lined with houses and gardens, was still free, though as one approached the village, it was more and more obstructed by fleeing inhabitants and troops. Every time the crowd surged forward, she managed to squeeze past by pressing herself close to the wall. With her slight figure, unobtrusive in its dark dress, her fine fair hair and small face half hidden beneath a black lace scarf, she attracted little attention, and walking lightly and silently she hurried on.

But at Balan the road was blocked by a regiment of marines; a dense crowd of men, waiting for orders in the shade of the tall trees that hid them from sight. Even by standing on tiptoe, she could not see the end of them. Nevertheless, she tried to make herself smaller still in order to slip past them. But their elbows jostled her and she could feel the butts of their rifles in her ribs, and before she had gone very far they began to protest. A captain, who happened to catch sight of her, lost his temper.

"You must be mad, woman. . . . Where d'you think you're going?"

"To Bazeilles," she replied, at which there was a burst of laughter, and everyone began pointing at her and making fun of her. The captain, who was also laughing, went on :

"If you're going to Bazeilles, my dear, you'd better take us with you! We were there not long ago, and I hope we shall be able to get back. But I warn you, things are pretty hot there."

"I'm going to Bazeilles to be with my husband," Henriette insisted in a quiet voice, though her pale blue eyes maintained their calm determination.

The laughter died away, and an old sergeant, taking her aside, forced her to turn back.

"Surely you can see it's impossible for you to get through, you poor kid. . . . For the present, Bazeilles is no place for a woman. . . . You'll find your husband later on. Come on, now, be sensible !"

227

She had to give in, though she still stood there, trying to see over their heads and obstinately determined to continue on her way. From what was being said around her, she managed to pick up some information. Officers were bitterly complaining at having been ordered to retreat from Bazeilles at a quarter past eight, when General Ducrot, as MacMahon's successor, had decided to try and concentrate all his forces on the Illy plain. The worst of it was that the 1st Corps, having withdrawn too soon, had left the valley of the Givonne to the Germans, with the result that the 12th Corps, already under fierce attack from the front, had been overrun on its left flank. But then, when General de Wimpffen replaced Ducrot and reverted to the earlier plan, they had been ordered to reoccupy Bazeilles at whatever cost, in order to drive the Bavarians back to the Meuse. Wasn't it simply ridiculous, ordering the 1st to abandon their position, and then telling them to recapture it? They were prepared to sacrifice their lives, but not just for the fun of the thing!

There was a sudden stirring of men and horses, and General de Wimpffen appeared, standing up in his stirrups, his face glowing, shouting excitedly:

"We mustn't retreat, men, that would be the end of everything. . . . If we have to withdraw, we'll make for Carignan, not Mézières. . . . But we're going to win. You beat them this morning, and you can beat them again!"

He galloped off, and disappeared along the road that led to La Moncelle. Rumour had it that he and General Ducrot had just had a violent argument in which each had stuck to his own plan; one insisting that to fall back on Mézières was no longer possible, the other prophesying that, unless the army withdrew to the plain of Illy, it would be surrounded before the day was out; and both accused the other of knowing nothing about the lie of the land or the real position of the troops. The worst of it was that they were both right.

For a moment, Henriette found herself distracted from her intention of going on. She had just recognized a family of poor weavers from Bazeilles, who were standing at the side of the road; a husband and wife, with three daughters, the eldest of whom was not yet nine. They were so distraught, so overcome with exhaustion and despair, that they could go no further and had collapsed against a wall.

"We've lost everything, ma'am, everything," the woman kept saying to Henriette. "You know where we used to live, in the square by the church? Well, it was set on fire by a shell. I don't know how any of us managed to escape. . . ."

Whereupon the three little girls began sobbing and crying again, while the mother, gesticulating wildly, described the disaster in detail.

"I saw the loom burning like a faggot of dry wood . . . the bed and all the furniture went up in flames like bundles of straw. . . . I hadn't even time to take the clock with me."

"God in heaven!" exclaimed the man, his eyes full of tears, "what's going to become of us?"

Trying to calm them, Henriette said in a voice that trembled a little:

"But you're still together, both of you safe and sound, and you've got your children. What have you got to complain about?"

Then she questioned them, hoping to find out what was happening at Bazeilles, whether they'd seen her husband, whether her own house was still standing. But they were so shaken with fear that their replies were contradictory. "No, they had *not* seen M. Weiss." Yet one of the little girls insisted that she *had* seen him, lying on the pavement with a big hole in his head. Whereupon her father gave her a smack, to make her be quiet, he said, because she was quite certainly lying. As for the house, it must have been standing when they left; they could even remember noticing as they passed by that the doors and windows were carefully shut, as though no one was inside. Besides, at that time the Bavarians had only occupied the village as far as the Place d'Église, and they'd have to fight for it street by street, house by house. Still, by now they must have made good progress, probably the whole of Bazeilles was alight. And these wretched people went on describing what they had seen with stumbling, terrified gestures, evoking a monstrous spectacle of flaming roofs, flowing blood and dead bodies littering the ground.

"But what about my husband?" Henriette asked again.

They did not reply, but went on sobbing between their clasped hands. And she stood there, terribly worried, but refusing to give in, although her lips were trembling slightly. What was she to believe? It was no use telling herself the child had made a mistake. She could see her husband lying in the street with a bullet wound in his head. Then the thought of the hermetically sealed house began to worry her. Why should it be? Did it mean he'd already left? The certainty that he had been killed suddenly froze her blood. Yet perhaps he had only been wounded? And the longing to get there, to be there, gripped her so fiercely that she would have made another attempt to force her way through the crowd if, at that moment, the bugles had not sounded the advance.

Many of these young soldiers, who had come from Toulon, Rochefort or Brest, were practically untrained and had never fired a shot, yet since morning they'd been fighting with the bravery and determination of veterans. Men who had marched so badly from Rheims to Mouzon, bewildered by the unfamiliarity of everything, were proving themselves to be the best disciplined, the most closely united by bonds of duty and abnegation, now that they were facing the enemy. As soon as the bugles sounded, they were ready to start fighting again, to go over to the attack, despite the bitterness in their hearts. Three times they had been promised a division to support them, yet it had not come, and they felt themselves abandoned and betrayed. It was their lives they were being asked to give by going back to Bazeilles, after being ordered to evacuate it. They knew this, and they were ready to die, without mutinying, closing their ranks, leaving the protective shelter of the trees to face once more the shells and bullets.

Henriette gave a sigh of profound relief. At last they were on the march, and she followed them, hoping to reach Bazeilles with them, ready to run if they ran. But already they had halted again. At present there was a hail of projectiles; if they were to reoccupy Bazeilles, they would have to fight for every yard, capture every house and every garden. The leading ranks had opened fire, now they could only advance in short bursts, the slightest obstacle forced them to waste precious time. If she had to wait until victory had been won, she would never get there; and she decided to break away to the right, along a footpath between two hedges, that led towards the meadows.

Henriette's plan was to reach Bazeilles by way of the huge meadows that lie along the Meuse. But she was not very clear about it. Suddenly she was pulled up short, her way barred by a motionless expanse of water. Flooding had transformed these low-lying fields into a defensive lake, about which she had completely forgotten. For a moment she wanted to turn back, then, at the risk of losing her shoes in the mud, she pushed on along the bank, sinking up to her ankles in the wet grass. For a hundred yards or so this was possible, but then she came to a garden wall, where the ground sloped away and the water, beating against it, was six feet deep. To get through it was impossible. She clenched her fists, exerting all her strength to prevent herself bursting into tears. After the first shock, she succeeded, by hugging the fence, in reaching an alley which ran between the scattered houses. This time she thought she was safe, for she knew this maze of tangled lanes well, and that eventually they led to the bridge.

Here, however, shells were falling. Henriette remained rooted to the ground, very pale, deafened by a terrifying explosion, the blast of which swirled around her. A shell had just burst a few yards ahead of her. She examined the heights on the left bank of the river, where she could see the smoke from the German batteries rising into the air, and, realizing what had happened, set off again, her eyes fixed on the horizon, watching for the shells in order to avoid them. The crazy temerity of what she was doing was not without a considerable element of self-control, all the strength and courage of which her brave little housewife's soul was capable. She did not want to get killed, but to find her husband, take him back with her and once more settle down happily together. Shells were now falling incessantly, and she hurried along keeping close to the wall, throwing herself down behind kerbstones, taking advantage of the slightest shelter. But she came to an open space, a stretch of roadway already pockmarked with shell holes, and as she waited at the corner of a shed, through a hole in the wall she caught sight of a child's head, straight in front of her, and looking at her curiously. It was a little boy, ten years old, barefooted and wearing nothing but a shirt and a pair of ragged trousers, some street urchin, greatly entertained by the battle. His small black eyes sparkled, and at every explosion he exclaimed delightedly :

"Oh, that was a dandy one . . .! Look out, here comes another! Boom! That was a smasher . . .! Don't budge, don't budge!"

And every time a shell fell, he dived into a hole, reappearing the next moment, his head cocked on one side like a sparrow, and then disappearing again.

Henriette noticed that the shells were now coming from Liry, whereas the Pont-Maugis and Noyers batteries were only firing at Balan. At every discharge she could see the smoke quite clearly, and then, almost immediately after the explosion, could hear the shell whistling through the air. There must have been a short respite, for the plumes of smoke were slowly disappearing.

"They've stopped for a drink," shouted the little boy. "Quick, quick, give me your hand, and we'll make a dash for it!"

He seized her hand and dragged her after him; and, stooping

down, the two of them ran swiftly across the open space. Reaching the other side, they flung themselves down behind a heap of bricks, and looking over their shoulders saw another shell coming, which fell on the shed in the very spot they had just left. With a tremendous crash, the shed collapsed. Whereupon the urchin, who regarded this as a tremendous joke, began dancing with joy.

"Bravo! That was a corker . . .! We only just made it, didn't we?"

But, for the second time, Henriette found herself confronted by an insurmountable obstacle, a garden wall with no gate. Still laughing, her small companion insisted that there was bound to be a way if they were really determined. He climbed up on to the coping of the wall, helped to pull her up alongside him, and jumped down on the other side. They found themselves in a kitchen garden, amongst beds of haricot beans and peas, railings all round. The only way to get out was through the gardener's cottage. The boy, whistling and swinging his arms, ran ahead, surprised at nothing. He pushed open the door, found himself in one room, then went into another, where there was an old woman, probably the only person left. Apparently dazed, she stood by the table and watched these two unknown people passing through her house. She said never a word, nor did they speak to her. Once more outside, they found themselves in an alley, which for a time they could follow. Then further difficulties arose. And so it went on, for almost half a mile, scrambling over walls, struggling through hedges, seeking the shortest possible way, using stable doors or people's windows, whatever chanced to turn up. Dogs started howling, and they were almost knocked down by a madly galloping cow. Still, they must be getting nearer to the village. There was a smell of burning, and every now and again clouds of reddish smoke hid the sun. Suddenly the boy stopped, and stood there barring Henriette's way.

"Tell me something, ma'am. After all this, where are you really trying to get to?"

"Why surely it's obvious. I'm going to Bazeilles."

He whistled, gave a shrill laugh like some rascal playing truant and, thoroughly pleased with himself, said :

"To Bazeilles? Oh no, that doesn't suit me at all. I'm going somewhere quite different, so I'll say cheerio !"

Then, turning on his heel, he made off, just as he had come, without her being able to find out whence he came or whither he was going. She had found him in a hole in the ground, she watched him disappear behind a wall; and that was the last she was to see of him.

Left to herself, Henriette experienced a strange feeling of fear. It had scarcely been any protection, having this puny child with her, but his chatter had distracted her. And now, though naturally courageous, she found herself trembling. The shells were no longer falling, the Germans had stopped firing on Bazeilles, for fear of killing their own men now they had captured the village. For the last few minutes all she had heard was the whistle of bullets, that sound like the humming of huge flies, that people had told her about. In the distance, there was such an inferno of noise that she could not even distinguish the sound of firing amidst the general clamour.

Turning the corner of a house, she heard, close to her ears, the dull sound of falling plaster, which made her stop short : a bullet had just chipped off part of the coping, and she stood there, pale with fright. Then, before she had had time to ask herself whether she had the courage to go on, she felt something strike her on the forehead like the blow of a hammer, and she fell to her knees, stunned. A second bullet, which had ricocheted, had grazed her head just above the left eyebrow, making a large bruise. Raising both hands to her forehead, she saw that they were red with blood, but she could feel that the skull itself was not injured; and, in an attempt to encourage herself, she began repeating aloud :

"It's nothing, nothing. . . . See, I'm not frightened, no, I'm not frightened."

And it was true. She got to her feet and began making her way through the bullets, as unconcernedly as if she had ceased to reason and was ready to give her life. She no longer made any attempt to protect herself, but walked straight ahead, her head held high, lightening her stride in the hope of getting there sooner. Bullets were falling all round her, a score of times she was nearly killed without appearing to be conscious of it. Her light step and silent energy seemed to help her, enabling this slim, supple creature to meet danger and avoid it. At last she was in Bazeilles, and she cut across a field of lucerne to get back to the main street that led through the village. As she reached it, she could see her house, sixty yards away on her right; it was burning, though the flames were not visible in the bright sunlight, but the roof had already half fallen in and the windows were belching clouds of black smoke. Then she started to run, to run until her lungs were bursting.

At eight o'clock that morning, Weiss had found himself shut up in the house, cut off from the retreating troops. It was no longer possible to return to Sedan, for the Bavarians, pouring through the Montivilliers park, had cut the line of retreat. Left alone, with his rifle and the few cartridges that remained to him, he suddenly caught sight of a dozen soldiers in front of the house, who, like himself, had been separated from their comrades and were looking for some refuge where they could sell their lives as dearly as possible. He quickly went down and let them in, and from then on the house became a fortress; a captain, a corporal and eight men, all beside themselves with rage and determined not to surrender.

"What Laurent, so you're here!" exclaimed Weiss, astonished to see amongst them a tall, lean lad, carrying a rifle that he had taken from a dead soldier.

Laurent, wearing a blue linen jacket and trousers, was a gardener, who worked in the neighbourhood, a man of some thirty years, whose wife and mother had both died recently of the same fever.

"And why shouldn't I be here?" he replied. "My carcass is all I've got to offer. . . . Besides, being a pretty good shot, it amuses me. I shall enjoy wiping out one of these sods every time I fire!"

The captain and the corporal had already started inspecting the house. There was nothing to be done with the ground floor, except to barricade doors and windows as strongly as possible. They decided to organise the defence in the three small rooms on the first floor and the attics, and they approved the preparations already made by Weiss, the mattresses protecting the shutters, with loopholes between the slats. As the captain took a chance, and leaned out of a window to examine their surroundings, he heard a child crying.

"What on earth can that be?" he asked.

And suddenly Weiss saw, in the neighbouring dyeworks, poor little Auguste, his face flushed with fever between the white sheets, calling for his mother, asking for a drink, while she, lying on the floor with her head battered in, was unable to answer him. Seeing this, he made a despairing gesture, and said:

"It's a poor kid whose mother has been killed by a shell and who keeps on crying. Over there . . . next door!"

234

"Good God," muttered Laurent, "but we'll make them pay for all this!"

As yet, only occasional bullets were hitting the side of the house. Weiss and the captain, accompanied by the gardener and two of the soldiers, had gone up into the attics, from where they had a better view of the road, that ran at an angle as far as the square in front of the church. The square was already in the hands of the Bavarians, who could still only advance with the greatest difficulty and extreme caution. For almost a quarter of an hour, a handful of infantry had managed to hold them in check with such a murderous fire that their dead were already lying in heaps; and, beyond that, there was a house at the other corner of the square which they still had to take if they were to get any further. Every now and then they could see through the smoke a woman firing from one of the windows. It was the baker's house, in which some soldiers who had got left behind were fighting alongside the people of the village; and when at last the house was taken, amidst the shouting, jostling mob of people making for the house opposite, there were sudden glimpses of a woman's skirt, a man's jacket, white hair standing on end; then, as the squad fired, blood spurted as high as the coping of the walls. The Germans made no concessions : all those captured with arms in their hands were treated as not belonging to the armed forces, and were shot immediately, as though it were their own fault that they were not covered by the rules of war. Angered at the villagers' furious resistance and the terrible losses they had been suffering for the past five hours, they exacted monstrous reprisals. The gutters ran with blood, the road was choked with corpses, the cross-roads were little more than charnel-houses, filled with the cries of the dying. Into every house that had offered serious resistance, they threw bales of lighted straw; and while some of them ran about with torches, others poured paraffin on the buildings, so that before long whole streets were ablaze, and Bazeilles became an inferno.

Meanwhile, Weiss's house with its closed shutters was the only place in the centre of the village that still presented the appearance of a fortress, determined not to surrender.

"Look out, here they come!" cried the captain.

From the attics and the first floor a volley rang out, bringing down three of the Bavarians, who were advancing, hugging the walls. The rest of them fell back, taking cover at each turn in the road; and the siege of the house began, such a rain of bullets

235

striking the walls that it sounded like a hailstorm. The fusillade continued for some ten minutes, bringing down chunks of plaster, but otherwise doing little damage. But one of the men the captain had taken up to the attic with him was rash enough to show himself at a window, and was immediately killed, a bullet striking him in the forehead.

"For heaven's sake," growled the captain, "that's one short already. Take care, can't you? We can't afford to get killed just for the fun of the thing!"

He seized a rifle and began firing from behind a shutter, but it was Laurent, the gardener, who aroused his admiration. Kneeling down, the barrel of his rifle resting in the narrow slit of a loophole as though he was stalking an animal, he only fired when he was quite certain of his aim, and then he would announce the result beforehand.

"This one is for the little officer in the blue uniform, down there in the courtyard. . . . Now that tall, skinny one behind him, between the eyes. . . . Now that fat brute with a red beard, who keeps annoying me, in the belly. . . ."

And, each time, the man he designated fell to the ground, shot in the precise spot he had indicated. And he went on, calmly, without hurrying, having plenty to do, as he said, for it would take a long time to kill all of them like this, one by one.

"Oh, if only I could see properly!" Weiss exclaimed angrily.

He had just broken his spectacles and was in despair, for, though he still had his pince-nez, he couldn't keep them on properly because of the sweat pouring down his face, so that as often as not he was simply taking pot shots, his hands trembling feverishly. He was so angry that he had completely lost his usual coolness.

"Don't be in such a hurry," Laurent told him. "It's not the slightest use. Here, aim carefully . . . that bloke who's lost his helmet, at the corner of the grocer's shop. . . . There you are, you see! Very good, you got him in the leg and he's bleeding like a pig."

Weiss looked at the man and turned rather pale.

"Finish him off," he muttered.

"What, waste a bullet? Certainly not! Much better save it for another."

The attackers must have noticed that this redoubtable marksmanship was coming from the attic windows. None of them could advance without being hit. Fresh troops were therefore brought up, with orders to concentrate their fire on the roof; and before long

236

the attic became untenable. The slates offered little more protection than sheets of paper, and soon bullets were humming about the room like a swarm of angry bees.

"Come on," said the captain. "We'll go down to the first floor. We shall be better off down there."

But, as he was making for the ladder, a bullet hit him in the groin.

"Too late, damn it!"

With the help of the one remaining soldier, Weiss insisted on getting him downstairs, though he yelled to them not to waste time bothering about him: he was done for, they might just as well leave him to peg out up there as anywhere else. However, no sooner had they laid him on a bed in one of the rooms on the first floor than he insisted upon continuing to direct the defence.

"Shoot where they're thickest, don't worry about the rest. As long as you keep firing, they won't dare take any risks."

And, indeed, it looked as though the siege of the little house might continue indefinitely. For though again and again it seemed that it must fall beneath the hail of lead, nevertheless, as the smoke cleared away after each burst of firing, there it still stood, holed and slashed, with bullets spurting from every fissure. Exasperated at being held up so long by one ridiculous little house, and at losing so many men, the attackers kept blazing away at long range, not daring to rush the ground-floor windows and door.

"Look out there," shouted the corporal, as a shutter fell to the ground, wrenched from its hinges.

But Weiss immediately pushed a wardrobe in front of the window, and Laurent, taking cover behind it, was able to keep up his fire. One of the soldiers fell at his feet, his jaw shattered, bleeding profusely. Another was hit in the throat, and lay curled up against the wall, groaning hoarsely, every now and then giving a convulsive shudder. Apart from the captain who, propped up against the head of the bed and too weak to speak, continued to give orders by signs, there were only eight of them left. Like the attic, the first floor was rapidly becoming untenable, for the mattresses were torn to bits and gave no protection against the enemy fire: lumps of plaster kept falling from the walls and ceiling, all the furniture was chipped, and the sides of the wardrobe were split from top to bottom. Worst of all, they were running out of ammunition.

"What a bloody nuisance," growled Laurent. "Just when things were going so well!"

237

Weiss had a sudden idea.

"Hang on a minute!" he said, remembering the dead soldier up in the attic.

He climbed up the ladder, felt in the man's pockets, looking for the cartridges he was bound to have. A whole section of the roof had caved in, and the sight of the cheerful light streaming from a stretch of blue sky astonished him. To avoid being killed, he moved forward on hands and knees; then, having found some thirty rounds of ammunition, he hurried back down the ladder as quickly as possible.

As he was sharing his booty with the gardener, another soldier crashed forward on his face, uttering a loud cry. Now there were only seven of them; a moment later, there were only six, the corporal having been killed instantaneously by a bullet through his left eye.

From that moment onwards Weiss lost all sense of what was happening. He and the five others blazed away like madmen until the ammunition was exhausted, without the slightest thought of surrendering. In the three little rooms, the floor was covered with bits of broken furniture, the doors were blocked by dead bodies, and in one corner a wounded man was moaning horribly. Everything was sticky with blood, and a thin red stream flowed across the floor and trickled down the staircase. It was almost impossible to breathe, the air was scorching, thick with smoke and the acrid, sickening stench of gunpowder, and except for the flashes from their rifles it was almost dark.

"Christ Almighty!" shouted Weiss, "They're bringing up artillery!"

In a desperate attempt to dispose of this handful of madmen who were holding up their attack, the Bavarians were manoeuvring a gun into position at the corner of the Place de l'Église. Having razed the house to the ground, perhaps they would at last be able to advance. But the only effect of having this gun trained on them was to make the besieged men wildly cheerful, for they regarded it as an honour.

"What bloody cowards, having to bring up a gun!" they jeered scornfully, while Laurent, still taking careful aim, picked off an artilleryman with every shot.

So effective was he, that it was five or six minutes before the first shell could be fired. Even then it was too high, and merely knocked off another piece of roof. But the end was approaching. In vain they searched through the pockets of the dead men; not a single round of ammunition was left. Angered and exhausted, the six men felt about, trying to find something they could hurl through the windows to crush the enemy. Then, as one of them stood up, yelling at the top of his voice and waving his firsts, he was hit by a volley of bullets, leaving only five of them. What were they to do? Should they make their way downstairs and try to escape through the garden? But at that moment a tremendous hubbub broke out, the staircase was crowded with angry men; it was the Bavarians, who had at last succeeded in surrounding the house and broken down the back door. And amongst the dead men and bits of broken furniture that littered the rooms, a frightful struggle ensued. One of the soldiers was bayoneted in the chest, two others were taken prisoner, while the captain, who had just breathed his last, lay on his back with his mouth open, one arm still raised as though giving an order.

Meanwhile, however, a German officer, a big, fair-haired fellow with a revolver, whose bloodshot eyes were almost starting out of his head, had caught sight of Weiss and Laurent, one wearing his overcoat, the other in his blue linen jacket, and he shouted at them angrily, in French:

"Who do you think you are? What the devil are you doing, mixed up with this lot?"

Then, noticing their powder-blackened faces, he started swearing at them in German, stuttering with rage. But as he raised his pistol to shoot them, the soldiers under his command rushed forward, seized Weiss and Laurent, and carried them off downstairs. The two men, swept off their feet by this human tide, were flung into the road, almost as far as the houses opposite, amidst such a storm of shouting that their officers could hardly make themselves heard. Then, while the fair-haired officer was trying to detach them from the crowd in order to proceed with their execution, they managed to get to their feet and look around them.

Other houses had been set alight, before long the whole of Bazeilles would be one vast bonfire. Tongues of flame were already shooting from the high windows of the church. Some soldiers, driving an old woman out of her house, had forced her to give them some matches so that they could set fire to her bed and curtains. On every side, more and more fires were getting a hold, as the Germans poured paraffin on the buildings and flung bundles of straw into the flames; and now, enraged by the delay, the soldiers

239

were fighting like savages to avenge their dead, lying in piles and being trampled beneath their feet. Beneath clouds of sparks and smoke, bands of soldiers forced their way forward, yelling at the top of their voices, a terrifying clamour of shouting, groaning, firing and the crash of falling buildings. In the swirling fog of livid dust that hid the sun, it was almost impossible to see, and over everything hung an unbearable stench of sweat and blood, as though the air itself was charged with all the abominations of massacre. And still the killing and destruction continued on every side, with all the brutality, all the senseless anger and maddened fury, of man preying upon man.

And now before his eyes, Weiss watched his own house being burnt. Soldiers hurriedly brought torches, while others stirred the flames, feeding them with bits of broken furniture, till the ground floor began to blaze and smoke poured forth from all the jagged wounds in walls and roof. Soon, the nearby dyeworks were also aflame, and one could hear the heartrending sound of little Auguste, lying in bed delirious with fever, calling for his mother, while the flames licked at the skirts of the wretched woman who lay stretched out in the doorway, her skull crushed.

"Mummy, I'm thirsty. . . . Get me some water, Mummy . . . ."

The flames roared, the child's voice stopped, all one could hear was the deafening cheers of the victors.

Then suddenly, above the noise, louder than all the clamour, a terrible cry rang out. It was Henriette, who had just caught sight of her husband, standing against the wall, facing a squad of men who were preparing to fire. She rushed up to him, and, flinging her arms round his neck, cried out :

"Good God, what are they doing? They shan't shoot you, they shan't."

Weiss stared at her in stupefaction. It was she, the wife he had so long desired, whom he adored with such idolatry. He shuddered violently, mad with grief. What had he done? Why had he stayed behind, firing a rifle, instead of returning to her as he had sworn to do? In a moment of giddiness he saw his happiness destroyed for ever; then, noticing the blood on her forehead, he stammered in a mechanical tone of voice :

"Are you wounded . . .? You're crazy to be here . . . ."

She interrupted him with a passionate gesture.

"Oh that, why it's nothing, a mere scratch. . . . But what about you? Why are they keeping you here? I won't let them kill you!"

240

In the middle of the street the officer was struggling with the crowd in an attempt to make a little elbow room for his men. Catching sight of this woman embracing one of his prisoners, he burst out violently, in French:

"Come on now, none of that nonsense here . . .! Where are you from? What do you want?"

"I want my husband."

"Is this man your husband, then . . .? He's been condemned to death, and the sentence must be carried out."

"I want my husband."

"Come, come, be sensible, and get out of the way. We don't want you to get hurt."

"I want my husband."

Seeing that she had no intention of obeying, the officer was about to order one of his men to take her away when Laurent, who had so far remained silent, decided to intervene.

"Listen here, captain, it was me that did most of the killing. If you want to shoot me, that's quite all right. Besides, I've got no one, neither mother, nor wife, nor child, whereas this gentleman here is married. . . . Look, why not let him go, and then settle accounts with me . . .?"

Beside himself with rage, the captain roared:

"Enough of this talk. Do you think you can fool me . . .? Let's have a volunteer to take this woman away!"

He had to repeat the order in German, whereupon a soldier stood forward, a stockily built Bavarian, with a huge head and tousled red beard and hair, beneath which all that could be seen was a broad flat nose and large blue eyes. He was covered with blood and terrible to look at, like some great hairy bear, ready to crush its victim to death.

Again Henriette cried out despairingly:

"I want my husband. If you kill him, you must kill me as well."

Whereupon the officer began beating his chest, declaring that he was no murderer, that while some people might be prepared to kill the innocent, he was not. This woman hadn't been condemned to death, he'd rather cut off his hand than harm a hair of her head.

Then, as the Bavarian moved towards them, Henriette flung her arms round Weiss and clung to him with all her strength.

"Oh, my love, I beg you, keep me with you; let me die with you. . . ."

241

Weeping bitterly, but without saying a word, Weiss tried to free himself from the clutching fingers of his frantic wife.

"If you love me, you'll let me die with you. . . . Hold me tight, then they'll get tired of waiting and have to kill us both together."

He had managed to loosen one of her hands, and pressed it to his lips, kissing it, and at the same time doing his best to make her let go with the other.

"No, no, hold me, hold me, I'd rather die. . . ."

At last he succeeded in securing both her hands, and breaking his silence for the first time, he said simply:

"Goodbye, my dear wife."

And, with these words, he thrust her into the Bavarian's arms; and she was led away, struggling and screaming, while in an attempt to calm her the soldier spoke to her rapidly in a hoarse voice. But with a violent jerk she managed to break free, so that she saw everything that happened.

The whole thing scarcely took three seconds. Weiss, whose pince-nez had come off while he was struggling with her, hurriedly put them on again, as though determined to look death in the face. Then, folding his arms, he turned his back to the wall, and as he stood there in his torn clothes, his gentle face took on an expression almost of exaltation and of noble courage. At his side, Laurent merely thrust his hands into his pockets as though disgusted by the cruelty of the scene and the monstrous behaviour of these savages, who were prepared to kill a man before the eyes of his wife. He drew himself up, stared them straight in the face and, in a scornful voice, spat out at them:

"You dirty swine!"

But the officer had already raised his sword, and the two men fell like logs, the gardener, face downwards; the other, the book-keeper, on his side, at the foot of the wall. Before he finally lost consciousness, he gave one last convulsive movement, eyelids flutter-ing and mouth contorted. The officer walked up to him and turned him over with his foot, to make sure that he was really dead.

Henriette had seen everything, the dying eyes striving to find hers, the last agonised convulsion, that great boot prodding his body. In an effort not to cry out, she buried her teeth savagely in the only thing within reach, the Bavarian's hand. He uttered a hideous groan, then struck out at her, almost knocking her down; and for a moment their faces touched. Never would she forget that red beard spattered with blood, those staring blue eyes maddened with rage.

Afterwards, Henriette had no clear recollection of what happened next. All she could remember was her longing to get to her husband's body, to take it in her arms and cherish it. But, as in a nightmare, fresh obstacles kept getting in the way, hindering her at every step. Then once again a burst of rifle fire broke out, and the German troops occupying Bazeilles were caught up in a great surge of movement: it was the regiment of French marines, who had arrived at last, and the fighting was renewed with such violence that the young woman found herself thrust into an alleyway amongst a crowd of bewildered villagers. But it was too late for the marines to win back the positions they had abandoned, and the result of the struggle was never in doubt. Though they fought on for another half-hour, giving their lives with tremendous courage, the enemy were continually receiving reinforcements, who swarmed in from every side, through the meadows, along the roads, and from the park at Montivilliers. Nothing could now dislodge them from this village, so dearly bought, where thousands of their men lay dying amid the blood and flames. Before long destruction had done its work: nothing was left but a charnel-house of dismembered limbs and smoking debris, while Bazeilles, battered and overwhelmed, slowly burned itself out.

From a distance, Henriette had a final glimpse of her little house, with its floors collapsing in a whirl of flame, while opposite it she could still see her husband's body, lying beneath the wall where it had fallen. Then she was caught up in a fresh surge of people. The bugles sounded the retreat, and without knowing what was happening to her she was swept away by the retreating troops. She had ceased to be a living creature, and had become merely an object, flung about like a cobblestone by the trampling feet of the stampeding crowd. And she knew nothing more, until at last she found herself once again at Balan, in a house belonging to strangers, sitting in the kitchen sobbing, with her head sunk upon the table.

243

V

ON THE plain of Algeria, at ten o'clock that morning, Captain Beaudoin's company was still lying among the cabbages, in the field where it had been since much earlier. The crossfire from the batteries at Le Hattoy and the Iges peninsula, which was more violent than ever, had just killed two more men, and still no order to advance had arrived : were they to spend the whole day there, letting themselves be cut down without putting up a fight?

The men no longer even had the satisfaction of firing their rifles. Captain Beaudoin had eventually succeeded in making them stop their furious, but quite useless, bombardment of the wood opposite, where not a single Prussian seemed to be left. The heat was becoming intolerable, as they lay stretched out on the ground beneath the scorching sun.

Happening to look round, Jean was concerned to see that Maurice's head had fallen, so that his cheek rested on the ground. His eyes were closed, his face set and very pale. What could it be?

But Maurice had simply dozed off. Though death was flying on every side, the waiting and the fatigue had been too much for him. He woke up with a start, and as he opened his large, calm eyes, they were immediately filled with the troubled bewilderment of battle. He had no idea how long he had been asleep, and felt as though he were emerging from a delicious and prolonged oblivion.

"Why, that's funny," he muttered. "I must have gone off . . .! Still, I feel a lot better for it."

And, indeed, he was now less conscious of the painful pressure on skull and chest, that girdle of fear that crushes a man's bones. He started to make fun of Lapoulle, who was worrying about the disappearance of Chouteau and Loubet, and was talking of going to look for them – a marvellous excuse for lying under a tree and having a smoke! Pache thought they must have been kept by the ambulance, because of the shortage of stretcher-bearers. . . . Not a particularly pleasant job that, come to think of it, bringing in the

244

wounded under fire! And he recalled the country superstition that it was unlucky to touch a corpse: you could easily die of it.

"Shut up, for God's sake!" shouted Lieutenant Rochas. "Who's talking about dying?"

At which Colonel de Vineuil, still seated on his horse, had turned round and smiled, for the first time that day. Then he returned to his former position, impassive as ever amid the bursting shells, waiting for orders.

Maurice, whose interest in the stretcher-bearers was now aroused, was watching them at work. There must be a mobile ambulance sheltered by the bank, at the end of the sunken road. The crew had quickly put up the tent and unpacked the necessary instruments, apparatus and bandages, ready to give first-aid to the wounded before sending them on to Sedan as fast as they could find transport to take them. The ambulance only had assistant surgeons; it was mainly the stretcher-bearers that displayed such stubborn and inglorious heroism. In their grey uniforms, with the red cross on their caps and armlets, they could be seen tranquilly risking their lives under fire, trying to get to the men who had been hit. They moved forward on hands and knees, taking advantage of ditches, hedges or any other available cover, doing their best to avoid exposing themselves unnecessarily. Then, as soon as they found anyone lying on the ground, their difficult task began, for many of them had only fainted, and they had to distinguish also between the dead and the wounded. Some lay on their faces, in a pool of blood, at the point of death; others had their mouths full of mud, as though they had been biting the ground; others lay in huddled heaps, arms and legs twisted, chests almost crushed. Then, with the utmost care, the stretcher-bearers would disentangle those who were still breathing, straighten out their limbs, and, raising their heads, do their best to clean them up. They all carried water bottles, but they had to be sparing of the contents. And often they would spend a long time, kneeling beside a wounded man, trying to revive him, waiting till he opened his eyes.

Fifty yards away on the left, Maurice saw one of them attending to a young soldier, with blood slowly oozing from his sleeve. Eventually he discovered where he had been wounded, and managed to stop the bleeding by applying a tourniquet. With urgent cases, they simply gave first-aid, not attempting to set broken limbs, but binding them up securely so that they could get them back without danger. And this getting them back was the real difficulty : those who were able to walk they only had to support, but all the others had to be carried, either holding them in their arms like children, or hoisting them on their backs, with their arms round their necks; and, in some cases, two or three of them would link hands to make a chair or stretcher, on which the wounded man could sit or, if necessary, lie down. In addition to the regulation stretchers, they used all kinds of ingenious inventions, improvising stretchers by tying together a couple of rifles with the webbing from their packs. And all over that flat plain, churned up by shells, one could see them, singly or in groups, hurrying along with their burdens, crouching down, groping their way forward, cautiously, but none the less heroically.

Maurice was watching one of them, a thin, puny lad, staggering along under the weight of a heavy sergeant with both legs broken, for all the world like an ant carrying a grain of wheat too big for it, when suddenly a shell exploded, and he saw him lurch forward and disappear from sight. When the smoke cleared away, the sergeant could be seen lying on his back, while the stretcher-bearer was huddled up with his side ripped open. Whereupon another stretcher-bearer appeared, another busy ant, and having first turned his mate over and discovered that he was dead, proceeded to hoist the wounded sergeant on to his back and carry him off.

Turning to Lapoulle, he commented sarcastically :

"Look, if you're so keen on their job, why not go and give him a hand?"

For a minute or two the batteries at Saint-Menges seemed to have gone mad, and the hail of shells increased. Captain Beaudoin, who had continued to walk nervously up and down in front of his company, eventually went over and spoke to the colonel. It was a pity to wear down the men's morale, keeping them here for hours at a time, with nothing to do. But the colonel only replied stoically :

"I've had no orders."

Once again, General Douay galloped past, followed by his staff. He had just met General de Wimpffen, who had implored him to stand firm, and he had promised to do his best, but only on the formal understanding that the Calvary at Illy, to their right, would be defended. If this position was lost, he wouldn't answer for anything, retreat would become inevitable. General de Wimpffen assured him that the 1st Corps was about to occupy the position; and, indeed, almost immediately a regiment of Zouaves could be seen moving up. This so reassured General Douay that he agreed to send the Dumont division to support the hard-pressed 12th Corps. But a quarter of an hour later, when he returned from satisfying himself that the men on his left flank were in good heart, he saw that the Calvary had been evacuated; not a Zouave was to be seen, and the whole plateau, rendered untenable by the terrible bombardment from the Fleigneux batteries, had been abandoned. Disheartened, and scenting disaster, the general hurried back to the right flank, only to find himself caught up in the rabble of the Dumont division, which was falling back in wild disorder, mixed up with the remnants of the 1st Corps. The latter, after its earlier retreat, had been unable to recapture the positions it had previously held, and leaving Daigny to hold the XIIth Saxon army and Givonne to face the Prussian Guard, it had been forced back to the North, through the forest of Garenne, under fire from the batteries which the enemy had installed at every vantage point from one end of the valley to the other. The terrible ring of fire and flame was closing in : one part of the Guard continued to advance upon Illy, following the line of hills from East to West, while from West to East, behind the XIth Corps, which had already captured Saint-Menges, the Vth was still pressing forward; it had passed through Fleigneux, and was continually bringing up more guns with impudent temerity, so convinced of the ignorance and impotence of the French troops that it did not even wait until the infantry arrived to support them. It was midday, the whole horizon was ablaze, thundering away, keeping the 7th and 1st Corps under a constant crossfire.

At this point, General Douay, as the enemy artillery was preparing for the final attack on the Calvary, decided to make a last effort to recapture it. Having given his orders, he rode off into the midst of the routed Dumont division, where he succeeded in rallying a body of men whom he hurled against the plateau. For a few minutes they managed to hang on; but the deserted, treeless fields were swept by such a hail of whistling bullets, such a whirlwind of shells, that they were soon seized by panic and driven back down the slope like straw caught in a gale. Whereupon the general, refusing to give in, ordered further regiments to attack.

A dispatch rider, arriving at the gallop, shouted an order to Colonel de Vineuil through the monstrous din. And the colonel, his face glowing, standing up in his stirrups, waved his sword in the direction of the Calvary.

"At last, lads, it's our turn . . .! Forward, follow me!"

Carried away by his enthusiasm, the 106th began to move. Beaudoin and his company were amongst the first to scramble to their feet, cheerfully cracking jokes about the lead in their boots and the rust in their joints. But scarcely had they began to advance, when the enemy fire became so fierce that they had to fling themselves into a trench, and moved forward bent almost double.

"Look out, lad," Jean shouted to Maurice. "This is it. . . . If you so much as show the tip of your nose, you'll be for it. . . . And if you don't want to get left behind, get a move on. Anyone who manages to get through this lot will be a real hero."

What with the infernal din and the buzzing noise that filled his ears, Maurice scarcely heard him. He no longer knew whether he was afraid or not, but ran forward, borne along by those around him, urged on, not by his own will-power, but simply by the desire to get it over as quickly as possible. And to such an extent had he become a mere ripple in this surging torrent that, when a sudden check occurred at the farther end of the trench at the sight of the open ground that still had to be covered, the panic immediately transmitted itself to him, and he was ready to take to his heels. The reaction was purely instinctive, a revolt of his muscles in response to his laboured breathing.

Some of the men were already beginning to turn back, but the colonel rushed towards them.

"Come on, lads, you're not going to let me down like this, you aren't going to behave like cowards. . . . Don't forget, the 106th has never turned tail. . . . You'd be the first to bring shame on our colours . . . !"

He drove his horse in amongst them, barring the way, with a word for each individual, and in a voice trembling with tears spoke to them about France.

Lieutenant Rochas was so moved by his words that he became furiously angry, and started hitting the men with the flat of his sword.

"You lousy sods, if you don't keep going, you'll feel my boot in your backsides! The first man who refuses to obey orders, I'll knock the swine down!"

But, to the colonel, this attempt to drive men into action by force was repugnant.

"That's not the way, lieutenant! They're going to follow me, aren't you, lads? You're not going to let your old colonel take on the Prussians single-handed . . .! Come on now, forward!"

248

He set off, and all the men did, in fact, follow him; he had spoken to them in such a decent, fatherly way that they would have been ashamed to quit. Seated calmly on his big horse, he rode forward across the empty fields, while the men fanned out in skirmishing order, taking advantage of the slightest cover. In order to reach the Calvary, they had to cover a good five hundred yards of stubble and beetroot fields. Instead of the classical assault you see on manoeuvres, with the men advancing in orderly ranks, all you could see were rounded backs, hurrying along almost level with the ground, as the soldiers, single or in groups, scrambled uphill, hopping about like insects, using all their skill and cunning to reach the crest. The enemy batteries must have spotted them, for shells began churning up the ground in such rapid succession that the noise of detonations was continuous. Five men were killed, a lieutenant had his body sliced in two.

Maurice and Jean were lucky enough to find a hedge, behind which they were able to advance without being seen. It didn't stop one of their comrades being shot through the temple, however; he fell amongst the hurrying feet, and they had to kick him aside. But by now there were so many dead that it had become impossible to keep count of them. All the horrors of the battlefield, a wounded man, screaming, clasping both hands to his belly in an attempt to hold back his protruding entrails, a horse with its back broken still trying to drag itself along – all this frightful agony eventually ceased to affect them, and what they suffered from most was the overpowering heat of the midday sun, eating into their shoulders.

"God, but I'm thirsty!" stammered Maurice. "My throat feels as if it was full of soot. . . . Can you smell something burning . . . like scorched wood?"

Jean nodded :

"It was the same at Solferino. Maybe it's simply the smell of war. . . . Hang on, I've still got a drop of brandy left. We'll have a swig."

In the shelter of the hedge they paused for a moment, taking things easy. But instead of relieving their thirst, the brandy only burnt their throats. It was exasperating, this taste of scorching in their mouths. Besides, they were starving, they would have been only too glad to eat the half loaf that Maurice still had in his haversack; but how could they? Behind them, following along the hedge, more and more men kept arriving, pushing them forward. Then, with a final leap, they reached the top. They were on the

249

plateau, at the very foot of the Calvary, an old cross, battered by wind and rain, between two stunted lime trees.

"Well, here we are, then," Jean exclaimed. "Now the main thing is to hang on!"

He was right, it wasn't exactly the most agreeable spot, as Lapoulle remarked, in a lugubrious voice that made everyone laugh. Again they all lay down in the stubble, but not before three more men had been killed. Up here, it was as though a veritable hurricane had been let loose; from Saint-Menges, Fleigneux and Givonne, so many shells were poured in that the earth seemed to be smoking with them as it does in a torrential downpour. Clearly, they wouldn't be able to hold the position for long, unless artillery support was forthcoming pretty soon. There was talk of General Douay having given orders for two reserve batteries to be brought up; and the men kept anxiously looking over their shoulders, waiting in vain for the guns to arrive.

"It's ridiculous, perfectly ridiculous!" Captain Beaudoin kept saying, walking backwards and forwards in his nervous way. "You don't order a regiment to advance like this, unless you can provide immediate support."

Then, noticing a dip in the land on their left, he shouted to Rochas:

"Look, lieutenant, the company could get some cover there."

But Rochas, standing there motionless, merely shrugged his shoulders.

"Here or there, sir, it's no great odds! We should be in just the same pickle. . . . Better to stay where we are."

At which Captain Beaudoin, who never swore as a rule, lost his temper:

"But, for Christ's sake, do you want us all to be killed? We can't just stay here to be shot at!"

And he obstinately insisted upon reconnoitring the position himself. But, before he had gone ten yards, he was bowled over by a sudden explosion, his right leg fractured by a shell splinter. He rolled over on his back, uttering a piercing shriek, like a woman taken by surprise.

"It was bound to happen," muttered Rochas. "It's no use careering about like that, you just have to take what's coming to you."

Seeing the captain fall, some of the men got to their feet; and as he went on calling for help, imploring them to bring him in, Jean eventually ran towards him, quickly followed by Maurice.

"Don't leave me here, for God's sake! Get me to an ambulance."

While they were discussing the best way to tackle the job, they caught sight of two stretcher-bearers, who were sheltering behind the hedge, apparently waiting for a job. They waved to them to attract their attention, and the two men came over to them. If they could manage to get him to the ambulance without worse befalling, he would be saved. But it was a long way, and the shells were falling thicker than ever.

The stretcher-bearers, having bandaged his leg tightly to prevent it moving, made a chair for him by gripping each other's wrists, so that he was able to sit, supporting himself with one arm round each of their necks. But just as they were about to carry him off, Colonel de Vineuil, who had heard what had happened, arrived at the gallop. He had known the young man ever since they had been at Saint-Cyr together; they were friends, and it was obvious that he was very upset.

"Don't lose heart, my dear fellow. . . . You'll find it's nothing much, they'll pull you through. . . ."

The captain made a gesture of relief, as if at last he had found courage.

"No, no, this is the end, it's better like this. What's so exasperating, is having to wait for something you know is bound to happen."

They carried him away; the stretcher-bearers were lucky enough to reach the hedge without mishap, and they rapidly disappeared with their burden. As soon as the colonel saw that they had safely reached the clump of trees where the ambulance was, he gave a sigh of relief.

"But look, sir," Maurice suddenly exclaimed. "You're wounded yourself."

He had noticed that the colonel's left boot was covered with blood. The heel had been torn away, and a piece of leather had been driven into the flesh.

M. de Vineuil calmly leaned over in the saddle, examined his foot for a moment, which must have been smarting painfully, and murmured:

"Yes, yes, I got that some time ago. . . . It's nothing. Anyhow, it doesn't stop me riding. . . ."

And as he turned back to take his place at the head of the regiment, he added:

"As long as you're on horseback and can manage to stay there, things aren't too bad."

251

At last the two reserve batteries arrived. To the anxiously awaiting men this was an enormous relief, as though the guns were a rampart and protection for them, a thunderbolt that would silence the enemy's cannons. Besides, it was a heartening sight to watch the batteries in correct battle order, each gun followed by its limber, the drivers on the nearside horses holding the reins of those on the offside, the gunners seated on the limbers, and the officers and N.C.O.s galloping along beside them. Riding across the stubble at full speed, and making a tremendous clatter, they maintained their exact positions as carefully as if they were on parade.

Maurice, who had again lain down in a furrow, raised his head in a state of great excitement to say to Jean:

"Look, the one on the left is Honoré's battery. I recognize the men."

With the back of his hand Jean promptly pushed him down again.

"Stay where you are, and don't move a muscle!"

But though both of them lay quite still, keeping their heads close to the ground, they were determined not to lose sight of the battery. They watched its manoeuvres with intense interest, their hearts beating furiously as they saw the calm courage of these men, who, they were convinced, were bringing them victory.

Suddenly, to the left of them, the battery came to a halt on a naked hilltop: quick as lightning, the gunners leapt down from the limbers, unhooking the spades of the guns, while the drivers, leaving the cannon in position, wheeled their horses in a semi-circle and brought them to a halt, fifteen yards to the rear, facing the enemy. In less than no time the six guns had been drawn up in pairs, some distance apart, and each of the three sections was under the command of a lieutenant, while all six took their orders from a thin, very tall captain, who was laboriously checking the field of fire. Then, when he had rapidly worked out his calculations, they heard him shout:

"Range sixteen hundred yards!"

Their target was the Prussian battery to the left of Fleigneux, hidden amongst the trees, whose terrible fire was making the Calvary untenable.

"You see," Maurice started to explain, unable to contain himself, "Honoré's gun is in the centre section. There he is, leaning forward with the gun layer . . . young Louis, the lad we had a drink with at Vouziers, don't you remember? . . . And over there, the driver on the left, that one on the magnificent chestnut, is Adolphe. . . ."

Each gun had its crew of six men and a sergeant, and beyond that the limber with its four horses and two drivers; then came the ammunition waggon, with six horses and three drivers, and further on again, the spare horsemen, the farrier, a whole train of men, animals and supplies, that stretched out in a straight line extending a hundred yards to the rear; not to mention the reserves, the extra ammunition waggon, the spare horses and men, who were drawn up away to the right, in order not to be unnecessarily exposed in the line of fire.

Honoré was busy loading the gun. The two centre gunners had already brought the shell and cartridge case from the ammunition waggon, which was in charge of a sergeant, whereupon the two leading gunners, having put the cartridge case into position, with its charge of gunpowder wrapped in a piece of twill, carefully rammed it home, and finally introduced the shell, the flanges of which made a grating noise as they passed the rifling of the barrel. Determined to aim the first shot himself, Honoré stooped over the range-finder, turning the adjusting screw to ensure the right eleva-tion, while at the same time motioning with his hand to the gun-layer standing behind him, who, with the aid of the direction lever, turned the gun imperceptibly to right and left.

"That's about it," he said at last, straightening his back.

The captain, his tall body bent almost double, then checked the elevation, while the No. 2 of each gun stood ready, with the string that worked the striker-pin in his hand. When the captain was satisfied that everything was in order, he called out to each gun in turn : "No. 1 fire ! . . . No. 2 fire ! . . ." and so on.

One after the other the six shots rang out, the guns recoiled, and, as they were being manhandled back into position, the warrant officer reported that they had fallen considerably short of the target. Fresh instructions were given, and the same procedure was repeated once again in exactly the same way; and it was just this regular, cold-blooded carrying out of a mechanical task that sustained the men's morale. Each gun, like some pet animal, gathered round it a small family, drawn together by a common undertaking. The gun was the bond that held them together; everything else, limber, waggons, horses, men, existed simply to supply its needs. It was this that gave the whole battery its cohesion, the solidarity and strength of a well-ordered household.

The men of the 106th greeted the first salvo with acclamation :

now at last the Prussian guns were going to get their answer! But they were soon disappointed, for they realized that their shells were falling short, most of them exploding in the air without reaching the clump of trees where the enemy artillery was concealed.

"Honoré says the others are absolute crocks compared with his," said Maurice. "He thinks his is so marvellous, I shouldn't be surprised if he sleeps with it! Just look how carefully he looks after it, wiping it down all the time to make sure it doesn't get overheated!"

Both he and Jean were so cheered by the tranquil courage of the artillerymen that they began cracking jokes. But, with three shots, the Prussian batteries had found their target, and they were now firing with such precision that the shells were falling amongst the French guns, while the latter, despite all their efforts, found it impossible to extend their range. One of Honoré's gunners, the one on the left with the ramrod, was killed. They pushed the body aside, and went on loading the gun with the same careful, un-hurried regularity. From all sides now, shells were falling and exploding; yet around each gun the same methodical movements continued: loading, finding the elevation, firing, easing the wheels back into position, as though the men were so completely absorbed in their work that they could neither see nor hear anything else.

But what struck Maurice most of all was the way the drivers, fifteen yards in the rear, sat facing the enemy, upright and motion-less in their saddles. Adolphe was one of them, with his broad chest, and the huge, fair moustaches almost hiding his red face; and it must really have taken plenty of pluck to sit there without batting an eyelid, watching the shells coming straight towards you and not so much as moving a muscle. It was all right for the gunners, they had work to do, and they had to keep their minds on it. But the drivers just had to sit there, with all the time in the world to think about death, and await its coming. This was why they were made to face the enemy, for if they once turned their backs, men and horses would have been seized by an irresistible desire to run away. Seeing the danger, they were able to defy it. There is no greater, nor less conspicuous, heroism than this.

One man had just had his head shot away, two of the horses attached to an ammunition waggon were plunging in agony, their bellies ripped open; and the enemy fire remained so deadly accurate that the entire battery would inevitably be wiped out if it stayed where it was. Despite all the difficulties of changing their position, something had to be done to get out of the line of fire. At last, the captain made up his mind, and gave the order:

"Bring up the limbers!"

The dangerous manoeuvre was carried out at lightning speed: wheeling in a semi-circle, the drivers brought up the limbers, the gunners hooked up the spades of the guns. But the immediate effect of this movement was to offer the enemy a more extended target, and they immediately increased their rate of fire. Three more men were knocked out, then the battery made off at the trot, describing a wide arc in order to take up its position some fifty yards to the right, on rising ground on the other flank of the 106th. Once more the guns were unlimbered, once more the drivers found themselves facing the enemy and the battery started firing, all with so brief a pause that the ground seemed scarcely to have stopped quivering.

This time, Maurice uttered a loud cry. For once again the German batteries had succeeded in finding the range almost at once, and their third shell scored a direct hit on Honoré's gun. They saw him spring forward, exploring the damage – a great piece had been torn away from the bronze muzzle. But it could still be loaded, and as soon as they had removed the corpse of another gunner, whose blood spurted all over the gun carriage, the whole procedure was repeated once again.

"No, it's not young Louis," said Maurice expressing his thoughts aloud. "It's him laying the gun. He must have been wounded all the same, for he's only using his left arm. . . ."

At this point, Jean, who had hitherto remained silent, interrupted him with an agonized exclamation:

"They'll never stick it. They're finished!"

And true enough, in less than five minutes this second position was becoming as impossible to hold as the first, such was the precision of the stream of shells. One of them knocked out a gun, killing a lieutenant and two men. Not a round was wasted, so that, if they insisted on remaining there much longer, not a single gun or artilleryman would be left.

Then, for the second time, the captain's voice rang out:

"Bring up the limbers."

The manoeuvre was repeated, the drivers galloped up, making a half-turn so that the gunners could attach the gun to the limber. But this time, in the middle of the movement, a shell splinter tore open Louis's throat, smashing his jaw; and he slumped across the spade of the gun just as he was starting to lift it. At the same moment Adolphe was caught in the furious salvo that broke out as men and limbers drove across the line of fire. He was hurled out of the saddle, shot through the chest, arms flung wide. And, in a last convulsion, his arms closed round the body of his friend, so that they met their death locked in a ghastly embrace.

Yet, despite all the horses that had been killed, despite the confusion caused among the men by the deadly bombardment, the whole battery succeeded in getting up to the slope and installing itself further forward, a few yards from the spot where Maurice and Jean were lying. For the third time the guns were unlimbered, the drivers rode off and turned to face the enemy, while the gunners straight away opened fire with an obstinate and invincible heroism.

"This is the end of everything!" said Maurice, in a voice that could scarcely be heard.

And, in truth, it seemed as though earth and sky had become fused. Rocks were split open, at times the sun was hidden by dense smoke. In the midst of the terrifying din, horses could be seen, bewildered, stupefied, hanging their heads. The tall figure of the captain seemed to be everywhere at once. Then, all of a sudden, shot through the head, he crashed to the ground like a shattered flagpole.

But the struggle went on, stubborn and unhurried, concentrated around Honoré's gun. Despite his sergeant's stripes, he himself had to lend a hand, for there were only three gunners left. While they fetched the ammunition, loaded, handled the swab and the ramrod, he laid the gun and lit the fuse. They had sent for men and horses from the reserve, to take the place of those that had been killed; but they were a long time coming, and meanwhile they had to manage without them. The maddening thing was that they still couldn't reach their target, the shells they fired nearly all exploded in the air, without doing much damage to those terrible batteries on the other side whose fire was so effective.

Then, all of a sudden, Honoré let out a tremendous oath that could be heard above the thunder of battle : of all the bad luck, the right wheel of his gun had been smashed to pieces ! God in heaven ! With one leg broken, the poor bitch lay on her side, her nose in the mud, lame and useless ! Tears streaming down his face, he seized the barrel in both hands, as if hoping to get it back into position simply through the warmth of his affection for it. The best gun of the lot, the only one that had succeeded in finding its target with one or two shells ! Then a crazy notion took possession of him;

they would replace the wheel, then and there under fire. With the help of one of the gunners, he succeeded in finding the spare wheel amongst the baggage, and they started to carry out the most dangerous operation that could be performed on a battlefield. Fortunately, the men and horses of the reserve had at last arrived, and there were two fresh gunners to lend a hand.

But now, once again, the battery was to be moved, and they had to abandon their heroic attempt, for at any moment the order to retreat would be given.

"Get a move on, mates," Honoré kept saying. "At least we must take it with us; we're not going to let them have it!"

His one idea was to save his gun, like saving the regimental colours. And he was still urging them on, when he was struck down, his right arm shot away, his left side ripped open. He fell back on to the gun, and there he lay, as though lying in state, head erect, his face, unmarked and beautiful in its anger, turned towards the enemy. And in his clenched fingers he still clutched a letter, snatched from his torn uniform and stained by the steady drip of his blood.

Then the only lieutenant who had not yet been killed gave the order :

"Bring up the limbers!"

One of the ammunition waggons had been hit, and the shells were exploding like a succession of fireworks. Another had to be left behind, as the horses were needed to save a gun whose team had been killed. Then, for the last time, the drivers wheeled their teams into position, the four remaining guns were hooked up, and away they galloped, not stopping until they reached the outskirts of the Garenne forest, three-quarters of a mile away.

Maurice, who had been watching everything that happened, kept repeating in a mechanical voice, his teeth chattering with horror :

"The poor fellow! Oh, the poor fellow!"

This last blow only increased the gnawing at his stomach. His animal instincts were in revolt : he had reached the end of his tether, and he was faint with hunger. The world seemed to be swimming before his eyes, he was no longer even conscious of how dangerous their position had become, now that the battery had had to withdraw. At any minute, a major attack might be launched against the plateau.

"Listen," he said to Jean. "I must have something to eat. . . . Even if it's the last thing I do, I must have a bite!"

257

He opened his haversack, took out the loaf with trembling hands and started eating it voraciously. Bullets whistled around him, two shells exploded a few yards away, but for him everything had ceased to matter except the need to satisfy his hunger.

"D'you want some, Jean?"

Jean looked at him, his mind numbed, eyes staring, his belly wracked by the same longing.

"All right, I may as well. I've had as much as I can stand."

They shared out the bread and ate it greedily, without a thought for anything else until they had finished the last mouthful. And it was only then that they noticed the colonel, sitting on his big horse, dangling his bloody boot. The 106th was scattering in every direction. Some of the companies had already fled. And only then, forced at last to yield to the flood, did the colonel raise his sword and, with eyes full of tears, exclaim :

"God help you, lads. . . . He hasn't done much for us so far !"

Then, surrounded by fleeing men, he disappeared into a dip in the ground.

Hardly knowing what they were doing, Jean and Maurice found themselves behind the hedge with the remnants of their company. No more than forty men were left under Lieutenant Rochas's command. They had managed to save the colours, and the second-lieutenant who was carrying them had furled the silken flag round the haft, to make it less conspicuous. They hurried along as far as the end of the hedge, then fanned out on a hillside, crouching amongst the trees. Here Rochas decided to start firing again : strung out like this, and under cover, there was a chance of making a stand, especially as the cavalry on their right were preparing to attack, and some regiments of the line had been brought up in support.

Maurice was now becoming aware of the slow, irresistible grip that was closing in on them. First thing in the morning, he had watched the Prussians streaming through the Saint-Albert gorge, and capturing first Saint-Menges, then Fleigneux; now, from beyond the Forest of Garenne, he could hear the thundering guns of the Prussian Guards, and had already noticed new German uniforms coming from the direction of the Givonne. Before long, the Guards would link up with the Vth Corps, and the circle would be complete, trapping the entire French army within a living wall, supported by a ring of blazing artillery. It must have been with some desperate idea of breaking out of this wall, that a division of

258

the reserve cavalry, General Margueritte's, was massing behind a fold in the ground, ready to charge. But they would be charging to their death, for the honour of France; no other result was possible. And Maurice, forced to look on at this terrible spectacle, thought of Prosper.

Since early morning, Prosper had done nothing but ride backwards and forwards across the plain of Illy, in a succession of marches and counter-marches. They had been woken at dawn, one by one, to avoid sounding the bugle; and, in order to make coffee, had had to rig up their cloaks to hide the fires, so as not to alert the Prussians. From then on, they had had little idea of what was happening: they heard cannon, saw smoke, watched the infantry moving in the distance, without understanding the significance of the battle or its result, without engaging in any action, apparently forgotten by the generals. Prosper could scarcely keep his eyes open. Overwhelmed by an invincible lassitude, the result of all the suffering and broken nights, of the piled-up fatigue and the swaying movement of his horse, he was beginning to have hallucinations; he imagined he was lying on the ground, snoring away on a mattress stuffed with pebbles, or dreamt of being in a comfortable bed, with white sheets. For minutes at a time, he actually dropped off to sleep in the saddle, became simply an inert object, borne along at his horse's whim. Some of the men, indeed, had fallen off like this, so utterly weary that the sound of the bugle no longer awoke them, and they had to be kicked awake, dragged back from their sleepy limbo.

"They don't give a damn for us, not a bloody damn," Prosper kept repeating to himself, in an effort to shake off this irresistible torpor.

At six o'clock, the cannon had started blazing away. Riding up a hill, two of his mates had been killed by a shell, right next to him. Further on, three more had been flung from the saddle, riddled by bullets, without knowing which direction they came from. It was exasperating, this futile, dangerous parading backwards and forwards across the battlefield. Now, towards one o'clock, he realized that the authorities had decided that they should at least be killed decently. The whole of Margueritte's division, three regiments of Chasseurs d'Afrique, one of Chasseurs de France and one of Hussars, had been assembled in a shallow valley, on the left of the road, just below the Calvary. The bugles sounded the dismount, the officers' orders rang out:

"Tighten your girths, check your saddlebags!"

Prosper dismounted, stretched himself and patted his horse. Poor Zephyr, he was as tired as his master, fed up with the whole ridiculous business. And, on top of this, all the clutter he had to carry : a change of clothes in the saddlebags, tunic and breeches, on top of them the rolled-up cloak, a wallet filled with first-aid materials at the back of the saddle, with a bag containing rations on the other side, not to mention sheepskin, water-bottle and mess-tin. As he pulled up the girth, and made sure that everything was in order, the cavalryman pitied the poor brute from the bottom of his heart.

Things were beginning to look tough. Prosper, no more of a coward than the next man, felt his mouth so dry that he lit a cigarette. Whenever you're about to charge, you can't help saying to yourself : "This time, I've had it!" Five or six minutes passed. General Margueritte was said to have gone on ahead to reconnoitre the terrain. They waited. The five regiments were drawn up in three columns, each consisting of seven squadrons, one behind the other – a pretty good target for the guns.

Suddenly, the bugles sounded to horse, and almost immediately another call rang out : "Draw your swords!"

The colonels of each regiment had already ridden ahead and taken up their position twenty-five yards in front. The captains were at their posts, at the head of their men. Again the waiting began. Not a sound, not a whisper beneath the burning sun, only a beating of hearts. The final order was yet to come that would bring this motionless mass to life, streaming forward like a gale of wind.

But, at this moment, an officer appeared over the crest of the hill; he was wounded, with two men holding him up in the saddle. At first, no one recognized him. Then a groan went up, and broke into a wild clamour. It was General Margueritte. A bullet had pierced his cheek, and he was already dying. Unable to speak, he waved his arm in the direction of the enemy. The roar of voices grew louder.

"It's the general. We'll make them pay for this!"

Whereupon, the colonel of the first regiment, raising his sabre high in the air, yelled in a voice of thunder :

"Charge!"

The trumpets sounded, the whole formation moved off at the trot. Prosper was in the front rank, at the far end of the right flank. The most dangerous place is always the centre, where the enemy

260

instinctively concentrate their fire. As they reached the brow of the hill where the Calvary stood, and started to descend on the other side towards the huge plain, he could clearly distinguish, three-quarters of a mile away, the Prussian squares they were to fling themselves upon. Yet he trotted on as though in a dream; he had the lightness, the floating sensation, of being asleep, an extra-ordinary emptiness in his brain, that left him without a thought. The machine moved forward on its own, driven by an irresistible impulse. In order to keep the ranks as tightly closed as possible, to make them as solid as granite, they kept saying: "Feel the next man's boot, feel the next man's boot." Then as the pace increased, and the trot changed to a furious gallop, the Chasseurs d'Afrique started to yell like Arab horsemen, maddening their steeds with their wild, shrill cries. Soon they were charging hell-for-leather, their ferocious yelling accompanied by the sputter of bullets, rattling like hail against mess-tins, water-bottles and metal breastplates, and the swirling hurricane thundered past, making the earth tremble and leaving behind in the sunlight a smell of scorched wool and sweating beasts.

Five hundred yards on, Prosper was flung to the ground by a terrible surge that swept everything before it. He caught hold of Zephyr by the mane, and managed to get back into the saddle. The centre, pounded by the bombardment, had begun to give way, and the whirling flanks drew in upon one another, determined to main-tain the impetus of the charge. But the leading squadron had been almost wiped out, the ground was encumbered with fallen horses, some killed outright, others struggling in agony, while horseless men ran hither and thither, frantically looking for a fresh mount. Already the plain was strewn with dead, and the riderless horses went on galloping, returning of their own accord to take their places in the battle line as though drawn on by the smell of gunpowder. The fury of the charge revived as the second squadron advanced, the men crouching over their horses' withers, holding their sabres at the ready. Amid the deafening clamour they had succeeded in covering another two hundred yards, when once again the centre gave way before the hail of bullets; and and horses crashed to the ground, blocking the way in an inextricable confusion of dead and dying bodies. It was the second squadron's turn to be mown down, wiped out, making way for those behind them.

This time, as a third charge gathered force, stubbornly heroic, Prosper found himself surrounded by Hussars and Chasseurs de

261

France. The regiments had all become mixed up, in one vast wave, that kept breaking and endlessly reforming, sweeping away everything that lay in its path. Prosper had little idea of what was happening, and simply trusted to Zephyr, the horse he was so devoted to, that seemed to be maddened by a wound in the ear. Now that he was in the centre, all around him horses were rearing in the air and falling over backwards, men were hurled to the ground as though caught by a sudden gust of wind, while others, killed outright, remained in the saddle, still charging forward with staring, sightless eyes. And this time, beyond the two hundred yards they had freshly gained, the stubble fields could be seen covered with dead and dying. There were some with their heads buried in the ground. Others lay on their backs, staring up at the sun, their terrified eyes starting out of their heads. And a big black horse belonging to an officer, its belly ripped open, vainly attempted to get up, its forefeet tangled in its own guts. Beneath the ever-increasing fire, once more the two wings stormed on, wheeled to the centre, fighting desperately.

In the end, it was only the fourth squadron, charging for the fourth time, that succeeded in reaching the Prussian lines. Swinging his sabre, Prosper struck out savagely at the helmets and dark-coloured uniforms that he saw through a kind of mist. All around, the din was so tremendous that he could no longer hear his own voice, though he was yelling at the top of his lungs. But behind the first line of Prussians lay another, and another, and another. Heroism was useless, for the endless ranks of soldiers stood there like tall grass, engulfing horses and riders, and the more you mowed them down the more of them there were. The firing at blank range became so intense that uniforms were set on fire. Everything was swallowed up in a gulf of stabbing bayonets, smashed-in chests, split skulls. The French were to lose two-thirds of their men, and all that remained of this famous charge was the crazy heroism of having undertaken it. Then, suddenly, Zephyr, struck full in the chest by a bullet, hurtled to the ground, crushing Prosper's right thigh, and so acute was the pain that he lost consciousness.

Maurice and Jean, who had been watching the heroic charge intently, cried out angrily :

"God in heaven, what's the use of courage?"

And they went on firing their rifles, crouched amongst the bushes on the little hillock. Even Rochas had picked up a rifle and was joining in. But this time the plain of Illy was lost for good, and the Prussian troops were swarming across it from all sides. It was about two o'clock by the time the German Vth Corps eventually joined up with the Prussian Guards, closing the circle.

Suddenly Jean was flung backwards.

"I've had it this time," he gasped.

Something had struck the top of his head like a blow with a hammer, tearing his cap to bits and flinging it behind him. At first it felt as though his skull had been laid open, exposing his brain, and for several seconds he was afraid to touch it, convinced that he would feel a hole there. Then, taking a chance, he raised his hand, and saw that his fingers were covered with blood. And, so violent was the shock, that he fainted away.

At that moment, Rochas gave orders to retreat; a company of Prussians had advanced to within two or three hundred yards of them, and at any moment they might be taken prisoner.

"Don't be in a hurry now. . . . Turn and fire, then make for that little wall. . . . That's where we'll assemble!"

Maurice was at his wit's end.

"Surely we're not going to leave the corporal behind, sir?"

"If it's all up with him, what else can we do?"

"But he's still breathing, sir. . . . We must carry him. . . ."

Rochas merely shrugged his shoulders, as much as to say that in battle you can't bother about every man that gets wounded. Whereupon Maurice turned to Pache and Lapoulle:

"Here, give me a hand. I'm not strong enough on my own."

But they scarcely heard him, preoccupied with their own safety, concerned only by the instinct of self-preservation. Crawling on hands and knees, they were making for the wall as fast as they could. The Prussians were now only a hundred yards away.

Weeping with rage, Maurice, left alone with the unconscious corporal, took him in his arms and tried to carry him. But he was too weak, too worn out with exhaustion and strain. Almost immediately, he staggered and fell to the ground. If only he could find a stretcher-bearer! Desperately looking around, he thought he saw one amongst the fugitives, and waved violently. But no one came.

With a last frantic effort, he lifted Jean up again and managed to stagger another thirty yards, but a shell, exploding nearby, knocked him over. He was convinced his end had come, that he, too, was going to die with his comrade.

Presently, however, he got to his feet and, feeling himself all over, discovered that he was not even scratched. What was to stop him running away? There was still time, he could still reach the wall, where safety awaited him. Again he experienced a wave of panic fear, but as he was on the point of making a dash for it, something held him back. No, it was impossible, he couldn't abandon Jean! He would never forgive himself, the friendship that had sprung up between himself and the peasant had struck deep, to the roots of his being; it was something dating back, perhaps, to the very first days of creation, when there had been only two men in the whole world, neither of whom could let down the other without betraying himself.

If Maurice had not eaten that loaf of bread an hour ago, he would never have found the strength to do what he now did. In any case, afterwards, he found it impossible to remember just what happened. Somehow or other he must have got Jean on to his shoulders, then somehow dragged himself through the bushes and across the stubble, and finally managed to get to his feet. Some invincible determination sustained him, giving him strength enough to carry a mountain. Behind the wall, he found Rochas and the few men belonging to their squad that were left, still firing, still defending the colours, which the second-lieutenant clutched under his arm.

In the event of failure, nobody had thought of preparing a plan of retreat beforehand. In the utter confusion and lack of foresight, each general was free to do as he chose, and now, under the formidable pressure of the victorious German armies, they were all making for Sedan. The second division of the 7th Corps was withdrawing in fairly good order, whereas the remnants of the other two divisions, inextricably mixed up with the 1st Corps, were streaming towards the town in a pathetic rout, a torrent of fear and anger sweeping along both men and horses.

But, at this moment, Maurice saw with delight that Jean had opened his eyes again; and as he ran to a nearby stream, in order to get water to wash his face, he was amazed to see, on his right, at the bottom of a remote valley protected by steep hills, the same peasant that he had noticed earlier in the morning, still driving his plough, drawn by the big white horse. What was the point of wasting a day? The corn wouldn't stop growing or people living, just because there happened to be a battle.

264

IV

As he reached the platform outside the attic and looked around him Delaherche was more anxious than ever to find out for certain what was happening. It was clear that most of the shells were falling beyond the town, and that the three or four that had smashed the roofs of the nearby houses were merely in response to the slow, ineffectual firing from the Palatinate fort. But he could see nothing of the battle that was being waged, and his determination to obtain reliable information was accentuated by the fear that, in the catastrophe, he might lose both his fortune and his life. He decided to go indoors again, leaving the telescope trained on the German batteries.

When he reached the factory garden, however, he was taken aback by the sight that met his eyes. It was nearly one o'clock, the emergency hospital was already crowded with wounded, and an endless line of vehicles was still arriving at the gate. As regulation ambulances were by now in short supply, every kind of ammunition-waggon and forage-cart had been requisitioned on the battlefield, and before long these were joined by hay-carts from the farms, drawn by whatever horses that could be found. All of these were filled with men who had been picked up by the mobile ambulances and given first-aid; an endless stream of wretched creatures, some sickly pale, others purple in the face; many of them unconscious, others groaning with pain. There were men so utterly bewildered that they merely abandoned themselves to the care of the nurses, their eyes starting out of their heads, while some of them died of shock directly they were touched. This influx of patients had reached the point where every mattress in the huge, low room was occupied, and Major Bouroche had to give orders for them to be laid on the straw that had been spread out on the floor. He and his assistants, however, were still managing to cope with the operations; he had simply had another table installed in the operating shed, covered with a mattress and a sheet of oil-cloth. Swiftly, one of the assistants would sprinkle a pad with chloroform and hold it over the patients' faces, then thin, steel blades gleamed, saws made a sound like a carpenter's rasp, and there would be a sudden gush of blood, stanched immediately. As they brought in those to be operated on and carried them away, there was such a continual coming and going that there was scarcely time to sponge down the oil-cloth; while at the far end of the lawn, the mortuary that had been installed behind a clump of laburnums to take the corpses, was already beginning to fill up with amputated arms and legs, and all the bits of flesh and bone left on the operating table.

Seated beneath one of the tall trees, Mme. Delaherche and Gilberte were rolling bandages for dear life. Bouroche, who happened to be passing, cheeks aflame, his apron already scarlet with blood, flung a bundle of linen to Delaherche and called out :

"Come on, here's a job for you . . . make yourself useful."

But the mill-owner protested :

"I'm sorry, but I have to go and see what news there is. No one has the slightest idea what's going on."

Then, touching his wife's hair lightly with his lips, he continued :

"My poor Gilberte, to think that a single shell could set the whole of this place on fire ! It's frightening."

She was very pale, and as she raised her head and glanced around, she shuddered. Then, in spite of herself, the irrepressible smile came back, and she replied :

"Yes, it *is* frightening, all these men being operated on. . . . The odd thing is, how I can stay here without fainting."

Mme. Delaherche, who had seen her son kissing his wife's hair, made a gesture as though to stop him, thinking of that other man who must have been doing the same thing a short time ago. But the old hands trembled, and she muttered to herself :

"In the midst of all this suffering, one has to forget about one's own !"

Delaherche turned away, promising to be back soon with definite news, but as soon as he stepped into the Rue Maqua, he was surprised to see how many soldiers were already pouring into the town, unarmed, their ragged uniforms covered with dust. Yet he found it impossible to get any clear account of what had happened from the men he questioned.

Some of them, still dazed, simply said they did not know : others talked at great length, with such wild gestures and so incoherently, that they seemed to be out of their minds. Presently, scarcely realizing what he was doing, Delaherche set out once more for the

Sub-Prefecture, on the assumption that all news must eventually arrive there. As he was crossing the Place du Collège, two guns, probably all that was left of a battery, drew up against the pavement. In the Grande Rue he could not fail to realize that the town was rapidly becoming choked with fugitives: three horseless Hussars were sitting in a doorway, sharing a loaf of bread; two more were slowly leading their horses by the bridles, not knowing where to take them; distracted officers were hurrying along, apparently without any idea where they were going. In the Place Turenne, a second-lieutenant advised him not to hang about, as shells were beginning to fall more frequently; indeed, only a moment ago one had destroyed the railings round the statue of the famous soldier, conqueror of the Palatinate. And as he quickly turned into the Rue de la Sous-Préfecture, two more exploded on the bridge across the Meuse, with a terrible bang.

He was standing outside the porter's lodge, trying to think of some pretext for questioning one of the aides-de-camp, when he was hailed by a youthful voice:

"M. Delaherche, come inside, quick! It's risky standing out there."

It was Rose, whom he had forgotten all about, though she was one of his mill-girls. Thanks to her, he would now be able to go where he liked in the Prefecture; and he entered the concierge's room, glad of a chance to sit down.

"Just fancy, sir, all this has made mother so ill that she's gone to lie down. So, as you see, I'm the only one left, because Dad's gone to the Citadel with the National Guard. . . . A few minutes ago, to show he hadn't lost heart, the Emperor insisted on going out, and managed to get to the end of the street, as far as the bridge. Only then a shell fell, right in front of him, killing one of his orderlies' horses, and he had to come back. . . . What else could he do?"

"Then you must know what's happening. . . . What were these gentlemen talking about?"

She looked at him in surprise. In the midst of all this terrible upheaval, she remained fresh and cheerful, with her fine hair and bright, childish eyes, but without the slightest idea of what was happening.

"I've no idea. . . . about midday, I took up a letter for Marshal MacMahon. The Emperor was with him, and they stayed there talking for the best part of an hour. The marshal was in bed, and the Emperor sat on a chair beside him. . . . I know that, because I saw them with my own eyes, when somebody opened the door."

"Well, what were they talking about?"

Again she stared at him, and this time she could not help laughing.

"Why, however should I know? Nobody in the world knows what they were talking about."

It was true, and he made a gesture to apologize for asking such a stupid question. Nevertheless, the thought of this supremely important conversation bothered him : it was bound to have been of the greatest interest! What decision had they come to?

"Now the Emperor's gone back to his study," Rose continued. "He's in a meeting with two generals, just back from the battlefield."

She broke off, glancing quickly at the flight of steps outside.

"Look, that's one of them, there. . . . And that's the other one with him."

Quickly stepping outside, he recognized General Douay and General Ducrot, whose horses were waiting for them. He watched them mount and ride away. After the retreat from the Illy plain, they had both hurried back to warn the Emperor that the battle was lost. They gave him a detailed account of what had happened, explaining that both the army and Sedan were now surrounded on all sides, and that a terrible disaster was inevitable.

In his study, the Emperor, weak with illness, walked up and down for a minute or two in silence. The only other person in the room was an aide-de-camp, standing near the door. He went on pacing backwards and forwards between the fireplace and the window, his ravaged face twitching with a nervous tic, while his back seemed more bowed than ever, as if the weight of the whole world was on his shoulders; beneath their heavy lids the lifeless eyes expressed the resignation of a man who has gambled against fate and lost the final throw. Yet every time he came back to the open window, he paused there a moment, shuddering.

During one of these brief halts, waving a trembling hand, he muttered :

"Oh, those cannon, those cannon, they haven't stopped all day !"

Indeed, the noise from the batteries at La Marfée and Frénois could be heard unexpectedly clearly. It was like the rumbling of thunder, rattling the windows, a persistent, nerve-racking din. And he must have felt that, from now on, the struggle had become hopeless, that any further resistance would be criminal. What was

268

the use of more blood being shed, more limbs crushed, more heads
shot away? Of adding still more dead to those already killed in
the course of the campaign? Since they had been defeated, since
everything was now over, why call for further massacre? Have done
with this abomination, all this ghastly suffering that cried aloud to
heaven to be brought to an end.

Back at the window, the Emperor, who was trembling again,
clapped his hands to his ears.

"Oh, those guns, those everlasting guns!"

Perhaps it was the terrible thought of his personal responsibility
that had suddenly struck him, a vision of the thousands of bleeding
bodies that lay out there as a result of his mistakes; or perhaps it was
only the yearning pity of a dreamer's heart, of a man still haunted
by notions of humanity : but beneath this terrible stroke of fate, that
was destroying his fortune and sweeping it away like straw in the
wind, he still found tears for others, dazed by the senseless butchery
that was still going on, without strength to bear it any longer.

"Oh, those guns, those guns. Stop them at once! . . . At once, do
you hear?"

And this Emperor who no longer had a throne, having entrusted
his royal powers to the Empress, this leader of an army who could
no longer give orders, having handed over supreme command to
Marshal Bazaine, felt a sudden reawakening of authority, an
irresistible determination to assert himself for the last time. Ever
since Châlons, he had remained in the background, without issuing
a single order, resigned to being nothing but a nameless, tiresome
nonentity, a troublesome package, relegated to the baggage-train.
Only now, in the moment of defeat, did he feel himself once more
an Emperor : and so, in the bewildered pity of his heart, the first,
the only order he still had to give, was to run up the white flag over
the Citadel, to sue for an armistice.

"Oh, those guns, those guns. . .! Get hold of a sheet, a tablecloth,
whatever you can find. Take it to the Citadel as quickly as possible
. . . and tell them they've got to put an end to this!"

The aide-de-camp hurried off, the Emperor went back to his
shambling pacing, backwards and forwards between fireplace and
window, and the batteries thundered on, shaking the whole house.

Downstairs, where Delaherche was still talking to Rose, a duty
sergeant hurriedly approached them.

"Mademoiselle, if you please, I can't find anything suitable. . . .
Have you got such a thing as a piece of white cloth?"

"Would a towel do?"

"No, no, it wouldn't be big enough. . . . Maybe you could find a sheet?"

Obliging as ever, Rose quickly rushed to a cupboard.

"I don't seem to have anything white that would be big enough. . . . Wait a minute, would a tablecloth do?"

"Splendid, that'll be just the thing."

And as he was making off, he added: "We need it to make a white flag. It's to be run up over the Citadel, to sue for peace. . . . Many thanks, mademoiselle."

Involuntarily, Delaherche felt suddenly pleased. So at last there was to be peace! Then, realizing that his satisfaction was unpatriotic, he checked himself. Nevertheless, he could not help feeling immensely relieved as he watched a colonel and a captain, followed by a sergeant, hurrying away from the Sub-Prefecture. The colonel was carrying the tablecloth rolled up under his arm. He decided to follow them, and left Rose standing there, still proud of herself for having thought of the tablecloth. At that moment, two o'clock struck.

Outside the Town Hall, Delaherche was pushed aside by a bunch of haggard-looking soldiers, who were coming down from the Faubourg de la Cassine; and, having lost sight of the colonel, he decided to forgo the pleasure of seeing the white flag hoisted. He certainly wouldn't be allowed into the Keep and, besides, hearing that shells were still falling on the College, he was seized by a new anxiety: perhaps the mill had caught fire while he had been away. He rushed off once more, a prey to feverish fears and glad to have a reason for running. But the streets were blocked by groups of people, and every cross-road was cluttered up with obstacles. Only when he reached the Rue Maqua, and saw his vast building still intact, did he heave a sigh of relief. As he entered the gates, he shouted to his mother and wife:

"Everything's going to be all right! They're hoisting the white flag, demanding a cease fire."

Then he stopped short, for the emergency hospital was a truly terrible sight.

In the huge drying-room, the main door of which was wide open, not only were all the mattresses occupied, but there was now no room on the floor. They had started putting straw between the beds, laying the wounded men close together. There were already more than two hundred of them, and more kept arriving. And all this heaped-up misery was lit by the harsh light from the big windows. Now and then, at too sudden a movement, someone would give an involuntary yell. In the dank air, men could be heard choking in their death agony; and from the far end came a gentle moaning sound, like someone singing, that went on and on. Then silence would fall, deeper than ever, the numbness of resignation, stupor, the grim torpor of the death chamber, broken only by the nurses' footsteps and the sound of whispering. Wounds, hurriedly dressed on the battlefield, some of them still unbandaged, displayed their misery through ragged greatcoats and torn trousers. Feet, crushed and bleeding, could be seen, still wearing boots; arms and legs hung inert, from joints that looked as though they had been smashed with a hammer; and there were shattered hands, with the fingers dangling from a shred of skin. Fractured arms and legs seemed the most common injury, stiff with pain, heavy as lead, but it was wounds in the stomach, chest and head that caused the greatest anxiety, blood flowing from hideous wounds, entrails twisted beneath the swollen skin, bodies hacked and cut to pieces, twisted and contorted. Here and there lay men who had been shot through the lungs, the wound in some cases scarcely perceptible and hardly bleeding, in others, blood gushing from gaping holes; and men with internal haemorrhages that left no mark, who would suddenly break into delirium. But the most frequent wounds were those in the head : broken jaws reduced to a bloody pulp of teeth and tongue; eyes protruding from smashed sockets; skulls split open, exposing the brain. In those cases where the bullet had actually touched the brain, the men lay like corpses, in a complete coma; whereas others, those suffering from fever or a fractured limb, tossed about, pleading for something to drink.

In the shed where the operations were being performed, there was still more horror. In the frantic rush, they were only operating on the most urgent cases, where the desperate condition of the wounded made it essential. If there was the slightest fear of haemorrhage, Bouroche amputated immediately. Similarly, if the wound was in a dangerous place, the base of the skull, armpit, groin, knee or elbow joint, he started probing without delay, to extract the bullet. Other wounds, that could be left for further observation, were simply dressed by the nurses, under his instructions. He had himself performed four amputations already, spacing out such major operations by extracting a few bullets, in order to get a little rest; and he was beginning to feel tired. There were

271

only two operating tables, his and another where one of his assistants was at work. He had had a sheet hung up between them, so that the men being operated upon could not see one another. But it was no use washing down the tables, it was impossible to remove the traces of blood, while the buckets they kept emptying on to a bed of marguerites, a few yards away, appeared to be full of pure blood, for a single basinful was enough to turn a whole bucketful of clean water bright red. Though there was plenty of fresh air, a nauseating smell hung over the operating tables, bandages and dressings, mixed with the stale odour of chloroform.

Shuddering with compassion at this pitiable spectacle, Delaherche's attention was distracted by a landau drawing up beneath the portico. This genteel conveyance must have been all they could find, and it was filled with wounded men, eight of them, lying on top of each other. As the last one was helped out, the mill-owner uttered a cry of shocked surprise, for he had recognized Captain Beaudoin.

"Oh, my poor fellow . . .! Wait a minute, I'll go and find my mother and wife."

Leaving the bandages to two servants, they immediately returned with Delaherche. The nurses had already carried the captain into the drying-room, and were about to lay him down on a pile of straw when Delaherche noticed a soldier lying on a mattress, motionless, with ashen face and staring eyes.

"Look, that man over there, surely he must be dead?"

"Why, true enough," muttered one of the orderlies, "I reckon he can do without a mattress!"

He and his mate picked up the body, and took it away to the morgue that had been set up behind the laburnum tree. A dozen bodies already lay there, some stretched out as though in pain, others just flung down, twisted into hideous positions. Some of them seemed to be sneering, eyes blank, teeth bared beneath the drawn-back lips, with huge tears still streaming down the set, terribly sad faces. One of them, a small, skinny man, still quite young, with half his head shot away, was clasping the photograph of a woman to his breast, one of those faded snapshots taken in the outer suburbs, now spattered with blood. And scattered pell-mell around the dead bodies were piles of amputated legs and arms, of flesh and bone from the operating tables, like the sweepings of a butcher's shop.

Directly she caught sight of Captain Beaudoin, Gilberte had begun to tremble. Good heavens how pale he was, lying there on

272

the mattress, his face deathly pale beneath the mud and filth! And the thought that only a few hours ago, bursting with life and freshly shaven, he had held her in his arms, froze the blood in her veins. She knelt down beside him, murmuring:

"How terrible, my dear! How terrible! But everything's going to be all right."

Mechanically, she took out her handkerchief and wiped his face, for she could not bear to see him like this, streaming with sweat, his cheeks blackened by gunpowder. It seemed to her that by cleaning him up a bit, she would be comforting him.

"See? It's not going to be too bad . . . it's only your leg."

In a state of semi-consciousness, the captain opened his eyes painfully. He had recognized his friends, and was doing his best to smile at them.

"Yes, only the leg. . . . I didn't even feel it, I thought I must have tripped and fallen over. . . ."

He spoke with the greatest difficulty, but managed to ask for water. Whereupon Mme. Delaherche, who was standing on the other side of him, hurried away to fetch a jug of water and a tumbler, into which she poured a little brandy. And when the captain had avidly drunk what was in the tumbler, she shared the rest of the jugful between the wounded men on either side, who were imploring her to give them something to drink. A Zouave, who did not manage to get any, broke down and sobbed.

Meanwhile, Delaherche was trying to get a word with Major Bouroche, in the hope of being able to do something for the captain. Bouroche had just come into the room in his blood-stained apron, with his broad, sweaty face framed in its leonine mane of hair; and as he passed, the men dragged themselves up on their mattresses, tried to stop him, all hoping to be operated on next, so that they could know the worst. Everywhere he went, he was followed by muttered prayers, and fumbling fingers plucked at his clothes. But, completely preoccupied, breathless with exhaustion, he merely went on with his work, paying no attention to anybody. He was talking to himself, half aloud, counting them, giving them numbers, classifying them: this one first, next that one, then that one over there; a jawbone, an arm, a thigh. And the assistant who accompanied them listened carefully, doing his best to remember.

"Excue me, Major," said Delaherche, "there's a Captain Beaudoin here. . . ."

Bouroche stared at him:

273

"What, Beaudoin here . . .? The poor bastard!"

He went over to the wounded man, and stood looking down at him. But he must have seen at a glance that he was in a bad way, for he immediately went on, without even bothering to examine his leg:

"Right, they can bring him in next, as soon as I've finished the operation they're getting ready now."

And he returned to his shed, followed by Delaherche, determined not to let him out of his sight lest he forget his promise.

The next case was a dislocated shoulder, and was to be treated by the Lisfranc method; what surgeons call "a pretty job", quick and elegant, all over in less than a minute. They had already given the patient chloroform, while an assistant, gripping the shoulder with both hands, pressed his fingers into the armpit, thumbs on top. Whereupon Bouroche, armed with a long scalpel, told them to sit the man up, took hold of the deltoid and pierced the flesh, severing the muscles, then, with a backward movement, cut through the joint with one stroke, and the arm fell to the ground. Meanwhile, sliding his fingers along, the assistant pressed hard on the humeral artery.

"Lie him down again!" said Bouroche, starting to sew up the wound, and smiling involuntarily to find that he had only taken thirty-five seconds. All that now remained was to pull the tongue of flesh over the wound. It was "a pretty job" because of the danger, for in three minutes a man could lose all the blood in his body through the humeral artery, apart from the fact that there's always a danger of death when a wounded man is made to sit up while under chloroform.

Delaherche was so scared that he wanted to run away, but there wasn't time; the arm was already under the table, and the man who had been operated on, a powerful peasant recently recruited, was beginning to come round. Catching sight of the arm as one of the nurses was taking it away, he glanced at his shoulder, and realizing what had happened, burst out furiously:

"Why, for Christ's sake! That's a bloody silly thing to have done!"

Bouroche was too exhausted to reply. But presently, adopting a cheerful manner, he managed to say:

"I only acted for the best. I didn't want you to snuff it, my boy. . . . In any case, I asked you first, and you agreed."

"I agreed? I agreed . . .? How was I to know?"

Then, recovering his temper, he began crying bitterly.

"How the hell am I going to manage now?"

They carried him back to his place on the straw, while the table and oilcloth were vigorously washed down, and another bucket of bloody water was taken out to the lawn and chucked on the flower-bed, dyeing the marguerites a deeper red.

Meanwhile, to Delaherche's astonishment, the guns were still firing. Why hadn't they stopped, since by this time Rose's tablecloth must have been hoisted over the Citadel? As a matter of fact, the noise from the Prussian batteries seemed to be growing louder; you couldn't hear yourself speak, even the least nervous were getting worried by the continual rattle of the windows. There violent explosions, that took your breath away, were as bad for the surgeons as they were for the patients; they produced a state of feverish excitement throughout the hospital.

"It's all over, so why do they have to keep on?" exclaimed Delaherche, who was listening anxiously, hoping to hear the final shot at any moment.

Then, turning to Bouroche to remind him about the captain, he was amazed to see him stretched out on the ground, face downwards on a bale of straw, with both arms, naked to the shoulder, thrust into buckets of cold water. Morally and physically exhausted, the major was trying to relax, overwhelmed by sadness, a sense of enormous desolation, experiencing one of those agonizing moments when a doctor feels himself to be powerless. Though he was a strapping, stout-hearted fellow, and not over-sensitive, he had reached the point of feeling "What's the use?" and the realization that it was impossible to do everything had suddenly paralyzed him. And what *was* the use, if, in the end, death was bound to win?

Two nurses brought in Captain Beaudoin on a stretcher.

"Major Bouroche," Delaherche said nervously, "the captain's here."

The surgeon opened his eyes, took his arms out of the water, shook them, and wiped them down with a handful of straw. Then, getting to his knees, he said :

"Ah yes, damn it all, another. . . . Come, come, the day's work isn't finished yet."

And in a moment he was on his feet again, refreshed, shaking his lion's mane, having recovered his poise through long practice and unending discipline.

Gilberte and Mme. Delaherche had accompanied the stretcher; and when the captain was laid on the operating table, they remained standing nearby.

"Good, it's above the right ankle!" said Bouroche, talking energetically to distract the wounded man's attention. "Not a bad place at all, we shall manage very nicely. . . . But first, we'd better have a look at it."

He was obviously concerned at Beaudoin's state of torpor. He examined the emergency dressing, a single bandage, drawn tight and held in position by a bayonet sheath attached to the trouser leg. And he started grumbling to himself, asking what son-of-a-bitch could have made such a mess of it. Then suddenly he broke off, realizing what had happened : during the journey in the landau, the bandage must have worked itself loose and slipped down, leaving the wound exposed, and thus causing severe bleeding.

"Quickly, cut it away, you clumsy sod!" Bouroche shouted angrily to an orderly who was helping him.

Hurriedly, the nurse cut away the trouser leg, then the shoe and sock, revealing the naked pallor of the foot and the leg encrusted with blood. And there, above the ankle, was a ghastly hole, into which a shell splinter had driven a piece of red cloth. A lump of flesh, torn from the muscle, hung from the gaping wound.

Gilberte had to support herself against one of the uprights. Oh that flesh, that flesh, once so white, now all crushed and bloody! Yet, horrified as she was, she was unable to tear her eyes away from it.

"Blast!" exclaimed Bouroche. "They've fixed you properly!"

He felt the foot, but it was cold and there was no sign of a pulse. His expression had become grave, with an odd puckering of the mouth, which, with him, was always a sign that a case was worrying him.

"Jesus!" he repeated, "this foot's in a pretty pickle!"

The captain, whose anxiety had overcome his torpor, looked at him, waiting. Presently he said :

"D'you really think so, major?"

But it was Bouroche's way never to ask a patient's authorization when an amputation was necessary. He thought it was better for the wounded man to become resigned to it of his own accord.

"A pretty pickle," he muttered as though talking to himself. "I don't see how we're going to save it."

276

Nervously, Beaudoin said :

"Then the sooner we get it over the better. What do *you* say, major?"

"Why, that you're a brave man, captain, and that you're going to let me do what has to be done."

Captain Beaudoin turned paler still, and a kind of red film hovered before his eyes. He had understood, and though his voice was almost choking with fear, he replied with simple gallantry :

"Get on with it, then, major."

The preparations did not take long. The assistant, who had already sprinkled chloroform on the pad, held it over the patient's nose and mouth. Then, during the brief struggle that usually precedes complete anaesthesia, two nurses eased the captain down the mattress so as to leave his legs free, and while one of them held on to the left one, an assistant took hold of the other, and pressed his fingers tightly into the groin to close the arteries.

Seeing Bouroche advancing with the knife in his hand, Gilberte could bear it no longer.

"No, no, it's too terrible," she murmured, staggering back, only prevented from falling by Mme. Delaherche.

"Why do you stay here, then?"

Both of them did stay, however, though they turned away so as not to see what was happening, trembling, clinging to one another despite the lack of affection between them.

It must surely have been at this moment that the noise of the guns became loudest. It was three o'clock, and Delaherche, exasperated and disappointed, declared it was impossible to understand what was going on. There could no longer be the slightest doubt that, far from stopping, the fire from the Prussian batteries was growing heavier. Why? What was happening? The hellish bombardment shook the ground, lighting up the whole sky. Around Sedan, the iron girdle, the eight hundred guns of the German armies, were firing simultaneously, blasting the fields in their vicinity with their continual thunder, so that if they went on for another two hours or so the shells, converging upon the centre from all the surrounding heights, would completely pulverize the town. Worst of all, the shells were once more beginning to fall on the houses; the explosions could be heard more and more frequently. One burst in the Rue des Voyards, hitting the tall chimney of the factory, and bits of rubble fell just outside the operating shed. Bouroche glanced up and muttered :

"What on earth are they trying to do, kill all our wounded . . .? This noise is unbearable!"

But the orderly was already holding out Captain Beaudoin's leg; with a swift, circular incision below the knee, the major cut the skin, five centimetres below the spot where he intended to saw through the bone. Then, swiftly, using the same knife so as not to waste time, he cut away the skin and turned it back all round, like peeling an orange. But, just as he was about to sever the muscles, a nurse came up to him and said :

"No. 2's done for, sir!"

Unable to hear, the major said :

"Speak up, for God's sake, these damned guns have split my eardrums."

"I said No. 2's done for, sir."

"Which was No. 2?"

"The one with the arm."

"I see. . . . Right, then you had better bring in No. 3 next, the one with the broken jaw."

And, with extraordinary skill, he cut through the muscles right to the bone, laying bare the tibia and fibula and fixing a clamp between them to hold them in position. Then he sawed through both bones, and the nurse was left holding the foot.

Owing to the pressure that the assistant was applying higher up, there was little bleeding, and the ends of the three arteries were soon tied. But the major was shaking his head, and when the assistant removed his fingers he examined the wound.

"That's bad, the small arteries aren't bleeding."

Then, with a gesture of discouragement, he delivered his verdict :

"Another poor devil done for!"

And once more his sweating face displayed all the exhaustion and sadness he felt at the thought that he couldn't hope to save more than forty per cent of his patients. Wiping his brow, he started pulling the skin back into position and sewing it up.

Gilberte had just turned round; Delaherche had told her it was all over and that she could look now, but she could scarcely fail to see the captain's foot, which the nurse was taking away to the laburnum trees. There, the heap of corpses had grown bigger, there were two fresh ones, one with its mouth open, looking as though it was still screaming, the other, so shrunken by pain that it appeared scarcely bigger than a sickly, misshapen child. Worse still, the pile of limbs had overflowed into a nearby pathway. Unable to find a

278

suitable place to put the captain's foot, the nurse hesitated, but finally decided to throw it on the heap.

"There you are, then," the major said to Beaudoin, who was beginning to come to. "It's all over now. You've got through it all right."

But the captain experienced none of the joy of returning to consciousness after a successful operation. He tried to sit up, only to sink back again, and stammered almost inaudibly :

"Thank you, major. I'd rather it was all over."

Nevertheless he could feel the surgical spirit in the dressing beginning to smart, and as they brought up a stretcher to take him away, a terrible explosion shook the whole factory. The shell had fallen behind the shed, in the little courtyard where the pump was. It shattered some of the windows, and thick smoke was pouring into the hospital. The drying-room, where the wounded were lying on the floor, was seized with panic; everyone started shouting with fear, and trying to escape.

Delaherche rushed out to see what damage had been done. Were they going to set his house on fire, demolish the entire building? What on earth was going on? Since the Emperor was determined to surrender, why was everything beginning all over again?

"For God's sake get a move on," Bouroche yelled to the nurses, who were paralysed with fear. "Swab this table down, and bring in No. 3!"

They washed the table, and once more carried away the buckets of crimson water to the other side of the lawn, where the bed of marguerites was little more than a pool of blood. As soon as No. 3 had been brought in, the major, in an effort to relax a little, immediately began looking for the bullet, which, after smashing the lower bone of the jaw, must have lodged somewhere beneath the man's tongue. Blood was flowing freely, and his fingers were sticky with it.

In the big room, Captain Beaudoin was back on his mattress. Gilberte and Mme. Delaherche had accompanied the stretcher, and even Delaherche, despite his excitement, had looked in to chat with him for a moment.

"You must rest, captain. As soon as we've got a room ready for you, we'll take you home with us."

Despite his exhausted condition, the wounded man revived a little, and had a moment of lucidity.

"No, no, I know very well I'm going to die. . . ."

And he stared at the three of them, wide-eyed, filled with the fear of death.

"Oh, you mustn't talk like that, captain," murmured Gilberte, forcing herself to smile. "In a month's time you'll be up and about again."

He shook his head, and his eyes, now looking only at her, filled with an immense regret at the thought of dying like this, before he had had time to exhaust all the joy of living.

"No, no, I know I'm dying. It's terrible."

Then, suddenly, his eyes fell on his uniform, filthy and torn, and on his dirty hands, and the thought of appearing like this, in the presence of women, shocked him. Ashamed of having given way, the thought that he was behaving badly had the effect of restoring his gallantry, and, in a cheerful tone of voice, he managed to say :

"The only thing is, if I've got to die, I'd rather die with clean hands. . . . Perhaps you would be so kind, Madame, as to fetch me some water and a towel."

Gilberte hurried away, and coming back with a towel, insisted on washing his hands herself. From then on, he behaved with great courage, determined to meet his end in a becoming manner. Delaherche did his best to encourage him, and old Mme. Delaherche, seeing that both husband and wife were so concerned about him, felt her bitterness disappear. Once more she would hold her tongue, despite the fact that this time she had fully intended to warn her son. What was the point of upsetting them both, since the dead man's sins would soon be buried with him?

The end was not long in coming. Captain Beaudoin, rapidly growing weaker, returned to a state of torpor, forehead and neck soaked with ice-cold sweat. For a moment he opened his eyes, feeling for an imaginary blanket, making restless movements with his hands, as though trying to pull it up to his chin.

"I'm cold, I'm horribly cold."

Then, almost imperceptibly, he passed away, and on his tranquil face there remained an expression of infinite sadness.

Delaherche took care to see that the body, instead of being put with the others, was laid in a nearby shed. He tried to get Gilberte to go back to the house, but she was crying, utterly overwhelmed, insisting that she was too frightened to stay there by herself, and would rather be with her mother-in-law, where the bustle of the hospital would help her to forget her grief. She hurried away to take some water to a Chasseur d'Afrique, delirious with fever. Then she helped a nurse dress the wounded hand of a twenty-year-old recruit, who had succeeded in escaping from the battlefield on foot, despite the loss of his thumb; and since he was an amusing lad, who lightheartedly joked about his wound, she soon became as gay as he was.

While the captain was dying, a second shell had fallen in the garden, smashing the ancient lime trees to pieces. And a considerable fire having broken out in the suburb of La Cassine, people were beginning to say that the whole of Sedan was ablaze. If the bombardment continued much longer it would be the end of everything.

"This is quite impossible! I'm going back," said Delaherche, almost beside himself.

"Where to?" asked Bouroche.

"Why, to the Sub-Prefecture, to find out whether the Emperor was just making fun of us when he talked about hoisting the white flag."

For some moments the major stood there aghast, dumbfounded at the thought of the white flag and capitulation, coming on top of his own feeling of impotence, and at the impossibility of saving more than a small proportion of all the wretched maimed creatures that were brought to him. With a gesture of angry despair, he burst out :

"Go to hell! We're all done for anyway!"

Outside in the street, Delaherche found it harder than ever to force a way through the increasing crowds. All the time, fresh streams of disbanded soldiers were pouring into the streets. He questioned several of the officers he met : not one of them had seen a white flag flying over the Citadel. At last a colonel declared that he had seen it for a second, just long enough for it to be run up and down again. This explained matters : either the Germans had failed to see it at all, or, having seen it appear and disappear, they had redoubled their fire in the belief that the end was near. A story was even going the rounds that, immediately the white flag had appeared, a general, mad with anger, had rushed forward and torn it down with his own hands, smashing the haft and trampling the flag into the mud. And still the Prussian batteries kept firing, still the shells rained down on the roofs and in the streets, still houses kept bursting into flames; and at the corner of the Place Turenne, a woman had just had her head smashed in.

By the time Delaherche reached the Sub-Prefecture, Rose was no longer in the porter's lodge. Every door in the place was wide open, the rout had begun. He ran upstairs, but everyone he met was utterly bewildered, not one of them made the slightest attempt to question his right to be there. On the topmost floor, as he stood hesitating, he met the young woman.

"Oh, M. Delaherche, everyone's going crazy. If you want to see the Emperor, you'd better come quick."

And, indeed, through a door that had been left ajar, one could see the Emperor, once more pacing backwards and forwards between the fireplace and the window. On and on he walked, not pausing for a moment, despite his intolerable suffering. An aide-de-camp had just gone in, it was he who had left the door open, and the Emperor could be heard asking him in a nerveless, desolate tone of voice :

"Tell me, sir, why are they still firing, when I gave orders for the white flag to be hoisted?"

It was the ceaseless gunfire, continually becoming more violent, that caused him such unspeakable torture. He could not approach the window without feeling a fresh pang, at the thought that all the blood that was being spilt, all the lives that were being destroyed, were his responsibility ! Every moment the mounds of dead were growing higher, and all to no purpose. And in his anguished revolt, every time anyone came into the room he asked them the same hopeless question : Why was the firing still going on, when he had given orders for the white flag to be flown?

The aide-de-camp muttered some reply that Delaherche could not catch. Meanwhile, the Emperor resumed his restless walk, continually yielding to the temptation to gaze out of the window. He had become paler than ever, and his long face, drawn and dejected, carelessly made up, bespoke his agony of mind. At that moment, a lively little man in a dusty uniform, whom Delaherche recognized as General Lebrun, crossed the landing and pushed open the door without waiting to be announced. Immediately the Emperor could again be heard, asking the same question in that anxious voice. But the aide-de-camp came out, closing the door behind him, so that Delaherche was unable to hear the general's reply.

"Everyone's going crazy," Rose repeated. "I can tell from the look on these gentlemen's faces. Like my big tablecloth. . . . I shall never see it again, some people say it's been torn to bits. . . . What upsets me worst of all, though, is the Emperor. He's a much sicker man than the marshal, he'd be better off in bed instead of walking up and down his room all the time."

She was deeply moved, and her pretty, fair face expressed sincere pity. But Delaherche, whose Bonapartiste fervour had become distinctly cooler the last few days, found her rather stupid. Downstairs, however, he stayed with her for a minute or two, waiting for General Lebrun to leave, and as soon as he appeared he followed him.

General Lebrun had explained to the Emperor that, if they intended to ask for an armistice, a letter, signed by the commander-in-chief of the French army, would have to be sent to the German commander-in-chief. Then he had offered to write the letter himself, and to go in search of General de Wimpffen, who would have to sign it. He had it with him now, and his one fear was that he would be unable to find de Wimpffen, since he did not know what part of the battlefield he might be in. Moreover, in Sedan, the crowds had by this time become so dense that he could only ride at walking pace; which enabled Delaherche to accompany him as far as the Ménil gate.

On the way there, however, General Lebrun was able to gallop ahead, and was lucky enough, on arriving at Balan, to catch sight of General de Wimpffen. A few minutes previously, the latter had written to the Emperor:

"Sire, if you will come and put yourself at the head of your troops, they will look upon it as an honour, and they will force a way for you through the enemy lines."

As a result, the mere mention of the word "armistice" threw him into a furious rage. No, no, he wouldn't sign anything; he was determined to fight on. It was then half-past three, and it was shortly after this that an heroic and desperate attempt was made to drive a wedge between the Bavarians by once more attacking Bazeilles. In Sedan and the countryside round about, a lie had been circulated in an attempt to put fresh heart into the troops, and people were shouting:

"Bazaine's coming, Bazaine will soon be here!"

Since early morning, many people had been dreaming of this, and every time the Germans brought a new battery into action they imagined they could hear the guns of the army of Metz. Some twelve hundred men had been got together, disbanded soldiers from different army corps, a mixture of foot soldiers and cavalry; and this little column of men set out gloriously, marching at a smart pace along the road swept by machine-gun fire.

To begin with it was magnificent: the fact that many of them were being killed did not damp the enthusiasm of the others;

and, with the courage of madmen, they succeeded in advancing nearly five hundred yards. But before long, as the ranks began to thin out, even the bravest of them faltered. What could they do against such overwhelming numerical superiority? The whole thing was simply the crazy temerity of an army leader who refused to admit defeat; and, eventually, General de Wimpffen found himself alone with General Lebrun, on the road from Balan to Bazeilles, and the attack had to be abandoned. All they could do, was to fall back upon Sedan.

As soon as he had lost sight of General Lebrun, Delaherche had hurried back to the factory, obsessed by one idea, to go up to his observatory again so that he could follow what was happening in the distance. But no sooner had he reached the porch than he ran into Colonel de Vineuil, who had been brought back, lying on a pile of hay at the bottom of a farm cart, almost fainting from the pain of his wounded foot. The colonel had persisted in trying to rally the remnants of his regiment until he actually fell off his horse. Now he was at once taken upstairs, to a bedroom on the first floor, and Bouroche, who had immediately been sent for and had found nothing more than a fractured ankle, had been content to dress the wound after removing the pieces of leather. He was overwhelmed with work and on edge, and when he got downstairs again he protested that he would rather cut off one of his own legs than continue working under such filthy conditions, without proper materials or the necessary assistants. Indeed, there was no longer any room to put the wounded, and he had decided they would have to go out on the lawn. There were already two rows of them, lying out there in the open, with shells raining down all around them. During the day, more than four hundred men had been admitted to the hospital, and though the major had asked for more surgeons, the only one he had been sent was a young doctor from the town. It was quite impossible for him to do everything himself; he probed, cut, sawed, sewed up, almost out of his mind, heartbroken at the thought that they kept bringing in more cases than he could possibly cope with. Gilberte, drunk with horror, sickened by the sight of all this blood and so many tears, had remained with her uncle, the colonel, leaving Mme. Delaherche downstairs, to take water to those suffering from fever and wipe the moist faces of those at the point of death.

When he reached the platform Delaherche quickly set about trying to size up the situation. The town had suffered less than was at first thought, a single fire was sending up a huge column of black smoke from the suburb of La Cassine. The Palatinate fort was no longer firing, doubtless for lack of ammunition. Only the guns at the Paris gate were still firing single rounds, at longer and longer intervals; and what straight away attracted his attention was the white flag that had once more been hoisted over the Keep. But it must have been impossible to see it from the battlefield, for the firing continued as intense as ever. The neighbouring roofs hid the Balan road, so that he could no longer make out the troop movements there. But, looking through the telescope, which had been left pointing in the same direction, he discovered that the German general staff was still in the same spot where he had seen it earlier. The supreme commander, the tiny little lead soldier less than half an inch tall, whom he thought to be the King of Prussia, was still standing there in his dark uniform, slightly in front of the other officers, most of whom were still lying on the ground, their uniforms glittering with gold braid. With them there were foreign officers, aides-de-camp, generals, all armed with field glasses, who, from early morning, had been following the agony of the French army as though it was a scene in the theatre and the formidable drama was now reaching its climax.

From the wooded heights of La Marfée, King William had watched the junction of his troops. It was now complete. The Third Army, commanded by his son, the Crown Prince of Prussia, had made its way, via Saint-Menges and Fleigneux, to occupy the plain of Illy; while the Fourth, under the Crown Prince of Saxony, had reached the meeting point by way of Daigny and Givonne, leaving the forest of Garenne on its flank. In this way the XIth and Vth Army Corps had been able to join up with the XIIth Corps and the Prussian Guards. The supreme attempt to break out of this circle, at the very moment that it was finally closing in, the futile but glorious charge by Margueritte's division, had drawn a cry of admiration from the King: "Ah, what courage!" Now, the inexorable, mathematical process of envelopment was over. The jaws of the vice had closed, and he could see the immense wall of men and guns surrounding the defeated army. To the north, the grip was becoming tighter and tighter, driving the fugitives back into Sedan, beneath intensified fire from the batteries that formed an uninterrupted line as far as the eye could see. By midday Bazeilles, captured, empty and desolate, was still burning, filling the air with huge clouds of smoke and sparks; the Bavarians, having seized

Balan, had trained their guns on the city, at a range of three hundred yards; while the other batteries, those on the left bank, at Pont-Maugis, Noyers, Frénois and Wadelincourt, which had been firing without a break for nearly twelve hours, completed the unbroken girdle of flame, almost as far as where the King was standing.

Tired, King William dropped his field glasses, but continued to watch the scene with naked eyes. The sun, slanting towards the woods, was about to set in an almost cloudless sky. It gilded the whole vast countryside, bathing it in a light so limpid that the smallest detail took on an extraordinary vividness. He could see the houses in Sedan, the small dark oblongs of the windows, the ramparts, the forts, the whole complicated system of defence, the outlines of which stood out clearly. And all around, scattered amongst the ploughed fields, were villages gleaming with fresh paint like toy farms, Donchery to the left, at the edge of the flat plain, Douzy and Carignan to the right, standing amongst their meadows. It looked as if one could have almost counted the trees in the forest of Ardennes, that vast sea of greenery stretching away to the frontier. In the wavering light, the slow winding Meuse gleamed like a river of pure gold. And beneath the sun's last rays, the monstrous, blood-soaked battle, seen from above, was like some delicate painting : dead horsemen and disembowelled horses strewed the plain of Floing with patches of bright colour; on the right, towards Givonne, the fleeing men, in a final stampede, were no more than whirling black specks, scurrying hither and thither and tumbling to the ground; while on the peninsula of Iges, to the left, a Bavarian battery, its guns no bigger than matchsticks, looked for all the world like some well-mounted, theatrical spectacle, so clearly could one follow the clockwork regularity of its manoeuvres. This was victory unlooked for, overwhelming victory; and the King looked down upon it without any feeling of remorse, for these tiny corpses, these thousands of men, of no more account than the dust on the roads, this immense valley, the fires at Bazeilles, the massacres at Illy, the anguish of Sedan, could not alter the fact that, in this serene ending to a lovely day, impassive nature still remained beautiful.

Then, all of a sudden, Delaherche caught sight of a French general, wearing a blue tunic and riding a black horse, who was climbing the hill towards Le Marfée, preceded by a hussar carrying a white flag. It was General Reille, charged by the Emperor to convey his letter to the King of Prussia : "Sire and Brother, Since it has not been granted me to die amongst my troops, it only remains for me to deliver my sword into Your Majesty's hands. I remain, Your Majesty, your fellow monarch, Napoleon."

In his concern to stop the slaughter, the Emperor, since he had ceased to be in control, hoped to appeal to the victor by surrendering. Delaherche saw General Reille, unarmed and merely carrying a riding whip, halt within ten feet of the King, dismount from his horse, and then go forward to present the letter. The sun was setting in a blaze of rosy light, and the King, who was sitting on a chair, leaning against the back of another one on which one of his secretaries was seated, agreed to accept the surrender, pending the arrival of an officer empowered to make arrangements for the capitulation.

VII

BY THIS time, around Sedan, from all the positions that had been lost, from Floing, from the plain of Illy, from the forest of Garenne and the valley of the Givonne, from the Bazeilles road, a terrified flood of men, horses and guns was streaming towards the town. This fortress, which they had had the disastrous notion of relying upon, was becoming a fatal temptation, offering, in the universal state of demoralization and panic, shelter to the fugitives and, even to the bravest of them, a hope of safety. Behind its ramparts, they were convinced that they would escape at last from this terrible artillery that had been blasting them for nearly twelve hours; men had ceased to reason, ceased to be aware of what was happening to them, and had become a prey to the madness of their animal instincts, intent on finding some hole where they could lie down and go to sleep.

Behind the little wall, Maurice, who was bathing Jean's face with fresh water, saw that he had opened his eyes again, and exclaimed joyfully :

"Well, you old sod, I thought you were done for . . .! I'm not complaining, but, by God, you were damned heavy !"

Still bewildered, Jean seemed to be waking from a dream. Then he must have remembered where he was, for two large tears rolled down his cheeks. This frail man, whom he loved and had looked after like a child, had, thanks to the depth of his affection, found the strength to carry him here !

"Hang on a minute, while I have a look at your head !"

The wound did not amount to much, it had merely grazed the skin beneath the hair and caused considerable bleeding. The hair, clotted with blood, had formed a kind of dressing, and he was careful not to wet it, lest he reopen the wound.

"There you are ! Now you're cleaned up a bit, you're beginning to look quite human again. Wait until I find something to cover your head with."

288

And taking a cap from a dead soldier lying nearby, he carefully put it on his friend's head.

"Why, it's just your size. . . . If you can only manage to walk, we'll be all right."

Jean got to his feet, shaking his head to make sure that it was still there. It still felt rather heavy, but he would manage somehow. And overcome with the emotions of a simple man, he seized Maurice in his arms and pressed him to his heart. Yet all he could find to say was :

"Oh, my dear chap ! My dear chap !"

But soon the Prussians would be here. They couldn't hang about any longer behind this wall. Lieutenant Rochas, with the few men left to him, was already withdrawing, determined to save the colours, which the second-lieutenant was still carrying, rolled up under his arm. Lapoulle, who was very tall, was still able to reach up and fire one or two shots over the coping; whereas Pache had already slung his rifle over his shoulder, having doubtless decided that they had done enough and that it was now time to find something to eat and drink. Bending almost double, Jean and Maurice hurried to reach the others. They were unarmed, having been obliged to leave everything behind, haversacks and all, but this was easily remedied : plenty of rifles and ammunition were lying around that others had discarded, and all they had to do was help themselves. The wall extended as far as the Garenne woods, and the little band, thinking they were now safe, quickly made for a farm, from which they were able to reach the protection offered by the trees.

"Fine," said Rochas, whose self-confidence still remained unshakeable. "As soon as we've had a breather, we can take the offensive again."

No sooner had they set off again, however, than they realized that the place was an inferno; but there was no going back, they would have to push on, for this was their only line of retreat. The wood, by this time, was becoming terrifying, a scene of despair and death, for realizing that the enemy were using it as cover the Prussians were riddling it with bullets, saturating it with shells. It was as though it were being whipped by a gale of wind, all confusion and shrieking amidst the crashing of branches. The shells cut down the trees, showers of leaves fell before the bullets, while the split trunks seemed to moan, and tears oozed from the sappy branches. It might have been the agony of a vast crowd in chains, the terrified cries of thousands of creatures rooted to the soil, unable to escape from this hail of fire.

All at once, Maurice and Jean, who had caught up with their companions, became frightened too. They were now making their way through a clump of high trees, and it was possible to run. But the bullets whistling all around them seemed to be coming from every direction, so that it was difficult to take cover as they hurried from tree to tree. Two men were killed, the bullets that struck them coming both from behind and from in front. Just ahead of Maurice, a huge old oak tree, its trunk smashed by a shell, crashed majestically to the ground, like some antique hero sweeping away everyone around him. And as the young man sprang back, an enormous beech tree on his left, struck by another shell, cracked and splintered, hurtling to the ground like the scaffolding in a cathedral. How were they to escape? Which way should they turn? All around them there was nothing but the crashing of falling branches, as if they were in some huge ruined building where room after room was collapsing, buried beneath the crumbling ceilings. Then, as they plunged deeper into the undergrowth to avoid being crushed by the falling trees, Jean narrowly escaped being cut in two by a shell, though, fortunately for him, it did not explode. But now, so dense was the inextricable growth, they could go no further: creepers clung to their shoulders, their feet were entangled in the thick grass, thick walls of greenery suddenly brought them to a halt, while showers of leaves and branches, mown down by some giant scythe, fell all around them. Nearby, another man, shot through the forehead, remained standing, held upright by two young birch trees. Imprisoned in this thicket, again and again they felt the presence of death sweep over them.

"Christ Almighty," said Maurice, "we shall never get out of here alive!"

His face was livid, and he had begun to shiver again. Even Jean, who all day had been reassuring him so bravely, had now turned pale, struck by an icy coldness. It was fear, terrifying fear, contagious and irresistible. Once again they experienced a burning thirst, an unbearable drying up of the mouth, an acutely painful contraction of the throat, like being strangled, and, in addition to this, a feeling of uneasy nausea in the pit of the stomach and a tingling sensation in their legs, as though they were being pricked with needles. And, as part of this purely physical reaction to fear,

290

thousands of black specks danced before their eyes, as though they could actually see the swarm of flying bullets.

"A bloody set-up, this is," said Jean, "being stuck here, getting smashed to pieces for other people, while they just sit about comfortably smoking their pipes!"

To which Maurice added, white-faced and miserable:

"Yes, why us rather than anyone else?"

It was a purely personal revolt, the angry egoism of the individual, unwilling to sacrifice himself for the good of the species.

"If you could only see what the point of it all is," Jean went on, "what it's all for!"

Then, looking up at the sky:

"If only that damned sun would make up its mind to bugger off! When it goes down and darkness comes, maybe the fighting will stop."

For some time past, not knowing what the time was, he had been watching the slow decline of the sun, which seemed to him to have stopped moving, to have stuck up there above the woods on the left bank. And it wasn't just cowardice, it was an increasingly demanding longing to stop hearing the shells and bullets, to get away somewhere, to sink into the earth, be annihilated. If it weren't for your self-respect, for the need to do your duty in front of your comrades, you'd just lose your head, and make off in spite of yourself, as fast as your legs could carry you.

By this time Maurice and Jean were, however, beginning to get used to it again; panic terror was giving way to a kind of unconscious exhilaration, of bravado, and eventually they stopped trying to hurry as they made their way through that terrible wood. Yet amid this race of shell-torn trees, killed at their posts, falling all around them like vast, motionless soldiers, the sense of horror was intensified. For here in the shadows, in the gentle, greenish half-light, deep in mysterious retreats carpeted with moss, death whispered savagely, lonely springs were violated, and in secret haunts where hitherto none but lovers had wandered dying men drew their last breath. One man, shot through the chest, just had time to cry out "I'm hit", then plunged forward, dead. Another, both legs smashed by a shell, continued to laugh, not realizing that he was wounded, imagining that he had simply tripped over a root. Others, riddled with bullets, mortally wounded, still went on talking, even managed to run several yards before crashing to the ground. At first, the most serious injuries were scarcely felt, and it was only

291

later that their terrible sufferings began, bursting forth in cries and tears.

Gradually, the tragic slaughtered forest was filled not only with the sobbing or dying trees but also with the shrieking pain of wounded men. At the foot of an oak tree, Maurice and Jean saw a Zouave, his belly torn open, howling continuously like a slaughtered animal. Further on, another was on fire : his blue sash had caught alight, the spreading flame was singeing his beard, and, unable to move because of his broken ribs, he was weeping bitterly. Then it was a captain, his left arm torn away, the whole right side of his body ripped open, who was dragging himself along on his elbows, imploring someone to put him out of his misery, in a shrill, pleading voice. And so it went on, more and yet more hideously suffering men, sprawling all over the grassy paths so that it was almost impossible to move without trampling them underfoot. But the dead and wounded had ceased to count; if your mate was hit, you left him behind, forgot about him, without so much as a backward glance. It was all a matter of luck; maybe you, maybe someone else !

Suddenly, as they were nearing the edge of the wood, a cry for help rang out. It was the second-lieutenant carrying the colours, who had been shot through the left lung. He had fallen to the ground, spitting out mouthfuls of blood; and, seeing that nobody was stopping, he summoned up his strength and managed to shout :

"Help, help ! It's the colours !"

Rochas immediately turned back and, hurrying towards him, took the flag with its broken pole just as the lieutenant was gasping, in a voice half choked with blood :

"It's all up with me, damn it . . . but save the colours !"

And there they left him, alone in this woodland dell, writhing on the ground and plucking at the grass with groping hands, to endure an agony that would go on for hours.

When, at last, they emerged from this agony wood, the only members of the little band that were left, apart from Maurice and Jean, were Lieutenant Rochas, Pache and Lapoulle. But a little later, Gaude, who had disappeared, scrambled out of a thicket with his bugle slung over his shoulder, and ran to catch up his comrades. And for all of them it was an immense relief to find themselves once again in open country, able to take things easy. On this side of the valley, the whistle of bullets had died away, the shells stopped falling.

Presently, at the entrance to a farm, hearing somebody swearing, they caught sight of a general in a furious temper, riding a horse that was drenched with sweat. It was General Bourgain-Desfeuilles, the commander of their brigade, covered with dust, and apparently at the end of his tether. His coarse, highly coloured face, expressed all the exasperation he felt at the disaster, which he regarded as a purely personal misfortune. His men had not set eyes on him since the morning. Doubtless he had been wandering around the battle-field, looking for the remnants of his brigade, and quite capable of getting himself killed, so furious was he with the Prussian batteries that were sweeping away the Empire, and, with it, his own position as an officer in good standing at the Tuileries.

"For God's sake," he was shouting, "is there nobody about? Can't anybody give you any information in this blasted country?"

The owners of the farm must have taken refuge in the woods. But, eventually, an aged woman appeared in the doorway, a servant who had been left behind, unable to walk because of her bad legs.

"Come on, woman. . . . Where are we? Is this Belgium?"

She looked at him in bewilderment, as though she could not understand. Whereupon, losing the last vestiges of self-control, and forgetting that it was a peasant he was talking to, he started yelling at the top of his voice : he wasn't going to be caught like a rat in a trap by going back to Sedan, he'd clear out abroad, and pretty sharp, too ! Some soldiers who had come up overheard what he was saying.

"Excuse me, sir," said a sergeant, "but you won't be able to get through, there are Prussians everywhere. . . . This morning was the time to clear out."

Rumours were, in fact, already on foot that a number of com-panies, cut off from their regiments, had unintentionally crossed the frontier; and that, later on, others had bravely succeeded in getting through the enemy lines before the encirclement was complete.

Beside himself, the general shrugged his shoulders.

"Look here, with a bunch of decent fellows like you, we ought to be able to get through wherever we like. . . . I can find at least another fifty who'd be prepared to have a crack."

Then, turning back to the old peasant woman, he went on :

"Well, for God's sake answer, woman. . . . Are we in Belgium or not?"

This time she had understood, and waved a skinny hand in the direction of the woods :

293

"That way, over there!"

"What are you trying to say . . .? Do you mean those houses over there, beyond the fields?"

"Oh, further than that, much further. . . . Over there, right over there!"

At this the general could contain himself no longer.

"Oh it's fantastic, this bloody country! You never know where you are. . . . A short time ago, Belgium was just over there, and everybody was afraid of crossing the frontier without meaning to. But now we want to get there, it suddenly seems to have disappeared! Really, this is more than I can stand! Let them take me prisoner and do what they like with me, I'm off to bed!"

And clapping spurs to his horse, he galloped off in the direction of Sedan, bumping about in the saddle like an angry wineskin blown-up with wind.

The path twisted and turned, running downhill towards the Fond de Givonne, a suburb surrounded by hills, where the road leading to the woods was flanked with villas and gardens. At present, it was filled with such a stream of refugees that Lieutenant Rochas found himself, with Pache, Lapoulle and Gaude, more or less cut off outside a tavern at a corner of the square. Jean and Maurice had difficulty in getting to them. And they were all surprised when they heard themselves addressed by a thick, drunken voice:

"Well, well, well, if that doesn't beat the band. . . . Who'd have thought of fetching up with you lot after all this!"

It was Chouteau, seated in the tavern at one of the ground floor windows, very drunk and continually hiccuping. He went on:

"Come on, pals, don't look so upset. . . . If you're thirsty, we can still find a drop for a mate. . . ."

And, vaguely gesturing over his shoulder, he called to somebody at the back of the room:

"Get a move on, lazybones. . . . Bring these gentlemen a drink. . . ."

Whereupon, who should appear but Loubet, with a bottle in each hand, which he was waving about in the air. He was not as drunk as Chouteau, and he hailed them in his mocking, Parisian voice, speaking through his nose like the coconut sellers at a fair:

"Come on, lads, have a drink . . . it's on the house!"

Neither of them had been seen since they had disappeared, earlier in the day, on the pretext of taking Sergeant Sapin to the ambulance. Since then they had been wandering about, taking it easy, avoiding places where shells were falling. And they had ended up here, in this looted inn.

Lieutenant Rochas got on his high horse :

"Just you wait, you crooks, boozing like this while the rest of us have been slogging our guts out!"

But Chouteau was not prepared to be reprimanded.

"Oh, get along with you, you old crackpot. We've finished with lieutenants, we're all free men now. . . . Haven't the Prussians given you a good enough hiding without asking for any more?"

Rochas had to be restrained from knocking him down, but Loubet, still clasping his bottles, did his best to make peace.

"Come on now, stop that! After all, it's no use fighting each other!"

And turning to Lapoulle and Pache, his two pals, he went on :

"Stop playing the fool, you two, and come in and wet your whistle."

For a moment Lapoulle hesitated, feeling uneasily that it was somehow wrong to be enjoying yourself when so many poor bastards had just copped it. But he was so dead beat, so exhausted with hunger and thirst, that he suddenly made up his mind and, without a word, entered the tavern, pushing Pache in front of him, equally silent and equally tempted. And there they remained.

"What a bunch of crooks," Rochas kept saying. "They all ought to be shot!"

Now he was left with only Jean, Maurice and Gaude, and gradually, despite their efforts, all four of them were swept away in the torrent of fugitives streaming along the road. Soon the tavern was left far behind. They had become part of the great rout, surging towards the trenches protecting Sedan in a muddy stream, like the deluge of earth and rocks that a storm, breaking in the mountains, sweeps down into the valleys. From all the surrounding heights, from every hill, from every fold in the ground, along the road from Floing, from Pierremont, from the cemetery and the Champ de Mars, as well as from the Fond de Givonne, they all formed part of the same endlessly increasing throng, hurrying along in panic-stricken flight. And who could blame them, these wretched men, who, for the past twelve hours, had waited patiently beneath the deadly artillery fire of an invisible enemy, against whom they could do nothing? Now the batteries were firing at them from all sides, continually converging upon them as the retreating army drew nearer to the town, reducing them to a human pulp at the bottom of a ghastly pit, into which they were being driven. One or two regiments of the 7th Corps, especially those coming from Floing, maintained some sort of order. But, in the Fond de Givonne, men and leaders were huddled together in a crazy confusion of Zouaves, Turcos, Chasseurs, Fantassins; most of them had discarded their weapons, their uniforms were filthy and torn, their hands and faces blackened with smoke, their bloodshot eyes starting from their sockets, and from their scorched and swollen lips issued a stream of foul language. Now and then a riderless horse galloped through the crowd, knocking men down, leaving behind a trail of panic. Then guns drove by at breakneck speed, routed batteries, whose drivers, drunk with fear and without a word of warning, rode down anyone that got in their way. And the tramp of feet never stopped, a dense crowd of men marching shoulder to shoulder, a mass flight, in which the slightest gap was quickly filled, hurrying along instinctively, in an effort to reach shelter behind the walls of the city.

Again Jean turned towards the setting sun. Through the thick dust raised by the trampling feet, its rays still gleamed upon the sweating faces. It was a lovely evening, and the sky marvellously blue.

"All the same," he said, "it's a bit steep . . . this bloody sun that can't make up its mind to bugger off!"

Suddenly, Maurice was horrified to see a young woman, whom he recognized as his sister, Henriette, huddled against a house and in danger of being crushed by the human flood. For nearly a minute he stared at her, dumbfounded; and it was she, who, without the least appearance of surprise, spoke first.

"They shot him at Bazeilles. . . . Yes, yes, I was there. . . . When I tried to take away his body, I had an idea. . . ."

She did not refer to Weiss or to the Prussians by name. Everybody would understand . . . and indeed Maurice did.

"Poor darling!" he murmured, almost in tears.

About two o'clock, by which time she had come to herself again, Henriette had found herself at Balan, sitting bowed over a table, in a kitchen belonging to complete strangers, weeping. But her tears had soon stopped. Already, the heroic spirit of this quiet, frail creature had begun to revive. She was afraid of nothing, her spirit was firm and invincible. In her grief, her one desire was to get hold of her husband's body, so that she could bury it decently. Her first idea had been quite simply to return to Bazeille, but everyone had tried to dissuade her, pointing out the utter impossibility. Then she had decided to find someone who would either go with her, or else undertake the necessary arrangements; and her choice had fallen upon a cousin, a man who had been assistant-manager at the sugar refinery at the Chêne when Weiss used to work there. He had been very fond of her husband and would not refuse to help her. For the past two years, thanks to a legacy that had come to him through his wife, he had been living in retirement on a handsome property, the Hermitage, not far from Sedan, on the other side of the Fond de Givonne. And it was to the Hermitage that she was now making her way, despite all the difficulties, forced to stop every few yards, continually in danger of being trampled underfoot and killed.

Maurice, to whom she briefly explained her plan, approved of it.

"Cousin Dubreuil has always been good to us. . . . He'll do what he can for you. . . ."

Then he suddenly had an idea. Lieutenant Rochas was determined to save the colours at all costs. He had already thought of tearing them up, so that each of them could carry a piece under his shirt, or else burying them under a tree and noting the exact spot so that they would be able to find them later. But the thought of the colours being torn up, or buried like a corpse, was repugnant to him, and he was only too glad to find an alternative. When, therefore, Maurice proposed leaving them in the safe-keeping of a reliable person, who later on would return them intact, everyone agreed.

"Right then," the young man went on, turning to his sister. "We'll go with you, and find out if Dubreuil is still at the Hermitage. In any case, I don't intend to leave you."

It was not easy to extricate themselves from the crowd. At last they succeeded in doing so, however, and turned into a sunken road that led away to the left. Before long they found themselves in a veritable maze of lanes and footpaths, a whole district consisting of market gardens and country villas, a jumble of small properties; and these lanes, these footpaths, with their high walls and sudden corners and dead-ends, offered a marvellous opportunity for ambushes, places where a dozen men could hold off a regiment for hours. Already, there were occasional bursts of gunfire, for the district dominated Sedan, and the Prussian Guards were advancing from the other side of the valley.

Maurice and Henriette followed close behind the others, and after turning first left, then right between two interminable walls, suddenly emerged in front of the Hermitage gates, which stood open.

The estate, with its small park, consisted of three large terraces, one above the other, on one of which stood the house, a large, square building, approached by an avenue of ancient elm trees. Facing it, but separated by a narrow, thickly wooded valley were other estates on the outskirts of the wood.

Worried at finding the gates left open like this, Henriette said: "They aren't there ...! They must have gone away."

And indeed, the previous day, foreseeing the inevitable disaster, Dubreuil had resigned himself to taking his wife and children to Bouillon. The house was not empty, however, and long before they reached it, signs of movement could be seen through the trees. As the young woman plunged into the alley, she started back at the sight of a Prussian soldier's corpse.

"Hell!" exclaimed Rochas, "so they've beaten us to it."

Anxious to find out what was going on, they all crept forward, and what they saw explained everything: the doors and windows on the ground floor had been smashed in with rifle butts, the gaping holes revealing the pillaged rooms, while the furniture that had been thrown outside was scattered about on the gravelled terrace. What especially drew their attention was a complete suite of pale-blue drawing-room furniture, a sofa and a dozen armchairs, set out pell mell around a large table, its marble top split down the middle. And Zouaves, Chasseurs, infantrymen and marines were scurrying about, behind the buildings and in the alley, firing away across the valley at the little wood opposite.

"If you please, sir," a Zouave explained to Rochas, "it's these bloody Prussians. We caught some of them fair gutting the place, but we soon settled their hash. . . . Only now the bastards have started coming back, ten to one this time, so things aren't looking too healthy."

The bodies of three more Prussians were lying on the terrace. This time Henriette glared at them, thinking of her husband, lying over there covered in blood and dust, and as she stood there, a bullet struck the tree just behind her. Jean sprang towards her:

"Don't stay out here! Quick, quick, get into the house!"

Seeing her again, so changed, so stunned with misery, his heart ached with pity for her, remembering her as she had been only yesterday, with her gentle, homely smile. At first, he could find nothing to say to her, not even knowing whether she recognized him. Now he would have done anything to restore that tranquil happiness.

"Wait for us in the house. . . . If there's any danger, we'll find some way of getting you away."

But she shrugged her shoulders apathetically.

"What's the point?"

However, her brother insisted, pushing her up the steps. Inside the hall she stood for a moment, looking out down the alley, watching the fighting.

Maurice and Jean took up a position behind one of the elm trees, whose huge girth provided ample cover for two men. Further on, the bugler, Gaude, was crouching beside Lieutenant Rochas, who, insisting upon keeping the colours, as there was no one to whom he could entrust them, had put them down in front of him so as to leave his hands free to fire his rifle. Behind every tree in the alley men had taken cover, Zouaves, Chasseurs, Marines, and only raised their heads to fire their rifles.

In the woods across the valley, the Prussians must have been steadily reinforced, for their fire was becoming much heavier. But there was nobody to be seen save the occasional figure of a man running swiftly from one tree to the next. A villa with green shutters was occupied by a machine-gun squad, who were firing from the half-open windows on the ground floor. It was about four o'clock, the noise of the guns was decreasing and gradually they fell silent; yet here, in this remote spot, from which it was impossible to see the white flag that had been hoisted above the Keep, men were still killing one another, as though involved in some purely personal quarrel. Till darkness finally fell, stubborn pockets of fighting like this still persisted, despite the armistice, and from the Fond de Givonne and the gardens of Petitpoint the sound of rifle fire could still be heard.

For a long time they went on firing at one another across the valley, and every now and again, if a man was rash enough to expose himself, he would fall, shot through the heart. In the avenue leading to the house, three more men had been killed, and a wounded soldier lying on his face was screaming horribly, yet no one thought of turning him over on his back to ease the pain.

Chancing to look up, Jean saw Henriette calmly placing a sack beneath the wretched man's head for a pillow, and hurrying over to her he roughly pulled her behind the tree where he and Maurice were sheltering.

"D'you want to get yourself killed?"

299

Apparently quite unconscious of her crazy temerity, she replied calmly :

"Of course not. . . . It's simply that I felt frightened, all by myself in the house. . . . I'd much rather be here outside."

She stayed there with them, and they made her sit with her back against the tree trunk, while they went on firing their last rounds of ammunition right and left, with a furious anger that made them oblivious of fear and exhaustion. They were scarcely conscious of what they were doing, but acted quite automatically, without thinking, having lost even the instinct of self-preservation.

"Here, look over there, Maurice," Henriette suddenly exclaimed. "Doesn't that soldier, the dead one, belong to the Prussian Guards?"

For the last moment or two she had been staring at one of the corpses, a stocky lad with big moustaches, lying on his side on the terrace; he had been shot through the throat, and his pointed helmet had rolled a few feet away. And, true enough, he was wearing the Guards uniform : dark-grey trousers, blue tunic with white facings, rolled greatcoat slung over one shoulder.

"I'm certain he's a Guardsman. . . . I've got a picture at home. . . . And then that photograph that cousin Gunther sent us. . . ."

She broke off, and before either of them could stop her, calmly went over to the soldier and stooped to look down at him.

"Yes, yes, he's got red tabs, that proves it. . . . It's cousin Gunther's regiment."

From that moment, neither Maurice nor Jean could persuade her to keep under cover. She kept looking out restlessly, trying to see what was going on in the woods, completely preoccupied. Still busy firing, when she exposed herself too much they pushed her down with their knees. Clearly, the Prussians were beginning to think there were enough of them to attack, for a group of them could now be seen moving about between the trees, suffering terrible casualties, for all the Frenchmen's bullets were finding their mark.

"Look," said Jean, "maybe that's your cousin . . . the officer just coming out of that house with the green shutters."

And, sure enough, the man was a captain, recognizable by the gold lace collar of his tunic and the golden eagle on his helmet, which glinted in the slanting rays of the sun. Sword in hand, without epaulettes, he was shouting an order in a hoarse voice, and so short was the distance between them, scarcely two hundred yards,

300

that they could clearly distinguish the slim figure, the stern face with its pink cheeks and little fair moustache. Henriette watched him closely, with piercing gaze :

"It certainly is him," she said, without the slightest sign of surprise. "I'd know him anywhere."

"Our cousin is it?" said Maurice furiously, already taking aim. "God help him, then. . . . This will avenge Weiss."

But Henriette leapt to her feet, trembling all over, and pushed up his rifle so that it fired into the air.

"No, no, not one of our relations, not people we know. . . . That's too horrible !"

Suddenly she had become a woman again, and sinking down behind the tree she began sobbing helplessly, overwhelmed by terror and pity.

Rochas, however, was exultant. The men nearest him, whom he was urging on at the top of his voice, were firing so rapidly, now that they could actually see the Prussians, that the latter fell back, withdrawing into the wood.

"Stand firm, lads ! Don't give an inch ! Look, the cowards are running away. Now we'll settle our score with them !"

He spoke cheerfully, and seemed to have regained all his confidence. For him, defeat was simply out of the question; the handful of men in front of him was the whole German army, and he was about to destroy it. His tall, thin figure, his long, bony face, with its hooked nose and kindly, violent mouth, glowed with all the boastful gaiety and cheerfulness of the seasoned trouper, setting out to conquer the world between kissing his sweetheart goodbye and downing a bottle of wine.

"S'truth, lads, now we'll give the bastards such a hiding. . . . Just you see. Nobody's going to beat us now. . . . They haven't got a chance in hell. One more effort, boys, and they'll be running like rabbits !"

Yelling and gesticulating, carried away by the illusions of ignorance, he was such a good sort that the soldiers shared in his jubilation.

Suddenly he shouted :

"Come on, kick the bastards up the arse, kick the sods all the way to the frontier ! Victory ! Victory !"

But at that moment, just as the enemy across the valley seemed to be on the point of withdrawing, a terrible fusillade broke out on their left, and in a clever turning movement, a whole detachment of Guards was advancing on their flank along the Fond de Givonne. From then on, any defence of the Hermitage was out of the question, and the handful of soldiers still defending the terraces, finding themselves caught between two lines of fire, were in danger of being cut off from Sedan. Some of them were killed, there was a moment of utter confusion. Already the Prussians were swarming over the wall of the park, streaming along the paths in such numbers that only bayonet fighting was possible. Bareheaded, his tunic torn, a handsome, black-bearded Zouave was causing terrible havoc, stabbing the attackers in the chest, plunging his bayonet into their bellies, cleaning one man's blood from it by thrusting it into the side of another; and, when at last it broke off, he went on smashing in their skulls with the butt of his rifle, until finally they managed to disarm him; whereupon he hurled himself at the throat of a huge Prussian, with such force that the two of them rolled over and over across the gravel path, as far as the battered kitchen door, hugging one another in a mortal embrace.

Between the trees that grew round the lawns, the heaps of slaughtered men were growing. But it was on the terrace in front of the house that the struggle reached its height, around the pale-blue chairs and sofa, where a heaving mass of angry men were firing at each other point blank, or tearing at one another with nails and teeth.

It was then that Gaude, with the mournful expression of one who has suffered much in silence, was seized with heroic madness. In this final hour of defeat, knowing full well that the company was annihilated, that not a man could answer his call, he seized his bugle, and, putting it to his lips, blew the rallying cry with all the energy of a man determined to raise the dead. And even when the Prussians reached him, he went on blowing his tremendous fanfare, without giving an inch. A volley of bullets brought him down, and his last breath died away on a high note, that hung quivering in the air.

Understanding nothing of what was happening, Rochas made no attempt to escape. He just stood there, muttering to himself:

"What's going on, then? What's going on?"

It never even entered his head that this was another defeat. Everything was different, even the method of fighting. Surely these people should have stayed on the other side of the valley, waiting to be defeated? It was no use killing them, they still kept coming on. What kind of a damned war was this, anyway? You were expected to fight against ten times your own number, and then the enemy only showed up late in the evening, after blasting hell out of you all day. Dazed, bewildered, without the slightest understanding of the campaign as a whole, he felt as though he was being swept away by something stronger than himself, against which resistance was impossible, although, out of sheer obstinacy, he kept repeating mechanically:

"Courage, lads, we'll beat them yet!"

Meanwhile, however, he had quickly picked up the colours. His one idea was to hide them, to prevent the Prussians from capturing them, but the broken pole got entangled with his legs, and he almost fell. Hearing the bullets whistling around him, and feeling that death was near, he began tearing the silken flag to pieces, trying to destroy it completely. But before he could do so, struck in the neck, the chest and the legs, he sank to the ground, clutching the torn shreds of the tricolour. For a moment or two longer he still clung to life, staring wide-eyed, seeing perhaps for the first time the true image of war, the monstrous life and death struggle that can only be accepted, totally and with resignation, as an ineluctable law. Then, with a little gasp, he gave up the ghost, still childishly bewildered, like some poor, insignificant creature, some heedless insect, crushed beneath the weight of nature's vast and impassive necessity. And with his death, a whole legend came to an end.

Directly the Prussian attack had started, Jean and Maurice had begun retreating from tree to tree, doing their best to protect Henriette, pausing each time to fire another shot before hurrying on to the next. Maurice knew of a little gate at the far side of the park and they were lucky enough to find it open. Quickly slipping through it, the three of them found themselves in a narrow passage that wound its way between two high walls. But as they reached the end of it, a sudden burst of firing forced them to turn left, into another lane, which unfortunately turned out to be a cul-de-sac. They had to make their way back beneath a hail of bullets, and take the other turning. Afterwards, none of them could remember which way they had gone. At every twist and turn there was firing, battles raged at every gateway, the smallest obstacles were defended and carried by assault with bitter determination. Then, all of a sudden, they came out on to the road leading from the Fond de Givonne, near Sedan.

Once more Jean raised his eyes and gazed at the western sky,

303

now suffused with rosy light. And this time, with a sigh of immense relief, he exclaimed :

"Thank God, at last the bloody sun's going down !"

Meanwhile the three of them ran on and on, not stopping to take breath. All around them, the last wave of fugitives was pouring along the main road, faster and faster, like a river that had overflowed its banks. When they reached the Balan gate they were held up by a wild mob of struggling people. The chains of the drawbridge had broken, and the only way to cross was by the footbridge, which meant that neither guns nor horses could get any further. At the other gates, La Château and La Cassine, the confusion was said to be even worse; all the remnants of the army, plunging downhill, were sweeping into the city with the angry roar of water bursting from a dam. So strong was the fatal attraction of the city walls, that even the bravest could not resist it.

Maurice, who was holding Henriette in his arms, exclaimed angrily :

"Surely they aren't going to shut the gate before everyone's through !"

This was what the crowd was afraid of, and, already, soldiers were clambering up the ramparts on either side of the gate; while in the moat, whole batteries had come to grief, in a jumble of guns, limbers and horses.

But a succession of bugle calls rang out, soon to be followed by the high clear sound of the Retreat. It was a summons to the soldiers still lagging behind, and more and more kept arriving, running at full speed, while bursts of gunfire, isolated now and more and more infrequent, could be heard from the suburbs. On the inner slope of the ramparts, a few detachments were hastily drawn up to defend the approaches, and at last the gates were closed. By this time, the Prussians were barely a hundred yards behind; they could be seen moving about on the road from Balan, calmly taking possession of the houses and gardens. Maurice and Jean, keeping Henriette between them to shield her from the crowd, were amongst the last to enter Sedan. Six o'clock was just striking. For the past hour, the bombardment had ceased, and gradually the occasional bursts of rifle fire died away. Presently, all that remained of the deafening noise, of the deadly thunder of the guns that had persisted since dawn, was the emptiness of death, a sinister, terrifying silence that descended upon the city as darkness fell.

VIII

ABOUT half-past five, before the closing of the city gates, Delaherche had returned once more to the Sub-Prefecture, anxious to discover what was happening now that he knew the battle had been lost. He stayed there for nearly three hours, walking about the courtyard, watching, questioning every officer that came in; and in this way he heard of the rapid succession of events: the surrender dispatched, then withdrawn by General de Wimpffen, the plenary authority he had received from the Emperor to accept from the Prussian High Command the least onerous conditions he could get for the defeated army, and finally the summoning of a Council of War to decide whether they should continue the struggle by defending the Keep. While this Council, which consisted of some twenty senior officers and seemed to him to be going on indefinitely, was in session, the textile manufacturer climbed the steps outside the Préfecture a dozen times or more. Then suddenly, at a quarter-past eight, he saw General de Wimpffen coming out, scarlet in the face and puffy-eyed, followed by a colonel and two other generals. They leapt into the saddle, and made off in the direction of the bridge. This could only mean that the capitulation had been agreed to.

Delaherche felt reassured, and suddenly realizing that he was famishing, decided to return home. But no sooner did he find himself in the street, than he hesitated at the sight of vast crowds of people who had collected there. Streets and squares were so densely packed with men, horses, guns, that they looked like one solid mass of humanity, rammed together by some gigantic hammer. While the regiments which had withdrawn in good order were bivouacked on the ramparts, the scattered remnants from every other corps, fugitives from every branch of the forces, had submerged the town in a seething mob, a dense flood of people, quite unable to move. The wheels of innumerable guns and ammunition waggons, as well as every other kind of vehicle, became interlocked; the horses, thrashed and spurred in every direction, had no room to move

305

either forwards or backwards; and the men, heedless of threats, poured into the houses, devouring everything they could find, sleeping wherever they could. Many of them had collapsed in the doorways, blocking the entrance. Others, too weak to go any further, simply lay down on the pavement, where they fell fast asleep, refusing to move despite the trampling feet, preferring to be crushed to death rather than to make the effort to find somewhere else.

Seeing all this, Delaherche realized that the capitulation had been inevitable. In certain squares, where ammunition waggons were drawn up in serried ranks, a single Prussian shell falling on one of them, would have blown up all the others, and the whole of Sedan would have been set alight like a torch. Besides, what could be done with this mass of wretched creatures, broken with hunger and fatigue, without ammunition, without food? Merely to clear the streets would have taken the entire day. The fortress was not armed, the town was without food supplies. These were the reasons advanced by the wisest members of the Council of War, who saw the situation clearly despite their bitter patriotic grief; whereas the rasher spirits, those who insisted with passionate voices that an army simply could not be allowed to surrender like this, were reduced to silence, unable to produce any practical ideas for renewing the struggle next day.

In the Place Turenne and the Place du Rivage, Delaherche only succeeded in forcing a way through the crowd with the greatest difficulty. As he passed the Croix d'Or Hotel, he had a pitiful view of the dining-room, with the generals sitting silently around the empty table. There was no food to be had, not even bread. Nevertheless, General Bourgain-Desfeuilles, storming about down in the kitchen, must have found something, for he suddenly stopped shouting and hurried briskly upstairs, carrying some morsel in grease-proof paper. Such a crowd had collected, peering in through the windows at this melancholy, famine-stricken feast, that the textile manufacturer had to use his elbows to prevent himself from losing what little ground he had so far gained. But in the Grande Rue the wall of people became impenetrable, and for a moment he lost heart. A whole battery of guns seem to have been flung down, one on top of the other; and he decided to climb over the gun carriage, straddling the gun barrel, and then leapt from wheel to wheel at the risk of breaking a leg. Next, it was the horses that barred his way, and he had to crouch down, creeping under the bellies of the pathetic creatures that were scarcely able to stand for hunger. Then, after struggling for a quarter of an hour, as he reached the top of Saint-Michel, the increasing number of obstacles appalled him, and he decided to cross the road and make a detour through the Rue des Laboureurs, in the hope that the side streets might be less crowded. There he had the misfortune to find a brothel, besieged by a mass of drunken soldiers; and afraid of getting caught up in their squabbles, he retraced his steps. From that point on, he was determined to reach the other end of the Grande Rue as best he could, sometimes balancing on the shafts of a vehicle, sometimes clambering over a forage waggon. In the Place du Collège, he was carried along for some thirty feet on somebody's shoulders, and when he managed to get down he almost had his ribs smashed in, and only managed to save himself by catching hold of an iron grille. In the end, by the time he reached the Rue Maqua, pouring with sweat and his clothes torn to shreds, it had taken him more than an hour to make a journey that usually took less than five minutes.

To prevent the garden and emergency hospital being over-run, Major Bouroche had taken the precaution of posting two sentries at the gate. To Delaherche this was a relief, for it had just struck him that his house might well have been looted. In the garden, the sight of the hospital, barely lighted by a few lanterns and giving off an unpleasant smell of sickness, made his blood run cold. He tripped over a soldier, asleep on the flagstones, and was at once reminded of the 7th Corps' funds, which this man had been guarding since morning, and who now, forgotten by his officers, was so worn out that he had simply lain down on the ground. Moreover, the house appeared to be empty, the ground floor in complete darkness, the doors wide open. All the servants must still be in the hospital, for there was nobody in the kitchen, where the only light was one small oil lamp. He lit a candle, and quietly ascended the main staircase, taking care not to wake his mother or his wife, whom he had implored to go to bed early after their laborious and trying day's work.

But, on entering his study, he had a shock. A soldier was stretched out on the couch, where Captain Beaudoin had spent a few hours the previous day; and it was only when he recognized him as Henriette's brother, Maurice, that he realized what had happened. Turning round, he saw yet another soldier wrapped up in a rug: it must be the man they called Jean, whom he had run into just before the battle started. Both men were so exhausted that they lay there like corpses, and, without more ado, he hurried to his wife's room, along the passage. A lighted lamp stood on the corner of the table, and in the quivering silence Gilberte lay stretched out on the bed, fully clothed, as though fearing some emergency. She was sleeping peacefully, while close beside her, seated on a chair, her head fallen forward on to the mattress, Henriette, too, was trying to sleep, haunted by nightmares, with large tears trembling on her eyelashes. He looked at them for a moment, tempted to awaken the young woman in order to find out what had happened. Had she managed to get to Bazeilles? If so, perhaps she would be able to give him news of his dye works. Overcome with pity, he was about to withdraw, when his mother appeared in the doorway, and without saying a word, signed to him to follow her. As they passed through the dining-room, he expressed astonishment:

"What? Do you mean to say you haven't been to bed yet?"

She shook her head, then said in a low voice:

"I couldn't get to sleep, so I've been sitting up with the colonel. . . . He's got a very high temperature, and keeps waking up and asking questions. . . . But I don't know how to answer him. You'd better come and see him."

Colonel de Vineuil had already fallen asleep again. On the pillow, one could just make out his long red face, and the line of his moustache, white as snow. Mme. Delaherche had shaded the lamp with a newspaper, so that all this corner of the room was in semi-darkness, and the light fell full upon her as she sat down in an armchair, her hands hanging down beside her, her eyes far away, lost in sombre dreams.

"Wait a moment," she murmured. "I think he's heard you and is waking up."

The colonel did, in fact, open his eyes and, without moving his head, fixed them on Delaherche. Then, recognizing him, he at once asked, in a voice trembling with fever:

"It's all over, I suppose? We've capitulated?"

The textile manufacturer, intercepting a glance from his mother, was on the point of lying to him. But what was the use? With a disheartened gesture, he said:

"What else could they do? If you could see what it's like in the town . . .! General de Wimpffen has just gone off to meet the Prussian High Command, to thrash out the conditions."

The colonel's eyes closed again, and a long shudder ran through his body. Wearily he exclaimed:

"Oh my God, oh my God. . . ."

Then, still keeping his eyes shut, he went on in a jerky voice:

"Oh, if I'd had my way, this is what would have been done yesterday. . . . I know this part of the country, and I told the general what I was afraid of. But they wouldn't even listen to me. . . . All the high ground up there occupied, from beyond Saint-Menges as far as Fleigneux, their army threatening Sedan, the Saint-Albert gorge lost . . . and us just waiting there, our positions incapable of defence, and the road to Mézières wide open. . . ."

His speech was becoming confused. He muttered a few more unintelligible words, his vision of the battle becoming more and more mixed up as sleep gradually overcame him. Perhaps as he slept he was still dreaming of victory.

"Does the major think he'll recover?" asked Delaherche in a low voice.

And, as his mother nodded her head, he added:

"All the same, these foot wounds can be terribly painful. He'll be laid up for a long time, won't he?"

For a time she remained silent, as though she, too, were overcome with grief. She belonged to another age, and to that old, tough middle class, who had once proved themselves so ready to defend their towns. In the bright light of the lamp, her stern face, with its sharp nose and thin lips, betrayed all the anger and suffering through which she was going, a feeling of fierce revolt that prevented her from going to sleep.

Delaherche felt quite alone, overwhelmed with a terrible feeling of despair. Again he realized that he was intolerably hungry, and it struck him that perhaps it was this that was sapping his courage. Taking up the candle, he tiptoed out of the room, and went downstairs to the kitchen. But there it was more melancholy still, the fire out, the larder empty, dish cloths lying all over the place; and there, too, the wind of disaster had banished the vital cheerfulness of food and drink. At first he thought he wouldn't find a bite to eat; all the bread that was left had gone into the soup for the wounded men. Then, at the back of the cupboard, he discovered some haricot beans left over from yesterday, and he ate them, without butter, without bread, standing there, hurriedly devouring this wretched meal, in the middle of this dreary kitchen filled with the smell of paraffin from the flickering lamp. It was scarcely ten o'clock, and as he waited to find out whether the capitulation had finally been signed, Delaherche felt at a loose end. He was oppressed by a persistent anxiety, fearing that the struggle might break out again, terrified of what would happen if it did. The unspoken thought weighed on his mind like lead. When he went upstairs again to his study, where Maurice and Jean had not stirred, he vainly attempted to relax in an armchair : sleep would not come, and no sooner was he on the point of losing consciousness, than the sound of firing made him sit up with a start. But it was only the noise of the ghastly bombardment that had been going on all day, still ringing in his ears; and the thought that he could still hear it bewildered him, left him trembling, as he sat there in the silence that now surrounded him. Unable to sleep, he preferred to be on his feet, and he wandered through the dark rooms, avoiding the one where his mother was sitting up with the colonel, because the fixed stare with which she followed him about got on his nerves. Twice he went back to see whether Henriette was awake yet, and stood there, looking at his wife sleeping so peacefully; then, not knowing what to do with himself, he went on wandering about, from room to room, upstairs and down, until two o'clock in the morning.

It was impossible to go on like this, and eventually Delaherche decided to return once more to the Sub-Prefecture, convinced that it would be impossible for him to relax until he knew what had happened. But when he saw the congested street he felt utterly disheartened : he would never have the strength to get there and back, the mere thought of all the obstacles to be overcome made him ache all over. While he was wondering what to do, he saw Major Bouroche approaching, out of breath and swearing to himself.

"God in heaven, I thought I was damn well never going to get through."

He had been to the Town Hall, to urge the major to requisition some chloroform and have it sent before daylight, for his own supply had almost run out. There were urgent operations waiting to be done, and he was afraid, as he put it, "that he'd have to butcher the poor sods, without being able to put them to sleep first."

"And what are they doing?" asked Delaherche.

"Why, they don't even know if the chemists have got any left!"

But it was not the chloroform Delaherche was concerned about.

"No, no," he went on, "what I meant was, have they come to an agreement with the Prussians yet?"

With a violent gesture, the major shouted :

"None whatsoever! Wimpffen's just got back. . . . It appears

310

the demands these brigands are making are utterly impossible. . . . It looks as though the whole thing's going to start all over again, till they've finished off the lot of us!"

Delaherche turned pale as he listened to him.

"But are you sure all this is true?"

"I got it from one of the members of the Municipal Council, which is in permanent session. . . . An officer had come from the Sub-Prefecture to inform them."

And he went on to give details. General de Wimpffen's interview with General von Moltke and Bismarck had taken place at the Château de Bellevue, near Donchery. This Moltke was a terrible fellow, harsh and tough, with the smooth, clean-shaven face of a mathematician, who won his battles by sitting in his study working out algebraical equations!

He had insisted straight away upon making it clear that he knew all about the desperate position of the French army : no food supplies, no munitions, men demoralized and out of control, and no possible chance of breaking out from the encirclement; whereas the German armies occupied positions of strength, and could burn down the whole town in a couple of hours. He coolly laid down his terms : that the entire French army should hand over all arms and supplies and give themselves up as prisoners of war. Bismarck, who sat there looking like a good-natured dog, had been content to back him up. Whereupon General de Wimpffen had done what he could to get these conditions modified, the harshest ever to have been imposed upon a defeated army. He had talked about bad luck, about the heroism of the soldiers, the danger of pushing a proud people too far. For three hours he had threatened and implored, speaking with all the eloquence of desperation, suggesting that the Germans should be satisfied with interning the defeated army in some remote part of France, even in Algeria. But the sole concession he had succeeded in obtaining was that those officers who would undertake, on their word of honour given in writing, to play no further part in the war, might return to their homes. In the end, it was agreed that the armistice should be extended until ten o'clock the following morning : if, by that time, the conditions had not been accepted, the Prussian batteries would open fire again and the town would be burnt down.

"But that's absurd," exclaimed Delaherche. "You don't go burning down a town that's done nothing to deserve it!"

But what made him quite beside himself, was when Bouroche

went on to say that the officers he had spoken to at the Hôtel de l'Europe were talking of a mass break-out before dawn. As soon as the German demands became known, they had started to put forward the most extravagant projects. It did not even occur to them that to take advantage of darkness, and break the truce without warning, would be dishonourable! And some of the proposals had been completely crazy: to recapture Carignan by filtering through the Bavarian lines in the darkness; to win back the plain of Illy by a surprise attack, and free the road to Mézières; even, by a last irresistible effort, to force their way into Belgium. True, some of the officers had not been a party to these schemes, and were ready to accept everything, sign anything, frankly relieved that the whole business was over.

"So goodnight to you," Bouroche concluded. "I'm going to try and snatch a couple of hours' sleep, which I badly need."

Left to himself once more, Delaherche did not know which way to turn. Could it really be true that the fighting was to start again, that Sedan was to be razed to the ground? It would become inevitable, this terrifying thing would surely happen, once the sun was high enough above the hills to reveal the full horror of the massacre. Mechanically, he once more climbed up the narrow staircase leading to the attics, and found himself standing among the chimneys on the narrow platform overlooking the town. But at this hour of the night everything was shrouded in darkness, and at first he could make out nothing at all. Then, gradually, it became possible to distinguish the confused mass of the factory buildings he knew so well: the machine-shop, the building where the looms stood, the drying-room, the stores; and the sight of this huge block of bricks and mortar, the source of his pride and of his fortune, filled him with self-pity at the thought that in a few hours' time it might be reduced to ashes. His gaze turned towards the horizon, trying to pierce that black immensity where the menacing army still lay asleep. To the South, in the direction of Bazeilles, sparks were still floating above the smouldering houses; while towards the North, the farm in the Garenne woods, which had been set on fire the previous evening, was still burning, shedding a blood-red light over the surrounding trees. Apart from these two fires, there was nothing but a bottomless abyss, shot through with fleeting rumours of terror. Over there, perhaps a long way off, perhaps on the ramparts, someone was crying. In vain he peered into the darkness, trying to make out Le Liry, La Marfée, the batteries at Frénois and

Wadelincourt, that girdle of bronze monsters whose presence he could almost feel, with their outstretched necks and gaping mouths. And as he looked down on the town lying beneath him, he could hear the sound of its anguish rising towards him. It was not only the restless sleep of the soldiers as they lay in the streets, the muffled stirring of this vast mass of men, animals and guns. What he sensed, above all, was the sleepless anxiety of his fellow townsfolk, of his neighbours, lying awake like himself, feverishly waiting for the dawn. They, too, must know that the capitulation had not yet been signed, and they, too, would be counting the hours, shuddering at the thought that, if it was not signed, there would be nothing for it but to creep into their cellars, and there await death beneath the crumbling ruins. It seemed to him as though, somewhere in the Rue des Voyards, a frightened voice was shouting murder, amid a sudden rattle of rifles. He leant out into the thick darkness, alone beneath the foggy, starless sky, trembling so violently that the hairs on his body stood on end.

Downstairs, on the sofa, Maurice was woken by the early morning light. Aching in every limb, he made no attempt to move, but stared at the window panes gradually whitening in the livid dawn. Hideous memories of the lost battle and disastrous rout were coming back to him with all the sharp lucidity of awakening. He could see it all again, down to the slightest details, and the terrible echoes of disaster shook him to the very roots of his being, as though he himself was responsible for it. And he went over the ghastly incidents that had taken place, analysing himself with an ever more acute awareness of his own defects. Hadn't he himself been content to be merely a spectator? Better educated than most, no doubt, but utterly ignorant of everything he should have known, and, in addition, vain to the point of being blind as to what was happening, misled by his eagerness to enjoy life, and by the deceptive prosperity of the regime? And this made him think of his grandfather, born in 1780, one of the heroes of the Grande Armée, who had fought at Austerlitz, and Wagram, and Friedland; and of his father, born thirty years later, a minor official in the civil service, who had worn himself out as a tax collector at Chêne-Populeux; and then himself, born in 1841, brought up as a gentleman, called to the bar, capable of the greatest stupidity and the wildest enthusiasms, and now, defeated at Sedan, in a catastrophe so immense that it meant the end of an epoch. And this degeneration of the race, which seemed to explain how France, victorious only two generations ago, had

313

now been defeated, weighed upon his mind like some hereditary disease, which, slowly getting worse, leads to inevitable destruction when the hour strikes. Had they been victorious, how brave and triumphant he would have felt! Confronted by defeat, weak and nervous as a woman, he sank into a mood of deep despair, in which his whole world seemed to be foundering. There was nothing left, France was dead. He began to weep, and folding his hands began muttering a childish prayer, his voice choked with sobs :

"Oh God, take me. . . . Oh God, take all these miserable, suffering people. . . ."

Lying on the ground rolled up in his blanket, Jean began to stir, and presently sat up in astonishment.

"What's the matter, lad? Are you feeling ill?"

Then, realizing that this was just another of Maurice's "crazy notions", as he put it, he adopted a fatherly tone :

"Come on now, what's the matter with you? It's no good getting upset about nothing!"

"What a bloody mess it all is," exclaimed Maurice. "We may as well all make up our minds to become Prussians."

And when his friend, in his slow, uneducated way, expressed astonishment, he tried to explain how, when a strain becomes exhausted, it can only be revived by an injection of new blood. But the peasant, stubbornly shaking his head, rejected this point of view.

"What? You mean my land wouldn't belong to me any more? That while I'm still alive and kicking the Prussians would take it off me? Get away with you!"

Then he, in his turn, haltingly, finding the words with difficulty, explained how he saw things. True enough, they'd had a damned good hiding! But that didn't mean everyone had been killed. There were still plenty of people left to get things going again, provided everybody put his back into it, was ready to work hard and not spend all his money on booze. It was the same as a family; if you took enough trouble and saved a bit, there was always some way of getting out of a mess, however difficult things might be. Anyhow, a good clout round the earhole wasn't always such a bad thing : it could sometimes knock some sense into a man. And another thing, it is was true there was a good deal of rottenness about, then, like gangrene, the sooner it was cut out and buried, to stop it spreading, the better for everyone.

314

"Done for? Oh no, no," he repeated again and again. "I'm not done for, not by a long chalk. . . . I won't have that!"

Then, exhausted as he was, his hair still clotted with the blood from his wound, he drew himself up, determined to go on living, to get back to the plough and start tidying the place up, as he put it. He was part of the ancient soil, wise and stubborn, in a country that believed in common sense, hard work and thrift.

"All the same," he went on, "I can't help feeling sorry for the Emperor. . . . Things seemed to be going pretty well, corn was fetching a good price. . . . But the truth is he's made a mess of it, there was no need to go and get mixed up in this sort of business."

"Oh, the Emperor!" Maurice intervened, dejectedly shrugging his shoulders, "I suppose I liked him well enough, really, despite all my ideas about a republic and freedom. . . . It must have been something in my blood, inherited from my grandfather, I imagine. . . . But now that's all gone to pot, too. Where in God's name shall we end up?"

He looked so distraught, heaved such a heartbroken sigh, that Jean was worried about him, and he had just decided to get up, when Henriette came in. The sound of them talking in the next room had woken her.

"Good for you," said Jean, pretending to make light of it. "You're just in time to give him a good scolding. He's not behaving at all well."

But the sight of his sister, so pale and unhappy, gave Maurice a salutary shock of tenderness. He held out his arms to her, and when she clung to him his heart was flooded with sweetness. She, too, was weeping, and their tears mingled.

"Oh, my poor, poor girl, how I hate myself for being too cowardly to console you. . . . Dear, good Weiss, who loved you so much! What's going to become of you without him? You've always had so much to put up with, and never a word of complaint. . . . I must have caused you enough unhappiness in the past, and who can tell whether I shan't go on doing so!"

She was trying to silence him, putting her hand over his mouth to stop him talking, when Delaherche came into the room, almost beside himself. In the end, he had come down from the roof feeling suddenly ravenous, one of those nervous spasms of hunger brought on by exhaustion, and going into the kitchen to get himself a hot drink, he had found the cook talking to one of her relations, a carpenter from Bazeilles, who had just poured out some hot wine.

315

And this man, one of the last inhabitants to leave the burning village, had told him that his dyeworks had been reduced to a heap of rubble.

"The villains," he stammered, turning to Jean and Maurice. "Would you ever have believed it! This really is the end, and this morning they're going to set fire to Sedan, as they did to Bazeilles yesterday. . . . I'm ruined, ruined!"

Suddenly he noticed the gash on Henriette's forehead, and it reminded him that he had not yet had a chance to talk to her.

"So you really managed to get there, then? And were wounded? . . . Oh, poor Weiss!"

Then, realizing from the young woman's red eyes that she already knew about her husband's death, he revealed the ghastly details which he had just heard from the carpenter.

"Yes, indeed. Poor Weiss! It appears that they burnt his body. . . . Yes, they collected the bodies of all the civilians who had taken up arms, flung them into a burning house, and then poured paraffin on them."

Henriette listened to him, horrified. Oh, my God, now she wouldn't even have the consolation of being able to bury his dear body. Maurice took her in his arms, talked to her in a gentle voice, called her his poor little Cinderella, imploring her to try not to be so upset, to be brave.

After a moment or two's silence, Delaherche, who had been watching the growing light through the window, turned quickly and said to the two soldiers:

"That reminds me. . . . The reason I came up was to let you know that, in that shed where all the money's stored, an officer has started sharing it out amongst the men, to prevent the Prussians getting hold of it. You two had better go down . . . the money might come in handy . . . if we don't all get killed, that's to say."

This was a sensible idea, and as soon as they had persuaded Henriette to take her brother's place on the sofa, Maurice and Jean went down to the yard. As for Delaherche, he went off to Gilberte's bedroom, where he found her still sleeping peacefully as a child, having scarcely changed her position, despite the sound of talking and weeping. Next, he peeped into the room where his mother was sitting with Colonel de Vineuil; but she had fallen asleep in the armchair, while the colonel, worn out by the fever, was lying quite still with his eyes closed.

Suddenly, he opened them wide, and demanded:

"Well, it's all over, isn't it?"

Annoyed at being detained like this, when he wanted to get away, Delaherche nodded his head angrily, and in a choking voice added :

"Oh yes, it's all over . . . till it starts up again! Nothing has yet been signed."

In a scarcely audible voice, beginning to be delirious, the colonel continued :

"Good God, if only I could die before the end comes . . .! I can't hear any guns. Why have they stopped firing . . .? At Saint-Menges, at Fleigneux, we control all the roads. If the Prussians try to turn Sedan in order to attack, we'll drive them back to the Meuse. With the town behind us like this, it strengthens our position. . . . Forward! The 7th Corps will take the lead, the 12th will act as rearguard. . . ."

His hands began moving up and down on the sheet, keeping time with the trot of the horse he was riding in his dreams. Then, as his words became more and more indistinct, gradually they slowed down, and he dozed off. Presently, they stopped altogether, and he lay there, exhausted, hardly breathing.

"You must rest," Delaherche whispered to him. "As soon as I have any news I'll come back."

Then, having satisfied himself that he had not woken his mother, he slipped away.

Outside in the shed, Jean and Maurice had by this time found the officer, sitting on a kitchen chair, behind a small table of unpainted wood; an officer in the Pay Corps, who, without any attempt to note the amount or ask for a receipt, was dispensing fortunes. He simply thrust his hand into the bag full of gold coins, and without bothering to count them, filled up the caps that the sergeants of the 7th Corps held out as they filed past him. It was understood that they were to share out the money amongst the men in their platoons. The sergeants accepted the money awkwardly, like a ration of meat or coffee; then, embarrassed, stowed it away in their pockets to avoid being seen in the street with all this gold. Nobody said a word, the only sound was the tinkling of the coins, while the poor devils stood there, stupefied at the thought of this surfeit of wealth, when, nowhere in the town, was there a loaf of bread or a bottle of wine to be bought.

At first, when Jean and Maurice stepped forward, the officer withdrew the money he had in his hand.

"You two aren't sergeants. . . . Only sergeants are entitled to get any. . . ."

Then, fed up with his task, and in a hurry to get it over, he added :

"All right, corporal, I suppose you may as well have some. Get a move on. Next!"

And he dropped the gold pieces into the cap that Jean held out to him. Staggered by the amount, nearly six hundred francs, Jean insisted upon Maurice taking half of it. One never knew what might happen; they could easily get separated.

They divided it up in the garden, outside the ward; then they went inside, having recognized their company drummer, Bastian, lying on the straw near the door, a fat, cheerful fellow, who had been unlucky enough to get a bullet in the groin at about five o'clock the previous evening, when the battle was already over. He had been lying there in agony ever since.

In the pale, early morning light, the sight of the hospital horrified them. Three more wounded men had died during the night, without anyone having noticed; and the nurses were now hurriedly removing the bodies to make room for other patients. Those who had been operated on the previous day, still half asleep, gazed in wide-eyed astonishment at this huge chamber of suffering, where scores of desperately wounded men lay about on the straw. Some attempt had been made to sweep the place out, to clean up the bloody mess in the operating room, but it had had little effect : the ill-swept floor still showed traces of blood; a huge sponge, floating in a bucket of blood-stained water, looking like somebody's brain; a hand, with all the fingers crushed, was still lying by the door, unnoticed. Everywhere there were pieces of flesh, the ghastly débris of the previous day's slaughter, revealed by the sombre morning light. And in this heavy, feverish atmosphere, the usual stir and bustle of early morning was replaced by a sense of crushing despair; the only sound that broke the sticky silence was an occasional faltering groan, still heavy with sleep. Glassy eyes stared in bewilderment at the new dawn, gummy lips breathed in the foetid atmosphere, as the huge room settled down to the succession of endless days, livid, evil smelling, wracked with pain, which was what these wretched cripples had to endure, in the hope that, two or three months later, they might perhaps emerge with the loss of one of their limbs.

Bouroche, back on duty again after a few hours' rest, paused

318

for a moment at Bastian's bedside, then passed on with an imperceptible shrug of the shoulders; there was nothing he could do. Nevertheless, the drummer had opened his eyes; and, apparently revived, was anxiously watching the movements of a sergeant, who had had the good idea of bringing his capful of gold into the ward, and was looking for any of his own men who might be there. He did, in fact, find two, and gave each of them twenty francs. Then other sergeants appeared, and before long gold coins were raining down upon the straw. And Bastian, who had managed to sit up, held out his hands, trembling with pain.

"What about me? What about me?"

The sergeant was about to pass him by, as Bouroche had done. After all, what use could the money be to him? Then, yielding to a kindly impulse, he dropped a few coins into the outstretched hands, which were already beginning to grow cold. For a time, Bastian fumbled with stiff fingers, trying to pick up the money. Then he fell back, dead.

"Too bad," said his neighbour, a little wizened black-haired Zouave, "the poor bloke's snuffed it! A pity, just when he'd got himself the price of a drink!"

His left leg was supported in a wicker cradle. Nevertheless, he managed to get up and drag himself along on his knees and elbows; and, having reached the dead man, he collected the lot, taking the coins from his hands and the folds of his overcoat. As he got back to his place, he noticed that people were looking at him, and said:

"After all, it would be a pity for it to get lost, wouldn't it?"

Maurice, stifled by this atmosphere of human suffering, lost no time in drawing Jean away. As they passed through the operating shed, they saw Bouroche, who, despite his annoyance at being unable to obtain any chloroform, had nevertheless just decided to amputate a poor little twenty-year-old's leg. And they hurried away, to avoid hearing the lad's cries.

At that moment, Delaherche came in from the street. He waved to them, and shouted:

"Come on up, you're just in time . . .! We're going to have breakfast after all, the cook has managed to get some milk. It will do us all good to get something warm inside us!"

Despite himself, he could not conceal his joy, and lowering his voice he added:

"This time it's going to be all right! General de Wimpffen has just gone to sign the capitulation."

What an immense relief, his factory saved, the ghastly nightmare over, life about to start once more, miserably, maybe, but life all the same! As nine o'clock was striking, he had met Rose, hurrying along to get some bread from her aunt, the baker's wife, and she had told him what had been happening at the Sub-Prefecture. At eight o'clock General de Wimpffen had summoned a new Council of War, consisting of more than thirty generals, and had laid before them the harsh demands of the victorious enemy that were the only result of his futile efforts. His hands were trembling, and he was so moved that his eyes were full of tears. While he was still speaking, a colonel from the Prussian headquarters had arrived, sent by General von Moltke to remind him that if no decision had been reached by ten o'clock, the bombardment of Sedan would be renewed. Faced by this terrible threat, the Council had authorized the general to return to the Château de Bellevue and to accept the conditions in full. By now, the general would have got there, and the entire French army, with all its arms and equipment, would be prisoners of war.

Rose had then given him a detailed account of the extraordinary excitement that the news had caused in the town. At the Sub-Prefecture she had seen officers tearing off their epaulettes, and bursting into tears like children. On the bridge, some cuirassiers had thrown their swords into the Meuse; then a whole regiment had filed past, and every man had done the same. In the streets, the soldiers were seizing their rifles and smashing the stocks against the walls; while artillerymen were removing the mechanism from their machine-guns and throwing them down the drains. Others were burying or burning their regimental colours. In the Place Turenne, an old sergeant, climbing up on to a milestone, had started cursing the officers, accusing them of cowardice, as though he had suddenly gone out of his mind. Yet others, their eyes full of tears, appeared to be completely bewildered; and nevertheless it must be admitted, the vast majority of them were delighted, every gesture expressing their feeling of relief. At last their suffering was at an end, they were prisoners; after all these days of hardship, of forced marches, of empty bellies, they hadn't got to fight any more! Besides, what was the use of fighting, when they were so hopelessly outnumbered? If the generals had sold out, so much the better, it'd be over that much quicker! What a treat it would be, to eat white bread again and sleep in real beds!

Upstairs, as Delaherche was taking Maurice and Jean to the dining-room, his mother called out to him :

"I want you a moment. I'm worried about the colonel."

M. de Vineuil, wide-eyed, gasping for breath, had relapsed into feverish dreaming.

"What's the odds, even if the Prussians do cut us off from Mézières? . . . There they are, coming round the Falizette wood, and there go some more, following the Givonne upstream. . . . The frontier's just behind us. When we've killed as many as we can, we can slip across in no time. . . . That's what I wanted to do yesterday. . . ."

Just then his feverish gaze encountered Delaherche. He recognized him, seemed to pull himself together, to throw off his hallucinations; and, confronted once again by the terrible reality, he asked for the third time :

"It's all over now, isn't it?"

Unable to conceal his immense satisfaction, the mill owner at once replied :

"Yes, thank God, over and done with. . . . By this time the capitulation will have been signed."

Violently, despite his wounded foot, the colonel stood up, and picking up his sword from the chair tried to break it in two; but his hands were trembling so much that the steel slipped.

"Look out, he'll cut himself," cried Delaherche. "It's dangerous. Take it away from him!"

And Madame Delaherche succeeded in getting possession of the sword. Then, seeing M. Vineuil's disappointment, instead of hiding it as her son told her to, she broke it across her knee, with a strength of which she would never have believed herself capable. At this, the colonel lay down again, and staring at his old friend with a look of infinite sweetness, broke into tears.

Meanwhile, in the dining-room, the cook had served everyone with big cups of hot coffee. Gilberte, who had woken up refreshed by a good night's sleep, bright-eyed and fresh-complexioned, was sitting with her arm round her friend, Henriette, tenderly assuring her that she pitied her from the bottom of her heart. Maurice sat on the other side of his sister, while Jean, drinking his coffee rather awkwardly, found himself opposite Delaherche. As Madame Delaherche never came down to breakfast, a cup was taken to her, and she was glad of it. The breakfast party, after a silent start, soon livened up. Shabby and hungry as they all were, how could they not help feeling glad to be alive and well, when thousands of wretched men were still wandering about in the surrounding countryside? In the big, bright dining-room, the clean tablecloth was a pleasure to look at, and the hot coffee was delicious.

In the course of the conversation, Delaherche, who had recovered all his self-confidence as a wealthy industrialist and genial employer, who liked being popular and was only hard on failures, reverted to the subject of Napoleon III, whose face had been haunting his restless imagination ever since the previous day. He addressed himself to Jean, this simple fellow being the person nearest to him.

"Yes, I don't mind telling you, sir, that I can't help feeling the Emperor let us down. . . . After all, however much his admirers may prate about extenuating circumstances, he is the primary, indeed the unique, cause of our present disaster."

He was already forgetting that, only a few months ago, he had been doing his best, as an ardent Bonapartiste, to ensure the success of the plebiscite. Now, he felt no sympathy for "the man of Sedan", but accused him of every kind of iniquity.

"In the light of what has happened, it's clear that the man is utterly incapable. . . . He's one of those unpredictable people, for whom everything seems to go well, provided they have luck on their side. . . . It's no use, now, trying to make us feel sorry for him, by telling us that he's been let down, that the Opposition refused to vote the necessary men and credits. It's we who've been let down by his vices and mistakes, which have landed us all in the terrible mess we're now in."

Maurice, who preferred to keep out of this conversation, could not repress a smile; while Jean, embarrassed by such political talk and afraid of saying something stupid, contented himself with replying :

"All the same, people say he's a decent sort."

But these few modestly spoken words infuriated Delaherche. All the fears he had experienced, all his anguish of mind, exploded in an exasperated and passionate cry of hatred.

"A decent sort, indeed! That's easily said. . . . Are you aware, sir, that my factory has been hit by three shells? And it certainly wasn't thanks to the Emperor that it hasn't been burnt to the ground. . . . Do you realize that this imbecile business is going to cost me a hundred thousand francs. . . . Yes, sir, a hundred thousand francs? . . . Oh no, no! The country invaded, buildings burnt down, people exterminated, industry forced to lie idle, commerce destroyed ... that's rather too much of a good thing. If that's what being a decent sort entails, then all I can say is, God preserve us from such people! Now he's landed himself up to his ears in mud and blood, let him stay there!"

And he made an expressive gesture with his hands, as though he were holding down some wretched creature who was struggling to escape. Then he greedily drained the remains of his coffee. Meanwhile, Gilberte was smiling involuntarily at Henriette's air of distraction, treating her like a child. Though their cups were by this time empty, they all continued to sit there, enjoying the cheerful peace of the big, bright dining-room.

At that very moment, Napoleon III was sheltering in the poverty-stricken house of a weaver, on the road to Donchery. At five o'clock in the morning he had insisted on leaving the Sub-Prefecture, ill-at-ease at the thought of Sedan lying around him like a threat, tormented by the need to do something to allay his sensitive heart by obtaining better conditions for his unhappy army. Intent upon seeing the King of Prussia, he had taken a post-chaise, and set out along the wide main road, bordered with tall poplars, on the first stage of his exile, undertaken in the chill of dawn and deeply conscious of the fallen greatness he was leaving behind him. And it was in the course of this journey that he had met Bismarck, hurrying to meet him, dressed in his old cap and big, dubbined boots, and determined to prevent him from seeing the King until the capitulation had been signed. The King was still at Vendresse, eight or nine miles further on. Meanwhile, where was he to go? What roof would shelter him? Back there, lost in storm clouds, the Palace of the Tuileries had disappeared. Sedan itself seemed to have withdrawn many miles, cut off from him by a river of blood. For him, there were no more imperial castles in France, no more official residences, not even a corner in the home of the most despised of his officials, in which he dared to seek refuge. He had ended up in this weaver's house, a poverty-stricken dwelling he happened to see from the road, with its tiny orchard surrounded by a hedge, and its two storeys lit by small, dismal windows. Upstairs, the bedroom, with its whitewashed walls and check curtains, had no furniture, save for a plain wooden table and two rush chairs. And there he remained for hours, at first in the company of Bismarck, who only smiled when he spoke of generosity; later by himself, brooding on his misery, pressing his chalk-white face to the window panes that looked out over the soil of France, with the lovely Meuse flowing between its vast, fertile fields.

Then, for several days, there were further stages on this wretched journey : the castle of Bellevue, that smiling, bourgeois stronghold overlooking the river, where he spent the night in tears after his interview with King William; the cruel departure, avoiding Sedan for fear of the defeated, starving soldiers; the bridge of boats that the Prussians had thrown across the river at Iges; the long detour to the North of the town; the side roads through Floing, Fleigneux, Illy, all this miserable flight in an open carriage. And then, on the tragic plain of Illy, still littered with corpses, the legendary meeting, when the wretched Emperor, unable to stand the trotting of his horse any longer, struck down by some violent crisis, sat puffing mechanically at his everlasting cigarette, while a gang of haggard prisoners, covered with blood and dust, who were being taken from Fleigneux to Sedan, drew to the side of the road to let his carriage pass, at first in silence, then beginning to mutter, till presently their anger burst out in a storm of yells and curses, and they shook their fists at him in a gesture of contempt and hatred. Then, later on, there was the interminable journey across the battlefield, mile upon mile of ploughed-up roads, amidst all the wreckage of war, all the unburied dead with their staring, threatening eyes, mile upon mile of empty countryside and huge, silent woods, the frontier at the top of a rise, and beyond that, the end of everything, a road lined with pine trees running away into the distance at the bottom of a narrow valley.

And that first night of exile, in an inn at Bouillon, the Hotel de la Poste, where there was such a crowd of French refugees and curious onlookers that the Emperor felt bound to appear publicly, despite the catcalls and muttered insults. His room, with its three windows looking out across the square, was just an ordinary hotel room; chairs covered with red damask, a mahogany wardrobe, and a metal clock on the mantelpiece, flanked by sea-shells and artificial flowers under a glass case. On either side of the door stood small twin beds. In one of them, an aide-de-camp, worn out with fatigue, was already asleep by nine o'clock. But in the other, the Emperor twisted and turned, unable to sleep himself; and when he got up and walked about the room in an attempt to allay his misery, all there was to distract him were two engravings on either side of the fireplace, one of Rouget de l'Isle singing the Marseillaise, the other, The Last Judgement, with angels blowing trumpets, summoning the dead from their graves to bear witness before the throne of God.

In Sedan, the baggage-train of the imperial household, piled high with luggage, still stood outside the Sub-Prefecture, unable to get away. No one knew what to do about it or how to conceal it from the eyes of the starving crowds, whose angry insolence and savage irony became more and more unbearable. It had to wait for a specially dark night, so that the horses, the carriages, the waggons, the silver plate, the spits, the crates of priceless wine could be surreptitiously evacuated, and follow the Emperor into Belgium, with the stealthy tread of thieves.

THROUGHOUT the interminable day of the battle, Sylvine, who had stayed behind in old Fouchard's little farm on the hillside above Remilly, had kept her eyes fixed in the direction of Sedan, amid the din and smoke of the guns, trembling at the thought of what might have become of Honoré. By the following day, owing to the impossibility of obtaining any precise news, her anxiety had increased, for the Prussians who were guarding the roads refused to say anything, and, indeed, they had little idea themselves of what was happening. The bright sunlight of the previous day had given way to showery weather, and the valley looked grey and depressing.

Towards evening, old Fouchard, as worried as she was beneath his grim silence, scarcely thinking of his son but anxious to find out how other people's misfortunes would affect him, was standing in the doorway watching what was going on, when suddenly he noticed a tall fellow in a blouse, who, for the last minute or two had been wandering along the road. He was so surprised when he recognized who it was, that he called to him at the top of his voice, despite the fact that three Prussians happened to be passing at the time.

"Why, if it isn't you, Prosper?"

Violently signalling to him to be quiet, the Chasseur d'Afrique came towards him, and said in a low voice:

"Yes, it's me all right. I've had enough of fighting for nothing, so I beat it. . . . Here, Monsieur Fouchard, what about taking me on as a farmhand?"

The old man had quickly recovered his normal cunning. He was, in fact, looking for someone. But it would be a mistake to admit it.

"What, take someone on in times like these? Not on your life. . . . Still, come in and have a drink. I wouldn't want to leave you out there, if you're in trouble."

In the kitchen, Sylvine was preparing the soup, while little Charlot clung to her skirts, playing and laughing. At first, she did not recognize Prosper, despite the fact that he had once worked with her, and it was only when she brought some glasses and a bottle of wine that she saw who it was. She uttered a startled cry, for all her thoughts were of Honoré.

"Why, you must have been there . . .! Is Honoré all right?"

Prosper was about to reply, but hesitated. For the past two days he'd been living in a dream, a succession of strange and violent happenings that had left no clear impression upon his mind. True, he felt pretty certain he'd seen Honoré's dead body lying across a gun barrel. But he couldn't swear to it, and what was the use of upsetting people when you weren't absolutely sure?

"Honoré?" he muttered. "Why, I don't really know. . . . I wouldn't like to say. . . ."

She stared hard at him, insisting:

"So you didn't see him, then?"

He made a vague gesture with his hands, and shook his head.

"It's hard to say with such a lot going on! With all this blasted fighting, I'm damned if I know what really did happen. . . . All the different places I've been in . . . why it makes me feel completely barmy!"

Then, having swallowed a glass of wine, he sat there peering distractedly into his shadowy memories.

"All I can remember is that, when I came round, night was already falling. . . . In the middle of the charge, when I came off, the sun was still shining, but I must have lain there for a couple of hours, with my right leg caught under poor old Zephyr, who'd been hit in the chest. . . . I don't mind telling you it was no joke, finding yourself like that surrounded by dead comrades, not a living soul in sight, convinced that I'd peg out too, unless someone turned up pretty soon. I did what I could to free my leg, but not a chance; it felt as though Zephyr weighed a couple of ton. He was still warm, so I began talking to him. But that's something I'll never forget – the way he opened his eyes and tried to lift up his head. Then I just talked to him. 'Poor old chap,' I said to him, 'I know it's not your fault, but unless you manage to shift yourself it looks like both of us have had it.' Of course, he couldn't answer. But I could tell from the way he looked at me that he didn't like the idea of leaving me behind. Then, what actually happened I don't know, maybe it was just his death agony. Anyhow he gave a sudden heave, and that rolled him over. I found I was able to stand up, but what a bloody mess I was in, legs as heavy as lead. . . . But I didn't worry. I lifted up Zephyr's head and tried to tell him what I felt. . . ."

What a good horse he'd been, how fond of him I was, and how I'd always remember him. I'm sure he understood, because he looked kind of pleased. Then he gave another twitch, and it was all over . . . and him lying there, staring at me with those great empty eyes. . . . It's a funny thing, you know, and I don't suppose anybody'll believe me, but I swear there were tears in his eyes, and that's the honest truth. . . . Just imagine, poor old Zephyr, crying like a human being . . ."

Prosper was so overcome with grief that he had to break off. Tears ran down his cheeks, and he drank another glass of wine before continuing his story, in broken sentences that he couldn't finish. It had begun to get dark, the last rays of the sun were throwing great long shadows. He must have stayed a long time sitting beside his horse, unable to move on account of his leg. Yet presently he forced himself to walk, suddenly afraid of being left alone, longing to be back with his mates, to feel less scared. And then from all around, from ditches and thickets, any kind of hole and corner, other wounded men who had been left behind like him began dragging themselves along, trying to catch up, forming themselves into little groups of four or five, so that if they had to die it wouldn't be so hard to bear. That was how, on reaching the Garenne woods, he came across two other fellows belonging to the 43rd. Though they hadn't even got a scratch, they were lying curled up on the ground like hares, waiting for night to come. As soon as they discovered he knew the way, they told him they were planning to get to the frontier and slip over into Belgium under cover of darkness. At first, he had refused to act as guide, preferring to make straight for Remilly, where he was sure of finding refuge; the only thing was, where was he to get hold of a peasant's blouse and trousers? Besides, how could they hope to get from the Garenne woods to Remilly, right from one end of the valley to the other, without passing through the Prussian lines? Eventually, he had agreed to show them the way. His leg was becoming swollen, but they were lucky enough to be given a loaf of bread at a farm. As they set out again, nine o'clock was striking from a clock tower in the distance. The only serious danger they were in was at La Chapelle, where they landed right in the middle of an enemy outpost, that started firing into the darkness. But by crouching close to the ground, and running hell for leather, they managed to get back to the undergrowth, despite the hail of bullets. After that they had stuck to the woods, feeling their way, and always on the alert.

328

Once, at a sudden turn in the footpath, they had surprised an isolated sentry, but they sprang on him from behind and cut his throat from ear to ear with one stroke. From then on, they saw no more of the enemy, and cheerfully continued on their way. Then, towards three in the morning, they reached a small Belgian village, where they woke up a friendly farmer who let them into one of his barns, and there they at once fell asleep among the bales of hay.

By the time Prosper woke up again, the sun was already high in the heavens. While his comrades were still snoring, he looked out and saw their host harnessing a horse to a big cart, loaded with bread, rice, coffee, sugar and all kinds of provisions, hidden beneath sacks of charcoal. The farmer told him that he had two married daughters at Rancourt in France, and was taking this food to them as they were bound to have been robbed of everything by the Bavarians. That morning, he had managed to obtain the necessary safe conduct. Prosper at once had the crazy idea of going with him, and so returning to the one spot on earth for which he felt home-sick. Nothing could be simpler; the farmer would have to go through Remilly, and could put him down there. Everything had been fixed up in no time : the farmer had lent him the trousers and blouse he so badly needed, and told everybody they met that he was his son. With the result that, by six o'clock, he had finally been put down by the village church, having only been stopped two or three times on the way by German outposts.

"No, I've had as much as I can stand!" Prosper repeated after a silence. "It would have been different if they'd made the slightest attempt to make any proper use of us, like they used to in Africa! But just to be shoved about all over the place, first this way, then that, makes you feel you're no damned use. In the end, you simply get fed up with it . . .! Besides, now poor Zephyr's dead I should be all on my own, so I may as well try to get work on the land again. That's better than being taken prisoner by the Prussians. Don't you agree . . .? You've got horses, Monsieur Fouchard. Why not give me a chance? I'll soon show you how well I can look after them!"

The old man's eyes lighted up. He clinked glasses again, and said slowly :

"Heaven knows, if it's going to be of any help to you, I'm pre-pared to take you on. . . . Though, of course, as regards wages, it's no good talking about them till the war's over. The truth is, I don't really need anybody at present, with times as bad as they are."

329

Sylvine, who was sitting with Charlot on her lap, had never taken her eyes off Prosper; and as soon as she saw him getting up, ready to go off to the stables to see to the animals, she asked him again:

"So you didn't see Honoré, then?"

Coming so suddenly, her question made him jump, as though it had suddenly lighted up some dark corner of his memory. He hesitated a moment, but eventually made up his mind.

"Listen, I didn't want to upset you just now, but I'm pretty sure Honoré got left behind."

"What d'you mean, left behind?"

"I think he was killed by the Prussians. . . . I saw him lying across one of the guns, wounded in the chest."

There was a silence. Sylvine turned terribly pale, while Fouchard, listening attentively, put down his glass, having just emptied the bottle.

"Are you quite sure?" she asked, in a strangled voice.

"Why yes, as sure as you can be about anything you see. It was on a little hillock, with three trees nearby. . . . I believe I could find my way there with my eyes shut."

For her, it was as though the world were falling about her ears. This man, who'd forgiven her, who'd given her his word, and was going to marry her as soon as the war was over and he was demobilized! And now they had killed him, and he was lying out there with a bullet through his heart! Never before had she loved him so deeply. And so great was her need to see him once more, to have him for herself in spite of everything, even if only to bury him, that she was aroused from her usual calm.

Sharply putting down Charlot, she exclaimed:

"All right, but I shan't believe it till I've seen it for myself. If you know where it is, you must take me there. And if it's true, if we find him, we'll bring him back here."

Tears choked her. She collapsed on to the table, shaken by long-drawn sobs, while the child, puzzled by his mother's roughness, also started crying. She picked him up again, clasping him to her breast, muttering in a broken voice:

"My poor child, my poor child."

Old Fouchard was badly shaken. In his own way he was fond of his son. Memories of the old days, the days when his wife was still alive and Honoré was still at school, came back to him; and the tears welled up in his bloodshot eyes, and trickled down his tanned cheeks. It was ten years or more since he had wept. He started

330

swearing, feeling annoyed with this son of his whom he would never see again.

"Good God, if that isn't about the limit, for a man to lose his only son!"

But presently, when they had all calmed down a little, it began to annoy him to hear Sylvine keep talking of going to look for Honoré's body. She had stopped crying now, but so obstinately did she stick to her proposal that he no longer recognized the docile creature he was accustomed to, resignedly going about her duties: the great submissive eyes were filled with obstinate determination, while beneath the thick brown hair her cheeks were deathly pale. She had torn off the red scarf she usually wore round her shoulders, so that now she was dressed all in black, like a widow. In vain he pointed out to her all the difficulties, the dangers she would be bound to encounter, the little chance there was of finding the body. She made no attempt to reply, and it soon became clear that, unless he was prepared to do something about it, she would set off on her own and might well do something silly that would get him into trouble with the Prussian authorities. In the end, he decided to go and see the mayor, who was a distant relation of his, and between the two of them they worked out a story: they would say that Sylvine was in fact Honoré's widow, and Prosper her brother. The result was that the Bavarian colonel, who was staying at the Croix de Malte hotel at the far end of the village, eventually agreed to give the brother and sister a pass, authorizing them to bring back her husband's body if they succeeded in finding it.

By this time darkness had fallen, and the only concession they could obtain from the young woman was that she would wait for daylight before setting out. Next day, Fouchard refused to let them take one of his horses, afraid lest he might never set eyes on it again. How could he be sure that the Prussians wouldn't confiscate his horse and trap? In the end, however, he agreed, with a bad grace, to lend them a little grey donkey and cart, which would be just big enough to take the corpse. He insisted upon giving lengthy instructions to Prosper, who, although he had slept well, was now getting more and more worried as to whether he would remember the exact spot. Then, at the last moment, Sylvine fetched a blanket from her own bed, which she folded up and put in the cart, and, before leaving, ran back to kiss Charlot goodbye.

"Listen, Monsieur Fouchard, I'm leaving him in your charge. Whatever you do, see that he doesn't play with matches."

331

"Yes, yes, you needn't worry!"

All these preparations had taken time, and it was nearly seven o'clock before Sylvine and Prosper finally set off behind the little donkey-cart, down the steep slope leading from Remilly. During the night it had rained heavily, transforming the roads into rivers of mud, and the sky was filled with great livid clouds.

Intending to take a short cut, Prosper decided to go through Sedan, but when they reached Pont-Maugis a Prussian outpost stopped the cart, and kept it there for over an hour. Then, when the pass had been examined by four or five different authorities, the donkey was released, on condition that they went round through Bazeilles, taking a side road that led away to the left. No reason was given, but probably they were afraid of allowing anyone else into the already overcrowded town. As Sylvine was crossing the Meuse by the railway bridge, the wretched bridge that had not been blown up and had cost the Bavarians so dear, she saw an artilleryman's body floating casually downstream. It got caught up in a clump of reeds, and for a moment lay there without moving. Then, turning on its face, it set off again.

In Bazeilles, through which they slowly made their way from one end to the other, they saw nothing but destruction, all the hideous ruin left behind by the devastating hurricane of war. The dead had already been taken away, and not a corpse was to be seen in the village streets, but the rain, though it had washed away the blood, had left pools of reddish water, in which could be seen gruesome shreds of skin, with hair still adhering to them. But the utter destruction of what, only three days ago, had been a smiling village, with cheerful houses standing amidst their gardens, and that now lay prostrate, obliterated, nothing left but empty walls, scorched by the flames, struck a deep chill in their hearts. The church was still burning, a huge bonfire of smoking beams in the middle of the square, from which an endless column of black smoke rose into the sky, and hung there like a black plume of mourning. Whole streets had disappeared, leaving nothing on either side but heaps of calcined stones, strewn along the gutter in a sludge of soot and ashes, a thick, inky mud that oozed in every direction. The houses at each of the four corners of the square had been razed to the ground, as though swept away by the fiery wind. Others had suffered less; one was still standing, cut off from the rest, while those on either side of it looked as though they had been battered to pieces by machine-gun fire, leaving nothing but gaunt skeletons.

332

Everywhere there was an unbearable stench, a sickening smell of burning, and strongest of all the sharp tang of the paraffin with which the houses had been soaked. And, on top of this, there was the mute desolation of all those things that people had tried to save, pathetic pieces of furniture, flung out of the windows and smashed to pieces on the pavement, ricketty tables with broken legs, cupboards with the doors torn off, from which hung household linen, torn and fouled, all the sad bits and pieces left behind after the looting, and now soaked with rain. Through a gaping hole in the front of a house, between the smashed floorboards, a clock could be seen, unharmed, still standing on the mantelpiece.

"Oh the swine!" Prosper snarled, his soldier's instincts returning and making him furious at all these monstrous sights.

He clenched his fists, and every time they passed a sentry, Sylvine, white with anger, had to calm him down with a look. As a matter of fact, the Bavarians had posted sentries outside all the houses that were still burning; and these men, standing there with loaded rifles and fixed bayonets, appeared to be protecting the fires, so that the flames could complete their work. If anyone, either out of curiosity or because they were personally involved, attempted to approach, they drove them away with threatening gestures and guttural shouts. Groups of inhabitants stood trembling with the effort to restrain their anger. One woman, quite young, her hair falling round her shoulders, her dress fouled with mud, persisted, despite the sentry's warning, in trying to rake over the glowing ashes of a small house, where her child was said to have been burnt to death. And suddenly, as the Bavarian was brutally pushing her away, she turned upon him, giving vent to her wild despair in a stream of insults and obscene words, which seemed to calm her a little. He could not understand what she was saying, and fell back, gazing at her anxiously. Then three other soldiers hurried up, and dragged the woman away, screaming. Before the ruins of another house, a man with two little girls was sitting on the ground, exhausted with fatigue, sobbing bitterly, not knowing where to turn now that everything they possessed had gone up in flames. But a patrol came by, and drove away the onlookers, so that once more the street became deserted, with only the sentries, sad-faced and grim, keeping a sharp look-out to see that their orders were obeyed.

"The swine, the filthy swine," Prosper repeated dully. "There's nothing I'd like better than to get my hands on one or two of that lot!"

Again Sylvine told him to be quiet. She was shivering. In a shed that the fire had spared, a dog, which had been shut up there for two days, was howling continuously, the pathetic sound dying away in the lowering sky, from which a thin, grey rain had begun to fall; and it was just then, in the Montivilliers park, that they came across three big carts, drawn up in a line, and filled with bodies. They were garbage carts, which normally went round the streets every morning to collect the piles of rubbish, but which were now making the rounds of the village, stopping every now and then to pick up a corpse, then rumbling on again until they were full to overflowing. Now they were drawn up by the roadside, waiting to discharge their loads into the public rubbish tip. Feet stuck out, pointing up at the sky; and a head could be seen, hanging down, almost severed from its body. And as the three carts moved off again, jolting through the puddles, a livid hand, dangling over the side, began rubbing against the wheel, gradually wearing away the skin and exposing the bone.

By the time they reached the village of Balan, the rain had stopped. Prosper persuaded Sylvine to eat some bread, which he had had the foresight to bring with him. It was already eleven o'clock, but as they were approaching Sedan, they were stopped by another Prussian outpost; and this time it was most alarming, for the officer lost his temper and refused to give them back their pass, insisting in the most correct French that it had been forged. On his instructions, soldiers took the donkey and cart into a shed. What were they to do? How would they be able to continue their journey? Then, almost desperate, Sylvine had an idea. She remembered that Fouchard had a cousin, a Monsieur Dubreuil, whom she knew, and whose estate, *The Hermitage*, was quite near, beyond the narrow streets, looking out over the suburb. Perhaps, as he was a bourgeois, the Germans would listen to him. Since they themselves had been allowed to go free, on condition that they left the cart behind, she took Prosper with her. Hurrying along as fast as they could, it was not long before the found *The Hermitage*. The gates were wide open, and as they turned into the avenue of elm trees, the sight that met their eyes astonished them.

"Hell," said Prosper, "this is a fine set-up, and no mistake!"

On the gravelled terrace at the bottom of the steps, a merry party appeared to be in progress. Round a marble-topped table, a sofa and armchairs covered with pale-blue satin had been set out like some open-air drawing-room, and two Zouaves, ensconced at

334

either end of the sofa, were roaring with laughter. A little infantry-man leant forward in his chair, clasping his stomach, three others lolled at their ease, while a Chasseur was reaching out his hand to take a glass from the table. Obviously, they had emptied the cellars and were enjoying themselves.

"How on earth do they come to be here?" muttered Prosper, more and more surprised the further he advanced. "They don't seem to give a damn for the Prussians."

But Sylvine, who had been staring at them wide-eyed, suddenly gave a gesture of horror, at the same time uttering a cry. None of the soldiers had moved; they were dead! The two Zouaves, bodies already stiff, hands clenched, were faceless, their noses torn away, their eyes pecked out. The grin on the face of the man clasping his belly was the result of a bullet that had hit him in the mouth and smashed his teeth. But what was really ghastly was to see these wretched creatures, frozen forever in the awkward attitudes of broken mannequins, with glassy eyes and wide-open mouths, apparently chatting away to one another. Had they, while still alive, dragged themselves to this spot so that they might all die together? Or could it be that the Prussians had collected the bodies, and then, for a joke, sat them up like this to make fun of the ancient gaiety of the French people?

"A bloody poor idea of a joke, if you ask me!" said Prosper, turning pale. Then, as he looked around at the other corpses scattered about the alley and under the trees on the lawn, these thirty or so brave men, amongst whom was the body of Lieutenant Rochas, gaping with wounds and still wrapped in the regimental colours, he added in a sober, respectful tone of voice : "There must have been a proper mix-up from the look of things! I somehow don't think we're going to find the folk you're looking for here."

Sylvine had already gone into the house, and was standing there in the dank air that blew in through the gaping windows and smashed doors. It was obvious there was no one there, the owners must have left before the battle started. Obstinately, however, she persisted, and as she reached the kitchen she again uttered a cry of horror. Two bodies had rolled under the sink, a handsome Zouave with a black beard, and an enormous red-haired Prussian, locked together in furious struggle. One man's teeth were sunk in the other's cheek, and they still clung to one another with their stiffened arms, their bodies so inextricably interlocked that they would have to be buried together.

Then, since there was nothing more to be done in this doomed house, Prosper quickly led Sylvine away, and by the time they got back to the guard post where they had had to leave the donkey and cart, they were lucky enough to find, in addition to the officer who had treated them so roughly, a general who had come to inspect the battlefield. The latter insisted upon seeing their pass, which he handed back to Sylvine with a gesture of pity, as much to say that this poor woman with her donkey should be allowed to continue her search for her husband's body. Without more ado she and her companion, followed by their little cart, made their way back towards the Fond de Givonne, having been forbidden once again to go through Sedan.

To reach the plain of Illy, they took the road to the left that led through the Garenne woods. But here again they were slowed down by the increasing number of obstacles that presented themselves. At every step they found the road barred by giant trees, felled by gunfire. Beneath the bombardment, the centuries old forest had stood firm, allowing itself to be hacked to pieces like a veteran regiment of the guards, so that on every side the huge trunks lay splintered and shattered like human bodies, the sap still oozing from the wounded branches, in a terrible replica of a human battlefield. And among the trees were more dead soldiers : a lieutenant with a bloodied mouth, still clutching a handful of earth that he had torn up in his agony; and further on a captain, lying on his belly, his head twisted in a final scream; while others seemed to be asleep beneath the bushes, a Zouave, whose blue sash had caught fire, had his beard and hair completely burnt away. And again and again as they made their way along the narrow forest path, they had to pull a body out of the way so that the donkey could get by.

Then all of a sudden, in a little valley, the scene of horror came to an end. The battle had passed elsewhere, leaving this charming spot untouched. Not a single tree had so much as been grazed, not a drop of blood stained the moss. There was water-weed trailing in the little stream, and the footpaths running along its banks were shaded by tall beech trees. And the freshness of the murmuring water, the trembling silence of the leaves, held all the charm of enchanted peace.

Prosper, who had stopped to let the donkey have a drink, uttered an exclamation of relief :

"Oh but it's good here !"

Sylvine looked around her in wonderment, surprised that she, too, could feel so relaxed and happy. Why should this little corner have remained so content and peaceful, when all around was only grief and suffering? Desperately she pulled herself together.

"Quick, quick, we must get on . . . ! Where was it? Where was the place you remember seeing Honoré?"

Fifty yards further on they came out at last on to the Illy heights, with the flat plain suddenly lying in front of them. This time it was the real battlefield, the bare land stretching away to the horizon beneath a vast, wan sky, streaming with continual showers of rain. Here there were no longer heaps of dead lying about; the Prussians must have been buried, for there was not one of them to be seen amongst the scattered corpses of the French that still lay along the roadside, in the stubble fields, between the furrows, wherever they had fallen. The first one they came across, propped up against a hedge, was a sergeant, a superb fellow, young and powerful, whose lips seemed still to smile from his calm face. But a hundred yards further on was another, lying across the road, horribly mutilated, one side of his head shot away, the brains spilling down over his shoulders. Then, beyond these single bodies, here and there were little groups : in one case, seven men in a row, kneeling down with their rifles to their shoulders, who had been killed in the act of firing; while, not far away, lay a non-commissioned officer, his hand still raised in a gesture of command. Further on, the road ran along a narrow ravine, and here they were once more overcome with horror at the sight of a whole company which seemed to have fallen into a kind of ditch, mown down by machine-gun fire : the ditch was full of corpses, a monstrous huddle of men, lying broken and higgledy-piggledy, whose hands had scrabbled at the yellowish earth in a futile attempt to check their fall. Overhead wheeled a flock of cawing rooks; and already swarms of flies were buzzing around the bodies, thousands of them, persistently returning to gorge themselves on the blood that flowed from their wounds.

"Where was it?" Sylvine asked once more.

They were now making their way along the side of a ploughed field, strewn with haversacks, that some hard-pressed regiment must have thrown away in a fit of panic. The nature of the debris that was scattered about recalled the various episodes in the fighting. For instance, in a beetroot field, the fallen caps, looking like huge red poppies, the torn uniforms, the discarded epaulettes and belts bore witness to one of the rare hand-to-hand encounters that had occurred in the course of the formidable twelve-hour artillery duel. But what most struck them were the discarded weapons – swords, bayonets, rifles – lying about in such profusion that they seemed like some monstrous kind of vegetation, some ghastly harvest. Messtins and water-bottles, too, were strewn all over the place, mixed up with the rice rations, brushes and ammunition that had spilled from men's packs. And the fields succeeded one another in a scene of vast devastation, fences torn down, trees burnt, the very soil itself so rent by shells, so trampled and ravaged by thousands of feet, that it looked as though it must remain forever sterile. Everything was drenched by the steadily falling rain, and everywhere was that same persistent stench, the stench of battlefields, that consists of fermented straw, burnt cloth, gunpowder and putrescence.

Sylvine, weary of these fields of death, through which she seemed to have been tramping endlessly, gazed around her in growing dismay.

"Where could it be? Wherever could it be?"

And Prosper, growing more and more uneasy, made no attempt to answer. What upset him even more than the corpses of his comrades was the great number of wretched horses they encountered, lying on their sides. Some of them were really pathetic, stretched out in monstrous attitudes, their heads shot away and the guts streaming from their bellies. A lot of them, swollen to an enormous size, lay on their backs, with their legs sticking stiffly in the air like distress signals. Some were still alive after two days of agony, and at the slightest sound they would raise their heads, turning them this way and that before letting them fall again; while others, unable to move, would now and then make the shrill, unmistakeable moaning sound of a horse in its death agony, so terrifyingly mournful that the air seemed to quiver with it. And each time he heard it, Prosper was overcome with grief, thinking of Zephyr, wondering whether perhaps he might see him again.

Suddenly, he felt the ground tremble beneath the thunder of charging hooves; and, turning round, he only just had time to call out to his companion :

"Look out, look out . . . ! Get behind that wall !"

Five or six score of riderless horses, some of them still with their saddles and bridles on, were streaming towards them down a neighbouring hill, going hell for leather. They were animals that had got lost during the battle, and had now instinctively formed themselves into a herd. After two days without hay or oats, they had grazed the fields bare, raided the hedgerows, stripped the bark from trees, and now, spurred on by hunger, they were galloping wildly over the empty, silent countryside, crushing the dead bodies with their hooves and finishing off the wounded.

As the whirlwind approached, Sylvine just managed to drag the donkey and cart beneath the shelter of the wall.

"Heavens," she cried, "they're going to smash everything to pieces!"

But the horses cleared the obstacle, and with a noise like the rolling of thunder were already galloping away on the other side, plunging into a sunken road that led to a spur of woodland, behind which they disappeared.

When Sylvine had led the donkey back on to the road, she pressed Prosper for an answer:

"Come on now, where was it?"

"All I know is that there were three trees," he replied, gazing round in every direction. "We must find those three trees. . . . While a battle's going on you don't have time to notice much, and afterwards it's difficult to remember exactly which way you went."

Then, catching sight of some people away to the left, two men and a woman, he decided to question them, but as soon as he approached them the woman took to her heels, and the men drove him away with threatening gestures. He saw some more. But they, too, made off, disappearing hurriedly into the undergrowth like suspicious animals, dressed in unspeakably dirty clothes, shifty-looking as poachers. Then he noticed that none of the dead bodies left behind by this shady bunch had any boots on, and realized that the wretched creatures were thieves, who followed in the wake of the German armies, preying on the wounded and stripping the corpses. One of them, a tall, thin fellow, dashed past with a sack slung over his shoulder, his pockets bulging with watches and silver coins stolen from the dead and dying.

However, a lad of thirteen or fourteen stood his ground when Prosper went up to him; and when the latter, seeing that he was French, began cursing him, the lad protested. Where was the harm? Everybody had to get a living somehow or other, and he was simply looking for rifles, for which he got paid five sous apiece. That morning, having had nothing to eat for the past twenty-four hours, he had run away from his village, and he had been offered the job by a dealer, a man from Luxembourg, who had come to an arrangement with the Prussians for collecting rifles from the battlefield.

The fact was, the Prussians were afraid lest the peasants on the frontier might take the rifles over into Belgium, and from there hand them back to the French; and, as a result, they were paying this bunch of wretched creatures five sous apiece to collect them.

"A bloody fine job!" grumbled Prosper.

"Well, damn it all, a fellow's got to eat," replied the lad. "I'm not robbing anybody."

Then, as he was a stranger to these parts and could not direct them, he pointed to a neighbouring farm where he had seen some people.

Prosper thanked him, and was about to rejoin Sylvine when he noticed a rifle, half-buried in the ground. His first impulse was to say nothing about it, then suddenly he turned back and, almost in spite of himself, called out :

"Look, there's one here. That'll be another five sous for you!"

As they drew nearer to the farm, Sylvine noticed some other peasants engaged in digging trenches, but these were acting on the orders of Prussian officers, for two or three of them stood supervising the work, stiff and silent, unarmed except for the canes they carried. They had requisitioned all the inhabitants of the villages to bury the dead, fearing that the wet weather would quickly decompose the corpses. Nearby stood two cartloads of bodies, and a team of men was unloading them, hurriedly laying them side by side in the common grave without even going through their pockets or looking to see who they were; and, behind them, came three men armed with shovels, who covered the bodies with a layer of earth so thin that the rain was already beginning to wash it away. So hurriedly was the job done that in less than a fortnight's time each of these burial places would become a source of infection. Sylvine could not help pausing at the edge of the ditch to examine the pathetic bodies as they were unloaded from the cart; and as she looked into each new face, she was trembling with fear at the horrible thought that it might prove to be Honoré's. Could that be he, the poor wretch with one eye missing? Or that one with the broken jaw? Unless she could find him, sooner or later he was bound to be thrown into a common grave as these had been. She turned away, and hurried to catch up with Prosper who had gone on ahead.

"For heaven's sake, find out where it is. . . . You must ask them, question them."

The only people in the farmhouse were some Prussians, and a

340

servant girl who had brought her child back from the woods where they had almost died of hunger and thirst. It was a scene of patriarchal simplicity, of honest rest after the grim toil of the preceding days. Some of the soldiers were carefully brushing their uniforms, which were hung on the clothes-line; another had just finished skilfully mending his trousers; while the army cook had lighted a big fire in the middle of the yard, where he was heating a great cauldron of soup that gave off a pleasant smell of bacon and cabbage. The victors were settling down with perfect discipline; sitting there smoking their long pipes, they might have been well-to-do peasants who had just got in from the fields. On a bench by the door, a fat man with red hair was nursing the servant's child, a kid of five or six years old. He was dancing it up and down, talking to it gently in German, amused to see the child laugh at the sound of this harsh foreign tongue, which it did not understand.

Fearing some fresh misadventure, Prosper had quickly turned away, but these Prussians were obviously decent folk. They smiled at the little donkey, and did not even bother to ask them for their passes.

From then on, their journey became stranger and stranger. The sun shone out for a moment from behind the clouds, already low on the horizon, and it seemed as though night might fall before they could escape from this endless charnel-house. Then another shower blotted out the sun, and once more they were shut in by an endless curtain of rain, obliterating everything, roads, fields, trees. Prosper was completely lost, and admitted as much. Behind them the donkey trotted along steadily, head down, pulling the little cart with docile resignation. They climbed uphill, to the North, then turned back towards Sedan. They had lost all sense of direction, and twice they found themselves covering the same ground, recognizing places that they had passed earlier; they must be going in circles. Eventually, worn out and disheartened, they pulled up at a point where three roads met, drenched by the rain and without the strength to continue their search.

Then, hearing the sound of someone groaning, they pushed on again, until they came to a small, isolated house, where, in one of the rooms, they found two wounded men. All the doors were wide open, yet during the two days they had been there, shivering with fever and with no dressings on their wounds, they had not seen a single soul. Though they could hear the rain beating against the window panes they were tortured by thirst, for they were unable to move. And they immediately called out: "Water, for God's sake, water!" – the heartrending cry with which, at the slightest sound of footsteps, the wounded appeal to anyone who happens to go by.

While Sylvine was fetching them something to drink, Prosper, who had recognized in the more badly wounded of the two a Chasseur d'Afrique belonging to his own regiment, realized that it must be somewhere near here that the charge had taken place. Eventually, in reply to his questions, the wounded man managed to make a vague gesture: yes, it was over there to the left, on the other side of a big field of lucerne. And as soon as she heard this, Sylvine immediately insisted on setting off again, having first summoned some men who were looking for dead bodies to come and take care of the wounded. She quickly seized the donkey by the bridle and began dragging it through the mud, anxious to reach the other side of the field of lucerne.

Suddenly, Prosper came to a halt.

"It ought to be near here. Look, there are the three trees, over there on the right. . . . Here are the wheel tracks, and that's the foundered gun, over there. . . . We're there at last!"

Trembling from head to foot, Sylvine rushed up to two dead artillerymen lying at the side of the road, and anxiously examined their faces.

"But it isn't him, he's not here . . .! You must have made a mistake, you must have imagined it!"

And a crazy hope, a feverish joy, began to take possession of her. If Prosper was mistaken it meant that Honoré might still be alive! Yes, yes! That must be it, he was still alive!

Then suddenly she uttered a low cry, for as she turned round she found herself on the actual gun emplacement. It was an appalling sight: the ground churned up as if by an earthquake, debris everywhere, men's bodies flung in all directions, lying in ghastly attitudes, arms twisted, legs doubled up beneath them and heads awry, their gaping mouths revealing the gleam of white teeth. A dead corporal lay with his hands still pressed to his eyes as though to blot out the terrifying sight. Some gold coins, fallen from a lieutenant's pouch, glittered among his bleeding entrails. Lying on top of each other, Adolph the driver and Louis the gun-layer, their eyes starting from their sockets, remained tightly clasped in one another's arms. And there at last was Honoré, stretched out on the crippled gun, as though lying in state, with one shoulder and all the side of his body shot away. But the face was unscathed, splendid in its wrath, still gazing out towards the Prussian batteries.

"Oh, my love," sobbed Sylvine, "my love . . ."

She had fallen to her knees on the muddy ground, clasping her hands in a passion of crazy grief. And in the one word she spoke was all the tenderness she felt for the kindly man she had lost, the man who had forgiven her, the man who, in spite of everything, had promised to make her his wife. Now her hopes were at an end, her life was over, for this was the only man she had ever loved, and she would love him always. It had stopped raining. Overhead a flight of crows wheeled above the three trees, casting a menacing shadow. Did they want to take him from her, to rob her of the beloved body it had cost her so much to find? She dragged herself forward on her knees to drive away the voracious flies that were buzzing around the wide-open eyes, and leant forward, still striving to meet their gaze.

Then suddenly she caught sight of a piece of blood-stained paper clenched between Honoré's fingers, and, overwhelmed with anxiety, began tugging at it gently, trying to take it from him. But the dead man refused to give it up, clinging to it so tightly that it was impossible to take it away from him without tearing it to pieces. It was the letter she had written to him, the letter he had kept beneath his shirt, close to his body, and which now, in his death agony, he held fast in a last farewell. And when she saw what it was, a profound feeling of joy burst through her grief, as she realized that in the moment of death his last thought had been for her. Yes, yes, of course she would let him keep it, since he was determined to take it with him to the grave. Then a fresh outburst of tears brought her relief, and getting to her feet she kissed his hands and forehead, and with infinite gentleness repeated again and again.

"Oh, my love . . . my love. . . ."

Meanwhile, as the sun was beginning to go down, Prosper fetched the blanket from the cart, and between them they reverently wrapped Honoré's body in it and carried it to the cart. It had started to rain again, and as the sad little procession set out on its homeward journey across the desolate plain, they heard once more the distant thunder of hoofs.

"Look out, the horses!" Prosper shouted again.

This time the charging horses were bearing down upon them across a huge, flat stubble-field, a dense mass of animals, manes floating in the wind, muzzles covered with foam, lit up by the slanting rays of the setting sun. Sylvine immediately flung herself in front of the cart, waving her arms in a desperate attempt to ward them off. Fortunately, however, thanks to the slope of the field, they swung away to the left, otherwise they would have been crushed to death. But as they galloped past, shaking the ground, a stone flung up by the thundering hoofs, struck the donkey, wounding it in the head. Then they disappeared from sight, over the brow of a ravine.

"It's hunger makes them do that," said Prosper. "Poor brutes!"

Sylvine, having tied up the donkey's ear with her handkerchief, once more took it by the bridle, and the gloomy procession retraced its steps across the plain on the six-mile journey to Remilly. But every now and then Prosper would stop to examine a dead horse, his heart heavy at the thought of having to leave the neighbourhood without having seen Zephyr again.

A little beyond the Garenne woods, as they turned to the left to regain the road, a German sentry demanded to see their pass. And this time, instead of being turned away from Sedan, they were instructed to go through the town under pain of arrest. There was nothing they could do about it, it was an order. Besides, it would shorten their journey by a mile, and this cheered them up, for by this time they were almost exhausted.

When they reached the city, they found the way impeded by yet another obstacle. For no sooner had they passed the fortifications than they were assailed by a formidable stench, and they found themselves walking through muck up to their knees; the streets were like open sewers, streaming with the litter and excrement of the hundred thousand men who had spent the last three days there. And in addition to this human filth, there was all kinds of other rubbish, straw, hay, horse dung and, above all, the carcasses of animals that had been slaughtered and cut up in the open streets. Their guts had rotted in the heat of the sun, and heads and bones, swarming with flies, were strewn all over the pavements. Unless this terrible layer of filth, which in some of the principal streets, rue du Ménil, rue Maqua, Place de Turenne, was already nearly a foot deep, was soon washed away into the drains, an outbreak of plague was inevitable. Meanwhile, the Prussian authorities had posted up notices, requisitioning the inhabitants for the following day, ordering everybody, workmen, merchants, shopkeepers and magistrates, to set to work with shovels and brooms, and imposing the severest penalties unless the town was cleaned up by the evening. Indeed, the President of the Law Courts himself was already to be seen, shovelling up the muck outside his house and wheeling it away in a barrow.

As Sylvine and Prosper turned into the Grande Rue, they had the greatest difficulty in making their way through the stinking muck. Moreover, the whole town was in such a state of turmoil that it continually added to their difficulties. The Prussians were ransacking the houses, looking for soldiers who had refused to surrender and had taken refuge in them. The previous day, when General de Wimpffen had returned from the Château due Bellevue after signing the capitulation, a rumour had spread that the whole of the captured army was to be shut up in the Iges peninsula, until such time as arrangements had been made for taking them to Germany. Only a sprinkling of officers had taken advantage of the agreement that they would be allowed to go free, provided they gave a written undertaking to play no further part in the war. Only one general, it was said, General Bourgain-Desfeuilles, had given this undertaking, on the grounds that he was crippled with rheumatism; and, that very morning, he had been greeted with boos as he set out in a carriage from the Hotel de la Croix d'Or. The order to lay down their arms had been enforced since early dawn; the soldiers had to file through the Place Turenne, and there throw their rifles and bayonets on to the rapidly growing pile in one corner of the square. A Prussian detachment, under the command of a young officer, a tall, pale-faced lad in a sky-blue uniform, with a plume of cock feathers in his helmet, had supervised the proceedings, looking on with a well-behaved, superior air, and all wearing white gloves. And when one Zouave, seized by a sudden feeling of revolt, had refused to give up his rifle, the officer had ordered him to be led away, saying in a voice without a trace of German accent:

"Have that man shot!"

The others continued to file past gloomily, flinging their rifles down automatically, glad to get it over with. But many of them, those whose rifles had been left behind on the battlefield, were already disarmed! And many more were in hiding, desperately hoping that they might still find some way of disappearing in the inconceivable confusion! The houses were full of these stubborn men, who had gone to ground and refused to come out. The German patrols who were scouring the town even found some of them crouching behind the furniture; and as many of them, even when they were discovered, refused to leave the cellars, the Germans had begun firing through the ventilators. The result was a sort of monstrous man-hunt.

As they reached the bridge across the Meuse, the donkey was stopped by the dense crowd. The sergeant in charge of the guard protecting the bridge, suspecting that they were attempting to smuggle in bread or meat, insisted upon examining what was in the cart. But having pulled back the blanket, and stared at the corpse for a moment in bewilderment, he signed to them to proceed. It was still impossible to make any headway, however, for the crowd was swollen by one of the first convoys of prisoners, being marched away to the Iges peninsula by a detachment of Prussian soldiers. It seemed to go on interminably, the men bumping into one another, treading on one another's heels, in ragged uniforms, hanging their heads, hardly daring to look anyone in the face, as they slouched along with dangling arms . . . beaten men, with not even a knife to cut their own throats. The voices of the guards, harsh as the crack of a whip, drove them forward through the confused silence of the crowds, broken only by the splashing of their heavy boots in the mud. It was raining heavily again, and nothing could have been more pathetic than this herd of defeated soldiers, trudging along through the downpour, like an army of tramps and vagabonds.

All of a sudden, Prosper, whose heart was pounding with stifled anger, nudged Sylvine with his elbow to draw her attention to two of the passing soldiers. He had recognized Maurice and Jean, tramping along side by side; and, as the little cart was now able to move forward again in the wake of the prisoners, he was able to follow them with his eyes as far as the suburb of Torcy, along the level road that leads to Iges, between gardens and allotments.

"After all," murmured Sylvine, looking at Honoré's body, "maybe the dead are better off!"

Night was falling as they reached Wadelincourt, and by the time they arrived at Remilly it was quite dark. Seeing his son's corpse, old Fouchard was completely taken aback, for he had been convinced that they would never find it. As for him, he had spent the day making a very satisfactory deal: the officers' horses caught on the battlefield were fetching twenty francs apiece, and he had managed to buy three for forty-five francs.

II

As the column of prisoners left Torcy there was so much confusion that Maurice became separated from Jean. It was no use hurrying after him, he only got more and more lost. And when, at last, he reached the bridge over the canal that separates the peninsula of Iges from the mainland, he found himself mixed up with the Chasseurs d'Afrique and unable to find his own regiment.

The bridge was defended by two guns, trained on the peninsula. Just beyond the canal, the Prussians had set up a guard-post, in a well-to-do house, under the command of an officer who was responsible for receiving and looking after the prisoners. The formalities, however, were minimal : the prisoners were simply counted, like so many sheep, without worrying too much about their uniforms or regimental numbers; and as the swarms of men poured across the bridge they settled down wherever they could find room.

Maurice decided to approach a Bavarian officer, who was sitting astride a chair, peacefully smoking.

"Excuse me, sir, but which way do I have to go for the 106th regiment of the line?"

Whether the officer did not understand French, or whether it just amused him to misdirect some wretched prisoner, he merely smiled, and, raising his hand, pointed straight ahead.

Although Maurice came from this part of the country, this was the first time he had ever been on the peninsula, and he had no more idea where he was than if he had suddenly found himself on some remote island. He turned to the left, and continued along which the Prussians had advanced, ran along the curve of the river which flowed to the right at the bottom of a steep embankment, and then gradually led uphill, twisting and turning, till it reached the small hillock occupying the centre of the peninsula; and here there were narrow footpaths that disappeared into the ancient quarries and excavations. Downstream, in the distance, was a mill. Then the road turned sharply, leading down to the village of Iges, built on the slope, where, opposite the Saint-Albert cotton mill, there was a ferry across the river. Beyond this, ploughed fields and meadows stretched away into the distance, a huge expanse of flat, treeless fields enclosed within the curve of the river. In vain Maurice scanned the broken slopes of the hill : all he could see were cavalry and artillery regiments already beginning to settle down. Once again he asked his way, but the sergeant-major of the Chasseurs d'Afrique to whom he spoke could not help him. It was beginning to get dark, and he sat down on a milestone to rest his weary legs.

Seized by a sudden feeling of despair, he could see, on the other side of the river, the accursed battlefield where, only two days ago, they had been fighting. In the dying light of this rainy day, the muddy sweep of country, stretching away to the horizon, was a dreary sight. The Saint-Albert gorge, the narrow roadway along which the Prussians had advanced, ran along the curve of the river as far as the whitish scree of the quarries. Beyond the Seugnon slopes clustered the treetops of La Falizette. But what chiefly caught his eye was Saint-Menges, straight ahead of him, a little to the left, with its road running down to the ferry; right in the middle was Le Hattoy, with Illy far away in the distance, Fleigneux almost hidden by a fold of the ground, and, nearer to him, Floing on the right. He recognized the field where they had spent hours lying amongst the cabbages, the high ground that the reserve artillery had tried to defend, the hill crest where he had seen Honoré shot down beside his foundered gun. And all the horror of the disaster surged up afresh, overwhelming him with pain and disgust until he felt like vomiting.

However, the fear of being caught in the dark drove him to renew his search; perhaps the 106th would have settled down beyond the village, lower down. But, encountering no one but one or two soldiers on the scrounge, he decided to make a tour of the whole peninsula, following the curve of the river. As he crossed a field of potatoes, he took the precaution of pulling up one or two haulms and filling his pockets. The potatoes were only half formed, but he had nothing else to eat, for, as a crowning misfortune, Jean had taken charge of the two loaves that Delaherche had given them as they were leaving. What impressed him particularly was the large number of horses he came across in the bare fields that sloped down from the central heights towards the river. Whatever was the point of bringing all these animals on to the peninsula? How were they going to feed them?

By the time he reached a little wood at the edge of the water it

348

was quite dark, and he was surprised to find the Emperor's household cavalry there, already settling down, drying themselves before blazing fires. These gentry, who held aloof from the rest of the prisoners, had proper tents, dixies already on the boil, a cow tethered to a tree. In his ragged infantryman's uniform, plastered with mud, he felt that they were eyeing him with contempt. They allowed him to bake his potatoes, however, in the ashes; after which he withdrew to some distance, and ate them sitting under a tree. It had stopped raining, the sky had cleared, and the stars were shining brightly through the bluish haze. He realized he would have to spend the night there, ready to continue his search first thing in the morning. He was completely fagged out, but at least, if it started to rain again, the tree would afford him some protection.

But he could not sleep, he was haunted by the thought of this huge prison, exposed to the night air that seemed to shut him in. It had been a singularly intelligent idea on the part of the Prussians to send the eighty thousand prisoners, all that remained of the army of Châlons, to a place like this. The peninsula was about three miles long by three-quarters of a mile wide, plenty of room to accommodate this vast horde of men. And Maurice was only too well aware that they were completely surrounded by water, the great bend of the Meuse running along three sides, with the canal cutting across on the fourth to join it at either end. That was the only way out, across the bridge; and that was guarded by the two guns. Thus, despite the extent of the camp, it was perfectly simple to guard it. He had already noticed the line of German sentries on the other bank, spaced out along the water's edge at fifty-yard intervals, with orders to fire on anybody who tried to escape by swimming across. And, behind them, were Uhlans, galloping backwards and forwards to keep the sentries in touch; and beyond them again, spread out through the vast countryside, the dark lines of the Prussian regiments, a triple girdle, alert and continually on the move, hemming in the army of prisoners.

For the time being, however, Maurice, wide-eyed with insomnia, could see nothing but the camp fires gleaming in the darkness, while beyond the pale ribbon of the Meuse, it was still just possible to distinguish the motionless figures of the sentries. There they stood, beneath the light of the stars, black, upright figures; and, at regular intervals, he could hear the threatening sound of their guttural voices as they called out the pass-word, dying away in the distance, drowned by the roar of the river. Listening to these harsh foreign

349

syllables, uttered on French soil, beneath a starry sky, the whole nightmare of the past few days revived, all he had seen an hour or two earlier, the plateau of Illy covered with dead bodies, the accursed city of Sedan where a whole world had collapsed. Lying in the damp undergrowth, his head propped against the root of a tree, he relapsed into the same despair that had gripped him yesterday as he lay on Delaherche's sofa; and what was now torturing him, aggravating his sense of wounded pride, was the question of the future, the need to plumb the depths, to realize the extent to which that world of yesterday had collapsed. Surely, since the Emperor had surrendered his sword to King William, this abominable war was at an end? Yet he recalled what two Bavarian soldiers had said when they were escorting the prisoners into Iges: "All of us in France, all of us to Paris!" And as he lay between waking and sleeping, he had a sudden vision of what would happen: the Empire overthrown, swept away amidst universal execration, and a Republic proclaimed in a feverish outburst of patriotism as the legend of 1792 aroused the ghosts of the past, the soldiers of the mass uprising and the volunteer armies, to purge the soil of the fatherland of foreigners. And in his poor sick mind everything became confused: the exactions of the conquerors, the bitterness of defeat, the determination of the conquered to shed their blood to the last drop, the captivity of these eighty thousand men, here on the peninsula to begin with, later on in the fortresses of Germany, for weeks and months, maybe for years. Everything was beginning to crack, everything was collapsing, in a disaster whose limits could not be foreseen.

The shouting of the sentries was gradually growing louder, then died away in the distance. He was suddenly awake, was just turning over on the hard ground, when a shot broke the silence. It was immediately followed by the cry of a dying man; and there was a splashing of water, the brief struggle of a body sinking like a stone. Doubtless some poor fellow, shot through the heart as he was trying to escape by swimming across the Meuse.

Next day Maurice was up at sunrise. The sky was clear, and he was in a hurry to get back to Jean and the rest of the company. At first he thought of searching the interior of the peninsula once more; then he resolved to complete his tour. And as he reached the edge of the canal again, he saw the remnants of the 106th, a thousand men huddled on the bank, with no other protection than a straggling row of poplars. On the previous evening, if only he had turned left instead of going straight ahead, he would have caught up with the regiment at once. Nearly all the regiments of the line were drawn up here, along the bank of the canal that runs from the Tour à Glaire to the Château of Villete, another handsome country estate on the Donchery side, surrounded by a few tumbledown cottages; and they had all settled down as close as possible to the bridge, the one possible exit, with the same instinctive longing for freedom that makes a flock of sheep crowd round the gate of a sheep-pen.

Jean gave a cry of pleasure.

"So here you are at last! I thought you must have fallen in the river!"

With him was all that remained of the squad: Pache and Lapoulle, Loubet and Chouteau. The latter, having spent the night at one of the gates of Sedan, had been reunited with the others in the course of the big round up. As a corporal, Jean was the last officer left in the company, since Sergeant Sapin, Lieutenant Rochas and Captain Beaudoin had all been killed. And although the Germans had abolished all ranks, on the principle that as prisoners the French owed obedience only to German officers, the four of them had decided to stick by the corporal, knowing him to be a sensible and experienced man on whom they could count when things got difficult. So this morning everything was smiles and good humour, despite the stupidity of some of them and the insubordination of others. In the first place, he had found them a dry place to sleep, between two drainage channels, where they had all huddled up under the only waterproof sheet they had. Then, later on, he had managed to get hold of some wood and a dixie, in which Loubet had brewed some coffee, the warmth of which had cheered them all up. The rain had stopped, it looked like being a fine day. They still had a few biscuits and a bit of fat bacon, and besides, as Chouteau said, it was a treat to be able to take it easy and not to have to obey orders from anybody. It was better than being shut up indoors, there was plenty of room; and, in any case, in two or three days' time they'd be leaving. In short, this first day, which happened to be a Sunday, passed happily.

As for Maurice, who had pulled himself together now that he was back with his comrades, what worried him most were the Prussian military bands, which played all afternoon on the other side of the canal. Towards evening they organized choirs. Beyond the line of sentinels, they could see the Prussian soldiers walking

351

about in small groups, singing in their slow, high-pitched Sunday voices.

"Oh these bands!" Maurice exclaimed in exasperation. "They get on my nerves!"

Less easily upset, Jean merely shrugged his shoulders.

"Why, dammit, they've got plenty of reason to be pleased with themselves. Besides, perhaps they think they're giving us a treat. . . . We shouldn't complain, things haven't been too bad today!"

But as darkness began to fall the rain started again, and the result was disastrous. Some of the prisoners had taken over the few abandoned houses, others had succeeded in putting up tents; but the great majority were without any kind of shelter, without even blankets, and had to spend the night in the open, beneath a steady downpour. Towards one o'clock, Maurice, who had fallen asleep exhausted, woke up to find himself lying in a regular pond. The drainage channels, swollen by the rain, had overflowed, submerging the ground where they were lying. Chouteau and Loubet were cursing with rage, while Pache was shaking Lapoulle, who, in spite of the growing flood, was still asleep with his fists clenched. At this point, Jean proposed that they should all take shelter under the row of poplars along the canal, and there they spent the rest of this appalling night, their backs chafed by the bark, their legs drawn up underneath them, trying to avoid the drips from the trees.

The next two days were really terrible, with continual squalls of rain, so heavy and frequent that their clothes never had time to dry. They were beginning to suffer from hunger, not a biscuit was left, not even a bit of cold bacon or a drop of coffee. The whole of the Monday and Tuesday they lived on potatoes, stolen from a nearby field; and even these were getting so scarce that, by the end of the second day, those who had any money were paying five sous a piece for them. True, the bugles still went on sounding "Rations", and each time the corporal hurried across to a big barn at the Tour à Glaire, where rumour had it that bread rations were being issued. But, the first time, he waited for three hours to no purpose, and the second, he became involved in a quarrel with one of the Bavarians. As their own officers weren't allowed to do anything, it was beginning to look as though the German command had decided to leave the whole defeated army out here in the rain to die of hunger. No arrangements whatsoever seemed to have been made, not even the slightest attempt to feed the eighty thousand men, and they were beginning to suffer serious hardship in this

352

damp hell, which the soldiers nicknamed "Misery Camp" – a name that even the bravest of them could never recall later on without a shudder.

Despite his usual calm, by the time Jean returned from these long, useless expeditions he was in a furious temper.

"What the hell do they think they're playing at, blowing the bugle when there isn't any food? I'm damned if I'm going to bother any more!"

Nevertheless, at the first note, he would dash off again. These regulation bugle calls were utterly inhuman; and they had another effect, which almost broke Maurice's heart. Every time they sounded, the horses the French had left behind on the other side of the canal would gallop up and plunge into the water, in an attempt to get back to their regiments, but they were so exhausted that most of them were dragged under, and only a very few got across. So many of them were drowned, that before long the canal was choked with their swollen, floating bodies. As for those that did get across, they behaved like mad creatures, galloping away across the empty fields till they disappeared from sight.

"More food for the crows," Maurice said sadly, remembering all the horses he had encountered on the first day. "If we stay here much longer, we shall all end up by eating each other. . . . Oh, the poor brutes!"

Tuesday night was especially horrible. And Jean, who was beginning to be seriously worried about Maurice's feverish condition, insisted upon wrapping him up in a torn blanket they had brought from a Zouave for ten francs, while he himself sat huddled up in his soaking greatcoat, exposed to the drenching rain that continued throughout the night. Beneath the poplars, things were becoming quite impossible: a stream of thick mud, the ground so saturated that the water lay in deep pools. To make matters worse, they had nothing in their stomachs, for their evening meal had consisted of two beetroots between six men, which they hadn't even been able to cook for lack of dry wood, with the result that the sickly taste soon produced an intolerable sensation of heartburn; not to mention the fact that they were already beginning to suffer from dysentery, brought on by exhaustion, bad food and persistent damp. A dozen times, Jean, propped up against the same tree trunk, his feet in a pool of water, stretched out his hand to make sure that Maurice hadn't thrown off his blanket in his sleep. Since his friend had saved his life on the plateau of Illy, by carrying him off in his arms,

353

he had repaid his debt a hundredfold. Without a thought, he gave himself completely, utterly forgetful of himself; yet this simple peasant, so close to the earth, could find no words to express the deep, obscure affection that he felt. Again and again he had "given him the food out of his own mouth", as the others put it; and he would gladly have given the skin off his back if it would have protected him from the rain or kept him warm. And, in the midst of all this savage egotism, surrounded by this little group of human beings, tortured by the pangs of hunger, it was perhaps to this complete self-abnegation that he owed the unforeseen reward of maintaining his health and cheerful tranquillity, for he was the only one of them who stood firm and never lost his head.

It was as a result of this terrible night that Jean made up his mind to carry out a plan that had been haunting him.

"Listen here, kid. Since it doesn't look as though they're going to give us anything to eat, that we've just been forgotten in this damned hole, the sooner we start doing something for ourselves the better, unless we want to die like dogs. . . . Do you think you can still walk?"

Fortunately, the sun had come out, and Maurice felt warmed through.

"Yes, of course I can."

"Right, then we're going to see what we can find. . . . As we've still got some money, it's a damned poor look-out if we can't find something to buy. And we're not going to worry about the others, they aren't worth it. . . . Let them shift for themselves."

The fact was, he had gradually become revolted by the selfishness of Loubet and Chouteau, who scrounged whatever they could without sharing it with their comrades; and he had long ago given up expecting anything from the brutal Lapoulle, or the canting humbug, Pache.

So the two of them, Jean and Maurice, set off together, following the road along the Meuse, which the latter already knew. At La Tour à Glaire, both the park and house had been laid waste and looted, the lawns looked as though they had been swept by a hurricane, trees uprooted, buildings broken open. A crowd of ragged soldiers, covered with mud, hollow-cheeked, eyes glittering with fever, had turned the place into a kind of gypsy encampment, fouling the rooms like animals, afraid to go outside lest someone else should steal their place for the night. Further on, on the surrounding slopes, they passed the cavalry and artillery, and they,

354

too, formerly so correct, had also given up, disorganized by the torturing hunger that was maddening the horses and driving the men to roam about the fields in devastating bands. On the right, outside the mill, they saw an endless queue of artillerymen and Chasseurs d'Afrique, slowly advancing : the miller was selling them flour, charging them a franc for a couple of handfuls, which they wrapped up in their handkerchiefs. But fearing they would have to wait too long, they decided to push on, in the hope of finding something better in the village of Iges. But what a terrible setback when they finally got there ! It was as bare and desolate as a village in Algeria after a plague of locusts had passed : not a scrap of food to be found, no bread nor vegetables nor meat, and the poverty-stricken hovels looking as though someone had been through them with a toothcomb. It was said that General Lebrun had called on the mayor, in a vain attempt to organize a system of vouchers, payable after the war, in order to facilitate the feeding of the soldiers. There was nothing left, money had become useless. The previous day it had still been possible to buy a biscuit for two francs, a bottle of wine for seven, a small glass of brandy for twenty sous, a pipeful of tobacco for ten sous. But now officers were obliged to guard the general's house, as well as the neighbouring hovels, sword in hand, because of the endless bands of men, who were prowling about, breaking into houses, even stealing the oil from the lamps and drinking it.

Three Zouaves shouted to Maurice and Jean : five of them could make a good job of it, they said.

"Come and give us a hand. . . . We know where there are some dead horses, all we need now is some dry wood. . . ."

Then they rushed off to a peasant's hut, smashed the cupboard doors, tore the thatch from the roof. But they were driven off by some officers, who arrived at the double, threatening them with their revolvers.

When he saw that the few inhabitants of Iges who had not already left were as poor and hungry as the soldiers, Jean regretted having disdained the flour at the mill.

"We'd better go back, perhaps there's still some left."

But Maurice was beginning to be so weary, so exhausted by hunger, that Jean left him behind, sitting on a rock in a sheltered part of the quarry, where he could look out towards Sedan. After waiting in a queue for three-quarters of an hour, he got back at last with a small bag of flour. All they could do was to eat it as it was, scooping it up with their hands. It wasn't bad, but almost tasteless, like eating macaroni. However, it made them feel a little better. They were even fortunate enough to find a pool of rainwater amongst the rocks, clean enough to drink; and it was a delight to quench their thirst.

When Jean suggested spending the afternoon there, Maurice protested violently :

"Oh no, not here . . . ! It'll make me ill if I have to look at this for long. . . ."

And, with a trembling hand, he indicated the vast horizon : Le Hattoy, the plains of Floing and Illy, the Garenne woods, these hateful scenes of slaughter and defeat.

"Just now, while I was waiting for you, I had to turn my back to it, or I'd have started howling with rage. Yes, howling like a dog. . . . You can't imagine what it does to me, it drives me crazy !"

Jean stared at him, amazed by this display of wounded pride and worried to see once again the same look of madness in his eyes that he had noticed earlier. He tried to make a joke of it.

"All right, then, that's easy enough. We'll change the view."

So for the rest of the day they wandered about, taking the first path they saw. They went to the flat part of the peninsula, hoping to find some potatoes; but the artillerymen had already ploughed up the ground and gathered the lot. They retraced their steps, making their way once again through the listless, desperate crowds, where starving soldiers walked up and down, utterly exhausted, or lay around in the hot sunlight. Every now and then, they themselves succumbed, and had to sit down. Then a nagging feeling of irritation would drag them to their feet again, and they would wander on once more, driven by the animal instinct to find food. It seemed to go on and on for hours, yet the minutes quickly slipped away. Out in the ploughed fields, towards Donchery, they were afraid of the horses, and had to shelter behind a wall, where they spent a long time crouching on the ground, at the end of their tether, vaguely watching the maddened animals galloping about against the crimson background of the setting sun.

As Maurice had foreseen, the thousands of horses that had been taken prisoner with the army, and which it was impossible to feed, were becoming an increasing menace from day to day. They began by stripping the bark off the trees, then they attacked hurdles, fences, any piece of wood they came across, and now they were beginning to devour one another. They would attack each other,

356

tearing out the hair from each other's tails and chewing it furiously, and the air would be filled with flying foam. But it was especially at night that they were terrible, haunting the darkness like nightmares. A few of them would gather together, then, attracted by the straw, charge down upon the tents that were still standing. To keep them away, the men lighted great fires, but it was no use, it only seemed to excite them all the more. Their neighing was pitiful, but as terrifying as the roaring of wild beasts. If they were driven off, they would only return in greater numbers, and more ferocious; and every now and then, in the darkness, one would hear the last agonized cry of some soldier, crushed beneath the galloping feet.

The sun had not yet sunk beneath the horizon, when, on their way back to the camp, Jean and Maurice were surprised to see the other four men belonging to their section, squatting in a ditch, and obviously up to some mischief. Loubet immediately hailed them, and Chouteau said.

"We're planning a meal for this evening. . . . We're just about starving, we haven't had a bite to eat for the last thirty-six hours. . . . So we thought, with all these horses about, a bit of horseflesh wouldn't be so bad. . . ."

"We thought you'd like to be in on it, corporal," Loubet interrupted. "With such a huge brute, the more of us there are the better. . . . Look, there's one over there we've been keeping our eye on for the last hour, that big roan. It looks pretty sorry for itself . . . it shouldn't be difficult to finish it off."

And he pointed to a horse, dying of hunger, at the edge of a ravaged field of beetroot. Lying on its side, from time to time it raised its head and gazed sadly around, painfully drawing its breath.

"My God, but he doesn't half take his time," said Lapoulle, hungrily. "What do you say I go and put it out of its misery?"

But Loubet restrained him. No thanks! They didn't want any trouble with the Prussians . . . they'd given orders that no horses were to be killed, for fear of the abandoned carcasses spreading the plague. They must wait till it was properly dark. This was why the four of them were in the ditch, watching the struggling animal with shining eyes.

"Here, corporal," said Pache, his voice trembling slightly. "You're a sensible bloke, d'you reckon there's some way of killing it without making it suffer?"

Jean rejected the idea with a gesture of revulsion. His first instinct had been to clear off and have nothing to do with this

357

horrible butchery. But seeing how pale Maurice was looking, he reproached himself for his squeamishness. After all, wasn't that what animals were for, to feed human beings? You couldn't just let yourself die of starvation when there was meat available. And he was glad to see that Maurice had cheered up a little at the thought of getting something to eat. In his good-humoured way, he said :

"Christ, I haven't the slightest idea, but if you want to kill it without making it suffer. . . ."

"Oh bugger that," interrupted Lapoulle. "Just you leave it to me !"

The two new arrivals had by this time taken their place in the ditch, and the waiting started again. From time to time one of the men got up to make sure that the horse was still there, stretching out its head towards the fresh breeze from the Meuse, as though its life depended upon it. Then, as twilight slowly turned to darkness, all six of them got to their feet, impatient of the laggard night, looking around anxiously to make sure that no one could see them.

"Come on," shouted Chouteau, "now's our chance !"

It was still just possible to see in the treacherous half-light, and Lapoulle ran ahead, followed by the five others. He had picked up a big round stone, and flinging himself on the horse, he began battering its head, holding the stone in both hands, his arms stiffly extended like a club. But, at the second blow, the horse struggled to get up. Chouteau and Loubet caught hold of its legs, trying to prevent it, and shouted to the others to help them. The horse whinnied, its bewildered, mournful voice sounding almost human, and struggled so violently that, if it hadn't already been nearly dead, it would have crushed them both. But it was still able to move its head about, so that Lapoulle's blows kept missing, and he could not finish it off."

"Christ Almighty, his skull must be made of iron . . .! Hold him still, so that I can fix the sod !"

Jean and Maurice were horrified. They did not answer Chouteau's appeal for help, but just stood there, their arms hanging nervelessly at their sides, not knowing what to do. And suddenly Pache, moved by some instinct of pity, fell on his knees, clasped his hands and began muttering prayers, as though he were at a death bed.

Once again Lapoulle struck out and missed, tearing off one of

358

the wretched animal's ears as it turned over on its side, neighing loudly.

"Hang on a minute, we've got to finish him off now, or we shall all get nabbed. . . . Don't let go, Loubet!"

He had pulled out his knife, a small one, with a blade no longer than your finger; and, sprawled across the horse, with one arm round its neck, he plunged it again and again into the quivering flesh, hacking away until at last he found the artery, and severed it. Then, as he leapt aside, the blood spurted out like the jet of a fountain, while its legs beat the air and its body was seized with a convulsive shuddering. It took almost five minutes for the horse to die, and its huge, sad eyes, filled with terror, were fixed on the haggard man awaiting its death. Then they flickered and began to glaze over.

When at last it had stopped moving, none of them knew how to cut it up properly. Loubet, the jack of all trades, had some idea, but, being a clumsy butcher and having nothing but this small knife, he soon lost his way in the huge carcase, still warm and quivering. And when Lapoulle grew impatient and tried to give him a hand, opening up the belly without the slightest necessity, the result was the most hideous carnage, as he hastily tore at the entrails, covering himself with blood, like a wolf devouring its prey.

"I don't know what kind of a joint you'd call this," said Loubet at last, straightening his back, and clasping a huge lump of meat in his arms. "Still, it ought to be enough for us all to have a good blow-out."

Jean and Maurice had turned away, overcome with horror, but so acute was their hunger that when the others made off at the gallop, in order not to be caught with a slaughtered horse, they followed. Chouteau, delighted with his find, was carrying three large beetroots that someone had overlooked. Loubet, in order to free his arms, had slung the slab of meat across Lapoulle's shoulders, while Pache was carrying the section's dixie, which they had brought with them in the hope of finding something to eat. And the six of them ran and ran, without stopping to take breath, like hunted men.

Suddenly, Loubet stopped them.

"This is bloody silly, we ought to have decided where we were going to cook it!"

Jean, who by this time had pulled himself together again, suggested the quarries. They were not more than three hundred yards away, and there would be plenty of places where they could

359

light a fire without being seen. But when they got there, a succession of difficulties arose. First, there was the problem of wood; and they were lucky to find a roadman's barrow, which Lapoulle kicked to pieces to make firewood. Then, there was the question of finding water that would be fit to drink. During the day the heat of the sun had dried up all the pools of rainwater. True, there was a pump, but it was a long way off, at the Tour à Glaire . . . besides, they'd be queuing up till midnight, and then, probably, someone would upset your bucket. As to the one or two wells in the district, they'd run dry two days ago, and all you'd get was mud. The only other possibility was to fetch water from the Meuse, which was just across the road.

"I'll take the dixie," suggested Jean.

But they all protested :

"No, no, we don't want to be poisoned, it's full of corpses."

And, indeed, the Meuse was simply choked with the bodies of men and horses. You could see them floating by all the time, their swollen bellies already turning green and beginning to decompose. Several of them had got caught up in the reeds on the bank, where they lay, rocked by the current and giving off a putrid stench. And almost all the soldiers who had drunk this foul water had suffered from nausea and dysentery, or were wracked with colic.

Still, there was nothing else for it, and Maurice tried to reassure them, pointing out that, as long as the water was boiled, there would be no danger.

"Right, then I'll go and get some," Jean repeated, taking Lapoulle with him.

By the time the dixie was finally on the fire, filled with water and lumps of meat, it was pitch dark. Loubet had peeled the beetroots, and put them in the pot to cook – they'd have a meal that would be out of this world, as he put it. And they all kept stirring up the fire, pushing pieces of the barrow under the dixie, while their long shadows performed a fantastic ballet on the surrounding rocks. Presently, they could wait no longer, and flinging themselves upon this revolting stew, they began tearing the meat apart with trembling fingers, without troubling to use the knife. But, despite their hunger, the lack of salt sickened them, and the tasteless beetroot, the lumps of sticky, half-cooked meat, tasting of clay, made their gorges rise. Almost immediately they began vomiting. Pache could not go on, Chouteau and Loubet cursed the wretched stew they had taken so much trouble to cook, and which now only gave

360

them the belly-ache. Only Lapoulle went on eating ravenously. But, later that night, when, with the other three, he was trying to get to sleep beneath the poplars, he thought he was going to die.

As they made their way back, Maurice, without saying a word, caught hold of Jean's arm and drew him down a side turning. Their companions filled him with a kind of furious disgust, and he suggested that they should go and sleep in the wood where he had spent the first night. It was a good idea, and when at last they were stretched out on the sloping ground, in the dry and sheltered by the dense foliage, Jean heartily approved. They stopped there until the sun was high in the sky, and as they both slept very deeply they felt a little restored.

The next day was a Thursday. But they had lost all sense of time, and were content simply to feel that the fine weather had returned. Despite Maurice's repugnance, Jean persuaded him to return to the canal, in order to find out whether their regiment was due to leave. By this time, prisoners were leaving every day, a thousand or twelve hundred men at a time, on their way to fortresses in Germany. Only a couple of days previously they had seen, outside the Prussian guard-room, a convoy of officers and generals on their way to catch the train at Pont-à-Mousson. It was the same with everybody, a passionate longing to get away from this terrible Misery Hole. Oh, if only their turn had come! And when they found the 106th still encamped on the bank of the river, increasingly disorganized by all they had been through, they almost lost heart.

Still, at last it looked as though Jean and Maurice were going to get something to eat. Since early morning a regular market had been established between the prisoners and the Bavarians on the far side of the canal : the former would throw some money over, wrapped up in a handkerchief, which the latter would return with a loaf of coarse black bread or some poorly cured tobacco. Even those soldiers who hadn't any money had found a way of doing business by swapping their regulation white gloves, which the Bavarians seemed to have a weakness for. For the past two hours, all along the canal, this barbaric mode of barter had resulted in a continual stream of packages. But when Maurice threw over a five franc piece, wrapped up in his neckcloth, in exchange for a loaf, the Bavarian, either through clumsiness or as an ill-natured joke, threw the loaf so that it fell into the canal, to the accompaniment of loud guffaws from the German onlookers. Twice Maurice repeated the manoeuvre, and twice the loaf fell short. Whereupon,

361

attracted by the sound of laughter, some officers appeared, and forbade the men to sell anything more to the prisoners on the pain of severe punishment. This put an end to the market, and it was all Jean could do to calm Maurice down, for he began shaking his fist at the thieves and shouting to them to return his five franc pieces.

Despite the fine weather, it turned out to be another terrible day. There were two alerts; twice the bugles sounded, and each time Jean hurried off to the barn in the hope that rations were being issued. But, on both occasions, all that happened was that he got pushed around in the general scrimmage. The Prussians, though themselves so highly organized, continued to display a brutal negligence with regard to the defeated army. As a result of protests from Generals Douay and Lebrun, they had finally agreed to provide a few sheep, as well as waggon-loads of bread; only the arrangements were so poor that, no sooner had they crossed the bridge, than the sheep were stolen and the waggons pillaged, with the result that those regiments who were camped a few hundred yards away still got nothing. Pretty well the only ones to obtain any food were scroungers who managed to rob the convoys. In the end, realizing what was happening, Jean took Maurice with him, and they stationed themselves near the bridge to await the arrival of food.

It was already four o'clock, and they had still had nothing to eat on this fine, sunny Thursday, when suddenly, to their great delight, they caught sight of Delaherche. A few of the middle-class people in Sedan had, with the greatest difficulty, managed to obtain permits to visit the prisoners and bring them provisions : indeed, Maurice had frequently expressed surprise at hearing nothing whatsoever from his sister. Directly they caught sight of Delaherche in the distance, carrying a basket and with a loaf under each arm, they hurried over to him. But again they were too late, for such a surge of men bore down upon him that his basket and one of the loaves had been spirited away before the wool merchant had the slightest idea of what was happening.

Having arrived with a cheerful smile, and the friendly expression of a man who likes to be popular, he was now so upset that all he could do was mumble :

"You poor fellows ! Oh, you poor fellows !"

Jean managed to get possession of the last loaf, however, and while he and Maurice seated themselves at the side of the road and began greedily wolfing it down, Delaherche told them his news. His wife, thank God, was well; only he was worried about the colonel, he had had a great setback, although his mother was still looking after him day and night.

"And my sister?" asked Maurice.

"Yes, of course, your sister . . .! She came with me. It was she who brought the two loaves. But she had to stay on the other side of the canal, the guard wouldn't dream of allowing her to come any further. . . . You know how it is, the Prussians have strictly forbidden any women to visit the peninsula."

And he went on to tell him about Henriette, how she had vainly attempted to get in touch with him and do something to help him. Then, by pure chance, she had run into her cousin Gunther in Sedan, the captain in the Prussian guards regiment. But he had simply passed her by, pretending not to recognize her, while she, furious at the thought that he might have been one of the men who had killed her husband, had started to hurry away; but then, with an abrupt change of heart that she was unable to explain even to herself, she had turned back and told him all about Weiss's death. Yet, despite this, all he had said was that, in war, such things were just a matter of luck, and he himself might well have been the one to get killed. His face had shown scarcely a trace of feeling. And when she told him about her brother being a prisoner, and implored him to arrange for her to see him, he had refused to assist in any way. Their orders were perfectly clear; and he had talked about Germany's plans with almost religious conviction. By the time they parted, she was quite convinced that he considered himself to be in France merely to administer justice, with all the intolerant insolence of an hereditary enemy, intensified by hatred for the people on whom he was inflicting punishment.

"Anyhow," Delaherche concluded, "at least you'll have something to eat this evening. Though I'm very much afraid I shan't be able to obtain another permit!"

He asked them if they had any commissions for him, and obligingly undertook to deliver the letters, hurriedly scrawled in pencil, which some of the soldiers handed over to him, having previously seen the Bavarians laughing and lighting their pipes with those they had promised to pass on.

Then, as Maurice and Jean were accompanying him to the bridge, Delaherche exclaimed:

363

"But look! There's Henriette, over there . . . ! You can see her, she's waving her handkerchief."

And, indeed, there in the crowd, beyond the line of sentries, it was just possible to distinguish a small, slim figure, a white spot shimmering in the sunlight. And both of them, moved to tears, raised their hands and waved wildly.

For Maurice, the most atrocious day of all was the following one, the Friday. Nevertheless, after spending another peaceful night in the woods, he was fortunate enough to get some more bread; Jean had discovered a woman at the Château de Villette, who was selling it at ten francs a pound. But, later in the day, they were to witness a terrifying scene, which, for a long time, haunted them like a nightmare.

The previous evening, Chouteau had noticed that Pache had stopped grumbling, and had the satisfied, faraway look of a man who has eaten his fill. He immediately concluded that the artful rascal must have some food hidden away somewhere, especially as that morning he had disappeared for almost an hour and, when he returned, had a sly smile on his face. Clearly, he must have been in luck, managed to scrounge some food somewhere. His behaviour annoyed Loubet and Lapoulle, especially the latter. Hell! If he'd found something to eat, what a lousy bastard not to share it with his mates!

"I'll tell you what, this evening we'll follow him. We'll find out if he's got the cheek to stuff his guts, when us poor sods are starving."

"That's right, we'll follow," Lapoulle insisted angrily. "We'll find out what he's up to!"

The mere thought of getting something to eat nearly drove him out of his mind, and he clenched his fists. His tremendous appetite made him suffer more than the others, he was so hungry that he had even tried chewing grass. Since the day before yesterday, when the horseflesh and boiled beetroot had brought on that terrible attack of sickness, he had had nothing to eat. For, despite his great strength, his huge body was so clumsy that, in the general scrimmage, he always failed to get hold of any of the looted provisions. He would have given his right hand for a loaf of bread.

As night was falling, Pache slipped off into the trees, and the other three followed him, keeping out of sight.

"He mustn't suspect anything," Chouteau whispered. "Take care he doesn't turn round."

364

But when they had gone a hundred yards or so, it was obvious that Pache was satisfied that he was quite on his own, for he began walking quickly, not even troubling to look behind him. They had no difficulty in following him as far as the quarry, and just as he was pulling away two big stones and taking out half a loaf of bread, they caught up with him. It was all that was left of his private cache, but enough for a meal.

"You rotten bastard," yelled Lapoulle. "So this is what you've been sneaking off for. . . . Just you hand that over, it's my share!"

Give them his loaf, why should he? Puny as he was, anger dragged him to his feet, and he stood there clutching the loaf with all his strength. He, too, was hungry.

"Bugger off, the lot of you! It's mine!"

Then, as Lapoulle raised his fist, he took to his heels, making for the bare ploughed fields that stretched away towards Donchery. The three others ran after him as fast as they could, gasping for breath. But, being lighter on his feet, he began to gain ground, so terrified was he, so determined to hang on to what belonged to him, that he seemed to be borne on the wind. He had covered half a mile, and was nearing the wood on the river bank, when he met Jean and Maurice, who were just settling down for the night. As he passed them, he called out in distress : while they, astonished by this furious manhunt, remained rooted to the ground at the edge of a field.

As bad luck would have it, Pache tripped over a stone and fell full length. Almost immediately the three others arrived, swearing and yelling, excited by the chase, like wolves pursuing their prey.

"Give me that," shouted Lapoulle, "or by God I'll fix you!"

Then, as he was raising his fist again, Chouteau slipped him the knife that he had used to bleed the horse, with the thin blade already open.

"Here you are, take this!"

But, at that moment, Jean sprang forward to prevent the tragedy, and losing his head like the others, threatened to shove them all in clink. Whereupon Loubet, laughing savagely, accused him of being no better than the Prussians, for as there were no officers now, only the Prussians could give orders.

"God in heaven," said Lapoulle, "will you give me that loaf?"

Though he was livid with terror, Pache was still hugging the loaf tightly to his chest with all the obstinacy of a hungry peasant refusing to surrender his property. "No!"

Then suddenly, it was all over. Brutally, Lapoulle plunged the knife into his throat, with such force that the wretched man did not even have time to cry out. His arms went slack, and the hunk of bread fell to the ground in a pool of blood.

Confronted by this crazy murder, Maurice, who had so far remained motionless, suddenly seemed to go out of his mind. He shook his fist threateningly at the three men, accusing them of murder, with such vehemence that it made him tremble all over. But Lapoulle did not even seem to hear him. Squatting on the ground beside the body, he began devouring the bread, which was soaked with blood; he looked ferociously stupid, as though bewildered by the sound of his own jaws; while Chouteau and Loubet, terrified by his monstrous greed, were afraid to demand their share.

Darkness had now fallen, a fine, clear night, beneath a sky bright with stars. Maurice and Jean, who by this time had reached their wood, could only see Lapoulle, prowling beside the river; the other two had already disappeared, probably making for the canal, scared by the thought of the body they were leaving behind. Lapoulle, on the other hand, seemed afraid of joining his companions. Shocked by the thought of the murder, his mind dulled by the effort of digesting the huge piece of bread, which he had eaten too quickly, he was obviously in a state of panic which kept him on the move, afraid to go back along the road where the corpse lay, walking backwards and forwards on the river bank, with a shambling, irresolute gait. Could it be that some feeling of remorse was stirring in the depths of that dark soul? Backwards and forwards he paced like a caged animal, and the growing longing to flee was as painful as some physical illness, which he felt was bound to kill him if he could not assuage it; a longing to run and run, anywhere, if only he could escape from this prison where he had just killed a man. Then suddenly he collapsed, and for a long time he just lay there, sprawled on the ground.

In his revulsion, Maurice, too, was saying to Jean :

"Listen, I can't stay here another minute. I shall go mad, I tell you. . . . What amazes me is that my body can stick it, that it still seems to be all right, though my head's splitting. . . . Yes, honestly, I'm going out of my mind. If I have to spend another day in this hell, I'm done for. . . . Let's get out of here, I implore you, immediately!"

And he started to expound the wildest plans for escaping. They would swim across the Meuse, throw themselves on the sentries and

366

strangle them with a piece of string he had in his pocket; they'd stun them, by hitting them on the head with a stone; or perhaps they could bribe them to exchange uniforms, so that they could escape through the Prussian lines.

"Here, chuck it, lad," Jean kept saying despairingly. "It puts the wind up me to hear you talking such nonsense. Where's the sense in saying such things, it's all rubbish . . . tomorrow we'll see. So just shut up!"

Though he, too, felt overwhelmed with anger and disgust, he still kept his head, despite being weak with hunger, despite the nightmare of their existence, which had plumbed the very depths of human suffering. And when his companion, growing more and more violent, tried to jump into the river, he had to restrain him violently, scolding and beseeching him, his eyes full of tears. Then, all of a sudden, he exclaimed :

"Here, look !"

There was a splash, and they were just in time to see Lapoulle, who had at last made up his mind. He had taken off his overcoat so as not to impede his movements, and his white shirt was clearly visible against the dark, moving water. He was swimming, gradually making headway, looking for some spot where he could scramble ashore; while, on the further bank, they could distinguish, quite clearly, the slight, motionless shadows of the sentries. A sudden flash pierced the darkness, and the sound of a volley rumbled away towards the Montimont rocks. For a moment the water seethed and bubbled, as though someone were rowing furiously. Then it grew still, and all they could see was Lapoulle's body, floating away, borne along by the current.

The next day, Saturday, as soon as it was light, Jean took Maurice back to where the 106th were encamped, hoping once again that at last they would be leaving. But no order had come through, the regiment seemed to have been forgotten. Many of the prisoners had already left, the peninsula was gradually becoming deserted, and those that were left behind were falling into black despair. After eight long days in this hell, everywhere there was a growing feeling of insanity. Though the rain had ceased, the heavy, leaden sunlight had only brought a different kind of torture. The excessive heat weakened the men still more, and the number of cases of dysentery threatened to become an epidemic. The evacuations and excreta of this army of sick men were poisoning the atmosphere with their deadly infection. The stench of the dead

367

soldiers and horses, rotting amongst the reeds, was so foul that it was no longer possible to walk anywhere near the river or the canal. And in the fields, so serious was the threat of plague from the decomposing bodies of the horses that had died of starvation that the Prussians were beginning to be concerned for their own safety, and, having distributed picks and shovels, were forcing the prisoners to bury them. That same Saturday, however, there was no longer any shortage of food. As the number of prisoners had decreased and provisions were now arriving from all directions, extreme destitution was suddenly transformed into superfluity. There was as much bread and meat, even wine, as anyone could wish, and the men did nothing but eat from dawn to sunset. When night fell they were still gorging themselves, and they went on until the following morning. A good deal of the men died of it.

Throughout the day, Jean's one concern had been to look after Maurice, for he felt he was capable of the wildest nonsense. No sooner had he had a drink, than he began talking of punching a German officer in the face, if only someone would fetch him one. And that evening, having discovered amongst the outbuildings of the Tour à Glaire a spare place in one of the cellars, he thought it would be a sensible idea to stay there with his friend, in the hope that a good night would calm him down. But it turned out to be the worst night they had spent, a night of terror, during which they dared not close their eyes. The cellar soon filled up with more soldiers, and two of them, who lay down beside them, were dying of dysentery; as soon as darkness fell, they started uttering a succession of deep groans, inarticulate cries, that gradually turned into the death rattle. And, in the shadowy darkness, this sound became so terrible that the men on either side who were trying to get to sleep, lost their temper and shouted at the dying men to be quiet. But they could not hear, and the death rattle grew louder and louder, until at last nothing else could be heard, except the drunken laughter of the men outside, who were still eating, unable to allay their hunger.

Meanwhile, Maurice was becoming more and more distressed. He had tried to escape this terrible sound of suffering that made him sweat with fear, but as he got up, feeling his way in the darkness, he stumbled over his outstretched limbs, and fell right on top of the dying man. And, this time, he gave up trying to escape. The whole ghastly disaster, from the time they left Rheims to the final tragedy of Sedan, appeared before him. It seemed to him as though

368

the suffering of the army of Châlons was now culminating in the inky darkness of this cellar, where the death rattle of two soldiers was preventing their comrades from sleeping. This army of despair, driven to the holocaust, was paying for everyone's mistakes with the scarlet river of its blood. And now, ingloriously murdered, spat upon by their enemies, it was suffering this undeserved martyrdom. It was too much. He was overcome with anger, hungry for justice, passionately longing to revenge their fate.

By the time dawn broke, one of the soldiers was dead, the other was at his last gasp.

"Now then, lad, come on," Jean said, gently. "Let's go and get a breath of fresh air, it'll do you good."

But when they found themselves outside in the bright, fine morning, as they walked along the bank of the river towards the village of Iges, Maurice became even more agitated, shaking his fist in the direction of the vast, sunlit battlefield, opposite them the plateau of Illy, Saint-Menges to the left, the Garenne woods to the right.

"No, no, I can't go on, I can't bear to look at it any more. Seeing this always before my eyes is bursting my heart, splitting my skull. . . . Get me out of here, get me out of here at once!"

Once more Sunday had come round, once more the sound of bells was floating towards them from Sedan, and already, in the distance, a German band could be heard. But the 106th had still received no orders, and Jean, scared by Maurice's growing delirium, decided to make an attempt that he had been brooding upon since the previous day. Drawn up on the road, outside the Prussian guardroom, another regiment, the 5th, was preparing to leave. The column of men was in a state of great confusion, and an officer, who spoke French badly, was vainly trying to take the roll call. Suddenly, the two of them, having torn the badges and buttons from their uniforms, slipped into the midst of the crowd, crossed the bridge and found themselves outside. Chouteau and Loubet must have had the same idea, for they caught sight of them at the rear of the column, looking behind them uneasily, like murderers.

Oh, what an immense relief, this first moment of happiness! Once outside, they felt as though they had been raised from the dead . . . the bright light, the limitless air, the reawakening of all their hopes! Whatever misfortune they might still have to face, they were no longer afraid, and as they left behind the terrifying nightmare of the Misery Camp, they both began to laugh.

III

THAT morning, Jean and Maurice heard the cheerful sound of
French bugles for the last time; now they were on their way to
Germany, a column of prisoners, marching along with a platoon of
Prussian soldiers preceding them and another bringing up the rear,
while others, with fixed bayonets, guarded the flanks. Now, when
they passed the German guardposts, all they could hear was the
shrill, sad notes of German trumpets.

When he noticed that they had turned left and would be passing
through Sedan, Maurice cheered up. He might be lucky enough to
catch a glimpse of his sister, Henriette. But the two miles from Iges
to the town were enough to spoil the pleasure of getting away from
that sewer, where, for the last nine days, he had felt himself to be
on the point of death. It was simply another form of punishment,
this pitiful convoy of prisoners, of unarmed soldiers, driven along
like sheep, with hurried, frightened steps. Clothed in rags, befouled
with their own excrement, emaciated by a week of starvation, they
had the appearance of a bunch of tramps, of sinister vagabonds,
rounded up on the highways by the police. When they reached the
suburb of Torcy, and the men began to stop, as women came to
their doors as a token of sympathy, Maurice felt overwhelmed with
shame and bitterness, and hid his face.

More practical, not so thin-skinned, Jean was simply thinking
what fools they were not to have brought a loaf of bread with them.
In the excitement of departure, neither of them had bothered to
eat, and now, once again, hunger was beginning to sap their
strength. Some of the other prisoners must have been in like case,
for several of them were holding out money, pleading with the by-
standers to sell them food. One of them, a great big fellow who
looked desperately ill, was waving a gold coin in the air, reaching
out over the heads of the guards, desperate at finding nothing to
buy. And it was at that moment that Jean, who had been keeping
a sharp lookout, happened to spy a dozen loaves piled up outside

370

a baker's shop. Immediately, before anyone else had noticed them, he flung down a five franc piece, and started to pick up two of the loaves. When the Prussians shouted at him, and brutally tried to restrain him, he insisted obstinately on at least getting his money back. But already the captain in charge of the column, a short, bald man with an insolent expression, was hurrying to the scene. Threatening Jean with the butt of his revolver, he swore he would knock down the first man who dared to move. And they had all shrunk away, with lowered eyes, submitting like frightened animals, as the column continued on its way.

"Oh, what I'd give to hit that fellow in the face," Maurice muttered angrily, "to knock his teeth down his throat!"

From then on, the mere sight of the captain, with his sneering expression, became unbearable to him. Meanwhile, they were entering Sedan, crossing the bridge over the Meuse; and similar scenes of brutality were repeated again and again. A woman, his mother probably, who tried to kiss a youthful sergeant, was driven back with a blow from a rifle butt, so violent that it knocked her down. In the Place Turenne, where some middle-class folk tried to throw food to the prisoners, they were roughly thrust aside. In the Grande Rue, a soldier slipped as he was trying to take a bottle of wine that one of the ladies held out to him, and was kicked and punched to make him get up again. Although, for the past week, the people of Sedan had been watching these miserable herds of prisoners being driven through the streets like cattle, they had not yet grown accustomed to the sight, and as each fresh column filed past they were stirred by a sullen fervour of pity and revolt.

Jean, who was also thinking about Henriette, suddenly remembered Delaherche.

"Here," he said, giving his friend a nudge with his elbow, "keep your eyes open, in case we pass the factory!"

And sure enough, as they reached the Rue Maqua, they saw a number of people standing at one of the decorated windows. They recognized Delaherche and his wife, leaning on the sill, and, behind them, the tall, grim figure of Madame Delaherche. They had a basket of loaves, which the millowner was throwing to the starving men, who reached up with trembling, imploring hands.

Maurice had immediately noticed that his sister was not with them, while Jean was anxiously watching the shower of loaves, afraid lest there should be none left for them. He waved frantically, calling out at the top of his voice:

371

"Hi! What about us? What about us?"

At the sound of his voice, the Delaherches were completely taken aback. Their faces, pale with pity, lit up, and they waved back cheerfully. Gilberte insisted upon throwing the last loaf to Jean, but she threw it so awkwardly that it made her laugh merrily.

Unable to restrain himself, Maurice looked back over his shoulder and called out anxiously:

"Where's Henriette? What's happened to her?"

But Delaherche's lengthy reply was drowned by the noise of tramping feet. He must have realized that Maurice could not hear him, for he began gesticulating violently, continually pointing to the South. By this time the column of men was already turning into the Rue du Ménil, the factory was almost out of sight, and all he could see was a hand waving a handkerchief.

"What did he say?" asked Jean.

Almost beside himself, Maurice still continued to look back, but it was no use.

"I don't know, I couldn't hear. . . . I shall be worried to death unless I can get some news."

On and on they trudged, while the Prussians, with all the brutality of conquerors, speeded up the pace, so that by the time the prisoners finally left Sedan, by the Ménil gate, they were drawn out in a long, straggling line, almost running, as if they were being pursued by dogs.

As they passed through Bazeilles, Jean and Maurice thought of Weiss, and tried to distinguish the ruins of the house he had so bravely defended. They had heard all about the destruction of the village, the incendiarism, the massacres, while they were in the Misery Camp, but the horror of what they now saw exceeded anything they had imagined. After nearly a fortnight, the heaps of ruins were still smoking, crumbling walls had fallen in, scarcely a dozen houses remained intact. But it was at least some consolation to see the barrows and carts, piled high with the helmets and rifles of the Bavarians that had been picked up after the battle, for at least it proved that many of these incendiary gangsters had been killed.

The first major halt was at Douzy, to allow the men to have a meal; but it had cost them dear to get there. Weakened by starvation, the prisoners had soon tired. Those who had been gorging themselves with food the previous night felt dull and stupefied, and suffered from attacks of giddiness; far from restoring their energy and strength, their greediness had only served to weaken them still further. When they halted in a meadow on the left of the village, the wretched creatures flung themselves on the ground, but were unable to face the thought of food. There was no wine to drink, and when kindly women tried to bring them some they were driven off by the sentries. One of them was so scared that she lost her footing and fell down; and amid all the shouting and tears that ensued, it was disgusting to see the Prussians drinking the wine they had just confiscated. Similar examples of this generous sympathy, on the part of the peasant towards the ordinary soldiers being marched off into captivity, occurred again and again; whereas they treated the officers with savage hostility. Only a few days previously, the people of Douzy had booed a convoy of generals, on their way to Pont-à-Mousson after being released on parole. Indeed, the roads were not safe for officers: peasants, escaped soldiers, even deserters, were liable to spring out upon them, brandishing pitch-forks and threatening to kill them as cowards and traitors. It was this that gave rise to the legend of betrayal, as the result of which, even twenty years later, anyone wearing epaulettes was still held up to execration in this part of the country.

Maurice and Jean ate half their loaf, and were lucky enough to be able to wash it down with a few mouthfuls of brandy, which a good-natured farmer had managed to put in their water bottles. But starting again was very hard. They were to spend the night at Mousson, and though the distance was not great, the effort required to get there was formidable. The short rest had made them so stiff that men cried out with pain when they tried to get up. A lot of them, whose feet were cut and bleeding, took off their boots in order to keep going. They were still ravaged by dysentery, and when one man fell out before they had gone half a mile, all they could do was to prop him up against a bank. A little further on, two more collapsed under a hedge, and had to lie there till evening, when they were found by an old woman. Nearly all the men were limping, and hobbled along, supporting themselves on sticks, which the Prussians, perhaps out of mockery, had allowed them to cut from a copse. The whole contingent looked like a swarm of beggars, covered with sores, haggard, breathless; and the brutality was incessant. If anyone fell out, even to relieve himself, one of the guards would start hitting him with a stick. The platoon that constituted the rearguard had been given orders to use their bayonets, and prod the laggards in the ribs. And when a sergeant refused to

373

go any further, the captain ordered two of his men to drag him along by the arms until the poor fellow started to walk again. But what they particularly resented was the way a little bald officer, taking advantage of his fluent command of French, abused the prisoners, using expressions in their own language that stung like a whip lash.

"Oh, if only I could get my hands on him," Maurice repeated furiously. "I'd bleed the devil to death, drop by drop!"

He was almost at the end of his tether, and this anger turned in upon itself, made him suffer even more than his exhaustion. Everything infuriated him, and the shrill sound of the Prussian bugles got on his nerves till he could have howled like a dog. How would he ever reach the end of this cruel journey without going out of his mind? Already, as they passed through the smallest hamlet, the thought that the women were looking at him stung him to the quick. What would it be like when they got to Germany, and the people in the towns crowded around, jeering and insulting them? And he kept thinking of the cattle trucks into which they would be herded, of all the suffering and filth of the journey, and the grim existence, shut up in fortresses, beneath wintry skies heavy with snow. No, no, better to finish with it all now, better to run the risk of being shot down at the side of a road, on French soil, than to rot in a dark German dungeon, maybe for months!

"Listen," he whispered to Jean, who was trudging along beside him, "we'll wait until we get to a wood, then jump over the hedge and make a bolt for it. . . . The Belgian frontier isn't far from here. We're bound to find someone who'll show us the way."

Jean began trembling with excitement, for though he was more far-sighted and cooler-headed, he, too, could not help thinking of escaping.

"Are you mad? They'd just shoot us down, and that'd be the end of it."

"But there's a chance they might miss," said Maurice. "And, in any case, even if it was the end, it couldn't be much worse than this!"

"All right, so what?" Jean went on. "What d'you think we should do afterwards, dressed up in these uniforms? You know damn well the whole place is lousy with Prussians . . . if nothing else, we should have to get hold of some other clothes. . . . No, no, lad, it's too dangerous. I won't let you risk it."

And he caught hold of his arm to restrain him, hanging on to

374

him as though they were helping one another along, doing his best to calm him in his rough gentle way.

At that moment they heard someone whispering behind them, and looked round. It was Chouteau and Loubet, who had also escaped from the peninsula that morning, though hitherto they hadn't noticed them. Now the two scoundrels were almost on their heels. Chouteau, who must have overheard Maurice planning to escape, took him at his word.

"What about it, then?" he muttered. "I reckon it's not a bad idea. Some blokes have got away already, and we certainly don't mean to let these swine drag us off to their lousy country like dogs. . . . So what about it? Suppose the four of us were to have a go, make a run for it?"

Maurice was beginning to get worked up again, and, to get rid of the tempter, Jean turned round and whispered angrily :

"If you're in such a damned hurry, why don't you beat it then? . . . What are you waiting for?"

Unable to withstand the corporal's steady gaze, Chouteau came out with his real reason for approaching them :

"Why, damn it, if there were four of us it'd be that much easier. . . . There'd be a chance for one or two of us to get through."

But Jean merely shook his head, refused point blank. He distrusted the fellow, and was afraid he would let them down, but it was all he could do to prevent Maurice from yielding, for just at that moment an opportunity had presented itself. They were passing a wood, with nothing between it and the road but a field covered with dense overgrowth. All they had to do was to dash across this field and disappear into the bushes, and they would be safe.

So far, Loubet had not spoken. Anxiously, he seemed to be sniffing the air, his restless, crafty eyes continually on the look-out for a favourable opportunity, determined at all costs not to rot away in Germany. He would rely on his speed and cunning, which in the past had served to get him out of many a tight corner. Then, all of a sudden, he made up his mind.

"Hell, I can't stand this any longer. I'm off !"

And he was off over the hedge, closely followed by Chouteau. Immediately, two of the Prussian guards set off in pursuit, before anyone thought of shooting. It had all happened so quickly that at first no one realized what was happening. Zigzagging between the bushes, Loubet seemed certain to escape, but Chouteau, not nearly so agile, was already on the point of being caught. Then, with a supreme effort, he managed to catch up with his mate, but in so doing he tripped him up, and while the two Prussians flung themselves on the fallen man, Chouteau disappeared into the wood. Some of the other guards, suddenly remembering their rifles, fired one or two shots, and even pursued him amongst the trees, but it was useless.

Meanwhile, the two soldiers who had brought down Loubet, had begun knocking him about, and when the captain arrived, beside himself with rage and shouting about making an example, the two German were encouraged to go on punching and kicking their victim. When, eventually, they dragged him to his feet, it was found that his skull was fractured and one of his arms broken, and they had to put him in a peasant's cart. But before they reached Mouzon he was dead.

"So you see," was all Jean said.

From the way they looked at the wood, it was clear that he and Maurice were disgusted that this crook had managed to escape; whereas they could not help feeling sorry for Loubet, who, in spite of being a good-for-nothing scrounger, was nevertheless a cheerful fellow, and certainly no fool.

Despite the terrible lesson they had had, when they reached Mouzon, Maurice was still haunted by the thought of escape. The prisoners arrived in such a state of exhaustion that the Prussians had to help them to put up the few available tents. The place where they were to camp was on low-lying, marshy land near the town, and, to make matters worse, another convoy had spent the previous night there, so that the ground was covered with filth, little better than an open sewer. The only way they could protect themselves at all was to put down some large flat stones that they were lucky enough to find near by. Later in the evening, however, things improved a little, for once the captain had disappeared, having presumably found himself a bed at the inn, the Prussians relaxed their vigilance. For instance, the sentries raised no objection to the children throwing apples and pears to the prisoners They also allowed the inhabitants of the town into the camp, so that before long a crowd of men and woman were selling bread, wine and even cigars, so that those who had any money were able to eat, sleep and smoke. In the falling dusk, the scene took on something of the noisy animation of an open-air market.

But Maurice's state of nervous excitement had returned. Behind their tent, he kept saying to Jean:

"Look, I can't stick it any longer. As soon as it's dark, I'm going to make a dash for it. . . . By tomorrow, we shall be a long way from the frontier, and it will be too late."

And eventually, unable to hold out any longer, Jean gave in:

"All right then, we'll take a chance. Maybe we'll get away with it."

But he now began taking stock of the people selling food. Some of the prisoners had managed to obtain smocks and trousers, and it was rumoured that some of the better-off inhabitants of the town had set up a regular clothing depot, with a view to helping the prisoners to escape. Before long, his attention was drawn to a fine-looking sixteen-year-old girl, with superb eyes, who had a basketful of loaves for sale. She was not crying her wares like the others, but stood there, hesitantly, with an attractive, uneasy smile. He stared at her hard, she raised her eyes, and for a moment they stood there, gazing at each other. Then she came towards him, with the shy smile of a pretty girl offering herself.

"Do you want any bread?"

Instead of answering, he made an almost imperceptible sign. Then, as she seemed to nod, he decided to take a chance, and asked very quietly:

"Have you got any clothes?"

"Yes, they're under the loaves."

Then, raising her voice, she began to call out: "Bread for sale, bread for sale! Who wants to buy?"

But when Maurice tried to slip a twenty franc piece into her hand, she withdrew it abruptly and went off, leaving him with the basket. However, they noticed that once or twice she turned back, and smiled at them tenderly with her splendid eyes.

No sooner had they got hold of the basket, than Jean and Maurice found themselves in difficulties. They were a long way from their tent, and by this time they were so nervous that they couldn't find their way back. What were they to do? How were they going to change their clothes? Jean felt awkward holding the basket, for he was sure that everybody could see what it contained. Eventually, they made up their minds, and going into the first empty tent they came across, they hurriedly put on the trousers and smocks, concealed their uniforms under the loaves, and left the basket behind. But they had only found one cloth cap, which Jean

377

insisted upon Maurice wearing. He himself, exaggerating the danger of being seen without a hat, was convinced he would be detected. While he was looking round for some kind of headgear, he noticed a filthy old man selling cigars, and decided to try to buy his hat.

"Best Brussels cigars! Two sous apiece, two for three sous!"

Since the battle of Sedan the customs had broken down, and all sorts of Belgian goods were entering the country free of duty. The ragged old man had already made a handsome profit, but as soon as he realized that they wanted to buy his hat, a greasy old felt, full of holes, he was determined to do even better for himself. Loudly complaining that he was bound to get a cold in the head, he refused to let it go for less than ten francs. But this gave Jean another idea: he would also buy the rest of the old man's stock, two or three dozen cigars. No sooner was the transaction completed than, pulling the hat well down over his eyes, he started to call out in a whining voice:

"Two for three sous, two for three sous. Best Brussels cigars!"

This proved to be their salvation, and he signed to Maurice to go on ahead. By good fortune, Maurice had picked up an umbrella that somebody had dropped, and as it was just beginning to rain, he calmly opened it and sauntered through the line of sentries.

"Two for three sous, two for three sous. Best Brussels cigars!"

In less than no time, Jean had sold out, for the men crowded round, delighted to find someone who was reasonable and wasn't trying to rob them. Indeed, so cheap were the cigars that some of the Prussians also approached him, and he was obliged to do business with them. Before long he had made his way past the sentries, having sold his last two cigars to a huge, bearded sergeant who could not speak a word of French.

"For Christ's sake don't walk so quickly," Jean whispered, as he caught up with Maurice. "You'll give us away."

Yet, despite themselves, they couldn't help hurrying, and they had to make a tremendous effort to stop for a moment amongst the crowd of people standing outside an inn. A number of middle-class people were chatting to the German soldiers, and they pretended to listen, even risked joining in, despite the rain, which seemed to have settled in for the night. One fat man was watching them so persistently that they were scared, but when he smiled at them in a friendly way they decided to take a chance, and asked him quietly:

"Is the road to Belgium closed?"

"Yes. But go through this wood, then turn off to the left across the fields."

Once they were in the wood, in the huge, dark silence, where nothing stirred among the motionless trees, they felt they were safe, and with a feeling of extraordinary exhilaration they threw themselves into one another's arms. Maurice was sobbing as though his heart would break, and even Jean was in tears. After all they'd been through, it was a relief to give vent to their emotion, to feel that, at last, perhaps fate had taken pity on them. They clung together, united in the fellowship of suffering, and the kiss they exchanged seemed to them sweeter and stronger than any they had yet experienced, different from those they had received from women, a pledge of eternal friendship, given in the absolute conviction that henceforward the two of them would be as one.

"Here, lad," said Jean in a trembling voice, as they broke away from one another. "It's all very fine to have got this far, but it's not the end by a long chalk. . . . We'd better sort ourselves out a bit."

Maurice was familiar with this part of the frontier, and maintained that if they kept going they would be all right. So, once more, they set off, one behind the other, cautiously heading for the outskirts of the wood. When they got there, remembering the fat man's instructions, they intended to turn left and cut across the stubble. But, as they came out on to a road bordered with poplar trees, a short way ahead they could see the fire of a Prussian guardpost, blocking the road. They could see the gleam of the sentry's bayonet, and soldiers chatting as they finished their meal. They quickly turned back, making for the depth of the wood, terrified lest anyone was following them. They kept thinking they could hear voices, footsteps, and for nearly an hour they wandered about, losing all sense of direction in the dense thickets, running round in circles, fleeing like wild animals, occasionally brought to a halt, sweating with fear, as they mistook the silent oak trees for Prussian soldiers. Eventually they came out on to the same road, only ten yards away from the sentry and almost on top of the soldiers, who were peacefully warming themselves at the fire.

"No luck," muttered Maurice. "This wood must be enchanted!"

But this time the Prussians had heard them. There was a sound of breaking branches and rolling stones. And when the sentry challenged them they made off at full speed, pursued by a burst of rifle fire.

"Christ Almighty!" Jean swore, stifling a cry of pain. A bullet had hit him in the calf of the left leg, and he staggered against a tree.

"Did they get you?" Maurice asked anxiously.

"Yes, in the leg . . . it's all to hell!"

They listened carefully, holding their breath, dreading at any moment to hear the clamour of pursuit close behind them. But the firing had ceased, and there was no sign of movement in the whispering silence that had closed in upon them once more. Apparently the Prussians were not at all keen on venturing into the wood.

Jean, struggling to get to his feet, stifled a groan. Maurice went to his help.

"Can't you walk?"

"I don't think so."

Usually so easy going, Jean felt a sudden excess of rage, and clenched his fists.

"God Almighty, if this isn't a bit of bad luck! Fancy letting yourself get hit in the leg when you're on the run! That just about puts paid to everything . . .! You'll just have to go on by yourself."

Maurice's only reply was to say cheerfully:

"Get along with you, you're barmy!"

He had taken him by the arm, and was helping him along, both of them anxious to get away as quickly as possible. They had not gone far, however, each step demanding an heroic effort, when a new cause for anxiety presented itself: a small farmhouse, just ahead, at the edge of the wood. There was no light in the windows, the gate into the yard was wide open, the whole place seemed dark and deserted. When they had plucked up enough courage to enter the yard, they were astonished to see a horse standing there, ready saddled, but without the slightest indication of how or why it came to be there. Perhaps the owner would soon be back, or perhaps he was lying behind a bush with a bullet through the head. They were never to find out, for Maurice suddenly had an idea which seemed to cheer him up immensely.

"Listen, the frontier's too far away, and, in any case, we should certainly have to have a guide. . . . On the other hand, if we were to go to Remilly, where my Uncle Fouchard lives, I could take you there with my eyes shut. I know every lane and footpath for miles round. It's a marvellous idea. If I can hoist you up on to this horse, we can rely on my uncle taking us in."

380

First, however, he insisted upon examining Jean's leg. The bullet had gone in one side and come out the other, breaking the tibia, but the bleeding was not serious, and it was sufficient to bind it up tightly with his handkerchief.

"Listen, you'd much better go on alone!" Jean repeated.

"Shut up, you're barmy!"

Once Jean was safely in the saddle, Maurice took the horse by the bridle and they set out. It was about eleven o'clock, and he reckoned the journey would not take more than three hours, even at walking pace. An unforeseen difficulty suddenly struck him: how were they going to get across the Meuse? The bridge at Mouzon was bound to be guarded. Then he remembered that, further downstream, at Villers, there was a ferry; and clutching at this straw, trusting that their luck would hold, he set off across the meadows and ploughed fields, making for the village. To begin with everything seemed to be going smoothly, though for a quarter of an hour they had to hide behind a wall to avoid a cavalry patrol. It had started to rain again, and, for Maurice, the going became difficult as he trudged along, leading the horse over the sodden ground. Fortunately, it turned out to be a quiet, well-behaved animal. As they approached Villers, luck really was on their side: late as it was, the ferryman had just brought a Bavarian officer over from the other side, and he was quite willing to take them back. It was only when they reached the village that the real difficulties began, for they almost fell into the hands of the sentries who were strung out all along the road to Remilly. Once again they had to take to the fields, relying on narrow lanes and almost invisible footpaths. But the slightest obstacle obliged them to make tremendous detours, scrambling over hedges and ditches, forcing their way through almost impenetrable thickets. In the steady drizzle, Jean was becoming feverish, and he sat slumped in the saddle, almost unconscious, clinging to the horse's mane with both hands; while Maurice, holding the reins in one hand, had to hang on to Jean's leg with the other to prevent him falling off. Mile after mile, for the best part of two hours, they continued like this, growing more and more weary, jolting and slithering about, struggling to keep their balance, in constant danger of the horse falling and bringing them both down. Before long they were reduced to a pitiful state, plastered with mud, the horse scarcely able to keep on its feet, the man on its back inert and helpless, while his companion, haggard and half dazed, only managed to keep going by a tremendous effort

381

of friendship. By the time they finally reached Remilly, it must have been nearly five o'clock, for dawn was already breaking.

In the yard of his little farm, overlooking the village, Fouchard was loading his cart with the carcasses of two sheep that he had killed the previous day. He was so taken aback to see his nephew in this sorry pickle that, once the first explanations were over, he shouted brutally :

"What? D'you expect me to keep the two of you here . . .? Just imagine all the trouble it's going to cause with the Prussians. . . . Why, it'd be as much as my life is worth !"

He made no attempt, however, to prevent Maurice and Prosper from lifting Jean down, and laying him on the big kitchen table; while Sylvine hurried away to fetch a bolster from her bed, which she slipped under the head of the wounded man, who was still unconscious. But annoyed at seeing Jean lying there on his table, the old man kept grumbling away, insisting that this wouldn't do at all, they'd much better take him straight to the first-aid post, since there happened to be one at Remilly, next to the church, in the old school-house, where there was plenty of room.

"The first-aid post !" exclaimed Maurice. "So that the Prussians can send him off to Germany as soon as he gets better . . .? What the devil d'you take me for, uncle. I haven't brought him all this way just to let him fall into the hands of the Germans."

Matters seemed to have reached an impasse, and Fouchard was beginning to talk of throwing them out, when someone happened to mention Henriette's name.

"What's that?" asked the young man. "Henriette?"

And eventually he discovered that, two days ago, his sister had arrived at Remilly, so overwhelmed with grief for her husband's death that she had found it impossible to stay in Sedan any longer, since everything there reminded her of how happy she had once been. As a result of a chance meeting with Dr. Dalichamp, an old acquaintance from Raucourt, she had decided to take a room in Fouchard's house, so that she would be able to devote herself to the wounded in the Remilly hospital. It was the only way she could forget about her own unhappiness, she said. As she was paying for her board and lodging, her presence brought such a note of sweetness to the farm that the old man had come to look upon her with a kindly eye. As long as he was making money, everything was always all right.

"So this is where she's got to?" said Maurice. "That must have been what M. Delaherche was trying to make me understand, when he kept pointing in this direction . . .! Well, if she's here, there's nothing more to be said : we're staying."

Tired as he was, he immediately insisted on going to find her at the hospital, where she had spent the night; while his uncle became more and more annoyed at the delay. Until this damned business he'd been landed with was cleared up, how was he to get on with his work? There were customers waiting for the two sheep he'd got in the cart.

When Maurice and Henriette got back from the hospital, they found the old man carefully examining the horse, which Prosper had led away to the stable. Though it was in pretty bad shape, it was a devilish fine animal all the same, and he was delighted. Jokingly, Maurice said he would give it to him as a present, while Henriette, taking him aside, pointed out that Jean would pay for his board and she would be responsible for looking after him. He could have the little room behind the stables – the Prussians would never think of looking for him there. And old Fouchard, still grumbling and by no means convinced that there would be any profit in it for him, nevertheless eventually climbed up into his cart and drove off, leaving her a free hand to do as she thought best.

In less than no time, with the help of Sylvine and Prosper, Henriette had prepared the room, and soon Jean was lying in a nice clean bed. So far, the only sign of life he had given was to mumble a few indistinct words, and even now, as he opened his eyes and looked around, he seemed unable to see anybody. Maurice, who, now that he could relax, suddenly seemed to be on the point of collapse, was just drinking a glass of wine and eating the remains of some cold meat, when Dr. Dalichamp arrived, on the way to pay his usual morning visit to the hospital; and the young man, anxious to find out how Jean was, somehow managed to accompany the doctor, who was about to examine the patient.

The doctor was a man of medium height, with a large, round head, greying hair and side whiskers. As a result of spending most of his life out of doors, hurrying from patient to patient, he had the high colour and rough skin of a peasant, but his keen eyes, determined nose and kindly mouth betokened an existence devoted to acts of kindness, the life of an honest doctor who, though maybe no genius, had, as a result of long experience, become an excellent healer.

Having examined Jean, who was still unconscious, he murmured :

383

"I'm rather afraid it may be necessary to amputate."

To Maurice and Henriette this came as a shock. But he added :

"It may just be possible to save his leg, but he'll need great care, and it'll take a long time. . . . For the time being, he's in such a state of physical and moral collapse that the only thing to do is to let him sleep. . . . Tomorrow, we'll see."

Then, when he had dressed the wound, he turned to Maurice, whom he had known as a child.

"And what about you, my dear fellow? You'd be a lot better off in bed than sitting there."

As though he had not heard him, the young man stared straight ahead, seeing nothing. Drunk with fatigue, he was becoming increasingly feverish, a state of extraordinary nervous excitement, due to the suffering and revulsion that had been building up since the start of the campaign. The sight of his friend lying there in pain, the sense of personal defeat, unarmed, naked, useless, the thought that so much heroic effort had ended in such misery, aroused in him a frantic urge to rebel against fate. At last he said :

"No, no ! I'm not done for yet ! I must get away from here. . . . Just because he's stuck here for weeks, maybe for months, it's no reason for me to stay. I must get away immediately. . . . You'll do what you can for him, doctor, won't you? And you'll help me to escape, and get back to Paris?"

Trembling, Henriette took him in her arms.

"Whatever are you saying? After all you've been through, all you've suffered, you're going to stay here with me. I'll never let you go . . .! Haven't you paid your debt? You must think of me as well. Surely you couldn't leave me alone, now that I have no one else."

They were both in tears, and they clung to one another desperately, with all the passionate tenderness of twins. But he was becoming more and more worked up.

"I tell you, it's essential for me to go. . . . People are waiting for me. If I stayed here, I should die of shame. . . . You can't imagine how the idea of staying here, doing nothing, makes my blood boil. I tell you, it can't be allowed to end like this, we've got to avenge ourselves, against whom or what I don't know, but somehow or other to avenge ourselves for all this suffering, so that we can still have the courage to live !"

Dr. Dalichamp, who had been watching what was happening with the greatest interest, made a sign to Henriette not to reply;

384

when Maurice had had some sleep he would probably be calmer. And, indeed, he slept through the whole of that day and the following night, more than twenty hours, without stirring. Nevertheless, next morning, no sooner was he awake than his determination to go away immediately revived, and nothing would make him change his mind. The fever had left him, but he was restless and gloomy, determined to avoid the temptation to relax induced by his surroundings. Though his sister was in tears, she realized that she must not insist; and when he came to see him again, Dr. Dalichamp promised to help him to escape, by procuring for him the papers belonging to a stretcher-bearer at Raucourt, who had just died. Maurice was to put on his grey jacket, with the red-cross armband, cross the frontier into Belgium and then make his way back to Paris, which as yet had not been cut off. All that day he remained hidden in the farm-house, without going out, waiting for nightfall. He scarcely opened his mouth, except to try to persuade Prosper to go with him.

"Surely you wouldn't mind another chance to have a crack at these Prussians?"

But the one-time Chasseur d'Afrique, who was munching bread and cheese, only waved his knife in the air and said:

"Well, from what I've seen of it up to now, I reckon it's scarcely worth while. . . . Since the only use they make of the cavalry is to send them in to get killed when it's too late, why should you expect me to go back again . . .? Hell no! After the way they've played me up, I'm damned if I'm prepared to do any more!"

For a while there was silence. Then he went on, trying hard to stifle his uneasy conscience as a soldier:

"Besides, there's too much work to be done here. We'll be starting ploughing directly, and after that there'll be the sowing. You've got to look after the land, you know. Fighting may be all very fine, but what would become of us if everyone stopped ploughing . . .? I can't just pack up the job, you see. It's not simply old Fouchard I'm worried about, though it wouldn't surprise me if I never saw the colour of his money . . . but the animals have begun to get fond of me. Why, only this morning, when I was up there in the Old Orchard, I was looking at bloody Sedan over there, and, honest, it did my heart good to think that here I was, all alone in the sun, with my plough and the horses!"

As darkness was falling, Dr. Dalichamp arrived in his gig. He had decided to drive Maurice as far as the frontier himself.

Fouchard, glad to be getting rid of one of them at least, went down the road to make sure that no patrol was on the prowl; while Sylvine finished mending the former stretcher-bearer's old tunic. Before Maurice left, the doctor examined Jean's leg again, but he couldn't promise that he would be able to save it. The wounded man, still hopelessly drowsy, was unable to recognize anybody, and did not say a word. But just as Maurice was preparing to leave without saying goodbye, and was leaning over to kiss him, he opened his eyes wide, his lips began to move, and in a weak voice he murmured :

"So you're off, then?"

And, seeing Maurice's astonishment, he added :

"I heard what you were saying while I was lying here. You'd better take all the money, feel in my trouser pocket."

Each of them still had two hundred francs left from their share of the regimental funds.

"Money!" exclaimed Maurice. "Why, you'll need it more than I do. After all, I can still walk! Two hundred francs will be plenty to see me as far as Paris, and after that it's not going to cost me anything to get killed. . . . I'll be seeing you all the same, old chap, and thanks for all you've done for me, for if it hadn't been for you I should be lying out there in the fields somewhere, dead as a door nail."

Jean shook his head.

"You don't owe me anything. We're quits. . . . The Prussians would have had me for certain, if you hadn't managed to get me out of it that time. It was the same yesterday, it was you who saved me from their clutches. . . . No, no, you've paid for two rounds; next time it'll be my turn. But I shan't half worry, not having you along with me !"

His voice was trembling and there were tears in his eyes.

"Give us a kiss then, lad."

And they embraced, and as they had done the previous night in the wood, with this kiss they expressed the brotherhood of all the danger they had undergone together in these few weeks of shared heroism, which bound them more closely to one another than years of ordinary friendship could possibly have done. The days without food, the nights without sleep, the utter exhaustion, the continual presence of death, these were the measure of their affection. Can two hearts ever be the same again, once they have become completely fused? But the kiss they had exchanged in the darkness of the forest had been full of the hope that their escape held out to them; whereas this one held only the sadness of farewell. Would they meet again one day? And if so, under what circumstances? Of grief, or of happiness?

By this time Dr. Dalichamp had already climbed into the gig, and was calling to Maurice. Once more he fondly kissed his sister, who gazed at him with eyes full of unshed tears, very pale in her widow's weeds.

"Don't forget it's my brother, doctor. . . . Look after him as carefully as I would!"

It was a big room, with tiled floor and whitewashed walls, that had once been used for storing fruit. It still had a pleasant smell of apples and pears, and the only furniture in it was an iron bedstead, a plain deal table, two chairs and a walnut-wood cupboard. But it was calm and peaceful, and all that could be heard were muffled sounds from the nearby stables, the faint stamping of hooves, the mooing of cattle. Bright sunlight streamed in through the window, which faced South, and one could just see the slope of a hill, with a cornfield running along the edge of a wood. And this snug, mysterious room was so well concealed that no one would have dreamt of it being there.

Henriette immediately set about putting it in order : it was understood that, to avoid suspicion, nobody but she and the doctor were to be allowed to visit Jean. Even Sylvine was to keep away unless Henriette sent for her. First thing in the morning, the two women made the bed and tidied the room; for the rest of the day the door was kept shut. If the invalid needed anything in the night, all he had to do was to tap on the wall, for Henriette's room was next to his. Thus, after his recent turbulent existence, Jean suddenly found himself completely cut off from the world, seeing no one but this gentle young woman who came and went with scarcely a sound. Meeting her again, she seemed to him now, as she had done that first time in Sedan, rather like a ghost, with her large mouth, delicate features and corn-coloured hair, looking after him with an air of infinite kindness.

For the first few days his temperature was so high that Henriette scarcely slept. Each morning, on his way to hospital, Dr. Dalichamp looked in on the pretext of calling for Henriette; and he would examine Jean's leg and dress it. Since the bullet that had smashed the tibia had passed right through the leg, the unhealthy appearance of the wound surprised him, and he began to suspect that the presence of some splinter, which he had failed to locate, might necessitate a resection of the bone. When he mentioned this to

Jean, the latter was horrified at the thought of being left with one leg shorter than the other : no, no, he'd rather die than become a cripple. For the present, therefore, after inserting a rubber tube to drain away the pus, the doctor contented himself with dressing the wound with lint soaked in olive oil and carbolic acid. Only he warned him that, if he did not operate, the wound might take a very long time to heal. However, by the second week, the temperature began to go down, and there was every indication that, provided he kept it absolutely still, the condition of his leg would improve.

Meanwhile a considerable intimacy inevitably developed between Jean and Henriette. Before long, they had become so accustomed to one another that it began to seem as though they had always lived like this, and always would. All the time she was not engaged at the hospital she spent with him, bringing him drinks, seeing that he ate regularly, helping him to change his position, with a strength one would scarcely have suspected in those slender arms. Occasionally they would talk to each other, but more often, especially to begin with, neither of them said a word. Yet they never seemed to be bored with one another, shut away in this profound quiet; life flowed gently along, he still tortured by memories of the fighting, she is mourning, her heart broken by the loss she had sustained. At first he had felt some embarrassment, for he regarded her as being above him, almost a lady, whereas he had never been anything but a peasant and a soldier, scarcely able to read or write. But gradually, seeing that she treated him as an equal, he began to gain confidence, was encouraged to reveal himself as he was, intelligent in his own way, sensible and unflustered. Besides, he was surprised to find that somehow or other he seemed to have become freer, lighter, full of new ideas. Could it be that, for the last two months, all the physical and moral suffering he had undergone had in some way refined him? But what impressed him most of all was the discovery that she was not so very much better informed than he was. After her mother's death, while she was still quite young, she had become the Cinderella of the family, the little housekeeper, responsible, as she said, for three men, her grandfather, father and brother, so that she had had little time to study. Reading and writing, a few simple sums, these were the sum of her accomplishments. And if she still intimidated him, still seemed to him to stand far above the other women he had known, it was because he recognized, behind the appearance of this retiring little creature, preoccupied with everyday matters, a woman of extraordinary courage and genuine goodness.

Whenever they talked about Maurice they understood one another immediately. If she devoted herself to Jean like this, it was because he was Maurice's friend, his brother, a brave man in need of help to whom she was repaying a debt of feeling. The more she got to know him, the more her gratitude and affection for him increased, the more she appreciated his simplicity and wisdom, his robust intelligence; while for his part, as she continued to look after him like a child, he felt so grateful to her that he longed to kiss her hand every time she brought him a bowl of soup. Living in this profound seclusion, a prey to the same worries, the tender bond of sympathy between them grew stronger every day. When they had exhausted all his recollections, all the details of that pitiful journey from Rheims to Sedan, about which she was never tired of asking, they always came back to the same questions:

What was Maurice doing? Why hadn't he written? Could the fact that they had received no news mean that Paris was now completely cut off? So far, they had only had one letter from him, posted from Rouen three days after his departure, in which he had explained, in a few words, that he had just arrived there, after having to make a wide detour on his way to Paris. And then for a week, nothing more, complete silence.

In the mornings, after he had finished dressing Jean's leg, Dr. Dalichamp would stay on for a time. Occasionally, he would even come back in the evening for a longer visit. And in this way he became Jean's sole link with the outside world, as it staggered to disaster. He was their only source of news, and, as an ardent patriot, each new defeat filled him with grief and anger. He scarcely mentioned the Prussian invasion, which, since Sedan, had gradually swept across France like a black flood. Each day brought its own quota of sadness, and he would sit there beside the bed, huddled up on one of the two chairs, discussing the worsening situation in a voice that often trembled. Frequently his pockets would be bulging with Belgian papers, which he would leave behind. And it was thus, weeks in arrears, that the echo of each fresh disaster reached this remote room, drawing the two unhappy creatures who were shut away there still closer together in their common grief.

From these out-of-date papers Henriette read aloud descriptions of what had happened at Metz, of the heroic battles that had ensued on three successive days. It was five weeks since they had

390

taken place, but this was the first he had heard of them, and now his heart grew heavy as he discovered that they, too, had been through all the misery and defeat he knew so well. In the quivering silence, as Henriette carefully formed each sentence in her lilting, school-girlish voice, the sorry story was gradually unfolded. How, after Froeschwiller and Spickeren, the routed 1st Corps caught up the 5th in its retreat, and how all the other Corps, drawn up in echelon between Metz and Bitche, had, after a moment's hesitation, been sucked into the confusion caused by these disasters, eventually to be concentrated in front of an entrenched position, on the right bank of the Moselle. But what valuable time they had lost, instead of rapidly falling back on Paris, a retreat which was later to become so difficult! It was then that the Emperor had handed over the command to Marshal Bazaine, to whom everyone looked for victory. But, on August 14, had come the battle of Borny. At the very moment that the army had at last decided to cross over to the left bank, it had been attacked by two German armies; one, under Steinmetz, threatening the entrenched position, the other, commanded by Frederick-Charles, who, having crossed the river further upstream, advanced along the left bank to cut off Bazaine from the rest of France. Borny, where the firing had only started at three o'clock in the afternoon; Borny, that victory which had led to nothing, since it had left the French army in command of the position, but straddled across the Moselle and incapable of movement, while the second German army had completed its encirclement. Then, on the 16th, Rézonville, with most of the French forces at last on the left bank, only the 3rd and 4th Corps being left behind, delayed by the terrible confusion at the point where the roads from Étain and Mars-la-Tour intersected; the bold attack by the Prussian cavalry and artillery, cutting these roads first thing in the morning; then the slow, confused battle which, until two o'clock in the afternoon, Bazaine could still have won, since there were only a handful of men still holding him up, but which, nevertheless, he eventually lost because of his inexplicable fear of being cut off from Metz; a tremendous battle, extending over miles and miles of hills and plain, in the course of which the French, attacked from the front and from the flank, had performed prodigies but had not advanced, thus allowing the enemy time to concentrate his forces; in fact, the French themselves contributed to the success of the Prussian plan, which was to force them to retreat from the other side of the river. And then, on August

391

18, back again in front of the entrenched position, the final struggle at Saint-Privat: an attack along a front of seven miles, two hundred thousand Germans with seven hundred guns, against a hundred and twenty thousand French with only five hundred guns; the Germans facing towards Germany, the French towards France, as though the invaders had become the invaded and were involved in a strange pivoting movement; and, from two o'clock onwards, the most ferocious fighting, the Prussian Guards repulsed and cut to pieces, Bazaine, strengthened by the steadfastness of his left wing, for a long time victorious, until that moment towards evening, when his weaker right wing had to abandon Saint-Privat, amid ghastly slaughter, drawing in its wake the entire army, defeated, thrown back upon Metz, and there shut up for good within a ring of iron.

As Henriette read, Jean kept interrupting:

"And just imagine, there were we, after Rheims, waiting for Bazaine to arrive!"

The marshal's dispatch, dated August 19, after Saint-Privat, in which he spoke of recommencing the general withdrawal by way of Montmédy, the same dispatch that had led to the advance of the army of Châlons, appeared to be little more than the report of a beaten general attempting to explain away his defeat; and when later, but not until August 29, the news reached him through the Prussian lines that an army was on its way to relieve him, though he had indeed made a final effort on the right bank at Noiseville, it had been so feeble that, by September 1, the very day on which the army of Châlons was defeated at Sedan, the army of Metz had fallen back, completely immobilized as far as the rest of France was concerned. Up till this time, it was still possible to regard the marshal as being simply an incompetent commander, who had failed to advance when the road was still open to him, and who was later prevented from doing so by superior forces; but now, dominated by political considerations, he was about to become a conspirator and a traitor.

But, in the papers brought by Dr. Dalichamp, Bazaine was still the great man, the brave soldier to whom France looked for her salvation. And Jean got Henriette to re-read certain passages to him, in an attempt to understand how it was that the third German army, under the Crown Prince of Prussia, had been able to drive them back, while the first and second armies, blockading Metz, were both so strong in men and guns that it had been possible to

392

recruit from them that fourth army which, under the command of the Crown Prince of Saxony, had achieved the disastrous victory over the French at Sedan. And when, eventually, he realized what had happened, lying here as he was, helpless and in pain, he nevertheless forced himself to go on hoping.

"Well, there it is, they were just stronger than we were . . .! Never mind, look at the figures: Bazaine's still got a hundred and fifty thousand men, fifty thousand rifles and more than five hundred guns. . . . I don't mind betting he's got a plan up his sleeve that'll fix them yet."

Henriette, unwilling to depress him still more, nodded her head in agreement, for though she was completely bewildered by these vast troop movements, she could sense that disaster was inevitable. Her voice was still clear, although she must have been reading to him for hours, happy simply to keep him entertained. Now and then, however, when she came to the description of some massacre, she would begin to stammer, and her eyes would suddenly fill with tears. Inevitably it reminded her of her husband, struck down back there, lying on the pavement, with the Bavarian officer prodding him with his foot.

"If it upsets you too much," Jean said, "you mustn't read any more of these accounts of the fighting."

But she pulled herself together, gentle and obliging as ever.

"No, no, I'm sorry, you must forgive me. Honestly, I enjoy it as much as you do."

One evening, towards the beginning of October, when the wind was howling outside, she came back from the hospital, in a state of excitement, crying:

"Look, a letter from Maurice! The doctor's just brought it for me."

For days now they had been more and more concerned at not hearing from him, especially now, when for a week or so there had been rumours that Paris was completely invested; and they had been desperately hoping for news, wondering what could have become of him since leaving Rouen. Now his silence was explained: the letter, which he had sent to Dr. Dalichamp from Paris on the 18th, the very day when the last trains were leaving for Le Havre, had only reached him by a miracle, having gone astray a dozen times or more on the way.

"Oh, the dear fellow," exclaimed Jean, delightedly. "Quick, read it to me."

The wind blew louder than ever, rattling the windows, and putting the lamp on the table beside his bed, Henriette started to read, sitting so close to him that their heads were almost touching. It was very cosy here, in this peaceful room, with the storm raging outside.

It was a long letter of eight pages, in which Maurice began by explaining that, when he arrived, on the 16th, he had been lucky enough to be accepted by a regiment of the line that was being brought up to strength. Then he went on to tell them the news, describing with the greatest excitement all he had learnt about the events of this terrible month : how Paris, having calmed down after the grievous shock of Wissembourg and Froeschwiller, had begun to have hopes of revenge, ready to indulge in new illusions, to accept all kinds of legends about the army's victories under Bazaine's leadership, the mass uprising, the imaginary victories, with enormous Prussian losses, that the ministers themselves proclaimed from the tribune. Then, suddenly, on September 3, Paris had been struck by yet another bolt from the blue; their hopes crushed, the ignorant, trusting city utterly disheartened, crowds on the boulevards shouting, "Resign, resign"; the short, gloomy session of the Chamber, the night when Jules Favre had read out the proposals for the reconstitution of the government that the people were demanding; then, next day, the 4th, the collapse of their whole world, the Second Empire swept away in the swirling torrent of its vices and mistakes, the whole population out on the streets, half a million men swarming into the Place de la Concorde in the bright sunlight of that Sunday morning, surging around the railings of the Chamber, protected by a mere handful of soldiers, smashing down the gates, invading the Chamber itself, from which Jules Favre, Gambetta and other left-wing Deputies had already fled to the Hôtel de Ville to proclaim a Republic; while, in the Place Saint-Germain-l'Auxerrois, one of the doors of the Louvre had quietly opened, and the Empress, dressed in black, had slipped out, with only one companion, crouching in the back of a hired cab, and bumped away over the cobbles, leaving behind the palace of the Tuileries, into which already the crowd was beginning to stream. And, on that same day, Napoleon III had set out from the inn at Bouillon, where he had spent the first night of his exile, on his way to Wilhelmshöh.

At this point, Jean, looking extremely grave, had interrupted the reading of the letter.

"Does it mean that now we are a Republic . . .? That's all right, as long as it helps us to beat the Prussians!"

But nevertheless he was shaking his head. As a peasant, he had always been brought up to fear the Republic. Besides, with the country still at war, it didn't seem a very bright idea for people to be quarrelling amongst themselves. Still, all the same, there had to be a change, for the Empire had definitely gone to pot, and everybody was fed up with it.

Then Henriette had finished reading the letter, which concluded with a reference to the approach of the German army. On the 13th, on the same day that a delegation had set up the Government of National Defence at Tours, Prussians had been seen to the East of Paris, and on the 14th they were at the gates, at Créteil and Joinville-le-Pont. But, by the 18th, the day he had written, Maurice seemed to think that Paris would not be completely cut off, and felt confident that the siege would prove to be merely an incident, a risky attempt, that was bound to fail within three weeks, by which time reinforcements would have arrived from the provinces, not to mention the army that was already on the way, via Verdun and Rheims. Yet, nevertheless, the links in the iron chain had eventually been forged, and now Paris was encircled, cut off from the world, nothing but a vast prison for two million men and women, shut away in deathly silence.

"Oh, heavens," Henriette murmured, "how long is it going to last? Shall we ever see him again?"

In the distance, a sudden gust of wind, sweeping through the trees, made the ancient timbers of the farm groan. If there was a hard winter, how terrible it would be for the poor soldiers, fighting out there in the snow, without fires and without bread.

"Well," concluded Jean, "I reckon that's a very nice letter. It's a real treat to get some news. . . . We mustn't lose hope."

So, day after day, October ebbed away beneath the sad grey sky. Jean's wound was healing extremely slowly; there was still too much pus for the doctor to remove the draining tube : but, though the wounded man had grown much weaker, he still refused to have an operation for fear of being left a cripple. It was a period of weary resignation, occasionally interrupted by sudden anxiety, during which the little room seemed to have fallen asleep, and what news they heard was as remote and vague as a half-remembered nightmare. Somewhere out there, the ghastly war, the massacres, the disasters, were still going on, but they could never discover what was really happening, all they could hear was the muffled sound of their country being slowly done to death. Beneath the livid sky, the wind swept the leaves from the trees, and in the bare countryside there were long, deep silences, broken only by the cawing of the rooks, announcing a hard winter.

The hospital, which Henriette scarcely left except to be with Jean, had now become one of their chief subjects of conversation. In the evening, as soon as she got back, he would begin to question her, for he had come to know each of the wounded men individually, and liked to hear which ones were getting better, which were dying; and since her heart was full of these matters, she was always ready to talk, describing the smallest details of her daily life.

Now that the battle had receded, the hospital was no longer a place where blood flowed freely from freshly amputated limbs. Instead, it had become the haunt of slow decay, smelling of fever and death, a stifling atmosphere of lengthy convalescence and interminable agony. Dr. Dalichamp had had the greatest difficulty in procuring the necessary beds, mattresses and sheets, and even now it was only by a daily miracle that he was able to provide bread, meat and vegetables, not to mention the bandages and dressings required for his patients. And the Prussians in charge of the military hospital at Sedan refused to let him have anything, even chloroform; he had to procure everything from Belgium. Yet he had accepted German casualties as well as French; in particular, he was looking after a dozen Bavarians who had been brought to him from Bazeilles. These men, who, so recently, had been striving to kill one another, now lay side by side, reconciled in mutual suffering. And the two long rooms of Remilly's one-time school, each containing some fifty beds and lit by the light falling from the high windows, had now become a refuge from fear and misery.

Ten days after the battle was over, they were still bringing in wounded men who had been found left behind in some forgotten corner of the battlefield. Four of them had been discovered in an empty house at Balan, where they had somehow managed to keep alive, despite the lack of medical care, thanks to the kindliness of one of the neighbours; but their wounds were swarming with maggots, and they had died, poisoned by the ghastly condition. There was no way of checking this atmosphere of festering disease; directly one opened the door, the stench of putrefying flesh caught one in the throat, and the foul pus dripped steadily from the draining-tubes. Often a new incision had to be made, to extract a splinter that had escaped notice. Then abcesses would form, spreading the infection still further. Exhausted, reduced to skin and bones, their faces deathly white, the wretched creatures endured incredible torture, some of them spending the whole time lying flat on their backs, scarcely breathing, their eyes closed like those of corpses, already half decomposed. Others, unable to sleep, twisted and turned in their restless insomnia like madmen, drenched with sweat. But however peaceful or violent they might be, once the infection struck, it was all over; the triumphant poison, spreading from one to the other, swept them all away on a wave of conquering putrescence.

Worst of all, though, was the room of the damned, of those suffering from dysentery, typhus and smallpox. They tossed about, continually shouting out in delirium, sitting up in bed like ghosts. Some, whose lungs were affected, died of pneumonia, while others shrieked aloud, and were only relieved by the stream of cold water with which their wounds were continually bathed. This was what they all waited for, the time when their wounds were dressed, the only time that brought them a little peace, when the beds were aired, and the bodies, cramped by lying so long in the same position, were able to relax for a moment. But it was also the time they dreaded, for not a day passed without the doctor, as he examined their wounds, noticing on some poor devil's skin the bluish spots that betokened the spread of gangrene; and next day they would have to be operated on, part of an arm or leg amputated. Sometimes, even, the gangrene spread still further, and the operation would have to be repeated until eventually the whole limb was cut away. Then there were men whose whole body was affected, who had to be taken away, gaunt and quivering, to the room of the damned, where finally they succumbed, the flesh already dead before the final agony. Every evening when she came in, Henriette would answer the same questions from Jean, in a voice trembling with the same emotion :

"Oh, the poor fellows, the poor fellows."

And it was always the same details, all the daily torments of this hell on earth : a dislocated shoulder, a foot to be amputated, the resection of a humerus to be performed. Or else one of the patients had been buried, usually a Frenchman, occasionally a German. Not many days went by without a furtive coffin, hurriedly knocked together, having to be taken from the hospital, at dusk, accompanied by a single nurse, often Henriette herself. In the little Remilly cemetery two trenches had been dug, and there the coffins were laid, Germans on the left, French on the right, reconciled in death.

Though he had never seen any of them, Jean had come to take an interest in some of them, and would make enquiries about them.

"How's 'poor boy' getting on?"

This was a young soldier, belonging to the 5th regiment of the line, a volunteer, not yet twenty years old. The nickname had stuck to him, because this was how he always referred to himself; and when one day somebody had asked him why, he had said it was because that was how his mother always used to speak to him. And the name was appropriate enough, for he died of a pleurisy, which developed as a result of a wound in his left side.

"Why, 'poor boy's' not doing at all well," said Henriette, who felt a motherly affection for him. "He's been coughing all day. . . . It's really heartbreaking to hear him."

"And what about your old bear, Gutmann?" Jean would ask, smiling weakly. "Does the doctor think he's improved at all?"

"Yes, there's a chance we shall manage to pull him through. But he's in terrible pain."

Though they were both sorry for him, neither of them could mention Gutmann without a feeling of kindly amusement. The first day she had been on duty in the ward, Henriette had been taken aback when she recognized him as the red-bearded Bavarian, with the big blue eyes and broad, flat nose, who had carried her off in his arms when her husband was shot at Bazeilles. He, too, had immediately recognized her, but he could not speak to her, because the bullet, which had struck him in the back of the head, had sliced away part of his tongue. And though, at first, she had been unable to pass his bed without a feeling of revulsion, an involuntary shudder, she had gradually been won over by the haunted, gentle look in his eyes every time he glanced in her direction. Surely this couldn't be the monster, with blood-spattered hair and furious, glittering eyes, who haunted her dreams? Seeing him now, so kindly and well-behaved, despite the atrocious pain he was suffering, she could hardly believe it. Everyone in the hospital was touched by the very unusual nature of his case. It was not even certain that his name really was Gutmann; he had been given it because the only sound he was able to utter was a two-syllable grunt, that sounded like that. The only other thing they had been able to find out about him was that he was married, and had children : he must have understood a few French words, for in reply to questions he would sometimes nod or shake his head. "Are you married?" Nod, nod. "Any children?" Nod, nod.

One day, the sight of some flour had made him so agitated that it seemed likely he might also be a miller. And that was all. But where was his mill? In what remote Bavarian village were his wife and children now weeping for him? Could it really be that he would die like this, nameless and unknown, leaving his family in a distant land, ignorant of his fate?

"Today," Henriette told Jean one evening, "Gutmann started blowing kisses to me. . . . Every time I gave him a drink, or did the least thing for him, he would raise his fingers to his lips, desperately trying to express his gratitude. . . . It's nothing to laugh about. Just imagine how terrible it must be, like being buried alive."

Meanwhile, as October drew to an end, Jean's condition improved. The doctor agreed to remove the rubber tube, for though he still felt some anxiety, the wound appeared to be healing well. Before long the convalescent was able to get up, and he would spend hours walking about the room, or sitting at the window watching the clouds drift overhead. He began to get bored, and talked of getting something to do, of making himself useful on the farm. One of his private worries was the question of money : he felt sure his two hundred francs must all have been spent in these last six weeks. If he still seemed to be in old Fouchard's good books, it could only be because Henriette was paying for him. The thought of this upset him, but he was afraid to have the matter out with her; and it was a great relief to him when it was agreed that he should help Sylvine with all the inside jobs, so that Prosper could devote himself to the farm work.

Despite the terrible conditions, Fouchard was doing so well that he could do with another hand. While the country as a whole was at its last gasp, he had extended his business as a travelling butcher so successfully that he was now slaughtering three or four times as many animals as before. It was said that, already by August 31, he had started trading with the Prussians on a large scale : the very man who, only the previous day, had threatened to shoot some of the men belonging to the 7th Corps when they had come to his house, who had refused to sell them as much as a loaf, swearing that there was nothing to eat in the house, had, as soon as the first enemy soldiers appeared, opened a general store, unearthing all kinds of provisions from his cellars, rounding up sheep and cattle that he had hidden away in various places. Since then, he had become one of the biggest suppliers of meat to the German armies, showing the greatest skill, not only in finding outlets for his goods, but also in getting paid, despite two general requisitions. While the other traders often suffered from the savage demands made by the victorious army, he had not supplied a bushel of flour, a gallon of wine or a quarter of beef without being paid hard cash for them. This had given rise to a good deal of talk in Remilly. People felt that it was a shameful way of carrying on, especially for a man who had just lost his only son in the war, and had never even bothered to visit his grave. Yet, at the same time, they also respected him for being able to make a fortune at a time when some of the sharpest dealers were merely getting swindled. As for the old man himself, he just shrugged his shoulders and laughed, growling in his stubborn way:

"Patriotic? Why, I'm a better patriot than any of them. . . . Surely there's nothing so bloody patriotic in feeding the Prussians for nothing? I damn well make them pay through the nose. . . . Just you wait and see!"

On his second day at work Jean stayed up too long, and the doctor's unspoken fears were realized: the wound opened again, a serious swelling developed in his leg, and he had to go back to bed. Dalichamp was convinced that there must be a bone splinter there, and that the exercise had worked it loose. He decided to investigate again, and this time succeeded in extracting it. But the shock of the operation brought on a violent fever, which so exhausted Jean that he felt worse than ever. And the faithful Henriette went back to her post in the little room, now saddened by the winter cold. It was the beginning of November; an east wind had already brought the first flurries of snow, and the sparsely furnished room, with its bare, tiled floor, was very cold. As there was no fireplace, they brought in a stove, which did something to cheer the place up. The days followed one another monotonously, and for Jean and Henriette this first week of his relapse was certainly the dreariest of their long, enforced intimacy. Would the pain never stop? Was there always to be this danger of it starting up again? No hope of his suffering coming to an end? Again and again, her thoughts returned to Maurice, from whom they had received no further news. Other people were said to have received letters, brief notes that came by carrier pigeon. Perhaps the pigeon that had been bringing them a word of comfort and affection had been killed on the way by a stray German bullet. News of the war only reached them at long intervals. The occasional papers that they continued to obtain from Dr. Dalichamp were often already a week out of date, and much of the gloominess they felt was due to their ignorance, to what they did not know but merely guessed, to the whisper of death that reached them nevertheless through the wintry silence surrounding the farm. One morning when the doctor dropped in to see them, he was very much upset, his hands were trembling. Pulling out a Belgian paper from one of his pockets and throwing it on the bed, he exclaimed:

"See here, my friends, this is the end of France! Bazaine has betrayed her!"

Jean, who was dozing, propped up against the pillows, woke with a start.

"What d'you mean, he's a traitor?"

"He's surrendered Metz, and his entire army! It's Sedan all over again, and this time it's more than flesh and blood can stand."

Then he picked up the paper and began reading:

"A hundred and fifty thousand prisoners, one hundred and fifty-five regimental colours, five hundred and forty-one guns, seventy-three machine-guns, eight hundred siege guns, three hundred thousand rifles, two thousand military vehicles, equipment for ninety-five batteries . . ."

And he went on reciting the details: Marshal Bazaine shut up in Metz with his army, reduced to impotence, making no attempt to break out of the iron encirclement; his persistent approaches to the Crown Prince Frederick-Charles, his dubious, hesitant intervention in politics, his ambition to play a decisive role, which apparently he had not properly thought out; then the succession of tortuous negotiations, the dispatch of unreliable and dishonest emissaries, to Bismarck and King William as well as to the Empress, who, in the end, had refused to treat with the enemy if it involved ceding any territory; and then the ineluctable catastrophe, the fulfilment of destiny, the outbreak of famine in Metz, the forced capitulation, by the terms of which both officers and men had to accept the onerous conditions laid down by the conqueror, with the result that France was now without an army.

"God in heaven," Jean swore under his breath. Though he did not understand the position at all clearly, until this moment he had regarded Bazaine as the one great leader, the only possible saviour of the country. "So what's going to happen now? What'll become of them all in Paris?"

The doctor was just coming to the news from Paris, which was disastrous. He pointed out that the paper was dated November 5, whereas Metz had surrendered on October 27, and the news had not reached Paris until the 30th. Following on the setbacks already sustained at Chevilly, Bagneux and Malmaison, and the loss of Le Bourget, this news had come as a bombshell to the people of Paris, who were already disheartened and angered by the weakness and impotence of the Government of National Defence. As a result, on the following day, October 31, there had been all the signs of a new uprising : vast crowds, swarming into the square in front of the Hôtel de Ville, had broken in and seized the members of the Government, who had eventually been freed by the National Guard, afraid lest the revolutionaries, who were proclaiming the Commune, would prove triumphant. And the Belgian paper's account concluded with humiliating reflections upon the city of Paris, torn by civil war at the very moment when the enemy was at the gates. What else could it mean, but that the present regime was collapsing in a torrent of mud and blood?

"And they're not so far out, either," muttered Jean, who had turned very pale. "We don't need to start knocking each other about with the Prussians right on top of us !"

Henriette, who always avoided talking politics, had so far not spoken, but now, as she thought of her brother, she could not help saying :

"My God, I only hope Maurice doesn't get mixed up in all this business. He's always so rash !"

There was a silence. Then the doctor, who was an ardent patriot, went on :

"It can't be helped, if we've got no more soldiers, we'll just have to grow some. Metz has surrendered, now perhaps it is Paris's turn. But that doesn't mean France is done for. Oh no, France was built to last, as the peasants round here say. We'll keep going somehow !"

But it was clear that he was hoping against hope. He talked about the new army that was being formed on the Loire; though its first efforts at d'Arthenay had not been too successful, it would soon find its feet, then it would come to the assistance of Paris. He was particularly enthusiastic about Gambetta, who, after escaping from Paris in a balloon on October 7, had arrived in Tours the following day, and had issued an appeal to all citizens to take up arms, couched in such bold and sensible language that the whole country was bound to accept a dictatorship in the public interest. Besides, wasn't there talk of another army being formed in the North? And yet another in the East? This showed that the provinces were stirring, that there was an indomitable determination to create everything that was required to carry on the struggle to the last penny, the last drop of blood.

"Why," he concluded, getting up to leave, "I've many a time seen patients I'd already despaired of, up and about within a week."

"Right then, doctor," said Jean with a smile, "hurry up and get me better, so that I can get back to the regiment."

Yet both he and Henriette were deeply depressed by the news.

That same evening there was a heavy fall of snow, and next day, when Henriette returned from the hospital, shivering, she announced that Gutmann was dead. The severe cold was decimating the wounded, emptying the rows of beds. The poor tongueless creature had hovered on the point of death for two days, and, as the end drew near, had gazed at her so imploringly that she had not left his bedside. His tear-filled eyes had tried to speak to her, to tell her his real name, and the name of the distant village where his wife and children were waiting for him. And he had died, still unknown, clumsily trying to blow her a last kiss to thank her for the care she had taken of him. She had been the only person to accompany his body to the cemetery, and the lumps of frozen earth, earth of a foreign land, had fallen on the deal coffin with a dismal sound.

The following day, Henriette had another announcement to make, and this time there were tears in her eyes:

"Now 'poor boy' has died, as well. If only you could have seen him! He was delirious, and kept calling me 'Mum', reaching out his hands so pitifully that I had to take him in my arms. . . . 'Poor boy' had lost so much weight from all he'd been through that he was as light as a child. . . . And I rocked him in my arms, so that he should die happy. Yes, me, whom he called his mother, though I'm only a year or two older than him. . . . And he cried so, that I couldn't help crying myself."

Even now the tears still choked her, so that for a moment she could not speak. Then she went on:

"When he was dying, he kept murmuring his nickname over and over again, 'Poor boy, poor boy . . .' And how many poor boys there are, my God, some of them mere kids, that this filthy war has

403

robbed of arms and legs, causing them such horrible suffering, before finally laying them in the ground!"

Every day, now, she was coming home like this, upset by some new death. And the sympathy they shared for the dead and dying brought them still closer together, during the long, desolate hours alone in this tranquil room. Hours of happiness, too, though, for as these two gradually came to know each other an affection had sprung up between them, a tenderness that they still believed to be that of brother and sister. He, so serious and deliberate, had gained in confidence from their continued intimacy; while she, finding him always so kind and sensible, never even thought that, before he was in the army, he had driven a plough. So well did they get along together that Sylvine used to say, with her grave smile, "they'd make an excellent couple". Yet there was no feeling of constraint between them. She went on nursing him, still in her widow's weeds, without another thought in her mind, almost as though she had ceased to be a woman.

Nevertheless, lying there by himself through the long afternoons, Jean could not help dreaming. What he felt towards her was a sense of infinite gratitude, a kind of religious respect, that made him dismiss any thought of love as sacriligious. Yet he said to himself that to be married to a woman like her, so tender and sweet, so attractive, would be like living in paradise. All this unhappiness, all the miserable years he had spent at Rognes, the failure of his marriage, his wife's violent death, this whole past welled up in him in a regretful longing for affection, a vague hope, as yet scarcely formulated, that it might still be worth attempting to achieve happiness. Shutting his eyes, drifting away into a state between waking and sleeping, he would imagine himself living at Remilly, married once more, with sufficient land to rear a family of decent, undemanding children. But the dream was too vague, too evanescent, ever to become real. He did not believe that he could ever again be capable of anything more than friendship, and, if he loved Henriette, it was simply because he and Maurice were like brothers. In the end, these dreams of marriage had become simply a kind of consolation, one of those aspirations one knows to be unachievable, with which one can soothe away the hours of sadness.

As for Henriette, she had not the slightest inkling of all this. Her heart was still ravaged by the ghastly tragedy at Bazeilles; and if now she was beginning to experience some assuagement, some new tenderness, she was completely unaware of it; what was happening to her was as imperceptible as the subtle modifications that take place in a germinating seed, a process that remains invisible to the closest observer. She was even unaware of the pleasure she derived from the hours spent sitting at Jean's bedside, reading aloud to him from the papers that so much upset him. If her hand happened to encounter his, she was not even conscious of feeling its warmth; thoughts of the future never set her dreaming, never aroused the faintest longing to be loved again. And yet, nevertheless, it was only here, in this room, that she was able to forget a little, to feel some consolation. When she happened to be there, quietly carrying out her duties, her heart was at peace; it seemed to her that her brother would soon be coming back, that everything would work out satisfactorily, that eventually they would all be able to live happily together. And so natural did she feel all this to be, that she would talk about it without the slightest trace of embarrassment, without it ever entering her head to seek any further, yet surrendering her whole heart, chastely and unwittingly. But one afternoon, as she was setting out for the hospital, the sudden pang of terror that froze her blood, at the sight of a Prussian captain and two other officers in the kitchen, brought home to her how deep was the affection she felt for Jean. It seemed obvious that these men must have found out about his being at the farm, and had come to take him away, which could only mean that he would be sent to Germany, to some remote fortress. And as she listened, she found herself trembling, and her heart beat violently.

The captain, a tall man who spoke French, was loudly reproaching Fouchard.

"This sort of thing can't be allowed to go on. You're just making fools of us. I've come here myself to warn you that, if it happens again, I shall hold you responsible, and I can assure you that I shall know what to do about it!"

Unperturbed, the old man assumed an air of complete bewilderment, waving his hands about as though he did not understand what was going on.

"But what on earth are you talking about, sir? What's the matter?"

"Come on now, don't try to kid me. You know very well that the three bodies of beef you sold us on Sunday were rotten . . . absolutely rotten, stinking. Why, the meat actually poisoned some of my men, and by this time may well have killed two of them."

At this, Fouchard immediately displayed disgust and indignation.

"What? Me sell rotten meat? Why, it's the very best quality, the sort of meat you'd give an invalid to build them up!"

And he began to grovel, beating his breast, insisting that he was an honest man, that he'd rather cut off his right hand than sell meat that wasn't wholesome. Good God, he'd been in business for the last thirty years, and in all that time no one had ever accused him of selling short weight or poor quality.

"I tell you, that meat was as healthy as a new-born babe, sir. And if your men have got the bellyache, it's probably because they ate too much of it . . . unless, of course, some rascal managed to poison the dixies . . ."

And he would have gone on for ever, pouring out a stream of fantastic explanations, had not the captain suddenly lost his temper and cut him short.

"I don't want to hear another word! You've been warned, so you'd better look out! . . . And there's another thing, we've reason to believe that some of you in this village have been assisting the guerillas in the Gourlay woods, and were responsible for killing one of our sentries the day before yesterday. . . . I tell you, you'd better look out!"

As soon as the Prussians had gone, Fouchard shrugged his shoulders, chortling disdainfully. Of course he'd been selling them rotten meat; that was all they'd ever get out of him! Any old crock the peasants liked to bring him, sick beasts that could scarcely stand on their feet, were good enough for these lousy sods!

And turning to Henriette, who was now feeling greatly relieved, he winked at her and, with an air of triumphant mockery, proclaimed :

"Just imagine, my dear, and yet there are some people trying to make out I'm not patriotic . . .! Well, let them talk. I'd like to see some of them selling the Germans rotten meat and getting away with it. Not patriotic, indeed. Why, I reckon some of the meat I've sold them must have killed more of their men than a regiment of soldiers could have done with their rifles!"

When Jean heard what had happened, however, he was upset. If the German authorities suspected that the people of Remilly were helping the guerillas, they might at any moment decide to search the place, and he would be discovered. The thought of compromising his host, of creating the slightest difficulty for Henriette, was unbearable. But she implored him to stay on for a few days longer; his wound was taking a long time to heal, he was not yet strong enough to join one of the regiments that were still fighting in the North or on the Loire.

The following days were the worst he had experienced in all the period of enforced solitude. By the middle of December, the cold was so acute that the stove was not enough to heat the big, empty room. When they looked out of the window and saw the thick snow covering the ground, they thought of Maurice besieged in Paris, cold and hungry, for they had still received no definite news. Endlessly they asked themselves the same questions: What could he be up to? Why did he give no sign of life? Both of them were afraid to speak of the fear at the back of their minds, that he might be ill or wounded, perhaps dead. Such vague information as they managed to elicit from the papers was scarcely reassuring. Reports of various successful attempts to break the siege were denied almost at once. Then came the rumour that General Ducrot had won a great victory on December 2 at Champigny; but soon it became known that, on the following day, he had had to give up the positions he had conquered and retreat once more across the Marne. Day by day the noose around Paris was being drawn tighter. There were growing indications of famine: all cattle being requisitioned, then potatoes, the gas being turned off in the houses, then all public lighting suppressed, so that the only light in the darkened streets came from an occasional bursting shell. And every time the two of them warmed their hands, or ate a mouthful of food, they were haunted by the thought of Maurice, shut up with two million other people in that giant tomb.

Meanwhile, on all sides, in the North as well as in the Centre, the news was getting worse. In the North, the 22nd Army Corps, consisting of Mobile Guards, garrison troops and men and officers who had managed to escape from the disasters of Sedan and Metz, had been obliged to abandon Amiens and retreat towards Arras; and next, it was Rouen's turn to fall into the hands of the enemy, without any serious opposition from the handful of disbanded, demoralized men who were defending it. In the Centre, the victory of Coulmiers that the army of the Loire had won on November 9, gave rise to the wildest hopes: Orléans recaptured, the Bavarians fleeing, the advance upon Etampes, the expected release of Paris. But, by December 5, Prince Frederick-Charles had retaken Orléans and cut the army of the Loire in two, forcing three army corps to fall back upon Vierzon and Bourges, while two others, under the command of General Chanzy, were driven back as far as Le Mans after an heroic retreat, and a whole week of marching and fighting. The Prussians were everywhere, at Dijon and Dieppe, at Le Mans and Vierzon. And almost daily there was news of yet another fortress capitulating. As early as September 28, Strasbourg had succumbed, after a forty-six day siege and thirty-seven days of bombardment; its walls breached, its public buildings battered to pieces by more than two hundred thousand shells. Already the citadel of Laon had been blown up, Toul had surrendered, and this was followed by a sombre succession of defeats : Soissons with its one hundred and eighty guns, Verdun with one hundred and thirty-six, Neufbrisach with a hundred, La Fère eighty, Montmédy seventy-five. Thionville was burning, Phalsbourg had only opened its gates after nearly three months of furious resistance. It seemed as though the whole of France was ablaze, crumbling into ruins beneath the monstrous bombardment.

One morning, as Jean was insisting that he must leave, Henriette seized hold of his hand, and clung to it desperately.

"No, no, I implore you, don't leave me here alone. . . . You're still too weak, wait just a little longer, only a few days. . . . Listen, as soon as the doctor says you are strong enough, that you can start fighting again, I'll let you go . . . I promise."

V

One cold December evening, Sylvine and Prosper were sitting in the big farm-house kitchen, alone with Charlot, she sewing, he engaged in making himself a whip. It was seven o'clock. They had finished their evening meal without waiting for old Fouchard, who must have been delayed at Raucourt, where there was a shortage of meat; and Henriette, who was on night duty at the hospital, had just left, having reminded Sylvine not to go to bed without making up the stove in Jean's room.

Outside, the sky was very dark above the white snow. No sound came from the village, and, inside the room, all that could be heard was Prosper's knife, busily carving the dogwood handle of his whip with squares and circles. Every now and then he would pause, and look up at Charlot, whose fair head was already beginning to nod sleepily. Presently the child dozed off, and the room became even more silent. Gently, Sylvine took away the candle so that the light should not fall on his eyes; then she went back to her sewing, and fell into a deep reverie.

It was at this moment, after some hesitation, that Prosper made up his mind to speak:

"Listen here, Sylvine, there's something I ought to tell you. . . . I had to wait till we were alone. . . ."

Anxiously she raised her eyes.

"It's like this. . . . I'm sorry if it upsets you, but I think it's best for you to know. . . . This morning in Remilly, just near the church, I saw Goliath as plain as I can see you. I couldn't possibly have been mistaken!"

She turned deathly pale, her hands trembled; almost under her breath she murmured:

"Oh, my God!"

Choosing his words carefully, Prosper told her what he had managed to find out during the day, by questioning people. Everybody was now convinced that Goliath was a spy, who had settled in the neighbourhood earlier on in order to get to know the roads and the local gossip. They remembered how he had worked for Fouchard, how abruptly he had left, and then all the other places he had taken later on, around Beaumont and Raucourt. And now, here he was back again, occupying some vague position in the Sedan administration, and once more visiting the villages, apparently responsible for denouncing some of the people, taxing others, and ensuring that the requisitions, which were such a burden on all the villagers, were effectively carried out. Only that morning he had been terrifying the people of Remilly, because of some delay with regard to a delivery of flour.

"I thought I ought to warn you," Prosper concluded. "Like that, you'll know what to do if he comes here . . ."

She interrupted him with a cry of terror.

"Do you really think he'll come here?"

"Well, it seems fairly likely. . . . He's bound to be curious, considering he's never seen the child. Though he knows all about it. . . . Besides, there's you. You aren't such a bad looker, you know, I dare say he wouldn't mind seeing you again."

With a quick gesture, she implored him to stop. Charlot, woken by the sound of their voices, had raised his head. Gazing vaguely around, as though he had been dreaming, he remembered the insulting words, taught him by some village lout, and with all the grave solemnity of a three-year-old, answered:

"The Prussians are pigs!"

Anxiously, Sylvine caught him up in her arms and sat him on her lap. Oh, this poor little creature, her joy and her despair, whom she loved with all her heart and could scarcely look at without weeping, how it hurt her, when he was playing with the other children, to hear them call him "The Prussian". She kissed him on the mouth as though seeking to wipe away the words.

"Who's been teaching you to say such naughty things? You know I've forbidden you to, my love."

But bubbling over with laughter, Charlot repeated obstinately: "The Prussians are pigs!"

Then, seeing that his mother was in tears, he flung his arms round her neck, and he, too, began to cry. Heavens, what new misfortune was threatening her? Wasn't it enough that she had lost Honoré, and, with him, her only hope in life, her one chance to forget the past and be happy again? The reappearance of this other man was simply the last straw!

410

"There, there, darling," she murmured, "come to bed. Mummy loves you, she knows you don't mean any harm."

And for a moment she left Prosper alone, who, not wanting to embarrass her, looked away, pretending to be busy with his carving.

Before putting Charlot to bed, however, Sylvine took him as usual to say goodnight to Jean, for he and the child had become good friends. As she opened the door of his room, candle in hand, she noticed the wounded man was sitting up in bed, gazing wide-eyed into the darkness. So he hadn't been able to sleep, then? Just imagine all the things he must have been brooding about, lying there alone, in the silence of this winter night! And while she was making up the stove, he played with Charlot, who was lying on his bed, curled up like a kitten. He knew Sylvine's story, and felt kindly disposed towards this decent, submissive girl, so hardly done by, mourning the one man she had ever loved, left with this poor child whose birth still tormented her as her only consolation. And now, having closed the stove, as she stooped down to pick up the child, he could see that her eyes were red from weeping. What could have happened? Had someone been upsetting her again? But she didn't want to answer his questions; later on, perhaps, if it seemed worthwhile, she might tell him. Good God, wasn't her life just one long worry, these days?

Then, as she was taking Charlot to bed, they heard voices and the sound of footsteps, outside in the yard. Taken aback, Jean strained his ears, trying to make out what was happening.

"Who can it be? It certainly isn't Fouchard, or we should have heard the wheels of the trap."

Hidden away in this isolated room, he had come to know exactly what was going on in the house, familiar with the slightest sound. Listening intently, he went on :

"That's it! It's those men from the Dieulet woods, the guerillas who come here for food!"

"Quick," whispered Sylvine, as she went out, leaving him once more in darkness, "I must hurry up and get them their loaves."

And indeed, they were already banging on the kitchen door, for Prosper, worried at being left on his own, was in no hurry to open it. When the master was out, he never liked to admit anyone to the house, in case they did any damage and he was held responsible. Luckily for him, just at that moment Fouchard's trap could be heard coming down the road, the horse's hooves making a muffled

411

sound in the snow, so that it was the old man who spoke to the men:

"Ah, good, so it's you three. . . . And what have you got for me today?"

Sambuc, his thin bandit's figure enveloped in a blue woollen shirt, much too big for him, did not even hear what he said; he was too annoyed with Prosper, his "respectable brother", as he called him, who had only just decided to open the door.

"Who the hell do you think you are, leaving us standing out in the cold as though we were beggars?"

But while Prosper, calmly shrugging his shoulders and not bothering to reply, was leading away the horse and trap, Fouchard peered into their barrow and exclaimed:

"Two lousy sheep . . .! Well, it's a good thing it's freezing, or they'd stink the place out."

Whereupon Cabasse and Ducat, Sambuc's two lieutenants, who accompanied him wherever he went, protested.

"Steady on," said the first, a noisy, excitable southerner, "They aren't that old. We got them from Raffin's, where there's an outbreak of foot-and-mouth. They only died three days ago, he told us."

"*Procumbit humi bos*," declared the other, an ex-usher, whose taste for little girls had cost him his job, but who still liked to use Latin tags.

Shaking his head, Fouchard went on disparaging the carcasses, insisting that they were too far gone. But, as he entered the kitchen with the three men, he concluded:

"Still, they can damn well put up with them. . . . Fortunately, there's not a chop to be had in the whole of Raucourt, and if people are hungry enough they'll eat anything, won't they?"

Inwardly delighted, he shouted to Sylvine, who had just finished putting Charlot to bed:

"Bring some glasses; we'll drink to Bismarck's perdition!"

In this way, Fouchard kept on good terms with the guerillas, who, for the past three months, had been in the habit of emerging from the impenetrable Dieulet woods at dusk, scouring the highways, killing and robbing the Prussians if they could take them by surprise, or else falling upon the farms and holding the peasants to ransom. They were the terror of every village in the neighbourhood, for whenever a convoy was attacked, or a sentry had his throat cut, the German authorities would take their revenge on the

412

inhabitants, accusing them of connivance, levying fines on them, gaoling the mayors and burning down the cottages. And if the peasants did not betray Sambuc and his band to the Germans, which they would have been only too pleased to do, it was simply because they were afraid that, if things went wrong, they would end up at the side of the road, with a bullet in the back.

Fouchard, however, had had the extraordinary idea of doing business with them. Ransacking the countryside for miles around, searching every ditch and barn for sick and dying cattle, they had become his principal source of supply. Within a radius of ten miles, there wasn't a dead steer or sheep that they failed to discover and bring to him; and he paid them in kind, especially bread, the batches of loaves that Sylvine baked for the purpose. Besides, even if he didn't particularly like them, he nevertheless had a secret admiration for the guerillas, cunning rascals that didn't give a damn for anybody; and though he was making a fortune out of his dealings with the Prussians, whenever he heard that another of them had been found, lying at the side of a road with his throat cut, he would laugh to himself, savagely.

"Here's to you," said he, clinking glasses with the three men.

Then, wiping his mouth with the back of his hand, he went on :

"Here, there's the hell of a row about those two Uhlans they found near Villecourt, the ones with their heads cut off. . . . You know they set fire to Villecourt yesterday? It's what they call 'passing sentence on the village', for befriending you lot. . . . You want to look out, you know . . . keep away from there for a bit. *I'll* see you get bread."

Sambuc gave a loud, sneering laugh, shrugging his shoulders. To hell with them, the Prussians could go and chase themselves! Then, suddenly becoming angry, he banged his fist on the table :

"It's all right about the Uhlans, but, by God, it's that other swine I'd like to get my hands on! You know the one I mean, the spy, the one that used to work for you. . . ."

"Goliath," said Fouchard.

Utterly flabbergasted, Sylvine, who had taken up her sewing again, stopped, listening intently.

"That's him, Goliath . . .! The rascal knows the Dieulet woods like the palm of his hand, he could easily get us pinched one of these days; especially as I hear that, this morning, in the Maltese Cross, he was boasting he'd settle accounts with us before the week's

413

up. . . . He was the lousy bastard that showed the Bavarians the way to Beaumont. That's right enough, isn't it, lads?"

"As true as that there candle's alight," Cabasse confirmed.

"*Per amica silentia lunae*," added Ducat, who sometimes got his quotations mixed up.

But Sambuc, banging his fist on the table once again, exclaimed :

"He's been tried and condemned, the swine . . .! If you happen to know where we can find him, just you let me know, and we'll serve him like we served the Uhlans! Oh yes, I'll guarantee that, by God!"

There was a sudden silence. Sylvine was gazing at them, wide-eyed, and very pale.

"That's the sort of thing it's best not to say too much about," Fouchard said cautiously. "We'll have another drink, and then I'll be saying goodnight!"

They finished the second bottle. Prosper, who had come back from putting the horse away, gave them a hand, loading their barrow with the loaves, which Sylvine had put into a sack. But he still refused to speak to them, and when Sambuc, his brother, disappeared into the snow with the two others and their barrow, he turned away, muttering to himself :

"Good night to you, and a bloody good riddance!"

Next day, after the midday meal, when Fouchard happened to be alone in the kitchen, Goliath arrived in person, a tall, stout, pink-faced man, with an easy smile. Even though the old peasant was taken aback by this sudden apparition, he certainly did not allow it to be seen. Screwing up his eyes, he peered at the visitor, who came forward and shook him heartily by the hand.

"Good-day to you, M. Fouchard."

Only then did he seem to recognize him.

"Why, it's you, my boy. . . . Still as hefty as ever; but you've put on weight!"

And he looked him up and down. He was dressed in a sort of cloak, made of thick, blue material, with a cap to match, and he had a well-to-do, self-satisfied air. He spoke without an accent, but in the slow, heavy manner of the local peasants.

"Yes, it's me all right, M. Fouchard. . . . As I happened to be in this part of the world, I thought I'd drop in and say hello."

The old man was still suspicious. What could the fellow be doing here? Could he have heard that the guerillas had been here yester-

414

day? He would have to find out. Still, as he was behaving quite politely, he might as well be friendly.

"That's very decent of you, my boy. We'd better have a drink."

He went off to find a bottle and a couple of glasses. Drinking all this wine went against the grain, but, if you were in business, you had to offer a chap a drink. And yesterday's scene was repeated; they clinked glasses in just the same way, said precisely the same things.

"Well, here's to you, M. Fouchard."

"And the same to you, lad."

At this, Goliath began to make himself at home, looking around like a man delighted to be recalling familiar things. Yet he made no reference to the past, nor for that matter to the present. Instead, he talked about the weather: this cold spell was bound to hold up work on the farm, but at least there was one good thing about the snow, it would kill all the insects. He did, however, allow himself to express some concern at the concealed dislike, the suspicious fear, that he had met with in all the other houses in Remilly. After all, everyone put their own country first, didn't they? Naturally, you did what you could for your country when you had the chance. But here in France, the people had some funny ideas about some things. And as the old man watched him, listened to his sensible, conciliatory words, he came to the conclusion that this fellow, with his broad, cheerful face, had certainly not come to see him with any evil intentions.

"So you're all on your own, then, today, M. Fouchard?"

"No, no, Sylvine's just feeding the cows. . . . Would you like to see her?"

Goliath started to laugh.

"Indeed, I would. . . . Quite frankly, I don't mind telling you that's really why I came."

Immediately, Fouchard got up, greatly relieved, shouting at the top of his voice:

"Sylvine! Sylvine! . . . There's someone to see you!"

And off he went, satisfied that now the girl would be there to look after the house.

When Sylvine came into the room, she was not surprised to see Goliath sitting there; and, without getting up, he looked at her with a kindly, almost diffident smile. She had been expecting him, but no sooner had she crossed the threshold than she stopped short,

415

her whole body taut. And Charlot, who had run after her, hid his face in her skirt, amazed to see an unknown man.

For a few seconds there was an embarrassed silence.

"So this is the kid, then?" Goliath asked eventually, in a conciliatory tone of voice.

"Yes," Sylvine replied grimly.

And again they fell silent. She had been seven months gone when he left the farm, and though he knew he had a child, this was the first time he had ever set eyes on it. Now he was anxious to justify his conduct, convinced, like the practical minded fellow he was, that there had been good reasons for it.

"Look, Sylvine, I realize you feel fed up with me. But it's not quite fair, all the same. I know I went and left you, that I treated you badly, but you must have known it was because I wasn't my own master. When you are responsible to others, you've got to do as they tell you, haven't you? If they'd sent me three hundred miles away on foot, I should have had to have gone. And, naturally, I couldn't talk about it : but it nearly broke my heart, clearing off like that, without even saying goodbye to you. . . . God knows, I'm not going to tell you, now, that I was sure I'd come back. Nevertheless, I always meant to, and as you see, here I am. . . ."

She had turned away, and was staring out at the snow in the yard as though determined not to listen. And he, upset by her scornful but obstinate silence, broke off his explanations to say :

"You know, you're prettier now than you used to be !"

And, indeed, with her pale face lit up by those superb great eyes, she was very beautiful. Her heavy black hair seemed to fit her like a widow's cap.

"Come on, now, be friendly ! Surely you must feel that I don't wish you any harm. . . . If I didn't still love you, I certainly shouldn't have come back. . . . But since I have, and since everything's going to work out all right, we'll go on seeing each other, won't we?"

With an abrupt movement, she shrank back from him, and looking him straight in the face, she declared :

"Never !"

"Why ever not? Aren't you my wife? Doesn't the child belong to both of us?"

Without taking her eyes from him, speaking very slowly, she said :

"Listen, it will be best to put an end to this straight away. . . .

416

You knew Honoré. Well, I loved him, I never loved anyone else, and now he's dead, and it's you who killed him. . . . I'll never have anything more to do with you, never!"

She had raised her hand, as though swearing an oath, and her voice was so full of hatred that, for a moment, he was completely taken aback, and could only mutter :

"Yes, I heard Honoré was dead. He was a very nice chap. Only, what's to be done about it? He's not the only one that's dead. It's the war. . . . Besides, it seemed to me, just because he was dead, there wouldn't be anything to prevent us; for after all, Sylvine, don't forget, I never treated you brutally, you consented . . ."

But she did not let him finish. Utterly distraught, pressing her hands to her face as though she could have torn out her eyes, she broke in :

"But that's just it, that's just what's driving me mad! Why *did* I consent? What *made* me, when I didn't love you at all . . .? I can't remember, I was so sad, so upset about Honoré going away . . . maybe it was because you used to talk to me about him, and seemed to be so fond of him. My God, the nights I've spent thinking about it all, crying my heart out! It's terrible to have done something you didn't want to, and not to be able to explain to yourself afterwards what it was that made you. . . . But he had forgiven me, he promised me, if these filthy Prussians didn't kill him, that he'd marry me just the same, as soon as he got back from the army. . . . And you really believe I'd go away with you? Why, if you threatened to kill me, I'd say, No, no, never!"

By this time, Goliath was scowling. Once, she had been prepared to give in to him; now he could feel that nothing would ever make her do so. Easy-going as he was, now that he was the master, he wanted her, even if it meant using force; and the only thing that prevented him from trying to impose his will upon her there and then was his innate caution, an instinctive cunning. This huge, heavy-fisted colossus did not like violence. Besides, he had thought of another way of making her submit.

"All right, so you won't have anything to do with me. . . . Then I shall take the child."

"The child? What do you mean?"

She had forgotten about Charlot, who was still clinging to her skirt, trying not to cry. Now, getting up from his chair, Goliath came towards them.

"Yes, you belong to me, then, sonny. You're a little Prussian

417

boy, aren't you . . .? Come along, I'm going to take you with
me!"

But Sylvine, trembling from head to foot, had already seized him
in her arms and was clasping him to her bosom.

"Him, a Prussian? Oh no, he's French. He was born in France!"

"A Frenchman? Why, you've only got to look at us both. He's
the spit and image of me, not like you in the slightest!"

All she could see was this huge, fair giant, with his curly hair
and beard, fat, pink face and great china-blue eyes. For, sure
enough, the child had the same shock of yellow hair, the same
plump cheeks, the same light blue eyes, whereas she, with her long
black hair escaping from her bun and falling in disorder over her
shoulders, was, as she knew, quite unlike either of them.

"But it was I that bore him, he's mine!" she exclaimed furiously.
"He's French, I tell you! I'll never let him learn a word of your
filthy language, and when he's grown up he's going to kill you
Germans to revenge all our lads killed by you."

Charlot had begun to cry, clinging to her, calling out:

"Mummy, mummy, I'm frightened. Take me away!"

Whereupon Goliath, anxious to avoid a scene, drew back and
contented himself with declaring in a harsh voice:

"All right, but just listen to me, my girl. . . . I know all about
what's going on here. You're in contact with the guerillas from the
Dieulet woods, and you supply that bandit, Sambuc, the brother
of the fellow that works here, with bread – and this bloke Prosper,
he's a Chasseur d'Afrique, a deserter, who belongs to us. What's
more, I know all about the wounded man you're hiding, another
soldier; it only needs a word from me, and they'd take him off
to Germany and lock him up. . . . So, you see, I'm pretty well
informed!"

She was listening to him now without saying a word, terrified,
while Charlot kept whispering in her ear:

"Mummy, mummy, take me away, I'm frightened!"

"Still," Goliath went on, "I'm not a quarrelsome bloke, and you
can tell him from me I don't like trouble. But this I swear, if you
don't let me into your bedroom on Monday night, I'll have them
all arrested, old Fouchard and the whole bunch. . . . And I'll take
the child away. I'll send him to my mother's, she'll be delighted to
have him. For once you decide to break with me, he belongs to me.
. . . Do you understand? There won't be anyone else here by then.
I shall just come and take him away. . . . I'm the boss here, and

418

I mean to have my own way. . . . So you'd better make up your mind."

She made no attempt to answer, but clung more closely to the child as though afraid he might take him away at once, and her huge eyes were filled with terror-stricken loathing.

"So there it is, and I'm giving you three days to think it over. . . . You'll leave the window of your room ajar, the one that looks out on the orchard. . . . And if, at seven o'clock on Monday, I don't find it open, I'll have the lot of them arrested the next day. And I'll come back and fetch the child. . . . So long, Sylvine."

He turned away and calmly left the room, leaving her standing there, rooted to the spot, her head buzzing with such frightful thoughts that she felt stupefied. And all the rest of that day she felt as if a storm was raging within her. Her first instinct was to snatch up the child in her arms, and take him away, no matter where. Only what would become of them when night fell? And how on earth could she earn a living for the two of them? Besides, the Prussians were always watching the roads, they would arrest her, perhaps bring her back. Then she decided to speak to Jean, to warn Prosper, even old Fouchard. But again she hesitated: could she count on them all to stand by her? Might they not decide to sacrifice her, so long as they were left in peace? No, no, she wouldn't talk to anybody. It was up to her to find a way out of the danger, since it was she who had brought it upon them by her stubborn refusal. But what was she to do, good God? How could she prevent this disaster? The thought that, through her own fault, she might bring suffering on all these people, especially Jean, who had always been so kind to Charlot, revolted her sense of decency; she would never be able to forgive herself as long as she lived.

Slowly the hours passed; tomorrow came, and still she had not decided what to do. She went about her work as usual, sweeping out the kitchen, seeing to the cows, cooking the meals. And in the absolute silence, that terrifying silence which she still refused to break, her hatred of Goliath began to mount within her, poisoning her more and more as the hours went by. He had been her sin, and was becoming her damnation. Had it not been for him, she would have waited for Honoré; and Honoré would have still been alive, and she would have been happy. How brutally he had made her realize that now he was the master! For nowadays it was certainly true that only might was right; there were no longer police or judges to whom one could turn. Oh, if only she had the power, so

419

that when he turned up again she could have him arrested, as he talked of arresting others! For her, the one thing that counted was the child, flesh of her flesh. The child's father meant nothing to her, had never meant anything. She was not married to him, the mere thought of him filled her with anger, the bitterness of defeat. Rather than let him have the child she would kill it, and then herself. She had told him to his face, this child that he had begotten was a gift of hatred: she only wished he was already grown up, able to protect her; that she could see him, rifle in hand, shooting them down, another Frenchman ready to kill Prussians!

And now there was only one day left, and she must make up her mind. Right from the start, a monstrous idea had vaguely presented itself to her poor, muddled mind; to warn the guerillas, to give Sambuc the information he wanted. But it had been no more than a fleeting notion, and she had dismissed it as too horrible to consider: after all, this man was the father of her child, how could she let him be murdered? Yet the idea had recurred again and again, gradually becoming more urgent, more obsessive, until now it was imposing itself with all the strength of simple finality. Once Goliath was dead, Jean, Prosper and Fouchard would have nothing to fear; she would be able to keep Charlot, and no one could dispute her right to him. And there was something else, a feeling so profound that she was scarcely conscious of it, surging up from the very depths of her being: the desire to efface, once and for all, the fact of his paternity by ridding herself of the father, the wild joy of feeling herself cleansed of her sin, the sole parent of her child, unshared by any man. Throughout the day she kept mulling the project over in her mind, powerless to dismiss it, coming back again and again to the details of the ambush, foreseeing precisely what she would have to do, until finally it became an obsession, deeply implanted, beyond the reach of reason. And when, at last, the time came to act, to obey this ineluctable urge, she went about it like a sleep-walker, as if she were dominated by someone else, and whose existence within herself she had never even suspected.

On Sunday, old Fouchard had felt worried, and sent word to the guerillas that he would have their sack of loaves delivered to them as the Boisville quarry, a lonely spot about a mile from the village; and, as Prosper was busy, he had sent Sylvine with it. To her this seemed decisive, as though the voice of fate had spoken. And when she met Sambuc, and made arrangements with him for the following evening, her voice was as clear, as dispassionate, as if she had no choice. And the next day there were other signs, which seemed to prove conclusively that not only people, but even inanimate objects, were set upon his death. In the first place, Fouchard, unexpectedly called away to Raucourt, left word that they were not to wait dinner for him, as he probably would not be back before eight o'clock. Then, late in the afternoon, Henriette, whose spell of night-duty was usually on Tuesdays, was informed that one of the nurses had fallen sick, and that she would therefore have to take her place that evening. And since Jean never left his room on any account, the only person left who might possibly intervene was Prosper. True, he wasn't the sort of man who approved of murder. But, when his brother turned up with his two lieutenants, the disgust he felt for them increased his hatred of the Prussians. In any case, he wasn't going to raise a hand to help one of the lousy sods, even if this was a pretty rotten way of knocking them off; he preferred to go to bed, and bury his head in the pillow, so that he wouldn't hear anything or be tempted to behave as a soldier.

It was a quarter to seven, and Charlot still refused to go to sleep; usually, as soon as he'd had his milk, his head began to nod. Sylvine picked him up and took him into Henriette's room.

"There, now," she said. "Go to sleep, love. Look what a lucky boy you are, sleeping in auntie's bed!"

But the child was so delighted at this treat that he wriggled about, laughing until he was choking.

"No, no, mummy. . . . Let's play a game. . . ."

She tried to conceal her impatience, patting him gently, saying over and over again in a coaxing voice:

"Go to bye-byes, darling. . . . Go to bye-byes, just to please mummy!"

And at last the child fell asleep, a smile still on his lips. She had not bothered to undress him, but she wrapped him up warmly, and he usually slept so soundly, that she left the room without locking the door.

Never in her life had she felt calmer, her mind so clear and alive. So swiftly did she make up her mind, so light were her movements, that she felt as if she had left her body behind, as if she were acting on the orders of that other person, the unknown stranger. Soon, she had let Sambuc into the house, with his two mates, and urging them to be very careful she took them to her room, where she placed them on either side of the open window. The room was in darkness, lit only by a faint glow from the snow outside. From the

421

surrounding countryside came a deathly silence; time dragged intolerably. At last, hearing the sound of approaching footsteps, Sylvine crept from the room and went into the kitchen, where she waited, sitting motionless, her eyes fixed on the flame of the candle.

She seemed to wait a long time. Goliath was prowling around the farm before making up his mind. Thinking he knew Sylvine inside out, he had come out with only a revolver stuck in his belt. But now he was beginning to feel uneasy. Pulling the window wide open, he put his head into the room and called softly:

"Sylvine, Sylvine!"

The fact that the window was open meant she had decided to do what he had told her to. He was delighted, yet he would have preferred her to be there, waiting for him; he would have felt safer. Old Fouchard must have called her back to the kitchen. He raised his voice a little:

"Sylvine, Sylvine!"

There was no answer, not a sound. He put his leg over the sill and climbed into the room; it was so cold he decided to curl up under the blankets and wait for her.

All of a sudden there was a wild rush, a scurry of feet, stifled oaths. Sambuc and the other two had hurled themselves upon Goliath, but despite the fact that they were three to one they were unable to overpower the giant, whose strength was increased tenfold now he realized the danger he was in. In the darkness you could hear their joints creaking as the panting men struggled to hold him. Luckily, the revolver had fallen from his belt. In a strangled voice, Cabasse kept muttering:

"Some rope . . . get some rope!"

Ducat, who had had the foresight to bring a coil with him, handed it to Sambuc; and a savage struggle ensued, as, beating and punching him, they proceeded to tie him up, first securing his legs, then binding his arms to his sides, till at last, so many knots and twists were there, he looked as though he had been caught in a net. He kept shouting for help, with Ducat swearing at him to shut his mouth. Then suddenly his voice died away: Cabasse had savagely thrust an old blue scarf into his mouth. And at last, stumbling and panting, they lugged him into the kitchen, and lifted him on to the table.

"Bloody Prussian," swore Sambuc, mopping his forehead, "he didn't half play us up . . .! Here, Sylvine, bring another candle so that we can have a proper look at the swine."

422

Sylvine got to her feet, the huge eyes staring from the pallor of her face, and, without a word, lit a candle, which she set down on the table close to Goliath's head. For a moment their eyes met: desperate with fear, he was mutely imploring her, but she seemed not to understand; and turning back to the dresser she stood there staring at him, her face set in a cold, sullen expression.

"Hell," growled Cabasse, whose hand was bleeding, "the sod's bitten off one of my fingers! Just let me get at him!"

But as he raised the revolver, which he had picked up from the floor, Sambuc snatched it from him.

"Oh no, we're not having any of that nonsense . . .! We're not just a bunch of crooks, we're judges. . . . You hear that, you lousy Prussian? We're going to put you on trial! But you don't have to worry, I'll see your rights are respected. Of course, you won't be defending yourself, because if we took that gag out you'd shout the place down. But you'll get a lawyer all right, and a damned good one!"

He drew up three chairs and placed them in a line to form what he called "the bench", himself taking the middle one, with his two lieutenants on either side. Then, rising to his feet, he began to speak, at first in a slow, bantering manner, which gradually gave way to savage anger.

"I'm acting as judge, and also as prosecuting counsel. I know that's not quite how it should be, but there aren't enough of us. . . . I therefore accuse you of coming to France as a spy, thus repaying our hospitality with the dirtiest kind of treachery. For it was you who were responsible, in the first place, for us being defeated; it was you, during the night following the battle of Nouart, who showed the Bavarians the way to Beaumont through the Dieulet woods. Only a man who had spent a long time in the neighbourhood could have known all the paths and bye-ways; and we know it was you, because you were seen with their artillery, showing them the way along roads that were little better than rivers of mud, where it took eight horses to pull every gun. To see those roads now, it's incredible, you'd never believe it was possible for an army corps to use them. . . . Without you, without your dastardly crime of worming your way into our lives and then selling us out, our troops wouldn't have been taken by surprise at Beaumont, wouldn't have had to fall back on Sedan, and might well have ended up by giving the Prussians a hiding! And I'm not going to say anything about all the dirty tricks you've been up to since then, having the damned nerve to show yourself again in these parts, throwing your weight about, denouncing and terrifying everybody. . . . You're just a low-down swine, and I demand the death penalty."

There was a silence. He sat down again, and presently announced :

"I call upon Ducat, who will act as your defence counsel . . . he's been a bailiff, and if it hadn't been for his weaknesses he'd have done well in his profession. You see, I'm giving you a chance, we're treating you properly."

Goliath, who was unable to move a finger, rolled his eyes in the direction of his improvised lawyer. Beneath his livid forehead, drenched with sweat despite the cold, only his eyes were alive, burning with passionate entreaty.

"Gentlemen," began Ducat, rising to his feet, "my client undoubtedly belongs to the foulest dregs of society, and I wouldn't have undertaken to defend him, were it not that I feel bound to admit on his behalf that everybody else in his country is just the same. . . . You've only got to look at him, and you'll see from his eyes how completely astonished he is : he just doesn't understand the nature of his crime. In France, we wouldn't touch one of our own spies with a pair of tongs, whereas, with them, spying is an honourable career, a meritorious way of serving your country. . . . And I will allow myself to observe, gentlemen, that perhaps they are right. For though our noble sentiments do us honour, the worst of it is they've beaten us. If I may so express myself, *quos vult perdere Jupiter dementat*. . . . You take the point, gentlemen !"

And with this he sat down again, while Sambuc demanded :

"What about you, Cabasse? Have you anything to say, for or against the accused?"

"Only this," yelled the man from Provence, "that this is a bloody long-winded way of settling accounts with the sod. I've had a good deal to put up with in my time, but when it's a question of justice I don't believe in fooling about, it only brings bad luck. . . . So let's bump him off, and have done with it !"

Solemnly, Sambuc once more rose to his feet.

"I take it, then, you're both agreed as to the verdict? That he should be sentenced to death?"

"Yes, yes, the death penalty !"

They pushed back their chairs and, turning to Goliath, Sambuc announced :

"So that's that. You've been condemned to death."

424

The two candles with their guttering wicks shone down upon Goliath's ravaged face. In his efforts to plead for mercy, to utter the words that were choking him, he struggled so violently that the blue scarf in his mouth was drenched with spittle; and it was a terrible sight, to see this man, already reduced to silence, dumb as a corpse, with a flood of unspoken explanations and prayers stuck in his throat.

Cabasse cocked the revolver.

"Shall I shoot him?" he asked.

"No, no," cried Sambuc, "shooting's too good for him!" And turning to Goliath, he went on : "As you're not a soldier, you don't deserve the honour of a bullet through the head. Oh, no, we're going to kill you like the dirty spy you are."

He turned away, and in a polite tone of voice said :

"I'm sorry to bother you, Sylvine, but I wonder if you could let me have a bucket."

Throughout the trial, Sylvine had not stirred. She had simply stood there waiting, her face rigid, her thoughts elsewhere, pre-occupied with the obsession, which, for the past two days, had completely dominated her. And now that she was asked for a bucket she merely obeyed, disappearing for a minute into the cellar and returning with the big one she used for washing Charlot's clothes.

"Good, put it under the table, near the edge."

She put it down, and, as she straightened her back again, her eyes once more met Goliath's. In the wretched man's gaze was a last entreaty, the expression of a man who does not want to die. But she felt no trace of womanly pity; at that moment, all she desired was his death, which for her meant freedom. She retreated once more towards the dresser, and there she stood.

Sambuc had opened the table drawer, and now produced a large kitchen knife.

"As you've behaved like a pig, I'm going to bleed you like a pig."

Apparently in no hurry, he discussed with Cabasse and Ducat the best way to perform the operation. They even began arguing, Cabasse maintaining that, in Provence, they hung the pigs up to bleed them, Ducat indignantly insisting that this was a clumsy and barbarous method.

"Pull him to the side of the table, over the bucket, so that everything doesn't get splashed."

They did as they were told, and Sambuc set about his task, calmly and skilfully.

With a single stroke he opened up the side of the throat, and immediately the blood began to flow from the severed carotid into the bucket, making a faint sound, like water falling from a fountain. He had made the incision as small as possible, so that only a few drops of blood, under the pressure of the heartbeats, missed the bucket. Though death was slower this way, there was no sign of convulsions, for the rope was strong, preventing the slightest movement of the body. Not a spasm, no sound of the death rattle. All the anguish was concentrated in the face, a mask etched with terror, from which the blood drained, drop by drop, leaving the discoloured skin white as a sheet. And slowly the eyes, too, emptied; then clouded over, and went out.

"Here Sylvine, we could do with a sponge."

She did not answer. She simply stood there, rooted to the spot, her arms crossed over her breast, her throat contracted, as though gripped by an iron collar, watching. Then, suddenly, she realized that Charlot was there, clinging to her skirt. He must have woken up and managed to open the door, and no one had noticed him steal into the room, filled with childish curiosity. How long had he been there, half hidden behind his mother? For he, too, was watching. With his big, blue eyes beneath the mop of yellow hair, he was staring at the blood, that thin, red stream, falling slowly into the bucket. Perhaps it amused him. Perhaps, at first, he hadn't understood what was happening. Then a wave of horror seemed to sweep over him, as though, instinctively, he had become aware of the abomination that was taking place, for he uttered a sudden bewildered cry.

"Mummy, mummy, I'm frightened, take me away!"

And the shock of his voice was so violent that Sylvine shuddered from head to foot. She was on the point of collapse. At last, horror overcame the obsessive energy and excitement that had kept her going for the past two days. The woman in her revived; she burst into tears and, picking up Charlot, she clasped him frantically to her heart. Then she rushed from the room, hearing nothing, seeing nothing, driven by a desperate need to hide herself away wherever she could find refuge.

At that moment, Jean opened the door of his room. As a rule, he took no notice of the noises he heard from the farm, but he had finally become worried about the continual coming and going, the

426

sound of people talking. So that it was in his room, that room of peace and quiet, that Sylvine eventually collapsed, dishevelled, sobbing, overcome by such a frenzy of despair, that at first he could scarcely make out the flood of stammering words. Again and again she made the same gesture, as though trying to drive away some atrocious vision. And at last he understood, could see it all, the ambush, the murder, the mother standing there with the child clinging to her skirt, watching the blood stream from his father's throat; and his blood froze in his veins, his peasant's heart stood still. Oh this war, this monstrous war, turning these wretched people into wild animals, sowing hatred on every side, spattering the son with his father's blood, perpetuating enmity, exacerbating hatred, sowing the seed of yet more terrible harvests.

Huddled in a chair, covering Charlot with frantic kisses as he clung, weeping, to her neck, Sylvine kept repeating the same words over and over again, a cry from her ravaged heart :

"Oh my poor child, no one shall ever call you a Prussian again. . . . No one shall ever call you a Prussian again!"

Meanwhile, Fouchard had returned. He had knocked at the door in such peremptory fashion that eventually they had let him in, and the sight of the dead man, lying on the table with a bucket of blood underneath it, had come as such a shock that he had immediately flown into a rage.

"What's going on here, you blackguards? Why the hell couldn't you have done your dirty business outside? D'you take my house for a dung heap, ruining all the furniture like this?"

And when Sambuc began making excuses, explaining what had happened, the old man was so scared that he became angrier than ever.

"It's nothing to do with me if you decide to kill someone. What sort of carry-on is this, dumping a corpse in somebody's house, without even asking yourselves what he's going to do with it . . .? Supposing a patrol turns up, a pretty mess I shall be in! A fat lot any of you care what happens to me. . . . Well, I'm bloody well telling you, if you don't get this bloke out of here, and pretty smart, too, you'll have me to deal with . . .! Come on now, one of you take him by the head and the other by the feet. And take care you don't drop him, I don't want blood all over the place. Get a move on, you've got exactly three minutes!"

Eventually Sambuc persuaded Fouchard to let them have a sack, though it almost broke the old man's heart to give away anything.

427

He picked out the worst one he could find, anything was good enough for a Prussian. Then Cabasse and Ducat had the greatest difficulty in getting Goliath's body into it, it wasn't big enough, and the feet stuck out. But at last they managed to get him outside, and heaved him into the barrow.

"I give you my word," declared Sambuc, "we'll dump him in the Meuse."

"And above all," insisted Fouchard, "make sure you tie two big stones to his feet, so that the sod doesn't float!"

And with that the little procession set off, disappearing into the darkness, and the only sound that could be heard was the faint, plaintive creaking of the barrow on the hard snow.

Later on, Sambuc always swore he really had tied to stones to the feet. Nevertheless, the body rose to the surface and, three days later, was found by the Prussians at Pont-Maugis, caught in the reeds; and when they took the body out of the sack and found that it had been bled like a pig, their anger knew no bounds. Probably some of the villagers talked too much, for one evening Fouchard and the mayor of Remilly were arrested, on the grounds that they were in contact with the guerillas, to whom the crime was attributed. In these difficult circumstances, old Fouchard behaved admirably, displaying all the staunchness of an old peasant who knows when to keep his mouth shut. He allowed the soldiers to lead him away, without the least sign of panic, without even demanding an explanation, convinced that everything would turn out all right. It was said that, on the quiet, he had already made a huge fortune out of the Prussians, and had stacks of gold hidden all over the place.

When she realized all that had happened, Henriette was terribly worried. Once again, not wishing to compromise his hosts, Jean was anxious to get away, although the doctor still considered him to be too weak; and she insisted on his waiting a fortnight, being very upset in any case by the thought of their approaching separation. At the time of Fouchard's arrest, Jean had been able to keep out of harm's way by hiding in the barn, but if, as was probable, there was a further search, he was almost certain to be caught. And as she was also worried about the fate of her uncle, she decided one morning to go to Sedan to see the Delaherches, for she had heard that they had a high-ranking Prussian officer billeted on them.

"Now, Sylvine," she said as she was leaving, "take good care of our invalid. Give him his broth at midday, and see that he takes his medicine at four o'clock."

The servant, once again busy about the house, had become as courageous and willing as ever, and in Fouchard's absence she was now looking after the farm, while Charlot played happily in the yard.

"Don't you worry your little head, ma'am, I'll take care of him. I like making a fuss of the poor man!"

VI

MEANWHILE, in the Rue Maqua, after the terrible shock of the battle and capitulation, for the Delaherches life had resumed its course; and, for the last four months, the days had succeeded one another under the grim weight of the Prussian occupation.

But there was one spot in that huge block of buildings that always remained cut off; the room that looked out on to the street, at the far end of the private apartments, where Colonel de Vineuil was still living. While the windows in the rest of the house were opened, letting in the noise and bustle of life outside, in this room they always seemed dead, and the blinds were invariably closed. The colonel complained that the daylight hurt his eyes, and though there was no way of telling whether this was actually the case, a lamp was always kept burning day and night. For two whole months he had been confined to bed, despite the fact that all Major Bouroche had been able to diagnose was a fractured ankle: the wound refused to heal, and there were complications. Now, he was able to get up, but he was in such a state of moral collapse, a prey to some ill-defined illness, stubborn and all-pervading, that he would spend the entire day stretched out on an invalid chair in front of a blazing fire. He had grown much thinner, a mere shadow of his former self, yet the doctor who was looking after him was, to his great surprise, unable to discover any definite cause for this slow decline. He was like a flame that was gradually burning itself out.

Right from the start of the occupation, old Madame Delaherche had shared his isolation; they seemed to have come to a decision between themselves, once and for all, that, as long as there were any Prussians billeted in the house, they would both remain aloof. Several Germans had spent two or three nights in the house, and now a captain, Herr von Gartlauben, was more or less living there. Yet neither the colonel nor the old lady made the slightest reference to the matter. Despite her seventy-eight years, she would be up at dawn, then settle down in her armchair beside the fire, facing her friend; and while she, in the steady light from the lamp, busied herself knitting socks for the children of the poor, he would sit there, doing nothing but stare at the burning logs, apparently pre-occupied with his thoughts, in a state of deepening stupor. Certainly they never exchanged twenty words in a day, and if ever, as she came and went about the household, she unthinkingly let drop some reference to what was happening outside, he would stop her with a gesture; so much so, that not a word about the siege of Paris, or the defeats on the Loire, or the daily anguish of the invasion was ever allowed to penetrate their self-imposed silence. And yet all the colonel's efforts to shut out the light of day and stop up his ears proved to be unavailing : somehow or other, through cracks in the walls, in the very air he breathed, knowledge of the terrible disaster must have seeped in, all the same, for he was poisoned by it, and it steadily drove him a little nearer death.

During this time, Delaherche, feeling in need of some kind of activity, tried to open his factory again, but such was the confusion, affecting both workmen and customers, that he only managed to get one or two departments working. To occupy his enforced leisure he had therefore conceived the idea of carrying out a complete inventory of his establishment and drawing up plans for improve-ments that he had often dreamt about. To assist him in his work he had taken on a young man, the son of one of his customers, who had turned up in Sedan after the battle. Edmond Lagarde, brought up at Passy, in his father's draper's shop, had risen to the rank of sergeant in the 5th regiment of the line, and, at the age of twenty-three, though scarcely looking more than eighteen, after fighting with great bravery, had had his left arm smashed by a bullet. This had happened about five o'clock, shortly before the cease-fire, and he had been taken to the hospital at Delaherche's factory. Later, when the rest of the wounded had been evacuated, the wool merchant had good-naturedly kept him on. Edmond had thus become more or less one of the family, and now that his wound was practically healed was acting as Delaherche's secretary until it was possible for him to return to Paris. It was due to the latter's protection, as well as his own promise not to attempt to escape, that the Prussian authorities had not interfered with him. Fair-haired, with blue eyes and almost girlish good looks, he was so shy that he blushed at the slightest word. He had been brought up by his mother, who had worked her fingers to the bone for him, devoting all their savings to keep him at school. He adored Paris, and loved to talk about it to Gilberte, who, having nursed him through his illness, had become attached to this wounded Cherubino.

Later on, the Delaherche household was joined by a further guest, Herr von Gartlauben, a captain in the reserve, whose regiment had taken over the garrisoning of Sedan from the front-line troops. Despite his modest rank, he was a person of some importance, for his uncle had been appointed Governor-General of Rheims, in charge of the whole region. The captain, too, prided himself on his passion for Paris, having lived there for a time and acquired something of its polish and refinement; and, indeed, he did his best to conceal his native uncouthness behind the airs and graces of a man-about-town.

Tall and fat, his uniform always tightly buttoned, he lied about his age, desperately anxious to pass himself off as less than forty-five. Had he been more intelligent he would have been frightening; but, thanks to his preposterous vanity, he was always so pleased with himself that it never dawned on him that anybody was laughing at him.

Eventually, he was to prove Delaherche's saviour. But in those early days, after the capitulation, the situation was appalling. Everyone in Sedan, which was swarming with German soldiers, dreaded the thought of looting. Then, when the victorious troops marched away towards the Seine, leaving behind only a garrison, the city assumed the deathly peace of a necropolis : houses all shut up, shops closed, streets emptied at dusk, only the heavy footsteps and raucous shouting of enemy patrols. Not a letter or a newspaper was to be had. It was like being shut up in a dungeon, completely cut off from the world, vaguely aware that new, unknown disasters were on the way. And to fill their cup of misery, the threat of famine was becoming acute. The city woke up one morning to find itself without bread or meat, the surrounding countryside stripped bare, as though a swarm of locusts had passed by, thanks to the hundreds of thousands of men who, in the course of a single week, had swept through it. Only two days' food supply was left, and they had to rely on Belgium for everything they required, which entered the country without paying duty, since the customs had broken down in the general catastrophe. They were also faced with endless difficulties, a continual struggle that broke out afresh every morning between the Prussian high command, installed at the Sub-Prefecture, and the Municipal Council, which remained in permanent session at the Town Hall. In vain did the latter heroically

432

dispute the ever-increasing demands; in spite of steady resistance the city's inhabitants were subjected to ever more fantastic and frequent requisitions.

At first Delaherche had to put up with a great deal from the soldiers and officers that were billeted upon him. Men from every part of Germany would turn up, puffing away at their pipes. Every day, without warning, two thousand, three thousand troops would arrive in the town, infantry, cavalry, artillery; and although these men were only entitled to a roof over their heads and a fire, often enough the people were expected to supply them with food as well. They left the rooms they slept in in a state of disgusting filth, and often the officers would come in at night dead drunk, and behave worse than the ordinary soldiers. Nevertheless, thanks to the harsh discipline that was enforced, looting and acts of violence were rare; in the whole of Sedan, only two cases of rape were reported. It was only later, when Paris refused to yield, that they really began to make their domination harshly felt, infuriated by the prolongation of the struggle, worried by the attitude of the provinces, and, above all, dreading a mass uprising, that savage type of warfare declared by the guerillas.

Delaherche had just managed to get rid of a cavalry commander, who used to go to bed with his boots on and had covered his room with rubbish, so that it went right up the chimney, when, one wet evening towards the end of September, Captain von Gartlauben turned up. At first, things threatened to go badly : he talked at the top of his voice, insisted upon having the best bedroom, and strode about the house, clanking his sword behind him. But as soon as he caught sight of Gilberte his manner changed; he kept himself to himself, stood aside to let people pass, acknowledging them with a polite bow. Everyone curried favour with him, knowing that a word from him to the colonel commanding the Sedan garrison was enough to ease a requisition or obtain a man's release from prison. Recently, his uncle, the Governor-General of Rheims, had issued a savage proclamation, decreeing a state of siege and the death penalty for anyone attempting to help the enemy by acting as a spy, giving false information to the German troops, destroying bridges, or damaging telegraph lines and railway lines. The "enemy", of course, referred to the French, and the people of Sedan were filled with indignation when the huge white notice was pinned up on the door of the German headquarters. It was already bad enough to learn about the German army's latest victories from the garrison's cheers. For each day brought its quota of grief, as the soldiers lit bonfires in the streets, and spent the night drinking and singing, while the people, obliged to be indoors by nine o'clock, could only listen from their darkened houses, overwhelmed by their feeling of uncertainty and the fear of fresh disaster. It was in these circumstances that, towards the middle of October, Herr von Gartlauben showed, for the first time, some measure of consideration. From early morning the city had been experiencing a renewal of hope; there was a rumour that the army of the Loire, on its way to relieve Paris, had met with a great success. But, as so often in the past, the good news had proved to be the prelude to bad; and, by evening, it was learnt that Orléans had fallen to the Bavarians. In the Rue Maqua, some soldiers in a house opposite the factory, thereupon began kicking up such a shindy, that the captain, concerned at seeing how much this was upsetting Gilberte, went over and ordered them to be quiet.

As time went by, Herr von Gartlauben was induced to perform a number of similar services. The Prussian authorities had re-organized the municipal administration, installing a German as Assistant Prefect, but although he himself proved to be comparatively reasonable, this arrangement had not prevented a succession of vexatious incidents. One of the most frequently recurring difficulties between the military authorities and the Municipal Council arose from the requisitioning of vehicles; and there was a tremendous to-do one morning because Delaherche's barouche and pair had not been allowed to draw up outside the Sub-Prefecture. The Mayor himself was arrested, and both he and Delaherche would have been hauled off to the citadel, had it not been for Herr von Gartlauben's intervention, who quickly succeeded in smoothing matters out. On another occasion, it was thanks to him that the city obtained a reprieve, after being sentenced to a fine of thirty thousand francs for a so-called delay in rebuilding the Villette Bridge, which had been destroyed by the Prussians. But it was following the surrender of Metz that Delaherche became specially indebted to his guest. To the people of Sedan, the terrible news had come like a bolt from the blue, the final destruction of all their hopes, and during the ensuing week, the city was once again overrun by troops, swarming in from Metz; the army of the Crown Prince Frederick Charles on its way to the Loire, General Manteuffel making for Amiens and Rouens, and the other army corps that had been sent to reinforce the army besieging Paris. For several days, every house

434

in the place was packed with soldiers, the butchers' and bakers' shops were cleaned out, and the streets were full of the smell of damp, greasy wool, like that left behind by a great flock of sheep. The only place in the city that was spared this influx of human cattle was the factory in the Rue Maqua; thanks to the friendly efforts of the captain, it was set aside as a billet for a few decently behaved officers.

Thus Delaherche had gradually come to abandon his attitude of cold aloofness. Whereas the majority of bourgeois households avoided all unnecessary contact with the officers billeted upon them, he, with his sociable nature and continual need for company and conversation, had found it difficult to sustain this stand-offish attitude; and his huge, silent house, with everyone living separate lives in a state of watchful hostility, became an increasing burden to him. One day, therefore, happening to meet von Gartlauben on the staircase, he decided to thank him for all he had done for them. And, from that moment, the two men gradually fell into the habit of exchanging a few words whenever they met, with the result that the Prussian found himself one evening sitting in the merchant's study, in front of a blazing fire, smoking a cigar and amicably discussing the latest news. For the first fortnight, Gilberte did not put in an appearance, and the captain pretended to be unaware of her existence, although, at the slightest sound, he would glance swiftly in the direction of her room. He did everything he could to avoid the impression of being a "conqueror", adopted a free and easy manner, and was always ready to laugh about the more ridiculous demands of his countrymen. For instance, when one day a coffin and a bandage were commandeered, he treated it as a joke. And, for the rest, whether it was a question of coal, oil, milk, sugar, butter, bread, meat, not to mention clothing, stoves, lamps, or any of the other necessities of life, he merely shrugged his shoulders. Damn it all, what could you expect? Of course it was a nuisance, he even agreed that they expected too much; but, after all, this was war, and even if you were in enemy territory, you still had to live. Delaherche, who was exasperated by these incessant requisitions, was prepared to discuss them quite frankly, and every evening examined them in detail, as though he was going over the household accounts. There was one occasion, however, when the discussion became heated : this was the question of a million francs levy, imposed by the Prussian Prefect of Rethel on the Department of the Ardennes, on the pretext of compensation for the losses caused

435

by the French navy and the expulsion of Germans domiciled in France. Sedan's share of this sum amounted to forty-two thousand francs, and Delaherche was at pains to make his guest realize how iniquitous this was, considering the exceptional position of the city as a result of what it had already suffered. Still, the upshot of this discussion was that they were on even better terms than before, for Delaherche was delighted by the flow of his own confused eloquence, while the Prussian was satisfied that he had behaved with truly Parisian urbanity.

One evening while they were talking, Gilberte came into the room with her usual air of heedless gaiety. She stopped short, pretending to be taken aback. Von Gartlauben sprang to his feet, and almost immediately withdrew. The following evening, however, finding Gilberte already installed, he took his usual place beside the fire. This proved to be the first of many pleasant evenings, and the fact that they were spent in the study, and not in the drawing room, represented a subtle distinction. Later on, even when the young woman consented to play for him, and he adored music, she would simply go into the neighbouring drawing-room by herself and leave the door open. In that bitter winter, with great oak logs from the Ardennes burning brightly in the high fireplace, tea would be brought in towards ten o'clock, and in the agreeable warmth of the huge room, they would go on chatting. And before long it was obvious that Herr von Gartlauben had fallen madly in love with this smiling young woman, who was flirting with him, just as she used to at Charleville with Captain Beaudoin's friends. He took more pains with his personal appearance, behaved with exaggerated gallantry and, desperately anxious not to be taken for a barbarian, some vulgar woman-chaser, he was content with the slightest favour.

Thus, in the great dark house in the Rue Maqua, life proceeded on two different levels. At meal-times, Edmond, looking like a wounded Cherubino, responded to Delaherche's endless chatter with monosyllables, blushing if Gilberte so much as asked him to pass the salt, and, in the evenings, Herr von Gartlauben sat in the study listening, with a rapturous expression, to the young woman playing Mozart sonatas, while the room in which Colonel de Vineuil and Madame Delaherche spent their time, with its drawn blinds and permanently lighted lamp, remained as silent as the grave. December had buried the city in snow, and the piercing cold seemed to stifle the disheartening news. After General Ducrot's

436

defeat at Champigny, and the loss of Orléans, the only hope that remained was that France might become a land of avengers, of exterminators, and swallow up its conquerors. If only it would snow harder, if only the frost would split open the ground so that it became a vast grave for the entire German army! But, for Madame Delaherche, there was a new cause for grief. One evening, while her son was away in Belgium on business, as she was passing Gilberte's room, she heard voices and the sound of stifled kisses, mixed with laughter. Rushing to her own room, she was aghast at what she suspected : it could only be the Prussian officer. She had already noticed the surreptitious glances that passed between them, but this was the final shame! Oh, this woman whom her son had brought into his home against her advice, this pleasure-loving creature, whom she had already saved once, by remaining silent at the time of Captain Beaudoin's death! And now the same thing was happening again, only, this time, how much more infamous! What was she to do? To allow such a monster to remain under her roof was impossible. The thought of it intensified the unhappiness of being shut away from the world, and for days she endured a terrible sense of conflict. And now, when she entered the colonel's room, and he saw her more sombre than ever, sitting there for hours, speechless, her eyes full of tears, he felt convinced that France must have suffered yet another defeat.

It was in the midst of all this that, one morning, Henriette arrived in the Rue Maqua, hoping to interest the Delaherches in the fate of her uncle Fouchard. Knowing that everyone was talking about Gilberte's dominating influence over von Gartlauben, she was somewhat disconcerted, therefore, when the first person she met was Madame Delaherche, on her way upstairs to visit the colonel, for she felt obliged to explain the purpose of her visit.

"Oh, Madame, it would be so kind of you if you could do something about it . . .! My uncle is in a terribly difficult situation, there's even talk of him being sent to Germany."

Despite her affection for her, there was anger in the old lady's voice, as she replied :

"But I'm in no position to do anything, child. . . . It's no use appealing to me. . . ." Then, seeing how upset Henriette was, she went on : "You've come at the worst possible time, my son is off to Brussels this evening. . . . Besides, he's as powerless as I am. . . . It's my daughter-in-law you should speak to; for her, nothing is impossible!"

And she turned away, leaving Henriette standing there speechless, convinced that she had arrived in the middle of a family
quarrel. On the previous day, Madame Delaherche had made up
her mind to tell her son everything before his departure for
Belgium, where he was going in order to buy a large amount of
coal, with a view to getting his looms started again. She was determined to prevent any recurrence of this shameful business during
his absence. She was therefore waiting to speak to him until she
could be quite sure that he was not going to put off his journey
yet again, as he had been doing for the past week. It would mean
the end of everything, the Prussian dismissed, the wife turned out
of the house and her name publicly denounced, which is what
people had threatened to do if any Frenchwoman gave herself to
a German.

When she saw Henriette, Gilberte gave a cry of joy.

"Oh, how lovely to see you . . .! It seems ages since you were
here. What with all these wretched goings-on, I feel as though I
was getting old!"

She drew her into her room, and made her sit beside her on the
couch.

"You must stay and have lunch, but first of all, you and I will
have a chat. You must have lots of things to tell me . . .! I know
you've had no news of poor Maurice. I'm so sorry for him. Just
fancy, being in Paris, without gas or firewood, perhaps without
food . . .! And what about this fellow you've been nursing, this
friend of your brother's? You see, a little bird's been talking to
me. . . . So it's him you've come about?"

Henriette was too upset to answer immediately. In fact, wasn't
it really on Jean's account that she was here? To try to ensure that,
once her uncle was released, nothing would happen to her dear
invalid? It embarrassed her to hear Gilberte talk about him, and
she was afraid to mention the real motive for her visit, for the
thought of Gilberte using her sordid influence on his behalf was
repugnant to her.

"Come, now," Gilberte insisted spitefully. "It's this fellow you
need help about, isn't it?"

And when Henriette, feeling herself driven into a corner, at last
began to tell her about Fouchard's arrest, she went on :

"Why, of course it is! I'm not an utter fool, my dear. I was
talking about him only this morning . . .! Indeed, it's just as well
you're here. We must do something about your uncle at once, for,

438

from all I hear, things aren't going too well for him . . . they intend to make an example of him!"

"Yes, it's true," Henriette continued, hesitantly. "I did think you might be able to advise me, that there might perhaps be something you could do. . . ."

Gilberte laughed gaily.

"Why, you silly, I'll get your uncle released in no time! Haven't you heard we've got a Prussian captain in the house, who does just what I tell him. . . . He simply can't refuse me a thing . . . !"

She laughed louder than ever, naïvely delighting in the power of her charms, and, seizing her friend's hand, kissed her. But Henriette, filled with uneasiness, tormented by the thought that this amounted to an admission of guilt, could find no words to thank her. Yet how serene she remained, how frankly pleased with herself!

"Leave it to me, and I'll send you home happy."

When they went into the dining-room, Henriette could not get over Edmond's delicate good looks. She had not met him before, and he enchanted her like some charming toy. Could this young lad really have taken part in the fighting, and been wounded in the arm? The legend of his courage added to his attraction, and, throughout the meal, Delaherche, who had welcomed Henriette like a man delighted to see a fresh face, never stopped praising his secretary, who, he declared, was as efficient and well-behaved as he was handsome. And as the four of them sat there, eating their lunch of cutlets and baked potatoes, in this pleasant dining-room, she felt herself gradually yielding to the atmosphere of cheerful intimacy.

"I suppose you've come to ask us if we can do anything about old Fouchard?" Delaherche went on. "Unfortunately I have to go to Belgium this evening. . . . Still, my wife will see to everything. She's quite irresistible, manages to get anything she asks for."

He laughed cheerfully, referring to his wife's influence with the utmost good humour, simply flattered that she exercised such power, and by the glory that this reflected upon himself. Then, changing the subject abruptly, he said:

"By the way, my dear, has Edmond told you about his find?"

"No, what find?" Gilberte demanded gaily, turning a melting gaze upon the young sergeant.

Whereupon the latter, blushing with pleasure, exclaimed:

"Heavens, madame, nothing really . . . it's simply that that lace you were talking about, for trimming your mauve dressing-gown. . . . Yesterday, I was lucky enough to find five yards of

Bruges point, quite lovely, and very cheap. The shopkeeper will be here presently to show it to you."

She was so enchanted she could have kissed him.

"Oh, how sweet of you! I shall have to find some way of rewarding you!"

Then, as the maid handed round a jar of foie gras, bought in Belgium, the conversation turned, by way of the fish that were dying of poison in the River Meuse, to the subject of the plague, which threatened to break out as soon as it started to thaw. Already in November, one or two cases of the epidemic had been diagnosed. The six thousand francs that had been spent upon cleaning up the town, burning all the haversacks and cartridge pouches and everything else that might harbour infection, had proved to be unavailing : it had done nothing to prevent the whole surrounding countryside from being filled with a nauseating stench whenever the weather was at all damp, as a result of the thousands of corpses buried there, beneath only a few inches of soil. Every field was full of graves, and the odour of putrefaction seeped out through the cracks in the ground. And now, only the other day, it had been discovered that the Meuse was another source of infection, despite the fact that twelve hundred horses' bodies had been fished out of it. It was generally assumed that all the human bodies had already been removed from the river, when a gamekeeper, noticing a number of white objects lying at a depth of five or six feet, which he at first took to be stones, discovered that they were, in fact, layers of human corpses, so badly mangled that they had not floated to the surface. These had been lying beneath the water for more than four months, caught in the weeds. Arms, legs and heads had been raised with hooks; occasionally a hand would be broken off merely by the strength of the current, and borne away; and the stirring up of the water caused great bubbles of gas to rise to the surface, where they burst, filling the air with a poisonous stench.

"It's a good thing it's freezing," remarked Delaherche. "But, as soon as it thaws, the whole place must be thoroughly cleaned up and everything disinfected, or there's bound to be an outbreak of plague."

And as his wife laughingly begged him to talk about something more agreeable while they were still eating, he merely concluded : "Hang it all, it's going to put a stop to any fishing for a good long time !"

But they had finished their meal and were drinking coffee, when

440

the parlour-maid announced that Herr von Gartlauben was asking if he might join them for a moment. This caused quite a stir, for it was the first occasion on which he had put in an appearance at this time of the day. Thinking, however, it would be a good opportunity of introducing him to Henriette, Delaherche told her to ask him in at once. And the captain, noticing the presence of another young woman, immediately redoubled his politeness. He even accepted a cup of coffee, which he drank without sugar as he had seen people doing in Paris. And he then announced that the reason he had asked to be received was simply that he wished to inform Madame straight away that he had been successful in obtaining the release of one of her protégés, an unfortunate workman who had been thrown into prison on account of a row with a Prussian soldier.

Gilberte thereupon seized the opportunity to refer to old Fouchard.

"Captain, may I introduce one of my dearest friends. . . . She's the niece of that farmer at Remilly who's been arrested in connection with that business with the guerillas, and she is anxious to obtain your help."

"Ah, yes, that spy affair, the wretched fellow that was found in a sack. . . . It's a serious matter, you know, very serious! I'm afraid there's nothing I can do about it."

"But I should regard it as a great kindness on your part, captain!"

She looked at him appealingly. Whereupon, assuming a blissful expression and bowing gallantly, he assured her that he would be delighted to do what he could.

"I shall be extremely grateful, sir," Henriette said hesitatingly, suddenly overcome at the thought of her husband, shot down at Bazeilles.

At that moment Edmond, who had discreetly left the room when the captain came in, now reappeared, and murmured something in Gilberte's ear. She promptly rose from the table, repeated the story of the lace, which the shopkeeper had just brought, and, making her excuses, followed the young man from the room. Whereupon Henriette, finding herself left alone with the two men, withdrew to the window embrasure, while they continued their conversation in loud voices.

"Let me give you a glass of cognac, captain. . . . There's something I want to talk to you about, and knowing how broad-minded you are, I don't propose to beat about the bush. The fact of the

441

matter is, your Prefect is making a great mistake in attempting to extract another forty-two thousand francs from people of Sedan. . . . Just think of all the sacrifices we've been called upon to make, right from the very start! To begin with, even before the battle began, there was the whole French army, already worn out and starving. Then there were all your people, and they were pretty peckish too, I may say. Why, the mere presence of so many troops, with all the requisitions, reparations and other expenses involved, cost us at least a million and a half! And if you reckon as much again for all the ruin and destruction caused by the battle, that makes three million. Then, on top of that, I assess the losses sustained by our industry and commerce at at least another two millions. . . . You see what I mean . . .? Five million francs, provided by a city with only thirteen thousand inhabitants! And now, on some pretext or other, yet another forty-two thousand francs are being demanded. I ask you, is it fair, is it even reasonable?"

Herr von Gartlauben nodded his head, but all he could find to say was:

"Well, there it is, my dear sir! That's war, that's war for you!"

There was a pause, and Henriette, sitting by the window, felt her head beginning to hum with vague, unhappy thoughts that nearly lulled her to sleep, while Delaherche gave his word of honour that Sedan would never have been able to cope with this financial crisis had it not been for the issue of paper money by the Commercial Bank, which had saved the town from disaster.

"Let me give you another glass of cognac, captain," he concluded, quickly broaching another subject.

"It was not the people of France who declared this war, it was the Empire. . . . Yes, the Emperor has greatly disappointed me. We've finished with him for good, we'd rather see the country dismembered. . . . The only man who saw things clearly in July was Monsieur Thiers, and the visits he's at present paying to the capitals of Europe constitute an act of great wisdom and patriotism. He has the good wishes of every sensible person in the country. May he prove successful!"

He ended his speech with a gesture, since to express a desire for peace in front of a Prussian, however sympathetic, would hardly have been decent. But this was precisely what he most ardently desired, like the majority of the old conservative bourgeoisie. Before long, the country would be drained dry of blood and money, and would have to surrender; and, in all the occupied provinces, a sullen bitterness was developing against the stubborn resistance of Paris. He therefore added, in a lower tone of voice, referring to Gambetta's impassioned proclamations :

"No, no, we don't want any truck with these crazy madmen. It would be sheer massacre. . . . For my part, I stand by Thiers, and his demand for elections; and, as for their Republic, it's not that that worries me, by God. We'll manage with it somehow, till we get something better."

With the greatest politeness, Herr von Gartlauben kept nodding his head in approval, repeating again and again :

"True enough, true enough. . . ."

Henriette, who was beginning to feel more and more uneasy, could sit there no longer. Without knowing precisely why, she was filled with anger, and longed to be gone; and presently she got up, and went off to look for Gilberte. But, on entering her room, she was amazed to see her friend lying on the sofa, overcome with emotion and weeping bitterly.

"Whatever's the matter? What's happened?"

At first, Gilberte did not answer, but went on crying, her cheeks flushed with embarrassment. Presently, however, when Henriette held out her arms, she flung herself into them, stammering :

"Oh, if only you knew, my dear. . . . I can hardly bring myself to tell you. . . . But you're the only person I can turn to, the only one who can perhaps help me. . . ."

And, trembling violently, she went on :

"Edmond was here with me, when who should come in but Madame Delaherche, she actually saw us. . . ."

"But what were you doing?"

"He had his arms round me, and was kissing me. . . ."

And, still clinging to Henriette, she confessed everything.

"Oh, don't think too hardly of me, my dear, I couldn't bear it . . .! I know I promised you I'd never do such things again, but you've seen Edmond . . . so brave, so handsome! And then, just think of it, the poor young fellow, wounded, ill, with no one to turn to! Besides, he's always been so poor, his family sacrificed everything to keep him at school. . . . I tell you, I simply couldn't refuse him."

Henriette listened to her in bewilderment, scarcely able to conceal her astonishment.

"What? You mean to say it was the little sergeant . . .? But, my dear, everybody assumes it's the Prussian you're in love with!"

At this, Gilberte leapt to her feet, protesting, drying her eyes.

"The Prussian? Oh, good God, no! He's frightful, I can't bear him. What do they take me for? How on earth could anyone believe I'd be guilty of such infamy? No, no, never. . . . I'd rather be dead!"

For a moment, the feeling of revulsion suddenly made her serious, transfigured by a kind of sad, scornful beauty. Then her mood changed abruptly, and as her coquettish gaiety once more gained the upper hand she broke into laughter.

"Oh, I admit . . . of course I amuse myself with him. He simply adores me. I only have to look at him, and he'll do anything I ask him to. . . . If only you knew what fun it is, teasing the huge creature, with that ridiculous expression on his face, as though he was convinced I'm in love with him."

"But that's playing with fire," Henriette said gravely.

"Why? Where's the danger? When he finds out that he's getting no further, the worst he can do is to lose his temper and go away. . . . But he never *will* find out. You just don't know him. He's one of those men that women can go as far as they please with, without the slightest risk. That's something I can always tell, you know. He's much too vain, he'd never admit I'd made a fool of him. All he'll get out of me are pleasant memories, and the consolation of being able to say to himself that he always behaved perfectly correctly, like a gallant gentleman who's accustomed to living in Paris."

And she added gaily:

"Meanwhile, he's going to arrange for your uncle Fouchard to be set free, and all he'll get for his pains is a nice cup of tea, poured out by my own fair hands."

But all of a sudden, remembering how she had been caught, her fears revived and the tears once more started to her eyes.

"Heavens, I was forgetting all about Madame Delaherche. What d'you think she'll do? She's never liked me, and she's quite capable of telling my husband everything."

Henriette had now recovered, she wiped away her friend's tears and insisted upon her tidying herself up.

"Listen, my dear, I haven't got the strength to scold you, although I can't forgive what you've done! But I was so upset by all I'd heard about you and the Prussian, it sounded so ugly, that upon my word this other business comes as quite a relief. . . . If you'll only keep your head, we'll somehow find a way out."

This was sound advice, especially as Delaherche and his mother came into the room almost immediately. He explained that he had just ordered the carriage to take him to the station, since he had made up his mind to catch the train for Brussels that evening. He had therefore come to say goodbye. Then, turning to Henriette, he said:

"You can put your mind at rest. Before he went, Herr von Gartlauben promised me he would take up your uncle's case, and although I shan't be here, my wife will see to everything."

As Madame Delaherche entered the room, Gilberte's eyes never left her, and her heart was constricted with fear. Was she going to tell her son what she had seen, and try to stop him leaving? Standing erect in the doorway, the old lady's gaze returned that of her daughter-in-law's, but stern though she was, she too must have experienced the same feeling of relief that had made Henriette tolerant. After all, since it had been with this young man, a Frenchman who had fought bravely, why shouldn't she forgive her, as she had previously done in the case of Captain Beaudoin? Her eyes softened, and she looked away. Though her son would not be here, Edmond would protect his wife from the Prussian. She even smiled slightly, she, who had not known a moment's happiness since the good news from Coulmiers.

"Goodbye, my dear," she said, as she kissed Delaherche. "Settle your business, and come back to us as soon as you can."

And, turning away, she walked slowly across the landing, towards the silent room where the colonel sat, staring vacantly into the shadows that lay beyond the pale circle of light from the lamp.

That evening, Henriette returned to Remilly and, three days later, she had the satisfaction of seeing her uncle calmly walk into the house as though he had just got back from concluding a deal in the village. He sat down and ate some bread and cheese. Then he replied to all her questions, without the least sign of haste, like a man who had never known what it was to be afraid. Why had they kept him in prison? He'd done nothing wrong. After all it wasn't he who had killed the Prussian. All he had said to the authorities was:

"Search the place if you like. I know nothing about it."

And since they had no proof, either against him or against the mayor, they had had to let them go. But his sly, mocking peasant's eyes gleamed, and he sat there, silently enjoying the pleasure of having got the better of those filthy bastards, whom, in any case,

445

he was beginning to get fed up with, now they'd started complaining about the quality of his meat.

As December drew to an end, Jean longed to be off. His leg was now completely healed, and the doctor declared that he was fit to fight. To Henriette, this came as a great blow, though she did her best to hide it. Since the disastrous battle of Champigny, no news had reached them from Paris. They had merely heard that Maurice's regiment, after a terrible bombardment, had lost a great many men. Then, once more, the endless silence had fallen again, without any letters, without even a message, although they knew of families at Raucourt and Sedan who had managed to obtain news by roundabout means. But what worried them most of all was the fear that Maurice might be dead. The silence of the great city, gripped in the embrace of the besieging army, had become for them, waiting in anguish, the silence of the grave. They had lost all hope of finding out what was going on, and when Jean told her that he had finally decided to leave, Henriette had stifled her grief, murmuring to herself :

"Oh my God, this is the end; now I shall be all alone !"

What Jean intended to do, was to join the army of the North, which General Faidherbe had recently succeeded in recruiting. Since General von Manteuffel's army corps had pushed on to Dieppe, this army had been left to defend the three Departments that were cut off from the rest of France, Nord, Pas-de-Calais and Somme; so Jean's idea, which he expected would be easy enough to carry out, was simply to get to Bouillon, and from there make his way through Belgium. He knew that the 23rd army corps had just been reformed, from the men who had managed to escape from Sedan and Metz, and he had heard that General Faidherbe had gone over to the offensive. Thus, when news arrived that the French had almost won the indecisive battle of Pont-Noyelle, he fixed his departure for the following Sunday. Again, Dalichamp offered to drive him to Bouillon in his gig. The doctor was a man of inexhaustible courage and kindness. At Raucourt, which was ravaged by typhus brought by the Bavarians, he had patients in every household, in addition to the two hospitals for which he was responsible, one at Raucourt, the other at Remilly. His ardent patriotism, his insistence upon protesting against useless violence, had twice led to his being arrested by the Prussians, and later released. Thus, when he arrived to fetch Jean, he was brimming over with delight at the thought of being able to help yet another victim of Sedan to escape, those "poor, brave fellows" as he called them, whom he looked after, and helped financially. Jean, who had been worrying about the question of money, knowing how hard up Henriette must be, gladly accepted the fifty francs the doctor offered him for his journey.

For the farewell party, old Fouchard really put himself out. He sent Sylvine for two bottles of wine, and insisted upon everybody drinking "Death to the Germans". Having made his pile, and carefully hidden it away, he now regarded himself as a man of some consequence; and feeling much safer now that the guerillas had disappeared from the Dieulet woods, all he wanted was to be allowed to enjoy the forthcoming peace. In a sudden fit of generosity, he had begun paying Prosper wages, hoping to keep him on the farm; though, in any case, Prosper had no intention of leaving. He drank his health, and also wanted to drink Sylvine's, having for a moment thought of marrying her, so sensible was she, and such a good worker. But what was the point? He felt sure she was in no hurry to leave, and would still be there by the time Charlot was grown up and ready to become a soldier. So, having toasted the doctor, Henriette and Jean, he declared:

"Here's to you all! And may everyone do as well for himself as I have!"

Henriette had insisted upon accompanying Jean as far as Sedan. He was in civilian clothes, wearing an overcoat and a bowler hat, lent him by the doctor. It was a bitter cold day, with sunlight glittering on the snow. They had intended to drive straight through the town, but when Jean discovered that his old colonel was still with the Delaherches, he insisted upon paying his respects to him, and at the same time thanking the wool merchant for all his kindness. This was to prove his last experience of unhappiness in that city of mourning and defeat, for when they reached the Rue Maqua, they found the whole household deeply upset. Gilberte was beside herself, Madame Delaherche was weeping silently, and her son, who had just got back from the factory, was profoundly shocked. The colonel had just been found, lying on the floor, dead. In the sheltered room, with the single lamp still burning, the doctor, who had been hurriedly summoned, had been unable to discover the cause of death; the colonel had simply been struck down, and no one knew whence the blow had come. It was not until the following day that someone found part of an old newspaper, that had been used to wrap up a book, which contained an account of the surrender of Metz.

"Just imagine, my dear," Gilberte said to Henriette, "when Herr von Gartlauben came downstairs just now, he took off his hat as he passed the room where my uncle's body is lying. . . . Edmond saw him. Don't you think it was very considerate of him?"

Hitherto, Jean had never so much as thought of kissing Henriette. Before climbing up into the gig beside the doctor, he was determined to thank her for all she had done for him, for the way she had looked after him like a sister. But unable to find anything to say, and choking with tears, he simply took her in his arms and kissed her. And so flustered was she that she returned his kiss. As the gig set off, he looked back over his shoulder, and they waved to one another, calling out in faltering tones :

"Goodbye, goodbye."

That night, back at Remilly, Henriette was on duty at the hospital, and during the long vigil she was again overcome with a fit of weeping. And there she sat, with clasped hands, sobbing bitterly, trying to stifle her grief.

448

VII

FOLLOWING the battle of Sedan, both German armies had renewed their headlong advance upon Paris; the army of the Meuse, following the valley of the Marne, reached the North of the city, while the army of the Crown Prince of Prussia, after crossing the Seine at Villeneuve-Saint-Georges, passed to the South, and made for Versailles. And on that warm September morning, when General Ducrot, in command of the recently formed 14th Corps, decided to attack the latter, Maurice, who was encamped with his new regiment, the 115th, in the woods to the left of Meudon, only received the order to attack when defeat was already certain. A few shells had been enough to create terrible panic in a battalion of Zouaves, which consisted almost entirely of new recruits, and quickly spread to the rest of the troops, resulting in such a frantic stampede that the fleeing army was driven back behind the fortifications of Paris, where it caused tremendous alarm. All positions in front of the forts in the South were lost; and, that same evening, the last link with the rest of France, the telegraph line along the Western Railway, was broken. Paris was cut off from the rest of the world.

For Maurice, this was a day of terrible sadness. Had the Germans been bold enough they might have spent that night in the Place Carrousel. But, being an essentially cautious people, and having committed themselves to a classic siege, they had already worked out the exact lines of the blockade : to the North, the army of the Meuse was to form one cordon, from Croissy to the Marne, passing through Épinay, the other, consisting of the third army, stretched from Chennevières to Châtillon and Bougival, while the high command, King William, Bismarck and General von Moltke, reigned at Versailles. This huge blockade, which no one had believed possible, was an accomplished fact; and Paris, with its surround of eight and a half leagues of fortifications, including fifteen forts and six detached redoubts, was one vast prison. And all the defending army consisted of was the 13th Corps, which General Vinoy had

449

managed to save, and the 14th, still in course of formation under the leadership of General Ducrot, between them amounting to eighty thousand men; to which must be added fourteen thousand marines, fifteen thousand volunteers and a hundred and fifteen thousand Mobile Guards, not to mention the three hundred thousand National Guards, divided up between the nine sectors of the fortifications. Although the total number was considerable, there was a marked shortage of disciplined and seasoned troops. Men were still being equipped and drilled, Paris was becoming one huge military camp. Preparations for her defence went on ceaselessly, all the main roads were cut, the houses in the fortified zone were demolished, two hundred large calibre guns and two thousand five hundred smaller ones were brought into action, while still more were being cast – a whole arsenal being created almost out of nothing, thanks to the patriotic leadership of the Minister Dorian. When, after the collapse of negotiations at Ferrières, Jules Favre announced Bismarck's demands – the cession of Alsace, the imprisonment of the Strasbourg garrison and an indemnity of three thousand million francs – there was an outburst of anger, and the continuation of the war was proclaimed to be a necessary condition for France's existence; even if there was no hope of victory, Paris must be defended in order that the country could go on living.

One Sunday, towards the end of September, when Maurice was sent on fatigue to the far side of the town, the streets and squares he passed through filled him with new hope. Ever since the defeat of Châtillon, it seemed as though men's hearts had been rising to meet the demands of the situation. Paris, where he had once found it so hard to enjoy himself, so close was it to the ultimate infamy, now appeared to be filled with a gay, simple courage, prepared to accept every sacrifice. Uniforms were to be seen on all sides, even those who were least committed wore the cap of the National Guard. Like a gigantic clock, whose mainspring has broken, all public life, industry, commerce, business had come to an abrupt halt; and all that remained was the passionate determination to win, the one subject that everyone was talking about, that stirred men's hearts and minds at public meetings, during spells of guard duty, among the endless crowds blocking the pavements.

The illusions men shared swept them off their feet, created a tension in which they were prepared for the most generous-hearted acts. Already there were signs of neurosis, of a feverish contagion that exaggerated both fear and confidence, exposing the masses to

450

every kind of influence. A scene Maurice witnessed in the Rue des Martyrs moved him deeply : a furious mob hurling itself upon a house, because a lamp had been left burning all night in one of its upper windows, an obvious signal to the Prussians at Bellevue, above Paris. Scared middle-class people would spend their whole time on the roof, spying on their neighbours. The previous day there had even been an attempt to drown some wretched man in one of the Tuileries fountains, simply because he had been seen studying a map of the town, spread out on the bench beside him.

In the general collapse of all his previous beliefs, even such an independent-minded man as Maurice was afflicted by this disease of suspicion. He was no longer despondent, as he had been during the panic caused by the defeat at Châtillon, anxiously wondering whether the French army would ever recover its will to fight : the various attacks that had been launched – on September 30, against Hay and Chevilly; on October 13, when the Mobile Guards had seized Bagneux; and finally, on October 21, when his own regiment had temporarily captured the park at Malmaison – had completely restored his faith, and the flame of hope, which a single spark had been enough to set alight, now burned brightly. Though the Prussians had succeeded in holding off these attacks, the army had nevertheless fought bravely, it could still win. But what worried Maurice was the way this great city, haunted by the fear of treachery yet desperately longing for victory, continually swung between the extremes of wildest hope and utter discouragement. Might not General Trochu and General Ducrot, like the Emperor and Marshal MacMahon before them, turn out to be feeble leaders, the unconscious architects of defeat? The same movement that had swept away the Empire, the impatience of violent men to seize power in order to save France, was now threatening to bring down the Government of National Defence. Already Jules Favre and the other members of the Government were more unpopular than Napoleon III's ex-Ministers. Since they were not prepared to fight the Prussians, let them make way for others, for revolutionaries who were sure to win, by calling a mass uprising, by giving a free hand to the inventors, who were proposing to mine the suburbs or to annihilate the enemy with streams of liquid fire.

Thus, on the eve of October 31, Maurice was torn between his dreams and his doubts. He was ready to accept fantasies that previously would only have made him laugh. And why not? Was there any limit to the crime and stupidity he saw around him? Wasn't it possible, in a world so shaken by calamity, that some miracle might occur?

Ever since he had first learned of the defeat at Froeschwiller, back there at Mulhouse, bitterness had been accumulating in his heart. Sedan was a scarcely healed wound that the slightest reverse was enough to re-open; he still felt the shock of each new defeat, his body weakened, his head swimming from the long succession of days without food and nights without sleep, overwhelmed by this nightmare existence, no longer knowing whether he was alive or dead; and the thought that all this suffering might lead to a still greater, an irremediable, disaster haunted him, transforming an educated man into a creature of instinct, at the mercy of every transient emotion. Anything, even destruction, extermination, would be better than to give up a single penny of France's wealth, an inch of her territory! The gradual change of view, which, at the first sign of defeat, had destroyed the appeal of the Napoleonic legend, his sentimental Bonapartism, which he had derived from his grandfather's epic tales, was almost complete. Already he was shedding his sensible republican theories, and turning to revolutionary violence, to a belief in the necessity of terror as the only way to get rid of the traitors and incompetents who were ruining the country. Thus, on October 31, he sided with the revolutionaries as a result of the news of one disaster after another which was pouring in : the loss of Le Bourget, which the journalist volunteers of the Press had so heroically captured on the night of the 27-28th; the arrival of Thiers at Versailles after his fruitless journey to the capitals of Europe, from which he had returned, it was said, to treat in the name of Napoleon III; and, finally, the surrender of Metz, another and more shameful Sedan of which Thiers had brought definite confirmation amid all the wild rumours that were already going round. And the following day, when he heard what had happened at the Hôtel de Ville – how the revolutionaries had momentarily been victorious, with the members of the Government of National Defence held prisoner until four o'clock in the morning and only saved by a sudden change of heart on the part of the masses, who, although at first disgusted with them, had then become worried at the thought of the insurrection being victorious – he regretted the abortive attempt to set up the Commune, which might perhaps have led to victory with its calls to arms and its "the country in danger", all those traditional cries of a free people determined not to die. Thiers had even been afraid to enter Paris, and when negotiations were broken off, the people had been on the point of illuminating the city.

Then came November, a period of feverish impatience, with a number of small engagements in which Maurice took no part. He was now stationed near Saint-Ouen, whence he escaped at every possible opportunity, driven by his insatiable longing for news. Like him, Paris, too, waited anxiously. With the election of mayors in all the arrondissements, political passions seemed to have calmed down; though the fact that nearly all those who were elected belonged to extremist parties was a warning of what was to come. And what Paris was waiting for during this period of calm was the mass sortie there had been so much talk about, which was to lead to victory and deliverance. Now, once again, no one doubted the outcome : the Prussians would be overthrown and trampled in the dust. Preparations were made in the Gennevilliers peninsula, the spot regarded as being the most suitable for a sortie. Then, one morning, the people suddenly went mad with joy at the good news of Coulmiers, Orléans recaptured, the army of the Loire on the march, and already encamped at Étampes, it was said. This changed everything, all they had to do now was to join hands across the River Marne. The military forces had been reorganized, forming three armies : one consisting of the battalions of the National Guard, under General Clément Thomas; another formed out of the 13th and 14th Army Corps, reinforced by the pick of all the other troops, which General Ducrot was to lead in the main attack; and the third, the army of the reserve, made up entirely of Mobile Guards, commanded by General Vinoy. On November 28, as Maurice settled down for the night with the 115th regiment, in the Bois de Vincennes, he felt complete confidence. All three army corps of the new second army were there, and everyone was saying that, next day, they were to establish contact with the army of the Loire at Fontainebleau. Then, all of a sudden, there was a succession of mishaps : on top of all the usual mistakes, an unexpected flood prevented them from throwing a pontoon bridge across the river, and their movements were delayed by tiresome orders. The following night, the 115th was one of the first regiments to cross the river; and, by six o'clock, Maurice had entered the village of Champigny, in spite of a terrible bombardment. He was firing like a madman, so that his rifle burnt his fingers despite the terrible cold. From the moment they set out, his one desire was to keep advancing, on and on, until they joined up with the army from the provinces. But, beyond Champigny, they found themselves held up by the high walls surrounding the parks of Coeuilly and Villiers, walls that extended for a quarter of a mile and which the Prussians had transformed into an impregnable fortress. This was the point at which their courage broke down. From then on, there was nothing but hesitation and retreat : the 3rd Corps was delayed; the 1st and 2nd, already brought to a standstill, defended Champigny for two days, but, on the night of December 2, having to abandon it after a sterile victory. That night the whole army returned to its camp in the Bois de Vincennes, which was white with frost; and Maurice, his feet numb with cold, pressed his face to the frozen ground and burst into tears.

Oh, the sad and dismal days that followed the failure of this tremendous effort ! The mass break-out they had been preparing for so long, the irresistible thrust that was to deliver Paris, had failed; and, three days later, a letter from General von Moltke announced that the army of the Loire had been defeated and Orléans recaptured. The ring of invading troops had been drawn tighter, so that now it became impossible to break it. Yet, in its passionate grief, Paris seemed to have discovered a new determination to resist. The danger of famine was becoming more severe. Since the middle of October food had been rationed : by December, of all the herds of cattle and sheep that had been put to graze in the Bois de Bologne not a single animal was left, and they had begun slaughtering horses. Supplies of wheat, later on eked out by requisitioning, were enough for four months, but when the stocks of flour gave out, mills had to be built in the railway stations, and coal and wood, also in short supply, had to be kept for grinding corn, baking bread and manufacturing weapons. And Paris, without gas, lit only by an occasional oil lamp, Paris shivering beneath its mantle of snow, Paris with its rations of black bread and horse meat, nevertheless still went on hoping, still talked about Faidherbe in the North, Chanzy on the Loire, Bourbaki in the East, as though by some miracle they were soon to achieve victory beneath the very walls of the city. Outside the butchers and bakers, the long queues waiting in the snow still managed to raise a smile now and then at news of some imaginary victory. After the despondency of each defeat, illusions revived, burned even higher amongst the crowds of people, hallucinated by suffering and hunger. In the Place du Château d'Eau, a soldier who talked of surrendering, was almost massacred by the passers-by. And while the disheartened army, feeling that the end was near, called for peace, the people still demanded a mass break-out, a tremendous sortie that was to include women and even children, and would hurl itself upon the Prussians and sweep everything before it.

Maurice held aloof from his companions, more and more disgusted at being in the army, since it kept him at Mont Valérien, idle and useless. He seized upon every excuse to get away, to return to the city where his heart belonged, for it was only when he was with the crowds, whose hopes he was determined to share, that he felt at home. Often he would go to watch the balloons, which set out every couple of days from the Gare du Nord carrying pigeons and despatches. They rose into the sad winter sky and disappeared; and if the wind drove them towards Germany the crowds looked on with sinking hearts. Many of them must have been lost. Twice, he himself had written to his sister Henriette, without being able to discover whether she received his letters. His sister and Jean seemed so remote now, out there in the big world, utterly cut off, that he rarely thought of them; it was as though they belonged to some other existence, while he himself was too absorbed in a perpetual struggle between despair and exaltation. Then, as the first days of January drew on, the German shelling of houses on the left bank became a new reason for anger. He had come to attribute the Prussians' slow advance to humanitarian reasons, whereas in fact they were simply due to organizational difficulties. But now that a shell had killed two little girls at the Val-de-Grâce, he was filled with savage scorn for these barbarians, who were prepared to murder children and threatened to burn down the museums and libraries. After a day or two of terror, however, the shelling only served to revive the stubborn heroism of the Parisians.

After the setback at Champigny there was one more inneffectual attempt to break out, at Le Bourget; and that evening, when, with the big guns battering away at the forts, the plateau of Avron had to be evacuated, Maurice shared the violent anger that spread throughout the city. The growing wave of unpopularity, threatening to sweep away Trochu and the Government of National Defence, reached such a point that they were forced to undertake a supreme and futile effort. Why did they still refuse to throw into the firing line the three hundred thousand National Guards, who were continually offering, demanding, to share the common danger? What the people wanted was the massive sortie they had called for at the start, that surging tide of people, bursting through the city's banks

455

and overwhelming the Prussians. Despite the certainty of yet another defeat, the Government had to give in to this demand for a display of gallantry; but, to keep down the losses, it was content to employ, in addition to the regular army, only the fifty-nine battalions of the National Guard that had already been mobilized. And, on the eve of January 19, the whole town was in holiday mood : vast crowds lined the Boulevards and the Champs-Élysées to watch the regiments march past, with bands playing and singing patriotic songs. Women and children ran alongside them, men stood on benches and cheered them on to victory. Then, next day, the entire population surged towards the Arc de Triomphe, crazed with hope, as the news arrived during the morning that Montretout had been captured. Epic stories were told of the National Guards' irresistible spirit : the Prussians had been overwhelmed, Versailles itself was about to fall. But as night fell, and news of the inevitable setback spread, how terrible was the dismay ! Though the troops on the left had occupied Montretout, the centre column, after forcing its way through the outer wall of the park of Buzenval, had flung itself in vain against the second, inner wall. It had started to thaw, a fine, persistent rain turned the roads to mud, and the guns, those same guns that Paris had bought by subscription, could not be brought up. On the right, Ducrot's column, having been thrown in too late, remained in the rear. The whole enterprise began to lose its impetus, and General Trochu gave the order for a general retreat. Montretout and Saint-Cloud were in turn abandoned, the Prussians set fire to them, and, as darkness fell, all that could be seen was this immense conflagration.

This time, even Maurice felt that it was all over. For four hours, under a murderous stream of fire from the Prussian trenches, he had been with the National Guard in the Buzenval park; and afterwards, when he got back to Paris, he could not speak too highly of their courage. They had, indeed, displayed the greatest gallantry. Wasn't it obvious, therefore, that the defeat was due to the stupidity or treachery of their leaders? In the Rue de Rivoli, crowds were shouting : "Down with Trochu ! Long live the Commune !" This was a revival of the revolutionary mood, a new surge of left-wing opinion, so disturbing to the Government of National Defence that, in an attempt to save itself, it insisted upon General Trochu's dismissal and replaced him by General Vinoy. The same day, at a public meeting at Bellevue which he attended, Maurice heard the speakers renewing the demand for a mass attack. He knew it was a crazy idea, yet such determination made his heart beat faster. When everything else fails, a miracle still remains possible.

Another week dragged by. Though on the point of death, Paris still uttered no complaint. The shops remained closed, not a carriage was to be seen in the deserted streets. Forty thousand horses had been killed for food, and by now dogs, cats, even rats were fetching a high price. Since the stocks of wheat had run out, the bread, made of rice and oats, was black, sticky and hard to digest; and outside the bakers' shops, long queues waited interminably to obtain their ration of three hundred grammes. Oh, the agony of this endless waiting, the wretched women shivering in the rain as they stood in icy mud, all the heroic suffering of a great city that refused to surrender! The death rate had increased threefold, the theatres had been turned into hospitals. From dusk onwards even the wealthiest parts of the city were sunk in darkness, enclosed in gloomy silence, like the outskirts of a town ravaged by the plague. And in this silence and darkness, the only sound to be heard was the endless din of the bombardment, the only light to be seen the flashes from the guns in the winter sky.

Then, all of a sudden, on January 29, Paris heard that Jules Favre had already begun negotiations with Bismarck for an armistice; and, simultaneously, that there was only sufficient bread for ten days, scarcely time to revictual the town. This meant that a savage capitulation would be imposed. Paris, dumbfounded by the facts, which it was now hearing for the first time, was shocked into silence. On the 28th, at midnight, the bombardment ceased. Then, next day, after the Germans had occupied the forts, Maurice was sent back with his regiment to the camp at Montrouge, inside the fortifications. For him, this was the beginning of a strange kind of existence, feverish and idle. Discipline was greatly relaxed, and the soldiers, split up into groups, lounged about, waiting to be sent home. Maurice felt utterly bewildered, he was in a state of nervous anxiety that quickly turned to anger at the slightest thing. He studied the revolutionary papers avidly; and the three weeks' armistice, which had been concluded for the sole purpose of enabling France to elect an Assembly that would be prepared to make peace, seemed to him to be a trap, the final betrayal. Even if Paris was forced to capitulate, he supported Gambetta, who was for carying on the war on the Loire and in the North. The defeat of the army of the East, which had been forced to cross over into Switzerland, enraged him. But even more maddening were the

457

elections : just as he had foreseen, the cowardly provinces, exasperated by the resistance put up by Paris, were in favour of peace and the restoration of the monarchy under the protection of the Prussian artillery. After the first meetings of the Assembly at Bordeaux, Thiers, who had been elected in twenty-six Departments and acclaimed as leader of the Government, was in his eyes the villain of the piece, both a liar and a criminal. And his anger was in no way assuaged by what followed. The peace that was concluded by the pro-monarchist Assembly seemed to him infamous, the mere thought of the harsh conditions it imposed infuriated him : an indemnity of five hundred million francs, and Metz and Alsace ceded to Germany, to become an open wound through which the country's blood and gold would endlessly pour.

Eventually, towards the end of February, Maurice decided to desert. Under the Peace Treaty, all soldiers stationed in Paris were to be disarmed and sent home. But his mind was made up : the thought of leaving this glorious city, which only hunger had been able to force to its knees, seemed to him the final ignominy; and he simply disappeared, renting a small furnished room in a six-storey house in the Rue des Orties, high above Les Moulins, looking out over the endless sea of roofs that stretched from the Tuileries to the Bastille. A friend in the Faculty of Law lent him a hundred francs; once he had settled in, he would join a battalion of the National Guard, and the thirty sous he would be paid would be enough to live on. The very thought of leading a selfish, placid existence in the country horrified him. Even the letters he received from his sister Henriette, to whom he had written directly the armistice was signed, in which she begged him to come to Remilly for a rest, angered him. He refused, but promised to come later on, when the Prussians had gone.

So Maurice idled away his life in a state of growing disgust. He was no longer suffering from hunger, and it was a treat to be able to eat white bread again. Paris, where there had never been any shortage of brandy or wine, was now living on the fat of the land, in a state of continual intoxication. Yet it remained a prison, with German sentries at the gates, and complicated formalities that made it impossible to get out. Life was still far from normal, for there was still no work and business was at a standstill; the whole population hung about with nothing to do, gradually going to pieces in the bright spring sunshine. During the siege, there had at least been military service to exhaust your body and occupy your mind;

whereas now, everyone lived in complete idleness, cut off from the rest of the world. Like everyone else, Maurice lounged about from morning till night, in an atmosphere poisoned with the seeds of madness; the unlimited freedom everyone enjoyed eventually became a source of infection. He read the papers and frequented public meetings, sometimes shrugging his shoulders at the more fantastic propositions, but nevertheless returning home haunted by thoughts of violence, prepared to act desperately in defence of what he believed to be truth and justice. And in his little room, looking out over the town, he still dreamed of victory, still told himself that, so long as the peace was not actually signed, France and the Republic could still be saved.

The Prussians were supposed to enter Paris on March 1, but so widespread was the anger and bitterness that it was impossible to attend a public meeting without hearing the Assembly, Thiers and all the other men of September 4 condemned, for having inflicted this ultimate shame on the heroic city. One evening, Maurice himself was so carried away that he made a speech, insisting that everyone in Paris should be prepared to die on the ramparts rather than admit a single Prussian. The people, distraught by months of hunger and misery, and now enduring the nightmare of unemployment and torn with suspicion of the ghosts they themselves had summoned up, welcomed the idea of insurrection, for which they were openly organizing. It was one of those moral crises that always tend to occur after a long siege, when the patriotism that had inflamed men's souls has been disappointed, and is transformed into a blind desire for vengeance and destruction. The Central Committee of the National Guard had protested against any attempt to disarm them. A great demonstration was organized in the Place de la Bastille, with red flags and angry speeches, in the course of which a wretched policeman was tied to a plank, thrown into a canal and stoned to death. Two days later, during the night of February 26, Maurice, who had been awoken by the sound of the tocsin, watched bands of men and women dragging guns along the Batignolles Boulevard; and, as soon as he heard that the people were taking them to the Place Wagram in order to prevent the Assembly from handing them over to the Prussians, he too went out and helped pull one of them to safety. There were one hundred and seventy of them, and as there were no horses, the people dragged them along with ropes, handling them with their bare hands, with the furious energy of a horde of savages saving their gods. And when March 1 arrived, the Prussians had to be content with being allowed to occupy the Champs-Élysées for a single day, drawn up behind barricades, while the people of Paris never so much as stirred, but left the streets empty and the houses shut up.

During the next two weeks, heedless of the passage of time, Maurice awaited the vast, vague events that he felt sure were about to take place. Peace had finally been concluded, and on March 20 the Assembly was to be installed at Versailles; yet nevertheless he could not believe that it was all over, he remained convinced that some terrible vengeance was about to strike. On the 18th, as he was getting dressed, a letter arrived from Henriette, in which she again implored him to join them at Remilly, threatening to set out for Paris herself if he delayed much longer. She went on to speak of Jean, describing how, after leaving them at the end of December to join the army of the North, he had fallen seriously ill, and had been taken to a hospital in Belgium; and now, only a week ago, he had written to say that, weak as he was, he intended to get to Paris to play his part. She ended her letter by begging her brother to let her have news of Jean as soon as he turned up. Having read it, Maurice found himself musing about his beloved sister, and Jean, his adopted brother, thinking how remote they both were from the tempest of ideas that endlessly pursued him! Then, as Henriette had warned him she had been unable to give Jean his address, he decided to go in search of him that very day. But scarcely had he left the house when, in the Rue Saint-Honoré, he met two men belonging to his battalion, who told him what had been going on during the night at Montmartre, and all three of them set off as fast as they could go.

For Maurice, March 18 was a thrilling experience, though afterwards he found it difficult to remember at all clearly what he had done and said. To begin with, he remembered hurrying through the streets, furious at the attempt that had been made to disarm Paris by recapturing the Montmartre guns. It was clear that, during the two days since his return from Bourdeaux, Thiers had been planning this surprise attack in order that the Assembly at Versailles might be emboldened to proclaim the restoration of the monarchy. Then he recalled being in Montmartre, about nine o'clock, and hearing stirring stories of the victory; the furtive arrival of the soldiers, their fortunate delay in finding horses, which had given the National Guards time to arm themselves, then the troops not daring to shoot down women and children, firing their rifles in the air and fraternizing with the people. Then he remembered wandering about the city, and realizing that, by midday, almost without a fight, the Commune had taken over Paris; Thiers and his ministers fleeing from the Ministry of Foreign Affairs, where they had held a meeting; the whole Government setting out for Versailles post-haste; the army of thirty thousand men hurriedly forced to evacuate Paris, leaving behind them more than five thousand, scattered about the streets. Then, about half-past five, at the corner of a street on the outer Boulevard, he saw himself once again, standing with a group of excited people, listening, without a trace of indignation, to an account of how two generals, Lecomte and Clément Thomas, had been brutally murdered. After all, why should he worry? He remembered the generals at Sedan, mere playboys and incompetents, so that one more or less could scarcely matter! And he spent the rest of the day in the same state of exhilaration, while the insurrection, which the streets themselves seemed to have decreed, grew and spread, until by ten o'clock that night, as its final triumph, it delivered the Hôtel de Ville into the hands of the Central Committee, astonished to find themselves installed.

But there was one memory that remained very distinct in Maurice's mind: his sudden meeting with Jean. The latter had been in Paris for the past three days, having arrived without a penny in his pocket, still pale and exhausted from the fever that had kept him in a Brussels hospital for two months. Luckily for him, he had run into an officer from his old regiment, the 106th, Captain Ravaud, who had immediately signed him up in his own company, the newly formed 124th regiment, and given him back his corporal's stripes. Now, he had just left the Prince Eugene barracks with his squad, and was taking them over to the left bank where the army had been ordered to assemble, when they were stopped by a crowd of people on the Boulevard Saint-Martin. There was a good deal of shouting, and someone suggested disarming them. And as Jean was calmly explaining that he was simply doing his duty, and harming no one, there was a sudden cry of surprise, and Maurice rushed up to him and flung his arms around him.

"Why, if it isn't you . . .! Only this morning I got a letter from Henriette and ever since I've been meaning to make enquiries about you at the War Office."

Jean's eyes filled with tears of joy.

461

"Well, well, well, my dear fellow! What a treat to set eyes on you again . . .! I've been looking for you all over the place, but what a hope in this bloody great town!"

The crowd was still threatening, and Maurice turned to face them:

"Citizens, just give me a chance to talk to them. They're a decent bunch of fellows, and I'll be personally responsible for them."

Then, seizing his friend's hands, he muttered under his breath: "That's right, isn't it? You're on our side?"

Jean looked at him in complete amazement:

"What on earth d'you mean, on your side?"

For a moment, he listened to him raving against the Government and the army, reminding him of all they had been through together, explaining that now they were the masters they were going to punish the incompetents and cowards, and save the Republic. But the more Jean tried to understand, the more his expression revealed his growing dismay.

"Oh no, my lad, if that's what you're up to, I'm off. . . . The captain ordered me to take my men to Vaugirard, so that's where I'm going, and nobody's going to stop me!" And he added with a laugh: "You'd do better to come with us!"

But with an angry gesture Maurice drew back, and for a moment they faced one another: the one carried away by the wave of madness that was sweeping through Paris, the other strong in all the commonsense and healthy ignorance of a man who had grown up in the countryside, accustomed to thrift and hard work. Yet they were still friends, they were still united by strong bonds of affection, and when a sudden surge of the crowd forced them apart they were both utterly dismayed. A regiment, the 79th, had emerged from a side turning and forced the crowd back on to the pavement. There was another outburst of shouting, but this time no one dared to bar the way, for the soldiers were accompanied by officers. And Jean's squad was allowed to follow in their wake, without further interference.

"So long, Jean!"

"So long, Maurice!"

They raised their hands and waved to one another, accepting their separation as an act of fate, yet nevertheless both deeply moved by their brief encounter.

During the next few days Maurice soon forgot about it, borne along by the swift stream of events. On the 19th, Paris awoke to

462

find itself without a government, more surprised than alarmed to discover that, during the night, the army, the public services and the ministries had all left for Versailles in sudden panic; and in the brilliant sunshine of that March Sunday, the people of Paris calmly sauntered about the streets, looking at the barricades. The large white notices, signed by the Central Committee and calling for elections, seemed sensible enough, though they were surprised to find that none of the signatories was known to them. In those first days of the Commune, Paris, embittered by all it had been through and haunted by suspicion, was firmly opposed to Versailles. Moreover, there was complete anarchy: the mayors at odds with the Central Committee, the former making futile attempts at reconciliation, while the latter, as yet not fully assured of support from the federated National Guards, was content to claim its municipal rights. It was the shots fired against a peaceful demonstration in the Place Vendôme, and the blood of the victims reddening the streets, that really roused the first shock of terror throughout the city. And when the triumphant rising of the people finally took over all the ministries and public offices, Versailles was seized with such fear and anger that the Government hastily assembled enough troops to repulse the expected attack. The best regiments of the armies of the North and of the Loire were hurriedly summoned; in less than ten days' time, some eighty thousand men had arrived and, so quickly was confidence restored, that by April 2 hostilities had begun, and Puteaux and Courbevoie were captured from the National Guard by two divisions.

It was only next day that Maurice, setting out with his battalion to capture Versailles, suddenly remembered how sad Jean had looked as he waved goodbye. The attack by the army of Versailles had shocked and angered the National Guard. Three columns of them, some fifty thousand men, had set off next morning, by way of Bougival and Meudon, to seize the monarchist Assembly and the murderer Thiers. It was like the mass sortie that had so frequently been called for during the siege, and Maurice could not help wondering whether, next time he saw Jean, it might not be amongst those fallen in battle. But defeat came all too soon. His own battalion had scarcely reached the plateau of Bergères, when all of a sudden a succession of shells, coming from Mont Valérien, burst amongst them. The effect was stupefying: some of them thought that the fort was still occupied by their side, others maintained that the commander had undertaken not to fire. The men were seized with crazy terror, whole battalions broke and fled headlong back to Paris, while the head of the column, caught in a flanking movement by General Vinoy, was massacred at Rueil.

Maurice, who had managed to escape the slaughter, was now more than ever consumed with hatred for this so-called government of law and order, which, though defeated by the Prussians at every encounter, was bold enough when it came to fighting against Paris. For the German armies were still there, from Saint-Denis to Charenton, enjoying the spectacle of a people's downfall! Consequently, in his present grimly destructive mood, he approved the violent measures that were taken now, the erection of barricades in the streets and squares, the seizing of the archbishop, priests and ex-officials as hostages. Already both sides were beginning to commit atrocities : Versailles was shooting prisoners, while Paris decreed that for every prisoner shot three hostages would be executed; and, in the general collapse of decency, what little reason still remained to Maurice was swept away by the prevailing anger. To him, the Commune appeared as the avenger of all the shame they had endured, a liberator armed with fire and sword. This was not something he had thought out at all clearly, but simply the memory of things he had once read, of free, triumphant cities, of federations of wealthy provinces imposing order upon society. If Paris won the day, he saw her as an aureoled figure rebuilding a France of freedom and justice, creating a new society, after sweeping away the last rotten remnants of the old. True, when the results of the elections were declared, and he saw the names of the members of the Commune, he was somewhat taken aback by the extraordinary mixture of moderates, revolutionaries and socialists of every kind, to whom this noble task had been entrusted. He knew several of these men, and regarded them as being pretty second-rate. Weren't even the best of them bound to be overwhelmed in the confusion of such conflicting views? Yet, on the day the Commune was solemnly constituted, in the square outside the Hôtel de Ville, with cannon thundering and red flags streaming in the wind, he forgot all this, uplifted once again by a surge of boundless hope.

Throughout April, Maurice was in action in the Neuilly neighbourhood. The swift advance of spring had brought out the lilac; and, after fighting all day in gardens bursting into leaf, the National Guardsmen would return at night with bunches of flowers stuck in the barrels of their rifles. By this time, so many troops had been assembled at Versailles that two new armies had been created, one under the command of Marshal MacMahon, the other, the reserve, under General Vinoy. As for the Commune, it had mobilized almost a hundred thousand National Guards, and almost as many militia men; though no more than fifty thousand actually took part in the fighting. And, every day, the Versailles army's plan of attack became clearer: after taking Neuilly, they had occupied Bécon, then Asnières, in order to shorten their front line; for they intended to enter the city by the Point-du-Jour, once they had breached the fortifications by a converging bombardment from Mont Valérien and the fortress of Issy. Mont Valérien was already in their hands, so that all their efforts were aimed at capturing the fortress of Issy, making use of the earthworks already thrown up by the Prussians. By the middle of April, the bombardment was continuous. At Levallois and Neuilly sharpshooters kept up sudden bursts of fire throughout the twenty-four hours. Powerful guns, mounted on armoured railway-trucks, moved backwards and forwards, shelling Asnières from the other side of Levallois. But at Vauves, and especially at Issy, so tremendous was the gunfire that every window in Paris trembled from the noise, as in the worst days of the siege. And, on May 9, when the fortress of Issy finally fell into the hands of the Versailles army, the Commune was faced by certain defeat and, in a moment of panic, resorted to desperate measures.

Recalling the history of the great Revolution, Maurice supported the setting up of a Committee of Public Safety, for if they still hoped to save the country surely the time had come to act with energy? Of all the acts of violence, only one filled him with secret dismay, the destruction of the Vendôme column; and even then he felt it to be a childish weakness, due to his memories of his grandfather's stories of Marengo, Austerlitz, Iéna, Eylau, Friedland, Wagram, Moscow, those epic tales that still made him tremble. But when they burnt down the house of Thiers, the murderer, when they seized hostages as a guarantee and a threat, these surely were just reprisals for the increasing savagery with which Versailles was bombarding Paris, destroying houses and killing women? And the black rage of destruction burned ever stronger in him, the nearer the end of his dream approached. If the idea of justice and vengeance was to be drowned in blood, then let the earth open, let it be transformed in one of those cosmic upheavals through which life has been renewed! Better that Paris should be destroyed, devoured in the flames of a vast holocaust, than that she should return to the vice and misery of the old order, ruined by injustice! And he conjured up yet another grim nightmare, the giant city reduced to ashes, both banks a desert of smoking ruins, healed by fire, by some nameless catastrophe from which a new race of people would emerge. And his fevered imagination was further stimulated by the stories that were current : parts of the town undermined, the catacombs filled with gunpowder and connected by electric wires that would explode them simultaneously; huge supplies of inflammable material, especially paraffin, that would turn the streets and squares into seas of flame. The Commune had sworn an oath, if the men of Versailles succeeded in entering the town, not one of them would get beyond the barricades, for the streets would open up, the buildings crash to the ground, and a whole world be consumed in the flames of Paris.

And the fact that Maurice indulged this crazy dream was a sign of his growing dissatisfaction with the Commune itself. He despaired of its leaders, felt it to be inept, torn apart by conflicting forces, becoming more and more incoherent and stupid the more the dangers of its position increased. Of all the social reforms it had promised, it had not succeeded in putting a single one into effect; and it was already clear that it would leave behind no lasting achievement. But what most troubled him was the rivalry that existed between the individual members of the Committee, their nagging suspicion of one another. A number of the more moderate members no longer attended its meetings. Others acted merely in response to events, feared the possibility of a dictatorship, had reached the point where groups from the revolutionary Assemblies were quarrelling amongst themselves, in order to save the country. One after the other, Cluseret, Dombrowski, Rossel became suspect. Delescluze, the civilian delegate to the Council of War, was unable to achieve anything on his own, despite his great authority. And, as a result, the great social undertaking they had embarked upon was falling apart, collapsing, as their growing isolation reduced its initiators to impotence and despair.

Throughout Paris, terror was gaining ground. The people, at first furious with Versailles and still suffering from the siege, were now beginning to detach themselves from the Commune. Compulsory conscription, a decree calling up all men under forty, had annoyed many people, and led to mass evasion; men were leaving the city in disguise, with false Alsatian passports, or lowering themselves over the walls at night, with ropes and ladder. The wealthy bourgeoisie had disappeared long ago. All the mills and factories were closed.

With no trade and no work, the people, condemned to idleness, anxiously awaited the inevitable outcome. All they had to live on was the National Guardsmen's pay, the miserable pittance, now paid from the funds requisitioned from the Bank, which had been one of the original causes of the uprising. Whole districts stood empty, with shops closed and shuttered houses. In the bright May sunshine, all one saw in the deserted streets were the grim funeral processions of National Guardsmen killed in action, the hearses, unaccompanied by priests, draped with red flags and followed by crowds carrying wreaths of everlasting flowers. The churches, closed during the daytime, were at night used as club rooms. Only revolutionary papers appeared, all the rest had been suppressed. It meant the end of Paris, of that unhappy city, which still, as the Republican capital, maintained its hostility to the Assembly, but where fear of the Commune, and a longing to be delivered from it, were steadily increasing, as terrifying tales of its doings spread – daily arrests of hostages, barrels of gunpowder in the sewers, with men with torches, so it was said, awaiting the signal.

Maurice, who in the past had never touched alcohol, found himself caught up in the craze for drinking. Now, during a spell of duty in the front line, or even if he had to spend the night on guard, he would accept a tot of brandy; and if he drank a second it would go to his head. This chronic drunkenness, a legacy of the first siege but aggravated by the second, was becoming an epidemic; and the people, short of food but with plenty of wine and spirits, all too easily drank themselves silly. On May 21, a Sunday, Maurice came home drunk for the first time in his life. He had spent the day at Neuilly, acting as a sniper, and in an attempt to overcome his exhaustion had been drinking with his mates. How he managed to get back to the Rue des Orties he never knew, it must have been by instinct. But as soon as he got upstairs, he flung himself on the bed, worn out and semi-conscious; and it was not until next day, when the sun was already high in the sky, that he was woken by the sound of drums and bugles. During the night, the Versailles troops had found the Point-du-Jour gate unguarded, and entered the city without difficulty.

Hastily throwing on his clothes, and slinging his rifle over his shoulder, he hurried downstairs, and, when he reached the Hôtel de Ville, found a group of scared National Guards, whose account of what had happened during the night was so confused that at first he had difficulty in following what they were saying. For nearly

467

a fortnight, the bombardment from the fortress of Issy, as well as from the batteries at Montretout and Mont Valérien, had been so heavy that the gate at Saint-Cloud had become untenable; and the assault was fixed for the following day. Then, towards five o'clock in the evening, a passer-by, happening to notice that the gate was unguarded, had simply beckoned to the Versailles troops, whose trenches were barely fifty yards away. Without more ado, two companies belonging to the 37th regiment of the line had entered the city. Shortly afterwards they were followed by the whole of the 4th Corps, under the command of General Douay, and the stream of invaders continued all night without interruption. By seven o'clock the Vergé division had reached the Grenelle bridge, and was pushing on towards the Trocadero. By nine, General Clinchant had taken Passy and La Muette. At three o'clock next morning the 1st Corps was bivouacking in the Bois de Bologne; while, about the same time, the Bruat division was crossing the Seine to capture the Sèvres gate and so facilitate the entry of the 2nd Corps, which, under the command of General de Cissey, was to occupy the Grenelle district an hour later. Thus, by the morning of the 22nd, the army of Versailles was in control of the Trocadero and La Muette on the right bank, and of Grenelle on the left; and all this had taken place to the utter bewilderment of the Commune, who, in their anger and confusion, were convinced that defeat was inevitable.

This was Maurice's first thought, directly he realized what had happened : the end had come, there was nothing for it but to get killed. But the peals of the tocsin rang out, the drums beat louder, women and children began strengthening the barricades, and soon the streets were full of National Guardsmen, hastily summoned, hurrying to their battle stations. By midday, hope had begun to revive in the hearts of the devoted soldiers of the Commune, who felt confident of victory as soon as they realized that the Versailles troops had scarcely advanced at all. This army, which they had feared would reach the Tuileries in a couple of hours, had learnt from its defeats; it was behaving with extreme caution, exaggerating the tactics it had been taught so harshly by the Prussians. At the Hôtel de Ville, the Committee of Public Safety, with Delecluze as delegate of the armed forces, was organizing the defence. It was said to have rejected a final offer of conciliation with disdain. This had raised men's spirits, once again it seemed certain that Paris would triumph; and in the state of hatred, intensified by lies and atrocities, that inflamed the hearts of both armies, it was clear that the resistance would be as savage as the attack would be implacable. Maurice spent the whole of that day in the neighbourhood of the Champs de Mars and the Invalides, slowly retreating from street to street, firing as he went. Unable to find his own battalion, he was fighting alongside unknown Communards, who had taken him with them to the left bank without his realizing it. At four o'clock, they were defending a barricade that shut off the Rue de l'Université from the Esplanade; and they did not give it up until dusk, when they discovered that the Bruat division had succeeded in capturing the Corps Legislative, by filtering along the Quay. They only just escaped being taken prisoner, and reached the Rue de Lille with great difficulty, by making a long detour through the Rue Saint-Dominique and the Rue de Bellechasse. By the time it was dark, the Versailles army occupied a line running from the Porte de Vanves, through the Corps Législative, the Élysées Palace, the church of Saint-Augustin and the Saint-Lazare station, to the Port d'Asnières.

The next day, Tuesday the 23rd, was warm and sunny, yet it was the most terrible Maurice had ever spent. The two or three hundred National Guards he was with, belonging to different battalions, still held the whole district from the Quay to the Rue Saint-Dominique. Most of them had spent the night in the gardens of the large houses in the Rue de Lille, and he himself had slept soundly on the lawn outside the palace of the Legion of Honour. He expected that, as soon as it was daylight, the enemy would emerge from the Corps Législative and drive them back behind the barricades in the Rue du Bac, but several hours went by without any sign of attack. Occasionally there were intermittent bursts of firing. The Versailles troops were carrying out their plan with extreme caution, determined to avoid a frontal attack on the formidable fortress that the insurgents had established at the Tuileries, in order to effect a two-pronged advance along the ramparts, first of all capturing Montmartre and the Observatoire, then doubling back so as to enclose all the central districts in one vast net. Towards two o'clock in the afternoon Maurice heard that the tricolour was flying over Montmartre : attacked by three army corps at once, whose men clambered up the hill on the North and West, along the three streets, Lepic, des Saules and Mont-Cenis, the important battery at Moulin de la Galette had been taken; and the victors swept down upon Paris, capturing the Place Saint-

Georges, Notre Dame de Lorette, the town hall in the Rue Drouot and the new Opera, one after the other; while on the left bank, a flanking movement, setting out from Montparnasse cemetery, seized the Place d'Enfer and the Horse Market. As news of the army's rapid progress spread, it aroused a shock of fear and anger. What! Montmartre surrendered after only a couple of hours' fighting! Montmartre, the glorious and impregnable fortress, the citadel of the insurrection! Maurice soon noticed that the ranks of the National Guard were thinning out, comrades slipping away without a word, hurrying to take off their uniforms and get washed for fear of reprisals. It was rumoured that their flank would be turned at the Croix-Rouge, where the enemy was already preparing to attack. The barricades in the Rue Martignac and the Rue de Bellechasse had been overcome, and more and more "red-pants" were to be seen at the far end of the Rue de Lille. Soon only Maurice and some fifty or so others were left, determined, resolute men, prepared to give their lives, but not until they had killed as many of the enemy as possible, those Versailles soldiers, who treated the National Guards as thieves and shot their prisoners. During the last twenty-four hours, hatred between the two sides had grown more savage; now it was war to the death, between the revolutionaries, dying for their ideal, and the army, stuffed with reactionary notions and annoyed at having to go on fighting.

By five o'clock, as Maurice and his comrades were steadily withdrawing behind the barricades in the Rue du Bac, retreating from door to door along the Rue de Lille, firing as they went, he suddenly saw a huge cloud of black smoke issuing from an open window in the palace of the Legion of Honour. This was the first act of incendiarism; and, swept away by an insane surge of anger, it filled him with savage joy. The hour had struck, let the whole city become a mighty pyre, whose flames would purify the world! But almost immediately he was shocked by a sudden apparition : five or six men, fleeing precipitately from the building, led by a great tall fellow whom he recognized as Chouteau, his one-time comrade in the 106th. He had run into him once or twice before, and knew that he had managed to get promoted and was now attached to the staff of some armchair general or other. He remembered a story he had heard, about Chouteau being installed in the palace of the Legion of Honour, where he kept a mistress and spent the whole time boozing, sprawling about on the luxurious beds in his boots and amusing himself by firing at the mirrors with his revolver. It was even said that his mistress, on the pretext of going shopping, used to set out each morning in the state carriage, stacked with bundles of stolen linen, clocks and furniture. So, now that he saw him running away with a can of paraffin in his hand, Maurice felt all his beliefs suddenly shaken by a hideous suspicion that it might be men like this who were in fact the instruments of the terror!

The hours dragged on, and though he went on fighting, he had lost all heart for the struggle and only longed for death. If he had been misled, at least he could redeem his mistake with his blood! The barricade in the Rue du Bac was strongly built, consisting of sandbags and barrels of earth, behind a deep ditch. He was defending it with at most a dozen other National Guardsmen, who crouched behind it, picking off every soldier who showed himself. And, when darkness fell, he was still there, gradually exhausting his ammunition, stubbornly refusing to give in. He could see the dense clouds of smoke billowing up from the Legion of Honour building, drifting across the street in the fading daylight. Another fire broke out in a nearby house. Presently one of his comrades came over to warn him that the soldiers, afraid of making a frontal attack, were forcing a way through the surrounding houses and gardens, demolishing the walls with pick-axes. This must be the end, at any moment now the soldiers would be here. And, sure enough, just then a burst of firing broke out from an upstairs window, and he caught sight of Chouteau and his men, hurrying frantically from house to house with their cans of paraffin and lighted torches. Half an hour later the whole square was alight, and Maurice, still crouching behind the barricades, took advantage of the brilliant light to shoot down any soldiers rash enough to show themselves in the street.

How long he went on firing he never knew. He had lost all sense of time and place, it might have been nine o'clock, ten perhaps. The whole hateful business made him feel sick, like the foul after-taste of wine when one has drunk too much. The heat from the burning houses was beginning to be unbearable, the air was stifling. The square, shut off by heaps of cobblestones, was like an entrenched position, protected by the burning houses. But wasn't this precisely what they had been ordered to do? To start fires wherever they were driven out from the barricades, to burn down every inch of Paris that they were forced to surrender? Only too well, he knew that the houses in the Rue du Bac were not the only ones that were on fire. Behind him, the whole sky was lit up by a huge red glow, and he could hear a distant roar as though the entire city was ablaze. To the right, all along the Seine, more gigantic fires were beginning to break out. It was a long time since he had seen Chouteau, running for dear life to escape the bullets. Even the bravest of his comrades were beginning to slip away, one by one, afraid of being completely cut off. And at last, when he was the only one left, crouching between two sandbags, still firing his rifle, the soldiers, who had been making their way through the courtyards and gardens, suddenly burst into the Rue du Bac and began to fall back.

In the excitement of this tremendous struggle, two whole days had elapsed without Maurice having given a thought to Jean. Similarly, Jean, who, after getting back to his regiment, had been sent to reinforce the Bruat division, had almost forgotten his encounter with Maurice. The day before he had been in action at the Champs de Mars and outside the Invalides. Today, it was not until midday that he left the Place du Palais Bourbon to clear away the barricades from the neighbourhood, as far as the Rue des Saint-Pères. Usually so easy-going, he was getting more and more fed up with this fratricidal war, when the one thing all his comrades wanted was to take it easy after all these months of fighting. The prisoners who had been sent back from Germany to rejoin the army were always railing against Paris; and then the stories he heard about the atrocities committed by the Commune infuriated him, offending his respect for property, his sense of law and order. He still remained the typical level-headed peasant, wanting peace so that he could get to work again and earn a living. But what made him most annoyed, wounding his deepest susceptibilities, was the incendiarism. To set fire to houses and burn down palaces just because you were being beaten, that was really too much! Only thieves and rogues would dream of such a thing! And now, already upset at the thought of yesterday's firing squads, he could no longer control himself, he was striking out wildly, yelling at the top of his voice, his eyes starting out of his head.

Forcing his way into the Rue du Bac at the head of his squad, and seeing nobody there, his first thought was that the barricade must have been deserted. Then something moved, and there, lying between two sandbags, was a Communard, still firing at the men in the Rue de Lille. In a surge of passionate anger he ran forward, and with a thrust of his bayonet, nailed the man to the barricade. There had been no time for Maurice to move. Throwing back his head, he uttered a loud cry, and suddenly in the blinding light from the burning houses, they recognized one another.

"Oh no, Jean – not you!"

He was ready for death, had even longed for it desperately. But to die at the hands of his brother, that was too much, that made a bitter mockery of death!

"No, no! It can't be you, not my friend Jean!"

Thunderstruck, completely brought to his senses, Jean gazed down at him. They were alone, the rest of the soldiers had hurried off in pursuit of fugitives. All around, the fires burned higher, the windows spewed forth sheets of crimson flame, and from the inside of the houses came the sound of blazing timbers crashing to the ground. Jean flung himself down beside his friend, sobbing, stroking his face, trying to lift him up in the hope that it might be possible to save him even now.

"Oh, my poor boy! My poor, poor boy!"

VIII

WHEN, after innumerable delays, the train from Sedan finally reached the station of Saint-Denis about nine o'clock, the sky to the South was already lit up by a huge red glow as if the whole of Paris was in flames. As darkness settled down it grew brighter, until gradually it filled the entire horizon, dyeing the clouds blood red as they drifted away to the East.

Henriette was the first passenger to jump down from the train. She was worried by the flames reflected in the sky, which she had been watching through the window as the train steamed across the darkening fields. In any case, there were Prussian soldiers on duty at the station insisting upon everybody getting out; two of them, standing on the arrival platform, were chanting in their harsh French : "Paris is burning. . . . You can't go any further, everybody out. . . . Paris is on fire, Paris is burning. . . ."

For Henriette this was a terrible setback. Did it mean she had arrived too late? Having had no reply from Maurice to her last two letters, and terribly worried by the increasingly serious news from Paris, she had suddenly made up her mind to leave Remilly. For the past two months, living there with her Uncle Fouchard, she had been growing more and more depressed : the longer Paris continued to hold out, the more exacting and harsh the German occupation forces had become; and now that regiment after regiment of them was being sent back to Germany, the endless streams of soldiers were once again stripping bare both the towns and the countryside. Only that morning, coming downstairs at dawn to catch the train for Sedan, she had found the farmyard full of cavalrymen who had spent the night there, sleeping as best they could, wrapped in their cloaks. Then suddenly a bugle had sounded, they had sprung to their feet without a word, and there they stood, draped in the long folds of their cloaks and so closely packed together that they looked like ghosts who had risen from some battlefield at the sound of the last trump. And now, here at

Saint-Denis, there were more of them, bawling out at the top of their voices:

"Everybody out, we're not going any further. . . . Paris is on fire, Paris is burning. . . ."

Completely bewildered, clutching her little suitcase, Henriette tried to find out what had happened. For the past few days there had been fighting in Paris and the railway had been cut, while the Prussians simply looked on. Determined to continue her journey, and noticing a captain who appeared to be in command, she hurried over to him and said:

"I am trying to find out what's happened to my brother, sir. I'm very worried about him. Couldn't you possibly give me permission to go on to Paris?"

Then, suddenly recognizing the captain, as the light from a gas flare fell on his face, she exclaimed:

"Why, it's you, Otto. . . . Fate must have meant us to meet again. Please, please do what you can to help me!"

It was, indeed, her cousin Otto Gunther, still as correct as ever in his guardsman's uniform, but at first he did not recognize this frail, timid woman, with her pale golden hair and pretty, gentle face hidden beneath her widow's veil. It was only when he noticed the brave, direct look in her eyes that he realized who she was, and acknowledged her with a barely perceptible shrug.

"You know my brother's a soldier," Henriette went on passionately. "He stayed behind in Paris, and I'm afraid he may have been mixed up in all this horrible fighting. . . . I beg you, Otto, help me to continue my journey."

At last, he condescended to speak:

"But, I assure you, there's nothing I can do. Since yesterday, no trains have been running. . . . I think they must have pulled up part of the line. I don't see how I can help you. I haven't got a horse or carriage available. I can't even spare a man to go with you."

She stared at him, so upset by his cold refusal to help her that all she could do was stammer out:

"Oh my God, if *you* won't help me, who else can I turn to?"

Oh, these Prussians, these all-powerful conquerors, who, at a word, could have requisitioned a hundred carriages, produced a thousand horses! Yet there he stood, with his smug, superior air, whose aim

475

was to refuse to get involved in the affairs of their victims, which he probably regarded in any case as dirty, and likely to tarnish his newly won glory.

"Anyway," Henriette went on, trying to speak calmly, "at least you know what's happened. Surely you can tell me that?"

He smiled grimly.

"Why, Paris is in flames. . . . If you come with me, you can see it perfectly."

He turned away and, leaving the station, walked a hundred yards or so down the line, till they came to an iron footbridge. They climbed the narrow staircase, and as they reached the top and stood there clinging to the railing, the huge plain stretched away before them.

"You can see for yourself, Paris is burning. . . ."

It must have been about half-past nine. The crimson glow in the sky was growing stronger. In the East, the last of the blood-red clouds had disappeared, leaving behind a huge arc of darkness, lit up by the distant flames. Now the whole line of the horizon was ablaze, with here and there splashes of brighter red bursting through dense clouds of drifting smoke. It almost looked as though the fires themselves were actually moving, like some great forest blaze with tree after tree catching alight, until the whole of Paris seemed to be one vast bonfire.

"See, over there," Otto exclaimed, "that great dark hump, standing out against the flames, that's Montmartre. . . . To the left of it, at Villette and Belleville, there aren't any fires so far. They must have started them in the wealthiest districts, but they're gaining ground. . . . Look, over there on the right, another one's just begun, a great burst of flame, and clouds of smoke hanging above it. . . . Everywhere you look, they're starting new ones !"

He neither raised his voice nor betrayed the slightest excitement, yet the very calmness of his enjoyment horrified Henriette. How could these Prussians simply watch all this going on? His tranquil, half-smiling expression seemed to her to be an insult, as though he had foreseen this unexampled disaster, had been looking forward to it for a long time. Now, at last, Paris was burning, whereas all the German bombardment had achieved was a few smashed gutters ! Here, at last, was satisfaction for all the bitter resentment he had felt at the long drawn-out siege, the terrible cold, the endless succession of difficulties that Germany was still smarting under.

476

Even the pride he took in the captured provinces, the five milliard francs indemnity, was not comparable with this spectacle of Paris, suddenly gone crazy, setting fire to itself and going up in smoke, on this clear spring evening.

"Of course, it was bound to happen," he added in a lower voice. "More strength to their elbows!"

Faced by the immensity of the catastrophe, Henriette was overwhelmed, choked by a passionate flood of grief. For several minutes she forgot all about her personal unhappiness, carried away by her sense of a whole people's suffering. The thought of this fire consuming human lives, the sight of the city ablaze from end to end, made her cry out involuntarily. Clasping her hands to her breast, she murmured:

"Oh my God, whatever can we have done to deserve such punishment?"

Otto raised his arm in a peremptory gesture. He was about to speak, with all the vehemence of his harsh, military, Bible-quoting puritanism. But, glancing at the young woman beside him, the calm intelligence of her gaze made him change his mind, though his gesture in itself had been enough to betray his feeling of racial hatred, his conviction that he was here in France as a judge, sent by the god of war to chastize a depraved people. Paris was being burnt down as a punishment for centuries of loose living, for the crimes and debauchery committed over the years, and once again Germany would save the world by purging it of the last traces of Latin corruption.

Letting his hand fall to his side, he said simply:

"This must be the end. . . . There's another district on fire, over there, to the left. . . . Look what a huge blaze, it's spreading out like a river of fire."

Appalled, they both fell silent. True enough, sudden bursts of fire kept shooting up, as if from a blast furnace, spreading across the sky in a huge, incandescent tide, emitting dense flames of smoke that hung above the city in a dark, copper-coloured cloud; then, stirred by the breeze, it drifted slowly away into the darkness.

Henriette shuddered, as though waking from a nightmare. Then, overcome with grief at the thought of what her brother must be suffering, she made a last appeal.

"So you won't do anything for me? You refuse to help me get to Paris?"

"What would be the point?" Otto replied with a sweeping gesture

477

that took in the whole horizon. "By tomorrow there will be nothing left but rubble!"

Realizing that there was nothing more to be said, she left him without even saying goodbye, and hurried away, still clutching her little case. But Otto stood there for a long time, slim and motionless in his tight uniform, plunged in darkness, feasting his eyes on the spectacle of Babylon in flames.

As Henriette was leaving the station, she happened to notice a buxom woman who was haggling with a cab driver to take her to Paris, to the Rue de Richelieu; and eventually, so earnestly did she plead, that she agreed to take Henriette along. Throughout the journey, the cabby, a little dark-haired fellow, urged on his horse, but never so much as opened his mouth. The stout lady, however, ran on and on, explaining how, two days ago, after closing her shop, she had come away, leaving behind some valuables, which she had hidden in a wall. And now, having watched the city burning for the past two hours, the only thing she could think of was how to get back and rescue them, even if it meant risking her life. At the city gate, there was only one sleepy sentry on duty, and he allowed them to pass without too much difficulty, especially as the stout lady invented a story about having been to fetch her niece, to help her nurse her husband who had been wounded by the Versailles soldiers. It was only when they found themselves in the streets of the town that their real difficulties began, for many of them were blocked by barricades, and they were obliged to make continual detours. In the end, having got as far as the Boulevard Poissonnière, the cabby refused to take them any further, and the two women had to continue on foot, making their way across the whole district of the Bourse. At first, while they were still near the fortifications, everything had been lit up by the burning houses so that the sky was as bright as day. Now, they were surprised to find how deserted and peaceful this part of the town was, and all they could hear was the distant roar of the flames. As they passed the Bourse, however, an occasional shot rang out, and they crept along, keeping close to the walls of the buildings. Once they reached the Rue de Richelieu, the stout lady was so delighted at finding her shop still intact that she insisted on accompanying her companion as far as the Rue des Orties. In the Rue Saint-Anne, they were delayed for a time by a battalion of National Guardsmen who had just taken over the street, so that by the time Henriette, worn out by all she had been through, finally reached the old house in the Rue des Orties, it was

478

past four o'clock and beginning to grow light. The door was open, and having climbed the dark, narrow staircase, she had to use a ladder, hidden behind the door, to get up to the attic.

Lying between the two sandbags, at the barricade in the Rue du Bac, Maurice had eventually managed to struggle to his knees, and Jean, who thought he had stabbed him to death, was suddenly seized by a desperate hope.

"What, lad, still alive, are you? That's more than I dared hope. Here, hang on a minute, and we'll have a look at you."

He examined the wound carefully by the bright light from the burning houses. The bayonet had passed right through his arm, close to the right shoulder, but unfortunately it had also penetrated his ribs, probably damaging the lung. However, the wounded man could still breathe without too much difficulty, though he could not move his arm.

"Don't get too worked up about it, old man! It's all right by me, I've had about as much as I can take. . . . In any case, you've already done quite enough for me; if it hadn't been for you I'd have pegged out long ago!"

Hearing him speak like this roused Jean to a fresh outburst of grief.

"Will you shut up! Twice you saved me from the Prussians, and that made us quits. Now, when it was my turn, I go and pretty well murder you. . . . Oh, for Christ's sake! I must have been drunk not to recognize you, aye, drunk as a pig. It must be all the blood I've had to drink."

And at the thought of how they had said goodbye to one another at Remilly, wondering whether they would ever see each other again, the tears sprang to his eyes. Had it all been for nothing, then? All those days they'd spent together, without food, without sleep, in constant danger of their lives? Had it simply been the prelude to this monstrous, senseless act? No, no, surely that was impossible!

"Here, do as I say, lad, and I'll pull you through yet."

The first thing to be done was to get him away, for the soldiers were killing all the wounded. As luck would have it, at that moment there was no one about, but there was no time to lose. Swiftly he slit open Maurice's sleeve, and pulled off his tunic. Then he hurriedly bound up the arm, with bandages made from the lining, applied a rough dressing to the wound in his chest, and, with a piece of string he happened to have in his pocket, tied the arm

479

firmly over the wound so as to immobilize that side of his body and prevent a haemorrhage.

"D'you think you can walk?"

"I expect so."

But it would be dangerous for Maurice to be seen like this, in his shirt sleeves. So, with a sudden inspiration, he ran into a nearby street where he had seen a dead soldier, and was soon back with a greatcoat and service cap. Throwing the coat round Maurice's shoulders, he helped him put his sound arm into the left sleeve, set the cap on his head, and exclaimed cheerfully:

"There you are, my boy, that's a lot better! Now you're one of us. . . . I wonder which way we'd better go?"

This wasn't an easy problem: where could he find a safe place to hide? The Versailles troops were searching the houses, shooting down every Communard they caught carrying arms. Besides, neither of them knew anyone in this part of the town, not a soul they could turn to on whom they could rely.

"The best thing would be if I could get home," said Maurice. "It's out of the way, and no one ever goes near it, but it's the other side of the river, in the Rue des Orties."

Desperate, unable to make up his mind, Jean cursed under his breath. It was no good thinking of trying to cross by the Pont Royal; the light from the burning houses was too bright there, and there was a continual exchange of shots from both banks. Besides, it would only take them to the Tuileries, which was already burning, or the Louvre, which was so strongly guarded that it would be impossible to get past.

"That's buggered it! He'll never get across," declared Jean, who knew his way around Paris from having spent six months there after the Italian campaign.

Then, suddenly he had an idea. If only there were still some boats tied up to the steps of the Pont Royal, as there always used to be, it would be worth taking a chance. It wasn't going to be easy, but he did not take long to make up his mind.

"Listen, lad, it's not safe here. We've simply got to get away somehow or other. . . . I shall just have to tell my lieutenant that I got captured by the Communards and then managed to escape!"

He took Maurice by his sound arm, and, half-supporting him, helped him across the Rue du Bac, where the houses were by this time flaring away like huge torches. A shower of burning embers was falling all round them, and so intense was the heat that it

480

scorched the very hair on their faces. Then, as they reached the quay, they were almost blinded for a moment by the brilliant glow that lit up the whole sky on both banks of the Seine.

"They certainly aren't short of candles," grumbled Jean, who would have preferred it to be pitch dark.

And it wasn't until he had got Maurice down the stone steps on the left of the Pont Royal that he began to feel safe, hidden by the great trees that grow at the water's edge. Even so, for the next quarter of an hour, they were worried by the black shadows they could see, moving about on the quay on the opposite side of the river. Suddenly, there was a volley of shots, and they heard somebody cry out, followed by a splash that sent the water spurting high into the air.

"What about spending the night in that shed?" suggested Maurice, pointing to a wooden hut.

"Not on your life! They'd be bound to find us in the morning."

Jean knew what he was about. He had already discovered a flotilla of little boats, but they were chained together. How were they going to get one loose? Eventually, he found an old pair of oars, and managed to smash a padlock; and as soon as he had settled Maurice comfortably in the bows he cautiously cast off and let the current take them, keeping close to the bank, in the shadow of swimming-baths and barges. Neither of them said a word, horrified by the ghastly sight that met their eyes. The further they floated downstream the more terrible it became, and by the time they reached the Pont de Solférino the quays on both sides of the river were in flames.

On the left, it was the Tuileries that was burning. Directly it was dark the Communards had started fires at both ends of the palace, the Pavillon de Flore and the Pavillon de Marsan. By now, the flames were rapidly spreading to the Pavillon de l'Horloge, midway between them, which had been turned into a powder magazine, from the dozens of barrels stacked in the Salle des Maréchaux. Clouds of reddish smoke, pierced by long tongues of flame, poured from the windows of the buildings on either side, and here and there great cracks appeared in the smouldering roof, through which the fire shot up from the furnace raging within. But worst of all was the Pavillon de Flore, where the fire had been started, and which was now ablaze, from the rooms on the ground floor to the topmost turret, and making a tremendous roaring noise. The floor-boards and all the hangings had been drenched with paraffin, with

481

the result that the heat was so intense that one could actually see the railings of the balconies bending and twisting, while the splendid chimneys, with their great sculptured suns, kept crashing into the glowing inferno.

Then, to the right, first came the palace of the Legion of Honour, which had been burning for the last seven hours and was now reduced to a mass of glowing embers; and, beyond that, the palace of the Council of State. Here the conflagration was at its worst, enormous and terrifying, with flames belching from the porticos on both storeys of the huge stone cube. The four ranges of buildings surrounding the great inner courtyard had caught fire simultaneously, and the paraffin, which had been emptied in barrelfuls down the flights of steps at each of the four angles, now formed a blazing river. On the side facing the river, the attic floor was still intact, a line of blackened masonry, with tongues of flame licking at its edges; while the colonnades and entablatures, with their sculptured friezes, stood out in brilliant relief against the blinding light. Such was the surging force of the flames that the whole colossal building, shuddering and groaning on its foundations, had been reduced to little more than the thick outer walls, while the molten lead spurted up from the roof like a volcano. Not far away, the D'Orsay barracks, one wing of which was already burning fiercely, thrust its tall, white column into the air. And yet further on, still more houses were on fire, seven in the Rue du Bac, twenty-two in the Rue de Lille, lighting up the whole sky, so that it looked like an endless sea of blood.

"My God, it's unbelievable!" Jean muttered in a choking voice. "The river itself will catch fire."

And, indeed, beneath the flickering reflections of this mighty conflagration, it almost looked as though the Seine was filled with red-hot coals; and as they drifted slowly downstream, between the flaming palaces, it was like travelling along some unending street in the city of death, whose gutters were filled with molten lava.

"What the hell!" said Maurice, half crazed at the sight of the destruction he had longed for. "Let the whole damned place go up in flames!"

But Jean signed to him to shut up, as though he was afraid that such blasphemy would bring them bad luck. How on earth could someone he loved so much, such an educated, sensitive fellow, have come to hold such ideas? And he rowed harder than ever, for he had left the Pont de Solférino behind, and they were now in a wide exposed stretch of the river. So brilliant was the light that it might have been midday, with the sun shining directly overhead. The smallest details were clearly visible : the swirling patterns of the current, the heaps of gravel on the bank, the trees growing along the quays. The bridges especially, dazzling white, were so clear that one could make out the individual stones; they looked like slender gangways, stretching unharmed above the glittering water. Now and then, amidst the ceaseless roar of the flames, a sudden crash could be heard, and clouds of soot fluttered down, filling the air with a foul stench. But the most appalling thing was the thought that other parts of Paris, far away and out of sight, no longer existed. On both sides of the river the monstrous force of the conflagration had created a black abyss, so that all one could see was a vast, shadowy emptiness, as if the whole of Paris, seized and devoured by the fire, had already disappeared into endless darkness. The very sky was dead, for the flames rose so high that they had put out the stars.

Maurice, still delirious, laughed crazily :

"A fine party they're giving in the Tuileries . . . everywhere lit up, chandeliers ablaze, women dancing. . . . That's the way, keep on dancing till your petticoats catch fire and your hair is alight. . . ."

He waved his arms excitedly, raving about the parties at Sodom and Gomorrah, the music, the flowers, the sensual enjoyment, the palaces vomiting debauchery, the naked bodies illuminated with such thousands of torches that eventually they burst into flames. Suddenly, there was an appalling explosion. The fire at the Tuileries, advancing from either end of the palace, had reached the Salle de Maréchaux, set alight the barrels of gunpowder and blown up the Pavillon de l'Horloge; and an immense plume of flames shot up into the surrounding darkness.

"Bravo ! Bravo !" yelled Maurice, as though this was the final curtain at some monstrous theatrical performance.

Again Jean pleaded with him to keep quiet : it was no good hoping for the worst, if everything was going to be destroyed, they too would perish. His main concern was to get ashore as soon as possible, but he had sufficient foresight to realize that they must get beyond the Pont de la Concorde, beyond the bend in the river, so that they could land at the Quai de la Conférence. And even then, despite the critical position they were in, his innate respect for other people's property made him spend several minutes tying up the boat, rather than let it drift away with the current. His plan

483

was to get to the Rue des Orties by way of the Place de la Concorde and the Rue Saint-Honoré. Leaving Maurice sitting on the bank, he climbed the steps leading up from the quay, but as soon as he saw all the difficulties that lay ahead of them, his misgivings returned. For just here was the Commune's strongest fortress, the terrace of the Tuileries, defended by guns, and the Rue Royale, the Rue Saint-Florentin and the Rue de Rivoli protected by high, solidly built barricades; and this explained the tactics of the Versailles army, which had advanced during the night to form a vast triangle, with its apex in the Place de la Concorde and its base, stretching from the goods yard of the Gare du Nord on the right bank to a point on the fortifications near the Arcueil gate, on the left bank. Then, just before dawn, the Communards evacuated the Tuileries and the barricades, and the army had occupied the district, where more fires were raging, twelve houses at the junction of the Rue Saint-Honoré and the Rue Royal, which had been burning since nine o'clock the previous evening.

By the time he got back to the river bank, Maurice was half asleep, as though dazed by all the excitement.

"I don't mind telling you, it's going to be pretty tough going. . . . D'you reckon you can still manage to walk, lad?"

"Yes, yes, don't worry about that. I'll manage to get there somehow, even if it kills me!"

What he found hardest was climbing the stone steps, but once he reached the quay he set off, walking slowly like a man in his sleep, supported by his companion. Though the sun was not yet up, the glow from the nearby fires lit up the huge square like a livid dawn. And as they made their way across the empty space, the grim sight of devastation that met their eyes was heartbreaking. At the two extremities of the vista across the Place de la Concorde, beyond the bridge and at the top of the Rue Royale, it was just possible to make out the ghosts of the Palais Bourbon and the Madeleine, riddled by gun-fire. The Tuileries terrace had been breached and part of it had collapsed. In the centre of the Place, bullets had pierced the bronze figures on the fountains, and the huge monument of "Lille" lay on the ground, cut in two by a shell, while opposite it the "Strasbourg" monument, hung with black crepe, seemed to be in mourning for the surrounding ruins. Near the obelisk, still upright on its pedestal, an exposed gas pipe had been pierced by a blow from a pick-axe, and the escaping gas, which someone had set alight, burned with a strident hissing noise.

Jean avoided the barricade across the Rue Royale, between the Admiralty building and the Garde-Meuble, for both of them had escaped the fire, and from behind the sandbags and barrels of earth he could hear the loud voices of soldiers. In front there was a ditch, filled with stagnant water, in which floated the body of a National Guardsman, and one could just see, through a gap, the houses in the Rue Saint-Honoré, which were almost burnt out, although fire brigades had now arrived from the suburbs. The trees and news-vendors' kiosks on both sides of the street had been riddled with machine-gun fire; the air was filled with screams, for the firemen had just dug out seven people from one of the houses, who had been buried in the cellar and were badly burnt.

Although the barricade across the Rue de Rivoli was higher and better built, and appeared even more formidable, Jean felt instinctively that it would prove easier to get past. Indeed, as it turned out, it had been completely evacuated, and so far the soldiers had not dared to occupy it. Abandoned guns lay about in confusion, but the only living creature behind this invincible rampart was a lost dog, which made off at their approach. But as Jean hurried on down the Rue Saint-Florentin, doing his best to support Maurice, who was rapidly growing weaker, the one thing he had been dreading happened : they ran smack into a company of the 88th regiment. Rapidly he explained to the officer that his mate had been wounded, and that he was taking him to an ambulance : the greatcoat he had thrown over Maurice's shoulders saved them, they were allowed to continue along the Rue Saint-Honoré, and Jean's heart leapt with joy. As dawn was breaking, there were occasional shots from one of the side streets, for fighting was still going on throughout the district. If they reached the Rue des Frondeurs without any more unlucky encounters, it would be a miracle. They were now moving at such a slow pace that the three or four hundred yards they had to cover seemed interminable, and when they reached the street they found it still occupied by a group of Communards. Fortunately for them, however, the latter thought they were the first of a whole regiment and took to their heels, so that now only the short Rue d'Argenteuil lay between them and the Rue des Orties.

For four hours now, Jean had been longing to get there, and it was a tremendous relief when at last they did so. The street was so dark, deserted and silent that the fighting might have been a hundred miles away; the tall, narrow house looked dead and uninhabited.

485

"The keys are in my pocket," muttered Maurice. "The big one for the outside door, the little one for my room, which is right at the top."

And with that he collapsed, fainting away in Jean's arms, to the latter's great anxiety. He forgot to shut the street door, and had to feel his way up the strange staircase, doing his best not to wake anybody by making a noise. Half-way up, he lost his way, and had to leave the wounded man on the stairs while he went ahead looking for the door of the room, which he found by striking matches. Then he had to go back for Maurice. But at last he laid him down on the iron bedstead facing the window, which he flung open to let in light and fresh air. Day was just breaking, and he fell on his knees beside the bed, sobbing unrestrainedly as he remembered how close he had been to killing his friend.

Several minutes must have elapsed, and when he suddenly caught sight of Henriette he was scarcely surprised : since it was her brother who lay there dying, what could be more natural? As he had not seen her enter the room, she had probably been there for hours. Now, slumped in a chair, he watched her stupidly, as she bustled about, horrified at the sight of her brother, stretched out unconscious and covered with blood. Presently he remembered something.

"Here, did you think to shut the street door?" he asked.

Completely taken aback, she nevertheless nodded her head; and when, eventually, she came towards him, holding out both her hands in her desperate need for affection and help, he went on :

"You realize? It's my fault. . . . I nearly killed him."

She didn't understand, she didn't believe him. He could still feel her hands lying calmly in his own.

"I tell you, I did it. . . . Yes, out there on the barricade. . . . We were fighting on opposite sides . . ." he went on, feeling her hands beginning to tremble. "It was as though we were both drunk, we didn't know what we were doing. . . . I nearly killed him. . . ."

Only then did Henriette withdraw her hands, shuddering, deathly pale, staring at him with terrified eyes. So this, then, was how it was to end, without a ray of hope to comfort her broken heart? Oh, Jean, Jean, whom she had thought about every evening, cheered by the vague thought that perhaps one day she would see him again ! And now it was he who had done this monstrous thing. Yet, all the same, it must also have been he who had saved Maurice, for who else could have brought him back here, despite all the

486

danger! And though she was too horrified to let him take her hands again, the cry she uttered expressed all the yearning of her desperate heart.

"Oh, but I shall get him better. I *must* get him better!"

During her long spells of duty in the hospital at Remilly she had become an expert nurse, and now, intent upon examining her brother's wound, she started undressing him. At first he showed no signs of life, but as she began to remove the dressing, he stirred slightly. Then, suddenly opening his eyes, which were burning with fever, he uttered a feeble cry. He recognized her at once, and murmured with a smile:

"So you've come? Oh, how glad I am to see you once more before I die."

"Die? But I'm not going to let you, I want you to live . . .! Don't try to talk, I've got a lot to do!"

When she saw, however, that the bayonet thrust had gone right through his arm and into his side, her face clouded over. Promptly she took possession of the room: found some olive oil, tore up an old shirt to make bandages, and sent Jean downstairs to fetch a jug of water. When he came back he said not a word, but watched her skilfully bathing and dressing the wound, incapable of helping her, overcome by the thought of her being there. As soon as she had finished, seeing how anxious she looked, he offered to go and fetch a doctor. But sensible as ever, she decided this would be a mistake: a strange doctor would perhaps betray her brother, better to wait for an hour or so and find one on whom they could really count. Eventually, as the time came for Jean to get back to his regiment, it was agreed that he would return as soon as he could, and do his best to bring a surgeon.

He did not leave immediately: it was as though he could not bring himself to quit this room, filled with the unhappiness he had caused. The window, which she had shut for a moment or two, was now wide open again, and the three of them stared out into the distance, while a heavy silence lay over them.

Here, from the top of the Butte des Moulins, a great part of Paris lay stretched below them, all the central districts, from the Faubourg Saint-Honoré to the Bastille, then the long ribbon of the Seine, with the densely crowded left bank, a sea of roofs, tree-tops, spires, domes, towers. The light was growing stronger; this dreadful night, one of the blackest in history, was over. Yet, in the clear rays of the rising sun, the fires still blazed beneath a rose-pink sky. Right in front of them, they could see the Tuileries, the d'Orsay barracks, the palaces of the Council of State and the Legion of Honour still burning; and the flames, though scarcely visible now in the bright sunlight, made the air quiver. Even beyond the burning houses in the Rue de Lille and the Rue du Bac there must have been other buildings on fire, for columns of flame rose into the air from the Croix Rouge and, further still, from the Rue Vavin and the Rue Notre-Dame-des-Champs. Nearby, to the right, the conflagration in the Rue Saint-Honoré was dying down, while to the left, the more recently lit fires in the Palais Royal and the Louvre sputtered and went out. But what at first they were unable to explain was the huge cloud of black smoke that the wind was blowing towards them. Since three in the morning, the Ministry of Finance had been burning, and as the vast quantities of paper accumulated in the low, plaster-covered rooms slowly smouldered away, they emitted, instead of flames, huge billows of sooty smoke. And though, as the great city woke to a new day, it no longer created such a tragic impression of utter destruction as it had during the night, nevertheless this dense, ever-growing cloud of smoke spread a sense of doom, of inevitable sadness, even over those districts that had been spared. Before long it had blotted out the bright morning sunlight, covering the reddish sky filled with a savage veil of mourning.

Maurice, who appeared to be growing delirious again, muttered incoherently:

"Isn't everything burnt yet? Oh, what a time it takes!"

Tears started to Henriette's eyes, as her own grief was deepened by the disasters engulfing her brother, and Jean, almost distraught, not daring either to take her hand again or to embrace his friend, got up to leave.

"So long," he muttered, "I'll be back as soon as I can!"

It was eight in the evening, however, before he returned, and already dark. Despite his anxiety, he felt more cheerful: his regiment, no longer involved in the fighting, had been charged with maintaining order in the district, and since his company was bivouacking in the Place du Carrousel, he hoped to be able to look in every evening to see how his friend was getting on. He was not alone. Happening to run into Major Bouroche, who had been in his old regiment, and despairing finding any other doctor, he had brought him along.

The quick-tempered major had no idea who it was he was coming to see, and grumbled about having to climb so many stairs.

When he realized that the wounded man was a Communard, he burst out angrily:

"For God's sake, what the hell do you take me for? . . . These fellows are nothing but a bunch of thieves and fire-raisers. It's obvious there's nothing wrong with the bastard that a bullet in the head wouldn't cure!"

But the sight of Henriette, sitting there, so pale in her black dress, with her fair hair falling over her shoulders, quickly calmed him.

"He's my brother, major," she said quietly. "And he fought for his country at Sedan."

He made no reply, but took off the bandages and silently examined the wound. Then, when he had put on a new dressing, he suddenly turned to the wounded man and asked him in his rough way:

"How the devil did you come to get mixed up with this pack of scoundrels?"

Maurice, who had been observing him ever since he arrived, without saying a word, now declared passionately:

"Because there's too much suffering in the world, too much injustice, too much shame!"

Bouroche shrugged his shoulders impatiently, implying that such matters were beyond him. He was on the point of saying something, but decided not to. Then, as he was making for the door, he called over his shoulder:

"I'll come and see you again."

Outside on the landing, he explained to Henriette that he could not accept any responsibility for what might happen; the lung was so seriously affected that, if there was a haemorrhage, the patient might well collapse.

As she re-entered the room Henriette did her best to smile, though the doctor's words had dealt her a bitter blow. Surely, somehow or other, she would be able to save him, to prevent this terrible thing happening that would part them for ever, just when they were together again? Throughout the day she had never stirred from the room, a kindly neighbour had done her shopping for her. And now she returned to her place beside the bed, and sat down again.

Meanwhile, in a state of feverish excitement, Maurice was questioning Jean, trying to find out how things were going. But the latter replied evasively, avoiding any mention of the savage hostility to the Commune that was being expressed on all sides, now Paris

489

had been delivered. Today it was Wednesday. Since Sunday evening, for two whole days, the people had been hiding in their cellars, sweating with fear. Now, as they ventured to emerge at last, the sight of the torn-up streets, the ruins, the blood, above all the terrible fires, aroused feelings of angry vengeance. They had begun searching the houses for suspects, turning over to the firing squads hundreds of men and women. From six o'clock in the evening, the army of Versailles had been in control of more than half Paris, from the Parc de Montsouris to the Gare du Nord; and the last members of the Commune, some twenty or so, had been driven to seek refuge on the Boulevard Voltaire, in the 11th Arrondissement.

A hush fell on the room, and presently, as they gazed out over the town, lying below them in the warm night air, Maurice muttered :

"And still it goes on, Paris is still burning!"

It was true. In the fading light, the flames could still be seen, reddening the sky with their monstrous light. During the afternoon, when the powder magazine in the Luxembourg had exploded with a terrifying roar, the rumour had spread that the whole Panthéon had collapsed and lay buried in the catacombs beneath. Throughout the day, moreover, the fires that had been started earlier had gone on burning. The palaces of the Council of State and the Tuileries, were still ablaze, and huge billows of smoke still poured from the Ministry of Finance. Again and again they had to shut the window, to keep out the half-burnt papers that fluttered about like swarms of black butterflies; in the end they covered the whole of Paris, and were even picked up as far away as Normandy. Moreover, now it was not only the western and southern districts that were on fire; the houses in the Rue Royale, at the Croix-Rouge crossroads, the Rue Notre-Dame, and the whole east end of the city seemed to be in flames as well, dominated by the vast bonfire of the Hôtel de Ville. And there, too, burning like torches, were the Lyric Theatre and the Town Hall of the 4th Arrondissement, as well as some thirty houses in the neighbouring streets, not to mention the theatre at the Porte Saint-Martin in the North, glowing far away in the distance. Some people were taking the opportunity to pay off old personal grudges, and criminals were doing their best to destroy the records of their crimes. It was no longer a question of the Communards trying to defend themselves, of holding off the victorious troops by setting buildings alight : the people were possessed by a vast surge of madness, and it was pure chance

490

that the Palais de Justice, the Hôtel Dieu and Notre Dame happened to be saved. To destroy for the sake of destruction, to bury the old, corrupt world beneath its ashes, in the hope that from them a new society would emerge, in all the purity and happiness of the earthly paradise of primitive legend!

"Oh this war, this ghastly war!" Henriette almost whispered, as she gazed down at the ruined city and all its suffering.

And, in effect, was not this the last, fatal act of madness, inherent in the defeats of Sedan and Metz, in the epidemic of destruction born of the siege of Paris? Was it not the supreme crisis of a nation threatened by death amidst all the bloodshed and ruin?

But without taking his eyes from the burning city, Maurice stammered:

"No, no, it's no use blaming the war. . . . What's happening is right, it's what had to be done . . ."

"Oh for God's sake!" Jean interrupted angrily. "When I look at you lying there, and realize it's my fault. . . . Don't try to defend it, war's a foul business!"

But with a vague gesture Maurice continued:

"Me? What do I matter, when there are so many others . . .? Maybe this bloodshed was necessary. . . . After all, you can't have life without death!"

And he closed his eyes, exhausted by the effort of speaking, while Henriette motioned to Jean not to go on arguing. Yet, in her anger at all this human suffering, she, too, wanted to protest, despite the self-restraint she imposed upon herself.

Two more days went by, Thursday and Friday, and still the burning and the slaughter continued. The din of gunfire was incessant, for the army of Versailles, after capturing the batteries at Montmartre, had turned them on those set up by the Communards at Belleville and Père-Lachaise; while the latter went on firing wildly, their shells falling as far apart as the Rue de Richelieu and the Place Vendôme. By the evening of the 25th the whole of the left bank was in the hands of the military. But, on the right bank, the barricades in the Place du Château-d'Eau and the Place de la Bastille still held out, veritable fortresses, whose defenders kept up an increasing stream of fire. Then, as the last members of the Commune broke up in disorder, Delescluze, in a final heroic gesture, picked up his walking-stick and strolled casually towards the barricade in the Boulevard Voltaire, where he was shot down in cold blood. Early next morning, the 26th, the Château d'Eau and the

Bastille were captured, and La Villette, Belleville and Charonne were the only districts still left in the hands of the Communards, now reduced to a handful of brave men, determined to die. And for two days longer they managed to hang on, fighting desperately.

On the Friday evening, as Jean was making his way from the Place du Carrousel to the Rue des Orties, he was forced to witness a summary execution. For the past couple of days, two court-martials had been functioning, one at the Luxembourg, the other at the Théâtre du Châtelet. Those who were convicted by the first were executed in the gardens, while the victims of the second were dragged away to the Lobau barracks, where a firing-squad, permanently on duty, shot them down in the inner courtyard, at point-blank range. It was here that the most terrible slaughter took place : men, even children, were convicted on the flimsiest evidence, because their hands were blackened with gunpowder, or because they were wearing army boots; innocent people, falsely accused by personal enemies, screaming out explanations which no one bothered to hear; and such crowds of wretched creatures were dragged in front of the firing-squad that many of them were not killed by the bullets, and had to be finished off by clubbing them to death with rifle butts. Blood flowed from morning till night, and the dead were carried away in cartloads. And throughout the conquered city, further victims of rage and vengeance were haphazardly killed in front of a barricade, against the wall of a deserted street, on the steps of public buildings. This was how it came about that Jean chanced to see the local inhabitants dragging a woman and two men to the guard post outside the Théâtre-Français. These middle-class people, incited by the newspapers which were now being published again, behaved with even greater savagery than the soldiers, and kept calling for the extermination of the Communards. A whole crowd of them were hounding their victims along, especially the woman, whom they accused of being one of those incendiaries, who, according to their frenzied imaginations, used to creep out at night, with cans of paraffin, and set fire to the houses of the rich. They had just caught her, they claimed, crouching beside a cellar window in the Rue Saint-Anne. And, despite her tears and protestations, they flung her, together with the two men, into a trench already filled with bodies, where the soldiers shot her down like a rat in a trap. Passers-by looked on, a woman and her husband stopped, while a baker's boy, delivering bread in the neighbourhood, whistled a hunting song.

492

Appalled, Jean was hurrying to get back to the Rue des Orties, when he suddenly remembered something. Surely that man in the worker's blouse, the one he had seen urging on the executioners, was Chouteau, who used to belong to his old squad? And knowing him for what he was, thief, traitor and murderer, for a moment he felt like going back and denouncing him, so that he, too, should be shot. It saddened him to think that the guilty could escape punishment, publicly flaunting their immunity, while innocent people were rotting in the ground!

Hearing his footstep on the stairs, Henriette came out on to the landing.

"Whatever you do, be careful," she implored him. "He's in an extraordinarily excitable state. Major Bouroche has been to see him, and I'm terribly worried."

Indeed, the major had not been at all encouraging. All he would say was that perhaps his youth might pull him through.

"So it's you at last?" Maurice said feverishly, directly he caught sight of Jean. "I've been expecting you. What's going on? How are things?"

And propped up with pillows, looking out of the window, from which he could see a fresh glow lighting up the darkening sky, he went on:

"Look, it's started again. Paris is still burning, surely this time the whole city must be consumed!"

No sooner had the sun gone down, than the flames from the burning Grenier d'Abondance lit up the farthest parts of the town, on the other side of the Seine. At the Tuileries and the Council of State the ceilings must have fallen in, causing the fire to flare up again, for every now and then flames and showers of sparks shot up into the air. For three days now, every time darkness fell, the fire seemed to get a new hold on the city, as though the very shadows were blowing on the embers, reviving them, scattering them on every side. And, tonight, so brilliant was the light coming from the burning docks at La Villette, that one could not help feeling that, this time, the entire city was to be swallowed up by the flames. Beneath the blood-red sky, a success of burning roofs stretched away as far as eye could see.

"This is the end," Maurice repeated. "Paris is burning!"

These words, which he kept repeating to himself, seemed to indicate a longing to speak, after the heavy stupor in which he

493

had lain for three days almost without saying a word. The sound of stifled sobs made him look round.

"What, my little sister crying, after being so brave? Surely you're not crying just because I'm going to die . . .?"

"But you shan't die, you shan't," she interrupted.

"Yes, yes, it's better that I should. . . . After all, it won't be much loss. Think of all the trouble I used to give you before the war, all the money and suffering I cost you, all the stupid, crazy things I did, that would have only landed me in prison or the gutter . . ."

She cut him short.

"Be quiet, will you? Be quiet. . . . You have more than paid for it!"

For a moment he was silent, considering what she said. Then he went on :

"If I die, yes, maybe then I shall have done. . . ."

And turning to Jean, he added :

"Perhaps, old man, when you stuck your bayonet into me, you were doing us all a good turn."

"Oh, don't say that," Jean protested, his eyes filling with tears. "You make me feel like shooting myself."

Maurice continued passionately :

"Don't you remember what you said to me after Sedan, when you were arguing that it was a good thing for everyone to get a smack in the eye now and then? And how you went on to say that, if part of your body was diseased, a limb for instance, it was better to have it cut off than to risk dying of gangrene? Many a time while I've been lying here, shut up on my own in this demented, miserable city, I've thought of what you said then. . . . Well, I'm that rotten limb. . . ."

He was growing more and more excited, and paid no attention to Jean and Henriette when they implored him to stop. With feverish energy he elaborated his theme, in a succession of symbols and striking images. It was the healthy part of France, the sensible, well-balanced peasants that had always remained close to the soil, which was now ridding the country of that other frantic, crazy element that had been ruined by the Empire, misled by its day-dreams and self-indulgence; and in order to get rid of it, it had had to cut deep, into the very flesh, without any very clear understanding of what it was doing. But this blood-letting was necessary; a grim holocaust, a living sacrifice on the altar of purification. The crucified nation was expiating its misdeeds, and would arise reborn.

494

"And it's people like you, Jean, straightforward, reliable fellows, who'll have to start tilling the soil again, rebuilding the houses . . . ! As for me, you were quite right to strike me down, for I was the ulcer eating into your flesh."

As his delirium increased, he insisted on getting up and looking out of the window.

"Paris is burning, and will go on burning till there's nothing left. . . . These flames are what I have been longing for, sweeping everything away, healing everything! Yes, yes, it's a good job they're doing. . . . Let me go, don't try to stop me carrying on the work of humanity and freedom. . . ."

It was only with the greatest difficulty that Jean managed to get him back to bed, while Henriette, tears running down her cheeks, kept talking to him about his childhood, begging him to calm himself. And high above the immense city the reflection of the flames grew brighter still, until the sea of fire seemed to be invading the darkness, and the sky was like the vault of some gigantic furnace, red and glowing. And in the savage glare of the conflagration, the dense smoke from the Ministry of Finance hung above them, a dark, slowly moving cloud of grief.

Next day, Saturday, Maurice's condition suddenly improved : the fever had diminished, and he had become much calmer. When Jean arrived that evening, he was delighted to find Henriette wreathed in smiles, dreaming once again of the possibility of happiness, all three of them united in some vague future relationship that she did not want to define. Was fate going to take pity on her at last? Night after night she had spent in this room, never going out, imbuing it with tenderness as she swiftly moved about attending to her patient. And for that evening Jean was able to forget himself, in the pleasure of being with his friends. During the day the army had captured Belleville and the Buttes-Chaumont, the only place that still held out was the cemetery of Père Lachaise, transformed into an armed camp. At last, it seemed to him, it was all over : he even maintained that people were no longer being shot; he spoke quite simply of the crowds of prisoners that were being led away to Versailles. That morning he had seen some of them on one of the quays, men in blouses, overcoats, shirt sleeves, women of all ages, some with hollow cheeks, others in the flower of their youth, children barely fifteen years old – a great tide of poverty and revolt, hustled along by the soldiers in the bright sunlight, to be met at Versailles, so it was said, by crowds of middle-class people, who booed them and struck out at them with their canes and umbrellas. But, for Jean, it was Sunday, the last day of this ghastly week, that proved to be the most terrible. From earliest morning, all through that bright, sunny day, he was haunted by a sense of supreme suffering. News of the repeated killing of hostages was only just getting about : the archibishop, the rector of the Madeleine and other priests, executed on the Wednesday, at La Roquette; the Dominicans at Arcueil, shot down as they were trying to run away, on the Thursday; then, on the Friday, more priests, and forty-seven policemen belonging to the Rue Haxo district. All this had led to a fresh outbreak of savage reprisals and mass executions of prisoners by the army. All through that lovely Sunday, the firing squads never stopped, the parade ground at the Lobau barracks, streaming with blood and smoke, echoed with the cries of dying men and women. At La Roquette, two hundred and twenty seven wretched creatures, arrested in the streets almost by chance, were mown down by machine-guns. At Père Lachaise cemetery, which had been shelled for four days, then captured, after a desperate running fight amongst the tombs, a hundred and forty-eight men were stood up against a wall and shot; and when three of them, despite being wounded, tried to escape, the soldiers caught them and finished them off. Of the twelve thousand people who gave their lives for the Commune, no one will ever know how many decent men and women were killed for every scoundrel! Although it was said that orders had come from Versailles to stop the executions, the killing still went on; and Thiers, despite his fame as the liberator of the country, was to remain the legendary murderer of Paris, just as Marshal MacMahon, who had been defeated at Froeschwiller, and one of whose proclamations now covered every wall, was now to be hailed as the victor of Père Lachaise. And all the time, beneath the brilliant sunshine, Paris appeared like a town on holiday : huge crowds swarmed through the streets that had been won back, people strolled about, idly gaping at the smoking ruins left by the fire, and mothers, with their smiling children clinging to their hands, stopped for a moment, listening attentively to the muffled sound of firing from the Lobau barracks.

That evening, at dusk, as Jean was climbing the dark stairs in the Rue des Orties, he felt a terrible presentiment. And as he entered the room, the first thing he saw was Maurice, lying back on the pillow, dead, choked by the haemorrhage that Bouroche had feared. The red glow of sunset shone through the open window, on the table beside the bed two candles were burning, and Henriette, on her knees and still dressed in her widow's weeds, was weeping silently.

Hearing a noise she looked up, and when she saw who it was, a shudder ran over her. Almost beside himself, Jean rushed forward, and, in an attempt to express his grief, seized hold of her hands. But he could feel them trembling, her whole body was quivering with revulsion and withdrawal. Now everything there had been between them was over. Maurice's death had driven them apart. And all he could do was to fall on his knees beside her, sobbing quietly.

At last, however, after a long silence, Henriette spoke.

"I had my back turned to him, preparing some soup, when suddenly he called out. . . . But almost before I could get to him, he was dead, trying to speak our names, yours and mine, though the blood was already choking him. . . ."

And this was her brother, thought Jean, the man she had adored since he was a child, whom she had brought up, who had been almost a part of herself, the one great love of her life, since she had seen her husband, lying in the street at Bazeilles, shot through the head. So the war had robbed her of everything, and now she would be left alone in the world, a widow with no one to love and cherish her!

"And to think that it was all my fault!" he sobbed. "That it was I, who was ready to give my life for him, who had to go and kill him . . .! What's going to become of us? Will you ever forgive me?"

As he was speaking, their eyes met, and they stood there, overcome with confusion, as they realized at last what it was they could read there. Suddenly the past sprang to life for them, the hidden room at Remilly, and all the sweetness and sadness of the days they had spent there. He remembered how he had dreamed, unconsciously at first, then gradually more clearly, of settling down with her, in a small house with sufficient land to provide a family with a modest living. But now it was a passionate desire, a profound conviction, that with a woman like her, so tender, so active and courageous, such a life could have been a paradise. And she, who, hitherto, in her modesty and ignorance of her own feelings, had been untouched by such a dream, now in this moment suddenly understood it too. Without realizing it, she too had vaguely longed for such a marriage. Unknown to her, the seed had been implanted, had germinated in silence, and now she was passionately in love with this man, to whom, in the beginning, she had turned purely for consolation. All this they saw in one another's eyes. Yet they knew that this moment of recognition must also be the moment of eternal parting. This was the terrible sacrifice they still had to make, their last farewell to a happiness that, only yesterday, had still been possible for them, but which, today, had been swept away on the stream of blood that had killed her brother.

After a long and painful struggle with himself, Jean rose to his feet.

"Goodbye," he said.

And Henriette, without moving, echoed him.

For a moment longer Jean remained standing by Maurice's body, looking down at the high forehead, the long, thin face, the eyes, so recently gleaming with an almost crazy light, now empty and at peace. He wanted to stoop down and kiss him, but dared not. He felt as though his hands were stained with blood, and shrank back from the horror of his fate. Oh, to have died like this, with the whole world falling about his ears, the final victim of the dying Commune! Still passionately longing for justice, the poor fellow had passed away at the very moment that his grim dream was being realized, that grandiose and monstrous conception of the old society being swept away and Paris burnt to the ground, so that, at last, from a land that had been purified, another golden age might arise.

Overcome with grief, Jean turned away, gazing out over Paris. On this fine Sunday evening, the red gleam of the setting sun, already sunk below the horizon, lit up the vast city. Thousands of window-panes glittered like burning embers; roofs glowed like red-hot coals; patches of yellow walls and tall, rust-covered monuments, like blazing bonfires, flung showers of sparks into the evening air. Surely this huge crimson inferno must be the final outburst, the whole of Paris, burning like a huge forest of ancient trees, filling the sky with tongues of flame and glowing embers? But still the fires burned, still the clouds of reddish smoke rose into the sky; and the distant murmur that could be heard might have been the dying groans of the prisoners being shot in the Lobau barracks, or perhaps the gay voices of women, and children's laughter, as they sat outside the restaurants enjoying a meal after their Sunday walk. From the looted houses and public buildings, from the gutted streets, from all this ruin and suffering, the roar of life still rose into the air, amid the splendour of this royal sunset, in whose glow Paris was finally burning itself out.

Suddenly Jean had an extraordinary feeling. As night slowly settled down upon the burning city, it seemed to him that a new dawn was already beginning to break. True, this was the end of everything, an accumulation of disasters, decreed by fate, such as no other nation had experienced : a succession of defeats, whole provinces lost, a huge indemnity to be paid, a terrible civil war drowned in blood, entire districts filled with nothing but dead people and ruined buildings, money and honour exhausted, a whole world to be rebuilt! And yet, somewhere beyond this fiery furnace, in the depths of the great peaceful sky, a living hope was even now being reborn, the inevitable rejuvenation of eternal nature and immortal humanity, the promise of renewal for all who dared to hope and work, the undying tree of life, that thrusts forth new and powerful shoots, when the withered branch that has been turning the leaves yellow with its poisoned sap has at last been cut off.

Through his tears, Jean once again uttered the single word "Goodbye", and Henriette, without raising her head, her face hidden in her hands, repeated it after him.

The ravaged fields had run to waste, the house had been burnt to the ground, and Jean, in all his humility and bitter grief, turned away, marching towards the future, to the harsh and bitter task of building a whole new France.